A Slip Between Realms

Darby Cox

Ever After Press

Published by Ever After Press

Cover and interior design by Mariyana Swisher

A Slip Between Realms is a work of fiction based on Scandinavian folklore. Names, characters, places, and incidents are the product of the author's imagination or are used fictitiously. Creative liberty was taken during drafting, and any resemblance to actual events, locales, or persons, living or dead, is purely coincidental.

ISBN:979-8-9939056-1-7
Printed in the United States of America

For the girl who dreamed of writing mysteries and fantasies at eleven...
this one's for you.

Chapter 1

I smacked my head for the fourth time this shift. How many times does someone have to smack their head to know that they should duck when leaving the kitchen? I cursed out loud as the cup of ranch on the basket of fries I was carrying tipped and spilled down my wrist, staining the side of my apron. Rachel, the bartender, held back an amused scoff as she poured a shot and slid it to her customer.

"Do I need to bubble wrap your head for you?" she asked, wiping her hands on a bar towel that had been soaking in a puddle of vodka for an hour.

I rolled my eyes and shook the ranch from my forearm. What I really wanted was for her to pour me a shot. I ducked back into the kitchen and grabbed another cup of ranch before dropping off the basket of fries at my table. As I slouched back over to the bar and propped my chin on my arms, I watched Rachel flip her customer the bird before flinging him a beer. The older man caught it with a devilish smile as she turned to print his check. She would get a great tip from this one. She always did. In the year since she'd started working here, I had seen her verbally abuse customers, and they would still thank her for their drinks. Perhaps it was the way her curly brown hair cascaded down her back perfectly or the golden hoop through her nose, but something about her brought in the kind of clientele that loved their beer to come with a side of verbal abuse. Perhaps I'd understand the psychology behind that if only I could be accepted into the program.

Rachel settled across from me, mimicking my chin prop and giving me an exasperated smile. "How'd the interview go?" she asked.

I shrugged. "Not sure. I was numb the whole time. I barely remember it. I'm not sure they'll want a stuttering mess of an orphan in their program." I tried to laugh it off, but the knot in my chest tightened. "Maybe I should just change my major to communications or something of the sort. I'd be a hell of a lot less stressed."

Rachel scoffed. "That's quitter talk, babes. I'm sure it went well." She pushed herself up from the bar and tossed her curls over her shoulder. "You can't be a server forever." Her eyes shone sweetly before she turned around to pour a beer for one of her regulars.

The dim lights in the bar accentuated her high cheekbones and plump lips, and I took a moment to admire her flawless skin, unlike mine, which was currently fighting off a breakout on my left cheek. Rachel giggled as the man in front of her cracked a joke, and she twirled a curl around her finger, every strand of hair perfectly in place. My auburn hair was wavy and frazzled from the shift, and I knew if I were in the same position as her, that man wouldn't tip me even a quarter of what he was going to give her. That just meant I had to work twice as hard. But if there was one thing I had that Rachel didn't, it was my freckles. They were my most complimented asset. Mama used to say I had a galaxy painted across my face. Granny would joke that I had stood behind a cow when it took a shit.

I sighed and straightened, making my way back into the kitchen. I couldn't help but think of Granny and Mama. It was times like this that I really missed them. Especially Granny, considering she was my last caretaker before I was dropped into the foster system. She always knew how to cheer me up, even during the most challenging times. If I showed up with a tear on my cheek, she'd shove a mug of hot chocolate in my hand and whip out the old photo albums. Billie Holiday would be playing in the background, and the smell of lavender potpourri and Bengay would fill my nostrils.

And then there was Mama. Eight years began to erase her face from my memory, but I could still remember her voice, hear her singing to me, and telling me stories of fairies, mermaids, and pirates. Something I remembered even more than her voice was the warmth she carried with her, the aura of whimsy she instilled within me. I may not recognize her face, but I would never forget her shine.

I opted to skip the drink Rachel tried to pour and decided a shift meal would be the better option for me, considering rent was due next week. I'd rather be fed for free than drunk for free, especially since I hadn't stocked my fridge since November, and we were going into April.

"Need some help cleaning?" I asked Rachel when my side work was done.

She turned to me with a confused expression. "I'll be here late, babes. Go home and get some sleep."

My shift ended with no more smacks to the head and no news from my interview.

I didn't know why I even applied to the psychology program in the first place. I was hardly qualified for it. I had only been in school for a year and didn't have time to participate in any extracurricular activities or internships that would enhance my qualifications for the program. I was too busy working. It's the unfortunate reality every orphan faces in college: no support system, having to pay my way because there was no generational wealth to back me up, so I was set up for failure because there just wasn't enough time in the day to work to support myself and study like I needed to. I didn't pity myself; I didn't have time for that or anything else. Applying to this program was a shot in the dark, and I missed my target by a mile, it seemed.

Being in the foster care system inspired me to pursue a career in psychology. Most people asked me that since the system was my inspiration, why not pursue a career in social work? Seeing how crappy social work was, particularly what our caseworker went through with the different incidents in the houses we were placed in, I wasn't eager to explore that field. Psychology would give me an outlet to help in the system while still keeping the hard memories at arm's length.

I also had my brother, Lucas, to thank for my high aspirations. He'd always been my number one fan. Even during high school, when all I wanted to do was drop out and run away from the foster home. He kept me there, saying that if I graduated, I could be a firefighter, a scientist, or a police officer. I remembered the night I actually tried to run away, and how selfish I had felt after deciding to stay. I had almost left him behind in that foster home and nearly abandoned him. The memory was hard to avoid, but I tried not to think of what would've happened if he hadn't woken up and seen me closing the bedroom door. I'm not sure I would have stayed. I don't know if I would even be alive. I liked to think that Lucas saved my life that night.

Lucas was still in the foster system, unfortunately. When I aged out, I was in no capacity to care for him, but luckily, he was reassigned to a foster home closer to me and the small college I attended. I visited him every few days, sometimes taking him out to see movies or get ice cream. I used to take him to the trampoline park, but he very blatantly told me that he aged out of that—Lucas was a bit precocious at times, and sometimes it felt like I was talking to a little man rather than my eight-year-old brother. My goal was to one day adopt him, but I knew that wasn't realistic for the moment, so for now, we had our visits.

Until then, home was a small, old house near downtown, within walking distance of the community college. It wasn't perfect, in fact, it was very run-down—there was definitely some mold growing in the walls that the landlord couldn't kill off, the back door barely fit in the frame, and I could only walk on certain spots of the front steps without my foot going through the boards. It was an undesirable living situation, but it was cheap, and the girls I lived with helped keep it clean and cozy.

Once I got home, I breezed past one of my roommates who had passed out on the couch, an open anatomy book splayed on the floor as if it were dropped when she nodded off. I had two roommates, but they might as well have been strangers, given how little I saw of them. The three of us met through a roommate finder site, a little over two years ago. Casey, the one who passed out before me, was working her way through nursing school. Between the late-night shifts at the family practice clinic, the clinical hours, and her classes, I saw her so little that I sometimes found myself struggling to remember what she looked like when she was awake. Leah, on the other hand, was studying business online, so she stayed confined to her room or the library.

I crept into my room and closed the door quietly, feeling my muscles droop and weaken at the sight of my bed. As I set down my stuff, my phone buzzed with a text from Lucas. He asked if we were still going out the next day. I closed my eyes and sighed, punching myself for forgetting. Tomorrow was my day off, and I was going to study, but it could wait. Anything could wait for Lucas.

I typed back that, of course, we were still going out the next day. We could do whatever Lucas would like. He mentioned the bookstore and that he wanted to get some new comics. He had leftover money from Christmas, and it seemed it was burning a hole in his pocket. Looks like we're comic book shopping tomorrow

Chapter 2

Lucas climbed into the passenger seat and gave a crooked smile as he buckled his seatbelt. I smiled back when he told me he missed me.

"I missed you too," I said and brushed a strand of his sandy blonde hair out of his eyes. As we pulled away, I tried to ignore his current and my former foster mom, Sarah, watching us from the front door. I wasn't sure Sarah fully trusted me not to take off with him. I knew I wasn't the easiest teenager to care for during the four months I stayed there, especially since I was so close to aging out. Our conflicting ideas about what was best for Lucas strained our relationship, and it was hard for both of us to forget the countless times we clashed.

I usually hid my annoyance about the matter pretty well, but it was getting harder to with how closely she'd been watching me. Sarah was an okay enough foster parent; she at least made sure Lucas knew how to tie his shoes before sending him off to kindergarten a few years ago. I didn't agree with all of her methods, but I trusted her enough to ensure Lucas received the care he needed.

"What kind of comics are you looking for today?"

He shrugged. "You ever hear of the Bone Chronicles?"

When I shook my head, Lucas's face lit up. He went on to describe the books in full detail, barely breaking to breathe. Hearing him talk about the comics reminded me of Mama telling me fantasy stories, both of which gave vivid descriptions that made me feel like I could be a part of the whimsical worlds. We got to the bookstore before he finished telling me about the first book.

Once we got inside, Lucas darted into the illustrated novel section while I stepped into the coffee shop and bought myself a latte and him a cinnamon roll. I had just spent at least three tables' worth of tips, but for Lucas, it was worth it. Besides, the cinnamon rolls here were his favorite. They were Mama's favorite, too. A few minutes later, he strode up to me with two books tucked under his arm, and he slid into the chair across the table. He thanked me for the sweet and gave it a good sniff.

"How did the interview go?" Lucas asked, shaking his shaggy blonde hair out of his eyes as he peeled his cinnamon roll apart.

I pressed my lips together. I didn't want to lie, but I really didn't want to tell the truth. "Um, it went okay," I answered.

He chewed and cocked an eyebrow at me. "That doesn't sound good."

I sighed. "It's just that...I don't think they'll want someone who isn't dedicated to school and extracurriculars." I paused. "I'd have to do some stuff outside of school before they'd accept me, I think."

He shoved another piece of cinnamon roll into his mouth. "They sound like idiots," he said, gazing over my shoulder at the books lining the wall. "Maybe you should just be a police officer."

I smiled. "Yeah, maybe." I paused as his fingers dug into the sticky part of the roll and dripped cinnamon onto his palms.

"Can I ask you a question?"

Taken aback, I answered, "Of course."

Lucas blinked, considering. "Did you know my dad?"

"Um," I stammered, unsure how to answer. He had never asked about his dad before. "Not really, buddy. He wasn't around a lot. Why do you ask?"

He shrugged.

Recovering from the odd question, I asked, "How's school going?"

Lucas sank a tiny bit in his chair, his cinnamon roll suddenly forgotten. "It's good."

I cocked my head and gave him a disbelieving look. "That doesn't sound good," I answered, mimicking his previous reply. "Are you having trouble with the work?" Lucas shook his head.

He swallowed his cinnamon roll and sat back. "They're having a spring recital."

I raised my brow. "Well, that sounds exciting!"

He shook his head while he played with the corner of one of the books he had chosen. His lower lip began to poke out. "Jacob Tarney's dad made him a really cool costume. He's going to be a grasshopper."

My eyes fell to the steaming cup of coffee in my hands as his words confirmed why he had asked about his dad. He thought it was unfair that everyone else had a dad to help them make a costume for the recital. I remembered in ninth grade, my art class had a final project showing in our gymnasium. Everyone's parents showed up, all except mine. I remembered feeling somber pride as a parent walked up to my art, smiled, and said my parents would be proud when they saw my work. I went home and cried into my pillow that night. It's not that I didn't miss Mama. I missed her every day. But that night, I wanted nothing more than for Granny to be there. She would've smiled at my work, pointed out the brush strokes, and complimented the novice technique I used.

Granny would've made Lucas the coolest costume on stage.

"Hey, buddy, it's okay," I said, but I knew it wasn't. "I'll be there cheering the loudest, I'll even make a sign. Have you asked Sarah to make you a costume?"

Lucas had begun toying with the dedication page of his book and accidentally smeared cinnamon goop on the paper. "It won't be as good as Jacob Tarney's."

I pressed my lips together. "Let's see what we can do. I'm sure we'll make it even better." When Lucas didn't answer, I asked, "What are you playing in the recital?"

Lucas scoffed. "A caterpillar."

"Hey, that's pretty cool!"

"Not as cool as a grasshopper! All caterpillars do is eat and sleep in their cocoons. I don't want to be a dumb caterpillar."

My teeth gnawed on my lower lip as I watched Lucas poke at his forgotten sweet. "But caterpillars turn into butterflies, and before you say that's girly, just listen to me." Lucas closed his mouth before he could get a word out. "Caterpillars don't *just* turn into butterflies. Some species turn into moths."

"Moths?" Lucas questioned, and the disappointment eased from his face.

"Yep, and moths are ruled by the moon. A lot cooler than butterflies, huh?"

My brother nodded. "I read somewhere that there is a mothman! Have you ever seen the mothman?"

I giggled. "No, but what do you say we go to the park and look for some caterpillars? Maybe we can get some inspiration for your costume."

We left the bookstore before I could finish my coffee.

In my haste to change the subject from Jacob Tarney's grasshopper costume, I forgot that there weren't many caterpillars out in March in Pennsylvania. But I was thankful for the time Lucas and I spent scouring the playground and the surrounding woods for moth caterpillars, not butterfly caterpillars, as he so adamantly reminded me. While there wasn't a bug in sight, Lucas still giggled and joked about the things we observed, occasionally taking a break to make little people out of the twigs we found.

The park was on the other side of town near our old foster home, the one I tried to run away from. The plastic playground equipment and worn benches had been a quick escape from the turmoil in our house, but it was easy to find us here when all we wanted to do was hide. When things got terrible, Lucas and I retreated to the woods behind that house, finding safety in the little shack someone had thrown together long ago. It wasn't the most stable place to play, but it was safer than the foster home.

It was a warm spring day, which brought a few people to the park, even though I had hoped it would be empty. The shouts and cries of delight from the other children playing filled my ears; however, I tried to avoid the rows of benches piled with parents chatting and warning their kids to behave on the equipment. I wasn't ready to have another conversation about our dead parents. And knowing Lucas, he would ask. So we stayed on the other side of the park.

It didn't stop a group of kids from wandering over to us.

"What're you doing?" a girl with black hair demanded.

"Hi, Stephanie," Lucas said with something close to resignation in his voice.

Despite the contempt I was already building for this little girl, I decided to be nice. First impressions could sometimes be wrong. "We're looking for bugs," I answered in a friendly tone that earned me a side-eye from Lucas.

The little girl exchanged a disgusted look with the other two girls she had brought with her. "Ew," they said in unison. "You should be looking for worms," Stephanie sneered. "That's what you're going to be in the recital, right, Lucas?"

My brother's nose wrinkled as his temper lit within him. I only knew it because the same thing was happening to me. And if there was one thing we both shared, it was a temper. While we both usually kept it in check, when someone jeopardized my brother, I had a hard time wrangling it.

"No, I'm not a worm, I'm a caterpillar," Lucas replied in a tone heavy with leveled anger.

Stephanie scoffed. "You *should* be a worm. It puts you closer to your mom, who is dead in the ground."

I stood suddenly, snapping the twig I had been fiddling with when the girls walked up. "That is not okay!" I exclaimed. "How *dare* you! What makes you think it's okay to speak to someone like that?" Stephanie shrank under my wrath, and her friends cowered behind her.

I didn't feel an ounce of regret as the little girl's face screwed together, and tears broke free from her eyes.

"What's going on?" A woman with black hair that matched Stephanie's demanded as she came rushing up to us. She knelt in front of the little girl with a worry-creased brow. "Sweetie, are you okay?"

By now, Stephanie had been reduced to shaking tears, unable to mutter a word through her sobs. Instead, she pointed to me.

"What is wrong with you?" Stephanie's mother demanded as she wrapped her daughter in her arms. "How could you yell at a little girl like that?"

I grit my teeth. "Maybe you should teach her to treat others with a little compassion, especially those who have less than she does."

Realization bloomed across the woman's face, like she suddenly realized who we were. She said nothing and instead corralled the rest of the girls away. Anger rippled through me as I watched them crowd around their parents, who were exchanging worried looks and pointing at us. I could only imagine what they were saying about us, but Lucas's voice stopped the thoughts before they could grow.

"I have less than they do," Lucas whispered behind me. I turned with a thudding heart. "I have less..." Lucas stammered. It wasn't a realization, but a fact that we both had been running from for years. A fact that I had tried to fight away from Lucas since he started school, and the kids found out he was an orphan. I had been able to protect him for a few years, as much as I could, given the circumstances. But now, it was becoming increasingly complex to keep him safe from that truth. I dreaded the day when it reared its ugly head and struck him like a snake.

I feared that day was today. And it was my fault.

Chapter 3

That night, I couldn't sleep, unable to get Stephanie's words out of my head. And even worse, I couldn't forget my own. I had said those words in front of Lucas, exposing him to the very truth I had fought so hard to protect him from. We had less than everyone else, and I wouldn't have enough to make up for it. There was only so much I could do to fill in those blanks for Lucas, especially when I could barely afford to keep *myself* alive. I would never be able to adopt him. He was my brother, but he always seemed just out of my grasp.

I hadn't realized I had fallen asleep until a phone call woke me up.

"Hello?" I answered as I wiped the sleep from my eyes.

"Layla?" came a shaky voice from the other line.

"Sarah?" I asked, quickly propping myself up on my elbows. "What's wrong? Is Lucas okay?"

The pause on the other end lasted an eternity. Everything had gone completely silent; the only sound in the room was my ticking clock echoing through my ears.

"Where is he?" was all Sarah said before my blood rushed through my ears and drowned out the clock.

"What do you mean?" I demanded as adrenaline launched me from my sheets and into action. "What's wrong? Lucas is gone?"

"Layla, if I find out you have him..."

Rage bit into my senses, and I fought the urge to smash my phone so that I wouldn't have to hear the rest of her threat. "I don't," I hissed. "Call the cops, Sarah. I'll be there in fifteen."

"I'd rather you kept your distance."

"He's my brother, Sarah..."

He's all I have left.

Sarah sighed. "Just stay out of their way, okay?"

I hung up the phone and hurried to the car.

Two police cars were parked in the driveway when I pulled up. The air was chilly as I crawled out and made my way to the front door, where Sarah greeted me, her blonde bob blowing in the breeze.

"The police just got here, they're upstairs."

I sat down at the kitchen table, and Sarah poured me a cup of coffee, then retrieved my favorite flavored creamer from the fridge.

"I hope your taste in coffee hasn't changed," she said and gave me a halfhearted smile. I gave her a gracious nod, but couldn't bring myself to say thank you.

"Tell me what happened," I asked. The warmth of the mug between my palms grounded me.

"He was quiet at dinner, but sometimes he's just like that. I didn't want to pry." She rubbed her forehead and adjusted her thick-rimmed glasses. "He said he didn't want dessert, but he wanted to watch a movie. Then he went to bed." She shook her head in disbelief. "I didn't hear a peep out of his room all night. The front and back doors were locked when I woke up this morning, and he couldn't have gotten through the windows, as they have screens on them. And not a single one had been knocked out."

I heaved a deep sigh, my fingers tapping on the mug. I hadn't told Sarah about what happened at the park, but now seemed like the worst time to say to her. But I weighed my options, and it was clear what I had to do.

"Something happened at the park yesterday," I began, and quickly explained the scuffle between the girls and us.

When I finished, Sarah pressed her lips together and shook her head, already frustrated with me. "Why didn't you tell me this last night?" she hissed, quiet enough that the police upstairs wouldn't hear.

I shook my head as my brow furrowed. "It was none of your business. This was about what happened to *our* family."

Sarah chuffed. "It *is* my business, Layla. When he is under *my* care, everything is my business. How many times do we have to have this conversation?"

11

I heaved a big sigh and stood when the urge to smash the mug of coffee became too tempting. "I'm all he has left, Sarah. He needs me."

At that moment, the police clomped downstairs and asked for Sarah's statement. I quickly gave Sarah the details of the girls involved in the argument yesterday so that she could explain it to the police, then stepped away and tiptoed upstairs.

Lucas's room looked the same as it always did. There was a Star Wars poster on the wall (even though he didn't like Star Wars, he just liked how it looked), a baseball bat from when Sarah tried to get him into baseball (he hated it), and on his desk was one of the two Bone Chronicle books he bought yesterday. The other one was missing.

My eyes wandered over the books and papers and colored pencils scattered on his desk, and I picked up a sketchbook to thumb through some of the pages. There were a few drawings of characters from some of the comic books he read, and others had pictures of characters from movies he had probably watched with Sarah. There was a sketch of a poster for the film I took him to last month, and I smiled softly at the memory. I couldn't help but marvel at my brother's work. He was a skilled artist, and each of his sketches showed a maturity beyond his age. Then again, not every eight-year-old grew up the way we did. I flipped through the last few pages when one drawing caught my eye. My finger paused on the page, and I squinted, scrutinizing the details. It was a man, his features dark and his hair long. The man seemed normal, just dark, as if he were drawn with charcoal instead of a colored pencil. Sketched in Lucas's large, blocky print was the name "Marcus."

Confused, I closed the book and turned on my heel.

"Did he have a key?" I heard an officer ask as I made my way back down the stairs.

"No," Sarah replied through burgeoning tears. She placed a bony hand over her heart, then fiddled with her necklace. "I got him a phone in case of emergencies, but he left that behind. The only thing he took was his backpack."

The officer scribbled something down in a small notebook, and I knew they would treat him as a runaway and not an abduction. They would issue an Amber Alert, but someone would have to see him for that to make a difference. Lucas wasn't going to be found because of anything the cops did.

"And there were no signs of any of the doors being opened or closed throughout the night?"

Sarah scoffed. "You tell me, officer. I have a security system, and it didn't go off once. Unless my system is faulty, then no, there were no signs of any open doors." At least she was just as annoyed with this procedure as I was becoming.

The officer offered placating hands. "Ma'am, we're just trying to get as much information as we can. We're going to contact CPS, and we'll need his dental records in case we find him."

Dental records? Oh god, dental records so that they could identify...

My stomach flipped, and I fled to the kitchen and out of earshot.

When I heard the front door close, Sarah stepped into the kitchen with her arms folded across her chest. I stood and gathered my things. "I doubt they'll do any good. I'd have better luck finding him myself."

Sarah huffed. "Stay out of it," she warned and pinned me with a look that was intended to scare me. Instead, it made me silently rise to the challenge. "I've had to put a lot of trust in you, and you're testing it."

Ignoring the underlying threat in her words, I asked, "Lucas didn't have any imaginary friends, did he?" The corners of Sarah's mouth tugged downward in confusion as she shook her head. "Did he happen to know anyone named Marcus?" I continued.

"Not that I know of, but it could be a classmate." She watched me carefully as I made my way to the door. "Why do you ask?"

"No reason, just saw he had a drawing of someone named Marcus, but don't remember him talking about anyone like that." I purposely left out the part that the drawing was of an adult, and a sketchy one at that.

I got into my car, disregarding Sarah's final caution to let the police do their job as desperation rose in my chest. Where could he have gone? It wasn't like Lucas to misbehave like this. Unless he remembered me trying to leave once things got tough and decided to do the same thing. I sank into my car seat and leaned my head against the steering wheel as a heaving sob escaped my lips. This was all my fault. I set a poor example for him, and if I hadn't said those things in the park yesterday, maybe he'd still be here. My brother was gone, and it was all my fault.

Chapter 4

I had driven around our town nearly four times before I pulled into the parking lot of the bar. There weren't many places I could think of that Lucas would go, but I still drove by his school, the bookstore, the park, and a few other places I knew he frequented with either me or Sarah. When I pushed the door of the bar open, the familiar wave of cleaner and whiskey washed over me. I trekked over to the bar where Rachel was leaning over, tapping on her phone. The place was empty, which was odd for a Thursday night.

"Hey, babes, you're not working tonight," she said without looking up. I pulled a chair out and slumped down. "Why're you here?" she asked concernedly, but she couldn't peel her blue eyes from her phone. When I didn't answer, she finally looked up. "Oh no, what happened?"

I pressed my lips together in an attempt to keep the lump in my throat down. "Will you pour me a shot?" I asked timidly, even though I wouldn't be able to afford it. I didn't care. Without a word, Rachel turned on her heel, grabbed a bottle of Dewars, and began pouring it into her shaker. A couple of ingredients and a few shakes later, and she handed me a green tea shot. I downed it and slid the glass over to her, gesturing for another. She picked up her shaker again, but I grunted and motioned for just the whiskey. Two more shots and I lowered my forehead to the bar, relishing the warmth that tickled my skin. It wasn't enough.

"Did you hear back from the program? Did you not get in?" Without lifting my head, I shook it. "Roommates?" Again, I shook my head. "Well, hun, then what's wrong?"

I raised my head, and it spun a little as I focused on Rachel. Then my eyes welled with tears. "It's my brother."

Rachel furrowed her brow, confusion spelling on her face. "You have a brother?"

I nodded.

"Why have you never mentioned him?"

I shrugged. "It's no one's business."

Rachel rolled her eyes. "What happened?"

I bit my lip and tried to keep my voice from shaking. "He's missing."

Her eyes widened. "Shit, dude." She made her way around the bar and pulled out the chair next to mine. "Do you know anything?"

I shook my head. "He just disappeared into the night." I scoffed. "He wasn't unhappy in his foster home. It's just...so out of the blue." I wasn't going to tell her what went down in the park. Again, it was no one's business.

Rachel shook her head in disbelief. "He's still in the system?"

I took a deep breath and let the whiskey open me up. "My mom died giving birth to him." I was thirteen.

My dad wasn't in the picture, never had been. Mama had dated here and there, nothing serious and nothing she really bothered to bring home. Then she met Dallas. Dallas was a sweet man, and he treated my mother well, but at the news of her pregnancy, he bolted, not even leaving a note behind. We never saw him again. Mama died nine months later because of an aneurysm during labor, and my newborn brother and I went to live with Granny. A year later, she died, too. Heart attack, according to the doctors. Except she had never had even the signs of an arrhythmia before. But I was young and knew nothing of cardiology, so I accepted the diagnosis of a freak cardiac incident.

And still, neither my father nor Lucas's came to claim us. After that, we were placed into the foster care system. The whiskey swirling around in my blood awoke feelings about their loss that I had overcome years ago. Or maybe just buried them so deeply I forgot about them until I got drunk. I couldn't afford to get drunk often enough to know the answer to that.

Rachel took a deep toke from her vape and puffed it out, then leaned back in her chair. "That's heavy, Layla." I remained silent. "I'm sorry that happened."

I shrugged, and the whiskey's warmth retreated and left a cold pit in my stomach. I shivered. Reaching across the bar and grabbing the bottle, I poured myself another shot and knocked it back. Now, four shots deep, it suddenly seemed pointless not to have told Rachel about my brother.

"For so long, it's just been me and Lucas. After my Granny died, we went into the system. Our first foster home had five kids, including us. We didn't stay very long because of the other kids, and our next foster home was somehow worse." I burped, and the sour taste of bile burned my throat, but it was nothing compared to the memories of that hell house. "Just before I graduated high school, we were placed with Sarah, and that's where Lucas has been ever since. But now he's gone."

"The cops couldn't find anything?" Rachel questioned, to which I shook my head. "And you have absolutely no idea where he could've gone?"

I chewed my lip in consideration. Lucas was a smart kid; he wouldn't just hop into some stranger's car after breaking out of Sarah's house. He would go somewhere he knew was safe, and because of the incident in the park earlier that day, that safety wasn't with me, which left only one other place. "There was this little shack in the woods behind one of our old foster homes. It was pretty far in the woods, and no one knows how it got there. It appears to have been a child's fort a long time ago. He and I used to go when we wanted to escape our foster parents for a bit. I don't even know if it's still there, but that's the only place I can think of."

Some of our best times together were spent in that shack. We used to pretend it was our own home, imagining that the bruises on our limbs came from gallant fights with trolls and not the swinging fists of our foster parents. In the shack, we could pretend we were the only family we needed, that I could take care of Lucas, and he could take care of me.

"I...I think I'm going to go to the shack," I said, the edges of my vision blurring as the shots sank me deeper into myself.

In a flurry of light brown curls, Rachel pushed her chair back, slid behind the bar, and flipped off the lights.

"What're you doing?" I asked and pushed my chair back as well, unstable for a second as my feet touched the ground.

"We're going to go to that fort," she said, then poured a shot for me and one for her.

"We?" I slurred with an edge of humor.

Rachel jabbed a manicured nail in my direction. "*You* are not driving. We can take your car, but I'm behind the wheel."

I couldn't help but scoff in amusement. "You're going to close the bar and go to the middle of the woods to find some old kids' fort with me?"

She gave me a look of obvious exasperation. "Duh." Rachel knocked back her shot and turned off the music, then a couple more lights as she headed for the door.

16

With the shake of my head, I swallowed the whiskey with a wince and followed her.

My hands shook as I climbed into her car, and I didn't remember much of the drive.

Rachel parked the car down the road from where our old foster home was, and I tried not to feel the memories and whiskey threatening to rise in my throat. The last time we were at this house, we were being taken away by our caseworker, and our foster mom was being shoved into a cop car. A new family had moved in, blissfully ignorant of the horrors that had occurred inside that house only a few years before.

Flashes of Lucas's little face and bright, scared eyes threatened to bring me to tears, but the cold air bit away the memories when I opened the car door. Shivering, Rachel and I took our first steps into the woods.

I pushed through the bramble of the woods, twigs snapping underfoot as I dodged a branch that threatened to smack me in the forehead. Rachel cracked a joke about my proclivity to hitting my head. I attempted a smile, but it hardly broke the tension like she had probably intended. I was too focused on discerning the trees in the shadows, the beams of our phone flashlights shedding only so much light. The sounds of Rachel stumbling and cursing echoed through the woods.

My memory also seemed to be failing me—I couldn't quite remember the track we used to take. Veer right at the dogwood, continue straight, then pass the giant sycamore and take a left. It was early spring, and the leaves still hadn't fully come out of hiding, so it was hard to discern which tree was which. We had just passed what I thought was the dogwood with the sycamore in our sights when the outline of a little shack began to form through the shadows. It looked smaller than I remembered. It felt like going back to your elementary school and seeing just how small it actually was now that you are looking at it with grown eyes.

As we approached, I scanned the shack for any evidence of my brother. There was a sudden flap of wings that startled me, and I nearly dropped my phone. There must have been an owl inside the shack, scared away by my flashlight. Part of the roof had caved in, and there were patches in the outer wall that had weathered away. Otherwise, it looked almost the same as it did before.

Heart pounding, I circled the shack until I came across the little door that still hung on its broken hinges like before. It screeched when I pushed it open. I shone my light into the dark space, but kept a careful eye on my periphery. The floor inside was covered with leaf scatter and snapped twigs, but still no sign of Lucas. I stepped in further, crushing an enormous dead sycamore leaf with my foot. I directed my beam of light onto the dilapidated walls, but there was

17

something I didn't recognize. Someone had painted on them, but it wasn't typical graffiti. Instead, it looked like someone had hand-painted the planks. Little figures danced across the wood, some carrying bows, and others shooting something out of their hands, like ice or magic. On the far left wall were hastily drawn figures, smaller than the others, and towards the short ceiling was a larger figure, one that looked to be the overseer of the smaller ones. Something told me that this wall was at war with the figures on the other wall.

"Hey, Rachel, come look at this," I called.

I was met with silence. I peered out of the window to find only the shapes of the scraggly trees and vines that had tried to ensnare us on our way here. I called Rachel again, but there was no response. I went to take a step towards the door to find my friend, when I stepped on something. Stooping down to investigate, my heart froze in my chest.

It was the other Bone Chronicle book Lucas bought just yesterday. The cinnamon sugar stain was still smeared across the dedication page.

A twig snapped at the door, and I stepped over to find my friend, only to retreat immediately into the shack. My knees trembled, and I let myself sink to the floor with my hand covering my mouth and nose to keep the sudden reek of rotting flesh from assaulting my nostrils. Another twig snapped, and then the sound of heavy footsteps circled the shack. The footsteps dragged across the leaves as if the person walking had a bad leg. Another second passed when my stomach dropped. The footsteps I was hearing weren't coming from two legs, but four. I swallowed, and my saliva was like glass against my throat. The thing sniffed at the window across from me, and two furry ears peeked over the sill. They would have been cute had it not been for the rotten stench that suddenly washed over me. I stifled my breath, trying to breathe in as little as possible.

It looked like it could've been a wolf, but there were multiple things wrong with that fact. For one, Pennsylvania lacked a native wolf population. And even in the unlikely chance there was a wolf in Pennsylvania, this thing sounded much larger, judging by the heavy steps it took. Besides, what wolf smelled so overwhelmingly like death?

The thing had made its way to the door and sniffed the threshold. In another second or two, it would find the open door, and I would be dead. Without another thought, I rose and slid through the window behind me, praying my sneakers would be quiet on the forest floor. As soon as my feet connected with the ground, the creature stepped into the shack. It filled almost the entire space inside. That was no wolf. No wolf's eyes glowed like this one's did. I took a step back, not taking my eyes off the beast as it sniffed the corners of the shack and tried to track my scent.

My foot snapped a twig.

And then the glowing eyes were on me.

Without another thought, I fumbled my phone and bolted.

I jumped over a fallen tree and ran until my lungs started to burn, not daring to look back. I wove in between the trees to throw the wolf off, but to no avail. I dared to take one look behind me, only to stumble at the sight of the massive thing hounding closer and closer, its glowing eyes locked onto me with deadly precision. A branch snagged my cheek and drew blood, and I ran my hand over the stinging skin. Without my phone's flashlight, I couldn't avoid the overgrown branches and sharp underbrush. The scent of death crept closer, but I kept going, sure that I'd find the road eventually. Or some form of civilization.

When the air in my lungs grew sharp, and no amount of gasping could give me enough oxygen, I slowed down even though it meant my death. It was almost poetic that running would be what ended my life, seeing as I nearly failed gym in high school. I could only maintain a quick jog until the inevitable happened.

I tripped.

My body hit the ground hard, and the thud vibrated the forest floor, like a web alerting the spider that the fly was stuck.

Only a few feet behind me was the wolf, circling me with slobber strings swaying from its jowls as it scrunched its muzzle and bared its teeth. I swallowed, too aware of my heart trying to beat through my ribs. Every breath I took stung, and my legs twinged, too weak to carry me any further. I prayed to whatever god would answer me that my brother be found and taken to safety, to make sure he grew up and became a fireman or a scientist or a police officer. He could grow up and become a moth, as long as he was safe. I prayed he would forgive me for not adopting him and for those things I said in the park. I begged him to forgive me for trying to leave that night.

"Don't move," a little voice said.

I froze.

Then an arrow shot down and struck the wolf in the eye. A second arrow was fired, not even a second later, and lodged in the wolf's side. It whined a pathetic squeal and took a step back, one glowing eye still locked on me. A third arrow launched and impaled the other eye. It planted a weak paw on the ground as if it were trying to take a step toward me, then gave a snarl that came off as a grunt. Its front paw gave out, and it fell to the ground with a thud, motionless. It was dead.

Relief couldn't stop me from gaping at the scene in front of me, especially with the way my blood thrummed through my veins. I stood and wiped my hands on my pants. Mud caked the knees of my jeans, and my once white sneakers were now an earthy shade of brown with bits of dead leaves clinging to them.

Another thud sounded to my right, and as I turned my head, I beheld a small boy sidling out of a tree a few feet away.

Lucas...

The boy's nearly white hair wiped that possibility from my mind, and my heart sank. He wore brown pants and a short brown tunic, covered with a leather vest. Boots covered his feet, and a quiver of arrows was slung over his shoulder. I eyed the bow clutched in his hands. The arch was inlaid with carvings painted with gold, and the tips curled inward to hug the string. It was beautiful.

"You're welcome," the boy said tightly, standing a little straighter.

I choked back a laugh of both relief and indignation. "I'm sorry?"

"It's not like I just saved you from the fenr or anything."

A look of confusion took over my face before I could stop it. "A what?"

The boy scrunched his nose in wonder. "A fenr..." he answered and gave me an expectant look. "Descendant of Fenrir, the wolf of Ragnarok?"

"Sounds like you've been watching a lot of Marvel, huh?"

It was his turn to look confused. "Huh?"

"Did you happen to see a taller girl come through here? Curly brown hair, wearing a green parka?" Really pretty and everything I wanted to be in life.

Confusion only deepened in his young features. "What's a parka?"

For heaven's sake.

"Isn't it a little late for you to be in the woods by yourself?" I asked. Realization dawned on me. "Was that your shack back there? Do you live there?" The boy only responded with another confused "huh?" When I pushed further about Rachel, he only shrugged and said I should be glad my friend missed being pursued by the wolf. Fenr, I guess.

"What's your name?" I asked, hoping that would be a question he would actually answer.

20

"Nilsen," he answered and slung the bow over his shoulder.

"Okay, Nilsen, my name is Layla, and I think I'm a little bit lost. Can you take me to your parents?"

Nilsen's eyes saddened a touch. "No, my parents are dead. But I have a brother I can take you to."

I nodded, unsure what else to do. Perhaps it was this sudden connection I had with Nilsen that pushed me to follow him. He reminded me a little of Lucas, the way his shaggy hair fell into his eyes, but the swagger in his step was where the similarities stopped. Maybe I decided to follow him because I understood the heaviness his features took on when he mentioned his dead parents. From one orphan to another, it was a feeling we were all too familiar with.

Nilsen gestured for me to follow, and after swallowing the screaming trepidation pumping through me, I complied. Our feet shuffled the leaves underfoot as we walked, and a faint night wind tickled my skin. Now that my blood was calming down, the night's chill was creeping through my muscles and permeating my bones. I rubbed my arms.

"You're lucky I was there to save you," Nilsen said. "Fenrs are vicious. They don't kill for survival like normal wolves. They kill for sport. They like the slaughter."

My stomach dropped. If it weren't for this kid, I would've been...slaughtered. I shuddered at the thought. I tasted whiskey as it rose in my throat at my next thought. Was Lucas...

No, I couldn't think like that. He was alive and safe, wherever he had run off to.

"I've been tracking this one for a while," Nilsen continued as he ducked under a low branch. "He's been killing off all of our game, and there's been a venison shortage for a week now." The longer we spoke, the more unmistakable the slight lilt in his voice became. It was a hint of an accent, where the final syllables of his words had a slight intonation, almost melodic.

I narrowed my eyes in puzzlement. "Do you guys like to live off the grid or something?"

"I don't know what that means."

I shook my head and waved my question away. "How do you know it was a he?"

Nilsen giggled. "The males are smaller than the females. Trust me, you'd know if it was a girl. Neither one of us would have survived."

I paused, worry settling into me. "Where exactly are you taking me?"

"To the village," he answered.

"A village?"

"My village."

I nodded slowly. "Are you...Is it like a religious village or something?" Images of the Heaven's Gate and Jim Jones documentaries I had to watch for class flashed in my mind, and I started to reconsider following Nilsen.

"No."

We walked for a little while longer in silence; the only noise was that of the forest. My mind swirled and tried to grasp what exactly had transpired in the last twelve hours. My brother went missing, Rachel and I went into the woods, Rachel was now missing or dead, some mystically large wolf chased me, this kid saved me from it, and now we're on the way to his "village." As unthinkable as this entire evening was, I just hoped Rachel was okay. We weren't close, but work would suck a lot more if she weren't there. I hated that the wolf gave me no time to search for her, but it was life or death. Maybe I drew it away from her, and she was able to make it back to the car. I clung to the thought and prayed it to be true.

"We're almost there," Nilsen assured, and I looked forward. In the distance, I could see the faint twinkling of firelight and the shapes of buildings.

"I just..." I began.

"Hallow..."

I stopped, and ice froze in my veins. It was not Nilsen who had spoken. The voice was cold, as if whoever had spoken had just crawled out of a frozen lake. Nilsen stopped as well and scoped the clearing. The voice spoke again, the repeated word dripping with chill. Nilsen began to tremble.

My breath clouded in front of me as if the temperature had plummeted below freezing. I shivered when the cold settled into the pit of my stomach. Then an icy pair of hands planted on the base of my back, and my insides turned to slush. My breath became shallow as it froze in my throat, coating it in hoarfrost. Staying awake was becoming increasingly complex—all I wanted was to curl up on the fallen leaves and cave into the growing fatigue. Sleep seemed inevitable now, and my eyelids drooped heavily. I was growing hollow, hollow, hallow, hallow, *hallow*...

Nilsen's small, grimy hand locked onto mine and pulled me out of my trance, toward the light of the village. Warmth flooded back into my body as if I had just plunged into a hot bath. As we ran, I began to feel invigorated. All around us, little shadows darted out of the trees, beady eyes watching us. A frigid chill followed us and hissed in my ears.

"Hallow..."

Little voices and giggles started closing in on us.

"Hey!" Nilsen shouted as the lights of the village grew brighter. "Hey! Get Aaren!"

As we approached, I saw two men congregating around a large brazier that billowed white smoke into the air. At the sound of Nilsen's voice, one darted away, quick on his feet. He moved as if he were made of air.

Nilsen's little hand was too sweaty to hold onto, and it slipped from mine, leaving me to tumble to the ground. My knees scraped across the leaf litter, and my palms slid into soft earth.

"Hallow..."

The biting chill returned and crept up my spine, every hair follicle on my scalp prickling. Goosebumps rose on my arms, and I could see my breath again.

"Take me..."

I pushed myself up again, wavering on my feet when something jumped on my back and wrapped its legs around my waist while its arms snaked over my shoulders. "Hallow," it said directly in my ear. My knees buckled under the weight as the thing's frozen breath tickled the side of my face. Hard ground met my knees, and jolts of pain shot through my legs as the night seemed to grow darker around me. There was shouting ahead, coming closer by the second. Nilsen was dragged away from me as a group of men sprinted forward.

"Hallow...Take me..."

Cold hands enveloped my throat, and the legs around my waist tightened as I pitched forward, reaching out to catch myself before my face hit the ground. My eyelids threatened to close, to give in to the cold exhaustion now settling into me. "Hallow..."

A man darted towards me, massive and bulky with muscle. His arms were outstretched as if to reach for me, but instead of grabbing me, he wrenched the thing that had attached itself to my back. Its grip broke, and life spilled into me once more, blood beginning to fill my veins again, warmth flushing my skin and pumping through me. I gasped when the cool forest air flooded my lungs.

I rolled over and propped myself up on my elbows, now aware of my surroundings. Nilsen was yelling behind me, not a fearful shout, but loud words of explanation, saying that he had found the fenr chasing me, that I was lost, and he was trying to help me. The muscular man who had detached the creature from me now held it out in front of him. The thing was just that: a thing. It was a mass of shadows that wriggled and writhed in his strong hands. It was about the shape and size of a small child, and it hissed and snarled at him. A muscle ticked in his jaw as he shook the creature.

"You have no place here," he commanded, and his voice was like a deep rumble of thunder. A vein protruded in his temple as fury smoldered across his high cheekbones, and the chilled air went static. "Leave!" The thing shrieked as he tossed it onto the ground, stepping towards it. "No hallow! Leave!"

The thing quickly skittered away on shadowy legs. Other creatures like it watched and hissed from the trees as the thing joined them. Within a matter of seconds, the things had all vanished. The clearing was warm once again and silent except for the crackle of electricity that kept the hairs on my arm at attention. It was like the brief moments before lightning strikes.

The humming energy in the air heightened, and I realized it was coming from the dangerously built man. He turned his attention to me, and my heart fluttered. He was very handsome. I'd never seen someone so handsome. I tried to note his features, examine the fine lines of his face, but my vision blurred, darkness encroaching on the edges. He studied me with a hardened face. "Who is she?"

Nilsen began to shout his explanations again, but before I could discern exactly what he was saying, my arms weakened as pure exhaustion set into me. My vision grew fuzzier, and my heart slowed as my eyelids drooped. I suddenly fell into one of the deepest sleeps I've ever had.

Chapter 5

The smell of something foul wafted to my nose and jerked me out of my dreamless sleep. Bile rose in my throat, and I coughed, moving to sit up, but a hand nudged my shoulder and eased me back onto the bed. A soft, hardy voice told me to lie back down. I cracked my eyes open to see a small woman standing over me, her hair covered in a white cap with gray strands spilling out. In her right hand was a jar filled with a dark green goop that bubbled and popped. A quick whiff in the direction of the smell told me it was coming from there.

My eyes shifted around me, mystified by my surroundings. I was in a room with single-pane windows where sunlight streamed through to illuminate the various gadgets and jars on the tables and shelves. On one table was a mortar and pestle, inside of which something emitted small orange flames. Next to it were jars filled with herbs of every color and shape, lined up neatly. There was a ledger open next to the jars, but I was too far away to see what was written in it. A fire crackled in a hearth off to the side with a pot sizzling in the middle. On the walls hung brooms, other tools I had never seen before, and the books on the shelves had titles in languages I had never known existed. I shifted my gaze to the windows and beyond, following the stretching trunks of the magnificent trees outside.

The horrid smell brought me back to the woman in front of me. The odor was overpowering as she rubbed it on my chest, and I studied her curiously. Her eyes bore crows feet and her smile lines ran deep on her red cheeks. A thin sheen of sweat covered her forehead as she worked, and I heard her taking shallow breaths to smell as little of the paste as possible. Her clothes puzzled me even more. The woman wore a dress that stopped just above her mid-calf, exposing her thick ankles, and on her feet, she wore flat, brown leather shoes. Covering the front of her dress was a dirtied apron smeared with the green liquid from the jar, among other things.

"What is this stuff?" I croaked, wincing at the tightness in my throat.

"It's luktrot," the woman answered. "Foul-smelling. However, it will help replenish your energy. We give this to mothers after they've given birth." She smeared a bit more on my chest. It reminded me of when Granny used to put Vicks VapoRub on me when I was sick. I would much prefer VapoRub to this stuff. "It speeds up healing and revitalizes. Good thing it's in season too, or you might have been out of luck."

"Where am I?" I questioned.

"Best leave the questions for later, dear," she said and placed the jar down. "You need to rest." The woman stoked the fire, fluffed my pillow, and stepped out into the bright sunlight.

I pushed myself up onto my elbows and realized what I was tucked into. Draped over my lap were smooth furs from animals I didn't recognize, mixed with some that I did. A couple were deer skins, and one looked like it could've belonged to a wolf, though, as I found out last night, it could be from something much different. I ran my fingers over one and felt the bristles tickle my fingertips. It was softer than I expected, and I kneaded my fingers into it, relishing the squishy texture under my palms.

I shed the furs from my lap and placed a foot on the ground, feeling the cold wood planks under my feet. I wore a soft nightgown that hung loosely around my frame, and I shivered at the draft. Embarrassment rose in my cheeks at the thought of someone removing my other clothes and dressing me in this. I stepped over to the fire to warm up. Kneeling before the hearth, I peered into the flames and savored the crackle as I watched them dance and flicker amongst the wood. It had been a while since I had seen an actual wood-burning fireplace. Granny had one, but towards the end, she never really used it, and Lucas and I were too young to start one. One of my foster parents had a fireplace, but it was gas-powered, so you couldn't enjoy the crackling and popping like the one before me.

The door opened, bringing in a cool breeze that felt more like a gale-force wind. Goosebumps rose on my arms as I froze, feeling suddenly naked in the nightgown.

A tall man strode in, his boots dancing lightly across the floor. His graying hair was pulled back out of his face, and the firelight illuminated his blue eyes. He wore clothes in hues of brown and green, mostly made of an unfamiliar fabric. He reminded me of a costumed educational interpreter, the kind of person you would find at a restored historical site. I went to a restored mansion in middle school, and the man who led our tour was dressed similarly to the one in front of me. But there was something more whimsical in the way this man was dressed. Maybe it was the intricate designs embroidered on his vest or the way his green shirt looked as if it had been woven from the very green of the forest. It looked like his clothes were made with magical fingers.

"Hello," he said softly with a slight nod of his head. In just one word, I could hear that same accent I heard last night from Nilsen.

26

I stood and hugged my arms around my middle.

The man straightened, his hands grasping behind his back as if he were at attention. I pressed my lips together politely and stepped over to the bed to sit, unable to find the words to greet him.

"I'm Rorik," he said, stepping over to the chair and sinking into it, his spine remaining tall. Deep laugh lines hid under his stubble, leading into a dimpled chin that curved up his square jaw and into an accentuated brow bone, his blue eyes underscored by small, aged bags. He appeared to be in his late sixties, but something about the way he carried himself suggested he was much, much older. I softened as I took in his kind face, and the hostile walls that had been building within me crumbled a little until there was just enough brick to hide behind should things turn south.

"I'm Layla," I answered, once again feeling the scratchiness in my throat.

"Very nice to meet you, Layla," Rorik replied. "I see Asta has given you some luktrot."

My hand grazed my chest in remembrance. The smell had worn off, and the paste had now hardened, beginning to crack and flake. The woman was right. I was feeling more restored, and the cut on my cheek had stopped throbbing. Rorik stood to grab a rag and dunk it in a washbasin by the fire. He handed it to me, and I began scrubbing the substance off my skin.

"I would first like to begin with welcoming you to our village," he paused. "We call it Skoghjem."

I blinked in confusion. "How far is it from Harrisburg?" I asked as I scoured a stubborn patch of luktrot that had caked hard on my collarbone.

Rorik furrowed his brow. "I'm not sure I follow," he answered. "Is that where you're from?"

"You've never heard of Harrisburg?" I demanded. He gazed at me in bewilderment. "It's...never mind. I need to get back there. I have things to do." And someone, now two someones, to look for.

Rorik's expression turned grim as he examined the bowl full of flames that somehow had not died out. He slipped a finger into the bowl where the flames circled his knuckles as if greeting him. I refused to let my wonderment show, a feat proving ever more difficult the longer I stayed here. "I'm afraid that is not permitted at the moment."

27

I tossed the rag onto the furs, and my temper crackled to life. "What do you mean it's not permitted?" I shook my head in puzzlement. "Are you holding me hostage?"

Rorik breathed a sigh through his nose, fingers leaving the bowl of flame. He rose with something like grace in his step as he glided to the fire and gazed into it. "Of course not. But we have some concerns about your arrival and our village."

I shook my head again. "I...walked. Actually, I ran, because a 'fenr' was chasing me."

Rorik inhaled deeply as if he were already trying to find the patience to deal with me. Turning to me, he explained, "Our village has very strict magical barriers around it. Barriers that have protected us for centuries. The founders of our kind erected them, and no human can cross them."

Magical barriers? Huh.

I nodded in mock understanding, deciding to humor him for the sake of getting some answers. "So you're wondering how I crossed them."

Rorik's expression softens. "Yes."

I couldn't help but laugh to myself. Something told me that this was a little more complex than me stumbling on a LARP convention. Do these people live like this? It reminded me of a movie I watched in high school, of a village that didn't know the modern world was beyond their borders. Did Harrisburg have its own closed-off society that no one was aware of? And if that were the case, I could be in danger. My mind ran through every scenario that could happen should I decide to leave, my heart sinking as each one ended poorly. For now, the best course of action would be to play along. Once night fell, I could sneak off and find my way back to town, where I could report Rachel's disappearance and keep looking for Lucas.

Although that didn't explain the massive wolf or the shadow that latched itself onto me, my psychology-educated brain rationalized that I was experiencing a stress-induced psychosis, my brain creating a delusion to hide the danger of what really happened to me. But it was all so real.

Blinking, I waved the troubling thoughts aside.

"Let me reiterate," he said. "*Humans* cannot cross."

I crossed my arms over my chest. "So." I smacked my lips. "You're implying I'm not human."

Rorik raised his shoulders in response. "That I have yet to figure out. If you were human, you couldn't have crossed our borders. Not to mention, a human hasn't been seen in our realm in thousands of years."

"So if humans cannot cross into your *realm*, what would that make you?"

Rorik chuckled. "That can be a tricky question. We're a hybrid race. Many confuse us with elves, but we descend from them. We are the Fraalver."

"The what?"

He repeated it: *Fr-all-ver.*

These guys were in deep character.

"Our realm is called Alveland."

This was already getting hard to follow.

"And what does that make me?" I demanded.

"If you were anything but Fraalver, you wouldn't be here." Rorik's pinched fingers found his chin as he took a moment to think. He muttered something under his breath.

"You wouldn't happen to be a full-bred elf, would you?"

I scoffed. "Wouldn't I have the ears to prove it?" I asked, trying to keep the joking out of my tone.

Rorik's lips thinned as he shook his head. "Ear clipping is not as uncommon as you would think amongst the elves. Particularly with elves that have been found to have a drop of Fraalver in them. If you're not an elf, then you must be Fraalver."

I shook my head slowly, trying to conceal the skepticism on my face.

The corners of Rorik's mouth tugged as he cocked his head. "You don't believe me." I bit my lip in answer. "Come," Rorik gestured to the door. "Let me show you the village."

I looked down at the thin nightgown. "Not wearing this, I'm not."

Chapter 6

Despite the warm clothes Rorik had provided me, I still felt naked without my bra—and I was very concerned about its whereabouts.

The bright sunlight blinded me as I stepped out of the warm hut. Before me lay a scene reminiscent of a fantasy television show; it almost looked like an episode of Vikings, but a lot cleaner and far less brutal. To my right was a sparring ring where two men clashed and clanged with swords while a crowd of spectators gaped and oohed as they dueled. To the left was a blacksmith toiling at a grindstone, white hot sparks flying from a crisp blade. Before me was a massive lodge constructed of sawn logs, with horn wall sconces framing the large double doors. Fraalver people walked here and there, some carrying baskets of vegetables, others sporting weapons strapped to their backs. Every single one of them was gorgeous.

A dog barked in the distance, and a herd of goats milled across our path. My eyes scouted the forest around me, overwhelmed by hues of green and brown and shining sunlight. Birds soared through the trees and deposited twigs amongst their nests as little heads poked up from branches to beg for worms from flapping mothers.

A group of children sprinted past us, giggling and clapping at each other. One girl had her hair pulled back into long blonde braids. Another had hers braided and pinned to her head. The boys had longer shaggy hair and all wore similar clothes to the ones I had seen Rorik and the other woman wearing. A twinge of doubt danced in my mind as I took in the scene in front of me. How likely is it that I really did stumble on a fantasy world?

Maybe it was a cult.

"Everyone here has a job," Rorik began as he led me down the path on the left. "Some Fraalver choose to follow the path their predecessors chose for them. We have a handful of farmers who not only provide for themselves, but also for the rest of the village at a small cost. We have two butchers..." he paused as we approached a stand attached to a small hut. Hanging from hooks were hocks of ham, chunks of venison, and slivers of beef laid out to be trimmed. Behind the stand was a small building with smoke swirling out of the top. I inhaled and relished the smoky scent of the cooking meat. My mouth began to water, and my stomach growled.

"Are you hungry?" Rorik asked when he heard my stomach's protestations.

I nodded when I realized I hadn't eaten anything since the day before. I had been too worried to eat. Rorik excused himself for a moment, then slipped into a larger structure with a wrap-around porch a few feet away. A few Fraalver lounged under the awning, sipping from pewter goblets as they laughed and joked. Rorik soon returned with a chunk of bread with cheese and a handful of blackberries, which he handed to me when we started walking again.

"That's the pub," he said, pointing to the building where he emerged. The Fraalver outside shouted and waved at him. Rorik beamed and waved back, but denied their invitations to sit and drink with them. "It's the main gathering place aside from the meeting hall for official matters. Inaborg serves a wonderful pigeon pie."

He veered us off to the left, explaining that there were two bookshops, both specializing in a particular genre they carried. One was for pleasure reading, and the other was for the history of their land and different kinds of recountings.

Bookstores and pubs—maybe this place couldn't be all bad. But I wasn't sure how I felt about pigeon pie.

The breeze picked up and sliced an icy chill across my skin, reminiscent of the dead hands that held me just last night. I shuddered as I remembered the hollow feeling...the hallow...

"Rorik?" I began. "What was that thing that attacked me last night?"

He paused and waited for a pair of women to pass before he spoke. "It was a myling." Tension rippled in his voice. "They are the souls of unclean children."

My skin prickled. I had a ghost child latch onto me last night. Its little hands wrapped around my neck, and I grew weary, as if it were sucking the life out of me.

"It kept saying something," I began, "hallow. What does that mean?"

Again, he paused as a lone Fraalver man passed. "Mylings are the souls of children that were not laid to rest properly. They seek the afterlife through a proper pyre burning, but they can never have that since their bodies were never found. They will latch onto a person and drain them until they are taken to the hallowed land." He exhaled. "Until last night, no one had seen a myling in these lands for hundreds of years."

And the first one to reappear was strapped to my back.

We meandered through the village on the dirt path while Rorik pointed out every feature he could. Most of the croplands were in the clearings on the outskirts, and the farmers were some of the more well-off people in the village. Rorik and Asta ran the apothecary, the hut where I woke up, and he also served as the advisor to Aaren, the village leader. The sparring ring was open to anyone who wanted to duel and practice, and some spectators placed friendly wagers. No one left bloodied, maybe only bruised, and most finished their fights in high spirits. The river was accessible by horseback a few miles away, but unless it was necessary, most people avoided it. Rorik said that certain entities and sprites plagued the shores, and it proved to be more of a risk to venture there.

After a full lap around the village, I retreated to the apothecary and settled back into the furs on the bed under the guise that I was going to rest a bit more, but I had other plans. Once Rorik closed the door, I darted over to the hearth and felt along the warm mantle for any evidence of modernity, whether it be a car key or a watch. But there was nothing, not even a single fleck of dust. When my search came up empty, I danced over to the table where the mortar and pestle that once held small dancing flames were sitting. The flames had died and smoldered at the bottom. Each jar was labeled in that same strange language. I picked one up and beheld its contents.

Blodreparsjon was scribbled on the label, and the herbs inside displayed hues of crimson red and deep brown. I shook it, and even though the herbs were dried and flaky, it gurgled.

I picked up another jar. *Slimavvisende* was the name of this concoction. The herb itself was a mix of white flowers and flakes of dark brown bark, and upon closer inspection, small mites crawled amongst the ruffage. I gently placed the jar back and shuddered.

The ledger on the table revealed nothing of importance, so I moved along to a shelf that held a couple of boxes, each of a different material. One box was made of clay, and as I went to pick it up, it cracked in my hands, and a few bugs crawled free. I placed it hurriedly back on the shelf and shook my wrists, trying to shake the feeling of the phantom insects crawling up my arms. I picked up a wooden box and cracked it open, only for a loud squeaking to emit from the darkness inside. Again, I placed the box back on the shelf. My search was yielding no results, and I was getting frustrated. And my hands were unusually hot and sweaty.

With a grunt of frustration, I stomped back to the bed. Before I could pull back the furs and climb in, the door opened and Nilsen trampled in. He slammed the door behind him and pressed his weight against it.

"Hey..." I greeted as I shoved my feet under the covers to warm them.

"Hi," Nilsen whispered.

I ducked my head and narrowed my eyes at him. "Why are you whispering?" I murmured.

Nilsen trudged over to the fire and held his hands out to warm them. "Because I'm in trouble," he answered nonchalantly. He dropped his hands and turned to me. "I wasn't supposed to go after the fenr."

"Well, thankfully, you did; otherwise, I'd be dead," I assured.

"That's why I don't care that I'm in trouble. Aaren can be mad at me all he wants, but I saved you, so I'm a hero."

I cocked my head. "Aaren...that's your leader," I inquired, remembering the unnerving energy the man exuded.

"He's my brother," Nilsen corrected.

I raised my brows in surprise.

Nilsen's eyes gazed around the apothecary. "I've only ever been in here once," he said. I asked him when. "When the visitor came. She carried a rake, and she didn't speak to anyone. I remember the colored cloak she wore. It was kind of green," he paused to think, "like the color of peas." I chewed my lip so as not to laugh. "Some people couldn't see her face. But my Far did. He said she was really pale. Mor saw it, too." His eyes circled the room. "They got really sick. Everyone who saw the visitor's face got sick." His eyes landed on me. "The last time I was in here was when they died."

My throat tightened.

He stepped over to the table where some of the jars were lined up and examined them. "She walked through the village and left. No one has seen her since." He picked up the jar of luktrot and toyed with the lid.

"Is that why your brother is in charge now?"

Nilsen nodded. "He doesn't want to be, but it's his duty to our people."

He twisted the top off the jar, and before I could warn him, he took a big whiff. His face turned green as he fell out of the chair with a howl and gagged at the scent. I couldn't hold back my laughter this time, and I threw my head back and cackled.

Nilsen picked himself up and shook away the smell. Then he froze. "Beans!" he exclaimed, his hands flying to his head in distress.

My brow scrunched. "Beans?"

"Beans! I'm supposed to be picking beans as punishment, and I forgot!" Nilsen scampered to the door. "If Aaren finds out, he said he'd string me by my toes and leave me for the Nokken!"

He uttered a rushed goodbye, and a second later, I was alone.

What the hell was a Nokken? And where in the actual hell am I? My head began to scramble with confusion as I added up all the things I knew about this place. They obviously had no idea what the modern world was like, and if they did, they hid it very well. They believed they were an ancient race of half-elves, and different creatures roam their "realm." I'd have to crack open my psychology textbook to put a label on the psychosis these people were suffering from.

It was terrifying how fast things could happen. Just this time yesterday, I was standing outside of Sarah's house. Lucas had been missing for a full twenty-four hours. Another twenty-four hours, and the likelihood of him coming home decreased.

I sank back into the bed as a wave of exhaustion washed over me. My eyes rested on the ceiling, tracing the strange lines carved into the wood above the bed. The swirls and curved lines circled in and out of each other, crossing here and there. It resembled an ancient Nordic symbol, one that would be found on a recreation of a Viking shield.

I was still staring at the ceiling, trying to make sense of things, when the door opened. Half expecting it to be Rorik, I casually sat up, only to stiffen when I glimpsed who it was.

I nearly gasped at the unnaturally yellow eyes that stared back at me. It was the man from last night, the one who had wrenched the myling off my back and sent it away with one fell swoop.

In daylight, I could examine his features more closely. He had a sharp nose and a straight jawline, a dimple in the middle of his chin. His features were set in a stern expression, and he lacked the laugh lines so many of the others possessed. His nearly white hair ended a little past his shoulders and was pulled back from his face. The firelight danced in his amber eyes, and I gaped at the size of his shoulders. I bet he crushed everyone in the sparring ring. His expression was one of harsh composure, unyielding as he roved over me. If it weren't for the furs that I had tucked myself into, I would feel exposed, the thought sending a rallying irritation in me. Behind the severity in his face, he was very attractive. So was everyone in this village, apparently, but there was something about him that set him higher than all the others in my eyes. There was a way he held himself, firm and threatening, as if no one had ever dared to challenge him.

34

I was ready to be the first. Even though I could feel the power rippling off of him. One wrong move, and I could end up in a chokehold. Or worse, a snapped neck.

The man nodded at me in greeting and pulled over a chair, sitting on the edge and resting his elbows on his knees.

"Hello," he said gruffly, the formal greeting lacking any pleasantry. His voice rattled in my ears—I didn't expect it to be that deep. And despite the levity the accent gave the others who possessed it, it had the opposite effect for him. It made his rigidity more concrete. "I'm Aaren. Aaren Skokjer."

I prayed my surprise didn't show on my face. *This* was Nilsen's brother? The leader of this village? They looked alike, sharing the hair color, though Nilsen lacked Aaren's severity. Where Nilsen was playful, Aaren was rough, stringent, and I knew at that moment I wasn't going to like where this conversation would go.

"I'm Layla. Layla Ashford," I said through gritted teeth.

"So I've heard." His imperious tone set my teeth on edge. "It appears Nilsen has taken a liking to you."

I pressed my lips together. For Nilsen's sake, cordiality won the battle over aggression, and I clenched my sweaty palms together. "Well, if it weren't for him, I'd be dead," I said, masking my growing uneasiness. "He's calling himself a hero." Aaren remained emotionless, not even the slightest facial twitch to acknowledge he heard me.

Then he shifted in his chair. "So tell me, Layla Ashford," he began, "exactly how you crossed our borders." His jaw tightened, and his eyes burned in the firelight.

I shook my head and rolled my eyes. "Look, I really don't know how I got here." I took a deep breath as my initial courage abandoned me. "I just remember I was...looking for someone in the woods and that wolf...uh, fenr, came after me."

"Who were you looking for?"

I paused, debating whether I should reveal my brother, when a thought dawned on me. What if Lucas were here in the village? What if he also stumbled upon this village and was taken in? Or what if he was just taken? Could it be that these people found my brother wandering the woods and kidnapped him? I shuddered, trying to erase the image of my brother shackled in a basement somewhere. My plan tonight still stood. I was going to get out of here and find my brother. I just had to keep playing along until sundown.

"I was looking for my friend," I answered bluntly.

Aaren sat back in his chair, rubbing his thumb and forefinger together as he examined me. I tried not to squirm under his gaze. "We've checked our borders numerous times since you arrived, and we cannot find a single hole or gap." He sat forward, and his stare intensified. "And as soon as you come close to our borders, you bring a horde of mylings to our doorstep. So I'll ask you again, *Layla Ashford*, how did you cross our borders?"

My blood sizzled. "For the last time, *Aaren Skokjer*. I. Don't. Know."

His eyes flared, but his expression remained flat. "I have ways to get the truth out of you," he threatened, "ways that would make you squirm. I don't know what your intentions are for being here, but I will learn them." He stood, his footsteps heavy as he crossed to the door. "For now, you are a guest in Skoghjem. But you will be kept under a watchful eye." He opened the door. "Tread carefully, *Layla Ashford.*"

The door closed behind him.

Chapter 7

Rorik set up a room for me on the second floor of the pub where I would stay for the duration of my time here, which wouldn't be as long as he thought. As he left, he explained that I was free to order whatever I pleased and that I should try the roast the barkeep was serving that day. I didn't want to accept the generosity, especially with all of the trouble I had caused thus far. But Rorik hurried away before I could protest, and left the barkeep to lead me to my lodging.

The room itself was small, but still bigger than some of the rooms I had in the foster houses. There was a small bed covered in furs and skins shoved in the corner, and mounted above the wall was the massive claw of a creature I'm sure I had never seen before. There was a short bedside table with an empty drawer and a dresser next to the door. On the other side of the small room was a squat bookshelf full of books that were written in a language I didn't recognize but, oddly, understood. I pulled one off the shelf and thumbed through the pages, reading the unfamiliar language as though it were one of my psychology textbooks. I wasn't entirely sure how to read the markings across the page, but they were clear as day, and I read with complete comprehension. The insane part of my brain attributed this to Rorik's crackpot theory that I wasn't fully human.

Every second I spent here, I felt less and less human. And more and more irritated.

The dresser drawer groaned when I pulled it open to rifle through the unusual clothes within. Instead of the polyester tops and leggings I was accustomed to wearing, there were soft cotton shirts and vests similar to the ones I had seen some of the villagers wearing earlier that day. The second drawer revealed leathers and a few neatly folded nightgowns like the one I had woken up in. It was strange to see such practical clothing—I was accustomed to clothing that could benefit me in ways beyond simply covering me. The tight pants I wore to work were intended to help me earn more tips, but they didn't work nearly as well as when Rachel wore something similar. I wondered what she'd say about these clothes. A hint of a smile pulled my lips when I thought of her picking up a cotton shirt and examining it between pinched fingers.

I started pacing. The longer I stayed in this room, the less time I was spending finding a way to Lucas. I ran through every detail I already knew about his disappearance. Sarah's security alarm hadn't been set off, nor were there any signs of exit from any point in the house. It was almost like he had disappeared magically. Which could mean he was here. But that also meant that I would have to admit that magic existed, and these Fraalver people weren't living in the delusion I thought they were.

Yeah, right.

But I had to get out of here, magical delusion or not, and that meant leaving this room.

The air outside was chilly yet warm in the sunlight, and a gentle breeze caressed my cheeks. The day reminded me of a Charles Dickens quote my high-school comp teacher had us write about: "When it is summer in the light, and winter in the shade." It was the kind of day that would typically have me giddy for spring, but instead, I was anxious to find Lucas.

As I passed Fraalver on the path, I expected to be confronted with sneers and side eyes, but instead I was greeted with soft smiles and friendly nods. The people of Harrisburg needed to take a page out of these people's book. I trekked the perimeter and took note of each guard stand marked by a large brazier. I counted four, separated by large gaps where I could easily escape into the forest. It seemed too easy.

I continued my walk until I came upon the sparring ring where two women were dueling, each with a thin sword gripped in her hands. I wondered how hard it would be to smuggle one on my way out tonight.

The woman with brown hair smirked as she puffed a stray hair out of her face. The blonde scoffed and readjusted her grip on the hilt of her weapon as they circled each other. The brunette made the first move. Metal clanged as they glided across the platform, twirling left and right, an elbow flying here, a punch thrown there, all in a spectacular dance of steel and leather. The blonde got the upper hand and plunged her sword into the brunette's gut. I gasped, looking for red to spill from her abdomen and pool onto the wooden planks below, but instead, the blonde pulled out the blade. It came out clean, and the brunette did not fall or kneel in agony, but simply bowed to her partner and stepped off the platform.

There was an amused chuckle beside me, and I turned to see a small woman beaming at my horror. "They're enchanted weapons," she explained as my shock dissipated. "Anytime the blade comes in contact with flesh, it becomes incorporeal. It cannot wound." I nodded in understanding. There was no point trying to steal a sword if it couldn't stop a myling. Or whatever else was out there.

"You're the stranger who brought the myling last night," the woman observed. "You've certainly caused some bustle amongst us, haven't you?"

I thinned my lips. "I suppose so," I answered, trying to avoid acknowledging last night.

The woman turned to me, wrapping her shawl around her as a sharp wind broke the crowd. "I'm Thea," she said. "I own one of the bookshops."

"Which one?" I asked.

Thea chuckled. "The one with the books people actually want to read. Do you really think Harald's shop is overflowing with visitors when all he sells is books on the Dwarf Wars and the Troll Executions?" She laughed. "I sell the good books." She turned back to the ring where two men stretched, then selected weapons for their spar. "I hope you learn to like it here," she says. "If you really aren't here for our destruction."

"Maybe I would like it, if I planned to stay," I blurted, wincing that my inside thoughts escaped.

We glanced at each other and burst into laughter, which turned heads. For the first time since Lucas's disappearance, I felt relief wash over me and fill my veins like a cool breeze. Thea's laugh was a booming melody that shook her bosom as she threw her head back. I took a moment to admire her mousy features that were relaxed in laughter. Her sharp nose gave way to lush lips that pulled back over white teeth. Her high cheekbones were dusted with a light rouge, and purple eyeshadow highlighted her brown eyes. She was beautiful. Her brown hair blew in the breeze as she wiped a tear from her eye and readjusted her shawl.

"Brave of you to assume Aaren would let you leave," she smirked. "He takes our security very personally."

Foolish of her to assume I cared.

Something small pushed into my hand, and I turned to see Nilsen standing behind me, his hand tugging at my fingers.

"I need to take you somewhere," he whispered with urgency.

Thea smiled pleasantly as Nilsen began tugging me away from her. "It was nice meeting you, Layla, bringer of mylings." I hid my grimace at the nickname. "Stop by my shop sometime. I'm sure you'll find a book you like."

Hesitantly, I followed Nilsen down the path away from the crowd. We weaved in and out of the buildings, and I skipped to keep up. Then I was following him outside of the village, gasping in the fresh forest air as I was now running so as not to lose Nilsen in the trees. I tried to keep track of the smaller landmarks in the forest to find my way back tonight, but he was pulling me too quickly to note anything of importance.

Nilsen slowed as we approached a large oak tree with stretching branches that towered into the sky. Nestled in the branches was a little treehouse made out of sawn logs, twigs, and a thatched roof. There was a little window where I saw a pair of eyes peering out at us. They disappeared when I squinted for a closer look.

We approached the tree, and Nilsen knocked three times. A knob appeared from the trunk, and he pushed it, the wood clicking under his palm. Up the side of the trunk, little divots just big enough for a foot began to carve themselves into the bark with a crunch. The divots reached all the way to the little house.

Nilsen began to climb, then paused midway to gesture for me to follow. I complied.

Hoisting myself up and bracing my foot, I felt the bark crumble and groan under my weight. As I took the next step up, the divot where my foot had been vanished. I began to climb faster.

At the top, we pushed through a trapdoor, and I gaped at the interior of the treehouse. It had looked small from the ground, but appeared larger as we moved inside.

The walls were made of smooth, shiny wood that curved gracefully around the window and the ceiling. Upon closer inspection, there were a few carvings etched into the sill. A large skin rug covered the majority of the floor, and throughout the room were wooden chests, some of which remained still while others emitted noises like chirps or gurgles. Posted in spots on the walls were little twigs and vines tied together to form obscure shapes, some even dangling from the ceiling. When I asked Nilsen what they were, he only said that they were for protection.

"We've already had one gnome problem," Nilsen shuddered. "We're not trying to have another."

Around the room, there were about twenty to thirty children, all of whom looked to be between five and twelve years old. Some sat in little chairs around the room, others played on the floor or ran in a game of tag. Nilsen raised his arms, and the treehouse fell promptly silent. Those not seated quickly found a chair or sank to the floor, and every pair of eyes was on me and Nilsen.

"I have brought Layla, myling hunter," Nilsen announced to the group. I bit my lip trying not to laugh. Something told me Nilsen embellished the story of the myling as he recounted it to his friends.

"Welcome, Layla, myling hunter," a girl spoke, her voice poised and regal. Trying not to chuckle, I turned to look at her and realized she was one of the girls I saw when Rorik showed me the village. She was the taller blonde with the braids.

Lucas and I used to play pretend when he was younger, and standing amongst this group of kids felt no different. His favorite game to pretend was a magic quest where we fought trolls and dragons, read enchanted books, and saved the princess from the tower. He would always play a knight and I an adventurer, and together, we embarked on endless journeys across the realm. My stomach panged in grief.

"Hello," I squeaked, feeling more intimidated by this group of kids than I did when I spoke with Aaren. Especially since the last time I was around a group of children, I yelled at them.

"I am Ingrid, leader of our gathering."

I nodded in recognition, clasping my hands in front of me in a polite manner.

Nilsen shuffled his feet next to me. "She's from a place called Harrisburg," he interjected. "It's not from our realm." A muffled chatter was emitted amongst the crowd, and a couple of children blurted out questions at me.

"And what do you do in Harrisburg?" Ingrid asked, her spine stiff as a board when she spoke.

"I go to school."

Ingrid scoffed. "You're too old for school."

"Well," I began, "it's a school for grown-ups. What is *your* school like?"

Ingrid considered my question, then dismissed it, choosing instead to ask her own. "What else is in Harrisburg?"

I paused to think of the fun places I got to go as a kid before Mama died. Places I wished I could've taken Lucas. "There is this huge place that is based on chocolate," I remembered Hershey Park fondly. Mama only took me once, but it was a core memory of mine. I was about six or seven, and she had gotten a bonus from work and decided to treat us to a trip. I don't remember everything, but I will never forget the build-your-own chocolate bar station. I made the most grotesque candy bar for any adult, but to me and my young taste buds, it was delicious.

"All for chocolate?" Nilsen asked, his eyes wide in amazement.

"Yep," I answered smugly. "And there are places called trampoline parks where you can go and jump on these things that make you bounce really high."

The kids stirred in excitement at this and began to chitter amongst themselves.

"Without jumping stones?" a kid asked.

I nodded, trying to think of what a jumping stone is.

The group quieted for a moment, but the children squirmed with too much excitement to maintain complete silence.

"What brought you to our forest?" Ingrid questioned.

Stick to the story you told Aaren, I reminded myself.

"I was looking for my friend." Ingrid remained quiet, awaiting more of my response. "I lost my friend, so I went looking for her. While I was in the woods, the fenr found me." I glanced at Nilsen. "If Nilsen hadn't been hunting it, I wouldn't be here right now." A few of the kids gazed up at Nilsen, who blushed in the spotlight. "He's a hero."

Some of the kids began to clap.

Before Ingrid could ask another question, a horn sounded in the distance. A symphony of moans and groans rose from the group as they all began to shuffle towards the trapdoor.

"What was that?" I asked Nilsen as we waited for the last of the kids to go through the door.

"That was the Hem horn. They blow it when the children need to come home. It can be heard for miles."

The setting sun outside confirmed the sound of the horn. I hadn't realized it had gotten so late.

Ingrid approached us, her braids trailing behind her. "Thank you for attending our meeting," she said, nodding her head in graciousness. "I hope you find what you're looking for." And with that, she turned and dropped through the trapdoor.

I bit my lip as I stifled a chuckle. "Is Ingrid always like that?"

Nilsen giggled. "No, only during meetings. She thinks she's this fearless leader, but she's not. You should have seen her during our gnome infestation. I've never heard someone scream like she did."

As our footsteps began to crunch along the forest floor, I heard the hoot of an owl in the branches overhead. With a rustle of feathers and branches, it took off into the night.

"That's Ugleverge," Nilsen said with his eyes trained to the sky where the owl had disappeared. "He guards our treehouse."

The sounds of the forest enveloped us as we trekked back to the village, allowing nature to fill my senses. Around us, crickets sang and leaves rustled in a cool breeze. The scent of wet moss and earth wafted into my nose. The first scents of spring I had smelled this year, and a quiet nostalgia stirred inside me. It was one of my favorite times.

As lovely an evening as it was turning out to be, I didn't let it distract me from scoping the natural landmarks that would help guide me through the dark tonight. I tried to find distinctive features, unlike the ones that led me to the shack. But I wasn't knowledgeable enough to identify a tree without its leaves.

As we approached the village, I noticed that the braziers had been lit, and light shone from old-fashioned sconces on each building. The village vibrated with a tense energy, the Fraalver exchanging furtive glances as they hurried home.

"I'm guessing they blew the horn for a reason other than nightfall," Nilsen observed as a Fraalver woman passed in a distressed rush.

Out of nowhere, Rorik stepped in front of us with a look of poorly masked disquiet on his face. "Nilsen, have Layla accompany you home; you don't need to be out any later."

"What's wrong?" Nilsen urged.

Rorik pressed his lips together, the firelight illuminating the strained shadows dancing across his aging skin. "Best I leave that to your brother to explain," is all he said before stepping away and muttering to a passing Fraalver. This one had a bow strapped to his back. The moment Rorik stopped muttering, the man dashed off, his black locks dancing over his shoulders as he moved.

Nilsen beckoned me to follow. We moved down a path, then turned right and left, passing by the medicine hut. As we passed, a scream sounded from inside, muffled, but loud enough to make my skin crawl. I tried to peer through the window as we passed, but what was once a clear windowpane was now murky and cloudy, making it nearly impossible to see through. I took a step further to move on when the door of the hut opened, and Aaren stepped out with a grave expression. His hair had been tied back in a hasty bun, and his sleeves were rolled up to reveal corded forearms that rippled when he crossed them over his chest. Aaren took one glance at me, and his jaw clenched. It seemed I was the last thing he wanted to see at the moment, which was just as well, because I shared that sentiment.

Nilsen stopped at the front door of a large house on the edge of the village. On the frame of the front door was another symbol that resembled two diamond goalposts with a line running down the middle. Nilsen waved his hand over it, and it shimmered, as if the grain within the wood were breathing. Then he traced his finger down the center line, and it vanished. The front door opened with a creak. I gawked at the symbol as it became solid once more.

"It's a door lock," Nilsen said. "They don't have those in Harrisburg?" I glanced down at the humor in his face and shook my head before taking a step inside.

I gazed around the room in awe. The ceilings high above were vaulted and hung with the skins of animals I had never seen. Each skin sported colors of forest green, aqua blue, ruby red, with spots and striations of other colors just as vibrant. They all had different textures as well; one of them, a scaly orange, caught my eye as it drifted lazily in the draft. On the walls were antlers, and upon closer examination, there were claws, tails, and fins on one plaque.

Stretched near the fireplace on the back wall was a long wooden table fashioned from sawn logs and smoothed to a shiny finish. Decorating the table was a runner of dried leaves that looked to be stitched together, and a bowl of bread and dried fruit was laid out, waiting to be eaten. The stone floor was neatly swept, and not a speck of dust or cobweb could be seen.

I strode over to the fireplace, where I inspected the carvings in the stone around the hearth. There was a minor etching of a man and a woman standing beneath a branch, their hands locked together in union. As my eyes moved along, more figures were added to the sketch until there were four of them. In between the new etchings were scenes of battle and valor. In one, the woman held a spear and faced off with a creature I did not recognize from any folklore I had ever seen. In another, the man stood over a crowd of misshapen figures, a head in his hands. Following the scene, a hooded figure was seen carrying a rake. At the end of the etchings, there were only two figures again, one small and one large. This was the story of Nilsen's family.

44

I swallowed, my throat raw from the heat, and as I turned away, my eyes caught sight of a small stone in the fireplace.

"What's the stone for?" I asked Nilsen as he sat down at the table with a small box in his hand.

"It's to keep the spirits away," he answered matter-of-factly, and he opened the box lid, pulling out its contents and placing them on the table in front of him.

I stepped away from the fireplace, already missing the heat, and sat down to study the pieces in front of me. "What is this?"

He had placed differently shaped figures made of something that resembled ivory, streaked with rivers of green. It reminded me of the crystals my roommate used to carry. Leah had been drawn to new age spirituality, and the house always smelled of incense when she was most stressed. She also collected crystals, sometimes clutching them tightly in the middle of a midterm. They must've worked because she got the highest grade in the class, either that, or the hours of studying paid off. But who was I to judge whether the crystals were actually magic? Apparently, I was surrounded by magic right now, and at this point, I was having trouble figuring out what was and wasn't real. Perhaps her crystals were effective, and maybe I was actually in a Tolkien book. The thought was laughable, but the voice in the back of my head didn't agree.

Looking into the box, I saw more figures, carved from a stone of deep ebony with red striations. I picked one up and saw that it was a little figurine of a man, oddly reminiscent of some of the fancier chess pieces I'd seen. I squinted to make out the details when it winked. I jumped, and the piece flew out of my hand and landed with a clatter on the table. Nilsen looked up from the box in confusion.

"What'd you do that for?" he demanded, reaching for the piece.

"It...it winked at me," I stammered.

"That means he likes you," Nilsen smiled. He placed the figure back on the table.

I shook my head and blinked. "But yours aren't moving."

Nilsen sighed in exasperation. "They only move if the player is touching them. By touching them, you give them life." He picked up an ivory and green piece. It wiggled in his touch and waved at him. "It's all part of the game."

Curiosity erased the hint of embarrassment I had previously felt. Crystal magic being real seemed less unlikely compared to the life in these game pieces.

"How do you play?"

Nilsen picked up one of his pieces, a particularly gleeful man who turned in Nilsen's hand and beamed at me. "This is Balder. He's the god of light and joy. He needs to be protected." I reached into the box and grabbed a second Balder piece. He came to life in my fingers and patted my hand to reassure me. I put him down, and he froze, the grin permanently etched into his face.

"Then you have two huldras." He slid over two pieces, both of which were beautiful women. I picked one up and watched the flowers in her hair flow in a wind I could not feel. She smiled sweetly and batted her eyes at me. I felt a tail poke through my knuckles. Nilsen snapped his fingers, and in an instant, her beautiful face shifted to that of a reptilian creature. Gone were the flora in her hair, replaced with twigs and dead leaves, and her tail that was once tufted with hair now ended in a sharp point. She bared tiny fangs at me, and a forked tongue poked through the corner of her mouth.

"You do *not* want to run into a huldra," he warned, and a faint shudder shook his body. "They will devour your piece in an instant." I gently set her back down, and her face returned to that of the beautiful woman set in stone.

"Then you have the troll." He slid the piece to me. It was a stout figure with ears that protruded from both sides of its head. Blemishes and craters dotted its face, and its teeth peeked out from its bottom lip. It looked like a smaller human, just...ugly. Despite the unappealing appearance, it had a kind face, and it cocked its head to consider me.

"You're lucky if you run into one of these," Nilsen lectured. "You get an extra turn. They're supposed to help you in real life, too, but no one has seen a troll for centuries." He paused, examining his piece. "Ingrid thinks they've gone extinct."

"The rest of the pieces are elves, dwarves, and humans. Elves will fight other elves, dwarves will fight dwarves and elves, and humans will fight everything." He began to arrange his pieces in front of him, and as I watched, I noticed that from behind, you couldn't tell which piece was which. Understanding dawned on me. I was supposed to find his Balder piece and destroy it before he could see mine. This game basically waged a miniature war.

I arranged my pieces around, hiding Balder next to one of the huldras who winked and blew me a kiss when I moved her. Nilsen indicated that I would go first. I placed a finger on the top of an elf's head and slid it across the floor. After a few inches, it stuck as if it were glued in place.

"I forgot to tell you, they're enchanted only to move a certain distance."

Nilsen placed his finger atop his own piece next to where I had moved mine. His piece revealed to be a dwarf, and before I could think of what to do next, my elf drew a bow and fired an arrow that fizzled as it hit Nilsen's piece. The pieces began to battle, my elf drawing a shortsword and dodging blows as Nilsen's dwarf drew its warhammer, and I struggled to keep my finger on the piece as it twirled and slashed. After a minute or two, my piece had won and advanced into the space where the dwarf had stood. The defeated piece had been knocked to a few shards, and Nilsen scooped him up and placed him to the side, where it began to fuse itself back together.

"Good fight," he said, nodding to me in congratulations. "Sometimes they take a while to battle. Aaren once had a piece that fought for an hour."

I laughed as I imagined that. Big Aaren is playing this game with little Nilsen and having to keep his finger on his piece for an hour.

Playing this game with Nilsen reminded me of playing board games with Lucas, and the loss returned with a heavy weight in my chest. We used to play a Simpsons-themed Monopoly with one of the kids in our second foster home. The fake money in the game had different Simpsons characters on it, and Lucas would rejoice whenever he had a stack of ones because Bart was on the one-dollar bills, and Bart was his favorite. He had never seen the show, but Bart was still his favorite. I sat in front of Nilsen, watching his brow furrow with concentration, and he reminded me of my brother. Lucas used to chew his lip when he was focusing. I swallowed a lump in my throat as I watched Nilsen move one of his pieces across the table to mine.

We played for a good hour, taking small breaks to eat the bread and dried fruit from the bowl on the table. Each piece after the initial battle took about five minutes to fight, and despite my efforts to discern a pattern in the winner, there was none. It was all up to the skill of the pieces. Nilsen was winning, however, having gained the upper hand when I ran into both of his huldras.

"What's the name of this game anyway?" I asked as two of our humans drew weapons and began taking swings at each other.

The front door opened before Nilsen could answer, and heavy footsteps stomped across the stone floor. I took my eyes away from the battle for a second to see Aaren striding toward us, his expression hard as he stepped over to the fire. He tousled Nilsen's hair but barely noted my presence as he turned his back on me to stoke the flames. Tension was set deep in his shoulders, and his movements were stiff and agitated. Maybe it was the fact that I was in his home, or perhaps it was what he had left in the medicine hut. Whatever it was that made him tense, one thing was for sure—I was not welcome here.

I felt a sharp pain in my cuticle, and when I turned my attention back to the pieces. My human had fallen, and Nilsen was trying to hack at my finger. I jerked back my hand and put my injured fingertip in my mouth.

"It's called Balderkrig," Nilsen answered, flicking his piece to the side to stop its attacks. "It means..."

"The War of Balder," Aaren finished gruffly from the fireplace. He turned to face us, his eyes focusing on me. "Our people worshiped Balder centuries ago. He's merely an old wives' tale now, just a legend."

Nilsen bristled. "You don't know that, he could be living amongst us for all we know!"

Aaren flicked his gaze to me for the briefest second before replying, "Save the fairytales for another time, *bror*. Focus on the basics, looks like she's still struggling with them."

Are you kidding me? Basic? I'll show him basic...

Nilsen's brow fell, and he turned back to our game with his arms folded across his chest.

Aaren approached the table, and my muscles tensed as if I was readying for a fight. Whatever was hidden behind his stony glare, it stirred my defenses, no matter how hard I tried to stay calm. He kneeled, whispering in his brother's ear. Nilsen smiled fiendishly and moved one of his pieces directly to my Balder, who turned and jumped in surprise, then raised his hands in surrender.

I furrowed my brow in annoyance. "How'd you know it was there?" I demanded.

Aaren's eyes glinted as he sat down next to Nilsen and poured himself a tankard of what looked to be mead. "Intuition," he answered bluntly, and irritation sank its claws into my nerves. There was no amusement in his demeanor, only harsh regard, and as he drained his mug and wiped his mouth on his sleeve, his eyes darkened and narrowed on me as if he were trying to see through my skin. I was used to dealing with bullies, and I wasn't going to back down. I stared back defiantly, my hands growing unnervingly warm in my lap.

Nilsen gave his Balder piece a high five with his pointer finger and laughed.

"Aaren, why did they blow the horn like that today?" he asked. The pieces clattered loudly as he swept them back into their box.

Aaren took a long drink, considering. "I'm not sure our...guest...would like to hear about it." He shot a warning glance at me, and I rolled my eyes. He didn't want to say anything in front of me in case I was an enemy to the village, but that's okay. I was leaving tonight anyway.

"I should get back to my room anyway," I said when the unwelcomeness began to weigh heavily in the air.

I stood, and Nilsen waved goodbye, but Aaren watched me walk to the door.

The walk to the pub was a confusing, winding hike, which set a bad precedent for my escape tonight. By the end of it, my teeth chattered with chill, and I was more than happy to accept a mug of hot mead once I entered. I sat at a table near the fire and sipped, savoring the sweet hints of honey and blackberry in the drink. As I stared into the flames, a shadow surged behind me, and I turned, my blood rising in defense, but it was only Rorik. In one hand, he held a plate of food; in the other, his own mug of mead.

"Did Nilsen make it back safely?" he asked, placing the plate in front of me.

My mouth watered as I observed the plate of food, and Rorik gestured for me to eat. There was a half-chicken with an herb crust, roasted potatoes, and a slice of soft white cheese wedged in a piece of hearty bread. I was thankful it wasn't pigeon pie. I didn't know where to start. I hadn't seen a meal like this in...I couldn't begin to think of the last time. I suppose it was before Granny died, and even then, she wasn't this much of a cook. She knew how to throw together a casserole, but a meal like this was fit for a king. Or elves.

God, I was confused.

"He did," I answered as I peeled the skin off the chicken and chewed. It was delicious. Whatever magic the Fraalver possessed, they used it in their food. I took another wondrous bite before asking, "What happened?"

Rorik sipped his drink and stared into the fire. "Layla, I'm going to tell you this because, despite what Aaren may believe, I do not think you are responsible for anything that is happening here." He rubbed his chin in consideration. "There was another myling attack today," he said gruffly, not taking his eyes from the hearth. "One of our hunters, Dagan, was attacked earlier this evening."

I took a steady deep breath as I chewed.

"All of that being said, we cannot ignore the fact that this attack comes only the day after you arrive here with a myling attached to you. I do not blame Aaren for believing you to be responsible for these mylings; however, I believe this to be bigger than your arrival."

"Aaren's a dick," I blurted, then immediately wished I had just shoved bread in my mouth instead of saying that.

Rorik's face hardened, the first amount of hostility I had seen in the man since we met. "Aaren is only looking out for his people," he said sternly. "Whether he is right in his assessment of the situation is neither here nor there. His priority is the village." He paused as a giggling couple passed, bubbly and red-faced from the drinks in their hands. "What is important at the moment is our safety and the matter of your presence here. *My* priority right now is to figure out how you crossed into the realm, as our security may rest on the reason why you are here now."

"I don't know why I'm here, Rorik," I began, feeling a sense of hopelessness settle in my chest. "All I know is that I don't belong."

I sat back in my chair, my belly full, and a heavy exhaustion settled into my muscles. I pushed the plate away from me and gazed dreamily into the fire. A heavy silence filled the air, broken only by the crackling of the fire and the laughter of passing villagers. Rorik watched the pub with pensive quiet. "You should head to bed," he suggested after a moment.

There was nothing to say, so I nodded. After I bid him farewell, I tromped up the stairs to my room, where I threw myself on the bed and snuggled into the furs.

My mind replayed everything from today, and the more I remembered, the less sense any of it made. I couldn't explain the things I had seen, like the game of Balderkrig and its moving pieces or the rune on the front door of Nilsen and Aaren's house, but I waved the thoughts aside, trying not to get distracted from the reason I wound up here. My focus was on finding my brother.

And Rachel, considering I had no idea where she had gone when I ran from the fenr. My head knew this wasn't my fault, but guilt still seeped into my mind. Rachel went into the woods to help me find Lucas, and I had no idea where she was. She would most likely be reported missing if she didn't show up for her next shift, which would've been tonight. Security camera footage would show that she and I closed the bar early and left. Police would probably trace my car to my old foster neighborhood and would be patrolling the woods for us. If I turned up and she didn't, I'd be a suspect, and I know my story of a large wolf hunting us down wouldn't hold up in an interrogation. *If* I could get out of here.

If anything, my disappearance coupled with Lucas's would raise red flags for the authorities—maybe it would encourage them to open a full investigation into it. At least then they would treat his disappearance more seriously. Or perhaps they'd conclude that I had kidnapped him myself, and I'm sure Sarah would perpetuate that theory, which would put me in even more trouble, especially if Rachel didn't turn up.

50

Escaping this village would be hard, but returning to Harrisburg and facing reality would be harder. I was going to stick to my original plan. I was going to leave tonight. I just had to sleep off this food.

My eyes fluttered closed, and I drifted off thinking of Granny's casseroles and Simpsons Monopoly.

Chapter 8

When I awoke, the pub below was silent. I rubbed my eyes and tried to shake the fuzziness from my head. I was wobbly when I stood from the bed, and I stretched to bring my muscles back to life. Giving myself a couple of taps to the cheeks to sharpen my senses, I opened the door and poked my head out to peer down the hall. Not a soul stirred, the only sound being the crackling fire in the hearth as it died into the night. I tiptoed down the hall and peeped over the balcony, watching my shadow move on the floor below in the flicker of the weak firelight, now mostly smoldering embers. The pub was empty, and as I passed a couple of the rooms I knew to be occupied, I didn't hear even a snore come from within. It was like everyone had disappeared.

I crept down the stairs and through the front door, where I was met with a cool air that bit my nose as I stepped outside. No one walked the paths, nor were there any lights inside the buildings and homes along the way. An unsettling silence had fallen on the village.

I padded down the path, heading towards one of the spots I knew was unattended, occasionally peeking around corners to see if anyone was lurking. Just like everywhere else in the village, the paths were vacant. The large building in the center of the town drew closer as I prowled along, and I saw that the structure was illuminated from within. Curiosity propelled me forward until I was crawling under a window and straining my ears for any sign of the Fraalver. To my relief, there were muffled voices inside, and I dared a glance through the window above and let my pupils adjust to the light.

Inside was every single Fraalver I had seen earlier today, plus nearly three hundred more. Standing tall in front of the gathering was Aaren, his sleeves still rolled up and his amber eyes shining in the bright light. The fire cast shadows on his face and highlighted a light dusting of stubble across his cheeks and jaw. Standing before his people, he was nothing but power and authority, a beacon of leadership and might. I didn't like him, but I could see why he was so respected. Behind him sat Rorik, who had slumped in his chair and was staring broodily past the crowd at the wall beyond.

"We can't just stop hunting," someone called from the crowd. "We'll run out of food before we figure out why the mylings are back."

"I'm not saying we should stop hunting," Aaren argued. "I'm saying no one should go alone anymore."

"It's that girl," someone called. "She's the reason for the mylings! We all know she brought them here!"

Rorik shifted in his seat and raised a calming hand to the crowd. "We don't know that, Alva," he began in a voice that was firm but gentle. "Layla's arrival and the myling attacks may be purely coincidental."

A man stood up. He clutched a hat in his hand, worry, if not desperation, etching his withered features. The room fell silent as he began to speak.

"Pesta."

A collective gasp rose amongst the group, then a sudden hush fell as the man's body quaked, as if containing something seismic within him. His features screwed up when he covered his face with the hat that was clenched in his wrinkled hands. "I lost my Lilja the last time a stranger broke our borders." A woman stood and placed a gentle hand on his back as he sank back into his seat, his sobs now muffled.

A heavy silence weighed the crowd.

Aaren sighed visibly and surveyed his people. "When Nils and Freya were taken from us, you stepped up to help my brother and me. In our hour of need, you aided me and helped me become the leader this village needed. This *fremmed*, Layla, needs our help. If we turn our backs on her, how are we any better than our ancestors when they turned away the trolls?"

That's something I don't remember Nilsen telling me. What happened with the trolls?

My heart fluttered with every word he spoke. He was defending me and my presence here. Why did he suddenly have such a drastic change of heart? Perhaps Rorik spoke with him and convinced him otherwise. From what little I knew of Aaren, it seemed more likely he spoke highly of me because there was an ulterior motive. There was no other reason for such a sudden switch.

I was still puzzling over Aaren's words when something clicked. The man, a few minutes ago, mentioned someone named Pesta and how he lost someone because of *Pesta.* Was this person the one whom Nilsen was talking about in the medicine hut? The woman who came carrying a rake, the woman whose presence killed his parents? The exact figure that had been carved into the fireplace.

"Until we learn more about Layla, she is a guest here and will be treated as such. If anyone takes issue with this, they can take it up with me." A heavy silence settled amongst the gathering again, this time out of respect for Aaren.

"In the meantime..."

His speech was interrupted by a shrill scream.

The spine-tingling screech came from a small shadow barreling toward the meeting house. It was a girl, her form small and unstable as she stumbled up the wooden steps, her blonde braids streaking behind her.

It was Ingrid.

The doors burst open with a loud creak as she slammed her body weight against them to shed light on her trembling form. She was pale-faced and sweating, her body vibrating with violent shakes as she sniffled on the steps.

"Hallow."

She dropped to the ground in a heap of nightgown and braids.

Chapter 9

Rorik sprang to his feet and sprinted to the doorway where Ingrid lay sprawled on the threshold, her brow glistening in the firelight. Aaren was close behind.

"What did she say?" Aaren demanded.

Rorik turned so his eyes met Aaren's and repeated Ingrid's single word. That same word the mylings had repeated over and over again in my ear. The thing they so desperately craved was hard enough to drive them to kill. Aaren paled and gritted his teeth.

"Ingrid!" a woman called from the crowd, and she began to shove Fraalver out of the way. A man grasped the arm of her dress, following her through the crowd. "Move! That's my daughter!" Dropping to her knees in front of Ingrid, the woman swept her hand over the trembling girl's forehead to examine her. "What happened, dear? What's wrong?"

Ingrid was catatonic, eyes distant and hazy. She lay limp as her mother scooped her into her arms, a disturbing sight from the little girl I had seen so lively just hours ago. What could have done something like this? I wouldn't let myself think of the possibilities, especially if it was a myling. That would make me responsible for her fate. But ultimately, I was liable—I brought the mylings here. This *was* my fault.

Rorik placed a gentle hand on the mother's shoulder and suggested that they take her to the medicine hut. She stifled a sob and nodded, then rose to her feet to pass her daughter to her father. The crowd parted as they made their way down the front steps.

Impulsively, I darted around the backside of the building as panic rose in my gut. Despite what Aaren had just said in the meeting, I had a feeling the finger would be pointed at me for this attack on poor Ingrid. I wasn't going to stick around to be blamed again, even though they were right. Besides, I still needed to find my brother, and this chaos provided me the perfect opportunity to slip away.

As quietly as I could, I hurried toward the spot I knew I could escape unseen and crossed over the village line. Once I was out of hearing range, I broke into a sprint, my feet slamming onto the ground below. My breath grew sharp in my lungs, the cold air icy in my throat, and I slowed once I saw that the lights of the village had faded to small pinpoints on the horizon. I heaved, dropping my hands to my knees as I gulped and gasped for breath, hearing a cold breeze rustle the leaves around me. I knew I was out of shape, but not this bad. It was like something sucked the oxygen from the woods, and what I was breathing was poisoned. My blood froze in my veins. All sound escaped the clearing, and I could hear nothing from the forest or the chaos in the village beyond. I could barely hear my own breathing. It was as if someone had hit mute on the scene around me. And I wasn't alone.

A twig snapped behind me, and before I could react, a pair of strong arms grabbed me and pinned me to my side. Then a hand snaked around and covered my mouth. Stiff muscles met my back, and the smell of forest and leather filled my nose. What was most peculiar was the odd buzzing emanating from the arms around me, as if a power line, not a person, held me. Untapped, metallic energy wreathed around me, coating my tongue with every panicked breath I took.

"Don't move," Aaren's rasping breath whispered in my ear, and it sent shivers across my skin. "Not a sound."

My lungs still ached from my run, and Aaren's hand covering my mouth was not helping.

"Hallow," a small voice said. "Hello, where are you?"

The temperature in the clearing dropped. As Aaren removed his hand, my breath pooled in front of me. A shadow darted in front of us, then there was a streak of black out of the corner of my eye. A little giggle sounded from behind us. Goosebumps dotted my arms, and without having to turn my head, I knew we were surrounded. My body broke out in violent shivers.

A small figure emerged into the clearing, draped in shadow, enough to conceal any strip of humanity the thing had left, but its features were still discernible in the light of the moon. It was a little boy, maybe five or six years old. Or at least, it was. Rot spotted its cheeks, and death clouded its small eyes. Flecks of earth clung to the rumpled strands of hair that stuck up at all angles, and Aaren's grip on me tightened as the thing smiled snakily to reveal teeth crusted with decay. Fatal gashes tore the gray skin at its neck, as if whatever killed it tried to rip its throat out. I cringed to think about what could have been done to a child.

"Are you hallow?" the myling asked, its voice rattling in its dead, mangled throat.

56

"There is no hallow," Aaren roared. "Why have you come here?"

The myling laughed a hoarse, harsh laugh. "We come to get what was promised to us."

"We promised you nothing."

It laughed again. "Give us our hallow..."

I cringed when Aaren's grip tightened around me, but I was grateful for his presence—I was finding that I wasn't as brave as I thought myself to be. No amount of time in the foster system could've prepared me for something like this. I could protect myself from a bully, but not the undead.

Voices all around us echoed the request, repeating the last word over and over again until the space was filled with a looping chorus of "Hallow, hallow, *hallow*." It sounded like a symphony of whispering insects, insects that had just crawled out of a rotting corpse. My ears began to ring as the pitch in the voices increased and reverberated amongst the trees until they created a vortex of screeches. It was a cacophony of despair.

"You were promised nothing, and you will get nothing."

Releasing one of my arms, Aaren circled his own above us, almost like he was rallying a whip. When he brought his arm down, he wielded a massive, thick vine. It cracked across the myling's chest and tore open rotten skin. It crumbled to the ground, where it howled and writhed. The clearing was alive with hisses and jeers from the hidden mylings, their shadows retreating from them as they slid out of their hiding spots. There were nearly fifty of them, all still shrouded in shadow to some degree, a sight that sent me into fearful tremors no matter how hard I fought them. My hands burned hot and sweaty as if I were holding them in front of a fire.

The myling on the ground continued to squirm, screaming for its hallow, crying out for mercy when that was the last thing such a monstrosity deserved. The dead leaves around my feet rustled, and I jumped, dancing on tiptoes before I realized that the source of the scuffling wasn't a myling, but more vines. They snaked around our ankles towards the sneering dead, children that were now drawing closer, close enough I could see the murkiness in their eyes. The closest myling succumbed to the vines, a choked gasp rattling from its throat as the vine wrapped around the ankles, then the torso, then coiled so tightly around the myling's neck that its eyes rolled back and the body went limp. Other mylings were suffering the same fate, the vines finding more creative ways to take them down until the remaining ones fled. The first myling, the one that had spoken to us, staggered to its feet, the gaping wound on its chest bubbling with black blood.

"We'll be back for our hallow," it said, and bared its teeth as it turned on its heel to retreat with the others.

Aaren released me. Astonishment had me weak in the knees, and I faltered, disbelief permeating the words that were ready on my tongue. But I couldn't speak, only gawk at the vine-wrapped bodies as the last victims choked on their final breaths.

"Why did you run?" Aaren growled, and I turned to see his features hardened into a scowl. That same buzzing energy thrummed around him, only intensifying the harder he stared at me. Aaren was powerful, and I would be stupid to cross him. That didn't mean I wasn't going to try.

"Answer me!" he barked, stepping close to me.

"I need to find someone!" I hollered back, seething at the way his lip curled in disgust. "And I can't look for them if I'm stuck here." With a renewed strength, I shoved him away with both hands on his chest, feeling an angry heat build inside me.

When Aaren retreated, shock evident on his face, hatred bubbled inside me. I wasn't going to stand for the disgusted way he looked at me.

Turning on my heel, I took off across the clearing, hoping to lose Aaren in the trees.

Weaving in and out of the towering oaks, I dodged branches and lost footing a couple of times, but to my surprise, I was putting a reasonable distance between myself and the village. And Aaren, who, to my cautious surprise, wasn't pursuing me in the slightest. I thought he would put up at least some chase before leaving me to the mercy of the forest. But he hadn't taken one step as I ran away, only glaring after me and shaking his head.

I wasn't sure where I was going, but anywhere was better than that village. If I kept running, I should find a road—the woods behind that foster home weren't *that* big. So I kept running and running. Running until my breath came like shards of glass in my throat and my pulse beat so hard I thought it would burst from my neck.

My pace slowed to a jog, the unnervingly quiet night settling around me. Then the leaves moved. My foot caught a root, and I tumbled to the ground, wincing, but also gaping, because that root hadn't been there seconds ago. And as I studied the protruding wood, it sank back into the ground and out of sight. Alarmed, I scrambled to my feet and broke into another run, only to be tripped by another sentient root. I only staggered this time, expecting another obstacle, and I huffed proudly as I regained my footing.

58

Then the wind picked up.

At first, it only began as a light breeze, one that worked well to cool my skin. Then it swirled around me, as if only me, it seemed, for the low-hanging branches nearby barely rocked in the increasingly aggressive wind. Dead leaves stirred to rise from the forest floor and circled my ankles, my knees, up my waist, picking up speed until a blustering gale surrounded me. Leaves broke across my vision, blocking out the moonlight and obscuring my surroundings. I was exposed, and if I didn't get out of this soon, I would pay for it. But I couldn't move.

And something was approaching.

I cursed under my breath, then tried to push through the wind, but thought better of it. It was howling so hard I wasn't sure what it would do to my hand should I try to break free.

The figure was drawing closer.

Panic rose in my throat as my eyes squinted through the raging leaves, but it was futile. I was trapped. The figure was feet away, and I opened my mouth to scream when it snapped its fingers. The tornado around me died instantly.

Aaren stood in front of me, radiating wrath as he took a step closer.

"Why are you doing this?" I demanded, my own anger rising to meet his, and suddenly, my body was smoldering again.

Something nudged my foot. Aaren continued his trek forward, fuming gaze never leaving me—a vine wrapped around my left ankle, then the right. I protested, but they banded quickly, trapping my legs within seconds. Aaren only watched as I fell to the ground, cursing his name as I writhed and tried to beat against the vines.

"What's wrong, Layla Ashford? You don't like my vines?" Aaren asked as he looked down on me. "If you're going to keep running, then get used to them."

Chapter 10

Aaren hauled me back to the village over his shoulder, enjoying the silence he had earned himself when he snaked a vine into my mouth as a gag. At first, I struggled, but when the vines held firm and Aaren showed no inclination to let me down, I resigned myself to returning to the village over his shoulder like a sack of grain. My arms were strapped to my body, and I had no choice but to yield.

I was thankful that the village was quiet and no one walked the paths, so there were no prying eyes to catch sight of my current predicament, except Rorik's when we got to the meeting hall.

Squinting against the bright firelight, I had no choice but to let Aaren haul me into the warm building. The entire way back to the village, I had been shivering, and my teeth chattered against the vine in my mouth. The warmth of the meeting hall gave me a little life back, but it also served to reignite my anger.

"By Himmelfjell, what happened?" Rorik's voice demanded as we passed.

Aaren grunted, and I felt him shake his head as he walked deeper into the room. The world spun when he dropped me into a chair, and I could finally gaze upon the two of them, body still quaking, but now it was with building fury.

"For Aesir's sake, Aaren, unbind her," Rorik spat.

Aaren shook his head and crossed his arms over his chest. "I don't trust her not to run."

Rorik closed his eyes and sighed. "Layla, do we have your word that you will remain in this room while we speak?" When my lip curled as my only response, Rorik sighed. "At least take the gag out."

Aaren complied, and I spat on the ground to get the woody taste out of my mouth.

"Explain," Aaren snarled.

"I..."

"Layla, remember, this isn't..." Rorik began.

"Quiet," Aaren barked, though his eyes never left mine.

He stared me down, eyes narrowing harshly as he leaned over me. "Start from the beginning and explain."

There was fiery rage inside me, unbridled, filthy anger, but something else was warring with it, and winning. Desperation, maybe hopelessness. Whatever it was, it was won, and the knot of this anonymous emotion was unraveling. Everything I had known was flipped backwards, upside down, and sideways, and there was nothing I could do but sit back and let it hit me in the face. I should be used to this feeling. It was all out of my control, but everything in my life was as well. And yet the helplessness won. My body was coming undone from sheer exhaustion, but I took a deep breath and started from the beginning.

"I lost my brother," I began with a hitched breath. "He went missing two days ago. My friend and I went looking for him in the woods when the fenr attacked." I hiccuped as I tried to steady my voice, wiping the thought of Lucas from my mind. I couldn't cry in front of them, I couldn't show such weakness. It was something I learned very early on in my orphanhood. "I wanted to look for him, them, but I can't do that when I'm here." I looked directly into Aaren's spitefully yellow eyes. "That's why I ran."

Aaren gritted his teeth, speaking as though his composure was a tight line about to snap. "I told you to stay put."

"Would you stay put if Nilsen was out there somewhere?"

The hardness in his face was unrelenting, but I caught the slightest twitch, and I knew he would've done the same. Rorik hummed, his chin resting on his fist contemplatively.

"Tell me about your brother," he requested calmly.

I blinked the damp out of my eyes before continuing. "We're orphans. Our mom died when I was thirteen, and we were raised in the foster system." A look of confusion crossed their faces, as if they didn't know what the foster system was. The likelihood of that being actual in Skoghjem became more evident the longer I stayed there. They didn't interrupt, though, and their steady attention urged me to continue—the following words jumbled in my throat, blocking the sound and damming my sentences. The more I divulged, the harder it was to hide my despair, until it was unbearable to keep in. A rumbling cry from my chest barrelled through my tight throat, and my apprehensive words spilled forth like a desperate river.

"I just wanted to protect him," I cried, sniffling to choke the sobs. "All I've ever wanted was to protect him."

"Aaren," Rorik whispered, then shot an obvious glance at me.

Aaren pressed his lips together as if fighting the argument ready on his tongue, but his face softened the tiniest bit when he looked back at me. He waved a hand, and the vine's grip loosened, then dropped onto the floor. Dried tears caked my cheeks, and I shook out my arms, massaging the sore muscle along my bicep where the vines had gripped me the hardest.

Rorik dug into his pocket and produced a small handkerchief to offer me. "Listen, Layla," he began. "When you're here, you're safe. We learned tonight that our village is in more peril than we believed it to be, and while it's not your fault, you *are* connected to it." He paused to deliberate his following words. "Learning of your brother tonight convinces me that he may be a part of this, too."

I glanced at Aaren, hoping to find an apology in his eyes, though I found myself disappointed. He clenched his jaw and avoided meeting my gaze. Instead, he studied the window and the woods outside. Annoyance struck a match inside me. Prick.

As I began to stew over his indignation, his following words surprised me.

"I was wrong to assume that you intended harm upon Skoghjem," Aaren said. His eyes shifted and met mine, locking me into an intense exchange. "You are safe here, and I believe it is wise that you remain here until the lungs are taken care of." His words said one thing, but his expression said another. He didn't really want me to stay, but it was smart to keep me here.

And to my astonishment, I agreed with him. Going back to Harrisburg would put me at risk of arrest, and it would be a lot harder to find Lucas from the inside of a jail cell.

I was helpless. Truly helpless. I had no idea where I actually was, in a culture vastly different from my own, whether magical or not. Lucas was still missing, and Rachel could still be wandering the nearby woods. Lucas had to be close by—I found his book in the shack. And the fenr and the horde of mylings were still out there. Nothing in my experience could have prepared me to face something like this, and I couldn't approach it with a psychology textbook. The best thing, and really the only thing, I could do was use Skoghjem as a base to continue searching.

Against both mine and Aaren's better judgment, staying here would be my best option.

At least we agreed on something.

Aaren, clearing his throat, broke the trance his amber eyes had lulled me into. They were such an unnatural color, like the shade of warm honey and firelight. "The search for your brother does not have to end."

My lips pressed together into a thin line, dropping my gaze to my lap as I felt a corner of despair wither away with the promise. I looked up.

"Now *I* need an explanation," I said.

Rorik nodded agreeably and drew a chair. Aaren did the same, though he spun it around and sat in it backwards, his corded forearms resting on the back nonchalantly. A soft ease permeated his rough exterior, though he was still guarded. No matter how much I disliked him, I understood why he kept those walls firm. It was the exact reason why, despite my agreement with them, I was still going to keep my cards close to my chest. I still wasn't safe here, and I was positive there were a few villagers who still had it out for me, even after Aaren's warning. Aaren had a village to protect, and more importantly, a brother. We could at least agree on that. So the wall in him could stay up, as would mine.

"What would you like to know?" Aaren asked gruffly. He perpetually sounded like he had just woken up.

Where to begin? As I thought over the day's events, the most important thing I could remember was Ingrid's scream, loud and piercing in my mind. "Is Ingrid okay? What happened to her?"

"We're not..." Rorik began.

"She's fine," Aaren cut him off.

It was obvious my invitation to stay still didn't grant me full transparency. Instead of arguing, I tried a different avenue.

"What's the deal with the vines?" I questioned. "How is it even possible?"

Aaren smirked. The first shred of positive emotion I had seen on his face since I met him. "As leader of the Fraalver people, I possess elemental gifts passed down through my ancestry."

He closed his hand to form a fist, then opened it to reveal a small patch of dirt with a sapling nestled in his palm. As he closed his hand, the window Aaren had been glaring through moments before bursting open with a wild wind shooting through. My hair rustled as it died down to a breeze, carrying that same woodsy scent as the tornado he had encased me in.

Rorik also explained that the average Fraalver possesses a small amount of domestic magic that has been passed down through the elf lineage. Magic as simple as starting small fires and filling empty ink pots with nothing but a flick of the wrist.

"The powers a leader possesses are advantageous to the location of the village," Aaren continued. "Skoghjem is in the forest, so the elements of the woodlands influence my magic."

I stared down at the motionless vines on the floor at my feet, waiting for them to stir and wrap me up again.

"Of course, there is some crossover," Rorik added, and Aaren agreed with a nod.

"So this isn't the only village of Fraalver?" I asked.

Aaren shook his head. He explained that small families of Fraalver spread throughout Alveland, but the highest concentration of them was gathered in the three main villages. "We have kin in the mountains and along the coast. Fiske and Helgi Sjøbrytt lead Kysthjem by the sea. Torsten and Ertha Felldatt rule Fjellhjem in the mountains."

"And what are their powers?"

Rorik chuckled. "We call Fiske the Fish King."

The smallest smile jerked at Aaren's lips as he said, "He's not particularly fond of that nickname. His power lies in controlling the sea and the creatures that inhabit it. I use the term 'control' loosely." Rorik sniggered. "Torsten and Ertha have the power to extract and shape rock at their will. Among other things."

I almost shuddered to think of what else those leaders could do with the earth.

"And you're...half elves?" The two of them nodded in confirmation. "Does that mean you live a long time?"

Rorik chuckled. "Compared to humans, yes. Compared to elves, no. I myself am four hundred and twenty years old."

Holy shit.

"How does that work?" I asked.

"When we're young, we mature at the same rate as humans," Rorik explained. "Nilsen is eight years old in both human and Fraalver years. Maturation slows down by the late teens, or for some, the early twenties. It takes a Fraalver about seven years to age what a human would in one."

My eyes widened, unable to control the shock that stunned my mind—the things I could accomplish if I could live to be that age. Rorik hid a sly smile and sat back, crossing his arms across his chest and relishing my bewilderment. Quickly composing myself, I nodded and sorted that information to think about later. "And Pesta?"

Any remaining amusement on Rorik's face vanished, replaced by a grim countenance that matched Aaren's perpetual scowl.

"How do you know about Pesta?" Rorik inquired.

Aaren rolled his eyes and scoffed. "Doesn't matter how she knows. She probably eavesdropped during the *sammenkomst*." My nose scrunched in annoyance, no matter if he was right. I had just shown some vulnerability, and he still regarded me like gum on the bottom of his boot. Arrogant, presumptuous bastard—

"Pesta is an entity that brings nothing but death with her," Aaren answered, still wearing that smug, infuriatingly knowing look on his face. "She travels from village to village spreading plague and sickness as she goes. If she carries a rake with her, only a few will perish. If she carries a broom, there will be nothing left of the village by the end of her stay." He watched his fingers twisting around each other before bracing the back of the chair. "She carried a rake when she arrived here."

"None of the Fraalver has seen her in centuries," Rorik explained. "Which begged the question as to why she decided to make herself known after all this time."

Aaren's eyes dropped to the floor and concentrated on the wood grain beneath his boots. "Pesta killed my mother and father," he murmured. "That is the only reason I am the leader of Skoghjem."

Rorik didn't waste any time launching into another explanation. For centuries, this branch of Fraalver had occupied these woods. When I asked how they were able to stay hidden from humans for so long, Rorik hesitated, exchanging unspoken words with Aaren before answering.

The Fraalver never needed to stay hidden from humans because the likelihood of a human stumbling across their village was nearly impossible. Me being the exception. The Fraalver people, as Rorik had mentioned before, lived in a realm called Alveland, or *Elven Land* in the common tongue. Alveland was a realm nestled in the branches of a tree called Yggdrasil. I nearly cackled with skepticism when they mentioned the tree—it reminded me of something Lucas used to talk about. I smiled a little at the memory. Lucas had borrowed a Thor comic book from one of his classmates a couple of years back. In his excitement after reading it, he checked out a library book on Norse mythology. For months, all he could talk about was the lore behind the creation of the comics. I had sat patiently and tried to match his enthusiasm as I listened, questioning him about everything he had learned.

Yggdrasil was the tree of life.

"So does that mean Asgard is real?" I asked, more ironically than curiously.

Aaren's eyebrow cocked in confusion. "How do you know of Asgard?"

Rorik politely cleared his throat. "Asgard existed long ago, serving as the home to all the Aesir, the gods."

"Like Odin?" I questioned.

"Like Odin," Rorik nodded, "but not as powerful as many believed the gods to be. Asgard disappeared from Yggdrasil long ago, and no one knows why. Some even claim it never existed in the first place, as there is no evidence to support its existence. Just spoken word."

There were other realms as well: Alveland, Midgard, where the humans lived, Nidavellir, and Himmelfjell. I was too tired to inquire about the other realms, and my brain began to ache from the overload of information. But I wanted to know about some of the things in this realm before the conversation was over, in case I encountered something else that could kill me.

"Are there...any other 'beings' in this realm? Mylings and a fenr have already attacked me." I inquired, wincing at the new vocabulary I struggled to use.

"There are plenty of other races and creatures in our realm," Rorik answered. "So many that we wouldn't be able to explain them all in one sitting. Harald's bookshop might be a good place for you to learn more about them." I remembered Thea mentioning Harald's bookshop, but I thought a visit to hers would be far more entertaining.

"What about the trolls? You said something about the trolls in the meeting—*sammenkomst*—earlier."

"The trolls are an ancient race that have not shown themselves in many years," Aaren elaborated. "They were once a helpful race, ready to aid in any conflict that the Fraalver, elves, and dwarves alike encountered." Rorik continued by explaining that four hundred years ago, they came into conflict with each other and required the help of their ancestors. Looking down on the trolls despite their previous aid, every race denied them help. The trolls faced their conflict alone and died off. Few have seen them since, and if one of the Fraalver encounters one of the few remaining trolls, it is an unfriendly exchange.

"Any other questions?" Aaren asked, his tone lighter than when the exchange first began. It was a pleasant shift, if not a little off-putting.

"No," I answered and rubbed my eyes as the adrenaline had depleted entirely from my body.

Rorik stood and placed a hand on my shoulder, suggesting that we all retire for the night and begin work tomorrow. What that work entailed, he did not reveal, and I did not bother to ask as I stepped into the cool night.

Sleep did not come as easily as I had expected, despite the fatigue that had enveloped my body. I couldn't take my mind off the complete flip in my world in only one day.

I had gone from a server and a psychology student to a bringer of mylings and a guest to an ancient half-elf village, which I was now helping to figure out what threatened their existence in exchange for their help in finding my brother. Adding to this, I might now be a fugitive in my own world; I most definitely was not going to hear back from the psychology program. The most inconceivable notion of it all was that I had believed every word these people told me. I *had* to think, especially with the evidence I had been presented with over the past forty-eight hours. This was going to take Stockholm Syndrome to a new level.

These people were my only hope of staying alive and finding Lucas, who would have loved this place. He would probably say it's like Harry Potter because of all the magic. He would get along really well with Nilsen. I closed my eyes and imagined the two of them playing Balderkrig together, seeing the wonder light up in his eyes as his piece came to life and danced around Nilsen's, swinging swords and clashing stone. Nilsen would still win.

Chapter 11

Waking up the next day was disorienting. At first, I thought I was in my apartment, and the sounds coming from outside my bedroom door were the regular mumblings of my roommates as they poured their coffee and packed their bags for the day. As the noises became clearer, I realized they were the sounds of a fire being made, people sitting down for breakfast, and morning songs being sung.

I sat up, remembering where I was, and a flood of information from the night before came rushing back. An uneasy rumble settled into my stomach as anxiety gripped the muscles of my back and shoulders. It didn't help that I was utterly starving, which kick-started my nausea into high gear.

Rolling out of bed, I padded over to the dresser where I pulled out a pair of brown pants and one of the loose cotton shirts that hugged my waist and wrists but flowed with every movement I made. A pair of tanned boots sat undisturbed at the foot of my bed, and I slid my feet in, shifting my weight to feel the leather hug my toes. As comfortable as these clothes were, I still felt exposed without my bra.

After I sat myself at the same table by the fire downstairs, a woman passed me a plate of food and a tankard of ale. She offered me a sweet smile, wished me a good breakfast, and departed to tend to her other patrons. Every pair of eyes in the pub watched my every move as I shoveled a forkful of eggs into my mouth. I wondered which Fraalver wanted to kill me.

Before I could take another bite, a stocky man sank onto the bench in front of me and busied himself with the heap of eggs and potatoes in front of him. The pub fell silent save for the slurps the man made as he gulped down his ale. After a beat, he noticed the hush and paused mid-chew to survey the other patrons at the surrounding tables.

"Why are you looking at her like she wears Pesta's cloak?" he demanded, his grip on his fork leaving his hands white-knuckled. "You heard Aaren. If he trusts her, then I trust her." He wiped his mouth on his sleeve, revealing unexpected muscles underneath, and rolled his eyes as he returned to his plate.

The conversation amongst the Fraalver slowly rose again as the pub returned to normal, only sending me a few glances here and there as they gossiped about my existence.

"Um, thank you," I offered the man as he tore into a piece of breakfast ham.

"Don't mention it," he said with his mouth full. I hid my recoil as food spilled back onto his plate. "The Fraalver are a kind people, but we're not used to visitors." He paused and scoffed. "Especially since the last visitor we had killed half of us." He took another swig of ale.

The man had a large, bulbous nose and small craters amongst his cheeks, bridging up to his dark green eyes, almost the color of pond scum. The bits of hair that escaped his cap were a light brown with soft highlights of blonde, and his ears poked dopily out of the sides of his head. He was not a very attractive man to behold, but he had charm in his character.

Placing my tankard down, I extended my hand across the table. "I'm Layla," I introduced myself.

The man examined my hand curiously, unsure of what I was offering him. Awkwardly, I closed my hand and retracted it to rest on my mug.

"Stieg," he responded as his eyes returned to his plate. "Stieg Trohjert."

"So what do you do here, Stieg?"

"I'm a whore," he answered.

I choked on my ale.

Stieg's mouth opened wide with laughter, showing every bit of the last bite he took. "I'm only kidding," he hooted, and he pounded the table as he howled with laughter. "*Godtroende*! Gullible little woman."

The outburst garnered more attention from the surrounding Fraalver. Such snide looks I was accustomed to, especially when I was in grade school, but that didn't make it any easier to ignore. Back home, I was an orphan. Here, I was a stranger. I swapped one oddity for another.

Stieg's chortling died down, and he sighed into his tankard as he took a long gulp. Wiping his mouth, he fixed his eyes on me and said, "I'm one of the scouts, a provisioner of sorts."

"Okay?"

"I go out in the woods and gather things that I think would benefit the village. No one told me to, I'm what you call self-appointed." He nodded matter-of-factly and patted his belly, smiling as he pushed his plate away from him.

I nodded and ripped a piece of bread before biting it. "And what kind of things do you find out in the woods?"

"All sorts of stuff. Mainly things that can be added to stews or can be sold to Kare, our trader here. Sometimes I find things that fall through the cracks of the realm."

I furrowed my brow. "There are cracks in the realm? Things can come through them?"

Stieg waved his hand and shook his head. "Not living things, see, but trinkets and small forgotten things. Like this." He reached into his pocket and pulled out a Kit-Kat wrapper.

"Oh, that's a..."

"Beautiful, isn't it?" Stieg asked. "I've got an assortment of them. No one wants them, so it's my own personal collection."

I stifled my laughter. I didn't have the heart to tell him what it actually was.

"But mostly when I'm out there, I look for food and certain ingredients for the apothecary. Rorik and Asta wrote me a list of things they need. I'm the only one who knows where they are, though. That's why I'm so important." He smacked his chest proudly.

An idea crackled to life in my brain.

"Stieg, I'm looking for something...someone. Would you help me look for them?"

Stieg raised his brows in consideration.

"I've got a list from Harald this morning. If you help me scout, I will help you look for what you've lost."

I nodded. "Deal."

We finished breakfast, then left the pub.

It was warmer today, and birds sang high above as Stieg and I began our foray into the woods. Neither of us spoke as we went; the only sound was Stieg's heavy breathing as we marched onward. His stocky body barreled through the bushes and created an easier path for me, whether he meant to or not.

The trees grew momentarily sparse as they opened to the clearing where the mylings had attacked me last night. Where Aaren had warded them off with lethal vines and chased me with harrowed gales. Just from the sheer size of him, I knew Aaren was powerful, but after last night, just the thought of what he was capable of sent shivers down my spine. Looking at him, one would think he could snap a person in half with just his thumb and forefinger. After what I saw last night, I knew he was capable of so much worse.

Don't move.

A treacherous shiver ran down my spine. It would be a long time before I forgot the feeling of his warm breath against my ear in the frigid night. Or the wall of hard muscle I backed into as I went to flee the encroaching mylings. I hated the feeling that stirred in my stomach, excitement, fear...arousal? Not for Aaren himself, but for the mystery of him. For the way his rumbling voice rattled through me last night as he pinned my arms to my side. I started to recoil at even the notion of such a feeling when Stieg's cackle shook me from my disgust.

"Looks like Aaren gave those mylings some hallowed ground, alright," Stieg laughed.

Peering down, I let out a startled yelp and danced away on the balls of my feet. A protruding root caught my foot, and I hit the ground with a curse of pain that made Stieg's eyes go wide. Raveled up in vines and sticking halfway out of the ground was the hardened face of a myling; its soft, decomposing skin had been replaced by hard, mossy wood. I shuffled away when I realized the root I had just stumbled on and now sat next to was another wooden myling, frozen forever into the ground. This root had already started to grow small sprigs of leaves.

Frightened, I shuffled away until I bumped into Stieg's boots, accepting his offered hand to bring me to my feet.

"Don't worry, they can't hurt you now," he said as I dusted myself off. He gave the rooted myling a glance before adding, "I think."

From my short distance away, curiosity was beginning to replace my startlement, and I squinted to observe the unmoving myling. The fear and sorrowful desperation that the myling must have felt as Aaren choked the unbreathing breath from its small form was frozen on its dead face. But the little sprigs of life blooming from it were, in a way, beautiful. Such a gift it was to give life from something so dead and rotten. But I wasn't eager to stick around and admire it any longer.

71

"What's on your list?" I asked Steig as I nudged him away from the scene of the mylings' devastation.

Stieg turned and led me onward, pulling a piece of parchment from a sack he had slung over his shoulder.

"Stinksaft from a grove of trees just ahead. Wicked foul stuff it is, but Harald uses it to bind his books together. Looks like he needs some more quills, which we'll get from the flock of treelskere birds that live in the sycamore near the river." He squinted his eyes at the scribbling on the paper. "And looks like a handful of pitch dirt." He huffed. "I thought this would be harder. I was hoping for a challenge."

I cocked my head. "Does Harald write all of the books in his shop?"

Stieg answered with a grunt. "I don't care for his books; no one really does. They're mainly used in lessons, but even then, it's not very often. He's very..."

"Prolific?" I suggested.

"Wordy."

"That's what I said," I replied.

"Huh?"

"Never mind."

A soft, woodsy breeze brushed my hair, the small wisps tickling my forehead. The scent was familiar yet foreign, like the opposite of deja vu. It was a smell like this, and the feeling it brought was unreal, fantastical, yet so familiar to me. It reminded me of Mama and the stories she'd tell me. Of Granny and the way she would tuck me close to her side while she cooked.

The wind blew again, this time stronger, carrying the scent even further. It was as if the forest was breathing, alive with something other than the nature within.

Was this Aaren's wind? A way to keep tabs on me while I wasn't in his sight?

"But he keeps writing them?" I asked before I dared to acknowledge my irritation and make it worse.

"I'm not in the business of figuring out why, I just get him what he needs," Stieg replied. Birds filled the silence for a moment before he spoke again. "Thea has some good books, though. I'll read hers any day."

Off in the distance, I could see the outline of the treehouse nestled in the branches of the massive oak. Even from far away, I could tell that it was empty.

"That little girl, Ingrid. Have you heard if she's okay?" I asked as the treehouse faded from view when Stieg took a sharp turn to the left.

He shrugged. "From what I heard, she just had a nasty nightmare."

Surely it wasn't that simple. Just a nightmare?

"Nightmares don't cause people to pass out like that," I replied.

Stieg shrugged. "There are nightmares and then there are nightmares." He chuckled at the confused noise I made. "Sometimes, when someone in Alveland has a bad dream, it's because a mare is tainting the dream. They sit on your chest until you can't breathe and make you see awful things."

Like a sleep paralysis demon.

"So you're saying that a mare attacked Ingrid?" I clarified.

"Not attacked, just visited. Mares can't do any real harm, except to scare you. Some say they can even be helpful to the right person. They can help someone see a hidden truth, as frightening as that might be."

I stewed in this information for a moment as we trudged on in silence. "So, what did it show Ingrid for her to come running and screaming of mylings?"

Stieg shrugged again. "Who knows? A myling to us is scary, but a myling to a youngin like Ingrid could feel like the end of the world."

We paused our walk about a half a mile from the village at the foot of a towering tree, its trunk big enough that not even Aaren and Stieg combined would be able to wrap their arms around. He snapped open his pack and retrieved a spigot that he hammered into the tree with his hand. I gaped at his ability to do so without a hammer, but waved the shock away as I assumed it might be a part of the Fraalver's physique. He held a small vial under the tree and blew out a heavy breath.

"You might want to cover your nose," he warned as he pulled out a handkerchief and pressed it to his face.

I cupped my hands over my nose and mouth, watching as a sticky sap oozed from the spigot and collected in the bottom of the vial in a sickly yellow slime. The odor seeped in through my fingers and assaulted my nose without apology. I reeled, quickly backing away, and Stieg chuckled, the sound muffled by the cloth concealing half his features.

I didn't come near the vial until it had been corked, and the spigot was replaced in his pack.

Then we were off again.

The woodsy wind picked up again, further raising my suspicions that Aaren was keeping breezy tabs on me.

"What can you tell me about Aaren?"

Stieg threw me a wondering look, then pondered for a moment before replying, his eyebrows moving as he thought through his answer. "His mother and father, Nils and Freya, were fierce warriors. Sadly taken from us by Pesta. Strong leaders, they were, and the reason we thrive today." He sighed. "It's a shame they died. The last thing Aaren wanted was to come into power. The only thing that occupied his mind was a sword and a woman."

"A woman?" I asked. I wondered what kind of woman could stomach him.

"He was promised to the daughter of Torsten and Ertha Felldat, the leaders of Fjellhjem." A sympathetic shake of his head. "Pesta hit their village, too, and took Aaren's bride with her."

I pressed my lips together, feeling guilty for a reason I couldn't quite place. "How long ago did she die?"

"Five years ago, but it still haunts Aaren. Not only were his parents taken by Pesta, but so was his betrothed."

Everything he loved had slipped through his fingers. It was a wonder he wasn't overbearingly protective of Nilsen. Or maybe he was and hid it very well.

"And what about Nilsen?"

Stieg chuckled. "Nilsen will likely never come into power unless Aaren gives it to him. The power of our village belongs to Aaren and his future wife. Together, the power is shared and full protection is granted."

"How does that work exactly?"

"Think of it as two doors." He stopped and held his hands up, his pinkies touching to mimic a set of doors. "When there are two, nothing can get in without granted access. If there is one..." he removes a hand, "There is still a doorway in which filth can slither in."

"Am I the filth that can slither in?" I retorted.

74

Stieg scoffed. "*Dumjente*," he muttered. "I didn't mean it like that. If anything, I'm ecstatic you're here. It's been a little quiet, just in time for someone like you to shake things up."

I pocketed Stieg's compliment for later, choosing instead to search for more answers.

"So without a wife, Aaren can't fully guard the village?"

Stieg nodded. "Yes."

Perhaps that was why I was able to cross their borders. Maybe Aaren was ready to find every other reason under the sun besides his lack of a wife to blame for my arrival. It still didn't explain how I had come to this realm in the first place.

"So do *you* have a theory of how I got here?"

Stieg pressed his lips together and shrugged. "No matter what, no living thing from outside our realm can cross over. But what already belongs in our realm will *try* to come and go as they please." He threw me a glance over his shoulder. "Guess you're not really from Midgard like you thought."

As if. My birth certificate says otherwise.

"If the village's safety is so important to him, has Aaren been looking for a new bride to fix this problem?" I doubted anyone in the village would volunteer for such a job.

Stieg made an amused noise. "No one in the village is fit for such a role."

Not quite my thoughts, but close.

Stieg continued. "Rorik has been aiding Aaren where he can, but it hasn't been enough. There is only so much he can do."

He paused for a moment and swept the brush around us. Then he changed direction and veered right. I followed quickly after.

"I know Rorik is the physician, but why is he helping Aaren so much?"

"The physicians in the Fraalver villages heal not just the people, but every branch that makes up our life. If you heal the home, you heal the people." He stepped over a fallen tree and helped me over it. "Helping Aaren is part of his job. Besides, Nils and Rorik were best friends."

Stieg held his hand out to halt me from another step forward.

75

"Quiet now, we don't want to attract a huldra."

He stepped forward lightly, his footsteps barely making a sound. I stayed where I was and watched him sidle up to a large tree, placing an ear against the trunk. With a meaty hand, he knocked twice against the bark, paused, then knocked twice more. There was a beat where nothing happened, then something orange cascaded through the air and onto Stieg's palm. It was a feather. Five more fluttered down, and he tucked them into his pack before stepping away and rejoining me.

Before I could ask, Stieg explained. "Treelskere birds. If approached properly, they will offer you their feathers as a token." He pulled one out so I could examine it. "Beautiful birds."

The feather was orange, but upon closer inspection, striations of red and yellow could be seen, and flecks of brown were woven throughout the strands. I could only imagine what the whole bird looked like.

"What happens if you don't approach them the right way?"

Stieg blew out a breath. "You don't want to know." When I gave him an expectant look, he made a gesture simulating something clawing his eyes out. My jaw dropped, and I shuddered to his satisfaction.

I moved to follow Stieg when something called out to me from across the river. But it wasn't my name being called that caused me to freeze. It was the voice that spoke it.

Lucas.

I whipped my head in the direction of the river, eyes widening at the sight of my brother with his pants rolled up around his ankles, wading in the shallows. His eyes lit up, and he stretched his arms out to beckon me closer.

"Lucas," I breathed.

Sense and better judgment abandoned me as I took off towards the bank, tasting sweet relief when my brother grinned. A breeze whipped his dark blonde hair, and Stieg's shouted warnings were white noise in my ears. I ignored the impossibility of it all, of how easy it had been to find him. He had slipped through the cracks just like I had, and now he was here, and he would be safe with me. He and Nilsen could play Balderkrig together. Hot tears pricked my eyes, and I sped up.

Just as I neared the bank, soft mud slid under my foot, and I fell, painting my palms dark brown. Stieg's heavy hand grasped my shoulder and wrenched me to my feet, where I focused on my brother still standing in the lapping waters. At this distance, Lucas's face was clearer and lacked the freckles that dotted the bridge of his nose. His skin held a doughy texture in the tree-filtered sunlight, like someone had molded him from the mud under my feet.

"Lucas?" I asked. Uncertainty strangled my senses, and I began to listen to the voice of reason in my mind.

Lucas smiled, revealing a mouthful of teeth that looked sharp enough to carve wood. Shock sent my heart into my throat, and my stomach wrenched as the thing in the water stepped forward with eyes that flashed with hunger.

"You don't belong here, *fremmed*," the thing said in a voice that was Lucas' mixed with the whispers of the river. The sound rang sharply in my ears. "He's coming for you."

I frowned. "Who?" I demanded. "Where is Lucas?"

The thing pretending to be Lucas hissed and, with a swift movement, it transformed into a slim, haggard creature with long fingers and a tail that swished into the swirling waters behind it. It looked identical to the huldra piece in Balderkrig.

"He has him. And now he comes for you."

The thing lunged toward us, and the hand that had been on my shoulder grabbed my wrist and hauled me away. I trailed behind Stieg, struggling to catch my footing. With one swift jump, I slung my weight onto his broad back and wrapped my legs around his waist tightly. The huldra maintained speed behind us, dodging low-hanging limbs and launching off of boulders to gain on us.

Stieg moved with surprising speed, considering his size and my extra weight strapped to his back. Before I could consider how far we were from the village, the tree house came into view. An owl shook the branches high in the tree, and its alarmed hoots carried through the trees. I pointed Stieg to the right and jumped off his back, trying to remember how to activate the ladder in the trunk. Nilsen had knocked once, then again... I knocked three times, and the knob appeared. Slamming my hand on it, the notches began to appear, and without another thought, I began to climb, calling for Stieg to follow.

The trap door was bulky and hard to lift, but it wasn't enough to stop my panicked strength from wrenching it open and hauling my weight through it. Stieg collapsed on the floor next to me.

Unlike earlier, the treehouse was now full of children. There were scuffling sounds, and then Nilsen appeared over me. "What in the name of the Aesir happened?" he demanded.

"Uh," I stammered, frantically waving my hands and pointing at the trap door. Words evaded me, and I could only speak in panicked grunts.

"Huldra," Stieg answered as he hauled himself to his feet. He knocked his head on the low ceiling.

Nilsen darted to the window and peered out, then gasped. "Shooters! Now!" Nilsen commanded, and the children jumped to their feet. Two boys began distributing small slingshots from a chest at the back wall, each inlaid with small, elegant carvings. For a child's slingshot, they looked deadly. A girl opened a cabinet and withdrew three large jars of stones, small enough to fit in a slingshot, but big enough to hurt. She distributed the stones, and the children lined up at the two windows on the left side of the treehouse. The place went quiet, save for the small pants of anticipation from the group of kids.

Nilsen waved his hand. "Light her up!"

The children with slingshots struck the stones on the windowsill as if they were matches, lighting them in a bright orange glow. Some of the kids tossed the heated stones between their hands before dropping them into their slingshots. Then they launched the stones.

I opened the trapdoor to see a barrage of burning rocks pummel the huldra. Upon impact, the rocks exploded, coating her in hot flames. She danced in surprise and flailed about to shake off the fire. The huldra spun around, frantically searching for a way up the tree, her claws carving into the base and shedding bark across her flaming skin. When it became evident she couldn't reach us, she fled through the trees as her wails echoed through the forest. When she was nothing but a rustle of leaves, birdsong replaced her screeches.

The children cheered and patted each other on the back as they tossed their slingshots back into the chest. The treehouse filled with whoops of glory and high fives, and I gave a relieved sigh. Nilsen beamed with pride, and a rosy tint flushed his cheeks. I stepped over and hugged him gratefully.

"That's the second time you've saved my life," I said. "Thank you."

Chapter 12

It was midday when Stieg and I made our way back to the village. The early afternoon sun warmed my cheeks as we trudged back through the woods, and nature carried on as if a huldra had not just attacked us.

"The huldra took the form of the person you're looking for," Stieg began bluntly.

I only nodded.

"Who is he?"

I sighed, as this was the third time I had to explain this to someone. "He's my brother. He went missing the day before yesterday. I went looking for him, and that is how I ended up here."

Before I could elaborate more, he gasped and dropped to the ground to rummage through the leaves. Something glinted in the foliage, and he extracted a Twix wrapper. The gold foil shimmered in the light.

"This is a new one!"

Stieg talked about his collection the entire way back to the village.

I had bid Stieg goodbye before I sat down at a table in the pub, ravenous from my excursion this morning. Adrenaline still twinged my limbs, and my hands shook as I began to eat, not tasting the food before I swallowed it.

"I'm glad to see you've decided to stick around," a smooth voice said behind me. I swallowed as Thea sat down in front of me with a knowing smirk on her face. In one hand, she held a mug of ale, in the other, something bright orange and soft. It was one of the quills from the treelskere birds.

"I thought those were for Harald," I voiced without thinking.

Thea puffed haughtily and raised a brow. "Sweet words can get you nice things." She cracked a smile. "It does help that Stieg is sweet on me." She sipped her ale. "I heard you got into some trouble last night." Her eyes sparkled.

"That I did," I answered curtly.

"And some trouble today?"

I blushed, hiding my eyes in my tankard as I took a sip. "How'd you know?"

Thea scoffed. "Nilsen has already told half the village, starting with Rorik." The food curdled in my stomach. If Rorik knew, then Aaren must have known. While I was thankful for Nilsen and his proclivity to save my life, I would have to have a conversation with him about discretion. If, or rather when, Aaren found out about today, I was going to be in deep shit. It was as if I had a parole officer to answer to, and I hadn't even committed a crime except maybe leaving Rachel for dead to that wolf.

Thea shook her head and picked at the bread that lay forgotten on my plate. "Aaren might finish you off since the huldra didn't."

Heat flushed my skin at the thought.

"So," I began, eager to change the subject. "I'm told you write the books in your shop."

Thea laughed. "Where else would I get my books?"

I shrugged. "Where I'm from, the booksellers don't write the books, they just sell them."

"That's obtuse."

I started to inquire more about her work when my heart stopped. The door to the pub opened, and Aaren's massive figure filled the frame. Patrons cheered as he strode in, and though he tried to greet every Fraalver that clapped him on the back or offered him a kind greeting, he moved forward with determination. He scanned the room, and I knew he was searching for me. Panic bloomed in my chest, and I sank into my chair in the hopes of disappearing suddenly. I wasn't sure what kind of lecture I was in for, but I wasn't about to find out.

"Thea, I'm going to have to leave you for a second," I said.

She winked and busied herself with picking at the remnants of my food.

Aaren hadn't spotted me yet, and if I moved deftly enough, I might be able to slip out of here unnoticed. I slid out of my seat and crept away towards the door on the other side of the pub. Seeing as my path to the front door was blocked by the person I was hiding from, I prayed that this other door also led to the forest outside. I slipped through it and closed it lightly behind me.

Unfortunately, it led to another room. The walls were lined with shelves of wine and kegs of ale ready to be rolled out and tapped. A large shelf on the back wall held massive wheels of aging cheese, and along the ceiling hung drying herbs and braids of spices. The aroma in the room was pleasant, similar to Christmas with notes of mulled wine, cinnamon, and warm spices.

My need to hide was forgotten as I stepped up to examine a bottle of wine with a dusty label with berries painted on it. It had been a while since I had a good wine, considering all the bar carried was cheap whiskey and vodka. My mouth watered at the prospect of this wine, especially if the food was any indication of what the Fraalver's quality of alcohol was like.

I had just reached up to pluck the bottle off the shelf when the door opened, and Aaren stepped in. The door closed behind him, and he rested his weight against the aged wood. His form covered the entire door. Anger rippled off of him as he crossed his arms over his broad chest and clenched his jaw, but there was something different about it this time. It wasn't the fiery rage I had experienced before, but something more catty, almost playful. This clever anger scared me more than his outrage. His amber eyes narrowed on me, but instead of shying away from the challenge, my spine straightened, and I squared up.

"Why must you find trouble with every breath you take?" Aaren sighed. There was an edge to his tone that bit harshly at my nerves.

I bristled and clenched my jaw in defiance.

"I didn't ask to be attacked by the huldra," I hissed.

"You had no business being in the woods in the first place," he said with an infuriating coolness. There was fire in his eyes, but ice in his voice. Every interaction with him made me grow even more frustrated—he was impossible to read —and as someone trying to pursue a career in reading people, it was maddening.

I squinted my eyes to scrutinize him. "I was helping Stieg scout for supplies. Is there a problem with that?"

"After the attack last night, I assumed you'd be smarter than to venture into the forest without either me or Rorik with you." He scoffed. "I suppose I shouldn't assume so highly of you, *fremmed.*"

I reared back, wanting to pull his perfect hair in response to that comment.

81

"Maybe you just need to keep a better eye on me then, huh? Send Rorik to spy on me, it'll give him a break from being up your ass all day."

The iron vise Aaren had on his composure loosened, and he let out an irritated growl. A muscle rippled in his forearm as if he were clenching a fist. "Whatever business I have with Rorik is none of yours. If what you're demanding is that I watch your every move, I regret to inform you that I do not care to know what you do behind closed doors." He smirked.

My lips pressed together, and I sighed as my anger began to rise. Years of standing up to bullies kept me from shrinking back when Aaren pushed himself from the door and closed the distance between us in three strides, reaching for my hand. My senses dulled as heat flushed my skin, but hot anger rushed to my fingertips and lit them back to life. A hot static crackled in my palms, like I was gripping a live wire. Aaren's fingers grazed my wrist and danced along the soft skin of my forearm as he traced a pattern I couldn't discern. I would have been alarmed by the sensation if it didn't feel surprisingly soothing. Before I knew it, he dropped my hand, but my skin continued to tingle as if a hundred ants crawled along my arm. As I held my hand up to my gaze, a small symbol materialized on my forearm. It was a rune, similar to the ones I had seen on his front door and on the stones in the fireplace. He had marked me.

"Consider yourself on restriction."

Chapter 13

The forest darkened as night crept in and the air chilled. The braziers were lit, though unlike the other nights, when the paths emptied, and everyone retreated to their homes, the Fraalver meandered the paths that led to the center of the village. Towards the meeting hall. I groaned as I pictured yet another village meeting where they would discuss me, who I was, and what my fate in their village would be. Another meeting where they were given a platform to gossip and propose theories about the destruction I was here to cause.

Instead of filing into the meeting hall, however, the Fraalver gathered around the sparring ring next to it. The Fraalver numbered eight deep to the ring, and I squeezed through the crowd, eager to see who was entering the ring.

Two men stood in the ring, the shorter one with cropped, dusty brown hair and a leather breastplate hugging his chest. He adjusted the bracers around his forearm, and I noticed the shin guards he had buckled around his legs. Whoever he was fighting must've been a perilous opponent. The other man stood across from him, rolling his shoulders and stretching his neck. White-blonde hair had been swept into a loose bun, and only a loose white shirt covered his torso. It was Aaren, and to my surprise, there was a devilish smile across his lips as he watched his opponent.

A woman, the same one I had seen battling just the day before, stepped into the ring and waved her hands in a cutting motion. The sounds of the crowd hushed instantly, as if sucked through a vacuum.

"There will be two rounds between Aaren and Sigurd tonight!" the woman bellowed, voice amplified by some unseen force. Must be part of the Fraalver's domestic magic. "Hand to hand first, then weapons." She turned to the two men, and Aaren smirked. "You two know the rules: no foul play and no magic." She gave Aaren a knowing side eye. "Both of you, play nice."

"Only if he's nice to me," Sigurd retorted playfully.

Aaren's sly smile deepened. "I always play nice," he replied. Then he swung.

Sigurd barely ducked in time, but the last knuckle of Aaren's fist caught him in the temple. The observing Fraalver collectively winced, but Sigurd recovered quickly and retaliated with two swift punches to Aaren's gut. The blows didn't faze him in the slightest, and he grabbed his opponent's arm and yanked. Sigurd stumbled forward, only for Aaren to wrap his arm around the smaller man's neck. His face went red, then purple, eyes going wide as he gaped for oxygen, breath that Aaren was not going to give him anytime soon. Desperate fingers fisted handfuls of white shirt and ripped it away from Aaren's body. His muscled back now exposed, Aaren released Sigurd, who dropped to his hands and knees and gasped. The crowd cheered, and the chilled air carried the sound deep into the forest.

"I said be nice to me," he hissed through strained breaths, and the color quickly returned to his face.

Aaren shook his head. "If you wanted nice, then you shouldn't have challenged me, *Venn*."

As quickly as the hand-to-hand round ended, the weapons round started. Sigurd selected two more miniature swords, one for each hand, and he knelt low in readiness. Aaren grabbed a broad sword, the harmless metal glinting in the light of the braziers. His breath pooled in front of him as he ripped the remainder of his shirt off, sweat gleaming across his skin. I marveled at the carved muscle along his body, but stopped when I saw the sheer number of scars flecking his skin, marking him as the brutal warrior he was. Smaller, dagger-shaped scars etched along his skin, too many to quickly count. There was a mottled bit of skin along his collarbone that looked like it had been a deep, jagged cut, and I didn't want to think of what could've given him such a scar. Aaren was a seasoned fighter, and I prayed that I would never encounter the things he had fought.

He turned his back to the crowd in which I stood, and I caught my gasp before it could leave my mouth. Along his spine was a stripe of scar tissue that followed from the base of his neck to where his pants hugged his waist. It looked like something had tried to rip his spine out, a feat that I'm sure none of his opponents in the rings dared try. Something very nasty gave him that scar. Something that Aaren was lucky to have survived.

There was no time left to dwell on his past injuries because Aaren launched into motion. Every movement was delicate, yet powerful, like a ballet dance fueled by power and might. Sigurd rolled forward and sliced his blades towards Aaren's Achilles heel. Aaren jumped to avoid the attack, then landed gracefully before giving Sigurd a swift kick to the stomach. He was only down for a moment before he surged forward, arcing his blade towards Aaren, who parried the attack and dipped left, his blade shimmering with magic. Sigurd didn't turn around before Aaren slid the enchanted weapon into his back.

Instead of dropping to his knees or gasping from pain, Sigurd pumped his fist in defeat and turned to Aaren, who nodded humbly.

"You were an excellent opponent, *Venn*," he said as he retracted the harmless sword from Sigurd's back and threw it onto the platform. "Perhaps another few weeks of training, and we can spar again."

The crowd thinned as Aaren helped the others clear the ring, handing each other weapons to put away and mopping the sweat and spit off the wooden planks. I went to turn away, but couldn't peel my eyes from his scars, those violent markings that served as reminders of battles he won, or battles he lost. How many battles had he lost? I couldn't imagine there were many, but something about some of those scars told me that they held more meaning to him than the triumphs. Especially the one on his back, the one that radiated pain even though it was fully healed. The way they etched deep into his skin, the memories behind them woven into the cleaner parts of him, was like a macabre art piece.

Aaren turned, and his eyes landed on me like he knew exactly where I was. I snapped out of my trance, remembering I was supposed to hate him, that I wasn't supposed to be admiring him. I scowled as I turned on my heel and stalked down the path back to the pub.

Inaborg, the barkeeper, filled me to the brim with chicken pie and potatoes, because I was "too skinny for a woman my age". She reminded me of Granny and the way she would shovel food into my mouth instead of a formal greeting. One day, she even shoved a piece of freshly baked bread into both mine and Mama's mouths before we had even crossed the threshold.

I sank onto the bench and twiddled with the handle of my mug, lost in memories of Granny and Mama, when Inaborg shoved another plate in front of me.

"I can't possibly eat another bite," I droned and rubbed my eyes.

"It's not for you, *dumt*, I need you to take it to Rorik. Poor chap has been locked in that hut for days now."

I couldn't argue with her, not after she had just fed me enough to satiate an army, so I nodded and rose with the plate in hand.

Regretting not grabbing something to break the brisk wind before I left, I hurried down the path, the steam from the food wafting onto my cheeks and giving a little relief from the cold. I had just ducked into the niche where the door to the hut was when the sound of gruff voices stopped my hand from knocking.

"It's getting worse, Rorik," Aaren's stern voice winced.

"You're stressed, Aaren. The pain is going to continue to flare if you don't *take it easy*," Rorik replied, and then there was a shuffling, like a removal of clothes. "You shouldn't have gone into that ring in the first place. You wouldn't be experiencing such a flare-up if you hadn't."

Aaren groaned. "Just give me the tonic, Rorik. I don't need any griping today."

Rorik sighed. "Your mother would've said the same thing."

"My mother is dead, so I don't see how it matters."

"Aaren, I..."

Aaren hushed him suddenly. "Someone is listening."

I nearly fumbled the plate of food as the door opened suddenly, and Rorik's furrowed brow greeted me. His expression softened when he realized who it was and what was in my hands, but the tall, lumbering presence behind him was not as welcoming.

Aaren stood shirtless by the table in the center of the room, and he gripped a small bottle full of dark blue tonic. I noted his wince at the slight movement he made to cover himself as if he were suddenly bashful to be in such a state in front of me.

There was a curtain around the bed I had occupied, but the firelight cast a shadow of the body lying there, unmoving, barely breathing. It was the hunter who was attacked. The one they called Dagan.

"Good evening, Layla," Rorik said, friendly but brief.

"Good...evening. Inaborg told me to bring you this," I stammered and shoved the plate of food forward.

Rorik took the plate and nodded his thanks before stepping away and closing the door. Neither of them spoke once the door shut, and I didn't linger to listen anymore, no matter how loud my curiosity was.

Rorik's words replayed in my head as I closed my eyes that night, and left me with more than questions than I had before.

The next morning, I planned on looking for traces of my brother on my own, despite Aaren's supposed close watch on me. I had suspected he was in Alveland—I was on the right track after finding his book in the shack. But the huldra's words confirmed my suspicions, and now I needed to see who the huldra was talking about. Who had Lucas? Suddenly, this was way beyond my brother, lost in the woods. And because of that, I wasn't going to let Aaren's "restriction" stop my search. Although I would stay away from the river this time.

I basked in the sunlight beaming through the morning canopy and inhaled deeply, enjoying the freshness. I wasn't used to such fresh air. In Harrisburg, the spring air was crisp, but nothing like this. It was due to this realm's lack of cars, planes, and factories that pollute the air, thereby plaguing the air quality. Just a hunch.

As I walked, my mind drifted to the huldra and a shudder rustled down my spine. I remembered the way it portrayed Lucas, still feeling the beady eyes drill into my own. Its slithery voice nestled in my ears when I recalled what it had said. *He* had Lucas, and *he* was coming for me, too. Who was *he*? And whoever he was, how did he get Lucas? I considered the fact that the huldra's words weren't truthful, but maybe a way to send me on a fool's errand and drive me deeper into the woods. But I couldn't shake the idea that this person, this *he*, was a lot bigger than a huldra's plan to have me for dinner.

And how did this all tie into the mylings? It was too coincidental for these events to be separate.

I stepped off the main path and traipsed over to one of the holes in the main village border. Something stopped me from crossing over, however, although I couldn't place what that something was. My right arm pulled me back, straining my shoulder, as if someone had grabbed hold and was keeping me in place. I scrunched my brow in confusion and attempted another step forward. When my arm yanked me back so forcefully that I flopped to the ground, and I felt the morning dew soak through my pants, I grunted in frustration.

Frustration that only worsened when a chuckle sounded behind me. I picked myself up and turned vehemently because I knew exactly who was behind this.

Standing on the path with a greatsword strapped to his back was Aaren, his lips pulled tight over his teeth as he let out a cocky laugh. A group of Fraalver behind him hooted and slapped their knees.

I was on an invisible leash, and Aaren held the end of it.

Rising, I brushed the dirt from my clothes and tried to salvage as much of my pride as I could. My cheeks reddened with embarrassment, and I thundered towards him, palms heating as I balled my hands into fists.

"You're a prick," I hissed at him as I passed.

"Not so fast," he said and stopped me with a rough hand.

I spun on my heel with a biting remark ready on my tongue. "What?" I demanded.

His amused smile faded, and his familiar severity settled across his face. "Before you go traipsing off again, I think it is wise if you learned how to defend yourself." His tone was clipped, as if the words he spoke were not his own. And something told me he was reciting the words a certain physician encouraged him to say. Aaren hated saying them as much as I hated hearing them.

"Defend myself?" I questioned. "From what? If I can't leave the village now, there's nothing I need defending from."

"So you want to stay stuck in the village?"

I grunted angrily.

"Why don't we make a deal?" he began, going off-book. He loosened and cocked his head to the side. "If you train once a day for three weeks, I will remove the rune I put on you, and you and Stieg can scout for garbage to your heart's content."

I rolled my eyes and shifted my weight from foot to foot. What could happen to Lucas in three weeks?

"Nilsen has saved you twice now," Aaren added with a disapproving scowl. "I have a village and my brother to protect. And no matter who you are, those come first."

It gutted me to admit he had a point. I couldn't face any of the creatures Nilsen, a *child*, had saved me from. I wasn't helpless, but I was close to it. If the fenr, mylings, and huldra were any indication of the dangers in Alveland, I wouldn't even make it out of the forest. The unfortunate truth was I was alone and grossly unprepared. And so far, no one has been helping me look for Lucas.

"And what would this training entail?" I demanded, crossing my arms over my chest. I didn't miss the slight glance his eyes gave to my chest, though I supposed it could've been from the slight flush that spread across my sternum as my palms grew sweaty. They were *hot*, and I didn't know why.

"One hour of physical conditioning, two hours in the sparring ring, two hours doing book work with Rorik."

I considered his proposal, unwilling to delay the search for Lucas, but knowing that if I went out there on my own, I wouldn't find him. I couldn't look for him if I were dead. Besides, I had endangered the village enough, and I couldn't fault Aaren for doing his job. Be that as it may, I wasn't going to make this easy on him. Not with the way he was staring down his nose at me.

I gave a resigned sigh. "Deal."

Chapter 14

Aaren suggested we get right to business and herded me to the sparring ring, where I began to peruse the selection of weapons laid out on the racks lining the fence. I selected a short-sword, its leather hilt sticky in my palm.

Aaren scoffed. "If you think we're immediately starting with weapons, you'd be gravely mistaken."

My eyes rolled so far, they could've gotten stuck in the back of my head. This was going to be the longest three hours of my life.

"Come here."

He curled his fingers to beckon me forward, and suddenly, my back straightened, and my arm tugged me to the center of the ring. I missed my bra now more than ever as my corrected posture forced my breasts against my shirt. And I hated how embarrassed I was when the sword that had been in my hand clattered to the wood.

Aaren cocked an eyebrow and smirked at my expression before dropping his eyes to my chest, then flicking them back to my face. "That rune allows me to not only keep track of you, but beckon you when I call. You're tied to me."

"All this rune is, is a weird power trip of yours, and I can't wait until it's off me so I can scrounge for garbage in the woods and dump it in your bed."

Aaren puffed out a breath as if to mock me. I gritted my teeth angrily, my jaw throbbing at the sudden pressure. I wanted nothing more than to spit in his beautiful face.

With one hand, Aaren reached out and shoved my shoulder. I stumbled, barely catching myself. Fire rose in my skin.

"Are you kidding me?"

"Lesson number one," he said and took a step back before I could return the gesture, "stance."

I scowled and stepped my feet hip distance apart to steady myself. I took a self-defense class as my physical education credit during my senior year of high school. Whatever knowledge I retained could be applied to our lessons. Maybe once I was trained enough, I would be able to beat up Aaren. It was wishful thinking, but I grinned at the thought.

Aaren scoffed and shook his head, then strode up to me to adjust my feet with his boot. "Jut out your foot like that, and you snap an ankle." His hands squared my hips, a gesture that had me breathing deeply through my nose so as not to curse out loud. He only replied with an unimpressed roll of his eyes. Aaren stood back to examine my stance.

"First thing. Bend your knees a bit," he said and tapped my right knee. "This allows flexibility and generates power in your blow. Straighten your spine," he said, and jerked me up with his invisible string. My spine aligned perfectly.

This damn rune made me his puppet.

"Stop doing that," I sneered.

Aaren ignored my warning and tapped my elbow. "Fists up."

The last thing I wanted was to look like a blundering fool, so I racked my brain for the best way to protect the face during combat. My instructor's voice was quiet in my ear, only loud enough to remind me of the fundamental posture. My arms covered my face, and I had just enough time to register the delight in Aaren's face as his fist came swinging towards me. My arms went weak upon impact and smacked me directly in the nose.

I cried out when a dull pain radiated across my face. My nose wasn't broken, but I might end up with a gnarly bruise tomorrow. I dropped my hands long enough to check for blood before my muscles clenched and the rune forced my hands over my face again.

"Don't drop your hands in combat, *fremmed*," Aaren said, pulling his fist back once more. Luckily, my senses were on high alert, a necessary adaptation when you share a room with other kids in the foster system and they get a hankering for punishing you for their problems. Lucas was lucky—he was too little to beat up. I, on the other hand, was the go-to punching bag for one of our foster brothers. After he gave me a particularly gnarly black eye, we were removed from that house and placed in one just as problematic. The house I tried to run away from.

The house I tried to abandon Lucas in.

"You still dropped your hands." Aaren snapped his fingers, and my arms tensed and assumed position over my face again.

"I said, stop doing that!"

Aaren's eyes shone. "Make me."

I stepped forward to shove him, but he gracefully side-stepped, and I floundered, cartwheeled my arms to regain balance. Breath puffed from me in frustration, and I whirled on my heels to find Aaren staring coolly at me, awaiting my next attempt. I strode up to him and rammed him with as much force as I could muster. His stance didn't budge, but I felt his chest ripple as he braced himself against me.

My anger began to burn hotter than before, and I flung my fists at him, unsure what else I could do except let my anger out. One punch was for using the rune on me moments ago, and another fist was for embarrassing me this morning. A third was for the damn kid in my foster home because I never got to hit him back. The next punch was for making me stay here even though it was the best thing for my safety, and I swung hard for the fact that I felt helpless, utterly clueless, like a newborn calf, and I didn't know who to be angry with about it, but Aaren seemed like a good source to blame.

Whatever punches he didn't deflect, he absorbed with grace.

I cried out in frustration. Why couldn't I land one painful punch? That's all I wanted.

I gave him one more push before I backed away, running my fingers through my hair in an attempt to cool down.

"Stop looking at me like that!" I roared.

"Like what, Layla? Tell me."

I didn't fight the words, instead letting them roar out of me, my shouts like a warning bark from an angry dog. "Like I'm a tiny mouse, like some stupid pet on a leash! All I want is to find my brother. I never asked to come here, I never asked for the mylings to follow me, and I never asked for you to train me!"

I shook out my arms and sighed loudly, feeling a release in my chest, a knot loosened, and my breath came easier. "I'm not stupid, despite what you may think of me. I am capable and strong, so stop looking at me like I'm a petulant child."

Fraalver had stopped on the path to watch my outburst, but I didn't care. Let this be a lesson that they should leave me alone. I was here to find my

92

brother, nothing more, nothing less. There was no free will in my being here. I was trying to make the best of it. My fists unclenched, and the air kissed my hot fingertips.

Aaren kept his gaze trained on me, studying my stance. He was watching me, deliberating his next move, should I decide to fly off the handle again. Should I choose to let loose more of the fury I had evidently held back?

My shoulders slumped, and I waited for Aaren to wave his finger and correct my posture.

He didn't. The rune was quiet for the rest of training.

Warm air enveloped me as I entered Thea's bookshop after leaving the ring, the smell of crisp parchment and burning candles greeting me. The walls were lined with small cases of books, some open faced to display a wide array of spines in every size and color, and others enclosed their books behind glass doors. Candles burned throughout the shop with pools of drying wax gathering underneath each holder. A small ladder rested against one of the shelves, and a pile of books had been stacked at its base. In the back left corner was a large counter strewn with torn books and loose pages, covered with scribbles and half-finished writings.

How on earth had Thea written every single one of these books? And how did she function when her space was riddled with scattered papers and torn scraps of notes?

I stepped fully inside and caught sight of Thea at the counter, her fingers flipping through the stiff pages of a thick book with a mahogany cover. Her eyes lit when they lifted to see me.

"I was wondering when you were going to visit my shop!" she beamed, grabbing the orange quill Stieg had given her and placing it in the crease as she closed the book. As I stepped into a stray sunbeam streaming through a window, Thea's face fell. "You look...unwell." Her lip curled. "And you stink."

I *felt* unwell. Not only did my arms feel obliterated from the pushups Aaren had me doing, but it was an active effort to keep my eyes open. Being a server helped me stay in some shape, but the laps Aaren made me run around the village taxed my remaining energy. Besides, being a server didn't require me to spar with a full-blooded warrior. I rolled my eyes as I remembered the smug look on his face as he used the rune to drop me to my knees and run me through a series of burpees and lunges. It was physically taxing, and by the end of it, I was nearing the edge of complete mortification—with nothing to hold my breasts in place, they had free rein. Aaren inevitably noticed, but refused to make any allowances.

I shook my head and groaned. "I was just training with Aaren. He did *not* take it easy on me." Dropping onto the stool in front of the counter, I grimaced as my muscles twinged and threatened to give out. One wrong move, and I'd be a pile of exhaustion on the floor.

After my humiliating outburst, Aaren had me rotate through a circuit of exercises that he claimed would help my balance and weight distribution in a battle. It was all about the feet, he had said, but everything was connected, relying on each other in case one part failed. Every part had to be up to snuff. By the end of the circuit, I had done two hundred sit-ups, a hundred push-ups, and then held a plank for two minutes. As miserable as it was, the physical activity helped me diffuse some of my angst.

It still hurts. And between the warmup workout and the circuit, I was sure Aaren was trying to torture me. And every sick part of him loved it. Perhaps he was operating under the guise of working me so hard that I spilled my secrets to him. Lost cause. Before he dismissed me, he tested my stance once more. I remained firm at his push and left the ring with a smug grin. Even Aaren was pleased, showing it in a way only Aaren could (a slight nod of his head and a grunt of approval before sending me off). I caught the slightest shine in his eyes as I turned, though, and even if he thought I didn't see it, I did. It was something I wouldn't soon forget.

But it was not literary curiosity that brought me to Thea's shop—I needed a replacement for my lost bra.

"Can I ask you a personal question?" I began.

With a curious look, Thea replied, "If you read any of my books, you'll know nothing is too personal."

"Can you help me find something to keep my..." I gestured to my chest, "...these in place for training?"

Thea laughed, her pleasant, melodic laugh filling the air as her hands rested across her chest. "I think I've got just the thing."

She ducked behind her counter, and a heavy trunk lid creaked open before she reappeared, clutching a thick piece of fabric. "I'm not daft enough to think I can squeeze you into a corset, but this might suffice." She passed it to me with instructions on how to bind my chest and pin the fabric to ensure it stayed put during training.

"I find it intriguing that he is taking the time to train you," Thea mused, "considering he has not taken an interest in a woman in years."

"Stieg told me about Aaren's betrothed; there's no need to dance around it."

Thea raised her brows in amusement and traced the wood grain of the counter with her finger.

"And he's not taking an interest in me," I retorted. "He's operating under some infantile need to assert dominance. Maybe prove something to the village. I don't know." Thea only replied by lifting her brow in evident disbelief. "The point is," I continued, "he's *far* from interested in me. I think he'd rather see me drawn and quartered than entertain anything else."

Thea blew a haughty breath. "Aaren is a lot more complex than some brute that picks up a weapon in the ring. There's a reason he's putting you through this."

It was my turn to make a haughty noise. "Only because Rorik told him to."

Thea smirked. "Be that as it may, see where this takes you. It might benefit you more than you think."

I opened my mouth to give her an incredulous retort, but a twinge of pain in my back distracted me. I rotated my shoulder and cringed when my muscles screamed in agony. I massaged my right bicep, feeling the muscles tighten with every dig of my thumb. My finger brushed the rune, and I placed my forearm on the counter for Thea to see. "Would you happen to know how to get rid of a rune?"

Thea chuckled. "Your naivete makes me laugh." She pressed her finger onto my forearm and examined it. "Only the imprinter of the rune can remove it. Whoever put this on you must be the one to erase it."

My head fell back, and I groaned. "Aaren put it on me to stay within the village borders. I'm stuck here."

Thea cocked an eyebrow. "*Venn*, you must be daft not to see what he's doing." When I replied with a simple shake of the head, Thea continued. "He's working, and I would say succeeding, to get a rise out of you."

A likely possibility, and one I knew Aaren was taking great pleasure in. The satisfied, almost wicked gleam in his eye when running me through the circuit was all I needed to confirm that suspicion.

I scoffed. "I thought you said there's more to it than him being a brute."

"And I'm right."

I shook my head in confusion, feeling the muscles in my neck stretch. "I don't follow."

Thea shifted in her chair and leaned forward as if she were about to divulge a secret. "Rorik and Aaren know you are not human; that much has been made clear to them. You wouldn't be here if you were. The question remains what you are, and since that is not human, it leaves it open to what kind of magic you possess."

My lips thinned to cut my laughter. The thought of me possessing magic was more than laughable: it was absurd. The idea that I was harboring secret magic was a ludicrous theory, and one that I would put absolutely no stock in. To even begin to think that someone as unremarkable as me could have magic...

Thea chuckled. "Aaren must be taunting you to see if anything escapes when you get emotional." She leans back. "That's usually when someone loses control of their magic."

So he planned for my outburst in the sparring ring. And I had played right into his hands. I'd have to compose myself when I was around Aaren in the future. Especially now that I knew he planned to rile me up and treat me like a science experiment. Not only a pet on a leash, but his guinea pig as well. Annoyance sizzled in my veins. This was going to be a lot harder than I thought.

"How did you piece all that together?" I asked, my tone piquing interest.

"I'm a writer, my job is to piece things together." She leaned forward on her elbows. "Would you like to check out my new book? I finished it just last week."

To be polite, I nodded and accepted the book she passed over the counter.

Chapter 15

The medicine hut was locked when I went to look for Rorik for my lesson; the windows were still cloudy, like the day the hunter was attacked. Resigned to finding Rorik elsewhere, I wandered back to the pub where, luckily, I found him sitting with a group of Fraalver, sharing a drink with them. Or many drinks as the glazed look in his eyes indicated. The group whooped and howled as someone recounted a bawdy story of a dwarf that had me scrunching my brow as they graphically exaggerated the size of a particular body part. Apparently, I was the only one who didn't find it funny.

I sat down next to Rorik, who grinned widely and wrapped an arm around my shoulder. He reeked of ale.

"And here we have Layla, bringer of mylings and deceiver of huldra."

The group cackled and threw back their ale, gulping and slurping as every one of them drained their tankards.

Rorik let out a satisfied sigh.

"You're drunk," I said pointedly.

"Yes, I am," he answered matter-of-factly. "It's my day off."

"As a physician, I didn't think you got days off."

He ignored my comment and gestured to me with his mug. "Someone get Layla some ale."

I pulled out of his arm and shook my head. "No, no," I protested. "I'm supposed to meet with you, Aaren's orders."

A hush settled around the crowd and some of the Fraalver turned and sipped their ale, obviously pretending not to listen. Rorik's eyes cleared for a moment. "I suppose it will have to wait until tomorrow." He hiccupped. "Or the next day." The drunken veil clouded his eyes once more.

I sighed and stiffly pushed myself up from the bench. At least I was off the hook for the day, and it wasn't my fault.

"Layla," Rorik slurred, letting out an airy burp.

I turned.

"You're going to be very powerful when you decide you're ready to be."

I searched for the right words to say, unsure where his thoughts had sprouted from. "Thanks, Rorik."

At least I was off the hook for today.

The next morning, I met Aaren in the sparring ring, my muscles stiff and aching. Every movement was agony, as if my limbs were slowly turning to rock. Aaren set me to stretching and I almost howled in pain as I extended my hamstring. I had barely made it halfway through the stretches before there was sweat on my brow and tears in my eyes.

"How was your lesson with Rorik?" Aaren questioned as he circled me, surveying my form.

I dipped and touched my toes with a wince. "I didn't go."

"What?"

I straightened, the blood rushing from my head, leaving me woozy for a few seconds. "I mean, I did go, but he was drunk."

Aaren dipped his head in resignation. "I should've remembered it was his day off." At my confused scowl, Aaren explained. "Fraalver people are hardworking, but we cherish our time and the pleasures we fill that time with."

"Interesting, because *my* time doesn't seem that valuable to you," I bit, thinking of Lucas.

"If it's any consolation, I don't ever get a day off. I'll give you a pass for yesterday, and you can start your lessons with Rorik today."

"How generous," I said sarcastically.

With a half-hidden, satisfied smirk, Aaren commanded, "On your knees," manipulating the rune until I complied. The gesture was a punishment for the sardonic glare I had sent his way, not because he was eager to start the training.

Aaren gave me the same circuit of exercises as yesterday, and as I neared the end of my last set, I was drenched in sweat and welcomed the cool, near-spring breeze. Throughout my workout, his eyes attentively studied my form and critiqued where he felt was needed. By the end, I felt there was not a single spot on my body he hadn't observed. At least my chest was bound today. I shivered, fighting the goosebumps freckling my skin as he adjusted my stance. Feigning irritation, I groaned that my stance was fine. Aaren responded by pushing me, and I toppled to the ground, cursing him and everyone who ever came before him.

For my foul language, he added an extra ten minutes of training to work on my stance again.

Aaren offered me a hand to pull me up from the ground after I finished his grueling set of crunches, and for a moment, we stood almost nose to nose, his eyes gleaming into mine. Striations of copper flecked his amber eyes, and I noted a hint of somberness, like the yellow of his irises was simply a mask for the swirling mess behind them. He blinked and pulled away.

"Take your stance."

Remembering the footing we had just adjusted, I assumed my wide stance, obediently awaiting instruction. Aaren held up a hand.

"Hit me."

I obliged. The shock of the blow reverberated up my arm, and my wrist sang in dull pain. When I shook my hand out, Aaren held out his own.

"Make a fist," he said, and when I complied, he shook his head. "No, curl your fingers like this." He played with my fingers until they were in the proper position, curling them inwards until my nails bit into my palms. "Good. Strike with this part of your knuckles."

He held up a massive hand and gestured for me to hit him again. As I did so, there was less pain and more power behind it.

"Better." His fingers danced up my arm as he directed the way my arm should rotate as I swung, and my skin flushed at the touch. "Again."

I did, hitting his hand again, and again, and again. He stepped away for a moment, instructing me to watch. He approached the straw-stuffed practice dummy and assumed his stance. His feet planted firmly on the ground, as if tree roots anchored him to the wooden floor of the ring. With a furious grunt, he struck the dummy's abdomen with a dull thud. His corded arm tensed at the impact, but no sign of pain stretched his features. Just grace and nonchalance.

Bits of straw dropped from the dummy, and Aaren turned, gesturing for me to approach.

I assumed my stance again, then launched my first punch at the figure. Straw scratched my knuckles, but the blow was satisfying.

"You're getting better," Aaren encouraged. "Let me walk you through it again."

He pushed me through a couple of slow-motion punches on the dummy, correcting my elbow when it flew out on the swing, then adjusted the way my fist landed. After ten minutes, I had an almost perfect punch.

"It takes practice, *fremmed*," Aaren assured. His softer tone surprised me, but I was too tired to linger on the thought. "Now, where is the best place to hit an opponent?"

Shrugging, I replied, "The face, I suppose." I knew there was probably a better answer, but I would say anything to make this lesson end faster.

"That's one of them," Aaren said, a few strands of silver hair spilling from his bun. "There is also the center of the chest," he traced a finger down his breastbone, "the stomach, and the cock."

Aaren froze for a fraction of a second, then cleared his throat. "The groin," he corrected. The blood in my veins heated momentarily. "What's that look on your face for?"

"So our next spar..."

I smiled in satisfaction as Aaren rolled his eyes. "No, you can't go for my co...groin!"

I stifled a chuckle.

Aaren shot me a warning look, telling me he didn't think it was that funny. "I'd like to keep my chances of having children later in life."

Rolling my eyes, I retook my stance. "I knew you weren't going to let me have any fun."

The rest of the lesson focused on dodging blows and the best ways to recover from them. I left the ring with the promise of more stretches and punching tomorrow, to my dismay.

Today, I tried the medicine hut again, but this time, the door was unlocked. Thinking Rorik was inside, I pushed the heavy wood open. The room was dark with only the weak sunlight streaming through the fogged windows. The fire in the hearth cracked softly, needing to be stoked. The little stones embedded in the ash shone weakly, as if the protection they gave the hut was faltering. Is that why the door was unlocked?

"Rorik?" I whispered into the gloom.

I took a step inside, scanning the room.

The hut was the same as it had been when I arrived a few days ago, except now there was a curtain surrounding the bed, shielding whoever lay behind it. Unable or unwilling to fight my curiosity, I peered around the drape and almost gasped at what I saw.

Nestled into the furs was the hunter, Dagan, who was attacked by the mylings on my first day. His skin was sallow, as if someone had drained the life from him and left behind a pale shell. He reminded me of when the cicadas would leave behind their shells in the summertime, and Mama would take me to the park to collect them.

Dagan's long hair had been braided back from his face, and his sunken eyes quivered under darkened eyelids, lost in a dream. As I drew closer, his features became more recognizable. He had been in the group of Fraalver at the border the night I arrived. The night I brought a myling to their village.

I moved closer to examine his still form, and a dull ache pumped in my chest. Twinges of guilt twisted in my gut as I tried not to blame myself, but it was no use. I brought the mylings here. Because of me, Dagan was tucked away in this bed, comatose from the myling's grasp. It should've been me. If it had just taken me at the beginning, none of this would have happened.

I shuddered as I remembered the feeling of those cold hands wrapped around my throat.

When I examined Dagan's neck, there were small handprints bruised into his blanched skin, spreading tendrils of red down his collarbone and onto his sternum. A half-used jar of luktrot sat on the end table near the bed, though the paste seemed useless in his case.

I reached down to adjust his pillow but froze. Dagan's eyes opened suddenly, and his hand wrapped my wrist in a deadly grip. His eyes were cloudy, no pupils or irises to be seen, only milky, swimming mire. The grip tightened on my wrist, and my hand quickly went numb, his fingernails digging into my skin, and his mouth spread into a sickly grin, baring his yellowing teeth. He hadn't looked like this the night he was at the border—it was almost like something was eating him from the inside.

"Sweet Layla," he rasped, and his voice sounded like a million voices compiled into one mouth. "I've been looking for you."

Panic danced in my muscles as I tried to pull my hand away.

"Lucas has been asking for you."

I gasped, wrenching my hand free from the man's icy fingers and backing up. He sat up with uncanny grace and turned to face me, his neck twisting at a gruesome angle.

"Where is he?" I demanded. "Where is Lucas?"

"I can take you to him," he answered. "All you have to do is let me in. Let me see where you are."

I shook my head, and my knees knocked into the table behind me, a glass jar shattering on the ground. The stink of potent herbs filled the room.

Dagan lithely swung his legs over the side of the bed and stood, that languid sneer imprinted into his features.

"Brother and sister can be reunited," he jeered, taking a firm step toward me. For a man who had just spent days in bed, he was strong on his feet. The smell of the spilled herb was becoming overpowering, and I stifled my breath to inhale as little as possible. Dagan extended his hand. "Show me," he whispered.

I dashed for the door and burst into the sunlight. After the darkness of the medicine hut, I squinted against the sun until my eyes adjusted. Thundering footsteps pounded after me as I sprinted down the path, dodging Fraalver as I passed. I shouted for someone to get Aaren as I bounded past a group of women, with curious and confused expressions on each of their faces.

"You can't run from me, Layla, you belong to me." The man's voice was clear, as if he weren't charging after me in a violent dash.

I skidded to a halt in the square in front of the meeting house and turned to see the man's sinister gaze focus on me as he took a step closer. His hand was still outstretched in offering. "It's *your* fault Lucas is gone." His cloudy eyes swam in the sun. "He remembers you leaving that one night. He saw you trying to escape, trying to leave him behind."

I shook in disbelief. How could he have known about that night? I wasn't even sure Lucas remembered it.

"I...I didn't try to leave *him*," I argued through hammering breaths. "I was trying to leave the house. I couldn't stay there anymore." As I said these words,

I prayed that Lucas could somehow hear them, and I begged whatever force was out there to bring my words to him. "I love you, Lucas." These last words were uttered under my breath.

"He remembers what you said in the park, Layla," the rasping voice hissed. "He has less than everyone. Why is that, Layla? What more could Lucas possibly need outside of you?" He sneered, exposing an eerily wide smile. "You can't take care of him when he's not there, Layla. Just let me in."

By now, a crowd had formed in a ring around the square, and instinctually, I shrank back, analyzing the best place to hide. There was no place to go. I couldn't let panic choke me, not when it had almost gotten me killed in the clearing with the mylings, so I stood tall and planted my feet firmly on the ground. Aaren's words rang in my head. A s*light bend in the knees generates power and flexibility.*

Dagan took one swift stride toward me, and I took a step forward, remembering the instructions for a perfect punch. With a deep breath, I swung my fist. It swooped through the air and landed square on the man's jaw with a sickening crack. He did not howl in pain nor did he stumble in recovery. Instead, he squared his shoulders, popping his jaw as his grimly foul smile returned to his face. I threw my fist again, and this time, he dodged.

He laughed wickedly as he straightened, rolling his neck as if he were readying for his own attack. "If you just take my hand, Layla, you can have your brother back. It's that simple." He offered his hand once more.

Fury rose in me, and I screamed, swinging punch after punch, kicking his legs with unyielding fire. My skin grew white hot as I whaled on him, the sweat on my brow doing nothing to cool me or the flames licking my insides. He deftly dodged each one, ducking and jumping out of the way. I was starting to tire, but I forced my strength into one last punch towards his face. He caught my hook in his hand and gave me a moment to stare into his opaque eyes. They were so empty, so...dead, and I reared back in panic, but my hand remained clenched in his. Then Dagan's eyes swirled with an unsettling fog that morphed into shapes of terror. I saw a crowd of people, all lined up in rows, each with varying degrees of decaying skin. The clouds transformed into a writhing snake. And then I saw Lucas, his face distorted as the clouds churned and roiled. I couldn't make out any details from the image, but it confirmed that he was still alive, and that meant I could still find him.

"Where are you?" Dagan wisped. His hold on my fist tightened with rage. "Where are you? WHERE ARE YOU?"

Dagan was cut short by something, a small choke coming from his throat. An almost black tongue slithered out of his mouth, chin dropping against his neck as he hacked. He dropped my hand and wavered as that haunting presence ebbed from his face. He coughed again, and his eyes cleared. The shape of blue irises surrounding a dark pupil returned. For a fraction of a second, there was actual life in those eyes. For the briefest moment, I saw Dagan for who he was before he careened and crumbled to the ground.

Pale hands clasped his throat as the tight skin across his face turned a slight blue, as if invisible hands were choking him from the inside. There was a slight breeze in the eerie silence of the square, filled only with the choking sounds of the hunter and the rustling of the leaves above. That familiar smell filled my nostrils, the same scent that embraced me that day in the forest with Stieg. I followed the breeze until I caught sight of Aaren at the side of the square, brow furrowed in concentration.

Dagan was being choked from the inside. Aaren was stealing the air from his lungs.

My stomach did sick flips as I backed away from the hunter, watching the clear eyes fade. A scream worked its way up my throat, but shock overwhelmed it, and I faltered before falling to my knees.

Dagan fell with a thud and did not move again.

I gasped, my hands flying to my own throat like I was scared Aaren would attack my lungs next. He didn't, though. Instead, he stepped forward and knelt next to the man he had just suffocated.

Thea was the next one to break the circle as she approached me cautiously, resting a gentle hand on my shoulder. I didn't react, couldn't react, as she pulled me up and led me through the crowd, shoving people away and murmuring calming words. As we withdrew, soft mutters washed through the crowd. I tuned them out, but I imagined what they were saying. The heavy weight of shame sank the ship of hope in my chest, a ship that was riddled with holes and filled with water every second I stayed here.

It seemed Thea's bookshop was becoming a haven of sorts for me, because as soon as the door closed behind us, I let out a sigh of relief. My feet moved of their own volition, and I sank into a chair and dropped my head into my hands, heaving a whimpering cry into my fingers. A warm washcloth heated the skin on my neck, and I trembled as that raspy voice still rang in my ears. I could still see that murky image of Lucas's misshapen face.

Thea cursed under her breath, the vulgar word such a stark contrast to her lovely voice. "Here they come," she sighed, and as I lifted my head from my hands, the front door of her shop swung open. Aaren thundered in, followed closely by Rorik.

"What happened?" Aaren demanded as he stomped through the bookshop, leaving pages flying in his wake. I wasn't sure if it was his stride or his untapped, forested power that caused such an upheaval. His tone was firm, even demanding, the rumbling bass woven with a territorial wrath that sent heat spiraling through my chest. Not because his towering frame flustered me, but from my own anger.

I stood fiercely, hands balling into perfect fists, and I wanted to grimace at how, because of Aaren, my combat readiness had already improved. "It wasn't my fault," I barked. He seemed to blaze like a raging forest fire as he took a step closer, and I craned my neck to keep him in my eyeline.

"What. Happened."

His eyes flared with anger, enough that I caught the warning to stand down, because if I didn't, it could get deadly. I grumbled agitatedly, and I wanted nothing more than to spit on him for the way he regarded me. Knowing by now that aggression would get me nowhere, especially with Aaren, I tried to dampen the malice in my chest. I wanted to fight back, but this wasn't the time or place. One of his villagers was dead, and yet again, all signs pointed to me. I sighed when I remembered his words in the pub a few days ago. Why must I find trouble wherever I go? It's not like I looked for it; it always just seemed to see me. It wasn't *my* fault; I couldn't find Rorik. And how was I supposed to know I was going to be chased through the village by a seemingly possessed man? The door to the apothecary should've been locked. That was no fault of mine.

"I was looking for Rorik," I began, "and I went to check the medicine hut for him. When I entered, the...man grabbed me. He said he's been looking for me." I paused to settle the remaining anger that had been threatening to build again. Brick by brick, I broke down the aggression and forced my tone to be less harsh, more diplomatic. "He knows where my brother is."

Aaren glanced at Rorik, who remained silent but narrowed his eyes in consideration.

"He said that if I touched him, he could find me." I furrowed my brow. "He caught my punch. Does that mean he knows where I am?"

Thea leaned down and grabbed my arm, pressing her thumb into the rune that now glowed brightly on my forearm. "This is the reason that he couldn't find you," she said. "This is the reason our village is safe now." She glanced at Aaren, but said nothing.

My eyes rose to Aaren's blazing, amber orbs. "He has my brother. Whoever *he* is."

Anger ebbed from Aaren's face, though nothing replaced it to my disappointment. I had at least expected a silent apology, a wistful, sorry look, or something. Instead, he turned on his heel and sighed. "Build the funeral pyre," he instructed Rorik. "The sooner we burn Dagan, the better. And find Nilsen, get him back home."

He turned to me, a minuscule hint of pride shimmering in his expression, a look that jarred me. "You fought well." He nodded to me, and a small swell of triumph rose in my chest, heat flushing my cheeks. Aaren then stepped out into the forest, leaving Thea and me alone.

Chapter 16

Nilsen beat me in Balderkrig again. His huldra demolished my trolls in a few turns, leaving my Balder vulnerable. I underestimated his strategy, and that led my small stone army into destruction. We sat at the table, chewing on dry bread, as we waited for the pieces to put themselves back together before starting a new game.

"Poor Dagan," Nilsen cooed as he pulled the crust apart in his hands and started rolling the bread into little balls.

"Did he have a family?" I asked, the bread like ash in my mouth. I took a sip of ale I had poured from the clay pitcher on the table.

Nilsen shook his head. "Pesta took his parents, and he didn't have a wife."

Guilt seeped into my chest once again, that same dread I had felt in the medicine hut before Dagan had awoken. Before I could ponder on the regret and blame myself, the door opened, and Aaren stalked in.

Having observed the broken players splayed in front of us, he asked, "Who won?"

I pointed a defeated finger at Nilsen, who grinned proudly.

"Excellent."

"She's getting better, though," Nilsen lied, reaching for another piece of bread.

"Well, like all good generals, you need to rest, Nilsen," Aaren said. "It must've been a very exhausting battle."

Nilsen dropped his head to the table in pretend fatigue, wiping his brow as if he had just fought in battle himself. I smiled—that was something Lucas would've done. Aaren scooped Nilsen up and threw him over his shoulder, ignoring the small punches and kicks from Nilsen as he giggled and squealed with delight, saying he wasn't even tired. I followed quietly, but stayed out of sight. Aaren kicked open the door to Nilsen's bedroom, where he flopped his brother's flailing form into the bed of furs. Nilsen nestled into bed, and I lingered just outside the door, smiling softly as Aaren ran a brotherly hand through Nilsen's hair.

"Aaren?" Nilsen asked as he wrapped an arm around something soft and stuffed. It looked to be a stuffed squirrel, only its tail was bushier and its eyes were larger, cartoonish in a way. "Did you kill Dagan?"

Aaren sighed and shifted on the bed. "He wasn't Dagan anymore, Nilsen. The mylings took that away from him." The regret was heavy in his voice, stirring undeniable guilt in my gut. Because, yet again, this was my fault. No matter what I did here, someone ended up hurt. It would be a long time before I forgot Dagan's pallid face and the remaining bit of his humanity that drained from his eyes.

"And he was about to hurt Layla. We don't want anything bad to happen to her." I blinked in surprise. Aside from his compliment in the shop earlier, that might've been the first nice thing I'd heard Aaren say about me.

Nilsen nodded innocently. "I wish the mylings would go away." He paused, twirling the tail of his stuffed animal. "And I hope Layla finds her brother."

Aaren paused with his lips pressed together pensively. "Me too, *bror*." Nilsen reached up and wrapped his small arms around his brother, getting lost in Aaren's bulky embrace. They stayed for a long moment, finding the only solace they could in each other before Aaren rose and pinched out the candle on the bedside table.

I tiptoed away before I was seen and danced back to my seat at the table, where I slurped a mouthful of ale. Aaren walked back into the dining area.

I beheld him for a moment, admiring not the warrior I was growing to know him as, nor the leader, but as Nilsen's brother. His protector. Aaren was all Nilsen had left. That's one thing Aaren and I had in common.

He nodded his head toward the door. "Come," he invited. "You'll miss the festivities."

I heard the drumbeat as soon as I stepped outside the house.

"Is this for Dagan?" I asked as we began our path to the square.

"Yes," Aaren confirmed. "Fraalver funerals are quite a spectacle." He went on to explain that the Fraalver viewed death as another stage in life, another adventure. They believed that after death, the soul embarked on a journey to Himmelfjell, the mountain of heaven. This mountain was also a realm on a branch of Yggdrasil. Everyone went to the mountain. If you could make it. According to common belief, the journey there was brutal, and many souls didn't make it, forcing them to wander the forest below the mountain for eternity. The Fraalver believed that the merrier the funeral, the easier the journey to Himmelfjell.

Once they reached the top of the mountain, they encountered three entities known as the Treskjebs. Each entity had one power to determine the soul's fate. If they were worthy, the first entity would allow the soul into the mountain. If they were not worthy, the second entity would dispose of the soul in a way no one knew until it happened. If the soul's destiny had yet to be filled, the third entity would send them back to the realm from which they came until they fulfilled their destiny.

"Has anyone ever come back?" I asked.

"No."

The drums boomed louder as we entered the square where a large funeral pyre had been erected. Dagan rested at the top. Surrounding his body were packs of supplies and weapons, all poised to be burned with him to assist in his journey to Himmelfjell. I couldn't look at his lifeless form for too long before guilt gripped me like an iron vice. If it weren't for me, he wouldn't be on top of that pyre. If it weren't for me, the drums wouldn't be playing. It would be a normal night. Right? A little voice in the back of my mind told me otherwise. It was telling me Dagan's fate was inevitable, just like my arrival here. But that wasn't something I was ready to dwell on.

Tables of food lined the square, one laden with a roast pig so large there was little room for garnish. On the others were trays of bread and cheese, smoked meats and roasted vegetables, and a massive keg of ale had been tapped and flowed freely. Next to the keg was a table with bottle after bottle of spiced wine. My mouth watered at the sight.

Each Fraalver was dressed in their best. One woman wore a dress of velvety scarlet with gold embroidered into the hems of her skirt and sleeves. Her lovely brown hair was woven into an intricate braid and pinned to her head with golden barrettes that sparkled in the flickering lights. The men wore beautiful jackets of rich colors, and their boots had been polished to shine in the firelight.

I tugged at my brown pants and dug my worn boots into the path, my cheeks flushing. "I think I'm a little underdressed."

As if my words summoned her, Thea appeared in a divine purple gown, stars of silver dotting the soft fabric. Silver suns dangled from her ears, and the rouge on her cheeks shimmered as the shadows danced across a face framed by cascading brown curls.

"I'll take it from here," she sang, looping her arm through mine and dragging me from Aaren.

Before I could protest, we wove through the crowd and back to her shop. The inside was dark save for the candle Thea had lit as she strode to the back corner. She kicked the rug away to reveal a trapdoor that creaked when she threw it open. I followed as she ascended the wooden stairs. Below her shop was a cozy apartment with a simmering fire and a large bed in the corner that looked soft enough to topple into. Near the bottom of the stairs was a small writing desk littered with papers, empty bottles of ink, and broken quills. Laying neatly on the bedside table was the orange treelskere feather. On the walls hung drying herbs and bouquets, and small pieces of parchment were stuck to the stone near her bed. I squinted to read them before I was caught, realizing they were love notes from the looks of them, but from whom, I could not tell.

Thea thrust open a trunk under the stairs and withdrew a long, light green gown with little wildflowers embroidered into the lacy layers of the skirts. The top was bunched in a corset, and there were light, flowy sleeves that cuffed at the wrists in a ring of delicate, white wildflowers. Putting on the dress was no problem, but lacing the corset proved too tricky for me to do on my own. Thea watched me knotting the strings, amusedly, before stepping in to help, pulling them tight. I clasped my abdomen as the corset squeezed the breath from me. How was I supposed to breathe the rest of the night?

"You don't," Thea replied to my musing and chuckled. "But your waist looks divine, *true.*"

Thea then set herself to work arranging my hair, weaving small buds through my auburn locks and fussing over the jewelry I had selected.

"You'd be better wearing these," she suggested and held up a pair of pearl earrings.

She applied rouge to my cheeks, tint to my lips, and a darkener to my lashes, claiming it wouldn't smudge during the night.

I slipped my feet into a pair of floral sandals and gaped at myself in the mirror. I was never one for dressing up, mostly because I couldn't afford it. If I had had the chance to wear a gown like this and go somewhere, I would've jumped on the first opportunity. One Christmas, Mama bought me a princess dress, and for three weeks after, I wouldn't take it off. Mama couldn't even convince me to take it off when I had spilled spaghetti sauce down the front. My high school threw a prom, but I never went because I knew I wouldn't have a dress, plus I didn't have a date, or friends for that matter, so I found no point in going. My roommates would sometimes dress up in their skinny jeans and sequined tops and go bar hopping, but I turned down every invitation until they stopped bothering to extend them to me. This was the first time I had seen myself in a lovely dress in years.

I seldom stopped to actually look at myself in the mirror, not for a very long time. Every time I did, I was disappointed by what stared back at me. An orphaned little girl grasping at the little bits of life she was able to live, starving for the scraps of freedom she was dealt. What looked back at me now was not a girl; she was something between a girl and a woman. I had grown into my curves, and the corset accented my chest in every proper way, breasts swelling with every strained breath I took. I admired the makeup Thea had applied, the rouge highlighting my supple cheekbones and small nose, and I gave myself a small smile. Whoever stared back at me was beautiful.

Now that I was appropriately dressed, we returned to the celebration. Following Thea to the drinks, I grabbed a mug of ale and drank deeply, enjoying the notes of honey and wheat. Thea sipped a small chalice of wine and surveyed the crowd.

"You look lovely tonight, *frue* Thea." I turned my head slightly to find Stieg leaning against the wine table, gazing dreamily at Thea, who cocked an eyebrow and smirked.

"And you look quite handsome tonight, *herr* Stieg."

Stieg reddened, even in the firelight, and wiped his sweaty palms on his loose pants. He had swapped his worn shirt for a clean linen one underneath a royal blue colored vest, fastened with gold buttons. His hair was combed back, and a small flower had been placed in the breast pocket of his vest.

"I finished your book this morning," Stieg told Thea sweetly.

"What did you think?"

He paused, his eyes dancing. "Riveting."

I was taken aback by the exchange, masking my surprise in my mug of ale. I wanted to kick myself for judging Stieg's character on face value, but after my morning in the woods with him, I didn't have him pegged for someone who read very many books, or someone who used the word "riveting." I suppose I should get to know him a little better. Maybe one day I'd get around to telling him the true function of his candy wrappers.

Rorik sidled next to me and smiled softly. "You look enchanting tonight, Layla."

I bowed my head in gratitude. "Thank you, Rorik."

"I am...sorry for this morning," he began, not taking his eyes off the crowd milling about in front of us. "If I had been more at your disposal, it might not have happened."

I curled my lips and shook my head. "It's not your fault, Rorik; you couldn't have known this was going to happen."

"That may be, but my apology still stands."

I thanked him.

"After your lesson with Aaren, I will happily meet you at Harald's. We can begin our first lesson there."

I agreed.

Scanning the crowd before me, I observed the interactions between the Fraalver. Not a single tear was shed over Dagan; in fact, many laughed and howled together in merriment, everyone sipping ale and munching bread and cheese.

I spotted Aaren across the square and my heart gave a slight flutter. Covering his muscled chest was a coat of deep green, embellished with gold accents that mimicked the forest around us. His hair was loosely tied back, half up, half down, with strands of hair that framed his face. He stood tall as he locked eyes with me, though I quickly broke his stare by pretending to need more ale. I swallowed heaping gulps to drown the harsh pounding in my chest. The square was hot, and I told myself it was because of the bonfire and all the bodies, not because of the way Aaren had just looked at me. When I was brave enough to look at him again, he had moved towards the pyre, and a hush fell over the crowd. His presence was a commanding one, his leadership a promise that every Fraalver held close to their heart.

He scanned the crowd momentarily with a clenched jaw. Was he nervous, or was that the look of an unyielding leader? His eyes revealed nothing, unfortunately, leaving me to continue to study him closely.

"Fraalver," he began. "We gather here to celebrate the journey of Dagan, hunter and loyal friend to us all." The only sound in the crowd was the crackle of the braziers. "Dagan died not only protecting his people, our people, but also giving us knowledge of what haunts our borders." His jaw rippled. "What threatens our safety?" A soft mutter swept across the crowd and then quickly died down. My mug became sweaty in my hand.

"We do not know the exact nature of the threat, but we need not insult his memory by casting hate and suspicion on those we do not know." A glance in my direction, but to my surprise, I was grateful for it. "Tonight, Dagan begins his journey to Himmelfjell. Be merry so his travels will be steadfast, and he will be welcomed into the mountain to meet our kin with open arms." He raised his tankard. "To Dagan!"

"To Dagan!" the crowd echoed.

I raised my own mug, and then I downed the rest before refilling it.

"Now, friends," Aaren continued. "Let's make sure he makes it to the mountain!"

A roar erupted from the crowd, and the drums proceeded with gusto. Someone began playing a flute, and another joined with a fiddle. I already needed another refill. I had decided tonight that I was going to get incoherently drunk. Dagan died for me; might as well help his journey as much as I could. Besides, after the events of the last few days, it would be nice to forget for a night.

A Fraalver approached Aaren and passed him a lit torch. Knocking back his arm, he tossed the torch in a magnificent arc, and it landed on Dagan's chest, sending the pyre into a flurry of outrageous flame. The crowd cheered and hooted as it blazed brightly.

I applauded and cheered with the Fraalver as the fire danced across the pyre, and the warm tingling that accompanied drinking settled into my limbs. I bounced and relished the looseness in my body, then took another gulp.

The Fraalver skirted the edges of the square, and pairs skipped in, bouncing to a jig the fiddle was hammering out. They laughed and spun and hopped to the beat, and for the first time in I didn't know how long, elation filled my veins. I sighed deeply as I swayed to the music. If I stayed here, I wouldn't have to do another assignment for school or work a single shift at the bar. When I found Lucas, he wouldn't ever have to go back to foster care. He could live with me, and I wouldn't have to fill out hills of paperwork or have wellness checks from CPS. He could be a kid here. He could run around with Nilsen and Ingrid and play Balderkrig and pretend in the treehouse, and I wouldn't have to worry about him because he would be here, safe like me.

Because right now, I felt safe. This ale must be magical.

I watched the crowd of dancers, surprised to see Aaren step into the center with a woman on his arm. The other dancers gave them space as the woman turned to face him, and his hand found her waist, pulling her close. I envied the ease with which they moved around the floor as I watched from my spot by the ale keg. Aaren moved effortlessly, the woman matching his movements with expert steps as the song progressed.

The music ended, and my mug was empty again. As I turned to refill it, a shadow crossed my vision. It was Aaren who towered above me, bemused.

"You look beautiful," he said over the noise.

Heat rose to my cheeks, and I wasn't sure if it was because of the ale. "Thank you."

Aaren extended his hand to me. "Care to learn the steps of the Fraalver?"

I hesitated because I couldn't remember the last time I had danced. About to shake my head, Aaren gave me an encouraging nod toward the crowd. "It's alright," he said, "Consider this part of your training." Still hesitant, I slid my hand into his rough palm and trailed after him into the square. Rorik cheered us as we found our place amongst the frivolity.

Aaren's hand settled on my waist, his touch lacking the severity he used in the training ring. I stood on my tiptoes to drape an arm over his shoulder with little success. He let out a small chuckle, a pleasurable rumbling that vibrated under my fingertips. It was almost like music to my ears. And that's how I knew I was far from sober. Aaren lifted me, then my sandaled feet landed on his boots as the first notes of the song were plucked. I glanced furtively to see what the other dancers did.

They all moved too quickly for me to count their beats and note their footwork; apprehension crept in. I was about to humiliate myself. Aaren lifted my chin with a finger until my eyes met the molten honey in his.

"Relax," he said, his eyes swimming in the firelight. Or maybe I was seeing things in my altered state. "Follow my lead. Just feel."

He took a step to his right, my left, and I was so focused on his next steps that I gasped when he whisked me across the square. My feet lost their footing as we moved, and I faltered at first, praying I wouldn't trip, but after a few steps, I caught my footing and glided through the crowd with him. I grasped Aaren's hand tightly as sweat tickled my brow and my cheeks ached with joy. The Fraalver around us called and cheered as they danced with us, around us. Aaren's back muscles worked as he held me, and we whirled across the square in spinning magnificence.

The flute sang as the drums pounded, and the ale that sang through my veins made me weightless. Aaren's hand clasped tightly on my waist, and he pulled me in closely as he spun, lifting my feet from the ground. My legs kicked out behind me as we twirled, and I squealed in jubilation, suddenly aware of the grip he had on me. The loose strands of his hair blew in the whirling breeze, and the firelight illuminated his eyes enough that I felt I could dive in and swim in them. Gone was the irritation that plagued his features and the furrowed brow. Aaren threw his head back and laughed, the sound of it reverberating in my ears. I blinked in awe—he was beautiful. He had let down a wall within him, a wall that harbored this looser version of him, the version that allowed him to be, not the leader of Skoghjem, but himself. Aaren. I hoped he wouldn't rebuild that wall after tonight.

Or maybe it was an ale-addled delusion.

The song ended, and Aaren gently placed me back down on my feet, bowing like the other men in the crowd. It took me a moment to steady my swirling head after such a spin and however many mugs of ale I'd had. I focused on Aaren's flushed face, on the sweat that beaded his brow. He didn't look like the stern leader who had interrogated me the first day. He looked human, or as human as a Fraalver can look.

"See?" he said through choppy breaths. "Easy."

I beamed, still a bit unsteady on my feet. Excusing myself, I scampered away to find another drink. Thea sidled up to me once I had refilled my tankard.

"You, madam, are quite the dancer," she cooed and knocked back the rest of her wine. Her painted lips glistened with the red liquid as her tongue swept her bottom lip. Her eyes were hazy as the effects of the wine set in. At least I wasn't the only one feeling good.

"I'd like to see you out there," I chimed, smiling cooly through heavy lids.

Thea chuffed. "Is that a challenge, *frue*?"

A fiendish smile spread across my lips. Wasting no time, I gulped down my mug and dragged Thea to the center. The tune was lively, and Thea grabbed my hands to hop across the square and cross paths with Fraalver locked in the same dance. Twirling in and out of each other's arms, we skipped away again, then lifted our arms for the dancers to prance underneath.

My head buzzed with gaiety and ale. I felt magical. Maybe I was magical. Mama always told me I was.

Clapping my hands, I hopped excitedly as I giggled with Thea, relishing her full-chested laugh. Everyone cheered, and a joyous howl erupted from the crowd around us. In a moment of clarity, I realized there was not a hint of distaste or poor regard, either towards me or the fact that we danced at a funeral and not a holiday feast. The Fraalver only smiled and cheered with me, more than happy to link arms and invite me into their dances. It was like I had lived here my whole life. Like I had never brought a myling to their borders. As the next song began to play, I started to believe that all of the disgust I had felt was directed at me wasn't actually from the Fraalver, but from myself.

Thea accompanied me to the table full of food as my stomach had begun growling at the final note of the song. I filled my plate, sat down, and watched the Fraalver mill about, glee electrifying the air. This was the best funeral I had ever been to. Especially since the only funerals I had ever attended were Mama's and Granny's.

I bit into a slice of the roast pig, and the strands of meat melted in my mouth in a blissful explosion of savory delight. A contented moan tumbled out of me as I chewed, and Thea choked on a laugh before stuffing her mouth with bread.

"So what's going on with you and Stieg?" I asked between mouthfuls.

"What do you mean?" Thea replied.

I shrugged. "I see how he looks at you."

Thea leaned back and sighed. "Stieg is a very kind man, and quite noble. I'm rather fond of him. But it would never work out."

The ale kept me from hiding my perplexity, though it came across more as incredulity. "Why not?"

Thea glanced over her shoulder, then lowered her voice as she said, "Rumor has it that Stieg isn't Fraalver."

I tilted my head, intrigued.

Speaking more into her goblet than to me, Thea continued. "Stieg and his father appeared on our borders sixty years ago. No one knows where they came from, but we let them in. You'll notice Stieg doesn't exactly look like a Fraalver." That fact I could not ignore. It wasn't that Stieg was unattractive, but he wasn't conventionally handsome by Fraalver standards.

Stieg was like me, an outsider and a mystery to the people. That explained why he was so quick to defend me in the pub a few days ago. I felt a little less alone.

116

"Who cares," I stuttered through a mouthful of potatoes. "You like him, he likes you, what's the big deal?"

I gave Thea a devious look, which she reciprocated with a cocked eyebrow to accentuate the wicked gleam in her eyes.

"Secrets *are* devilishly exciting," she snickered.

I swallowed the last bit of ale in my mug and stood, swaying. "I need more drink," I slurred and staggered to replenish my mug.

Only dregs of ale remained, but I gladly filled my cup to the top. A warm presence approached from behind, and I turned sluggishly to see Aaren pop the top of a bottle of wine, eyeing me with reserved amusement. Excitedly, I dumped the ale and offered my cup for him to fill.

"It looks to me like you've had enough," he observed, but I wasn't too drunk to notice the corners of his mouth twitch.

I rolled my eyes, which sent my head into a spin. "I'm supposed to make sure Dagan makes it to the Himagel."

"Himmelfjell," Aaren corrected, but I ignored him and jabbed a weak finger in his direction.

"You're not being a good leader if you don't let me help him."

He paused, brows raised in consideration. Then he poured my wine.

I took a sip and swayed on my feet, sighing delightedly at the new flavor. Catching sight of the rune on my arm, I brought it up to my blurred gaze. "I hated this rune," I slurred as I turned it to show Aaren as if he weren't the one who placed it on me. At first, it had been nearly invisible on my arm, but now it shone prominently, as if it had been burned into my skin. "But I'm growing to like it. It's pretty."

Smirking to hide his confusion, he replied, "I'm glad."

I took a deep gulp of the wine, now too drunk to register the subtle hints of strawberry and rhubarb. "I saw you tucking Nilsen into bed," I admitted, accepting that my filter was gone. I'd deal with it in the morning—if I remembered it. Isn't that what I was supposed to be doing anyway? Getting mindlessly drunk to make up for the fact that I got someone killed?

I jabbed a finger into Aaren's chest. "You're a big softy."

He chuffed, hints of amusement gone, something like arrogance taking its place. His lighthearted mood seemed to die as the night aged, and I wasn't fond of the returning rigidity.

"He's the only family I have left," Aaren replied as a protective glimmer crossed his face. It disappeared as quickly as the shadows from the fire.

My face fell. "I know what you mean."

Our conversation was cut off when Thea pulled me back into the dancing crowd, where we spent the following few songs stumbling across the square in a fit of giggles. But as much fun as I was having, my energy was fading, and I was very drunk.

I staggered out of the crowd to find a spot tucked away where I could sit and try to gather my bearings again. But the sound of voices a few feet away caught my attention.

"Despite it all, it's a lovely night," Rorik said, followed by the sound of him sipping his ale.

"No, Rorik, it's not," Aaren grumbled without a trace of the frivolity I had seen before. "I had to kill one of our own for the sake of the *fremmed*. Tonight is anything but lovely."

All my enjoyment in the night's festivities left me as I stomped over to them, lips pressed together and knuckles white around my mug. My drunken mood shifted when I saw the shock on the men's faces, and I dumped the remaining wine on their boots and offered a resounding "fuck you."

Aaren only stared at the puddle of wine at his boots, his chest rising in a calming breath.

The music wasn't as pleasant anymore, the drums sounding more like a pounding headache than a festive beat, and the fiddle's screech rang in my ears as I left the square.

My hands caught the side of a building as I stomped down the path, the toes of my sandals catching on the dirt path as I went. The wind rustled the shadowy branches above, but this wind was different from the breezes I was learning belonged to Aaren. This one didn't smell quite as pleasant, almost like someone had covered a body in flowers to hide the smell of decomposition, like the wind was trying to mask itself for something it wasn't.

Layla.

I froze, teetering on the path as I began to question if I was so drunk I was hearing things. It spoke again from around the corner.

Layla.

Something tugged in my stomach, something desperate and demanding.

Layla.

There it was a third time, accompanied by another sharp tug in my gut. I listened to it and rounded the corner, but it didn't let up; instead, it grew more intense the farther I chased it. I followed the winding path around the village, empty of Fraalver, as they left the celebration. The tugging turned into discomfort and was morphing into something akin to stomach pain, and no matter how far I chased the feeling, it wouldn't subside. The urgency to find whatever was calling my name was going to consume me.

The wind called my name again, and again, and again, but something interrupted it. My pace slowed by a fraction. There was a small hoot, followed by a shadow in the branches. Ugleverge, the owl guardian that protected the children. It hooted again, but the pain returned to my gut, and I threw myself forward, slamming into something hard.

There was that familiar smell, the forest and leather carried on a night breeze, and I grappled against what I hit, feeling a soft jacket and hard flesh underneath. And just like that, the pain was gone along with the phantom voice carried on the dead wind. The form I was pressed against let out a low chuckle.

"Going somewhere, *fremmed?*" Aaren rumbled.

My mouth went dry, the shock of everything muting the explanation I was grappling to say. There was a soft giggle a few feet away, a sweet melody that drifted through the air. Then a deeper voice groaned. Aaren swept me up, pressing me into the shadows of the nearest building and shielding me from whoever was moving this way.

The voices grew closer, landing somewhere just around the corner from where we hid. The softer voice sang again, and I bit my lip to catch the gasp that almost gave us away.

"Stieg..." Thea breathed.

A brief pause followed, soft giggles, then footsteps retreating into the forest beyond.

As entertaining as that encounter was, I was still pinned under Aaren's towering form in the cover of deep shadows. He could do anything to me. Strangle me, slit my throat, snap my neck...

His breath fanned over my face, warming my cheeks and tickling my lips.

He could kiss me.

The thought of any of those things happening sent me slipping through his arms and stumbling down the path once more, not chasing after a lost voice, but to get away from him.

Even though kissing him didn't sound all that bad right now.

I should've known better than to think I would get very far in the presence of Aaren Skokjer and his magic. The night had gone so still that I could hear Aaren's fingers snap. A root broke the path and snagged my foot, sending me tumbling to the ground. Dirt bit into my skin when I tried to break my fall, and I slid across the peat and gravel. Cursing the skirts that jumbled my legs, and cursing myself for drinking so much, I scuffled to stand, almost pitching forward when my legs straightened. Aaren didn't wait for me to find my footing before he stooped down and scooped me up, ignoring my pounding fists as he threw me over his shoulder. The movement was effortless, like I weighed nothing more than a bag of grain.

"What're you doing?!" I demanded.

"I think I should ask you the same."

"I was *trying* to get away from you, you lying asshole!"

He scoffed. "Did I hurt your feelings, *fremmed?*"

I echoed my earlier sentiment. "Fuck you."

There was no use in fighting, so I let out a resigned sigh and let him haul me through the dark village. The celebration was still in full swing, but to my dismay, we did not return. I wanted another drink after such a sobering tumble. Attempting to track the path Aaren was taking us, I closed my eyes as my stomach roiled and protested the idea of another mug of ale.

It wasn't until my feet hit the ground that my writhing stomach decided it had had enough. I keeled over and vomited on the ground at Aaren's boots, the second thing I dumped at his feet tonight. I would be lying if I said I wasn't a bit proud. Aaren only sighed and, to my dulled surprise, patted my back.

"I suppose I deserved that," he said.

I spit the foul taste out of my mouth, then straightened. My fingers grasped the building behind me at the sudden flush of blood to my head. Aaren steadied me even though I wanted to push him away and claim independence. I had been drunk before; this wasn't my first rodeo. But when I tripped on the first step into his house, it was evident I wasn't going to accomplish much on my own.

My vision blurred in the warm light, and I lost track of where he led me when I dropped onto something soft and warm. Sleep was consuming every other instinct, and I fell to my side where I snuggled into the furs of a bed and inhaled deeply. It smelled like Aaren, that rich scent of leather and rain, that same smell in the breeze. It was a musk that lingered in my nostrils, one that was proving to be increasingly hard to forget. A fire crackled in the background, and I hummed in bliss.

Aaren poured something into a pewter cup and placed it on the bedside table. His back turned as he went to leave the room, but something compelled me to grab his wrist.

Maybe it was the ale dulling my better judgment, or perhaps it was the panic of the spins setting in with every blink, but I really didn't want to be alone.

"Please stay," I breathed, my heart racing in panic as dizziness rattled my head.

Aaren hesitated as his gaze settled on my frame, buried in the furs on the bed. His expression was unreadable in his moment of hesitation, but he dropped into the chair next to the bed, keeping me under a careful watch. I told myself his vigilant eyes were because he was afraid I would bolt again, but the unfamiliar softness in his face gave me another idea. My mind shut down before I could give it another thought, and I fell into a fitful sleep.

Chapter 17

The next morning was agony.

My temples throbbed as I sat up in bed, the unfamiliar room striking unease in my chest. I had a fuzzy recollection of my conversation with Thea, and I had a painful reminder that I fell, judging by the state of my palms, but I don't remember much else. A wave of nausea had me clutching the wall as I moved to the door, and I retched as bile rose in my throat.

I opened the door to the familiar dining room where I played Balderkrig with Nilsen. I was in their house.

And I had slept in Aaren's *bed.*

Nilsen sat across from Aaren at the table near the fire, and surprisingly, Rorik was also present, straight-spined and sipping from a mug. The sight of a mug filled with any liquid made my mouth water with disgust.

"Layla!" Nilsen exclaimed when he spotted me. I didn't remember his voice being that shrill. I winced, but plastered on a weak smile as I sat down on the bench. Aaren pushed a plate of eggs and meat over, and I grudgingly pulled it closer.

Rorik nudged Nilsen. "Nilsen, I told Ingrid she should be well enough to play today. I heard that there might be a gathering in the treehouse to welcome her back."

Nilsen's eyes lit up. Aaren permitted him to go if he finished his breakfast, which resulted in Nilsen stuffing his cheeks full of bread and oatmeal, then dashing through the door. It slammed shut behind him with a booming thud.

The silence was heavenly.

Both pairs of eyes landed on me as I poked at my eggs, stifling a yawn. "What happened last night?" I droned, massaging my cheeks with sweaty, mangled palms.

"You got a real taste of Fraalver ale," Rorik chimed.

122

"I don't want it ever again."

Aaren let out something like a chuckle. "That's what I said after my first time."

"Did I fall?"

"You didn't just fall," Aaren answered. "You ate dirt."

The memory of running away from Aaren crept into my mind, then a foreign tree root. My jaw dropped.

"That was *your* fault!"

Rorik's brow raised to his hairline. "*Skam*, Aaren. Shame on you."

This time, Aaren did chuckle. "You were drunk, *fremmed*. Anything could've made you fall."

I grumbled a curse under my breath, avoiding eye contact with my breakfast plate as it was sending my stomach into somersaults. What else happened last night? I had the faintest recollection of throwing up on Aaren's boots, which put a satisfied smile on my face as Aaren got up to stoke the fire, and I saw that his boots were freshly polished. There was a fuzzy memory of hiding in the shadows, heat exchanging from Aaren to me, but why did he shove me against a wall like that? That was the question I needed to focus on, and not the molten heat at the memory of Aaren's lips so close to mine.

Moaning, I remembered someone moaning. *Stieg...*

Holy shit, Thea and Stieg...

"You ran away," Aaren said bluntly. "Or at least tried to. You were headed straight for the border."

My fingertips brushed the rune, and it burned dully. "That's ridiculous," I replied. "I know the rune won't let me leave the borders. I must've just been really drunk." But my stomach clenched, thrusting me back into the memory of that decayed wind and the compulsion to follow it. Something had driven me to run away without thought, and it terrified me that I didn't know what.

Aaren shook his head and gave me a concerned look. "You didn't seem like yourself." His eyes flicked to his advisor seated next to him. "You don't think this is..."

Rorik sat in heavy contemplation, his finger tracing the wood grain of the table. "It may be possible, but also a stretch."

I squinted in irritation. "Care to let me in on this? This is about me after all." I was getting sick of the omissions. And this hangover was killing my patience.

Rorik's eyes closed after giving Aaren a reproachful glance.

"She's right," Aaren chimed. "She deserves to know."

"It's a stretch," Rorik reiterated. "But if Aaren says you weren't yourself last night, then I'll take his word. You might be in danger." That was just what I needed to hear when fighting for control of my guts. "When Dagan attacked you, he was possessed by something. I'm not sure what, but—"

"But he acted a lot like you were last night. At least when you were running for the borders," Aaren finished. "Your eyes were almost like his."

Any other wandering thoughts I had been entertaining vanished in a puff of smoke, and I blinked. "My eyes were..."

Aaren nodded. "Empty. Like someone had sucked the color from your irises, they cleared when you bumped into me."

My face must've turned a shade too green because Rorik suddenly started fishing for something in his pocket. "Drink this," he said, pushing a small vial of clear liquid into my hand. "It won't help the ale withdrawal, but at least it will let you eat something."

I winced when the liquid burned on the way down, but Rorik was right; I had a mild appetite after taking it. I picked apart a piece of bread, and Aaren shoved a mug of juice across the table for me. "So, what does all of this mean?"

Rorik shook his head, as if he were debating whether he should elaborate on his thoughts. "Whoever it was that possessed Dagan, the one who has Lucas, had control of you last night."

And suddenly my nausea returned with a vengeance, along with my anxiety over my missing brother.

"And my intuition tells me that whoever it was would have succeeded in taking you if it weren't for this." Rorik tapped a finger to the rune on my forearm.

I had Aaren to thank for many things. I went to meet his gaze only to see his was already locked on me. I tried for a grateful look, softening my brow and pressing my lips into a small smile, but Aaren looked away and cleared his throat.

"Look into it, Rorik. We need to explore every possibility."

Rorik paused, debating if he should argue, then gave a short nod. "As you wish." He stood, gathering the small satchel he had slung over his chair and adjusting his shirt. "Take it easy in the ring today. You're too—"

"I will," Aaren interrupted. "Thank you."

Rorik hesitated, halting midstep as if he were going to say something, then thought better of it. "Take care, both of you." He shot me a wink at his last words.

Aaren stood after he finished whatever was in his mug. I looked away before I could gag at the sight. "Time to train."

I laughed indignantly. "I'm not training today."

Aaren scoffed and cocked an eyebrow. "Like hell you aren't."

Aaren wouldn't change his mind as he finished his ale and shoved through the front door.

I threw up in the sparring ring. Twice.

By the end of our training session, I had successfully sweated out two pints of ale, and I shook as I stumbled off the platform with a headache that was more pressing than the protestations of my muscles. I swiped my brow, smelling the alcohol oozing out of my pores. With the assurance that I was on my way to visit with Rorik, I took a brief pit stop at Thea's, welcoming the cool draft that greeted me.

"You smell, girl," she purred. She nudged a mug over to me. "Drink this."

I scrunched my nose. "Absolutely not."

"It's not what you think," she assured and pushed it into my hands.

The metal brushed my lips, and I took an exploratory sip. Something sweet dazzled my taste buds, and I groaned delightedly, taking a deep drink. It tasted like Granny's shortbread.

"What is this?" I inquired, struggling to pull the mug away from my lips as the warm taste lingered in my mouth.

"The best ale sickness cure I've ever found."

My stomach settled, and the tension in my temples eased as relief seeped into me.

She retrieved the mug and brought it to her own lips. I gave her an expectant look, which she responded to with blissful ignorance. "Out with it," she said with a wave of her hand as she took another sip.

"How was your rendezvous with Stieg?"

Thea choked.

I threw my head back and laughed. Astonishment settled on her sharp features, and she smacked her bosom to reset her breathing.

"How did you know?"

"I heard you two." Her eyes bulged with embarrassment as she licked the tonic from her lips. I shook my head. "I was...on a walk...When I heard you giggling around the corner."

Relief crossed her face, but a wicked gleam quickly replaced it.

"He was...delicious."

I grabbed the mug for another drink and to hide my discomfort.

"I wasn't sure at first, but... he knew exactly what he was doing." She stuck her tongue out.

I regretted asking.

"What about you, girl? Did you find a lucky Fraalver to romp?" She winked. "You and Aaren were very friendly in your dance."

I chuffed. "Hardly."

"Be that as it may, Aaren needs a wife. The village needs two leaders after all."

"I don't belong here, so whatever scandalous author fantasies you're plotting in your head can stay there."

Thea shrugged as if to say "suit yourself" and sipped.

I left Thea's with a groan when it was time for my next lesson. On my way to find Rorik, *he* found *me*.

"How're you feeling?" he inquired. When I lied and said I felt fine, he gave me a knowing look. I still looked like death, and I supposed I smelled like it, too. "We'll be spending our lesson with Harald today," he informed, and beckoned me to enter the bookshop I had unknowingly stopped in front of.

I wasn't sure what to expect from my sessions with Rorik, but I hoped they were more pleasant than the morning I had just endured. I wasn't ready to throw up again.

Harald's shop was stuffier than Thea's, and a subtle tickle settled into my lungs. Dim candles illuminated the dingy shelves, which displayed dull-colored books with withering spines. Each book looked as if it hadn't been touched in a hundred years—given that Fraalver lifespans were longer than a human's, that theory might be true. Thick flecks of dust clouded the air as a tall, graying man approached. His kind eyes held a comforting warmth that made me unclench my jaw a little. As stuffy as the bookshop was, Harald made it feel safe.

Even though I was about to sneeze three years off my life.

"Good morning, Harald," Rorik stuttered as he held back a cough. He cleared his throat. "We need volumes one, two, and three of Fraalver Beginnings."

Harald made an excited titter and scurried to a shelf, withdrawing three books. He seemed unaffected by the cloud of grime that erupted from the tomes as he piled them on top of each other and handed them to me. Rorik nodded in thanks.

The air outside was crisp and clean, and I welcomed breath after breath into my lungs. Rorik wheezed into his fist. He explained that not many people visited Harald's shop except for the times when someone would use a book to teach their child, but that was about the extent of his business. Harald never minded, though; he was doing what he loved.

We brought the books into the pub, and I cracked the first volume open, holding my breath as dust billowed from the pages. Like the books in my room, I could read the strange text as if it were my first language. Rorik began explaining the history of the Fraalver, and much to my disappointment, it was as dry as I had expected. The Fraalver people descended from the mixing of elves and humans long ago. The elves and humans had a mutual relationship until the humans broke away in search of a land of their own, pillaging as they went and eventually finding Midgard. After they crossed into their new realm, the way back to Alveland closed. No human was able to return, and the knowledge of Yggdrasil slowly faded to myth, hence the Norse mythology that existed in the books Lucas checked out of the library.

The elves that still occupied Alveland lived across the Stornish Sea, a good month-long journey between the two lands. After the humans left, the elves became bitter over their abandonment, growing to despise their hybrid offspring. They shunned the Fraalver, losing contact with them over two thousand years ago. None of the Fraalver felt inclined to reignite a connection with the elves, and their kinship died quickly. All knowledge of the elves was lost over the years, and some even questioned if the land they once occupied still existed.

Boredom kicked in as Rorik opened the second volume. He went on about the different leaders and worthy figures in Fraalver history, and as he droned on, I zoned out and started watching the various patrons in the pub. Two men with scraggly beards, one bald, the other with a full head of black hair, had their arms draped across each other as they swayed to a tune the bard's flute sang. It amazed me how they were still going after last night. A woman with her face smooshed against the bar draped her arm over her head, her eyes fluttering in and out of sleep as she tried to block out the music. At least there was one person who seemed to be just as worn out as I was. I felt a little better about my hangover.

"I believe we can stop there," Rorik said, clapping the book shut in a plume of dust. He slid it over to me and tapped the cover. "I want you to finish volume two tonight." I sank into my chair. Being here would grant me a pass from homework.

I grunted in anguish.

Rorik made a reprimanding face. "Relax, it's just a few chapters."

Chapter 18

It was *not* just a few chapters. It was over half the book.

My eyes blinked furiously as I struggled to keep them open, focusing on a grimy page of volume two. The words weren't registering as I read them. I didn't remember a single name of any of the leaders who ruled the village or any of the heroes who single-handedly defended the borders from huldras, giants, and other monsters whose existence still baffled me.

I had begun to nod in and out of sleep when a name caught my attention, and I shot up in bed.

Markus Sviker.

That name was so familiar, the memory on the tip of my tongue. I raked over the name inked into the page, noting the font and the swirl of the cursive. And then the memory of the name scrawled in blocky writing and colored pencil slammed me in the face.

Markus.

Change one letter, and the name becomes more familiar.

Marcus.

The same name that had been scribbled next to Lucas's drawing of the dark man that I found in his room the day after he disappeared.

I continued to read.

Markus, like me, was an outsider. He came to the Fraalver village to apprentice under the physician Quirinus. During his time with the Fraalver, Markus's magic manifested intensely. As an apprentice, he began to experiment more with dark magic, the kind used to resurrect the dead, possess others, and influence the unwilling. The more he learned, the harder it was to ignore his craving for power. Suspecting Markus's budding sinister intentions, Quirinus expelled him from his mentorship and banished him from the village, cursing him so that should he try to return, he would not remember the way or how to find it.

Rumors gathered that he had accrued a heavy following of elves and other creatures that desired the power he possessed, though no one in Skoghjem had heard from Markus since.

The book didn't mention what race Markus was, which gave me pause. If he wasn't Fraalver, could he still be alive?

My head swam with worry. This couldn't be a coincidence, not when this realm had quickly taught me that anything I had believed to be impossible was now within my grasp. Everything I had experienced in the last few days fit the description of Markus's dark magic. His possession of Dagan is my uncontrollable compulsion to flee the village. And Lucas had this man's name written all over his sketchbook.

I swung my legs over the side of the bed and thundered down the stairs of the inn, not caring who I woke up. When I flung the doors open to the frigid night air, I sprinted down the path and straight to Aaren's.

The race through the village was a race against time, and when I touched the first step of Aaren's house, I beat my fists on the door. When it didn't swing open immediately, I panicked and searched for another way in. The protection rune carved into the door shimmered. Without a second thought, I ran my finger down the center, and the door opened with squeaking hinges. I exhaled in relief and stumbled in, almost falling to the floor in my haste if Aaren hadn't been there to catch me.

"How did you...?"

"I know who it is," I blurted. "I know who has my brother."

Aaren's eyes were heavy-lidded with sleep, but the urgency in my tone seemed to shock him from his stupor.

"Wait here," his husky voice commanded, then the door slammed shut, and I was left to my own devices.

I sat down in front of the fire, my leg bouncing with impatience. One by one, my nerves settled when the fire started to warm me, and exhaustion took the place of my panic. The stone in the ash sizzled, the rune growing brighter than before, but I felt comforted by the protection it promised. No matter who Markus really was, I was safe in here.

A few minutes passed, then the front door creaked open. Aaren and Rorik entered, the latter kneeling at my chair in calm expectancy.

I didn't wait for him to ask. "Markus," I shuddered. "Markus Sviker. He's the one who took my brother, and he killed Dagan." When Rorik asked me how I knew, I explained the drawing I found in Lucas's room, including every minor detail of the sketch. Explaining the connections I made, I saw the skepticism shift to grim acceptance in Rorik's features. Aaren said nothing as I spoke, only glaring into the fire with a pensive intensity. Rorik shifted in consideration and scratched the scruff on his chin.

"Despite the years that have passed since I've heard that name, it's possible," Rorik said, his voice hoarse with distressed exhaustion. "If there were such a person to take revenge on the Fraalver, it would be Markus." He rose.

Aaren had begun to pace by the hearth, his corded arms rippling as he flexed and unflexed his hands.

"But why me?" I asked. "Why Lucas? It can't just be a coincidence."

"There must be something about you that he wants," Aaren said, his boot heels clicking with every stride across the stone.

A sigh from Rorik, and I turned to see resignation in his tired face. "Might I see your arm, Layla? The right one?"

Complying, I extended it and watched the warm light illuminate the rune, which seemed to have grown darker since yesterday. Then he grabbed Aaren's hand and examined his palm. Another sigh, then he said, "I was afraid of this.

"Markus is controlling you," Rorik explained, his thumb trailing my arm. "Last night, when you tried to run away, you were under his influence. Since Quirinus put the curse on him, he cannot remember where the village was, nor can he ever locate it through traditional means." He rubbed his chin again and continued. These myling attacks are not coincidental. Markus must be behind them.

"I did some digging today and found a bit of rare, fairly dark magic. The exact kind of magic that would get you dismissed from an apprenticeship and excommunicated from the village." Rorik, now lost in his explanation, pressed his thumb firmly to my rune. "When the myling attacked Dagan, it implanted a piece of Markus in him, likely in the hopes that contact with you would manipulate the curse, and he'd finally be able to locate us. But this rune," his finger dug into my skin further, and I bit down on a yelp, "stopped him. But when you touched the piece of Markus that was in Dagan, it transferred itself to you."

That was why his eyes went clear before his last breath, and he was able to return to himself. Dagan didn't have to die.

My skin crawled like a thousand tiny mites had suddenly invaded my body. "You're telling me that Markus is inside me right now?"

"I'm afraid, yes, Layla."

The abrupt urge to claw at my skin, to rip away the flesh and release that piece from me, threatened to consume me. "How do we get rid of it?" I asked almost frantically, and my heart rose into my throat. I felt sick.

"Give me the day," Rorik answered. "I'll have the answer by dusk."

I didn't want to wait that long, couldn't, but Rorik was already out of the door before I could argue.

Chapter 19

I didn't sleep the rest of the night. If Markus could put a piece of himself in me, what could he do to Lucas?

Aaren stayed up with me, though we hardly spoke. Between his restless fire stoking and frequent visits to Nilsen's bedroom door to check on him, it was hard to spark any conversation. So I worried my mind with other things, trivial things that no longer meant anything to me. I would be short on rent this month, considering how long I'd been out of work, and my roommates would certainly have plenty to say about the week-old spaghetti I had left in the fridge.

Mama used to make spaghetti, and she'd put olives in the sauce, saying they were actually spider eyeballs. When I threw a fit about eating them, she told me not to worry, they were good for me, even if they looked weird. I went to school the next day and told the girl beside me that I had spider eyeballs for dinner the night before, and she ran to the teacher crying. It wasn't my proudest moment, but it still made me smile thinking of how disgusted she—

Pop!

"Aaren, the fire is fine!" I exclaimed when the noise startled me from my thoughts. "Stop messing with it."

He threw me a frustrated glare over his shoulder and threw the stoker back on the hearth with a clang. Aaren kept quiet, striding on silent feet to check on Nilsen for the twelfth time tonight. When he returned, he took up the chair next to mine, crossing one foot over the other and grumbling.

Menial thoughts like the ones before didn't return. Instead, more complicated questions filled my mind, questions I didn't have the stomach to ask or answer. The loudest question of all blared like a siren and rang inside my head.

Why?

Why was this about me? A small girl, someone who hadn't accomplished anything in life. Why me? And why Lucas?

An impossible yet glaringly preposterous notion popped into my head, one that I either had to be drunk or stupid to ask about. Or utterly exhausted.

"I'm not completely human, am I?" I asked, feeling my throat tighten with the possibility.

Aaren sighed deeply through his nose. "No," he replied.

As idiotic as I felt asking the question, I felt even more foolish for believing it. "How do you know?"

"You wouldn't have been able to enter Alveland if you were."

I sat with that for a moment, reeling at the simplicity in his tone.

I wasn't human. Which meant either one or both of my parents was something otherworldly. A persistent feeling told me that if Mama were anything but human, she would have dragged me to whatever world she was from. That seemed to rule her out. Which meant that whoever my father had been was the one who gave me my inhuman blood.

If Lucas was in Alveland, that meant he wasn't human either. But I knew Lucas's father, Dallas, was the farthest from any magical being as he could be. And yet Lucas was here. Impossibly so, but still here. Just like me.

None of that should've been relevant to me. No matter what blood ran through mine or Lucas's veins, no matter the circumstances of our fathers, I was still going to find him. And I was going to gut Markus like a fish.

And since I wasn't entirely human, what was I capable of?

Motivation kicked my legs into motion, and I stood, stirring Aaren from his seat. He inquired after me as I marched to the front door and flung it open.

"I'm going to the ring," I answered resolutely. "I can't kill Markus if I don't know how to fight."

Aaren summoned Asta to keep an eye on Nilsen, then followed me out into the square.

The braziers surrounding the sparring ring lit as we approached, and my boots clicked on the smooth wood when I assumed my stance. Aaren shed his vest, leaving a loose white shirt that revealed a small V of carved chest underneath. The shirt shifted, exposing a bit more, and I couldn't help but try to peer inside for a better look.

I took a moment to braid my hair back and shake out my hands, antsy from the lingering uncertainty and heavy feelings of the night. And when Aaren started to circle me, our eyes met, and an unspoken agreement passed between us. He wasn't going to take it easy on me, and I didn't want him to. I needed to test what the other half of my genetics was capable of. My fingertips buzzed as I waited for him to strike, his continuous circling pushing me closer to the edge of attacking first.

Aaren swung his fist, and I ducked, his knuckles grazing the crown of my head. If I had taken the time to breathe, he would've caught my cheek, hard, and I celebrated with a delayed breath. On the rebound, I jumped up to brace my hands on his shoulders as I kneed him in the gut, though he hardly winced. Air was locked in my throat when he looped his arm around my neck and flexed his bicep. I smacked his arm in the hopes that he would loosen the chokehold to no avail. A couple more seconds of this and I'd be down for the count within the first minute of our spar.

It was infuriating. Anger drowned out all other emotions, and I began to see red.

"You're too slow, Layla," he panted, the hair falling from his bun, hanging down and tickling my brow.

Outrage burned in my throat when I roared, fury flooding my system like electricity, and I kicked him to break free. He stepped away and got back into a defensive position, hands by his face, ready to block my next throw. Amber's eyes focused on me and clocked every tiny move I made, even the heave of my chest when I gulped down a hefty breath of air. Aaren dodged a punch, and I jumped over a sweeping kick, each attack fueled by the presently raw emotions from our night. Every swing I landed dripped with rage for my brother and his captor. Aaren's movements were heavy with frustration, so much so that his attacks were getting sloppy, almost like he was distracted.

A wound-up punch pulled back too far had him wincing, losing track of his step, and my fist caught his jaw hard enough that he faltered. Aaren's hand cupped the spot under his chin where I struck, blinking in surprise.

"Well done," he grimaced. His hand rubbed the spot a moment longer, then he stretched his neck and shoulders. "Again."

By the end of our match, despite having a long way to go in combat, I began to feel the improvement. In a couple of months, I may be his strategic equal. I laughed quietly at my wishful thinking. It was a far cry, but my movements were steadier than before, our sparring coming closer to a dance than stilted movements. While my attacks were fury-driven, they were smooth, a kind of graceful savagery. Aaren's counterattack was steady, like a lion stalking its prey, smooth and calculating, then quick and destructive.

The sky turned into a warm pink as the sun broke the horizon, but we didn't stop fighting. By the time the sun had risen halfway through the sky, sleepy Fraalver milled about the square, some of them heading to the pub for breakfast.

I swung one last fleeting punch at Aaren, who caught it in his calloused hand, sweeping a leg under my boots and knocking me on my back, where he quickly pinned me to the wood.

Panting, I accepted defeat. A heavy sheen of sweat graced his brow, and his eyes drifted lazily over my pinned form. Heat simmered sweetly in my stomach as my chest heaved in desperation, wrenching for breath. As if snapping out of a trance, he blinked away, pushing himself up.

Aaren's hand was just as sweaty as the rest of him when he helped me to my feet, and I steadied myself, then brushed off my pants. Aaren shook his hair out of the bun and ran his fingers through the nearly white strands. I looked away before he caught me staring.

Rolling his shoulders with a quiet scowl, he stepped out of the ring. "Come on, *fremmed*," he beckoned. "Let's get some breakfast."

The pub was bustling when we walked in, and my stomach growled at the smell of bacon and fresh bread.

Inaborg served us breakfast and filled our mugs with juice that spread a blissfully tart feeling across my tongue. Hunger had escaped me until I saw the plate of food in front of me, warm and steaming in the drafty pub. Unable to contain myself, I scarfed it down, forgetting Aaren sitting in front of me and the manners Granny had nailed into my brain when I was younger. Once my belly was full, I sat back and took a sweeping glance around, and watched the Fraalver milling about with their own breakfasts. I gazed at a couple and realized who they were.

"What exactly happened to Ingrid?" I asked, keeping a discreet eye on her parents.

Aaren swallowed the bread he had been nibbling. "She never said what happened," he answered, looking briefly at the pair before returning his gaze to his plate. "After we took her to the medicine hut, she fell asleep. A deep sleep. By the next morning, she was awake and talking as if nothing had happened." He shrugged. "Rorik supposed it was a nightmare of the mylings."

My lips pursed, accepting the answer for what it was, recalling what Stieg had said about mares. "I'm glad to hear she's better," I mused, watching her parents laugh and drink with ease.

We returned to the ring after breakfast, vigor renewed and ready to pick up where we left off.

Aaren instructed me through a new circuit of exercises that had me reeling with exhaustion by the end of it. But I wasn't going to stop on account of lost breath and sweat. I had to kill Markus. I could keep going.

Ducking a punch, I lost my balance and landed on my bottom with a thud. Embarrassment and frustration stung my cheeks as I stood and began to warm up my joints. Aaren launched another swing, then grunted angrily when he missed. I moved around him to attack his vulnerable side, but he turned, knowing that was my next move. He looped an arm around my waist, and I gasped when he slammed me to the ground, knocking the wind from my lungs.

Gulping like a fish out of water, I had to lie there and pray Aaren didn't use this moment of weakness to his advantage. As the breath returned to my lungs significantly slower than I willed it to, I met Aaren's gaze. A fleeting look of hunger crossed his eyes, then something snapped in him, like he had realized that his tongue darted over his lips when my breath finally returned. He pushed off of me and extended his hand, helping me up. Then he retreated across the ring.

I rolled my neck and readied for his next attack. Before Aaren could advance, Rorik entered the ring.

We walked to the medicine hut in silence, and the air was heavy with grim implication.

Despite the hut's lack of occupants, the clouded window charm remained. I glanced at the bed and shivered, remembering Dagan lying prone in the furs, with Markus's raspy voice and wicked grin. The walls grew tighter around me as discomfort sank like cement in my stomach.

Asta sat by the fire, her hair tucked into the same cap she wore the day I woke up here. There was a silent exchange between her and Rorik, and she smiled politely before patting Aaren on the shoulder, letting him know where Nilsen was before exiting the hut.

Despite the apprehension jarring the remaining adrenaline from my system, I stepped further into the hut. The table that had previously held vials and jars of herbs was now scattered with notes and tomes from what looked like Harald's shop, if the dust was any indication. Aaren moved to sit at the table, then thought better of it and assumed a spot near the fire. Unsure where to go, I let Rorik lead me to an armchair not far from Aaren.

"We were right," Rorik began, skipping the pleasantries, much to my relief. "Markus implanted a small piece of him in you, but he has been unable to track you because of the rune." I became keenly aware of the marking on my arm. "The other night at Dagan's celebration, Markus tried to control you through that piece. I'm assuming the ale hindered the rune's influence, and that is why he was able to gain control momentarily." He cleared his throat. "We need to remove that piece of Markus, and I know how."

A pregnant pause, one where the cement in my gut solidified, and I felt like I weighed a thousand pounds.

"You're going to have to purge him from you."

The walls started to close in again, and the hut became sweltering and freezing all at once.

"How?" Aaren asked from the fireplace.

Rorik held up a small vial of swirling lilac. "With this. It will open an exit for Markus to leave. But it won't *leave* without a *push*."

Sweat pooled in my palms, and I rubbed them together, feeling the skin pull against itself. Chest tightening, I heaved a deep breath. "How?"

Rorik gave a grim shrug. "That's for you to decide. But you won't know until you take the potion."

Chapter 20

It was a half moon tonight, providing just enough light for me and Aaren to navigate around the path and to one of the holes in the barrier. Aaren had granted me a temporary passage outside the village with a short wave of magic over the rune per Rorik's instructions. The physician believed it wise to expel Markus into the forest so as not to risk the curse being manipulated any further within the village.

As Aaren led me outside the borders, he interrupted the heavy silence. "Are you...feeling okay?" he asked, holding a branch out of my way so I could pass.

I tried to be nonchalant, though my roiling stomach hardly granted me that luxury. "I'm fine," I lied. Though what I really wanted was to curl up by the fire in my room and pretend that I didn't have a magical piece of some wicked sorcerer inside me. But that wouldn't help me find Lucas.

"It's like you're off to your first battle," Aaren joked, hoping to ease the tension. He offered me a hand to help me across a small babbling creek.

"I suppose so," I answered, accepting his hand and taking the small leap across.

The awkwardness was agony.

"A long time ago, I got sick before my very first fight. The nerves got the better of me." He cleared his throat. "There was a giant who made a shelter a couple of miles away from the village. He kept attacking our hunters; giants have a taste for Fraalver flesh, you see. My mother told me to go and take care of it."

"Why are you doing this?" I asked, trying to understand the reasons behind my fear, anger, and exhaustion, which drove my blunt questioning. "I thought your dislike for me outweighed any obligation to politeness."

Aaren's silence told me that I was right, or at least, I think it did.

"I'm saying I know how it feels, the first time before you fight something. Whether it's fighting a giant or something internal, it never gets easier."

I blinked at the unfamiliar, empathetic side of the leader.

"And did you? Or did you chicken out?" I asked.

Accepting my silent olive branch, Aaren chuckled. "I took care of it, but not without a few bumps and bruises." He extended his arm where the faintest scar glinted in the moonlight. "Giants have massive claws, and I was lucky enough that he only grazed me. If I hadn't moved in time, he would've taken my entire arm off." He patted the scar lovingly. "Asta set me right."

I smiled, imagining a young Aaren facing off with a giant. Then I shuddered as I thought what such a giant would look like.

Overhead, Ugleverge hooted and tracked our movements as we continued forward.

"Is Ugleverge a regular owl?" I inquired, following the shadow of his flapping wings across the moonlit sky.

"In a sense, yes. But also, no." I prodded him to elaborate. "Ugleverge means *owl guardian*. He appeared a couple of centuries back, around the time my parents took up leadership. He watches over us whenever we leave the safety of the borders."

"And you don't know where he came from?"

Aaren shook his head.

My anxiety increased tenfold as we neared the clearing where I spotted Rorik pacing and tossing the potion bottle from hand to hand. His lips thinned when he caught sight of us, and he strode over, slipping the bottle into my hand. The glass was warm in my palm, and the liquid lapped at the sides as I held it up and examined the contents.

"Once you take it, Aaren and I can no longer help. We'll be here physically, but the struggle will be yours alone."

That was nothing new—I'd spent most of my life doing things on my own.

Rorik patted the hand that held the vial with a thin-lipped smile. "Good luck, Layla Ashford."

I uncorked the bottle and took a whiff. The smell was pungent, but pleasantly so, similar to the aroma I had smelled in the medicine hut earlier, like a lilac flower that had started to wilt.

"Let's get this over with," I sighed, then knocked it back like a shot.

The potion kicked in immediately. And my world shattered.

My chest stretched, feeling as if phantom claws ripped my skin and tore into my breast, and I threw my head back and screeched. I cursed Rorik loudly at the potency of his brew and dropped to my knees, pawing at my chest. Bosom stretching and aching, my heart felt exposed, displayed as an offering to the forest, and to the men standing along the edge of the clearing. The blades of my shoulders met in the middle of my back painfully. I couldn't remember feeling any pain like this. When I was younger, I had fallen out of a tree and broken my wrist, but that was a papercut compared to the torture that consumed my every breath.

Vicious pleas tumbled from my lips, begging them to make it stop, to take the pain away. I was willing to sell my soul to rid myself of the agony that held me in its fist. The two men at the edge of the clearing lost their familiarity, forested shadows shrouding them in anonymity.

"Please!" I cried out to the figures, reaching out a hand despite the arcing pain the motion sent through my chest.

The taller figure moved as if to take a step towards me, only for the shorter to halt him.

Tears stung my eyes, then a faint whisper brushed my ear. "You'll never get rid of me, Layla," it hissed, sending a harsh shiver down my spine despite the sweat beading along my skin. "I'm in your blood." I whimpered, hands clamped over my ears as if I could block out the voice that spoke from inside my mind.

"I am a part of you."

Howling, I slammed my hands on the scattered dead leaves, demanding the voice get out of my head, but it only laughed. Wickedly, spitefully, because it knew the control it had over me, over the spine-tingling agony that invaded my existence. Waves of pain washed over me, crashing on the empty shores of my body. Another figure emerged in the clearing, new but familiar.

It was Granny. But she wasn't in front of me; she was in my head.

In a miraculous moment of clarity, Granny's face took form. I pondered her features, quickly memorizing the bits I had forgotten. Her wrinkled mouth smiled, and for a moment, the pain was ignorable. Her blue eyes shone as she beheld me, keeled over and writhing. I reached out for her to feel her warm cheek in my hand once more. Desperation overwhelmed me because it had been so long since I had touched her, felt her warm hands stroke my hair as she sang to me. And as my fingers brushed the soft skin of her cheek, I was met with ice-cold flesh. The light in her eyes dimmed, her irises losing their color and

141

fading into a dull gray. Granny's cheeks hollowed, and her lips curled up to expose rotting teeth. She was turning to dust right in my hands, slipping through my fingers until she was nothing but ash.

I threw myself back and cried like I did the first time I lost her. The day I realized that I was really, truly alone in the world. Alone with a baby that I knew only I could truly raise. The baby boy who grew up to be the only thing that would ever matter to me. Then I was standing in the corner of a room, a swaddled baby in my arms, his features pinching as he cried. Across the room was a basic wooden casket, the only one Granny could afford to bury her daughter in. I avoided looking at it, instead doing my best to soothe my wailing newborn brother in my arms. But then someone called my name, and I had to look at the casket as Granny beckoned me forward, right to the side of the wooden box where Mama lay motionless.

"Give me your brother," Granny said. She rested her cane on a pew and let me drop Lucas into her arms. "Tell her good-bye."

"I don't want to, Granny," I whined, keeping my back turned to my dead mother in the casket.

"You'll regret it if you don't," she replied and turned to sit in the pew with a cooing Lucas tucked in her arms.

Fear clenched me as I turned on my heel and faced the casket. Faced my mother. My poor, dead Mama. She was pale, and her features looked painted on, as if the mortician had based her makeup on a Picasso painting, rather than the picture of Mama on the beach Granny had given him. My hands gripped the side of the casket, cold and unyielding, and I leaned over and brushed my lips across her forehead. I was met with ice-cold skin, so far from the warm, sunny woman she had been only days before, plump with pregnancy and alight with joy. I wasn't saying good-bye to my Mama, I was saying good-bye to the devastated body the hospital had left us with, the twisted image the mortician painted.

I said good-bye to Mama the day they wheeled her into the delivery room. The day she never came out of that room.

Shaking away the shudder that crawled up my spine like a thousand mites along my skin, I scooped Lucas from Granny's arms, admiring his small face, the way his little chin doubled when he yawned. I pressed my lips to his forehead, and he was warm and smelled like fresh baby soap. There was life in the baby in my arms. In my brother. Mama was in Lucas. And I would do everything to hold onto that one little piece of her.

Lucas.

All of this writhing and crying and endless pain was for Lucas. I would endure endless hours of torture, worse than this, if it meant that piece of Mama could still live. The love of Granny could carry on. So my brother could come home to me.

Hadn't that been my sole purpose in life?

It had been, until the night I tried to leave the foster home. When I almost left Lucas behind.

The baby in my hands squirmed and opened its small mouth, emitting a wail that shook every bone in my body. The scream morphed from a baby's to a boy's, the sound so familiar to me that it threatened to erupt every cell in my body.

"I have less than they do," Lucas's soft voice whispered in my mind.

"You should be a worm," Stephanie's snide voice jeered. *"It puts you closer to your mom, who is dead in the ground."*

Rage like I had never known rippled through me.

The scene in my mind changed to the darkened bedroom of that one foster home, the one that nearly broke us apart. I sobbed desperately as the image of Lucas's face on that night filled my mind. His pitifully hurt eyes glistened, and I beheld the sleep-tousled hair, the face of betrayal as I began to close the door.

No, I thought, *don't walk away. Do not walk away.*

I cried louder, protesting as my feet carried me through the doorway. I grappled for the frame, fingers biting into the painted wood, nails chipping as I fought my own body. The wood escaped my grip.

The door closed.

I shrieked, fists beating the earth. My body knocked back, and I writhed, my insides twisted into a thousand knots, and my limbs stretched until my joints popped. I was falling apart at the seams.

Mama.

Granny.

Lucas.

I said their names over and over again, hammering them into the earth with every beat of my heart.

Mama. Granny. Lucas.

I fought the force that pulled me away from the door, kicking my feet to gain a grip against the wall.

Mama. Granny. Lucas.

The unseen embrace faltered for a moment, its hold on me loosening. While it was weakened, I lunged forward, arms cartwheeled to keep me from tumbling. My hand clasped the cold brass doorknob, and the door swung open. Lucas was still nestled in the blankets. I pitched forward and staggered to him, noticing the tear streaks down his small red cheeks. Vigor and life returned to me when I wrapped my arms around him, and his small frame filled my embrace perfectly, like two pieces of a puzzle. I rocked him side to side and soothed him with tear-soaked words.

"I'm so sorry, Lucas," I sobbed, smoothing his hair as tears dropped into his curls. "I'm not giving up on you." I squeezed my eyes, and the tears flowed freely and carved wet trails down my own cheeks and onto my neck. "I will never leave you. I promise."

His wet eyes gazed into mine, his lower lip trembling. "I love you, Layla."

My body wrenched forward, fingers kneading my stomach and pulling at my shirt until the fabric tore. My knotted insides surged, and I lurched forward. Hot bile burned my throat and climbed up until my tongue was coated with a sickly, acidic flavor. It tasted like death, like rotting fruit left to decay, and the pathetic lunches my old foster parents used to pack me. It tasted like every bit of life I wasn't able to live, every core memory I was robbed of. I vomited onto the forest floor.

The relief did nothing to calm the shivers that wracked me as I hiccupped and leaned into my hands that were braced firmly on the ground. In the puddle of sick below me, a small black mass writhed and twisted, and I recoiled in disgust, moving away until something embraced me. Hard muscle tensed under my fingers as Aaren covered my exposed chest with his burly arms, and the shock of the experience masked my surprise when he stroked my hair, pulling me closely into his muscled chest. And there was that smell again, that comforting, life-giving scent. It brought me back to the branches above and the leaves beneath my feet.

The shorter figure at the edge of the clearing was Rorik, recognition returning to me fully as Aaren's breeze kept me anchored in the now. Rorik crossed to the center, where I shivered and knelt over the puddle of black sludge. He hummed, then poked the wriggling mass, calling for Aaren.

144

The cold night air replaced his warm body when he answered Rorik's summons. Aaren stood side by side with his physician as they both grimaced at the thing nestled in the leaves.

Aaren knelt over the puddle and shook his head. "Nice try, *fiende*. But you're going to have to try a lot harder next time."

The scrape of a match sounded, and a small light illuminated Rorik's grim features as he held the small flame. Aaren didn't move when the match dropped and engulfed the puddle in fire. He watched it burn, his jaw set firmly in place.

When the fire had reduced the sludge and the leaves beneath it to ash, Aaren made his way to me, scooped me up, and cradled me in his warmth. My head lolled to the side with weariness.

He didn't say anything as we moved through the forest, and I was too tired to speak. I nuzzled my face into his neck and closed my eyes, not caring that it was Aaren who held me. All I cared about was getting back to the village so that I could rest. The sooner I recovered, the sooner I could keep training and find Lucas. The sooner I could keep Mama and Granny alive.

The rune burned comfortingly on my arm when we entered the village again.

Chapter 21

I awoke swaddled in the skins of Aaren's bed once more, feeling lighter than I had the day before. The air was musky and pleasant as I breathed deeply and savored the open chest and clear sinuses I had been blessed with this morning. My shoulders felt loose and ease nestled into my bones, boosting me as I lithely glided to the door.

There were hushed voices in the hall, and I paused, straining my ears to listen.

"You *have* to stop pushing yourself so hard, Aaren. The progress you've made in your recovery will be for nothing if you don't take it easy." Rorik's voice was strained, corded with concern and annoyance.

Aaren groaned. "You don't think I know that, Rorik?"

"Drop your tone when you speak to me, *gutt*. I may not be your equal, but Nils and Freya did not raise you like this."

There was a pause, and then, "I'm sorry." Rorik hummed in acceptance. "But she needs training."

"And I can think of a hundred qualified Fraalver to teach her," Rorik retorted, to which Aaren let out a minor grumble. "I know that look," Rorik said

"I'm the most qualified to teach her. I only want her to learn from the best."

Rorik sighed. "Take. It. Easy. That's all I ask."

Aaren made an amused huff. "That may be difficult with how quickly she's learning. Faster than any half-breed I've ever seen."

"We don't know what the other half of her breed is," Rorik mused before I heard him take a sip of something. "For all we know, she could be half huldra. Or something more powerful." Another pause had me craning my head, as I was dangerously close to being exposed for eavesdropping. "Something with a strong possession of magic. She did exceptionally well last night, something that only a powerful magical being could've accomplished."

Aaren made a noise of agreement.

"Keep pushing her. We need to know just what she is capable of. It could be used to our advantage. Or disadvantage should she fall into the wrong hands."

Magic. It was still so foreign to me, even though I was surrounded by it here. The idea of me possessing any form of magic was laughable. But the slightest inkling of suspicion rooted deep in my gut because something had been stirring inside me since I came here, something that seemed to have been asleep for a very long time. And I couldn't explain the heat that radiated from my palms when my emotions ran high.

My stomach growled loudly enough that Aaren and Rorik looked up from their breakfast. I blushed, feeling suddenly naked under their gazes.

"Good morning, Layla," Rorik smiled and gestured for me to join them.

"Morning," I sighed, playing for nonchalance even though I was feeling anything but. When Rorik asked how I was feeling as I sat down, I responded with a half-hearted, "I'm fine."

Rorik looked taken aback. "No soreness or fatigue? Nausea? Any dizziness?"

I shrugged and shook my head as I grabbed a bread roll from the basket Aaren passed me. "No, I feel perfectly fine." And I was. More fine than I should feel after thirty-six hours of poor sleep and the soul-wrenching experience last night.

I didn't miss the sly look Aaren and Rorik exchanged, no matter how secretive they thought they were being.

"Speaking honestly, Layla, after such an...expulsion, you should be feeling...well, a longer recovery period might do you well."

I shook my head. "No, really, I'm fine. Well enough to keep training today."

My eyes flicked to Aaren, who hid a small smile in his mug. When he put it down and swallowed, he glanced once at Rorik, then back at me.

"Let's go, then," he said, ignoring Rorik's objections as we rose from the table.

Training was easier that day, and I even came close to besting Aaren.

Over the next week, I became more adept in my hand-to-hand combat, enough that my muscles ached a little less after each session, and Aaren looked

147

more weary as he left the ring. By now, I was able to spar for a couple of minutes before he bested me, an improvement from when I started, where I barely lasted twenty seconds. The amount of progress I had made in the last two weeks lent credence to the theory that my genes were definitely not human. Since the night in the clearing, some barrier that had held me back had been removed, and my progress in the ring was proof of that.

After my daily training, other Fraalver would occupy the ring, and I would find Rorik for my lesson. We had run out of history, so he moved on to the different types of creatures that occupied the realm. He briefly touched on the huldra, but since I was unfortunately familiar with them, we moved on to the Nokken. The Nokken were shapeshifters that lived in bodies of water and lured people by transforming into women, horses, and, oddly enough, a wooden boat. The only way to get rid of a Nokken was to say its name, and it would retreat.

Then we briefly touched on hudflasker, which were devious shapeshifters that delighted in carving people up and stringing them in the trees to dry. That is, if they were hungry for flesh. Their normal appetite was for energy and fear. They desired to leech good energy from a person and spit it out until the only thing left was raw, carnal fear. When I asked about the difference between a hudflasker and a huldra, Rorik shuddered.

"A huldra will change its skin to lure someone in to eat. A hudflasker can stay in a certain skin for years, if it means they can keep feasting on someone's fear."

Goosebumps crept along my arms as Rorik recounted the tale of Olana, a woman whose husband was replaced by a hudflasker. She grew so afraid of her husband that she never left the house, eventually dying before she ever saw the sun again. Legend had it the hudflasker still roamed the woods, wearing her husband's skin.

The monsters in this realm were nothing like the ones I grew up with. I started to miss the precautionary tales Granny would tell me about, like the Boogie Man or the ghost she claimed occupied the shed in her backyard. Of course, she would say these things when Mama wasn't around—because it was Mama who would have to deal with me crawling into her bed at night because I feared the goblins Granny told me were in my closet.

At night, Thea and I walked the paths of the village and admired the stars through the tree branches, and she introduced me to anyone who passed. By the end of the week, I had met nearly everyone in the village.

Aaren pushed me more and more in the ring, whether it was to actually challenge me or to see what magic came from it, I wasn't sure. It surprised me how unperturbed I was by his ulterior motive, but I myself was curious to see what would come of it. To his disappointment, not a spark of magic manifested during training.

As the end of that week approached, my training sessions with Aaren doubled in time. Instead of spending only two hours together, we spent four, filling every minute with different strength-building exercises, runs around the village to build my endurance, and countless hand-to-hand fights. As each session came to a close, my knuckles sang with pain, and my muscles were stiff and nearly useless. Eventually, Aaren thought I had progressed enough, and I graduated to a practice sword. Though it was only made of wood, I still found it satisfying when I smacked him with it, and by the end of our training each day, we were bruised and wincing.

His hardened exterior began to grow on me as I learned to enjoy the small smiles he tried to hide when I whacked him with the sword. Small words of encouragement were the only praises I received, but I found I didn't require more—I had made it this far without any form of reward. Although I did like the butterflies that flitted around in my chest and stomach when he complimented me on my form. Aaren seemed to let go of some severity, sometimes pausing to recount a story of battle that related to the combat we were learning for that day. I enjoyed his stories, even if a punch often followed them. It seemed he didn't dislike me as much as I thought. Perhaps I was growing on him, too.

After my lessons, I had decided to help out in the village where I could, to the delight of the Fraalver. It helped me keep my mind off of Markus and the images he had stirred the night I purged him, images I had worked very hard to keep buried. I spent two days helping a woman named Aurora plow her fields in preparation for planting. As the sun set on the first day of helping her, I felt at ease knowing my exhaustion was well earned.

Randolf, one of the butchers, obliged in putting me to work and taught me how to trim certain types of meat, and I learned how to dry the beef he cured. I trudged back to the inn, smelling of smoke and starving, as I was not allowed to try any of the meat we pulled from the smoker that day. I was still glad to help, and I learned a lot.

Wanting to say thank you for healing me after my first encounter with the mylings, I joined Asta in the medicine hut and helped her dry and sort her herbs, label tonics, and keep her ledger while Rorik was out. We exchanged stories about medical practices between our two realms, and I reveled in her astonishment when I told her of the different surgeries I had learned about in my Anatomy and Physiology class. She shook her head in disbelief, chiming how thankful she was for herbs.

"We've just now replenished our stores of pestmorder after years of growing it back," Asta hummed as she crumbled the dried flowers into the mortar. "We completely depleted our stores after Pesta."

I shrank at the thought of the woman hobbling through the village with her rake. "It's such a shame," I said, drizzling the flowers with a small dose of elderberry syrup. "What happened to Nils and Freya. And everyone, really."

Though Asta's brow was knit with concentration as she shook out three black seeds into the mix, she nodded. "They were quite the pair. Firm leadership. And fearless fighters. Why do you think Aaren is as deadly as he is?"

She screwed the lid back onto the jar of seeds and tapped the pestle on the rim before grinding the mix.

"What exactly did they fight?" I inquired.

"Lots of things," she replied and paused for a moment, her tongue poking through her lips as she twisted the pestle. "Nils took on Nix the Nokken in his youth. Nasty fight it was, he came home needing thirteen stitches across his belly." She nudged the mortar and pestle toward me. "You grind, I need a break." She puffed a loose strand of hair out of her face and sat back.

The pestle was warm in my hands as I began to mix. "And Freya?"

Asta smiled. "Freya killed the witch of Grimshade. The foul creature continued to curse our crops. You know some believe it was she who sent Pesta to us from the grave." I asked her if she believed that. "No," she answered. "No one controls Pesta."

"I'm sure Aaren has told you of a few fights he's been in." She moved to the fireplace and snatched the kettle from the flames.

"A few," I replied, shaking out my hand. Training this morning did not prepare me well enough to grind this many herbs in the span of an hour.

She laid out two teacups with herbally scented tea bags inside and poured the steaming water. "Humble man. Has he told you of the Grindelin giant?"

Was that the same giant Aaren started to tell me about that night in the woods?

"Gnarly fight, and an even gnarlier gash across his chest." Asta shook her head as she counted something on her fingers. "Eight stitches, and he was only thirty-eight. Let's see, then there was the horde of farljorts that snatched Kare's daughter fifty years back, *helvete*, he even wiped out the nest of hudflasker that took up in the caves a couple miles away."

150

Which one of those had given him that scar on his back? I thought about asking, but didn't know how well it would go if Aaren found out I was inquiring about his injuries. It might seem like I was worried about him.

"Not to mention he's dealt with every mercenary and thief that enters these woods with ill intent." Asta sighed and blew on her tea. "We owe him a lot."

Against my better judgment, I offered to help Harald in his bookshop, and he excitedly accepted my help, setting me to work shelving books and assisting with his research. While it was a pain looking through some of his older tomes, I learned a lot from them.

Alveland was not just home to the Fraalver, though they were the dominant race, but also to other civilized creatures. There was a race of nymphs called Andrefolk who lived sparsely throughout the realm, choosing not to concentrate heavily in one spot like the Fraalver did. Instead, many families spread throughout the land, owning taverns and inns that housed travelers across the different realms, serving those in need. Other smaller races existed across the realm, mainly made up of hybrids of different races, not enough of them to keep any decent account of them. Some of those hybrid races grew large enough to form small settlements to support themselves, though Harald had hardly taken the time to make note of them. He seemed to be more focused on history rather than demography.

Of the Fraalver, there were three main villages where the highest concentration of half-elves lived. Other large settlements were scattered across Alveland, where they mostly kept to themselves, though some had been known to move back to the villages.

My favorite person to help was Inaborg. After my sessions with Rorik and before the dinner rush, Inaborg and I would toil away in the kitchen, roasting potatoes and crushing spices. I learned how to properly knead bread, tap a keg of ale, and spatchcock a chicken, all while listening to her stories of owning the pub. She inherited it from her father, who died a few years ago after turning the ripe age of five hundred and twenty-seven.

Over the next few weeks, my days settled into a routine. Mornings with Aaren and Rorik, followed by helping whoever I could in the village. When I wasn't sharing a drink with Thea or helping someone, I was at Aaren's playing Balderkrig with Nilsen, who was surprised by how well I had begun to play. I adjusted my strategy a couple of times and tested him, and I won a few times, although he claimed he let me win. I played Aaren twice, and both times, I lost.

Evenings like these reminded me of when Lucas and I would spend our afternoons together after school. After helping him with his homework, we would spend our time lost in fantastical pretend battles or diving into the depths of stories we had read over and over together. I knew he was out there, and nothing could stop me from finding him, but I still wasn't ready to face whatever lay beyond the borders of Skoghjem.

At the end of one day, a day that started with a particularly grueling training session, Aaren joined me in the pub.

Inaborg slid him an ale as he sat next to me at the bar, turning to face the entirety of the pub. He leaned back with his mug to his lips, and watched his people holler and drink and eat, simply celebrating being alive. A couple crossed his view, holding hands while giggling and whispering to each other. A smile graced his lips, and he watched as they found a place by the fire, the woman placing a gentle kiss on the cheek of her lover. I averted my eyes, electing to give the couple some privacy, but Aaren couldn't seem to look away, something like unchecked longing in his face.

"Do you miss your mother?" Aaren asked when his stare finally shifted to the mug in his hands.

I faltered for a moment. An odd question, but I'd bite. I shimmied back onto my stool. "Every day," I answered. "Her and my Granny."

He considered me, then took a drink. "And you never met your father?"

I shook my head. "And I never care to. But Mama was...fantastical," I began. "Every minute we spent together was alive with magic." Aaren cocked a brow, asking if there was magic in Midgard. I chuckled and shook my head. "No, not that kind of magic. She was magical in the sense that she made you feel alive. She had a raging zest for life, like she was starving for every minute she could live." I smiled into my mug, heart slowly sinking into my stomach. "And then there was Granny."

I was puzzled when Aaren said, "Tell me about her."

There hadn't been an opportunity for me to talk about Granny in a very long time. Before I realized it, I had launched into talking about her, telling him everything from the bread she would make to how she used to eat the baby corn from a box of Chinese food. I laughed myself silly as I described her holding the tiny cob of corn and running her teeth over it as if she couldn't just eat the whole thing. Aaren's laugh came as a low rumble, a jarring yet welcome display of his amusement. He smiled, his Adam's apple bobbing, as his lips spread to reveal perfect teeth.

Inaborg refilled our mugs as our laughter quieted to small spurts of chuckles, and I wiped a tear from my eye. A light feeling filled me, and it wasn't the ale.

"What about you?" I asked. "I'm sure you think of your parents often."

Aaren sighed as he regained control of his low chuckles. "All the time," he answered, chasing his amusement with a deep gulp from his tankard. "It baffles me how they made running the village look so easy."

"My understanding is it's easier when there are two leaders. You can't fault yourself for struggling on your own."

"No, but it doesn't remedy the fact that I'm doing a piss poor job."

There was a beat of silence as we watched the couple leave the fireplace and traipse toward the door, one thing clearly on their mind. "But Nils and Freya, they were just...so in love." I marveled at the way his tone softened, unsure of this new territory we had entered. I was used to throwing punches and shouting at each other. Aside from my outburst when I first got here, Aaren didn't venture into vulnerability.

"They had this unbreakable bond. Obviously, because they were leaders, but also because it was evident between them. The way they spoke to each other, the way they made decisions." He blinked, his eyes glazing over. "It never faltered."

My eyes dropped to the bubbles in my drink, unsure how to answer. I began to wonder if he had stopped talking about his parents and instead spoke of his lost betrothed. Were they as unbreakable as his parents had been? Did Aaren mourn Solveig not only for who she was, but what she could have been, not only a partner in leadership, but a life partner?

Aaren's chuckle pulled me out of my thoughts. "And they couldn't keep their hands off each other." Another surprising laugh, then he recounted the story of Inaborg's father's funeral. Freya and Nils never left the dance floor, unable to rip away from each other's arms. They danced and swung and stepped until the weak morning light began to peek over the trees. They were fantastic dancers, he told me.

"A part of the village died when they did," Aaren said, setting his mug down on the bar behind him. "I want to give that missing piece back to my people."

"You will," I said, suddenly guilty for standing in the way of that. "I'm sorry for the chaos I've brought to Skoghjem."

Aaren said nothing, and I wished his eyes would give away what he was thinking. He cleared his throat.

"Rorik has been the biggest help I could ask for," he continued. "I owe him everything."

"Are Rorik and Asta together?" I asked.

"Oh no," Aaren replied. "They're cousins. Their family has been our physicians for centuries."

I nodded in understanding, though it still left a question I had been wondering for weeks now unanswered. "Why has Rorik never found a wife?"

Inaborg rounded the bar and began collecting abandoned drinks and half-eaten plates of food.

"Never found the right woman, I suppose. My parents tried to help him out, but Rorik preferred to keep his nose in a book instead of a woman's bosom."

I rolled my eyes. "Gross."

Inaborg stoked the fire and turned, placing her hands around the edges of her mouth. "Last call, *fylliker*," she boomed. "If any of you drunks want any more ale, now is the time to get it!"

I set my empty mug on the bar behind me. "I should get to bed. Especially if we're starting shield work tomorrow."

"Right, yes," Aaren said, then cleared his throat. He stood, towering over me as I stepped away from the bar.

"Good night, Aaren," I said.

"Good night, *fremmed*."

Chapter 22

As my third week in the village began, Aaren took me to the blacksmith.

Though I had met Borgil in passing, stepping into his forge was entirely different.

White heat blew in my face as we approached, and I saw Borgil hunched over his workbench, smoothing the limb of a bow and gingerly running his fingers over the wood to feel for any missed patches.

"Borgil," Aaren greeted.

Borgil flicked his eyes to us briefly before returning to his work. "Afternoon, Aaren," he said, his tongue poking through his lips in concentration. "What can I do for you?"

"I think it's time for Layla to be fitted for a sword."

"Oh?" Borgil placed the bow down gently and dusted his hands on his clothes. As he stood, his gentle features came into focus, and unable to stop myself, I smiled at his tentative approach. His hair was dark and curly, and the light wrinkles etched on his face hinted that he was in his fifties, at least in human years. I hadn't quite nailed the lifespan of the Fraalver yet.

He veered around the workbench and settled in front of me. "May I?" he asked politely, offering his palms to me. Perplexed, I nodded. Borgil lightly grasped my right arm and pressed the pads of his fingers into my muscle, stepping his digits down my arm and counting the length. Then he wrapped his soot-stained hand around my wrist, then my elbow, then my bicep.

After taking my measurements, he handed me a sword and instructed me to swing. It was odd swinging a real sword when I was used to wielding the practice wooden swords in the ring—I hoped I didn't look as uncoordinated as I felt when I swung. Borgil nodded, then stepped away, flinging open a trunk and tossing out a heavy ingot. It landed with a metallic thud at my feet.

"Good material to you?" he asked as he pushed himself to his feet again.

I looked to Aaren, unsure how to answer.

"Perfect," Aaren answered.

The next day when I met Aaren in the ring, Borgil stood by his side, his chin lifted proudly as he cradled a wooden box in his hands.

"What's this?" I inquired lightheartedly.

Borgil offered me the box. "Your sword, *frue*."

He opened the box and revealed a gleaming silver sword resting atop a bed of crisp green leaves. The hilt had been wrapped in smooth, treated leather with tendrils of ivy etched into it. The blade itself was sleek and shimmering, sharp and daunting. Beautiful and deadly. I blinked at my reflection in the blade as I gawked at it.

I swallowed and breathed, "It's beautiful."

Borgil nodded modestly.

I picked it up and adjusted it in my grip, feeling the weight shift perfectly with each movement, though I still wasn't used to the heaviness concentrated into one arm. This was significantly heavier than the wooden sword I had been using for training. It felt like an extension of my own arm, a heavy extension, but a part of me nonetheless. The longer I held the sword, *my* sword, the more excited I grew to use it. Excited at the possibilities this sword held. This could be the blade I plunged into Markus's gut for stealing my brother. This sword could be the weapon that could help me get Lucas back. I grabbed the hilt with two hands, anticipation shooting through me as the last ounce of my previous trepidation vanished. With every swing, the blade whistled through the air, the grip never shifting in my hand. I held it up and gazed proudly at the shimmering metal.

"I don't know what to say," I breathed.

"Nothing is needed then, *frue*," Borgil assured.

Aaren backed up in invitation, spreading his arms wide. "You think it's good enough to take me?" he challenged. He spun his own sword in his hand smoothly and planted his feet.

I cocked my head and strode towards him, my sword arm still adjusting to the new weight, tingling with anticipation. Circling me, Aaren's eyes glanced over my frame, assessing my form and contemplating the first move. He prowled, dangerously beautiful determination set into his features as he analyzed me, sized me up. A predatory stillness settled over the ring as he stopped, taking the smallest moment to glance at me, then a smirk. With a furious swing, he advanced, and I had just enough time to spin away before our blades clashed with a magnificent clang. Sparks flew from my fresh blade.

"I think I can handle it," I answered, my forehead inches away from his.

I was surprised by how quick my defense was, how flawless it felt. I had only been practicing with wooden weapons for a few weeks, but being in the ring, fighting, just felt right to me. Back in my old realm, I wasn't particularly good at anything, especially anything active, seeing as I almost failed gym. But being in Alveland, fighting with Aaren, it came naturally, like I had known it all along. I felt like it had been waiting idly in my blood, waiting to awaken and burn.

That night, Rorik gave me an unreasonable amount of reading. I had already run through twenty pages of another dusty book from Harald's when my patience stretched thin, and I slammed the book shut, waving away the cloud of dust. It's not that the books he assigned were terrible; they were just repetitive, and Harald was very long-winded. Thea was right, you can only read so much about the dwarf wars before you want to start clawing your eyes out. And I found that the dwarves were very hotheaded people, considering the number of wars they had over frivolous matters.

When yet another passage started with the words "and so war began," my annoyance had reached its peak. To make matters worse, I had another look at the stack of books I needed to read by the end of the week. I grunted loudly as my frustration grew to meet my annoyance, balling my hands into fists, knuckles cracking. I jumped as blue sparks stunned my palms when my knuckles popped. I shook out my hands in astonishment and disbelief. By now, magic was not a foreign concept to me, but it still stunned me every time I encountered it. Curiously, I pushed my fists again, waiting for them to crack, but they didn't. I pulled my fingers and stretched my joints, but when nothing happened, I sighed in defeat.

Almost laughing at the crazy notion that those sparks could be this hidden store of magic I was theorized to have, I ran through what had just happened. And just as Thea had said all those weeks ago, it had been a strike of heavy emotion that conjured it. Anger, frustration, annoyance. I just had to make myself feel that way again. An easy feat once I glanced at the stack of books again. Frustration rippled through me, and taking the opportunity, I snapped my fingers. I gasped when a small flame sputtered from my fingertip.

And then it all made sense. This was why my hands were getting hot amid high emotion. Whatever stores of magic I possessed were awakening the longer I stayed in Alveland, the more work I did in Skoghjem. My magic was another weapon to add to my arsenal against Markus.

I was too giddy to sleep that night, and it took a toll on my training the next morning.

Breath cut from my lungs as my back slammed the wood of the ring, Aaren's boot pressing into the space between my breasts.

"Bested again," he panted with a sly smile. "Don't give me that look, you're the one who stepped left."

I slapped the side of his boot angrily, and sweet breath spread through my chest when he moved it. I rose to my feet slowly, legs protesting after the last hour of fighting and defeat. Today felt different than all the other days Aaren and I had spent in the ring. I was off my game, wary even, especially since I planned on telling him about my blossoming magic after our session.

"Hands up, *fremmed*," Aaren instructed, and I didn't bother to quiet the groan that rumbled through my lips. He gave an amused grunt. "I'm not done with you yet."

Three more rounds of sparring, all ending in my defeat, and Aaren let me free for the day.

I watched him from across the ring as he racked his practice sword, trepidation rooting my boots to the planks. The sunlight caught underneath his light shirt and illuminated the ghastly scar on Aaren's back.

"You're staring, Layla," he said as he turned and shook out his hair from the hasty bun he had thrown it into before the session.

"Something happened last night," I said and started to cross the ring. When I was only a foot away from Aaren, I lowered my voice. "You know how when I first got here, you said I wasn't human, and Thea told me about ways young magic can manifest and—"

"Spit it out, *fremmed*," Aaren said with an impatient edge.

I took a deep breath. "I summoned magic last night."

I wasn't expecting surprise from Aaren when I broke the news, but I certainly wasn't expecting the nonchalance he gave me in answer. "Let's see it," he said and eyed my hands.

"What?"

"Do what you did last night."

Shit. If I had known he was going to ask for a demonstration, I would have prepared better. I'm not sure how I could have, but I would have found a way.

I blew out a breath and raised my hands, tracing my mind back to last night and the headspace I was in when I summoned my first flame—frustration and anger over my homework from Rorik. I dug into those feelings, letting them grow and fester in my chest, but it didn't feel like enough.

And it wasn't, because when I snapped my fingers, nothing happened. "Hang on," I said, and closed my eyes to focus on stirring agitation and annoyance, trying to think of all the things that annoyed me. Indecisive customers at the bar, the way Aaren pants in triumph when he shoves me to the ground in a spar, Markus, Sarah's voice as she argues with me over Lucas...

Snap!

And...

Nothing happened.

"Shit," I cursed. "It happened, Aaren, I swear it did."

Aaren didn't say anything; his eyes instead studied my hands. "Go find Rorik. You don't want to be late."

I was only a few minutes behind, but Rorik still reprimanded me, even though Aaren's last fifty pushups were to blame for my tardiness.

My fingers dug into my closed eyes as Rorik began his lecture on yet another dwarf war. There wasn't much I was learning from these lessons except the fact that the dwarves were short-tempered and fought over the stupidest things. I couldn't keep their wars straight, and I think it was unrealistic for Rorik to expect me to have them memorized.

"Am I boring you, Layla?" he asked, peering at me from under a raised brow.

I faked a smile. "No, I'm fine."

"This is important to remember." He said that about the last eight chapters.

"I know," I replied, readjusting in my chair to rouse myself from my stupor. "It's just...Aaren went pretty hard on me today. I'm worn out."

Rorik nodded kindly. "Perhaps a cup of vekkin root tea would do you some good."

My mouth soured at the thought—the last time Rorik made the tea for me, I almost spit it out on the first sip. It may help with muscle soreness, but it tasted like sour blackberries soaked in swamp water. Just as Rorik stood, the medicine hut door swung open, and I sighed in relief when Aaren's towering frame filled the door.

"Afternoon, Aaren," Rorik said from one of the herb shelves.

Aaren gave a polite grunt in greeting, then sat down in front of me. He smelled of sweat and forest, a pleasant musk I was becoming accustomed to when his weight wasn't incapacitating me in the ring. He glanced at the books splayed across the table, then gave me a sympathetic look.

"The ninth dwarf war, huh?" he asked. "Haven't made it very far into the dwarven history, have you?"

I gave him a pleading look, to which Aaren chuckled.

"Dreadful to study, but essential," Rorik replied as he returned with a steaming mug of what looked like bog scum. "Drink up, Layla. That should help with the soreness."

Aaren kept his gaze locked on me as I feigned gratitude when I accepted the cup. I took a small sip, barely letting the liquid touch my tongue before it went down my throat. It was just as awful as I remembered, but unfortunately, Rorik wasn't going to let me leave the hut until I drank the last drop.

"What brings you here, Aaren?" Rorik asked as he took up his spot next to me once more.

"Layla told me something interesting in the ring today," he said, leaning back in his chair. When Rorik gave him an expectant look, Aaren gestured to me. "Go on."

Wrapping my fingers around the warm mug, I said, "I summoned magic last night."

Rorik's brows flew to his hairline. "You did?"

I nodded. "I was feeling frustrated and then it just...happened."

"That's fantastic," Rorik said, and to my wondrous relief, started closing the history books. "What were you frustrated about?"

I shook my head. "Oh, that's not important."

160

"I'm here because now that we know she can, I think it's wise that we teach her how to use her magic properly."

"But I can't," I retorted after a quick, disgusting sip of tea. "I tried to in the ring and nothing happened."

Rorik waved a hand. "And it won't every time. Not at first. I think magic lessons are a great idea."

Great. Another lesson to add to my day. It was starting to feel like I was back in school again. Only the lessons here weren't as fun as the ones I sat through in college. At least those didn't involve me getting punched regularly.

"Fine," I said. "But no more homework. You already give me enough, Rorik."

Rorik opened his mouth to retort, but Aaren interrupted him. "Try summoning it again."

Just like in the ring, I tried to find that same headspace, burrow deep into the negative sphere of thinking. But Aaren broke my concentration by thumping me on the elbow. "What was that for?" I demanded. He shrugged and gestured for me to continue. I breathed deeply, sinking into annoyance, focusing on the long, thin text along the spine of the history book, thinking of the endless history of the dwarves and their hot temper and—

Aaren thumped me again.

"Stop that," I spat, swatting at him like a fly.

Dwarves and wars and fighting and—

Thump.

"Aaren, I swear to God, I'm going to—"

Thump.

Rorik's eyes flicked between the leader and me, a hint of quiet amusement in his face. The corners of his mouth tugged down as if he were hiding a smile.

Thump.

"I can't believe this isn't working," Aaren said, seeming to hide his own smile. Then he pinched me.

"STOP!" I said, my voice booming through the medicine hut. My hands were hot, but no sparks of flame erupted from my fingers. The air was alive with something static, a crackling energy, and I wondered if it had come from Aaren or me.

The traces of amusement were gone, and the two men sat back, seeming to study me as if they were formulating the best way to rile me up.

After many more attempts to summon my magic—which included startling me, more pestering, and a fair amount of harshly worded insults—we gave up for the day. Both men apologized for what they put me through, and I retreated to the pub and hid in the storeroom amongst the cheese and spices.

The continued magic training sessions yielded nothing—the more I tried to work myself up and force my emotions, the more my magic dug deeper inside me and hid. No amount of advice or tips and tricks from Aaren and Rorik could muster a single spark, and after the third day of trying, they decided to let me rest and let it come naturally. Since then, even in the privacy of my own room, I couldn't summon anything to stir my power.

On the bright side, I practiced with my sword for a week, and by the end, the weight of the weapon felt like the most natural thing I could carry.

I was fighting well and learning every day, but the better I got, the harder Aaren fought. After each spar, I thought the next one would be my victory. And by the next spar, he seemed to hit me harder, push me farther. It was infuriating. Though I had studied his footwork, mimicking his every graceful move, I still couldn't disarm him.

"You can't copy me, *fremmed*," Aaren said, his labored breathing puffing out the loose hair that had fallen from its hold. "I know my tactics. If you mirror me, you become predictable."

I huffed. "I'm sorry I can't be as good as you," I bit sarcastically, though in the back of my mind, I meant it. "It's not as easy as you make it seem."

Aaren chuckled, a sound I was slowly getting used to hearing, and his cheeks creased to accentuate his hidden laugh lines. I liked it when those laugh lines appeared.

"Drop your sword," Aaren instructed. Complying with a groan, I didn't shy away as he approached me, even though there was a high likelihood this was a trap. He had pulled something like this before, claiming to teach me a lesson in trusting your opponent, instructor or not. Thankfully, it wasn't some scheme to catch me off guard, and instead, he shook out my arms to loosen the muscles.

"Relax. You're overthinking it. The more you watch me, the less attention you give to your own fight."

I scoffed. "No offense, Aaren, but you're an excellent fighter. I might need to start fighting someone different."

Heat flashed through his eyes. Here one moment, gone the next. "No, you don't. We fight well together. Besides," he dropped my hands, "no other opponent will be as handsome as I am."

I scoffed. "You're insufferable."

Aaren's eyes darkened. "You want to fight another opponent, fine. I know exactly where you can start."

With a crook of his finger, he extended a challenge, and I accepted. Sliding my sword into the scabbard at my side, I trailed behind him and out of the ring as a thrilled curiosity thrummed through me. Aaren threw a mischief-filled glance over his shoulder to make sure I was following, then took off in a sprint. I cursed, still wiped out from our morning run.

"Aaren!" I shouted angrily, falling into a fast jog. I wasn't sprinting after him, not after the sit-ups he had me do this morning. The restriction rune tugged at my arm when I neared the border, sending me skidding to a halt. I was glad the rune gave me a warning, because I was not prepared to smack face-first into the mud puddle my boots splashed in.

Aaren, not too far ahead, jogged the distance back to me.

"Allow me," he said, somehow still breathing normally, even after such a sprint. I reminded myself that Aaren had probably been running laps around the village for decades while I had only been doing it for a little under two months. He waved his hand over the rune where it shimmered, and there was a pleasant tingling across my skin as it released the hold it had on me.

"Just for now," Aaren said almost reproachfully. "The moment you bolt, I'm leaving you to the vines."

I pressed my lips together. "Thank you."

My temporary freedom from the rune felt like a weight off my shoulders, and it filled me with a renewed vitality. I took my first step over the border since purging Markus. And yet when both of my boots crossed the border, the weight returned, almost like the freedom from the village I had craved wasn't actually what I had wanted. For some reason, the walls of the village called to me more than the rest of the forest did.

Aaren led the way, immediately veering left. Within a few minutes, we passed the treehouse, from which soft giggles could be heard above. Aaren picked up a pinecone and launched it at the tree, where it exploded on the side of the clubhouse. The muffled squeals from inside sent Ugleverge flapping away. Aaren grabbed my hand, and we ducked behind a small holly bush, peering through the spiked leaves at the treehouse window as little heads peeked through the opening. I chuckled at their puzzled faces and hurried theories as to what caused the sound.

When the treehouse died down, Aaren and I slipped away.

"Where are you taking me?" I inquired as we crossed a mossy log over a babbling stream. He offered me his hand as I jumped down.

"There is a trehag that has been stealing some of Aurora's crops. She's asked me to take care of it for her."

"A trehag?"

"It means tree hag," Aaren answered. "Very ugly and very deadly."

Fabulous, just what I needed to fight when I was completely obliterated from a training session.

"They were once Fraalver, long, long ago, but nature took them instead, molding them into the wretched things they are now."

"And...you want me to fight it?" I demanded.

"You wanted a different opponent, I'm giving you one," Aaren retorted bluntly.

There went my stomach. Suddenly, I didn't feel so good. Fighting with Aaren was one thing; taking on a whole creature I had never even seen before was another. Besides, fighting Aaren was skilled combat; it sounded like this trehag would be a nastier fight.

My breakfast began to climb in my throat, and my teeth were on edge as we trudged through the woods. Paranoia quickly dominated my good mood, and every sound other than our footsteps tensed the cords of muscle in my body. Something scuffled from the underbrush a few feet away, and I swiveled, hands grasping for the hilt of my blade.

Aaren scoffed. "It's a rabbit, *fremmed*," he assured, moving to scoop the fuzzy rodent up. The rabbit barely reacted as Aaren stroked its fur, not a single worry about its safety in his hands. This was Aaren's forest, and whatever nature lay within was keenly attuned to him, and only him.

I reached up and scratched the rabbit's head, heart melting at its big eyes and twitching nose. It licked its lips.

"How are you supposed to face a trehag if you're afraid of a mere rabbit?" Aaren goaded, letting the rabbit nuzzle his cheek before setting it back down on the ground. It darted back into the brush.

My eyes rolled, and Aaren dodged the punch I tried to send into his stomach. "I wasn't afraid of a damn rabbit, Aaren. I thought it was this trehag thing!"

"Don't be afraid of a trehag, they're nearly harmless. Except the claws. They're poisonous." Well, fuck.

My anxiety returned with a force rivaling the roaring rapids of the river a few miles away, and this time, there was no bunny to make me feel better.

The birds singing overhead grew quieter as we approached a ravine. Carved out of the rock within the ravine was a small cave, the entrance covered by a door woven together from twigs and vines.

"She's in there," Aaren pointed out, and my stomach sank. "I wouldn't go in and start hacking away. You won't be able to swing your sword in there. Lure her out."

"You're not going to help?" I whispered frantically. My trepidation was shifting into outright fear.

Aaren smirked. "You can do this, it's just a trehag."

Sure, just a creature I had never seen before, much less fought. A creature with poisonous claws and a love for cabbage. Not to mention, I had never faced any real combat where I was put in mortal danger. Puffing out a breath, I concentrated on cooling my nerves. I needed to go into this as level-headed as possible, and I was thankful Inaborg had poured me juice instead of ale with my breakfast this morning.

I took a hasty step forward, the leaves crunching underfoot sounding as loud as a bullhorn across a field. I might start playing the drums to announce myself. Nothing stirred behind the door, and I thanked the heavens the path had been cleared of leaves and pebbles that could crumble underfoot. Only mud squelched under my boots.

I was maybe four feet away from the door, nearly glued to the mud and starting to sink. If the trehag opened the door now, I should lie down in the mud and offer myself with a side of vegetables. Glancing over my shoulder, I searched for Aaren only to find he had vanished, most likely concealed behind a tree. I respected him for letting me fight this alone, but I also wanted to stomp him in the chest for it. A part of me believed he thought it was funny to send me off on what felt like a death sentence, and the lower I sank into the mud, the more likely that seemed.

I heaved a deep breath.

Chapter 23

It was now or never. My boots squelched as I pulled them free from the mud and tiptoed to the door. Lying myself flat against the rock wall an inch away from the makeshift door, I held out a hesitant fist and knocked. Air evaded my lungs as I waited for the door to burst open and a slimy, hideous creature to come crawling forth.

The ravine remained silent, and so did Aaren, wherever he was.

Confused and a little braver, I knocked again, snapping a dead twig under my fist. Still, nothing moved or answered the door.

"Aaren, I don't think she's..."

There was an ear-splitting screech, a sound not like a banshee or a pained animal, like I had expected, but a crying eagle. My eyes flew to the sky, intrigued by the noise, only to see a haggard woman standing on the rock above me in a tattered dress. Muddy green scales grew along her decrepit, sagging arms, and small clumps of hair clung to her otherwise bald head that glinted in the sunlight. Her features were sharp and slanted, almost like a bird. She looked like a harpy if one mated with a human and rotted in the forest for a few decades. Her sharp teeth were caked with mud and green goop, but they weren't what struck a lightning bolt of fear into me. It was her claws. Her long, knobbly fingers curled forward, ending in pointed talons ready to spear straight through me if I got too close.

Mud spattered my clothes as she jumped from the rock and landed in front of me, a sinister snarl baring those jagged teeth at me. Aaren was right. She was *ugly*.

With that same raptor cry, she swiped her talons, cutting through the air with a harsh swoosh. Mud caked to my shirt as I dodged and tumbled into the squelching muck to avoid the fatal bite of her claws. The trehag pivoted with a nasty snarl, and a sickly pointed tongue ran over her teeth.

"You look delicious," she crowed with a step towards me. "You'd taste divine with my leeks." The leeks she stole from Aurora.

I hurdled left as she bowed, but her claws grasped for my shirt and ripped the shoulder to shreds. As I narrowly escaped another swipe, I fell clumsily into the mud, cringing as it caked in my hair and sank into my scalp. No amount of bathing would get this feeling off me, and I silently cursed Aaren for sending me into this so unprepared.

There was a moment where I caught my breath and collected my thoughts, desperately running through every possible solution I could come up with. I shuffled away and pushed myself up, wobbly in the sinking mud. My palms smeared the filth out of my face, sure Aaren was laughing at me from afar. Prick.

I drew my blade, thankful the mud hadn't seeped into its scabbard. The sword glinted in the light, casting a blinding reflection on the trehag's face. She cried out and covered her eyes with her claws as I lunged. My sword arced towards the wretch, but the trehag caught on just in time and swiveled. When her claws raked through my bicep, pain seared through the muscle and streaked through my upper arm and shoulder: shit, shit, *shit.*

Those claws were poisonous, and she had just ripped into my arm. Burning fear dulled the pain as I waited for the poison to take effect, though I didn't have much time before she launched her second attack. Sword in hand, I charged her, ramming my shoulder into her slender abdomen. The trehag stumbled back a few paces and slammed against a tree with a breathtaking thud. She gasped, tatters of her dress ripping as she fought against my weight.

The pain in my arm grew harder to ignore, and my muscles throbbed as the blood leaked from the wound and stained my already filthy shirt. I would kill for some help right now, but I knew Aaren wouldn't. This was my fight after all. It still didn't make me want to kick him in the balls any less.

The trehag's dress ripped completely, the scraps falling around her ankles, and I backed up, gaping at the hideous figure against the tree. Disgust twisted my features, and I stepped away a few more steps, eager to escape the vicinity of the naked thing. She didn't give me that luxury, however, and sprang forward, talons flared as she tackled me into the sludge.

Her gnarled teeth gnashed at me, and I strained against her claws that were trying to carve my cheeks to shreds. I pushed away with all the strength I could muster, given the gash in my bicep, but she was just as strong, balancing out our efforts. The tip of her pointer claw brushed my cheek, barely breaking the skin, and her gruesome tongue licked the corner of her mouth excitedly.

I was not going to die underneath a naked trehag.

She screeched in pain, and then the smell of burning flesh filled the ravine. She pulled back, still attacking me, but shielding the spot where my hands had kept her at bay. Scorch marks in the shape of my hands marred her skin, blood weeping from the wound as she continued her attacks.

With the remaining ounce of strength I had, I wrapped my leg around her middle and rolled, the mud squelching underneath. In a swift movement, I grappled my sword and plunged it into her bony chest. There was a visceral crack as the blade broke bone, and the trehag groaned horrendously, twitching under the sword through her breast. She choked on a gnarled groan, and a sigh blew through my lips as I fell away from her. Breathing didn't come back to me easily, and I focused on settling my aching lungs and racing heart before I thought of anything else.

I had done it. I killed the trehag. Aaren was right, I *was* capable of it, I had fought a new opponent and came out triumphant. My adrenaline rush was cut short by the pulsing in my bicep, and I jolted forward, as the poison now coursed through my veins. How long would it take for it to take effect? I doubted we would get to the village in time for Rorik to concoct some form of antidote. I was going to die bleeding and muddy.

Aaren appeared at the top of the ravine, standing tall like one of the trees rooted along the top. "Well done," he called. Mud splattered when his boots hit the ground next to me. "You fought well, *fremmed.*"

"The poison!" I cried, showing him my mud and blood-coated arm. "She got me, her claws got me!"

There was no urgency in the look he gave me, nor was there an ounce of concern over the damage the trehag had done to my arm. "There is no poison," Aaren said through a stifled chuckle. "I just said that to scare you."

Relief washed over me, but it was brief before anger took its place. Without thinking, I swung my arm, aiming my fist straight for his face. Aaren ducked, and my punch connected with empty air. "Are you kidding me?" I demanded.

There was nothing sheepish about the smirk he gave me as he straightened, his full height making my mouth go dry. I almost punched the leader of Skoghjem out of anger. What kind of punishment did they reserve for such offenses here?

"I suppose it backfired a little bit, but you're alive?" Despite his words, Aaren didn't seem apologetic in the least.

Forgetting my wound momentarily, I stooped down and grabbed a handful of mud, smearing it across his chest. His jaw dropped as I spread the muck from his white shirt, up his neck, and painted his cheeks in dark brown.

"You deserve it," I spit, turning to step away.

"In Skoghjem, that could be noted as a criminal offense," Aaren rumbled from behind me. I couldn't tell if he was being serious by the way his tone had taken a grave turn. Seeing as I had done far worse to him in the sparring ring, smearing mud across his face hardly seemed like a prosecutable offense.

"Put it on my record," I retorted, still warring between whether I should worry.

Mud squelched behind me, then rough hands braced my hips and flung me backward. Barely missing the trehag's body, I splashed into the mud.

"I'll consider myself merciful for leaving that as your only punishment," Aaren said smugly, then took a step away.

He had just declared war, and unfortunately for him, I was in the mood to wage one. With my uninjured arm, I reached out and barely grasped the heel of Aaren's retreating boot. For such a ruthless warrior, he had horrible off-guard balance. That's something I'd use to my advantage next time we sparred. Aaren plunged into the mud, the muck a stark contrast across his silken white hair.

"Oh," Aaren almost whispered as he turned his head slowly, like a bear prematurely awoken from hibernation. "You're going to regret that."

The fiery glaze in his yellow eyes told me I was in dangerous territory, and I scrambled away, but my hands and feet couldn't find traction in the mud. Fingers circled my ankle and yanked me through the sludge, and to ready my offense, I grabbed a handful of mud. When I was close enough, I slapped my palm onto his head, satisfied at the grime that dripped from his crown, down his brow, and onto his cheek.

The corners of his mouth twitched, and I breathed a sigh of relief, giggling as he blinked the mud from his eyes. Aaren gave in to the smile he had been fighting and let it spread across his lips, then the low rumble of his laugh could be heard, growing louder. Then, to my astonishment, he threw his head back, letting that blessed laughter ring through the forest. And then I couldn't control my own smile, the laughter that joined his and filled the clearing. I wondered when the last time Aaren had let go and laughed like this. Had his hardened exterior been a facade he put up as leader, or was he truly as miserable and severe as he came off? With the way his laugh lines filled out with each breath of laughter, I started to believe it was the former.

Or maybe he grew to be like that after his parents died. Or his betrothed. I, of all people, should know what grief does to a person.

As our laughter fell to chuckles, the forest replaced our sounds of gaiety. The birdsong grew louder, and my eyes settled on the treetops, admiring the green and blue canvas painted above. Looking up at the forest canopy reminded me of an artist's rendering I had seen at the art museum Mama had taken me to one time. We spent hours roaming through the paintings and sculptures, pointing out which ones we liked and which ones we could probably create ourselves. There was a particular painting that looked just like the trees above me, and I remembered how I had marveled at each brushstroke and fleck of paint. I had gotten lost in that painting, in the woods the artist created. I wanted to be in that forest. It seemed now I was.

I turned my head and caught Aaren's amber eyes locked onto me, a softness rimming his pupils. Before I could delve further into that look, he blinked and looked away, then sat up. There was something about that look, something warmer, as if some of that hard stone had been chipped away and whatever was underneath was fighting to get out. But Aaren wasn't one to relent so easily, so I savored the moment for what it was—just a look, just a few brief seconds where he slipped away.

After helping me to my feet, Aaren surveyed the trehag's lifeless form slowly sinking in the mud. His eyes lingered on the hand-shaped scorch marks.

He didn't mention that he noticed the scorch marks, but he also didn't hold back his critiques of my fight with the trehag on the way back to the village, some accompanied by my gripes that it wasn't as simple as keeping my elbow tucked in. The pain in my bicep was throbbing by now, but I hid my wincing as we crossed over the border, right to the medicine hut. After Rorik patched me up and I had violently scrubbed the mud from my skin, I went downstairs for dinner.

The pub was bustling tonight, boasting double the numbers on a typical night, and I was tempted to offer Inaborg some help had she not already told me to rest for the evening. I wove through the tables until I found Aaren and Nilsen, who were pressed tightly to his brother's side, having barely touched his plate of food.

"Eat, *bror*," Aaren advised as he took a sip of ale. "You're not getting anything else tonight if you don't eat your food."

Nilsen caught my eye as I sat down, giving me a look that told me he knew that wasn't true. Aaren would cave and send Nilsen off to bed with a slice of bread and cheese if he begged hard enough. Inaborg placed a plate in front of me and poured me some ale.

"Are we going to talk about the magic you summoned today?" Aaren asked through a mouthful of shepherd's pie.

Nilsen's eyes went wide. "You used magic today?"

I took a bite of my food and shrugged. "I was scared," I answered. "I thought I was going to die from poison." Aaren chuckled and bent to whisper in Nilsen's ear.

Nilsen giggled. "You thought a trehag could poison you?" he asked incredulously.

I stuck my tongue out at him for making me feel stupid. Nilsen returned the gesture, then shoved a bite of pie in his mouth.

"We're going about the magic all the wrong way," Aaren said.

"How else am I supposed to summon my magic? You said it yourself, emotions rile them."

Aaren gave me a look like I was missing the point. And I was, because he may as well have been speaking in riddles. "There are other ways to use magic, that's just the easiest and most common way."

Nilsen finished his last bite and sank against Aaren, yawning. My chest went tight as I watched his eyelids flutter open and closed as he fought sleep, just like Lucas's when he wanted to stay up and keep reading. Aaren pushed his plate away and stood, holding his brother's now sleeping form against his chest.

"We'll work on it tomorrow before your lesson with Rorik."

Chapter 24

I won a couple of spars the next day, but the thought of my magic lesson distracted me in our later fights, and I yielded when Aaren's practice sword sliced across both of my limbs as if to maim me. When the swords were put away, Aaren met me in the middle of the ring.

"High emotions are good for summoning magic when you're scared or want to lash out, but it can be unreliable. When you summoned your magic, what exactly happened?"

"Flames," I answered. "I conjured a flame."

Aaren retreated to the side of the ring and brought back a lit brazier. The heat kissed my face, and I squinted as I looked into the flames.

"There are stores of magic inside us, which is what we use to conjure when we're feeling a certain way. But," he gestured to the brazier, "magic is found in other places. And it can be more powerful if sourced from the right place."

The flames licked wildly at the sides of the brazier, as if begging to be let free.

"Nature is our greatest asset," Aaren continued. "It gives us food, shelter..."

Rough wood scraped against refined wood, and vines began to creep over the edges of the sparring platform and curl lazily around our feet.

"...and power."

"Isn't that asking a lot of nature, though?" I asked, remembering the toll humans took on the earth. We took food, shelter, and a different kind of power, and it slowly evolved into a parasitic relationship.

Aaren shook his head. "It wants to give us these things, but we have to respect the balance." A vine slid up his leg and curled around his wrist. "It respects us if we respect it." He gestured to the flames. "But you have to be open to feeling it."

The heat seemed to withdraw when I looked away. "How do I do that?"

Aaren shrugged as his vines began to retreat. "That's for you to figure out." A lot of help he was.

I turned back to the brazier and welcomed the heat again, despite the warm spring air that surrounded us. The flames danced higher, as if they were waking up, and something tugged in my stomach. It wasn't like the tug I felt when Markus possessed me. That tug was painful and demanding. This tug was inviting and exciting, almost. It felt like expecting a guest and hearing them knock on your front door. There was a sense of familiarity, excitement, and potential.

I opened that front door, and the fire's life spilled into me, spreading warmth and energy and light across every inch of my being, from each hair follicle to the tips of my toes. I was invigorated, giddy, and my hands burned sweetly.

"Holy shit," I said, smiling down at my fingers in wonderment. The fire curled around my heart, making itself at home in my chest and filling me with a comforting buzz of power. When I snapped my finger, a bright orange flame danced across my nail and slid along my knuckle into my palm.

I did it. I had summoned magic, and I didn't have to get angry or upset.

The power was revitalizing, intoxicating, and suddenly, I knew precisely why Markus craved it so much.

Over the next few days, all parts of my magic took form. It was like unlocking my fire opened a door to all my other power. Suddenly, every bit of nature that surrounded me was reaching out and offering itself. I could barely walk by a trough of water without feeling that delightful tug in my stomach.

Working in the fields with Aurora became a lot more interesting, especially when the dirt that caked underneath my nails no longer disgusted me, but sent a thrill through me. After a couple of days, Aaren taught me how to quiet down the connections, or rather, ignore them politely. He said it was like turning down an overeager servant—you didn't want to take advantage of their eagerness to serve, but you also didn't want to lose the connection with them by cutting them off completely.

He taught me how to siphon off small amounts of the offered power, and I found that I could use them in everyday life. Need to start a fire in the hearth? I got it. The wind whipped the window open in the middle of the night. I'll use that same wind to close it from the comfort of my bed.

When I wasn't siphoning off small bits of power from the elements around me, I learned how to put up small blocks against them. Not a hard stop, but enough that I could function without being overcome with power. It reminded me of a screen door, enough to block anyone from coming through, but you could still feel a breeze through it. Shielding and siphoning were becoming second nature.

In the few weeks I had been working on my magic, it had sharpened significantly. The sense of accomplishment that accompanied the honing of my power was different than what I'd felt before. In school, I was proud of the work that I put in, but I saw no real gain, especially after applying to the psychology program and never hearing back. With this magic, it was something I saw come to fruition, something that came from within, not a book I had to read. The energy that thrummed in me was sheer power, and it was addicting to behold.

The shouts and hoots of merriment echoed around the halls of the pub as I accepted a mug of ale from Thea. Full of roast chicken and limp from training, I leaned back against the bar and observed the exuberance. My sword arm hung uselessly at my side, so I had to favor my left side for the rest of the evening, even though Aaren urged me to continue to use it. He said not using it would only make the soreness worse, and while he may have been right, I was done listening to him for the day. He'd been bossing me around in the ring more than usual, and I was grateful for a reprieve from his barking orders.

Thea sighed jovially and sipped from her mug. "As a Fraalver myself, I still wonder how they carry on so avidly." I had thought the same myself, especially considering half of the people carrying on so vibrantly had been in here last night, draining the dregs of the last keg of Inaborg's cherry cider. Thea turned to me expectantly, her eyes dancing. "I saw you practicing with Aaren today."

I groaned. "Please spare me your romantic theories."

Thea, taken aback, scoffed. "I was going to compliment you on your form, *frue*. You've improved. Not everything is about the glamor of love, despite what my books will have you believe."

I nodded, but I couldn't stop my brow from cocking in disbelief. Thea's sly comments over the past few weeks did nothing to prove her point, but it wasn't her words that seemed to put me on edge.

My own conflicting feelings had made me defensive in response to such comments and implications. Aaren was my friend, even though sometimes I believed he'd argue that fact, and my own admission of such a notion sent a jolt of surprise through me. But when you spend every day with someone, it's hard to fight the growing affection, whether platonic or otherwise. And I blamed my minimal experience with romance for my confusion about my present feelings.

I had never had a boyfriend growing up, as no one had ever shown me genuine interest. It didn't upset me, though; it was very easy to see why that was the case. There was nothing extraordinary about me—I wasn't devastatingly beautiful, nor was I particularly talented at anything. I had a high school crush on a boy named Tommy Porter, but a crush was all it remained. That's all I had ever had. My first crush was on Bran from The Goonies, and Mama and I used to fawn over Westley from The Princess Bride. However, as I grew older, I began to take an interest in the opposite sex, but they did not seem to take an interest in me. I came to accept the fact and instead focused my attention on my studies and work.

There had been one exception, though it was rather unpleasant. It had been a long night at the bar, and I had one customer who had stayed throughout the duration of my shift. He was kind enough, and he wasn't bad on the eyes, plus it had been a harrowing shift, so when I got off and took a seat next to him at the bar, I gladly let him buy me drinks until Rachel started shutting down. When both of us had drunk enough beer that we kicked a keg, he invited me back to his place, and I obliged. He had shown me to his bedroom, and three minutes later, I was putting my clothes back on, feeling grossly underwhelmed for my first time. I hadn't seen him since.

I didn't really care for sex after that. After such an underwhelming first experience, I never really understood why it was such a big deal. My roommates would bring home a guy occasionally, and I would smile through my envy as they recounted their time spent with said guys. It wasn't that I was jealous of them directly, but rather that I wondered when my time would come to bring someone home with me. I didn't blame the men who overlooked me as a viable partner. Why would anyone want me romantically when no one had even tried to adopt me? I didn't hold it against anyone. It was just an unfortunate truth I carried with me.

The sexual politics of the Fraalver were still a mystery to me, except for Thea and Stieg. The Fraalver were a lively people and carried on heavily in the pub, and I often wondered if their high-spirited gaieties carried over into the bedroom.

The memory of Dagan's funeral came into my mind, blurry and stomach churning. As fuzzy as the events were that night, I recalled one thing clearly, and that was the way Aaren's body felt against mine. I went to admonish myself for thinking such thoughts of my friend, then stopped. To hell with it, a little fantasizing didn't do any harm. And the thought of Aaren's lips so close to mine sent a warm flush to my skin.

"Did you even hear what I said?" Thea asked.

I coughed into my mug and a spray of ale shot out, sprinkling my shirt. I hacked, and Thea gave me a swift smack on the back before sighing in annoyance. Fantasizing would do me some harm.

176

"No," I wheezed. "What were you saying?"

"I said," Thea began, "that I think I might see Stieg again tonight."

"Oh!" I exclaimed when I had fully recovered. "That's great!"

Thea arched a brow mischievously. "He said he has a collection of treasures to show me."

Letting out a laugh, I imagined Stieg excitedly showing Thea his collection of candy wrappers. Finishing my drink, I bid my friend goodnight and padded up the stairs, snuggling into the bed. Contentment warmed me like the furs that wrapped my body, and my eyes drifted shut, enjoying the sizzles and pops of the fire in the hearth. Though Lucas still held a heavy presence in my mind, with a lingering guilt that could not be pushed aside, I had grown to love the life this village was teaching me to live. I was never in a rush anymore, living slowly through the life of the forest.

Even my appearance had begun to change, something I had noticed the other day as I washed the sweat and dirt from my face after a bout of training with Aaren. My face had filled out, and the faint freckles that bridged my nose and cheeks had darkened, painting a constellation across my face. Muscle had slowly wrapped my arms and legs, and the bags that I sported beneath my eyes from the long nights at the bar had vanished. I looked like a new woman.

Sleep enveloped me, numbing each sense one by one until all I could hear was my own satisfied breathing.

I hadn't been asleep long when I awoke abruptly, unable to breathe. Attempting a deep breath, my lungs constricted, as if someone had dropped a boulder on my chest. I thrashed, trying to shift my body upright, but cold filled my limbs. It was a feeling like a brain freeze, but instead of an aching head, it was filling the fascia of my joints, the cells of my skin. Before I knew it, I was as good as paralyzed. The weight on my chest only grew heavier, and my lungs were close to collapsing. There was only thick, inky darkness around me, and for a moment, I feared I had gone blind. It was impossible to determine what was hindering my breathing, so I focused on taking a shallow breath. Something soft brushed my cheek as if a furry hand brushed away the tears that streamed silently from my eyes.

"Your blood betrays you," a frighteningly raspy voice said, too close to my face. A pair of beady orange eyes blinked above me, flickering like the lights in a pumpkin in the fall. "What gave you life now seeks to extinguish it."

"Huh?" I wheezed, thankful I was able to work my vocal chords.

The thing sighed, almost as if whatever sat atop my chest grew annoyed with my confusion. "You're a threat to Markus's power." Breaths came in choppy spurts, the soft touch against my cheek brushing away another pained tear that had gathered at the corner of my eye.

It continued. "His power lies in his heir. But what he could not see in the first, he saw in the second. Your brother, who is now coming of age, stands by his father's side to be raised in the dark to cast a shadow on your growing spark." The thing blinked its lovely orange eyes, curiously watching my face. "One mustn't fret," it assured. "The heir lives."

A choked question sputtered from my lips, but the orange eyes winked out before I could finish. A corded breath rattled my lungs as I gasped in sweet, sharp air. I didn't give myself time to recover my breathing before shooting a small flame into the fireplace, reeling from what the thing had said.

What gave you life now seeks to extinguish it.

My mother...my father. The father, who was from this realm.

Dread flooded my stomach. The thing mentioned by Markus.

The dread rose to my throat.

Markus was my father.

"Oh god," I whispered. Then the dread spewed out of me, and I was sick before I could make it to the washbasin in the corner.

Markus was my father. His evil blood was in my veins.

A renewed guilt sang through me as I wiped my mouth and straightened. I wanted to hate the blood within me, hate it for killing Dagan and bringing the mylings and everything else that happened as a circumstance of my being. Even though that same blood gave me the ability to do wonderful things, I couldn't hate my magic or what it was helping me to become. I couldn't. I just hoped the others shared that sentiment.

The night was quiet as I sprinted silently down the path, barely noticing the shadowed wings in the trees keeping track of my movements. Ugleverge hooted overhead, and I sent a silent thanks for his protection. Upon bursting through Aaren's front door, I dropped my hands to my knees and tried to stop the shaking that rattled my entire body. Aaren and Rorik sat across from each other in front of the fire, murmuring in hushed tones. Aaren's eyes were cold, distant as Rorik muttered something in a tight voice.

My urgency was tangible, and both men shot to their feet.

178

"What happened?" Aaren asked abruptly. He didn't touch me, but his hand strained as if he were fighting the urge to reach out. His eyes darted to the partially open door behind me to search for anyone who could've been trailing.

"I'm so sorry," I breathed. "I'm so, so sorry." Panic built a dam in my throat and kept me from explaining, kept me from even catching my breath despite my frantic heaving.

Calloused hands caressed either side of my face, and my eyes rose to meet concerned amber irises. "Layla, calm down."

Beautiful things, I could do lovely things with the tainted blood in my veins. If I kept reminding myself of that, I'd eventually believe it.

"Breathe with me, *fremmed*," Aaren instructed, then led me through a three-second inhale followed by a five-second exhale. It helped, and another round sent a cooling calm through me.

Rorik strode and closed the front door. When my breathing evened out enough for me to straighten, I stepped away from Aaren and walked to the fire to stare into the writhing flames.

Beautiful things. I can create beautiful things with the evil I've been given.

"Markus is my father."

Only the crackle of the fire answered me, and I could only imagine Aaren and Rorik exchanging an alarmed look with each other, opting for silence should I reveal more.

"How do you know?" Aaren asked, the composure in his tone unnerving me.

When I turned and beheld both faces staring at me, I wished I could read what was going on behind their unflinching expressions.

"I was asleep," I began, overseeing their faces, "and something heavy sat on my chest. I couldn't breathe, but it told me..."

Breath left my lungs as the truth burned painfully in my throat. "It told me who my father is." I repeated the words the thing had said.

Finally, Rorik's face broke to reveal the same stunned astonishment that hit me upon learning of my parentage. "Impossible," he breathed.

"Not anymore," Aaren said, leaning against the table with a nonchalance that should have been impossible to achieve at a time like this. "A mare, fremmed, visited you."

I blinked. "A what? Like Ingrid?"

From my conversation with Stieg and Aaren, I knew a little about mares. Rorik filled in those gaps, explaining that what had pulled me so frightfully from my sleep was a mare, a creature that squats on a sleeping person's chest and delivers them bad dreams, restricting their movements so the person couldn't escape their altered dream state. In my old realm, it would be considered a sleep paralysis demon from a horror movie. The difference was that this mare hadn't seemed evil like it had been portrayed, but rather a helpful spirit, despite the news it divulged. But like a sleep paralysis demon, it couldn't be proved that it was real since no one saw one while awake.

"If it was a mare, then we have to question the validity of what it told you," Rorik added.

"If she says it's true, Rorik, then it's true," Aaren hissed, knuckles growing white as he gripped the table. Rorik shot him a look of reproach, and Aaren's jaw only clenched. "Ingrid, she must've also encountered this same mare."

Rorik lifted a brow in consideration. "It showed her the mylings, that they weren't just a freak occurrence. Which means..."

I stopped my lip from trembling. "I really am from this realm. And Markus is my father."

I couldn't bring myself to meet Aaren's eyes because of how much I was dreading the look on his face. Sinking onto the bench, I tried to focus on anything other than the towering presence that still gripped the table that now looked like it wanted to splinter under his grasp.

"So, my interpretation is," Rorik started, "that Markus fathered you, expecting *you* to be his heir. Then you turned twelve, and your magic couldn't manifest in Midgard. Markus saw that and found you an unworthy heir, so he sired Lucas. And now that Lucas is coming of age, Markus stole him to groom him into being the heir he desires."

There was no better way to put it. Everything started to click.

That meant that Dallas was Markus. Of course, Mama fell for him—he was the same man who won her heart thirteen years before.

Finally braving a look at Aaren, I was confronted not with the disdain I had been expecting but with a silent anger. It was a look that set his jaw, and the fire reflected in his eyes looked like a window into the pits of Hell.

My stomach bottomed out at that look, and I felt like I was going to be sick for the second time tonight.

"I believe it's wise you get some rest, Layla," Rorik said, rising from his seat. "There is much to discuss tomorrow." As he made his way to the door, Aaren followed, exchanging the last few muttered words of the night before closing the door behind his physician.

I stayed in front of the fire as Aaren closed the distance between us.

"Are you angry with me?" I asked bluntly, realizing the challenge in my tone before I could correct it.

"No," Aaren replied, "not with you."

I wanted to say I was relieved, but it wouldn't be true. Not when Aaren's eyes still burned like two collapsing stars.

"You're a pawn," he seethed in a tone painted with malice. "A pawn in Markus's twisted schemes against the Fraalver. I have many reasons to hate him. For the crimes he has committed against my people. For the countless lives he's taken in the name of power." Aaren's lip twitched as disgust shadowed his face. "But using you for his sick games...I despise him the most for that."

Beautiful things, I told myself again. I can make beautiful things.

Chapter 25

Aaren let me spend the rest of the night in the house, though I couldn't sleep. Shock kindled with dread had sunk its claws deep and kept my eyes glued to the ceiling instead of resting, as my body ached for.

I doubted Aaren got much sleep either, as I heard Nilsen's door creak open and closed throughout the night.

The morning sun had begun to break through the night sky, casting a faint light through the window. Abandoning the idea of sleep, I rolled over and pushed myself out of bed. Birds sang overhead as I strolled back to the pub, where Inaborg greeted me with a plateful of eggs and a kind smile. An unexplainable somberness settled into me as I ate, but I shoved it to the side and headed for the ring for my morning training.

Aaren wasn't there, and in fact, I noted a heavier presence of Fraalver out and about than usual at this hour. And they were all heading in the direction of the meeting hall.

"Is there a *sammenkomst* this morning? I don't remember anyone calling a meeting," I asked Kare as he passed with his wife, Sofie, in hand.

"Aaren called one early this morning," he replied. "Something about Kysthjem."

Kysthjem? The Fraalver village by the coast?

I followed the crowd into the meeting hall, fighting the chorus of yawns that resulted from my sleepless night. Aaren and Rorik stood at the front of the meeting hall, in the exact spot where the night I had tried to escape. Fraalver continued to trickle in, curiosity buzzing through the air as the room filled quickly. I surveyed the crowd, noting the familiar faces amongst them. Thea sat on the other side of the room from Stieg, though I saw the wandering glances exchanged between them. Borgil sat a few rows away from Inaborg, whose red face was visible through a sea of curious eyes and inquiring murmurs.

Not knowing where I should sit, I slid to the side and rested against a wooden pillar, the wood grain pressing into my back. The hushed murmurs in the room quieted when Aaren stepped up. There was a moment when he stood before his people, regality heavy on him, observing them as a king surveys his kingdom.

"Welcome, *venner*," he greeted, his spine rigid. "Late last night, Kysthjem sent a gull with word from Fiske and Helgi Sjøbrytt. They were attacked and have requested aid."

Attacked? Was it merely a coincidence that the attack came at the same time as my visit from the mare?

When someone asked what attacked, my heart nearly stopped when Aaren answered.

Mylings. Mylings had attacked Kysthjem. An image of the dead children crawling out of dark water sent a chill down my spine. A wave of gasps and whispers erupted, and I caught Thea's eye in the sea of murmurs. She gave me an inquiring look, silently asking if I had known. I shrugged in response as Aaren continued.

"A group of our men and I will leave tomorrow to aid our allies. In my absence, Rorik shall take my place. Any grievances can be taken up with him."

If Aaren was leaving Skoghjem, I could go with him. While he was busy helping Kysthjem, I could use the time away to look for Lucas or at least clues about where Markus had taken him.

The meeting was dismissed, and I wove through the bustling crowd so I could get back to the pub and pack when the rune on my arm burned suddenly. I bit down on a cry and turned on my heel to see Aaren still standing at the front, eyes focused solely on me. He lifted a finger and gestured a come-hither motion. I huffed, not wanting to come like a dog when called and turned away again. This was my first and last mistake. My arm yanked me back suddenly, and I slammed into Borgil. He laughed when I offered him a sheepish apology before seething in Aaren's direction.

He smugly regarded me with a cocked brow. "Growing rebellious, aren't we?" he jabbed, crossing his arms over his chest.

I smiled sardonically. "Yes, Aaren? How may I serve you?"

Something almost hungry flickered across his features before his smugness returned. "I expect you to keep up your lessons while I'm gone. Sigurd has agreed to take my place in the ring until I'm back."

"What?" I demanded. "No, I'm coming with you."

Aaren gave an incredulous laugh. "That is a brave assumption, *fremmed.*"

Rolling my eyes, I retorted, "You told me, when I first got here, that I could look for my brother. I've trained and proved myself trustworthy enough. I'm going with you because you need to hold up your end of our bargain. Besides, now that we know the mylings, Markus, and my brother are all connected, it only makes sense that I come with you."

There was a moment where we stood with locked eyes, frozen in silent challenge. Then he sighed and looked away, a muscle ticking in his jaw. "Fine," he conceded. "But the minute you step out of line, you're walking behind the horses the entire way."

I grinned. "Does this excuse me from training today?"

A high female voice scoffed behind me. "Wouldn't want you going soft on us, *frue*," Thea said. I beamed when I turned and saw her wearing her usual shade of purple. She smiled back, then averted her eyes to her leader. "Good morning, Aaren, I hope the night bode you well."

"Not as well as I had wished," Aaren admitted.

Thea hummed, deciding to get right to the point. "When do you leave?"

"Dawn," Aaren replied.

"I see, and do you plan to find a wife overnight?"

"Thea, it's not as simple as you make it out to be," Aaren replied as if this wasn't the first time they'd had this conversation.

Thea rolled her eyes and spoke as if he were a child. "You do not have a wife, Aaren; therefore, there is no dual leadership, and our borders remain weak. They decay every day there is no second leader. How will we fortify the borders when you are away, Aaren? It feels like we're barely keeping it together with you *here*. What is not simple about that?"

Damn. She did have a point, but why was this concern so pressing for her and not for anyone else in the village? No one else seemed to be as vexed as she was about this, not even Rorik, who was to be left in charge.

"What would you have me do before tomorrow, Thea?" His patience was slipping, and the breeze outside the hall picked up. "No one in Skoghjem possesses the magic necessary for leadership. There hasn't been anyone since..."

His eyes went distant for a second.

"...since Solveig."

Thea turned her attention to me. "It's no secret Layla has the magic necessary for the marriage. Marry her."

Hold the phone. What?

"Oh, I—" I stammered and shoved my heated hands in my pockets. I prayed they wouldn't burn a hole in my pants.

"Make a decision, Aaren. I won't stand by while more of us die because you can't swallow your pride."

Thea pressed her lips together, eyes squinting as if she were close to tears. "Good luck on your journey tomorrow," she said over her shoulder as she turned and made her way out of the meeting hall. "And try not to get yourself killed. Poor Nilsen doesn't need this responsibility, especially if you can't handle it yourself."

I was going to explode.

I stormed after her, sure that if I didn't move, I would combust into flames. The small elements around the village rose to meet my anger—the spring breeze, the fire from Borgil's forge, the flower beds outside of Harald's bookshop—but I kept my fleeing friend in my sight and put up my block like Aaren had taught me.

"Hey!" I called after her, and I knew she was ignoring me when she quickened her pace. I huffed and sped into a hasty jog, following her through the winding buildings. My outrage carried me forward until she slammed the door of her shop in my face. Ignoring her inclination to be alone, I burst in, howling with anger.

"What was that?" I demanded. "I know what you were doing back there, and it's pathetic!"

Indignation hit her like a slap to the face, and her cheeks began to flush. "And what exactly was I doing?" she challenged.

"You were trying to find a way to put me and Aaren together! Like one of your books, Thea. You're trying to orchestrate this grand romance between us when all you're doing is embarrassing yourself! I'm not one of your books. You can't just write a happy ending for me."

Her mouth dropped as she choked on a laugh. "You truly believe that I inquired about the safety of our borders because I want you two to get together?" She let out another exasperated laugh. "You must be the dumbest girl I've met in all my years. Did it ever occur to you that maybe I've been trying to get you two together because I want our safety to be restored? Maybe my story is a little deeper than being your side character, Layla." Her head shook, an air of disbelief and outrage clouding the bookshop like a brewing thunderstorm.

"Then enlighten me, Thea," I spat, the bite in my tone unintentional.

Her eyes went distant, and her skirts ruffled as she sat on the stool behind the counter. "I had a husband."

Had a husband. *Had.* And just like that, I was an asshole.

Of course, Thea was hesitant with Stieg. The matter of his bloodline and public perception was merely an excuse to conceal a more profound and harsher truth.

My hands had cooled enough that I could comfortably rest them on my arms as I leaned against the counter and encouraged my friend to go on.

"After Nils and Freya died and Aaren came into power, our village suffered a draugr attack." Her voice shook, so she took a steadying breath and continued. "With one leader, our barriers keep us safe from bigger attacks like the mylings, but something as simple yet dangerous as draugr can slip through the cracks. And Aaren was new to his leadership, still coming to terms with his parents' deaths and learning about his new power and responsibilities. Our borders were as weak as a fledgling's wings. Perfect for a group of draugr to slip in. They had escaped a crypt in the hills outside the forest. My husband, Lars, was at the border when they arrived. Three others perished with him." A small tear trailed her cheek, but no sob accompanied it. "Aaren blamed himself, understandably, but it wasn't his fault."

I placed a comforting hand over hers, an apology ready on my lips when she continued.

"Don't you ever pretend to know my motivations," Thea spat and retracted her hand as if she had touched a hot stove.

I blinked before managing to stutter, "I'm sorry."

There was a static pause where Thea kept her eyes on the hand I had just brushed. "I'm sorry too," she whispered to my surprise. "I should've told you sooner. Friends don't keep secrets."

Friends. We were friends. I've made a lot of friends since I arrived. Back in Harrisburg, having friends, even just one, was so far off my radar that I couldn't begin to fathom what being a friend—particularly a good one—would entail. Lucas was my only friend. He was the only person I ever needed. So, standing in front of Thea, hearing about her tragic past and actually caring about it was as much of a surprise to me as stumbling across this realm was.

I left Thea's with heavy thoughts, and the question that burned like acid on my tongue—how was I going to make this right?

Fraalver smiled and waved as I passed, and every face I recognized sent a pang of something unfamiliar through me. Guilt perhaps? But a positive side of guilt, because every smile I saw, every friendly greeting I received, made me realize that I cared about Skoghjem, and every Fraalver here. I passed Borgil as he returned to his forge, catching sight of me and asking if my sword needed sharpening. Fraalver filed into the pub, where merry voices had resumed their singing, and I meandered on with the taste of Inaborg's new cherry cider on my tongue.

Then the negative side of the guilt set in, because deep down, I knew there was something I could do to protect these people.

Children sped past me on the way to the treehouse with Nilsen and Ingrid in the lead. I could almost see Lucas mingling in the group as they disappeared, and my heart somehow grew heavier. I would need a place to bring my brother when I rescued him, and every day here convinced me that Skoghjem was the best place for him to grow up. There was a future here for both of us.

A future I was going to secure by solidifying the borders.

Dust kicked under my boots as I came to an abrupt halt, turned on my heel, and sprinted back to the meeting hall.

Aaren was the only person within, his gaze distant as he sat in the chair at the front of the room. His arms rested on his knees, fists clenched, and I knew that undeniable look in his face. It was desperation, hard and etched deep into the creases of his brow. I knew that feeling well, because every time I dropped Lucas back off with Sarah, it heated me like a shot of whiskey. It's what drove me to try to run away all those years ago. And it's what pushed me forward to stand in front of Aaren and say, "Marry me."

His eyes flicked to mine, and he gave an amused puff through his nose. "Very funny."

"What's so funny? Explain to me what happens when the sole leader of Skoghjem leaves the village," I replied. "What happens to Nilsen if the borders are not secured while you're gone? How vulnerable will the village be without you here to protect it?"

"*Fremmed*, I—"

I shook my head. "No, do not make excuses." Aaren gave me an incredulous look. "I need a place to bring Lucas when I get him back. We leave tomorrow. Marry me tonight and let it be done."

There was a moment where Aaren just stared at me, completely unreadable. I didn't need to read him to know what was going through his head, because they were probably the same thoughts going through mine. But his obligation to keep the village and his brother safe outweighed any pride that could make him say no to my proposal. Not to mention, he would be marrying me, the *foreign*, and not the woman he obviously wanted to be with. But she was dead, and he didn't have a choice.

Finally, he stood, towering over me with that same desperation emanating from him.

"Are you sure?" he asked.

No, but I didn't see any way out of it. "Yes."

Aaren dropped his eyes to my hands, where they were grasped nervously in front of me. He reached out, fingers dancing along my forearm, and there was a tingling as the restriction rune disappeared.

Rorik found me shortly after I left the meeting hall and headed to the pub, catching me on the path halfway there. Aaren must have intercepted him before I could.

"Spare me the argument, Rorik," I sighed when he opened his mouth to say something. "My mind is made up. You're not talking me out of this."

"I wasn't going to," he said as he fell in step beside me. "I know by now how strong-willed you are." His polite way to say I was stubborn as shit. "On the contrary, I was coming to fill you in on the details of the ceremony."

I gaped at him. "You threw a ceremony together that quickly?"

"Every Fraalver wedding is the same," Rorik explained. "A leader's wedding has some extra bits, but at the core, our weddings follow the same timeline. The village will gather in the forest at sundown. Asta will help you get ready. Do you have any questions?"

A million and none at the same time. "No," I replied.

"We can discuss the matters of consummation after the ceremony," he said as he took the path to the medicine hut to his right.

Wait...consummation?

"What do you mean—"

"Layla, is what I just heard true?" Thea asked from the pub door.

Shit, word traveled fast in Skoghjem. It would have been easier to follow Rorik as he disappeared around the corner, but I owed Thea an explanation, especially after the way I had behaved earlier today.

I turned slowly on my heel and said, "Depends on what you've heard."

Thea stepped onto the pub's porch, letting the door slam shut behind her. "You're marrying Aaren?" When my silence seemed answer enough for her, she asked, "Why?"

I took the first step onto the porch. "Because you're my friend. And I love Skoghjem. I can do something about the borders, and I'd be selfish if I did nothing."

When my boot landed on the top step, I was face-to-face with my friend. And close enough to see the silver lining in her eyes. "You don't know what this means." She slid her hand into mine and, feeling the squeeze she gave me, the grief-heavy gratitude behind the gesture, solidified my decision. If I had any doubts, any moment of second-guessing, the look in Thea's trembling features washed it all away.

"Come with me," she said, the steps creaking as she left the porch and led me away from the pub.

I followed her to her bookshop, where she closed the door behind us, flung open the trapdoor to her basement home, and descended the steps. I waited in a stray beam of sunshine through the window, stomping down the storm of emotions that was brewing inside me since I ran into Rorik.

The word consummation rang in my head, stirring butterflies in my stomach, followed by bubbling apprehension that morphed into fear and uncertainty. Did the Fraalver consummate marriage like humans did? Would Aaren and I have to...

And just as these alarming thoughts began to take over, I heard Thea rustling downstairs, and they all dissipated. I would do anything for the borders because it meant I could keep my friend safe and keep Nilsen safe. To bring Lucas back here. Anything. Including consummating with Aaren.

Thea was covered in dust and looked a little frazzled when she emerged from the trapdoor, carrying a large, tattered box. She dropped it into my hands and swiped a stray piece of hair out of her face, leaving a streak of dust across her cheek.

"Open it," she said with a small smile.

I complied and gasped.

Inside was a white dress of smooth satin that shimmered in the beam of light I stood in. Small beads had been sewn into the bust, which was embossed with lace, and the sleeves were adorned with lacy ribbons that met at the wrist in a circle of white flowers. It was a wedding dress. It was *her* wedding dress.

"Some think it's a little flashy, but I like it," she said, now smiling at the dress as her eyes went distant.

I ran my fingers over the fabric. "It's beautiful," I said and imagined her wearing it as she walked down the aisle.

"I want you to wear it."

Her jarring words shook me out of the image, and my eyes widened. "What? No, Thea, I can't. It's your *wedding dress.*"

"And my husband is dead." Her voice shook, but this time, it wasn't with grief, but conviction. "All it does is serve as a reminder of lost love. Give this dress another meaning."

My palms heated underneath the box as my throat tightened. "Okay," is all I could manage as a single, hot tear spilled from my eye. Thea nodded, fighting back tears as well, and swallowed.

"Okay," she repeated, her eyes squinting as she strained a smile. "Okay."

Asta found me early that afternoon and took me to a private room in the pub. Her and Thea helped me into the dress, the breath pinching from my lungs when the corset strings pulled tight around my middle. I couldn't breathe, but the dress was indescribably beautiful. Once the pub emptied, Inaborg joined to help me get ready. The three women bustled around the room, chatting quietly, if not excitedly, about the celebration to come. I watched myself in the mirror as Thea fiddled with my hair. She had woven strands of flowers into my styled auburn locks and pinned back the front strands with a white daisy. Inaborg fussed with the skirt and train of the dress, muttering when the material fought her ministrations.

If you had asked me a month ago when I thought I would get married, I wouldn't have said anytime in the next ten years, considering my current love life and my work-to-social life ratio. And yet here I was. I had stumbled across a hidden realm full of magic and horrifying creatures, uncovered the secrets of my parentage and suppressed magic, and was soon to be married to a half-elf lord. Shock rattled my mind as I realized just how much had changed. How much *I* had changed.

The woman who looked back at me in the reflection was unfamiliar. Gone was the girl who scurried around the bar, wishing to be more like Rachel, look like her, get as much male attention as her. The girl who hoarded psychology textbooks, hoping that the number of books she owned correlated with a higher likelihood of success. The girl who was orphaned at a young age, who never had any friends in school because she didn't fit in with the other kids. The girl that no boy would take an interest in, except for one underwhelming lover.

The woman who looked back favored Mama, sporting that same pointed nose and green eyes. She had the same magic that Mama had woven so many tales about, and could do so many wonderful things with that power. The woman in front of the mirror finally had a purpose. Mama would've been proud to see what was in the reflection.

An unexpected sadness settled into my mind as I watched Inaborg straighten and examine her work on the train of my dress. It was my wedding day, a day every girl dreamed of, or at least that was what I had been told. A day where the family could come together and celebrate the joy of the couple's union. Granny and Mama should be here on my wedding day, even if it were to a man I had just met in a magical realm in the forest. It was moments like this that held me in a tight grip, subjecting me to the cruelty of orphanhood.

Thea hummed in my ear, face creased with concentration as she wove the last flower into my hair. I smiled softly. Though my friend couldn't fill the hole that Mama and Granny had left behind, she played the maid of honor well. At least I had her.

Inaborg smiled at my reflection, gave my cheeks a loving pinch, then led us out of the pub. My heart was beginning to thud a little faster in my chest as the heat of fire brought a flush to my cheeks that rivaled the rouge Thea had applied. She stood back and sighed, eyes examining every detail of her dress that hugged me in all the right places. Thea had been right—it was a little flashy per Fraalver standard, but that made me like it more. Although I could do without the steep neckline that accentuated my breasts a little more than I would've liked.

"I never thought this dress would see the light of day again," she sighed, tucking in her bottom lip to keep it from quivering.

I turned and wrapped my friend in a hug so tight, I wondered if the sleeves around my shoulders would rip. "Thank you, Thea," I said in her ear, knowing the shake in my voice could be heard, even in a whisper.

Nerves had nearly consumed me as the moon reached mid sky. Fraalver women led the train in front of me, the sounds of crunching leaves consuming the otherwise quiet night. Before leaving the pub, Thea explained that it was a Fraalver wedding tradition for the women of the village to lead the way to the marriage site. It represented the feminine side of the union. This side properly balanced the masculine that so often threatened to take over, just as it had for the duration of Aaren's leadership. Inaborg took the lead, followed by Asta, then Sofie, and Aurora. It was uplifting to be led by these women, almost as if I were being led into battle, blessed by angels. It kept the anxiety at bay until we reached the clearing ahead of us.

My breath escaped me when I beheld what awaited. Woven into the trees were little fairy lights, drifting aimlessly through the branches. Benches were stationed in concentric circles around a clearing where a lone, mossy green branch hung low. In the story of Aaren's family, etched into the hearth, there was a carving of his parents united under a branch. This was that branch, likely another venerated Fraalver tradition. The shadows shifted in the branches above, and when I gazed up, a fairy light grazed by to reveal Ugleverge, clicking his beak at me. His eyes were of a deep ebony, and the feathers along the wings were striated with brown and tan, creating a pattern reminiscent of tree bark. He cooed softly as if the song were a blessing for the bridal chain ahead.

As we embarked down the center aisle, the women began to disperse and take their respective places on the benches. With a now uninhibited view of what awaited me under the branch, my heart stuttered when I saw Aaren. His hair was smoothed back into a clean bun, not like the ones he sported in the sparring ring, where sweat and exertion had his flyaways clinging to his forehead. He wore a crisp white shirt covered with a deep green jacket that clung to the contours of his muscular arms. Tight brown pants donned his legs, the cuffs covered by his brown leather boots that still had the scuff on the toe from when I stomped on his foot the last time we were in the ring. No matter how flattering the clothes were, the way he fidgeted suggested that he would rather be wearing one of the loose shirts he sported in the ring. Finery suited him, but he didn't favor it. Perhaps it was also that he seemed to be as consumed with nerves as I was. It's not every day you get married.

Especially since the last person he planned to marry was dead.

Thea took a seat in the front row, next to Nilsen, who was wearing his own set of fine clothes. His white hair, akin to Aaren's, was combed back neatly, vastly different from the usual rattiness he sported. He sat still on the bench with a look of hopefulness, a look that stirred those rumbling thoughts I had quieted in Thea's house.

Aaren's eyes were distant as I met him under the branch, his boots on the ground, but his mind somewhere far, far, away. I tried to ignore the unease the distance stirred in me, focusing instead on Rorik, who stood next to us. His velvet mahogany jacket was clean, and he smiled as I took a deep breath, hoping to center myself.

"Good evening, Layla," he said. I nodded politely, and already angry butterflies flitted furiously in my gut.

Rorik watched the crowd until the last person was seated, then began.

"This evening, we unite Aaren Skokjer, son of Nils and Freya, and Layla Ashford, daughter of..." He blinked momentarily, then cleared his throat. "Daughter of Midgard."

I sent him a silent praise with my eyes, and Rorik let out the smallest of chuckles. Aaren's mouth twitched like a smile was trying to break through.

"With this union, they pledge to establish and maintain protection for our village. Through strife and injury, they accept the duty to the people of Skoghjem, the ancestors before us, and the children after us. Together they are bound by the sanctity of our ancient magic, forged by our forebears." His gaze narrowed as he addressed Aaren and me. "If you would join hands."

I hesitated when Aaren didn't move immediately, and a quick glimpse into his yellow eyes told me he was still far from where we stood under the marriage branch.

"Hands, please," Rorik repeated, then gently grabbed my right hand and joined it with Aaren's.

His hand was warm in the cool night, and he seemed to come to the present at the touch. He examined my face like he was searching for something, as if whatever he was looking for was vital for his survival. Rorik wrapped our hands with a woven fabric engraved with a repeated rune. The symbol resembled a conglomeration of moons and tick marks, and a glance above confirmed that it was the same rune that had been carved into the green moss of the branch above us. When I returned my attention to Aaren, he seemed to have found what he was looking for in my face, and he blinked in near disbelief. I gave him a questioning look, but the scratchy texture of the fabric against my skin reminded me of exactly what I was doing.

I was getting married.

The absurdity of it all hadn't set in until now, when I was at the altar, standing in front of Aaren, about to make the vow to him. The warmth of his hand spread into mine, and something like ease grew from the touch. This was Aaren, the man I was marrying, my disgruntled friend, and out of everyone in the village, I was glad it was him. Despite our previous discourse and rough start, I knew I could trust him not to compromise my honor. The look in his eyes told me he shared that sentiment.

"Aaren, please repeat after me," Rorik instructed.

Aaren took a shallow breath and straightened.

"Under the eye of my people, I bond my magic with yours," Aaren said, his deep voice ringing in my ears.

As he spoke, my arm grew hot, as if someone had placed a warm mug against my skin. The heat intensified for a moment, and my skin prickled as if I were being branded. I twisted my arm subtly. Aaren's thumb brushed over the skin on the top of my hand, a comforting gesture that had me momentarily ignoring the odd pain in my arm. Then it receded, and I was left wondering if Aaren had felt the pain, too.

Rorik instructed me to repeat the vow.

I took a deep breath. "Under the eye of...my people," the words felt foreign on my tongue, "I bond my magic with yours."

Aaren's eye twitched, and his grip tightened slightly. Repeating the gesture, I rubbed my thumb across the top of his hand, hoping to give him the same comfort he gave me.

Rorik began muttering under his breath in a tongue I had never heard before, not even in the daily language of the Fraalver. It sounded archaic, ritualistic, and the longer he spoke, the tighter the fabric wound around our arms. A pulsating energy thrummed through my wrist, weaving from me to Aaren, from him to me, our magic touching, tentative at first like the first few raindrops of a summer storm. His magic prodded mine, and my palm heated as it stirred to greet his. That familiar-smelling breeze blew lightly through the clearing and brushed my loose hair against my cheek. A shimmer of light danced down from the branch and landed on the fabric, the runes glowing bright. Our magic twisted and molded together as if someone were kneading it like clay.

Rorik's murmurs quieted, and the cloth cooled as he unwrapped our hands. Scorched into my inner wrist was the rune from the fabric, twin to the fresh one growing darker on Aaren's skin.

"You are now united leaders of Skoghjem," Rorik pronounced.

Aaren entwined his fingers with mine, raising our freshly singed runes into the air. We were met with raucous cheers from our people.

When I walked back through the forest, I was hand in hand with my husband.

Chapter 26

The celebration that followed was somehow livelier than Dagan's funeral. A larger array of food had been prepared, and the fairy lights from the ceremony had followed us through the woods, illuminating the square. The lively music pulsed across the square, and the dancers that had already begun moving stomped their feet to the drum.

Thea wove her way through the mass of swirling bodies, her eyes closed, and head thrown back in rapture as she moved. Stieg watched her from the sidelines with eyes alight with a devilish hunger. He looked like a beggar whose last meal was a week ago, and Thea was a steaming tray of cinnamon rolls. I chuckled to myself, imagining Thea and Stieg standing under that branch, Thea wearing an even more elaborate dress than the one she lent me.

Aaren lingered by my side in a stunned silence as he watched the revelers, only opening his mouth to sip his ale, not to speak to me. His quiet wasn't unnerving; there had been many a time where we had sat in silence together, but there was an air of hurt to it, like he was wearing a coat of pain that only stillness could relieve.

Rorik found us after visiting the drinks table and bowed his head dutifully as he approached.

"Congratulations," he said in a courtly tone. When all I could offer him was a strained smile, he said, "You did our village a great service today, Layla. We will be forever in your debt."

"Thank you, Rorik. It means a lot."

He smiled, though there was something awkward behind the expression. "I have informed Aaren of the modified consummation. I'll leave him to inform you of the matter." He nodded politely once more, then stepped away, leaving my heart to drop into my stomach.

"Please tell me we don't have to drink each other's blood," I said, and to my relief, Aaren chuckled.

He shook his head and replied, "No, there will be no blood spilled tonight."

I had been joking, but a small seed of relief bloomed in me. When I looked at him again, he wasn't looking at my face, but at the bare expanse of chest the dress left exposed. My hand moved to shove his arm and snap him out of whatever trance he had lured himself into, but he blinked and looked away, jaw clenching.

"Then what do we have to do?"

"Perform a dance of sorts. Our movements mimic a traditional consummation and will reinforce the barriers. It's old magic." The corner of his mouth tugged as he eyed me. "You should be glad we eradicated the old ceremony. I would've had to fuck you in the middle of the square for all to see."

I couldn't stop the gasp that escaped me or the flush that colored my face red. I also couldn't ignore the uncontrollable rush of heat to the lower parts of me. I didn't dwell on it, instead choosing to fret over what such a dance would look like.

"Layla!" Thea called, bringing the sound back to my ears and feeling back into my fingers. She twirled and beckoned me into the square.

"Go," Aaren said, nodding to my friend in the square. "Have fun."

And I did, but not as much as I could have.

Unlike Dagan's funeral, I refused to drink a drop of ale, seeing as this consummation dance was still a mystery to me. I wanted to keep a sharp mind in case it entailed something other than footwork.

As the celebration died down and Fraalver began to depart with well wishes and drunken singing, Rorik lingered near the edge of the square, waiting to show us to the meeting hall. I helped Inaborg cart the rest of the untapped kegs into the pub before meeting Rorik and Aaren. Curiosity and nervousness filled the pit in my stomach where the ale should've been.

"Good luck," Rorik said, lingering on the last step before the door. "If you encounter any problems, you know where to find me."

Aaren nodded, then slipped his hand into mine before he pushed the doors open. Inside, the benches had been pushed back, and a large circle of lit candles had been set up in the middle of the room. I swallowed thickly, letting Aaren lead me into the middle of the candles, skirts in my free hand so that I would miss Thea's dress on fire.

"Relax," Aaren said, then shed his jacket and discarded it outside the circle. He stretched out his neck, then his shoulders, bulging muscles trying desperately

197

to break free from the shirt he had worn underneath. He worked his hands through his hair and shook out the bun. His light locks cascaded as he ran his fingers across his scalp. I wished I could do the same for myself, but I would drop an entire meadow on the floor with how many wildflowers Thea had woven into my hair.

Aaren let out a small, relieved sigh when he unbuttoned the top two buttons of his shirt. He finally looked comfortable, or at least as relaxed as he did during our lessons. A warrior at ease.

"Come closer," he said, curling his fingers as if to summon me. Unfortunately for him, he didn't have the restriction rune to force me to do what he said. It was my own free will that sent me stepping forward, stopping a foot away from Aaren.

He shook his head. "Closer."

I inched forward again, and it still wasn't enough. Aaren reached for my hand and drew me in until our noses brushed, our lips barely a hairsbreadth apart. The two of us lingered for a moment, sharing breath until something static sparked between us. It was when I flicked my eyes to his that something ignited in me, and I tried not to fall into the warm honey of his irises. Those beautiful amber eyes swam, and I nearly lost my balance as I fell further into them. It was like the impatient look he gave me sparked my magic to life, and an odd energy buzzed through me.

Aaren traced through the space between us with a light finger, barely touching me and yet sending an intense shiver down my spine. The fresh rune on my forearm grew hot as he backed away and began to circle me, much like the sizing up he had done in the ring, yet this was something different. There was a primal spring in his step, and his jaw was set hungrily as he prowled. Not only was he circling me, but it also appeared as if he was circling the village, allowing his movements to mimic the solidification of the borders. The electric buzzing within me intensified, and I squirmed as I grew antsy under his gaze.

Then he was crossing the circle to stand before me again, my arm pressed in his hand as a light finger circled my new rune. I suppressed a shiver, something in me going weak, and I wanted to fold under his touch, unsure how to feel about the gentleness. Aaren let out a sudden breath, as if some tight string of control snapped in him, and he pressed himself into me, his movements now broken and almost feral. My hand moved to rest on his bicep, the muscles rippling under my touch. Aaren's body pushed so firmly into me that my feet fell out from underneath me, and I braced for the hard floor, but his arm caught me and laid me down gently, skirts riding up to my knees. Aaren hovered over me, that powerful energy vibrating between us as something low in his chest growled.

Then it clicked—we were going through the motions of a traditional consummation without actually consummating. Our movements summoned this buzzing energy, the static power emanating from the meeting hall and extending to the borders. I couldn't imagine what kind of power an actual consummation generated.

My breath caught when Aaren dipped his head, lips hovering over the skin of my jaw, but never touching me. The contours of his chest molded to mine, and my breasts ached as I traced my hands over his arm, barely touching him even though everything inside me begged to make that connection. Aaren's body shifted just right that a strike of pleasure shot up my spine, eliciting an uncontrollable moan from my lips.

I gasped just as quickly as I had moaned, and my skin flushed with embarrassment.

"It's okay," Aaren whispered, though his weight never shifted from mine. "It's just a part of the ceremony."

As true as his statement was, there was more to it than that. But I wasn't going to acknowledge those conflicting feelings when all I wanted was for his breath to return to my skin. I rubbed my thighs together, ignoring the undeniable truth of what this was doing to me.

Aaren's hard hands grabbed my hips, and we flipped, my knees now pressing into the wooden planks as I straddled him. His hands brushed my hips, then he dropped them, as if it were against some internal boundary within him to touch me more than necessary. And perhaps that was true. Maybe there *was* something built up inside him that would keep him from feeling more than this should be.

This was for the sake of our borders and the safety of our people. Not some excuse to indulge in the strange feelings I had been bottling up for weeks. I took my hands off his chest, setting that same boundary within myself, and tried to ignore the evidence of Aaren's arousal underneath me.

But God, I couldn't ignore the size of him.

Heat burned at my fingertips, rivaling the warmth that was pooling in my stomach the longer I sat atop Aaren. A swell of something I had never felt before overcame me, and I couldn't help but move, even if it were the most minor shift of the hips. Aaren's breath caught, eyes darkening, and I didn't want to admit to myself what that look did to me.

I moved again, this time a little more obviously, earning me a slight growl as the hands at Aaren's side balled into fists. He wanted to touch me, and it looked like it might be the end of him if it didn't. And yet he kept his hands at his side, jaw clenched tightly as he watched me on top of him.

The electrical current was so potent in the room now that I could almost see it—either that or it was the need that was flooding my system so vehemently that I felt I would burst. I started to move my hips again, but my movements were stunted as Aaren sat up and drew his face to mine. Our noses barely brushed. His scent circled my nose, the rich leather and forest more distinguishable now than ever, as if our matching runes had attuned us to each other. Heat scorched my skin when he finally touched me, bringing his rune to its match on my arm.

A wave of electrified power burst from the circle, blowing out the candles and passing through the walls. As the borders finally solidified, so did my role as leader. There was no turning back now. I was magically bound to this village and to Aaren. I nearly laughed at how outrageous a notion that was.

Aaren peeled his forehead from mine and gently nudged me off him, turning away from me as he stood. There was slickness between my thighs when I rose to my feet, but now that the heat of the moment had cooled, I was embarrassed at just how much Aaren had affected me. He was my friend, to a degree, but friends weren't supposed to writhe on each other like that, much less enjoy it. I brushed off Thea's dress and hoped there weren't any smudges or stains on the soft silk.

The sleepy village was quiet when we made our way back to Aaren's, where I was to stay from now on. It would make me feel safer being closer to him, but I knew I would miss hearing the exuberant sounds of life in the pub. There was a quiet security laying low amongst the buildings that hadn't been there previously. The magic that lingered around the paths of Skoghjem had awakened, out of sight, but never out of mind.

When Aaren pushed the front door open, Nilsen, who had been sitting in an armchair by the fire, turned and smiled.

"You should be in bed, *bror*," Aaren chastised as his boots echoed when he crossed the room.

Nilsen shrugged. "Rorik said I could stay up until you got home." On the table next to the chair was a plate of cookies I had attempted to make a few days before. The plate was mostly empty, save for a half-eaten cookie and some crumbs.

"And Rorik needs to stop spoiling you," Aaren said, scooping his brother into his arms and giving him a reproachful look.

As I approached, Nilsen smiled softly at me. "Thank you, Layla," he said. "I knew I rescued you for a reason."

Chaper 27

The sun had begun to shine through the window of my new room when I heard a soft knock on my door. I groaned and rolled over, hoping I had dreamed the disturbance. Sleep overtook me again, and I was back in the meeting hall, spread atop of Aaren once more. It was a dream I couldn't stop having throughout the night.

Bang bang bang!

I jolted awake and nearly toppled out of bed. The furs had tangled around my legs, and I stumbled to the door, ignoring the slick that had pooled between my thighs as I dreamt.

When I swung open the door in irritation, I found Aaren filling the frame, his fist poised to pound on the door again.

"Finally," he grumbled. "Get dressed." At the direction of his gaze, I became wholly aware that the only thing covering my naked body was a pair of cotton shorts and a loose shirt that had slipped off my shoulder in my haste to answer the door. His eyes looked anywhere but below my neck, a muscle rippling in his jaw as he cleared his throat. "You have five minutes."

I groaned and rubbed my eyes as he turned with a grumble. After Aaren put Nilsen to bed last night, he showed me to my room, where he, before I could even thank him, wished me a good night and hastily closed the door. I wasn't sure if his sudden departure was related to the private ceremony or the fact that we were now married, and the last person he was to be married to died a tragic death. I wanted to believe the latter, but our rooms shared a wall, and the noises coming from his side told me it was the former—just the sounds he made sent my heart into a flutter. I wasn't sure I'd survive. I had to repeat Aaren's words to myself; the ones he told me when I had groaned from the building pleasure of our mock consummation.

It was just a part of the ceremony. It was a natural reaction to movements so similar to consummating.

Even though I was likely to hear those sounds in my dreams for months.

I dressed hurriedly and darted into the main hall, shoving bread and cheese down my throat and quickly washing it down with a mug of juice before finding Aaren outside the house, waiting for me, his wife. I wasn't sure I'd ever get used to such a title. Even though it seemed it was solely that to him, a title.

"I didn't pack anything," I said regretfully.

"Everything has been taken care of," Aaren assured as we took our first steps to the square.

A small group of Fraalver assembled in the center of the village, familiar faces dotting the crowd. Nilsen stood by Rorik's side with a small slingshot slung over his side. The smell of rose perfume filled my nostrils, and I turned to see Thea with a tattered book in her hands, striding to my side. She slid it into my hands with a wink.

"It's one of my bestsellers," she said, her lips spreading into a lovely smile. "To keep you busy when the road gets long." I caught sight of Aaren over her shoulder when she brought me in for a crushing hug.

Aaren knelt before Nilsen, the distance between us muffling his words. He reached up and adjusted his brother's tunic, his brow set sternly as Nilsen replied with a nod. He patted the slingshot proudly, and while I couldn't hear the conversation, I had an idea I could imagine what it sounded like. Nodding again, Nilsen threw his arms around Aaren, whose arms were so large around his brother that they seemed to consume him entirely. A strong hand braced the back of Nilsen's head, and Aaren placed a small kiss on his crown before rising.

Thea's rose scent left my nose as she released me and stepped away, giving me unfettered access to Nilsen, who strode towards me. I opened my arms, and he embraced me.

"I'm going to miss you," he said in my ear, and I smiled.

"I'll miss you too."

"Protect him," Nilsen said when he drew back, his voice dropping quiet enough that only I could hear him. "Promise me you'll protect Aaren."

Unsure what else to say, I nodded and replied, "I promise."

When Nilsen joined Rorik's side again, Aaren gave him a side eye. "Keep him away from the sweets, Rorik. And his bedtime is eight. Be sure he sticks to it."

Nilsen's lip curled in defiance. Thea brushed her fingers through his white hair, assuring Aaren that she would take care of it.

Aaren summoned the small group of Fraalver gathered in the square and ordered them to the stables to ready the horses. There were four of them, ranging in ages and sizes. I had met them all at some point during my time here, but never exchanged anything more than a smile or a brief nod. I looked forward to getting to know them on the road, especially now that they were *my* people.

Inside the stables, there were horses of every hue of brown that could be found in a handful of soil. Each horse knickered or chuffed as we passed, and hay crunched beneath my feet as I stopped outside a stall. Aaren grabbed the reins of a chestnut horse and guided her out into the sunlight. Then he handed them to me.

"This is Froki," he said and patted the horse affectionately. The horse snorted and bobbed her head in agreement, nearly snatching the reins from my hand. I watched nervously as the other Fraalver mounted their own horses—I was going to make a fool of myself when I tried to mount Froki.

"How long is this going to take?" I questioned, stroking Froki's mane, which earned me a chuff.

"About three days." Aaren paused and ran his fingers through Froki's coarse hair. "I hope you don't mind sleeping on the ground."

"Better than some of the beds I've slept in in my life," I replied.

Aaren's eyes went hard. "Whose bed were you sharing before you came here?" He asked in a joking manner, but there was ice behind the words. I nearly laughed—he was jealous. For some odd, mysterious reason, Aaren was envious of the nonexistent man that was warming my bed in my old realm. This was new territory now that I was his wife, I supposed.

I scoffed. "I was talking about yours, Aaren. It's a wonder how you sleep on that thing."

"If you're complaining about *my* bed, then the ground is really going to disappoint you."

With Aaren's help, I mounted Froki and adjusted to the saddle. I really hoped it wasn't apparent that I had never ridden a horse. I squirmed in the saddle and accidentally kicked Froki when I adjusted my feet in the stirrups. The horse gave me a side eye, and I stroked her mane in apology, which she didn't accept.

Chirps and trills sang overhead, and the village grew smaller behind us. A weird sense of homesickness struck me. It was a foreign feeling, one I hadn't felt since Granny died. The towering oaks and sizzling hearths of the village had instilled a sense of comfort for me, and it was hard to let the village fade from sight. The stale bread and hard jerky Aaren passed me wouldn't fill that hole in my stomach the way Inaborg's roast chicken could.

By noon, the forest had thinned out to reveal a grassy plain. Summer had swept through the land, bringing an unforgiving afternoon heat that had me wiping the sweat from my brow before shedding my vest, leaving me in my loose cotton shirt. I still wore the binding Thea had given me months ago, and I was thankful for the security it provided among my traveling partners. The plains stretched on for miles, giving me only bushels of grass and flat land to view. When the forest was utterly out of sight, I groaned, surrounded by nothing but a smooth horizon, broken only occasionally by a copse of trees. It was maddeningly dull, especially after traveling in silence all day. Our company was alert, perhaps a little on edge, which led to a quiet scene only broken by the hoofbeats and trampled grass. And my own damn thoughts are screaming way too loud in my head.

Froki continued to be snotty as the company slowed, and she blew through her nostrils and bobbed her head. I felt her pain, even though I had no idea what set her off. I had spent way too much time in the saddle, especially since this was my first time riding. Every part of my lower half was in ruins—my legs were tight, my bottom was bruised, and everything in between protested my movements when I dismounted.

Aaren had led our company into a stand of oaks, large enough for us to retreat into should something ambush us in the night. I helped the others gather firewood while Aaren snared a handful of rabbits, keeping us busy well after dusk. Once the fire was started, the rabbits were skewered and placed there to roast, filling our small camp with the smell of sizzling, gamey meat. I glanced around the fire and observed the men I traveled with.

Next to me was Axl, a tall, brooding male who was around a hundred thirty-two, which I had come to learn was the Fraalver age for twenty-three. I recognized him the moment he mounted his horse—he was on the border the night I went to the village. Axl was lean with muscle and shaggy-haired, a fact I was only able to confirm once, when he removed the dark hood he favored. The others had introduced him to me, seeing as it would be unlikely he'd do it himself.

Besides, Axl was his polar opposite. Despite his dark hair and harsh brow that could cut the hull of a ship, Ivar spoke enough for both of them. He was the archer of the group, possessing a quick draw and less than cunning wit. I had seen him around the village before, even introduced myself to him, but never made any connection after that. When Ivar commented that he didn't recall ever meeting me, the first time I introduced myself was in the pub, and I remembered him staring at me with crossed eyes—he whooped with laughter that scattered the birds from the trees.

Oswin sat across the fire from me, hocking insults and joking with Ivar back and forth like a tennis match. I had met Oswin the same night as I had Ivar, during which the two had drained half the keg of Inaborg's brew. Needless to say, Oswin didn't remember me either. He was a farmer with a knack for swordplay without a woman to occupy his free time. While Ivar had ratty black hair, Oswin didn't have any, sporting a shiny bald dome. What he lacked in hair, he made up for with his fiery red beard that he delighted in comparing with Ivar's shorter, yet just as impressive, facial hair.

Lastly, there was Von. Reminiscent of a clueless puppy, Von was a bit absentminded, to put it politely. When he had happily thrust his hand into mine and shook it before kicking his horse to the front of the group, Ivar joked that while Von's head may seem full of air, his knife work was impeccable. He was young like Axl, and easy on the eyes, which felt sinful to think, considering I was now a married woman.

This opened up a chest of uncertainty about what I was and was not allowed to do as a married woman. And since Aaren and I hadn't had time to have a conversation about anything, let alone what was allowed in our marriage, I had no idea if I was even allowed to look at other men in such a way. I had no idea about the implications of Fraalver unions.

Aaren plucked a rabbit from the fire and passed me the skewer.

"Tell us, Layla," Oswin began. He picked at the rabbit in his lap and bit into a leg, juice streaming through the tangled strands of his beard. "How was Aaren's bedding last night? It must not be up to snuff if you can still walk today!"

Ivar chortled, showing a full display of meat tucked into his cheek. "If what they say is true, he should have split her in half!" A bit of rabbit meat fell from his mouth and into the fire, where it sizzled and charred in the blazing coals.

"Shove it, Oswin," Aaren grumbled and placed a fresh rabbit over the fire. "I'm guessing you want to know for the next time you fancy your right hand?"

Von choked, which earned him a swift smack to the back from Ivar. Oswin burst into another fit of raucous chortles that reverberated around the trees and into the plains beyond.

"If you two don't quiet down, you'll attract a horde of ratatos," Axl chastised, having shed his hood for the evening.

"What's a ratato?" I asked. I had read the term somewhere in the weeks of reading Rorik had assigned, but with the amount I had read, that information got lost in the mess of dwarf history.

"They're descendants of Ratatoskr," Von explained. "He was the squirrel that would climb up and down Yggdrasil and ferry messages between the realms. He was helpful, but his descendants aren't as friendly. Axl, show her." With a sigh, Axl rolled up his right sleeve to reveal a large, mottled scar on his forearm.

Oswin chuffed. "My question was never answered, Layla. Did Aaren make a good farmer?"

"Farmer?" Aaren asked irritably.

"Yes, farmer, considering you ploughed her..."

A vine whipped up from the ground and slapped the rabbit out of Oswin's hands and tossed it into the fire. "Careful, or your face is next," Aaren warned. Oswin stared hungrily at his burning rabbit that was now fully consumed by the flames, but there was not an ounce of regret on his face.

"My apologies, Aaren, it was all in good fun."

Aaren seemed to accept his apology, and he placed the last rabbit on the fire to replace the one that had been removed.

"I did what was needed to reinforce the borders, and that is all you need to know."

I hoped my expression wasn't obvious when I processed his words. I knew that what we did in that meeting hall was part of our duty to the people. Part of my plan to find Lucas. But I wasn't going to discard that tiny, minuscule hope that what we did wasn't the result of something else that I thought was building between us. That the feral hunger that had clouded his eyes last night was because of some secret desire for me and not a natural reaction to such movements. I had known deep down it was just part of our service to our people, but it didn't hurt any less to hear it directly from his mouth.

Now irritated and feeling spiteful, I scooted closer to Von on my right. Aaren noticed immediately, glaring daggers at the closer proximity.

"So," I said to break the tense quiet that had settled amongst the circle. "Which way are we headed tomorrow?"

Ivar shifted and reached behind him, pulling a map from his back pocket. He spread it out over a nearby rock, and I left my spot next to Von to peer at it, knowing Aaren's glare was still laced with bitterness. The edges of the map were crinkled from being stuffed in his pocket, and the parchment on which the map was scrawled was faded and soft. Ivar pointed a grimy finger at a tiny cluster of woods. "We are right here."

The map expanded from the small clump of trees to an expanse of blank parchment, breaking away into broad sections. Skoghjem was situated in the center with small landmarks labeled nearby, then the woods gave way to sprawling mountains above. Fjelljem was scribbled above the highest peak in slanted writing. To the west of the mountains lay more open space, indicating an expanse of fields and plains. A small circle marked the spot on the map, surrounded by rocky terrain. When I asked what it was, Oswin replied, "Klartvan Lake."

"What's at Klartvan Lake?" I inquired.

"Nothing except murky water and a bunch of nymph brothels," Axl replied, and Ivar hooted. From the story they went on to tell, it seemed Oswin and Ivar were all too familiar with the brothels in the plains neighboring the lake. I begged them to spare me the details, and a quick bark of disapproval from Aaren shut them down before they could start.

Ivar tapped a chewed finger on the cluster of trees we occupied. "We still have to cross all of this," he said and traced across the vast emptiness between us and the sea.

Cursing under my breath, which seemed to surprise Ivar, I returned to my seat and resumed picking at my rabbit. Aaren spared me his mercilessly watchful gaze, and I spent the rest of the night listening to Oswin and Ivar goad each other with dirty jokes and silly stories, only to have Axl quietly remind them countless times to keep their voices down.

Full, but unsatisfied by the bland meal, my eyelids drooped. The crackle of fire had lulled me into an exhausted trance as I tried not to pay attention to the discomfort from being in a saddle all day. I would have dozed off had Aaren not stood up abruptly and dropped the last log into the fire. Blazing pieces of ash flew into the night as he stoked the fire one more time, flickering out into the treetops.

"Von has first watch," Aaren grumbled. "The rest of you should get some sleep. Axl, switch with Von at midnight. Oswin can take over after."

"Good luck getting any sleep if Aaren's bedding is as good as he says!" Ivar laughed as he stood and stretched.

I was thankful we had erected the tents before dusk, and the warm interior was a welcome sight to my aching bones. I almost groaned with disappointment that my rest would have to wait when Aaren's fingers brushed mine, and he gestured for me to follow him deeper into the trees. The tent flap fell from my hand as I stepped away, letting him lead me into the darkness and swallowing my trepidation as the crickets quieted the deeper we plunged into the woods. When Aaren finally stopped, the camp was a mere speck in the distance, but Oswin could still be heard cracking jokes.

"What the fuck was that back there?" Aaren demanded when he turned to face me with a fire that threatened to burn the trees around us to ash.

I simmered in satisfaction knowing I had made my point. "Don't pretend like you have any real obligation to me other than maintaining the barriers of the village."

Aaren took an angry step forward, then another, until he realized he was slowly backing me into a tree. Harsh bark bit into my palms as I braced against the trunk, heat rising to my skin.

"You're still my wife, Layla. You cannot throw yourself at whatever man you want because you're bored."

At least I got my answer—I wasn't allowed to seek out other male attention, all while being deprived of it within my own...marriage. Even though I had a hard time accepting it, I found it unfair, and I wasn't going to sit and take it. "Then who can I touch, Aaren?"

Aaren's lip twitched as the wind picked up, the trees above us swayed, and the branches groaned in the breeze. The smell of burning wood filled my nostrils and replaced the leather and forested scent that accompanied Aaren's breezes. I peeled my palms from the trunk and subtly shook them out, hoping Aaren wouldn't spy the hand-shaped scorch marks burned into the bark. His breath had picked up, and a small vine slithered through the leaves and started to curl around my ankle.

"Do it," I challenged and glared into his glowing eyes. "Go ahead, put me in my place."

Aaren's nostril flared, and the vine around my ankle receded as he took a steadying breath. "I will not have your behavior cast a shadow on my leadership, do you understand me?"

My lips pressed together as I tried to rein in the awakened magic that was building pressure in my chest. "Good night, Aaren," I said, then pushed off the tree. I left him in the darkness, not caring if he found his way back to the camp.

Once back at the tent, I tried to get some sleep.

The bedroll I had snuggled into was more comfortable than Aaren had professed it to be, but it did nothing to fight off the chill of an early summer night. Because of this, sleep evaded me as I stared vacantly at the canvas above instead of the inside of my eyelids. Aaren still had not come to bed, and there was no indication that he had even returned to camp. I hated the way I found myself worrying about him, considering I was the one who had left him behind in the dark.

I didn't regret my rebellion or what Aaren saw as an act of disobedience. I married him to help his people, and in doing so, I tied myself to him. But I'd be damned if I let him pull that chain too tight.

Finally, a hand pulled back the flap, and I closed my eyes and pretended to be asleep. Aaren's scent filled the tent, and I became aware of the rune on my wrist that prickled as I breathed it in, a pleasurable current buzzing in my skin. An odd, but comforting sensation, a feeling akin to the warm burning of a shot of whiskey. A thud told me he had kicked off his boots, and then a rustle of clothes, and no matter how mad I was at him, it was hard to fight the urge to watch him undress.

My heart fluttered like a startled butterfly when I took in his sculpted back, muscles creasing and flexing with every movement. Then there was the vicious scar along his spine, that same scar that made my skin prickle as I tried to fathom what in this realm could've given him such a marking. I shuddered.

Aaren scooted into his own bedroll and lay facing away from me. There was a slight twinge of disappointment, which I quickly stomped out, and I scooted away from him, eliminating the chance of any accidental touching. Finally, I fell asleep listening to the rhythmic breathing of my husband.

I hadn't slept the best though, and our wake-up call was far from pleasant.

"Wake up, lovebirds," came Oswin's voice from outside the tent. "The horses are growing antsy."

Blinking through the sleep that still dulled my senses, I helped pack the horses. I didn't want to cast a pall on the day's journey, but I had a feeling it would be dreadful considering the never-ending gray sky accompanied by a chilly drizzle of rain. My clothes had soaked through within the first hour of our ride, and no amount of mead passed around the group could chase off the chill that was soaking into my bones. Lunch was soggy bread and a handful of nuts and dried fruit. I barely ate since the bread fell apart in my hands, and the fruit was more seed than flesh. Dinner was the same, as the firewood we found was soaked, and we had to forgo a fire, despite my best efforts to start one. No fire to roast meat meant no hunting, so we resorted to chewing stale jerky and shriveled apples.

My petty attempts to shun Aaren backfired in the tent later that evening as I shivered in my bedroll. It took every ounce and whim of self-control not to curl into his chest and soak in his warmth. I would've tried to warm my bedroll with my magic, but I had a repeating image playing in my mind of accidentally lighting it on fire. I opted for safety and shivered throughout the night.

As the sun rose on the third day, my spirits lifted when the blue sky returned, and I promised never to take it for granted again. Everyone else seemed to share those high spirits, even Aaren, who sported a less intense scowl than he had yesterday. Only a few hours away from Kysthjem, according to Ivar's map, we rode on, Oswin and Ivar returning to their regular banter of dirty jokes and brainless remarks. Von even chimed in, though Axl shrank deeper into his hood.

The returned gaiety of our company ended abruptly when the beginnings of Kysthjem came into view. Or rather, what was left of it.

The village was situated about half a mile away from a gray beach, nestled into the green grasses of a short cliff. The coastal Fraalver had not constructed their layout as compactly as the forest Fraalver had, choosing instead to spread their buildings across the cliffs. What I could imagine had been sturdy, warm homes were now smoldering ruins, shells of the life they had once held. There was a moment of panic that flashed across Aaren's face before he schooled his features again and barked the order to tie the horses. As we fanned out to scout the area per Aaren's instructions, I was happy he didn't try to keep me close, and I stayed out of his sight for as long as I could.

The village square and the corresponding meeting hall were the most intact parts of the village, which was saying something, considering the way the door of the hall hung on its hinges. The floorboards groaned under my weight as I crossed the large meeting hall, stepping over overturned benches and crunching on broken glass.

"We've got bodies!" Von called from a distance, and the others hustled to meet him. Not wanting to see any dead body, I kept to the meeting hall, moving to a window at the far end.

The meeting hall was situated at the edge of the closest cliff, making the view from the window breathtaking. The distant waves crashed on the shore, deep blue water lapping and swelling as if what lay on the cliff above wasn't the most devastating thing I had ever seen. My eyes followed the expansive stretch of the beach, the sand curving around the cove and ending in a trail of boulders surrounded by foamy white water. There was an open hole in the side of the cliff, where the boulders tapered off, allowing water to flow in and out of the opening.

211

Curiosity carried me from the building and down the treacherous path until my feet hit cold, squishy sand, and the waves roared in my ears. From the path, it was a ten-minute walk across the beach to the sea cave.

As I walked, I counted the years that had passed since I last visited the beach, remembering that sunny, blistering day with a fondness that stirred a note of grief in my chest. Mama had been pregnant with Lucas, nearing the final days of the last trimester. Claiming she wanted one more adventure before her trip to the hospital—a stretch she would never return from—she packed me into the car and drove the hours-long journey to the nearest beach (against doctor's orders, I might add). I remembered the way she sank into the sand, eyes closed in rapture as she stretched her belly to the sky, red hair splayed across the beach towel. The pulled skin over her navel was etched with branches of blue veins, stark against her pale skin.

I eyed her stomach, watching intently for the rare moments when Lucas would stir.

"Be patient, love," Mama said. "He'll be here soon enough."

That was the last adventure I ever went on with Mama.

Having finally reached the edge of the cove, I watched the waves surge in and out of the sea cave, realizing that the path inside may be more treacherous than I thought. The climb over the sharp boulders wouldn't be challenging, considering the countless nooks for me to wedge my fingers and toes into. It was the short swim from the boulders to the cave that concerned me, but I wasn't going to let it stop me from trying. There was something in that cave, and I was going to find out what.

I shed my vest and shirt, shimmied out of my pants, and kicked off my boots. The calm sea air, mingled with the sea breeze, summoned goosebumps on my skin. The first part of the climb along the boulders was a learning curve as I tried to find my balance and searched for the best places to wedge my fingers. By the time I reached the edge, my feet were raw, and my hands were cut in the palms, and the salt stung as I stood, gazing into the dark churning waters outside the cave.

It was now or never.

Shivering, I dove into the water, and the current immediately carried me away from the cave. I floundered, head breaching the surface for the briefest moment before the current switched and threw me against the wall of the cliff. Panic flooded my system, followed by instant regret over my poorly thought-out decision. Then a foreign, surging energy accompanied my fright, awakening something in my veins. It was the ocean's power, strong, virulent, and ready to pulverize me. I had never tangled with a power bigger than the water barrels or troughs around the village. This magic was defiant, more alive than anything I had ever felt before. And it was going to kill me if I didn't take some of its control.

I gasped before my head went under the water again, carried out before the sea tossed me towards the rock. My body could only take so much, and my ribs were already singing with pain. That surge of energy surged again, and, unsure what else to do, I clung to it, letting it fill me with a thrum of life that intertwined with my magic. It wasn't like when I had practiced in Skoghjem. The elements around the village gave me the boost to perform domestic magic, but this was far more potent and deadly.

I grasped onto that power, willing the roiling in my blood to calm, and in turn, so did the current, as much as it could considering the small breadth I had honed my power into. In time, I knew I would be able to do more. With a better chance to concentrate and a few more months of practice, maybe I could've turned the whole cove into a whirlpool.

Wishful thinking, probably the product of the euphoric surge the water's energy was giving me. It was a new feeling, but I liked it. It felt like walking into a cold room after spending the day in the sun.

The current stilled, long enough for me to paddle to the small, jutting overhang inside the sea cave, barely big enough for me to hoist myself up and heave a gasp. Salt filled my lungs as I coughed, and the vibrant life of the water drained from me, leaving an emptiness that rivaled starvation.

Recovering just enough that I could stand, I started my trek into the sea cave. The waves echoed around the rock walls as I moved deeper, using what little bit of energy I had left to summon a small flame to light my way. The obvious uncertainty I should've felt the moment I saw the cave finally set in as I realized I had no idea what could be waiting for me at the end of this small, jagged path. Considering Rorik and I had barely touched on the aquatic creatures that dwelled in Alveland, I should've been more scared than I was.

Lost in my own head, I didn't see the looming cave wall rise before me until it was too late, and I smacked into the rock. Pain sang through my cheeks, and I knew a bruise would form within minutes, and I would have to explain that the damage on my body came from none other than myself. I groaned loudly, and it echoed around the walls until the sound was barely more than a whisper. Then a cry answered.

If I had hackles, they would've raised at the sound. I listened closely, trying to discern other sounds from the angry waves that lapped at the ledge on which

I stood. I didn't have to listen for very long before the sound came again, this time a little louder, and a little more frantic.

It was a baby.

"Hello?" I called, hand bracing against the harsh stone. I rapped my knuckles against the rock, not caring about the discomfort the rough edges brought to my fist. "Is anyone there?"

Nothing answered, and the crying ceased, leaving me to question if I had even heard it in the first place. Shivers started to take over my body as the adrenaline eased and took the heat with it. I turned to leave, then someone knocked back against me.

I froze, turning back to the wall, hand raised to knock back when a small piece of rock shifted, small enough for a fraction of a face to peer through. A piercing blue eye nestled under a harsh, gray brow caught mine and blinked into the weak light of my meager flame.

"You're not Aaren," a gravelly voice observed.

"No," I answered. No, I wasn't Aaren, but I was just as capable of helping them as he was. "But I'm from Skoghjem."

"Then who are you? How'd you find us?"

I swallowed, tasting salt. "I'm Layla, Aaren's...wife." The eye only blinked, and there was a muffled whispering that made it blink again. Then it moved to examine the flame in my hand, which was now flickering to nothing more than candlelight. I held up my dying flame to highlight the rune on my forearm. The faint light illuminated my magically tattooed skin, and I couldn't help but feel an unexplainable twinge of pride, a feeling I couldn't dwell on before the eye left the opening, replaced by that same stern voice warning me to stand back.

Careful not to fall back into the troubled waters inside the sea cave, I stepped away. The wall shifted, rock scraping against rock as wet pebbles rained down onto the slick floor beneath my feet. Bigger chunks of rock fell from the wall and splashed into the water, where they sprayed me with salt. Taking a couple more safe steps back, I watched as the wall I had collided with fell to pieces, revealing a large cavern behind it crammed full of trembling, shivering Fraalver.

Torchlight filled the space as I took in the state of the Fraalver before me, quickly finding the source of the young cries I had heard minutes before. A shaking woman cradled a writhing blanket, small hands reaching out as the crying resumed. Turning away from the chord of sorrow that cried plucked in me, I caught the blue eye that had pierced through the hole in the rock and tried not to gape at the person it belonged to.

In front of me stood a very tall, well-built man with a thick, gray beard and curved mustache. His bald head was sprinkled with drops from the cave ceiling, and his clothes indicated that, like the Fraalver behind him, he had been in there for days. Etched darkly into his forearm was the same rune I had on mine, matching the one on the forearm of the much smaller woman standing next to him.

If the man in front of me was Fiske Sjøbrytt, then she must've been Helgi. Quite literally half the size of Fiske, Helgi sported salt-and-pepper hair that had been tied back with a leather strap. Joyful wrinkles etched her face, curving over the small forehead and around her soft eyes. Her slightly upturned nose wrinkled as she breathed in the fresher air of the sea cave.

Stretching behind the leaders was a cavern large enough to fit roughly a hundred and fifty people. Nearly three hundred Fraalver shared the space. The cave was far from habitable and coupled with the smell of so many bodies crammed into such a small, dank space, the scene was gut-churning.

"I'll save the introductions for the beach," Fiske said, leaving little room for politeness in his expression. "Our people have suffered enough. It's time to get them out." I wasn't going to argue, so I shuffled to the mouth of the cave as quickly as I could, the sounds of Fiske's orders to his people blending with the sound of the waves.

As I braced to dive back into the water and brave the current, Fiske's approaching warning stopped me. "You'll be pulled out to sea before we even introduce ourselves," Fiske said as he joined my side.

I braced against the wall to watch the leader as he furrowed his already stern brow and layered his hands parallel with each other. Then, pulling his palms away from each other, he parted the water, leaving a path of soggy sand and limp seaweed. I shouldn't have been surprised, given the nickname the other leaders had given him. The Fish King wasn't a far-off title, no matter how much he probably disliked it.

Fiske was the first to dismount the ledge, then offered his hand to Helgi before helping me down. As Helgi and I trudged along the squelching, sinking sand, Fiske remained near the mouth of the cave, making sure each Fraalver made it to the sand safely. Lingering on the shore ahead was Aaren and our company, likely having spotted me trudging along the beach before delving into the cave.

As we drew closer to the shore, the wind picked up and bit at my skin, and I grew keenly aware of the wet clothes that clung to my frame, likely leaving nothing to the imagination. That was the first thing Aaren noticed upon my arrival on the beach, his eyes dropping to my breasts, then my bare legs, something hot simmering behind his golden irises. I ignored his lingering gaze that made my skin flush hot enough to keep away the chill, and moved to my sandy pile of clothes, with no other option than to put them on. I grit my teeth as the sand bit my skin and rubbed me in the wrong places.

Aaren's gaze was still on me as I returned to where the sea parted, watching as the Kysthjem Fraalver walked along the path and onto the beach. I lingered in silence until the last Fraalver climbed the bank, followed abruptly by Fiske. When the water had returned to its normal, turbulent state, Fiske joined Helgi to stand in front of us.

"You're a sight for sore eyes," Fiske said. "Though any sight is good for me. Been in there for days now."

Aaren replied with a sly chuckle. "And here I thought you were finally admitting I was the better-looking leader out of the lot of us. It's slim pickings with you in the mix."

Fiske broke into a loud wheezing laugh, clapping Aaren on the arm as Helgi closed the distance between them and wrapped her small arms around Aaren's massive frame.

"It's good to see you, *venn*," she said into his chest. "I wish it were under better circumstances." As she pulled away, she shot me a glance, then gave Aaren a sly smile. "She's pretty, Aaren. How'd you convince her to marry you with that scowl?"

Aaren was indeed scowling, though it was at a lingering Fraalver that eyed me with a sort of predatory curiosity.

"Josef, back to the cliff," Helgi barked, startling the man into action. He took off across the sand without a second glance back.

"It was...I guess luck was on my side the day she chose to be mine."

Chapter 28

The village was full of life once more as the remaining Fraalver bustled about, recovering their lost belongings and setting up shelter and a cook station in the square. Fiske and Helgi directed us into the meeting hall, where Helgi draped me in a wool blanket to Aaren's apparent relief. Dusk was on the horizon, and I shivered when I imagined another chilly night in the tent with Aaren. With the chill that took hold of my body today, I might have to use him for body heat.

Seated across from the other two leaders, Aaren and I awaited their explanation.

"I was out past the borders," Helgi began.

She had been out combing the beach, looking for a specific type of mussel that only inhabited the cove a couple of miles away. Seeing as Kysthjem didn't have Stieg to scout for them, Helgi gladly filled the role as she enjoyed the time for herself and the peace the walk gave her.

On the way back, there was a screaming, something like the distressed shouts of children in the distance. Without thinking, Helgi took off in pursuit of the sounds, unsure what fate those children would befall should she arrive too late. The source of the sounds was a small group of children that had been playing too close to a small quarry, abandoned by Fraalver long forgotten. A small girl was half-buried underneath a boulder, writhing and crying for help. Three more children milled about nervously, seemingly desperate for a way to help their friend.

There was something off about the children, about the darkness that gathered around them. It was like shadows were clinging to them in broad daylight. But Helgi wouldn't focus on that, not until they were safe. She called out to them, already running through ways to save the child, when her heart nearly stopped in her chest. The children halted, heads turning in unison where Helgi beheld the drooping, rotten flesh of their mangled faces. The girl under the rock ceased her writhing and dug her fingers into the earth and pulled, leaving her lower half under the boulder. Strings of viscera and intestines trailed behind her as she dragged herself towards the others, gnashing her teeth in a sickly grin.

"Hallow," the children said as one.

"By the fucking gods," Helgi whispered.

"No, *frue*," a girl sneered. "There are no gods here."

As Helgi took off in a sprint, so did the mylings, all except the girl who had cut herself in half. A mile went by, and they stayed close on her heels, and Helgi felt herself slowing, breath and life leaving her with every sprint she took. She wasn't as spry as she used to be, and gods, it was going to get her killed now. The sound of three sets of footsteps seemed to multiply, but she wouldn't look back, not until the village was in her sights, when she neared the border and finally glanced over her shoulder, her heart bottomed out in her stomach. There was an army of nearly twenty mylings, and counting, each child joining from over the cliffs, behind bushes, from under the crags in the rocky parts of the earth.

A horn blew in the distance, strong and fierce, but it wouldn't be enough to stop these things, and dread filled her until her feet slowed and life started to drain out of her. No, it wasn't dread that was stopping her, but the small hands that wrapped around her neck, sending ice into her and squeezing until the world grew darker, colder.

She crossed the border, unfortunately tainting their protection as she brought the myling into the village. That was the way the magic worked after all. Nothing could get in unless a leader allowed it.

A fact I wasn't aware of, and silently thanked her for divulging.

Because she had crossed the borders with the myling, she had just opened the doors for the entire fleet of the undead.

Helgi turned away from Aaren and me, her voice going quiet as the air went stagnant.

"I brought them here," she muttered.

Fiske grabbed her shoulders until she faced him directly, their eyes meeting. "It was not your fault, Helgi. We could not have been prepared for something like this. We will rise from this, *mitt hjerte*. All will be well."

Helgi blinked, then took a shallow breath and turned to Aaren and me with eyes lined with silver. She sniffled once, then regained herself. Fiske studied us as if he knew there was something we weren't telling him.

"You two aren't surprised about the mylings," Fiske observed.

Aaren inhaled deeply. "No," he replied shortly. "Not surprised in the slightest, seeing as we were also attacked. Not as devastatingly, but we were attacked."

Not as devastating was an understatement—the mylings that had attacked us only served to deliver a warning. These mylings were out for blood, carnage, attacking anything that moved, tearing down anything that didn't. The mylings that attacked Kysthjem had a different agenda.

It was Helgi's turn to study us, her soft eyes narrowing on Aaren, who, surprisingly, squirmed the slightest bit. Was he afraid of Helgi? She reminded me of Granny—smooth enough to nurture, but hard enough to reprimand when needed. I liked her.

"Aaren," she said sternly as if he were a child who had just lied about breaking a vase in the house. "You're not telling us something."

Aaren's jaw clenched, then he glanced at me.

"Do you remember Markus Sviker?" I asked out of turn.

Fiske's face dropped in astonishment as Helgi turned pale. "You don't mean..." she stuttered.

"He's back," Aaren said.

Fiske crossed his arms over his chest. "And why is he suddenly sending his little dead henchmen to pick us off? Aside from his distaste for our kind, what does he have to gain from this?"

"We don't know," Aaren answered, then nodded his head to me. "But Layla is the key to understanding why."

Fiske's face soured as if he had just popped a rotten grape into his mouth. Helgi, on the other hand, only cocked a brow.

"Why her?"

I cringed as I answered, "I'm his daughter. And he's taken my brother, and I'm trying to get him back."

Helgi glanced at Fiske, who was still stewing in uncertainty. When she urged him to say something, he uncrossed his arms and rested them on his knees, gazing at me and only me from under his harsh brow. "Start from the beginning," he said. "Tell us *everything*."

219

So I did. I told them about Lucas and my old realm, about the night I unknowingly brought the myling, and the fenr. Both silently listened, faces neutral, even at the craziest parts of my story.

Nearly ten minutes later, I finished and awaited their response. I wasn't afraid that they would reject me or renounce my presence and demand that I leave their village and name me an enemy of the Kysthjem Fraalver. Or maybe I was, but I knew it wouldn't be the worst thing to happen to me. The worst had already happened—I lost my brother. Anything above that, I could endure.

Finally, Helgi spoke. "Sounds like you've been through more than one should endure in a lifetime."

I let go of a breath I hadn't realized I was holding. "You have no idea," I muttered.

Fiske still watched me sternly, though it seemed his aggression was placed elsewhere. "If he's after you, then why attack us?"

"Again, we don't know," Aaren said. "But we would be foolish to assume none of this is connected."

"The fact that Markus is again at large remains." Helgi shook her head and shuddered. "And we don't know how many of those mylings he has awaiting the order for another attack. Every second we spend idly is time given to Markus."

"There is a target on all of our backs," Aaren said, his muscles straining against his shirt as he crossed his arms. "If both Skoghjem and Kysthjem have been hit, Fjellhjem could be next."

Helgi nodded to Fiske's apparent disdain. "Aaren's right, Torsten and Ertha must be warned."

Fiske shook his head incredulously. "No, I'm not leaving after an attack like this. We're too fragile."

I couldn't argue with that, but Helgi would. "I'm insulted that you think I can't handle it." She gave him a challenging look. Fiske sighed.

"That's not what I was implying, and you know that."

The two went back and forth for another minute or so, exchanging catty words and lovingly aggressive looks before Fiske finally relented and agreed to travel with us to Fjellhjem. The decision was made only on the condition that we would stay a day longer to ensure that we left Kysthjem in a slightly more stable state than it was now. We would leave at dawn the day after next, and Helgi agreed, though she had some mumbled words about it.

"Until then," Helgi started grimly. "We have loved ones to burn."

Chapter 29

A hundred bodies. There were *at least* a hundred bodies. And every one of them somehow looked like someone from Skoghjem. Or at least, at first glance. The first body I came upon was a short man with shaggy hair that looked too much like Stieg for my liking, until I blinked. The resemblance was gone after a second of examining him. But it was a grim reminder that these could have been my friends. *My people.*

I felt sick to my stomach when I dragged the man through the village, passing more bodies on my way. There was one that looked like Thea, and Inaborg, and Kare, and—

Fucking hell. There was a little boy.

He was face down on the side of the path, long black hair matted with mud and gravel, but the dark skin on his hands was raw and flecked with deep cuts. My heart stuttered not at the soggy, tattered clothes around his lifeless frame, but the little shoes he wore on his feet. He was the same size as Lucas. Those could have been my brother's shoes.

Seeing the destruction Markus sent to Kysthjem, the death and grief and havoc, lit my blood on fire. My father didn't just kidnap my brother or get Dagan killed. He almost wiped out an entire village with just a group of mylings. What was next?

I looked down at the dead boy again, and there was a powerful tugging in my gut, just like the feeling I got when I was in the water. It was the sea beyond the cliffs, answering my anger with a wrath of its own. Placing the man I had been carrying down carefully, I knelt by the boy and rolled him over, guts clenching at the smear of mud and blood across his pale cheeks. I ignored his features—I couldn't—as I let some of the sea's power into me. Cool water filled my palm, and I dipped the fingers of my other hand, using the water to wipe away the grime and blood until his face was clean. I couldn't dwell on how cold his skin was, or the fact that his empty blue eyes watched me as I worked.

An earthy breeze replaced the salty wind that kissed my cheeks, and I turned to see Aaren standing over me, knees covered in mud and dried blood flecking his cheeks. We stared at each other for a moment, the same silent thought passing between us. This little boy could have been either of our brothers.

Aaren knelt next to me, closing the boy's eyes with a wave of his hand. I wanted to say something, anything, but the words wouldn't come, and the inescapable, blaring truth kept ringing between us. It could have been our brothers. Aaren rolled the boy into his arms and stood. I followed him down the path where he laid the boy on the growing pile of bodies to be burned that night.

Kysthjem had basement stores of food and supplies in the meeting hall that the mylings had not found and destroyed; the ale and wine outnumbered any other store of supplies. It seemed the Fraalver would rather run out of food before they ran out of alcohol. I helped them roll out the kegs as the sun set, taking in a deep whiff of the swirling aromas of cooking meat, bonfire, and salty air.

All the dead were accounted for and piled in the center of the square, too many of them to create a single pyre like we had for Dagan. The surviving Kysthejem Fraalver gathered in the square, our company lingering on the outskirts as Fiske and Helgi stood at the front.

"Dagmar," Fiske said.

"Rayne," Helgi added.

"Hilda," Fiske continued.

Someone in the crowd let out a weak cry.

"Orman," Helgi said. "Hragmar. Sylva. Starla."

They were naming their dead. Every single one of them.

"Henrick, Kristiana, Gerthik, Jorn..."

And on they went. Until every last one of their dead had been called, and I wondered which one of those names belonged to the young boy that could have been Lucas or Nilsen.

Helgi raised a mug as Fiske retrieved a torch and dipped it into a lit brazier.

"To the peaks of Himmelfjell!" she cried.

The Kysthjem Fraalver answered her with a thundering roar, filled with grief, despair, and so much loss that I could hardly bear to hear the sound. Aaren tensed next to me, as did the rest of our company, as Fiske tossed the flame onto the bodies and sent them to the afterlife.

As I watched the flames reach into the night sky, I felt the tug of the fire's energy, and I knew two things for sure. That boy wasn't turning into a myling. And I was going to find Lucas.

As the dead burned, the living began to dance and sing and feast. There was such liveliness in the face of the brutality they had faced. I didn't know how the Fraalver could muster up the delight in their movements, the smiles on their faces. There was a great deal to learn from them. Not in magic or combat or history. But in living.

I accepted a mug of ale from Oswin and sat back, listening to the music as the instruments started to play. The melody was different from the music of the forest Fraalver, and as I sipped, I picked apart the subtle differences in the sounds. The music, I realized, represented the land in which the village was situated. While our music was steady and lively, like the trees of our forest, this music was smooth and powerful, much like the ocean below, swaying and calm, then crashing onto the shore.

In the center of all the dancing was Helgi, her cheeks flushed rosy from dancing, and her salt and pepper hair flowed wildly in the sea breeze. I smiled when she spun, drifting her arms into the air with an exalted sigh. Then she set her sights on me, and my stomach spun in a downward spiral because I knew exactly what she was pushing through the crowd to do. Barely giving me time to set down my drink, her sweaty hand clasped mine and pulled me into the bustling crowd. She sent me into a twirl, landing me in the center of the square where I swayed awkwardly, unfamiliar with the dances of Kysthjem Fraalver. A melodic waltz settled after a swelling intro, the notes long and smooth like the glassy surface of a still ocean. Helgi waved her arm into the air, arcing over us, then bowed deeply, pointing her toes. She reminded me of a graceful ballerina, stretching and waving across a stage. Her movements were agile, her feet nimble as she skipped across the ground and pulled me with her. I stumbled, waving my arms clumsily.

"Oh dear," she said as she paused in the middle of the flowing dancers. "You're overthinking, *frue*." She reached for my hands and shook my arms. "Loosen up."

I hadn't drunk enough ale for this, but I listened to her, taking a deep breath and sending it through my body. My limbs loosened a bit, but not enough to make up for the fact that I could feel countless eyes on me, including Aaren's, who watched me from the sidelines next to Fiske.

Helgi lifted my arm and spun me. "Think like the water, Layla. Flow." She swung her arms elegantly, and I mimicked her, but my cheeks reddened with embarrassment. I looked like a damn fool.

My eyes drifted from the dancing to the ocean beyond, the dark water rippling against the horizon. Granny had a painting nearly identical to the scene in front of me. The brushstrokes accentuated the small, insignificant waves against the brightly moonlit sky, and there was something about the way the artist found a way to paint a salty breeze into the scene. The painting hung next to Granny's bed, where I spent many nights after Mama died. Lucas slept in a bassinet next to us, and I would spend most of the night gazing into that painting and wishing I were being carried away by the waves instead of lying in bed with insomnia.

Now I was in that painting, and Mama would've killed to be where I was right now. She would've loved the way Helgi danced and would've made the moves her own, adding her own flourishes and bows. The smile would never leave her face, even if she missed one step or all of them. Mama just would've been happy to be here. How could I take advantage of that? How was I supposed to keep Granny and Mama alive in Lucas when he wasn't here?

Imagining I was standing in the shallows of the beach below, I let the waves lap at my knees and swayed my hips with the small swells. The rest of my body moved as the water's tempo picked up, surging and flowing as the waves crashed, then receded. A phantom hand slipped into mine, warm and soft, the body in which it belonged to smelling of sweet cinnamon and ginger. Just like Mama.

This time, when I danced, I danced for her. For the memory of her. Since she couldn't be here to see the beach from the painting, to see that I possessed the magic she had told so many stories about. Every move was for Mama.

Helgi and I danced for three songs, bouncing and skipping about, and the revelry embraced me like a warm summer breeze. Mama was with me the whole time, dancing in tandem with me, and I hoped that she was with Lucas, too, wherever he was. Was he able to dance like I was, or was he locked in some dungeon somewhere, living off stale bread and enduring whatever means of torture our father was putting him through?

The thought of Lucas shackled in some rusty cell broke my elation, and as the song ended, I excused myself to graze the food-laden table. The food was mostly preserved supplies that had been doctored up to be palatable, but I wasn't going to complain after days of hard jerky and nuts. I chewed on a piece of dried edible kelp, a Kysthjem specialty according to Ivar, when Aaren walked over with a full mug of ale in his large hand.

"You're glowing, *fremmed*," he complimented and tried for a casual smile. "The coast suits you."

I shrugged, going for nonchalance, but I knew it was unconvincing with how hard I had to chew the kelp. "It's beautiful, but I prefer the forest."

Aaren gave me a questioning look, almost playful. "And why is that?"

"It's easy to breathe," I replied, remembering that familiar scent the breezes in Skoghjem carried. "But it's not like it matters anymore."

Aaren paused, and the levity in his face washed away. "What do you mean?"

"Even if I liked it here more, I would never be able to stay. Choosing to marry you took away my choice."

"Never mind. I'll see you in the tent," I said, tossing the rest of the kelp on the ground and stepping away. There was a tugging in my rune, almost like the invisible string that tied Aaren and me together was pulled taut. I pushed against it, even though a foreign, pleading feeling filled me. I wasn't sure where that feeling came from or why it was suddenly coursing through me, but I pushed it away as much as I could and followed the path to the cliff and down to the beach.

The music and shouts could still be heard between the waves crashing on the shore. I swallowed, trying to get the souring flavor of ale and kelp off of my tongue. So many thoughts rattled around in my head, ranging from the insistent image of Lucas in a dungeon to Mama and Granny to that odd, lingering feeling of pleading that had somehow warped into something like desire in the span of my walk to the beach. Desire for what, I didn't know, but the answer was in the back of my mind, and it was going to stay there.

There was a full moon tonight, and it cast a shimmering reflection across the Stornish sea, illuminating the deep dwelling underneath. The thoughts continued to fight for center stage in my mind, creating a resounding echo. It was funny, back in Midgard, I was too busy and broke to have thoughts like these occupy my mind. And before I could entertain that notion, all noise was silenced in my head, leaving one lone, shocking realization.

It wasn't my realm, or even my old realm. It was Midgard. After a few months here, the idea of claiming Midgard as my realm was unsettling. How could I claim a realm that had only given me death and heartache and nothing but struggle with no avail? All Midgard did was take and take from me. From the first week I was in Alveland, it had given me a purpose, friends, and a home that was actually worth fighting for. It had shown me acceptance, something that I couldn't even get from a psychology program I wasn't sure I even wanted to be a part of. Deep down, acceptance into that program wasn't about the school or the career that would follow. It was about being accepted for the first time in my life.

Midgard was not my realm anymore. Alveland was.

Chapter 30

As I wandered the ruined paths of Kysthjem looking for some way I could help, Helgi caught sight of me and pulled me over to a ramshackle table near the edge of the square. The hastily pieced-together table was littered with crumbled sheets of parchment scrawled with faded ink, and as I studied them closer, I realized they were blueprints for some of the buildings lining the square. The small group of Fraalver that stood and deliberated over the prints with us looked like they had been tossed into the sparring ring with a group of hudflasker. After being trapped in a sea cave for that long, I know the last thing they wanted to do was rebuild.

"We'll need far more havstok than I expected," Helgi said. I answered her with a questioning look. "It's a sort of adhesive, stronger than any glue you'll ever encounter," she explained. "It's used in our construction, but it is difficult to obtain. Our only known source can be found at the bottom of a treacherous pit we call Farliggrop."

A Fraalver chuckled next to me. "It literally translates to 'dangerous pit.'"

Helgi nodded. "The Fraalver are crafty with everything but our words." She turned her attention to the smaller man next to me, his curly black hair appearing almost blue in the sunlight. He looked familiar, but I couldn't place him. "Isak, how do your stores of vanpust look?"

For fear of looking stupid, I refrained from asking what vanpust was.

Isak sighed. "Given that the mylings smashed most of my jars, I doubt there's much left."

"No need to fret, *venn*. I suppose a quick dip into the tide pools wouldn't do us any harm."

Isak nodded and scratched his nose. "Perfect."

Helgi nodded her head to the beach. "Come on, the tide should be going out soon."

I followed the others down to the beach, and breathed the salty air deep into my lungs.

The tide pools of Alveland weren't like the tide pools that populated the shores in Midgard. One look into the puddles of saltwater confirmed that I saw a small iridescent shrimp skimming through the water. I watched it curiously, following its movements as its little legs propelled it forward to climb out of the pool. Small wings sprouted from its back when it shook the droplets from its body, and I did my best to master my shock as it took flight. Knowing I looked like I was trying to catch flies with the way my mouth was hanging open (an expression Granny used when I didn't cover my mouth when I yawned), I snapped it shut, blushing when Helgi chuckled at me.

"Wing shrimp," she said, watching the shrimp flutter away. "They're good eating." When I asked if you eat the wings too, Helgi laughed. "The wings are the best part," she replied.

Isak and Helgi knelt beside me and peered into the tide pool, our reflections distorted by the swirling water. He reached into the pool and picked a handful of swaying purple moss and passed it to Helgi, who shoved it into a small satchel slung across her chest.

"What does this stuff do?" I questioned, not taking my eyes off the remaining patch in the pool.

"It helps you hold your breath longer," Isak explained as he swiped sweat from his dark brow. "It heightens your lung capacity, so you can go twenty minutes without needing to breathe. Plus, it makes it so you don't have to decompress when you come back up."

"We're going to eat it?" I asked, not even bothering to hide my disgust.

"We?" Helgi inquired with a spellbound confusion.

"I want to help," I replied, something like a plea almost leaking into my tone.

"And how does Aaren feel about this?" Helgi questioned.

"He's fine with it," I lied without an ounce of remorse. "He's off helping Fiske, why can't I help you?"

The smug knowing that permeated Helgi's features remained, but there was also a note of understanding in her eyes.

"Alright, *frue*," she sighed. "Come with me."

A short while and a change of clothes later, I followed that same group back down the path with a pair of goggles in my hand. When I asked why Helgi had slapped them into my hands, she explained that I would need them against the saltwater. I agreed, though none of the other Fraalver carried a pair with them. Helgi went on to explain that over the centuries, the Fraalver of Kysthjem had become accustomed to the salt and had developed a heightened sense of sight underwater. I envied the Kysthjem Fraalver—I'm sure the goggles looked ridiculous when I donned them.

Following Helgi and the others to the water, a slight tap on the shoulder stopped me. Standing behind me with a polite, yet timid smile was Isak, clutching a cloth-wrapped something in his hands.

"Here," he said and pushed it into my hands. "You're going to need it."

Isak had already made it halfway across the beach when I unwrapped the gift, stomach dropping as the sharp knife blade pressed into my fingertips. Certain muscles in my body went weak at the ominous gift and the realization that I would need it. When I said I wanted to help the village, I meant helping to prepare the communal dinner that the surviving pub keeper was planning for tonight.

There was a small strap of leather attached to the hilt, which I used the buckle to secure to my thigh as I met the rest of the group on the shore. I recoiled when Helgi dropped a slimy dose of vanpust in my palm, watching it jiggle as my hands began to shake. The Fraalver next to me chucked it into his mouth, throat working to swallow it as his lip curled in disgust.

"Are you supposed to chew it?" I asked, stalling.

"I wouldn't," he answered, followed by a shudder. "It tastes dreadful as it is. Chewing it only makes it worse."

Fabulous.

The man was right. My tongue was assaulted with the taste of wet leaves left to rot in a jar. Warm spit gathered in my mouth as my throat tried to send the moss back up, but I swallowed pridefully, keeping my lip from even twitching. The man watched me with surprise, then turned and mumbled to himself. I didn't catch what he said, but I'm sure it was along the lines of the dirty jokes I heard Oswin and Ivar crack.

Helgi gestured the group into the waves, more turbulent today than they had been last night when I watched them with a thoughtful eye. Securing the goggles tightly over my eyes, I watched Helgi dive under the waves, followed by each of the others until it was only me above the surface. Taking a huge gasp of air, I sprang forward and dove under the next crashing wave. Instead of the usual discomfort that accompanies holding my breath, a pleasantly cool softness comforted my lungs, unlike anything I've ever felt before.

Feeling less goofy and more thankful for the goggles now that I saw how murky the water was today, I discerned the fuzzy shapes of the group ahead. Seaweed brushed against my skin, tricking me into thinking a flock of wing shrimp was assaulting me. Or something worse. I kicked forward, eager to escape the tumbling flecks of aquatic flora the waves had pulled free from the sand.

The water's energy greeted me with a friendly, but adamant, tug in my gut. It was like a cat that was excited to see me but didn't want to show it. I invited some of it in and let it propel me forward, thankful for the break it gave me from paddling. The free-floating seaweed gave way to a swaying kelp forest, and the soft tips of the leaves tickled my legs as I moved past. The water had cleared a bit, but the bottom of the kelp was indiscernible, leaving my imagination to run far away from me. I propelled forward hurriedly as a sinking feeling told me something nasty crawled along the floor of the underwater forest.

A school of fish swam next to me, nearly uniform in color with shimmering scales of green. Green is not like the swirling kelp below, but the treetops in Skoghjem. A comforting reminder of my new home as I plunged further into the sea.

The kelp forest gave way as we swam into open waters, a menacing darkness shrouding the deep ocean floor. Five minutes passed before an aching discomfort hugged my lungs, just in time for the group to surface and tread in place. Cold air nipped my cheeks as I took in a deep breath, kicking to keep my head from being smacked by the lapping water.

"One more dose of vanpust before the plunge," Helgi instructed, passing out more sickly purple moss.

I held my breath when I swallowed it this time, but it barely helped.

"Right," Helgi said as she swallowed her share. "Layla, Olyn, Marsy, and I will make the descent. The remainder of you are to tread here and keep watch. Can't have a repeat of last time."

That was the last thing I needed to hear, considering the knife strapped to my thigh was pressing more evidently into my skin. I wondered how Aaren would react if he knew I was in the middle of the Stornish sea, about to plunge into Farliggrop. I didn't know, and frankly, I didn't care. Although the thought of what he might do when he found out sent a heat flushing from my rune. What could he do, tie me up with his vines again?

230

On second thought...

"Get ready!" Helgi shouted. There was a hint of excitement in her tone.

"Dive!"

Marsy, the Fraalver next to me, slid her hand into mine once the water closed over my head. Olyn grabbed my other hand, then linked with Helgi, creating a chain so we wouldn't lose each other upon plunging into the darkness. I kicked, careful not to knock Marsy beside me as we clung to each other. A swirling darkness slowly surrounded us. Pressure built in my ears, and soon I couldn't see anything that could swim through my line of sight.

Then something swished across my skin.

Loud bubbles flew from my mouth when I let out a muffled gasp and reared back, tugging on Olyn in my left hand and bumping into Marsy behind me. She took her free hand and placed it over my mouth, muting the bubbles and my distorted shout. Whatever had touched me was not something that should know we were here.

Shaken and deterred from going any further, I moved more carefully, keenly aware of every small current that swished near me. After nearly ten minutes of swimming directly downward, our chain leveled, and my feet brushed the slimy ocean floor. I shuddered as my toes wove into a drifting softness, praying it was only algae or a graze of sea moss.

A warm blue light blinded me momentarily, then I squinted to see that the gleam emanated from a glowing stone in Helgi's hand. I almost wished she hadn't lit that stone, so I didn't know what my toes gripped in the darkness. Below my feet was a dark blue algae-like grass, but stringier, almost like I had tangled my toes through a horse's mane. Every few seconds, the ground would pulse intensely, as if it were taking a big sweeping breath.

Little silver fish darted around us, their tiny razor-sharp teeth glimmering in the stone's light. I swatted two or three of them away, only for them to return with a vengeance and pester me like a swarm of hungry mosquitoes.

Helgi dropped Olyn's hand and swam over a small ledge, gesturing for me to come to her. Not wanting to comply, but seeing no other option but to obey, I swam to the ledge as trepidation filled me instead of the air I began to crave. She passed me the light, so her hands were free, and I held it close to the mud-coated rock face. Mud clouded around us as she dug her fingers in and pried the rock face up to reveal something hard and faintly yellow underneath. With one hand, she held the rock open while the other fished in her satchel for a sharp tool that glinted in the blue light when she pulled it out. Then, using the tool, she scraped it across the exposed jagged surface, working at the built-up gunk and collecting it in her satchel.

Starting to feel a little more at ease, I studied the rock Helgi was scraping, noting the grooves and lines that had been worked into it. It resembled teeth. Then the sea floor swelled, as if the mud were taking a deep breath.

Wait...breath, teeth...

My heart stopped.

The rock didn't resemble teeth. It *was* teeth.

And Helgi was extracting the dental plaque of some massive creature buried under the mud.

If there was any time to master my shocked fear, it was now, seeing as one wrong move could startle this monster awake, and then we'd all be screwed.

Helgi continued to work, features etched with concentration. Coupled with my now angry heartbeat, there was a growing discomfort spreading through my lungs, tightening as the need for air grew more pressing. The vanpust was wearing off. And those damn silver fish wouldn't leave me the hell alone. I waved my hand in my best attempts to shoo them away. Clearly tired of my swatting, one lone fish darted through my hand and sank its sharp teeth into my wrist.

I yelped, and as soon as the bubbles left my mouth, I knew it was over.

Helgi whipped around to look at me with alarm.

The mud shook.

Helgi fumbled with the satchel, frantic fingers snapping the clasp shut before she looped her arm through mine and pushed off with surprising force. Marsy, linked with Olyn, caught my hand as we shot past, ripples of water moving over us as the sea floor rumbled again. Flecks of glowing blue floated past as Helgi crushed the rock in her hands to better hide us from whatever stirred below. It did little good, however, as a green eye cracked open and a slitted pupil searched around. The ground rumbled when the eye locked on us, mud clouding around it as it rose. All that could be seen in the stirring murk now was that lone green eye that never lost sight of us as we swam away.

In any other circumstance, we were making good time, but as there was a massive creature that was beginning its ascent to swallow us whole, we weren't fast enough. Fear held me in a crushing grip, constricting my lungs as the need for air was becoming desperate. The light from the surface was growing brighter, but still not enough for me to see anything other than the swirling waters above.

Not enough for me to see what struck me before swimming away to get lost in the darkness, this time, however, I caught my cry of pain before even a bubble of precious air could escape me. Still, the salt water did nothing to help the violent pain that was now cascading along my shoulder and leaching into my back and along my collarbone.

The unblinking green eye followed us, growing bigger as it drew closer. The surface shrouded us with light, and the Fraalver bobbing above milled around as they searched for the danger that was now tangible in the water. Something shot past my face and landed with a gut-churning thud below. There was a muffled screech, then bubbles cascaded upwards, threatening to trap me in a column of disorienting ripples. The eye faltered for a moment and granted us just enough time to bask in the sweet sunlight and prepare for whatever attack it was going to hit us with. When it recovered, the eye shot through the water with a renewed ferocity that sent my heart into my stomach. Now bathed in sunlight, the monster could be seen in all its glory, a sight that made every muscle inside me clench in horror.

The dark blue moss coated its back, while the skin on its sides was jagged, with dark blue scales caked in mud. The thing looked like an overgrown tadpole, if a tadpole mated with an angler fish and lingered at the bottom of the ocean for a century. The glowing green eye dimmed as it followed us into lighter waters, the filtered sun shining a spotlight on its sickening teeth. What I hadn't seen in the dark was the bits of flesh and bones wedged into the grooves between its teeth, which ended in sharp spikes, honed enough that they could easily snap a boulder to bits.

My shoulder was now singing in agony as my blood clouded the water crimson. I was losing blood quickly, and with it, feeling in my left shoulder, resulting in Helgi's hand slipping from mine. Marsy dropped my other hand, and I fell into a slow free fall through the open water.

Without the extra propulsion from the others, coupled with my now-useless left arm, there was no way I was going to outswim this thing. My mind reached out to the ocean's energy, but it retreated. It seemed the sea decided to cap me on the amount of magic I could use at once.

As if answering my call to the ocean, something unnatural sang through me, something other than the water that I so desperately grappled for. It was like an adrenaline injection to the heart, and I kicked my legs, sending myself upward. Despite the chilled water, my rune burned hot, but there was no time to figure out why, not when my shoulder felt like it was going to detach itself from my body. Not to mention my foot had just brushed the jagged snout of the creature. Time froze, and I stood on the nose of the monster, blood circling me like an angry storm cloud.

Sense snapped back into me, and I braced my foot and kicked off, flying through the water. My efforts were short-lived. Something slimy coiled around my waist and yanked, leaving a trail of red through the beautifully blue water. One glance below me revealed it to be the creature's tongue twined around me, wrapping tighter with every second.

I fumbled for the knife strapped to my thigh, the hilt slipping from my fingers for a split second—a split second where all my hope was lost in the cloud of blood above me. Then my fingers grasped it, and the hilt rolled into my palm perfectly. I thanked whatever was in the heavens above, then sawed at the tongue. Black ichor spilled into the water and mixed with my blood as the thing wailed, the water doing nothing to drown out the deafening roar. The final strand of flesh unraveled from around me and left me to flail towards the surface. Underwater arrows zipped past me as I clumsily swam away, thanks to the panic overtaking my coordination.

Helgi kicked toward me, a spear clutched in her grip. The creature circled us, and Helgi pointed to her neck, made a stabbing motion, then pointed to me. Bewildered by what exactly she was trying to convey, I watched her kick away, her movements exaggerated as she tried to attract the creature's eye. It worked, and the slitted pupil honed in for the kill. Her plan clicked—she was the distraction, I was the killer.

Grimacing as I pushed my shoulder as much as the pain would let me, I lunged forward, grappling for purchase exactly where I needed to be: the gills. The flaps opened and closed as it tracked Helgi, and I took the brief moment when she dodged to count the pattern of breaths. Open for two seconds, closed for four. I waited for one second, then two, three...

On the fourth second, the gills opened, and I let the sharp intake of water pull my arm in until the blade found soft flesh. The gills closed, trapping my arm as the creature screeched again. Then I readjusted my grip on the hilt of the dagger for a fraction of a second, twisted, and felt my hand sink into the wound. Another four seconds went by, then the flaps opened, and I retracted my arm, only to plunge it into a different spot in the gills and slice through.

The creature thrashed to shake me off, but I wedged my fingers under the scales and held tight. The muscles of the gills faltered as the thing began to die. The steady breathing lost tempo, leaving my arm trapped for up to eight seconds before the gills opened. I planted my feet on the side, and when the gills opened one last time, I wrenched my arm and the knife free, then kicked off. There was no satisfaction in my kill. The pain in my shoulder wouldn't allow it.

As the monster sank to the bottom, the bright green eye faded until the darkness swallowed it completely.

Pain pulsed through me and tried to send me into the depths, agony bleeding into delirium as the remaining effects of the vanpust wore off. There were a few more good kicks in me, and I expended what was left of my energy to swim the last bit of distance until I reached Helgi, who looped an arm around me and dragged me upward.

I never breathed sweeter air in my life. As our heads breached the surface, I sucked in the largest breath I had ever taken, so desperate for air that I couldn't savor how crisp it was or how it filled me with life again. I was holding tightly onto Helgi since I couldn't tread water on my own.

"Slow your breaths, *frue*, there's plenty of air. I don't need you passing out on us."

"My shoulder," I winced, letting Marsy drape my left arm over her to take some of my weight off Helgi. "Why didn't you tell me *that* was where the havstok was?"

Helgi gave a laugh peppered with exhaustion. "It normally goes a lot smoother. If you hadn't woken it up, we wouldn't have had to kill it!"

With my air restored, the pain was manageable, if only for a few seconds. "Well, excuse me! I didn't plan to wake the...what was that thing?"

"A hagua," Helgi answered. "They burrow into the bottom of pits. The havstok we use is extracted from the plaque on their teeth."

I cringed as the water slapped into my shoulder with no remorse. "It nearly took my arm off!" I cried, gesturing to my still bleeding shoulder.

Helgi smacked her lips and examined my shoulder. "That didn't come from the hagua, that looks more like the sting of a usett."

"A what?"

"An usett. An unseen. They're invisible creatures with horrific barbed tentacles," she examined the bleeding welt pulsing on my skin. "Nasty stings, but you'll live, *frue*."

Chapter 31

The pain had become almost excruciating as we trudged back into the village. Helgi sent me to the meeting hall, so Isak could clean and dress my wounds, collapsing onto the window seat overlooking the cliff as he readied his supplies.

"I suppose we'll have to find another source of havstok in the future," Isak stated as he dabbed my shoulder with a warm cloth.

"Sorry," I said, but I didn't mean it. I was just relieved to be out of the water. "Thank you, by the way, for the knife."

Isak nodded and dunked the rag into a basin. "You'd be stupid to go into the water without one," he answered. "The creatures in the deep are stirring, like they're growing restless. We've had more attacks in the past year than we've had in fifty."

We both knew why; there was no use in denying it.

"It's bad, isn't it?" Isak asked, something that weighed down his features. Something all too familiar. It was grief.

"It's...it's not good," I replied, too distracted by the look on his face to give a better answer. I knew that type of grief well, the same feeling having weighed on *my* shoulders for weeks.

"I lost my brother in the myling attack," he muttered, pausing to steady his voice before continuing. "He was only eleven."

My throat constricted when Isak's dark hand tucked a black lock of hair away from his eyes. When he blinked silver tears from ice blue eyes, I saw those same irises, murky and clouded with death, in my memory.

The little boy I found was Isak's brother.

"I'm sorry," I barely whispered. It was all I could manage between the pain and the guilt and my own grief.

Isak couldn't meet my gaze, and a small part of me was thankful that I wouldn't have to see his blue eyes again, swimming with life when his brother's had been so dull.

"I let him out of my sight for five minutes. That was all the time I needed to finish my ledgers, and he wouldn't let me concentrate." Isak let out an exasperated, almost desperate chuckle. "I sent him outside to wait. And then the mylings came..."

He unknowingly squeezed the rag he had been cleaning my wound with, droplets of water raining on the floorboards at our feet. His nose twitched as he continued. "He thought it was his friends. But everyone was screaming and there was fire and...when I came to get him...it was too late."

His voice shook, but there were no tears on his cheeks, as if sorrow had left him, and all that was left was a bubbling rage that heated his cool irises. "If I hadn't sent him outside, he would still be here."

I understood more than he could know.

The crashing waves beneath the cliff below quieted, and there was a moment when our eyes finally met, and that understanding was exchanged between us. Nothing needed to be said because he recognized his own pain in my expression, the grief and blame we carried and could never truly reconcile.

And then Isak blinked and cleared his throat as he turned back to my wound. "It looks like it got you good, though," Isak observed, squinting at my shoulder with clearer eyes. "I've never seen a welt bleed like this before." Sure enough, a steady dribble of blood trickled from my shoulder with no sign that it had started clotting. "If there are still any barbs in here, there'd be no way of knowing, considering they'd be invisible."

I moved my shoulder the slightest bit, feeling pinpricks of pain along the welt. "They're in there," I said, after sucking in a sharp breath through my teeth.

Isak nodded and shuffled through a small medicine bag he had managed to salvage from his wrecked stores. "Only one way to get them out," he said, and produced a palm-sized bottle of dark brown liquid. "We're going to dissolve them."

"It's going to hurt like a bitch, isn't it?"

Isak gave me a sheepish look and nodded.

I blew out a steadying breath. "Alright, get it over with."

Just as Isak unscrewed the bottle, the meeting hall doors burst open, and Aaren thundered in, bringing in a fierce wind that blew the blankets and bandages across the room.

"What happened?" he demanded, and my rune burned furiously. Isak scooted away to move out of Aaren's path of destruction. When Aaren reached me, he grabbed my arm and examined the welt with a brow furrowed with fury.

My words jammed in my throat as I tried to grapple with the pain and the wind that just blew the meeting hall into chaos.

"What. Happened."

The wind died, but the pain remained. "I was helping Helgi," I stammered. "We had to get more havstok, but an unsert..."

"Usett..." Isak corrected.

"...got me and...I'm fine, Aaren, I promise."

Isak stood, dropping the washcloth into the basin, and awkwardly muttered that this seemed to be a private matter, then exited the hall.

Aaren shook his head as if it was the only thing he could do to keep from losing his grip on the anger bubbling inside him.

"Do you understand how dangerous your little excursion was?" he demanded. "You not only endangered yourself, but all of Skoghjem! We married to reinforce our borders. When you throw yourself at the mercy of a hagua, that negates the whole point of our union."

I frowned. "I'm fine, by the way, thank you for asking."

Aaren rolled his eyes, and another breeze blew through the hall. "This isn't something to be flippant about, Layla. Every one of our actions carries weight now that we're united. I beg you to keep that in mind next time you have the urge to go off on your own."

For the first time in my life, I shrank away from the fight. Because Aaren was right. I was being selfish when I chose my petty feelings over our village. All because Aaren made me angry.

Finally, Aaren sighed, a little calmer, and asked, "Are you actually okay?"

I nodded unconvincingly, features trembling as they fought to hide the grimace from the sting.

"No, you're not," Aaren said as he dropped to his knees in front of me. He was so tall that even on his knees, the top of his head would've met my collarbone had I been standing. I nodded, trying not to grimace when he moved my arm for a better look at the wound. "I know firsthand how much a usett sting hurts."

And just like that, the tough facade I was going for crumbled. I stopped trying to hide my wincing as he examined me, but the more I showed it, the harder it was to keep the pain under control. The heat in his eyes simmered to hot coals, much to my relief, but I couldn't shake the feeling of that furious wind. His fingers grazed my skin almost soothingly as a tenderness softened his features, a look I had only ever seen when he was taking care of Nilsen.

"Helgi had you going after a hagua for a little bit of havstok?" Aaren finally questioned, sitting back and cracking his knuckles.

"I was just trying to help," I said, letting out a shaky breath as I tried to steady the rising pain again.

Aaren plucked the bottle of brown liquid from the table where Isak had left it, mumbling that he would be having some words with the Kysthjem leader. I wasn't going to argue—I was starting to get nauseous with the way my arm was throbbing.

He uncorked the bottle, then met my eyes. "I know you're no stranger to pain..."

"Thanks to you," I scoffed through gritted teeth.

Aaren nodded once as he accepted the jab. "But this is going to hurt a lot worse than most of my punches." Even though he punched *very* hard. "Are you ready?"

A deep breath filled my lungs as I tried to ground myself. "Let's get this over with."

Aaren told me I had until the count of three to prepare myself. I pressed my lips together and braced for agony as my eyes turned to the window and the waves beyond.

"One," Aaren said, then dumped half the bottle onto the welt.

I screamed, back arching as my head dropped to the wall of the window seat. Acid burned my skin as it dissolved the invisible barbs from my arm and what felt like the flesh from my entire shoulder.

"You're okay, *fremmed*," Aaren said through the ringing chimes of pain blaring in my ears. "Breathe through it, Layla, it's almost over." Just as he said it, the stinging ebbed, enough that I could heave in a wavering breath and blink away the tears that filled my eyes. He continued to talk me through it, his voice a soothing rumble that sent a comforting flush to my rune. As the pain receded to a dull ache, I realized his fingers were woven with mine. Once he realized it himself, he pulled his hand away, clearing his throat as he retrieved a roll of bandages from Isak's medicine pouch.

Aaren's fingers began to unroll the fabric, and I asked a question I didn't know I had.

"How did you know I was hurt?" I asked, watching as Aaren's fingers fumbled with the bandages.

"I don't know," he answered truthfully and started to bind my shoulder. He worked expertly, and I knew this wasn't his first time patching someone up, whether it was himself or someone he pushed too far in the ring. "I just...felt your panic."

And I must've felt his when that rush of adrenaline filled me enough that I could finish the fight. Was it a product of the rune we shared, a way that not only tied us together but also synced our feelings?

"Sounds like Rorik forgot to tell us something about our marriage rune," I chuckled. It was a nice break from the tension. He pinned the bandage and had me rotate my shoulder to check the range of motion within the bindings. When he was satisfied, he eyed me almost sheepishly.

"Listen," he said, and for the first time since I'd met him, Aaren looked nervous. "I'm...sorry if things have been...different since the wedding," he said, gaze dropping to his hands, then through the window next to me. "I just...didn't expect to be married so soon after...after Solveig."

I understood, even though I didn't want to. I tried to fault him for feeling that way, to explain the tension between us as just him being a prick, because it would make me feel better about my childish behavior and spiteful thoughts. But I couldn't. I would likely feel the same way had the roles been reversed and I was forced to marry a stranger only a few years after losing my one true love. The thought of it clenched my stomach. No matter the reasons behind our marriage, I was not Solveig, and I never would be. I just hoped Aaren didn't hold that devastating fact against me.

"It's okay," I answered, following his gaze through the window. "I...I'm also sorry...about the other night. I was being childish."

Finally, our eyes met, and honeyed amber swirled with guilt and sorrow and...there was something else, something way too similar to affection for me to wave it away as anything else. He was holding something back. I just wasn't brave enough to inquire.

Instead, I asked him a different question. "Where did that scar along your back come from?"

Aaren's jaw tightened as he looked away, uncomfortable with the change in conversation. "Just one of the battles I lost," he replied, then stood, towering over me. "You should get some rest. We leave tomorrow at dawn."

Chapter 32

The rain returned the next morning and had soaked through my clothes by the time we had finished packing the horses. Swallowing my groan, I gripped Ivar's hand tightly as he helped me mount Froki, who seemed to be just as displeased with the rain as I was. She flicked her tail and nickered, and I patted her before nudging her forward to follow the train of horses ahead of me.

I hadn't slept well the night before, which added to the foul mood that seemed to be shared with everyone else in the group. I had tossed and turned late into the night while the pain of the sting engulfed my shoulder as the skin tried to heal. There was nothing in Isak's stores to ease the pain, so I resigned to quietly squirming all night. Aaren had stayed up with me for most of the night, checking the bandages and making sure my pain wasn't from complications with my wound. The circles around his eyes were just as dark as mine, but he kept his chin high and spine tall, the perfect image to lead his men.

Helgi followed us on horseback to the village borders, a brief twenty-minute ride across the open plain. The horses slowed so Helgi and Fiske could dismount and say their good-byes. I kicked Froki forward to give them as much privacy as the open plain could permit. Aaren lingered by my side, heaving a large yawn.

When Fiske climbed back onto his horse, Helgi gave me a quick kiss to the cheek, and we set off again, crossing over the Kysthjem borders and leaving the coast behind.

The plains stretched far ahead and into the horizon. The swaying grasses muted the horses' hooves, and I sighed, dreading another long stretch in the endless plains with nothing but my thoughts to keep me company. I became aware of my rune and the feeling it was evoking within me. Mischief? A desire to cause trouble? Whatever it was, I knew Aaren felt it too, or maybe he was the origin of the wickedness. I locked eyes with him for a moment, noting the playful spark.

"Are you ready, *fremmed*?" he asked.

"Ready for what?"

Aaren bounced his brows playfully, then kicked his horse into a canter. The others followed suit within seconds, whooping and singing—everyone except Axl and Fiske—as their horses' hooves thudded against the ground. I panicked and shoved my heel into Froki's side. She was more than happy to rise to the challenge, and I bent low on her back as she took off, passing Ivar and Von's horses with ease. She didn't stumble or falter on the uneven ground as her hoofbeats fell into rhythm. Within seconds, I caught up to Aaren and his horse.

Rain pelted my face like tossed gravel, but I didn't care, not when adrenaline thrummed through me, keeping the goosebumps that had been on my arms at bay. I was side by side with Aaren, and when he shot me a glance, I threw up my middle finger. He cocked a brow, giving me a devilish smile before veering to the right. Taking the bait, I followed him, spurring Froki until she was close on his tail.

I followed him as he circled the group, and the shouts of encouragement from the others sent a grin across my face. Oswin gave Ivar a friendly shove, which quickly grew into not-so-friendly shoves, then a game of tag between the two that seemed likely to end in blood. Von joined in, laughing as Ivar shouted a nasty curse at Oswin, who replied by blowing him a flirtatious kiss.

I was still on Aaren, just close enough that I could reach out and grab his shirt should I find myself brave enough. As if he read my mind, he yanked his reins, sending his horse into a skittering halt. Panic jolted me when his horse reared its front hooves and threw Aaren out of the saddle. He thudded to the ground with a grunt, and I circled Froki back to him and dismounted. Aaren lay motionless on the ground, and I was ready to scrap together whatever makeshift first aid I could as I ran to him. Then I kicked mud at him when I saw that he was laughing instead of nursing any injuries.

"You prick," I said.

He didn't argue with that as he shook off the mud and mounted his horse again.

The rest of the journey wasn't as lighthearted as our game of tag. In fact, the endless plains in front of us put everyone at each other's throats. Oswin and Ivar bickered over something so trivial I didn't bother to figure out what it was. Axl and Fiske began to argue over the route Fiske had chosen, as it added an extra half day. Fiske asserted that it was the safer way, though, as his men had encountered a recurring pack of farljorts on this path (I quickly found out that farljorts were a type of aggressive deer that ate Fraalver flesh, and a pack of them was deadly to a traveling company such as ours). Axl insisted that it was a risk we would have to take, but Fiske stayed firm on his decision. Aaren, surprisingly, was the only member who kept his spirits from sinking, commanding our troop onward through the squabbling and rain.

The skies cleared around noon, and I remembered I had Thea's book, and Froki enjoyed the loose reins I granted her as I lost myself in the first pages. After finishing the first three chapters, I strongly agreed with her when she said she wrote books worth reading. I squirmed in my bedroll that night as I read, trying not to make it evident to Aaren that I was reading smut right next to him.

My shoulder had healed enough that I could move it more freely, though Aaren insisted that we continue to clean and bandage it, much to my annoyance. I bit my tongue to control the urge to tell him to tend to his own wounds. Considering his reaction to my question about his scar in Kysthjem, I wasn't sure how that comment would be received.

The skies darkened again, and the rain returned.

Ivar's map curled at the edges from the poor weather but was still readable thanks to the rocks he put on each corner when he pulled it out to read. I hadn't realized just how large the vast expanse of blank parchment was when I examined the map that first night. There had been minor landmarks dotted across the space where we stopped to break up the trip, although the rolling plains seemed to go on and on. During the second day, a tall, dark figure broke through the unrelenting rain, stretching high into the clouds.

"What is it?" I asked as I gaped at the gigantic monolith towering over me.

"A shrine," Aaren replied, tying his horse to a nearby bush. "To the fallen gods of Asgard."

"People actually believe that Asgard existed?" I asked, observing the small tirnkets and flowers laid out in offering. It was hard to wrap my head around why anyone would travel this far out to make offerings to gods that, even if they had existed, had fallen from grace. There was nothing the gods could offer them.

"Not many, but the ones who do hold strong to that belief," Axl said as he led his horse to drink from an offering barrel that had filled with rain.

We traveled for three days until we saw the beginnings of the mountains. Large, jutting foothills gave way to towering mountains that were lost in the low-hanging clouds. The path wound up a hill, packed mud giving way to hard rock that produced a rhythmic clopping sound as our horses trudged forward.

Dusk was only an hour away when the horses slowed at Fiske's command.

"Torsten is another day's journey into the mountains," Fiske explained. "We should stop here for the night. The mountains can be treacherous without the light of day." We were in a nest of trees along a slender valley, wide enough that I could cross it within a ten-minute walk. A babbling creek cut through the center, rife with shimmering trout that Fiske promised to spear for dinner. I breathed a sigh of relief when I dismounted, my muscles screaming from three days in a saddle.

Oswin and Ivar eagerly went to work setting up camp while Axl and Aaren left to scout the perimeter. Von tended to the horses, brushing out their coats and cooing quietly as if they could understand his soft words.

"Would you like to help me, Layla?" Fiske asked as he turned towards the stream that was nestled in the trees a few feet away.

I nodded, eager for something to do.

My boots sank into the bank of the stream as I knelt next to Fiske, watching him roll up his sleeve. "Have you ever caught a fish before?"

I shook my head and watched Fiske smile. "They don't call me the Fish King for nothing." He paused. "Except for the fact that my name means *fish*."

Laughing, Fiske slipped his hand into the icy water, right in front of a trout that was lazily navigating the current. The trout regarded his hand for a moment, then slid into his fingers as if it were just another part of the creek bed. Then Fiske plucked it from the water and tossed it into his satchel, which he had flung open next to him.

"That feels wrong," I said, watching the fish flap and wriggle in the bag.

"You want to eat, right?" Fiske asked as he slipped his hand back into the water.

I didn't like it, but he was right.

Fiske plucked two more fish from the stream before I said, "So you can manipulate water and the creatures that live within. What else can you do?"

"It's not as cut and dry as you say," he replied, shaking the cold water from his hand. "I can manipulate water, but not the fish." He chuckled at my confused look that I directed towards the dying fish in his satchel. "Because of who I am, they don't recognize me as something apart from the water. To them, I'm just another stray current."

Fiske caught a couple more fish and then sat back. "There's only so much I can do, though," he said. "No one can tame the sea." I watched the water, admiring the trout that still pushed against the current, unperturbed by the loss of their brothers. "Give it a try," Fiske said. He gestured to the water, and I laughed at the thought of me chasing after a fish, but seeing as there was nothing else to do, I decided to give it a shot.

Rolling up my sleeve, I hovered my hand over a fish, hoping my shadow in the setting sun wouldn't startle it. Secure in my position, I dunked my hand in, and my fingers grazed the slippery scales before the trout swam out of my grasp.

"Not so easy, is it?" Fiske teased. "Glad I did the fishing; otherwise, we wouldn't be eating tonight."

Later that night around the fire, the crickets made the only noise, singing their chirps into the summer air that was growing warmer by the day. Fiske had cooked the fish to almost perfection, and when I meandered to our tent, I was full and content.

There was a comfortable silence between Aaren and me as we settled in, a welcome change from the brooding stillness he favored before we made our amends.

Aaren unbound his hair from the usual half-up, half-down and ran his fingers through the silver strands, a quiet groan rumbling from his chest. His half-lidded eyes shone in the small lantern light as he stretched, and a subtle wince shadowed his features. His shoulders tensed in obvious pain.

"You're hurting," I said, kicking off my boots before unwinding the base of my braid.

"I'm fine," he grumbled as another wince pinched his features.

"It's that wound on your spine, isn't it?"

Aaren crawled carefully into his bedroll and fought the next twist of pain that clenched his jaw. "I said I'm fine, *fremmed*. Leave it be."

I turned, unlacing the strings of my vest. "I was just trying to help," I muttered and threw the vest onto the floor next to my boots.

My skin prickled. A sixth sense told me Aaren's eyes watched me as I undressed to my underclothes, covering everything necessary, but leaving enough bare that Aaren's imagination could run wild should he let it. As I settled into the bedroll next to him, I pulled Thea's book from my pack and flipped to the last page I read.

Just as I found the words where I left off, Aaren scoffed. "Is that one of Thea's books?"

I peered at him from around the tattered cover, noting the amusement masking the pain on his face.

"It is," I replied, then flicked my eyes back to the page. "Why?

246

"I'm just...surprised."

Closing the book and dropping onto my bedroll, I turned and propped my head on my hand. "And what is so surprising about me reading a book, Aaren?"

"I didn't think such promiscuous subjects were your choice in literacy," he replied.

It was my turn to scoff. "She writes more than just romance," I retorted. It wasn't a total lie—her romance books just greatly outnumbered her other fiction.

"And is that one of the non-romance books you're reading?" he asked, gesturing to the discarded pages.

I rolled my eyes. "No, it's not, but I don't see why that's any of your concern."

Aaren chuckled arrogantly. "Defensive, aren't we?"

I wasn't defensive; I was annoyed because the two main characters had to share the same bed at the inn where they were staying, and instead of reading, I was having this conversation.

"I'm not a prude if that's what you're getting at," I spat, pushing myself up and crossing my legs.

"That's not what I meant," Aaren said. He shifted so that one arm supported him, the other draped over his knee, which he propped up. He looked like he was modeling for some seductive painting. "I'm sure there's more substance to her books than just sex."

My aggravation grew. "You haven't read any of her books, have you?"

"I have, actually," Aaren replied bluntly.

"Then why are you giving me grief for reading them?"

Aaren chuckled. "Because I wanted to watch you squirm."

I pressed my lips together, but my irritation eased, and left behind remnants of heat that I prayed Aaren wouldn't detect from the way my cheeks flushed.

"And what do you think of them?" I inquired, tucking my legs back into my bedroll, so I wouldn't feel as exposed.

Aaren shrugged. "They're fine, but she embellishes a lot."

"Like what?" I challenged.

He squinted his eyes, gaze going to the tent ceiling as he thought. "Sex is a lot different than how she writes it."

The answer took me by surprise, though I didn't know what I had been expecting. "And you would know?"

"I'm no stranger to a woman's body, if that's what you're implying, *fremmed*."

And why did that statement evoke a rush of jealousy in me? A jealousy for Solveig or whatever woman he had chosen to lie with before coming into his leadership, I didn't know, but the thought of him...

I wasn't going to complete that thought because the image it conjured drove my jealousy into sea green envy.

"But her books are mostly written from the female gaze. For all you know, her writing is very accurate."

Aaren's brows rose to his hairline as he gave me an inquiring look. "You would know?" he asked, recalling my previous question.

No, I wouldn't know since the last time I had sex, it was with a man who had thrust into me thrice before rolling over and passing out in a fit of drunk snores. But Aaren didn't need to know that.

"Yes," I answered sharply. "I would."

Aaren conceded. "Then my apologies, *fremmed*. I stand corrected."

Satisfied with my victory, I shoved the book back into my pack and turned away from Aaren, flustered and eager to hide it.

Summer had yet to arrive in the mountains, and the creeping chill settled into the tent and seeped through my bedroll. I curled in on myself and shivered.

My chattering teeth must've stirred Aaren, and he let out a sleepy groan and rolled over, scooting closer to me. Working solely on instinct in my sleeping state, I backed into him, and his warmth spread across my back. The shivering eased, and my limbs unfurled and stretched against him, relishing his warmth. A lazy arm snaked around my waist and pulled me closer, locking me in a tight embrace. There was no thinking behind the gesture, no subtext to read into, just warmth and a comfort I had never felt before. A comfort that soothed my soul and lulled me back into a pleasant sleep.

The sound of harsh growls pulled me awake, but Aaren's swift jump into movement jolted me into panic. Disoriented, I had barely kicked away my bedroll when Aaren slid on his boots and started strapping on his weapons, an impressive feat considering how many he had and how little time it took him to arm himself. He threw the tent flap back and disappeared, leaving me to dress with shaking hands.

When I emerged from the tent, the camp was in chaos.

Flashes of gray fur crossed my vision, as massive wolves, no, *fenrs*, tore apart the clearing. Oswin and Ivar's tent was in ruins, trampled and torn to shreds. Ivar stood atop a rock while three fenrs barked and scratched at the base. Their furious growls went unnoticed as he shot arrows at the pack pursuing Fiske a few feet away. Barks and yips came from the line of trees near the stream where Von spun with a knife in each hand, slashing through the ferns with ease. Oswin charged a fenr from across the clearing and bellowed a deep roar as his sword met fur and flesh.

It was Aaren who caught my attention despite the violent havoc the fenrs wreaked upon our company.

His blade swung with a crisp slice through the air before beheading a fenr, a sad yelp wrenching from its throat before it was severed completely. A throwing star found its place in the eye of an approaching foe, but Aaren had moved onto the next before that one had even hit the ground. He moved lithely, expertly, slashing through fenrs as if he were cutting through soft butter. His blade shone with crimson, in keeping with the flecks that stained his white shirt and leather boots. Hair clung to his sweat-sheened brow as he lunged into his next attack, eyes alight with the killer instinct that made him such a victorious warrior.

Distraction was a leading cause of death—a lesson Aaren had preached to me over and over again in the sparring ring, and one I was about to learn firsthand.

There was a growl on my right, and I had been so swept up in watching the battle that I forgot I was a part of it. My hand found the hilt of my sword just in time for a set of yellow, grime-caked teeth to come gnashing for me, accompanied by another growl identical to the one I heard my first night in Alveland. I rolled out of its path with only a millisecond to spare, and the whiskers of its muzzle grazed my cheek before I tumbled away to the side of the tent. The fenr growled, giving me enough time to draw my sword and assume my fighting stance.

Hackles raised and seething with primal hatred, the fenr lunged for me. My sword cut through the air when its gaping maw yawned wide enough to wrap around my throat. It met my blade with a pitiful whine, legs giving way from underneath it as I slid my sword from its side. Loose rock caught my boot as I backed away, and I fell to the hard ground, where my tailbone smashed painfully.

The fenr took what remaining life it had left to launch its final attack, using my now-compromised position as leverage. My hands flew up, eyes flying shut as the stench of the fenr's breath filled my nostrils, but it caught my sword, gutting itself as it made the dive for my face. Warm blood soaked the front of my shirt, then something heavier dropped onto my chest as the fenr let out one more choked yelp. When my eyes opened, I was face-to-face with the fenr, muzzle stuck in a permanent snarl. And lying on my chest was its steaming insides.

Partially digested trout rose in my throat as the smell of death and viscera reached my nose. I kicked the fenr off of me and tried not to gag as its guts fell away with a squelch. Standing proved too tricky with the way my legs were shaking, so I knelt on the rock and caught my breath.

The remaining fenrs were slowly being picked off by the others, quiet yelps and whines replacing the roars and snarls we had woken to. Von had jogged to the river to clean his knives while Axl helped Oswin drag the dead fenrs to a quickly growing pile at the base of the rock, where Ivar was knocking off the last few escaping fenrs with expert arrows.

My search for Aaren was short—he was already in front of me before I could start looking for him.

"Fuck, *fremmed*," he said as he took in all the blood on me. "Are you okay? Where are you hurt?"

I shook my head, but I felt like it barely registered with how much the rest of me was shaking.

Aaren tucked a strand of my blood-matted hair behind my ear, breathing as if it were a sigh of relief. "You really did a number on that fenr, didn't you?"

The clearing had been transformed into a bloodstained pit of fur and carnage.

"I don't think this was just some fenr attack," I said through a shaky breath. This was too coincidental for it to be that simple. Fenrs didn't come this far north, one of the few things I remembered from the reading Rorik assigned me on the creatures that occupied Skoghjem. If fenrs *did* come this far, it was rare. There had been too many rare occurrences happening lately for things to be written off as mere coincidences.

Mylings reemerged and attacked Kysthjem. We left our borders and were assaulted by fenrs in a region they aren't known to inhabit. Markus was the only apparent reason for these strange happenings.

Aaren only nodded, unbuckling my sword scabbard from my waist and tossing it onto the ground. "Okay," he said after ducking into the tent and grabbing my pack. "One thing at a time. Let's get cleaned up, and then we can talk about it, okay?"

"No, this can't wait. This could mean anything, this could mean that Lucas..."

I couldn't finish the thought, knowing that the images it would conjure would send me spiraling.

"Layla," Aaren said, stepping in front of me to block the view of the others and the blood-stained wreckage. "Breathe. It can wait, I promise. I'm not going to promise you that Lucas is alright. I don't want to make you false promises. But whatever this means, it can wait five minutes so you can clean yourself up."

Aaren instructed me to breathe again, and the bile in my throat dropped as I complied. With a soft hand on my back, he led me across the clearing and through the trees to the stream where Von was still cleaning his daggers. Aaren ordered him to scram, mumbling something along the lines of "make yourself scarce, and if I see any eyes this direction, you'll suffer the same fate as the fenrs."

I slid off my boots, ignoring the way the crimson shone in the soft light of the half-moon. Aaren dug in my pack and produced a fresh set of clothes—the last set I had—and turned his back as I peeled my soaked clothes off of me.

The water was icy against my skin, turning red as the current washed the viscera off me and carried it downstream. My scalp tingled as the cold spread across it, and I ran my fingers through my auburn hair, wincing as they caught on the tangles and knots. The stream probed my magic cautiously, but I shrugged it off and kept scrubbing. Aaren stayed with his back turned, broad shoulders hunched as his arms crossed over his chest. There was a small cloth on the bank that I used to dry myself, shivering but thankful nonetheless for the wash.

Once the last button was fastened on my vest, Aaren turned.

"Now, let's talk."

I launched into my explanation of the fenrs and why I thought this wasn't just a coincidence. This was all bigger than just a pack of fenrs stumbling across our camp.

Aaren remained quiet for a moment, but the disturbed look in his eyes told me of the trouble running through his mind. He took a deep breath.

"We need to get to Fjellhjem then," he said finally. "This is a lot more urgent than we thought."

After hastily packing up camp, we set out before the moon set in the sky. The horses trudged reluctantly up the mountain path and puffed in protest of their interrupted sleep. I shared that sentiment, yawning wide as the adrenaline from the attack left me aching and exhausted.

We rode without pause until midafternoon, opting for a mobile breakfast in which we passed around a waterskin and a few pieces of dried lamb. When the sun had risen to its highest point in the sky, the mountains stretched through the clouds and shrouded us in their looming shadows. I marveled at their majesty, in awe of the wondrous landscapes Alveland provided in every region. Froki was feeling the opposite, however, huffing and bobbing her head as she veered around a huge boulder that obscured part of the path. Chuckling, feeling lighter for the first time since the attack, I patted her mane lovingly.

My contented thoughts bled into worry as the path extended steeply uphill and the gravel started to crumble under the horses' hooves. Pebbles and dust slid down underfoot, a horse occasionally slipping after a miscalculated step. Von's horse whinnied in anger after stumbling for the third time since we began the ascent, and I held my breath until the path leveled out a few feet ahead.

Now higher off the ground than I ever wished to be, I surveyed the mountain range as the wind whipped my hair about. Low-lying clouds settled amongst the peaks, and my eyes followed the trail as it wound around and behind another mountain. Then I looked down and immediately felt the hurried lunch of bread and cheese churn in my stomach.

I was as stiff as a board by the time the beginnings of Fjellhjem came into view in the form of small scattered buildings bordering a bustling river. They increased in number the farther down the path we trekked, the river growing louder and wilder as treacherous rapids churned into white water. A large building sat at the edge of the bank, loud shouts and declarations of merriment coming from inside.

I was glad to find the pub so soon after such a rough ride. I needed a drink.

Next to the pub were the stables where we directed our horses and finally dismounted. My knees screamed as my feet hit the ground, and I let out a loud groan as I stretched my limbs. Oswin chimed in with his own groan, grabbing onto the side of the stable dramatically, begging for a drink before we found Torsten and Ertha.

"One drink," Aaren permitted. "Make it quick, we need to get inside."

"Inside where?" I asked, looking around for the meeting hall.

"Inside the mountain, *true*," Axl answered, removing the hood from his head. "Some of Torsten's people prefer the open air. But most of them reside within." Which explained why I had counted only twenty houses as we entered the village. Axl gestured his head to a gap in the rock face several hundred feet away. Large torches lined the inside of the rock, though I couldn't see far into the tunnel before a gravelly voice called from a few feet away.

"Well, well, if it isn't Aaren, King of Trees."

A stout, red-faced man with white chops on the side of his face waddled toward us. He held a large mug that sloshed ale with each drunken step. The buttons on his shirt looked ready to pop as his belly strained against them, and his greasy hair was slicked back in a short ponytail.

Aaren's shoulders tightened as he turned, his jaw clenched. He smiled, though it never reached his eyes. "Boden," he grunted.

"I see you're just as stiff as you used to be," Boden said, taking a loud swig from his tankard.

Aaren kept his strained smile despite his biting tone. "And you're just as fat and drunk."

Boden snarled as he sized up the group, who all straightened and squared up. Von's fingers tapped anxiously on the hilt of his knife, and the leather of Ivar's bow creaked as his grip tightened around it.

Boden looked at Fiske and scoffed. "I thought I smelled fish," he sniggered. "Or maybe it's your wife I smell on you."

Expecting Fiske to start swinging, I was surprised when he chuckled and stood a little taller. "I do hope that wasn't jealousy in your tone, Boden. I thought the pigs were treating you just fine."

Boden's lip curled, then he slid his slimy gaze to me. Not bothering to mask my disgust, I glared daggers at him, heart thumping a bit faster as I readied myself for a fight.

"And what about this one?" he asked, motioning to me with his ale. "She looks fresh, tight." He licked his lips like a cow would after drinking from a trough. "I'm going to enjoy stretching her out..."

One moment, Boden was on his feet; the next, Aaren had him in the air by the collar, snarling as Boden's limbs flailed. He slammed the drunk into the mud at the mouth of the stables. Whatever ale hadn't been dumped down his

253

front now spilled into the dirt. Boden gasped for air like a fish out of water and squirmed, his double chin growing as he struggled to roll over. He blanched at the way Aaren's eyes seared, jaw set, and features twisted into a look that was forged in the fires of malice.

Aaren's lip twitched. "Mine," he grumbled.

Boden's bravado snapped, and his face pinched as he began to plead like a fat coward, offering Aaren everything he owned if he would just let him go, but Aaren looked ready to do anything but release him.

"Apologize!" Aaren barked.

Boden wove his fingers together and shook them, begging my pardon before groveling for his life.

"Aaren!" a male voice called from the distance behind us.

Emerging from the tunnel into the mountain was a tall Fraalver man with dark brown hair and a matching well-groomed beard. He wore a humble slate-colored tunic and dark gray pants; his clothes were so similar to the mountains around us that he would have blended in if he had held very still. By his side was a woman of equal height, with flowing blonde locks and a confident smirk set into her beautiful, blossoming lips. Hugging her ample curves was a dress of midnight blue, with half sleeves that flowed with each step she took.

Aaren gave Boden one last snarl, then straightened, rolling out his neck and shoulders.

As the Fraalver couple approached, an exasperated smile danced across the man's lips. "You've been here for five minutes and you're already beating up my people. Have you no respect?"

Aaren huffed a breathy laugh. "He was speaking ill of my wife, Torsten," he replied tensely.

The man, Torsten, raised his brows. "Wife?"

A confused grunt sounded from Boden, who was still floundering in the mud puddle. Aaren slid to my side, his finger brushing the rune on my arm. "This is Layla, my wife."

Chapter 33

After the commotion with Boden, spirits were lighter. That was the dose of absurdity our company needed to break the tension left over from the fenr attack. Torsten shook his head as he led us down the tunnel, commenting on how the drunk's behavior had gotten worse over the years.

"When Boden was a babe, his mother must've dumped mead into his bottle to keep him quiet," the blonde woman in the beautiful dress joked as the outline of a door slowly came into view. "I suppose we should count our blessings that he has never sired a child," Torsten added.

"No woman would stoop low enough to share his bed," Aaren scowled.

Oswin and Ivar's stifled chuckles could be heard behind us before there was a thud, like one of them hit the other. Aaren cast a warning glance over his shoulder, chastising them like he would two children ready to brawl.

"Apologies for the sullied arrival, Layla, but it is a pleasure to meet you," Torsten said, offering me a polite nod. "This is my wife, Ertha."

The woman smiled sweetly, but a shadow of something else lay behind the expression, something deeper, something she held very close to her heart. "Such a blessing it is to see Aaren finally married." She blinked, then looked away, that heavy somberness easing as she turned her focus to Aaren. "How is Nilsen?"

"Growing bigger by the day."

The tunnel led us to a large, sweeping staircase that opened onto a small antechamber, which split into two directions. We took the right one, following a hall carved from the jutting rock that had been polished to a shine. Doorways were etched in the niches of the rock, some of them open to reveal their interiors. One room had a fireplace with sizzling embers and lit sconces across the walls. It resembled the medicine hut in Skoghjem, with its glass jars filled with dried herbs and multicolored bottles featuring different labels. Another room opened into a wide-mouthed cave with a roaring blacksmith pit in the middle and a massive, broad-shouldered man hammering at a sheet of metal.

Roughly ten minutes down the hallways, we turned left into a vast expanse of carved rock. Columns of polished rock rose to the towering ceiling where scenes of war and epic battles were etched. Across the massive room, there was a colossal fireplace, wide enough to fit our entire company inside and tall enough that I doubted Aaren would even be able to reach the top. The flames inside reached as tall as me, and the radiant heat was enough to roast a suckling pig from ten feet away.

Gathering around a large table in the center, Torsten sat and rested his elbows, looking at us expectantly. "Now then," he began frankly, "to what do we owe the honor of both yours and Fiske's presence, Aaren?"

Taking a seat across from Torsten after pulling out a chair for me, Aaren cleared his throat. "How're the mountains, Torsten? Are the peaks as quiet as I remember?"

The subtext underneath his statement was lost on everyone but the three leaders, and if it wasn't, everyone did a splendid job of hiding it.

"Relatively," Torsten replied tightly, his tone matching the growing caution in his features. Ertha shared the same expression, her eyes growing unwelcome. I wasn't sure if it was the way Aaren spoke or if she was choosing not to hide her evident disdain for me, but either way, she looked much less pleasant than she had before.

"Quiet if you don't count the increased burrower sightings," Ertha said, her voice just as tight as Torsten's. It seemed all formality and polite diplomacy were out the window. That same shadow still lingered on her face, growing clearer the more we spoke.

This was about Solveig. And the fact that I wasn't her.

"What're burrowers?" I asked, trying to shake off the discomfort that was closing its claws on me.

Torsten, seemingly forgetting that I had never been to the mountains of Fjellhjem, offered me a polite smile. "The burrowers are a race of *nisse*, goblins, you see. They have evolved, however, and no longer resemble their ancestors. Burrowers are nearly blind from their time spent within the mountains, and the darkness has altered their skin to a pale, nearly translucent hue. They mostly keep to their caves, but my men have faced ambushes while hunting." When he turned back to Aaren, Torsten tried for an air of nonchalance, rubbing his thumb and forefinger together. I would've believed him to be as unfazed as he was portraying if it weren't for the way his other hand gripped the table. Things here were a lot worse than they were letting on, but Torsten and Ertha weren't going to risk showing any weakness. They may be our allies, but this was a play of powers, and they seemed to have the upper hand.

For now.

"Why do you ask?" Torsten inquired.

Aaren and Fiske exchanged glances. "Mylings attacked Kysthjem, Torsten," Fiske finally said.

"Kysthjem is in near ruins. This attack comes just weeks after Skoghjem faced its own attack." Aaren wove his fingers together tensely. "There are far more dangerous forces at play, *venn*. We cannot face them alone."

Ertha shook her head in disbelief. "What greater forces are there, Aaren? There has been no mention of greater forces in Alveland since the Drapstre."

Warmth circled my rune as if warning me to brace myself. Deciding to listen to that feeling, I steeled my expression and clenched my hands in my lap.

"Markus Sviker," Aaren said.

Torsten's eyes widened. "Impossible."

"It's not."

"Oh, but it is, Aaren, because Markus Sviker was killed close to two hundred years ago."

The world stopped spinning, and I almost slid from my chair as shock barreled into me like a wave off the shores of Kysthjem.

If Markus were dead, then we were wrong about everything, and we would be back to square one. How could I have been so wrong?

I wasn't wrong. Markus wasn't dead; he was my father. I knew it just as much as I knew Lucas was my brother. I couldn't prove it, but this feeling had to count for something.

Fiske eyed Aaren momentarily, almost distrustfully, as he took in Torsten's words. This didn't seem to faze Aaren, however, and he took a steadying breath before saying, "He's not dead, Torsten."

Ertha raised a brow as if shocked Aaren would dare challenge Torsten. If Aaren didn't take offense to it, I certainly did—who was she to look down on Aaren's judgment? Aaren, her equal. My hands, which were clenched in my lap, started to drip water as my indignation grew, and I wiped them on my pants before I summoned more than could be written off as just sweaty palms.

"And what evidence do you have to prove otherwise?" Torsten challenged with an authority that shimmered in his eyes.

"A few weeks ago, a myling attacked one of my hunters and implanted a piece of Markus inside him. That piece was then given to Layla the second they touched."

Neither Torsten nor Ertha looked convinced. "And where is your evidence that it was a piece of Markus?" the former asked. "And why did he target her?"

I guess we couldn't put it off any longer. "Because I'm his daughter," I answered plainly.

Torsten masked his disbelief better than Ertha, whose closed lips curled as she began to shake. My own anger matched hers, growing like a tempest that was ready to tear down the mountain. First impressions aside, Ertha's angered trembling stirred something in me I had only felt a handful of times. Once in the ninth grade, a girl slammed me into a locker for no real reason, which resulted in the first and only school fight I had ever been in. The next time was when the little girl in the park spoke those hateful words to Lucas.

If there was one thing Ertha and I had in common, it was that we were both about to explode. Which one of us would do more damage?

"How. Dare. You," she seethed at Aaren. The burning pits of my anger spilled over and spread like wildfire through my veins. Ertha could insult me all she wanted, but the bite of the daggers she was glaring at Aaren was only kindling to my inner flames.

"Not only are you putting *every* Fraalver in jeopardy and insulting the pillars of life we stand on, you are defiling her memory!" *Her.* There she was again. The mention of the girl that Aaren once belonged to. The girl who seemed right in every facet where I felt wrong. Ertha shook her head and backed out of Torsten's calming touch, his soothing words lost to a menacing rumble in the cavern.

Putting every Fraalver in jeopardy.

When all I wanted to do was help.

Defile her memory.

All I was trying to do was live up to the standards she set before me. To be as good as her.

258

Not enough, never good enough, enough, enough, *enough...*

The cavern shook again, and pebbles rained down on the table as a fissure broke the rock directly above us. Torsten rushed to Ertha's side as her eyes, now lost in fright, shot to the damage in the ceiling.

"Calm down," Torsten warned softly as he brushed a finger along her cheek. "If you're not careful, you'll bring down the entire mountain."

Ertha shook her head, eyes finding me at the table. "This is not me," she muttered through a shaky breath.

Torsten followed her gaze, brows flicking to his hairline when he saw me trembling in my seat, red-faced and trying to rein in the swirling disaster of emotions inside me.

I blinked, releasing the tension that clenched my shoulders and fists. Warmth originating from my rune circled my forearm, and a wave of foreign calmness filled me. I invited the feeling in further so it could douse my raging fire and soothe the damage such an outburst had set in my nerves. Aaren hummed in quiet approval, only loud enough that I could hear. Then the rumbling ceased, and the cavern stilled.

"Evil blood," Ertha spat under her breath, and Torsten squeezed her arm in warning.

"Be that as it may, dearest," Torsten said, his eyes still watching me with a calculated coolness, "it may be wise to hear them out." His eyes rose to the ceiling, then dropped to the scattered traces of the ceiling along the floor. "Something tells me she may be worth the risk."

It was almost dinner time before the meeting finally ended, and Torsten had the barkeep bring in some pork and vegetables.

Ertha opted out of dinner with us, loudly expressing she'd rather enjoy a quiet dinner in her chambers without the risk of the ceiling caving in on her. Subtly rolling my eyes, I ignored the disdainful look she threw me before striding out of the meeting hall, her blonde locks trailing after her like wisps of smoke.

"You'll have to excuse her," Torsten said through a mouthful of pork later that evening. "Losing Solveig has been hard on both of us, but Ertha has had a far worse time coping than I." His gaze shifted directly to me. "She means well, Layla. After Pesta, her wariness towards strangers has grown. But she only wants what's best for her people."

A lie, I knew he was only telling me to ease my mind, and the tension Ertha had planted and watered like a spring garden. I knew the contemptuous look she gave me—it was the same one all of my bullies gave me in grade school. It was rooted in prejudice and disrespect, and it was unlikely I would earn any other look from her.

I chewed my roast pork and nodded anyway. I would accept Torsten's apology, but it wouldn't change the way Ertha and I felt about each other. "I would like to apologize for...threatening to destroy your meeting hall."

Oswin and Ivar chortled into their mugs, accidentally spewing ale over the sides.

Torsten offered me a forgiving look. "It is nothing we cannot fix in a day. But I would like to discuss what," he pointed to the ceiling, "...that was. Your magic is peculiar. Nothing like I've seen before."

Aaren scoffed. "You and I both, *venn.*"

I stomped his foot under the table, earning me a sly smile.

"I'm not sure how to describe it," I replied as I pushed a potato around on my plate. "A few months ago, I wasn't even aware I had magic. I was just an ordinary human in Midgard."

"Which, again, baffles me," Torsten said after draining his mug and refilling it with wine. "All those years ago, Markus wasn't Fraalver, but it was never documented where he came from or what race he belonged to. He just...was."

That certainly didn't make me feel better.

"There was no indication of magic when you were younger? No rogue fires or..." he pointed to the ceiling again, "surprise caved ceilings?"

Pressing a smile away from my lips, I shook my head. "Not a single spark nor boulder bent to my whim. I just...was." Funny, I was just like my father.

"Rorik and I suspect that her magic may have, in a sense, awoken once she crossed over into the realm," Aaren said and sat back, his remarkable eyes warm like hardened honey.

Torsten agreed, saying that it wasn't uncommon for magic to dilute or disappear entirely upon crossing realms.

"At least it tells us one thing," Aaren said as he pushed his plate to the side and cupped his mug. "At least we know what we're up against."

The dinner topics, much to my relief, shifted away from my parentage and onto other matters, such as the current growing season in each village, and how the changes in the weather promised a better bounty than last year.

Once dinner was cleared, Torsten stood and beckoned us to follow, leading us toward our rooms for the night. Oswin and Ivar excused themselves, explaining that they were promised *at least* one ale—to which Aaren gave them an annoyed side eye—and strode down the tunnel back to the valley. Torsten showed Axl and Von to their rooms, the former closing the door immediately behind him with a polite nod, the latter taking a quick look around inside, then skittering down the hall to join Oswin and Ivar.

Fiske's room was only a few doors down from Von's and promised a large bathtub, which Torsten joked would feel more like home. Now at the end of the hall, Torsten led Aaren and me up a stone spiral staircase that he claimed was only fifty stairs—but felt like two hundred—and onto a landing that led into another hall. Only a few feet away was a large bronze door that creaked loudly on its hinges when Torsten pushed it open.

I loved Skoghjem, and Kysthjem was terrific too, but this room made me miss my room at Aaren's a little less. Across from the main door were two glass balcony doors, plated with gold accents that highlighted the mountain range beyond. Ornate rugs covered the stone floor, and a hefty pelt of a large creature I had read about and couldn't remember the name of was spread out in front of the crackling fireplace to the left. Across the room from the fireplace and the two velvet armchairs in front of it was a massive bed covered with furs that made my skin tingle in anticipation of spreading out on them. The headboard was carved from fine marble, matching the two bedside tables positioned along either side, each adorned with bottles of wine and a spread of bread, cheese, and dried fruits. In the far left corner, a few feet away from the fireplace, was another bronze door that led to the bathing room.

"I hope this is to your liking," Torsten said.

"Wonderful, Torsten," Aaren replied before I could voice my stuttering realization: there was only one bed. Thea would be jumping for joy, knowing one of her romance book tropes had proven to be true.

"Excellent," Torsten chimed, then turned with his hand on the door. "Good evening to you two. I look forward to speaking with you more tomorrow."

And with that, the door closed behind him, and I was alone with my husband.

Aaren strode towards the bed, unstrapped his sword from his side, and threw it down on the furs. "What is with the perplexed look on your face?" he asked as he shed his coat and dislodged his handful of throwing stars from their holster across his chest.

I snapped my jaw shut after realizing it had been hanging open and moved away from the door. "Nothing," I answered, walking up to the glass doors and peering through them.

Aaren finished disarming himself and then hid his weapons in various places around the room, in case of another attack like the night before. It was unlikely, but never impossible, especially in these times.

"I need a bath," Aaren sighed in a voice gruff with exhaustion. He pivoted to the bathing room door and offered a sarcastically salacious smirk when his hand stopped on the handle. "Care to join?"

"Don't flatter yourself," I snorted, but the images that flashed through my head sent a blissful shiver down my spine.

Aaren huffed, then turned away from me with a look like he knew exactly what just went through my head. "Suit yourself."

As the bathing room door closed, I stepped outside onto the balcony, the mountain range a welcome sight considering I couldn't get the image of a naked Aaren out of my head.

The stars in the sky winked and flickered, and I leaned against the stone railing, basking in the cool breeze that brought a comforting shiver to my arms. My eyes traced the peaks in the distance, counting each one and following the dips and curves of the range. Could Lucas be hiding in these valleys, in the caverns or gorges in the land of Fjellhjem?

Of course, Lucas occupied my mind every day, more so lately, considering all I had time to do was think during our travels. But it still didn't feel enough, especially since every step I took towards him felt like a step back. How much further did I have to delve into Alveland to find him? I hoped he hadn't forgotten about me, or lost hope that I was coming for him. He had to know I was coming for him; he had to know that I would stop at nothing to find him, even if it meant I had to marry a foreign lord and train until I physically couldn't carry myself. He had to know that, but what lies was Markus telling my brother?

I sighed and dropped my forehead to the stone rail, taking a deep breath before my thoughts got the better of me.

The door of the bathing room creaked open, and I stepped through the open balcony doors, only to freeze in my tracks.

Aaren's back was to me, utterly naked.

The scar along his back was stark in this lighting, accented by the muscles that cut deep and ridged to meet at his spine. My eyes followed down, down, studying the cut lines at his base, the outline of his buttocks. He had let his hair down, and it fell below his shoulders, where the silken strands clung to the water droplets that freckled his skin.

"Enjoying the view?" Aaren asked without turning.

Words evaded me as I ripped my gaze from the gnarled scar on his back and, unsure what else to do, I scurried wordlessly into the bathing room and closed the door behind me. The heat from his bath still filled the space, and I breathed in the warm scent of lavender that had mingled with the musky, forested scent of Aaren. I loved that scent. It smelled like Skoghjem and the breezes he summoned along the pathways. It smelled like home. And that leather scent he carried with him, that second half of his aroma, I couldn't place why it had been so familiar. Wherever I knew it from, it sent a twinge of nostalgia when it filled my nostrils.

When I emerged from the bathing room after a much-needed bath, Aaren was clothed and sitting by the fire with a goblet of wine in his hand. He had placed a log strategically into the fire, waiting for the flames to catch, but was unsuccessful; instead, he stared at the simmering embers.

"Help me out?" he asked over his shoulder.

Heart still fluttering at the image of his naked backside ingrained in my mind, I sent that feeling to my hands. My palms heated, and then I shot a small tunnel of flame at the wood. The fire crackled delightedly as if it were happy to be revived.

I poured myself a goblet of wine and sank into the chair next to him, savoring the sweet notes of blackberry and sage that painted my tongue. My eyes darted around the room, inspecting the minor details of the rock and the small knick-knacks that decorated the mantle. Next to a large rat-like creature that had been crystallized in amber was a miniature painting of a young woman. I squinted to take in her blonde hair and blossom lips akin to Ertha's.

Discomfort made me shift in my chair when I realized who was in this painting.

"That's her, isn't it?" I asked when I realized Aaren's gaze had been avoiding the mantle. His eyes went vacant as he nodded stiffly. "What was she like?" I asked.

Aaren shot me a questioning look as he swallowed a mouthful of wine, his lips painted red, and his tongue darted out to clean them. I swallowed thickly and buried my eyes in my own goblet.

"She was very beautiful," he replied, "and kind. And just...right."

Jealousy stirred inside me, and guilt that I wasn't her, and I never could be. Perhaps it was a question I shouldn't have asked, but could I really be faulted for wanting to know the girl I was unfairly compared to?

"And she had these beautiful blue eyes. Blue like the waters of Kysthjem."

My eyes were green, green like the forest I now claimed as home.

Aaren's grip tightened on his goblet. "The last time I was in these halls, we were still betrothed."

I couldn't imagine how hard being here was for him. Maybe I could, if it was like the feeling I got the last time I was at Granny's house. It was the day after she died, and everything in there suddenly felt foreign, like all her things now belonged to someone else. That familiar aroma of leather swirled in my nose, either from Aaren or the memory of Granny's house, but before I could dwell on it, he spoke again.

"The last time I saw her was just before Pesta took my parents."

I didn't know what to say, so I let him continue.

"She had come to stay at the village to become acquainted with my people before the marriage." A reminiscing smile spread across his lips, displaying his perfect teeth. "She woke up one morning and walked the whole village five times to make sure she knew her way around as soon as possible." He chuckled. "She looked like a lunatic walking that path for hours. But she was determined.

"Then Pesta came to Skoghjem, and Solveig wanted to go back. She was so fierce when she got it into her head to do something, and she was going to help my people...her people. But I didn't let her. I couldn't."

I moved my hand to grab his, but stopped myself, my fingers instead gripping the arm of the chair.

"I had just lost my parents, I couldn't lose her, too." His smile had faded, hard guilt etching his features. "But Pesta came and took Solveig. And not only was I now the sole leader of Skoghjem, but I had just lost everyone who could ever help me. Everyone except Rorik."

264

Now I knew why Rorik was always with Aaren—it wasn't Rorik micromanaging Aaren, it was Aaren truly needing him.

"I sometimes wonder what would've happened to Solveig if I had let her come to Skoghjem. Maybe she would've survived."

"You know it's not your fault," I said, studying the way his eyes danced with the firelight.

"That's what they tell me," he replied and drained the rest of his goblet.

When he sat back down, he brought the pitcher of wine with him and topped off my drink.

"Enough about me," he said with a sigh, choosing the skin rug instead of the chair. I joined him, careful not to spill my full wine. "I know all about your Mama and Granny. Tell me about Lucas."

I smiled warmly as the wine opened me up. "There's so much to tell," I sighed, shimmying into a comfortable position on the rug.

"Tell me your favorite story of him," Aaren said in a deeper voice now that the wine was setting in.

My eyes rolled to the ceiling as I thought, but Aaren's gaze draped me in warmth. He watched me as I laughed to myself and drank deeply before beginning my story.

"Lucas used to be this really timid child. He hid from pretty much anyone that wasn't me and barely spoke until he was about five years old." We were in our first foster home, shortly before we were relocated to the one I tried to run away from. Lucas had just turned four, and another kid kept picking on him because Lucas was an easy target. He was smaller and younger than his bully, and he was pushed around when our foster parents' backs were turned.

It was one of the reasons why they discourage having multiple foster children from different families in the same house. Of course, fifty percent of the time it works out, but Lucas and I fell into the other fifty percent.

There was only so much I could do to stop it—I couldn't be around all the time to keep this kid at bay. To remedy this, I told Lucas he needed to stand up for himself, as much as a four-year-old could to a six-year-old. I promised him that I would never get mad at him if he fought back, even if our foster parents did. To him, my approval was the only thing that mattered.

One day, Lucas was in our room coloring when our foster brother came in, snatched the marker out of his hand, and scribbled across his picture. Seeing as he was already quite the artist for his age, this struck a chord in him that no other act of violence had. His bully could punch him, steal his snack, but the minute he messed with Lucas's pictures, it was war.

I was in the hallway, making my way to our room just in time to hear my brother let out a war cry, then push the kid to the ground before scribbling across his face with a permanent marker he had snatched from my school bag. By the time the kid had pushed him off, half of his face was covered in black lines and circles that took days to fade. Lucas, of course, lost his art privileges, but that foster brother never messed with him again. Besides, we had an agreement—if I snuck him colored pencils and paper, he could color at night after bedtime.

"I was so proud of him," I said, smiling into my goblet.

"What a little fighter you raised," Aaren grinned. "Maybe he could teach Nilsen a few things."

I swallowed my wine. "Hey, Nilsen can be quite the warrior, too. He's saved me twice, after all."

Aaren waved that aside. "Yeah, yeah, but don't let him fool you. You've never heard him squeal at the sight of a cockroach."

I threw back my head and laughed. Aaren joined me as our goblets emptied, and we poured the last of the pitcher.

"Can I ask you a question?" Aaren asked, the air of mirth around us blowing away with the smoke through the chimney.

Cautiously, I replied, "Sure."

"When you purged Markus, you were apologizing, but not to me or Rorik. Were you apologizing to Lucas?"

I bit my lip. If I had known this was the question he was going to ask, I wouldn't have agreed to answer. Aaren read the thought on my face.

"You don't have to answer..."

I shook my head. "You told me something about your past. It's only fair if I do the same." I took a deep breath, pressing down the coiling anxiety that was starting to wake up at the repressed memories I was about to unpack.

"We lived in a bad foster home," I began, taking a quick breath to steady my already shaking voice. This was the foster home we were sent to after the incident involving the marker. "Our foster mom was strict to a fault. Withholding meals was the most common punishment. She made me sleep outside in freezing

266

weather once because I mouthed off to her." Swishing the remnants of my wine in the goblet, I willed myself to continue. "We weren't bad kids, Lucas and I. He was young, still learning the difference between right and wrong. I was sixteen."

Aaren's brows quirked in understanding. "And we both know the desire to rebel as a teenager."

The tension eased at his comment, and I gave him a quick, awkward smile. "Exactly. I got into a lot more trouble than Lucas. But when he was punished, my world felt like it was ending."

Like Lucas with his bully, there were a lot of things I would let slide before I snapped. I gladly took any punishments if it meant Lucas was safe. But the minute he was in trouble, I lashed out.

My throat tightened as I remembered the stuffed rabbit Lucas towed with him everywhere. It came from Granny's house, something found in her bedroom after she passed away, and given to Lucas as a token of her memory. The thing was flimsy and matted with love, and it had to be pried out of his little hands to be washed. He would sit next to the washing machine and watch as the rabbit went round and round in the soap. One day, Lucas had a particularly rowdy fit as every child his age does, and knocked over a lamp, shattering it on the hardwood floor. Our foster mother flew into a blind rage and snatched the rabbit from the crook of his arm, and I could still remember the devastation on his face as she decapitated it and threw it into the fireplace. Poor Lucas dirtied his hands trying to piece the ashes back together once the fire died.

I hadn't noticed it, but Aaren's hand had balled into a fist, veins protruding along his forearm and up to his rune.

"I tried to run away," I continued, swallowing that overwhelmingly large lump in my throat. "I thought that if I ran away, I would find us a way out of that house."

I could find a job or beg for money—I would take anything to make sure I could keep Lucas safe. "I couldn't do it with him, though. That foster home was still safer than coming with me. At least he would be fed and have a bed to sleep in. If I took him with me, then we both would suffer."

"And did you?" Aaren asked, his eyes like pools of honey. "Did you run away?"

I shook my head. "No. He woke up before I could slip out. How can you tell a child that you're leaving them behind like that?" I finished my wine and wiped my mouth on my sleeve, not caring how uncouth I looked. "The night I

267

purged Markus, he tried to use that night against me. To convince me that Lucas hated me for trying to leave."

Tears stung my eyes that threatened to pool over onto my cheeks, but Aaren's warm hand draped over mine stopped them.

"Don't you ever blame yourself for that, do you hear me?"

I blinked at the disparity between the soft gesture of his hand holding mine and the intensity in his voice, his eyes, boring into me with something like hardened pride.

"Don't ever blame yourself for trying to take care of your family. Even if no one else can see it for what it is. Never apologize for that."

Isn't that what both of us had done when we married each other? We joined together and solidified the borders so that he could protect Nilsen and his people. So that I could be one step closer to finding Lucas.

"We're going to find him, Layla. I will stop at nothing to make sure he is brought back untouched."

I wasn't sure what I expected when I asked him why, but the answer made my heart flutter.

"Because you deserve to have him back. After everything you've sacrificed for him."

Aaren wiped a tear away with his thumb, then circled my cheek as he gazed into my eyes. The wine must be affecting his judgement—he had never been so tender with me or spoken so sweetly. I must've been just as drunk because I wanted more of whatever it was he was giving.

I blinked, about to fall into his eyes, when cold air bit my cheek as his hand left me.

"I...I think we finished all the wine," he said, holding up the empty pitcher.

Shaking myself out of this stupor, whatever trance he had lured me into, I let out an awkward chuckle and moved away. Standing proved to be a lot harder than I expected, and Aaren guided me to the bed where I nestled into the furs with a delighted sigh.

When I opened my eyes, the spot next to me was barren and cold, and I searched for Aaren. Through the darkness, I saw his sleeping form on the floor next to the fire.

The night was not long enough for Ertha to change her mind about me, though I can't say I expected otherwise. She at least attended breakfast with us and agreed on the strategy meeting scheduled immediately after, but it didn't stop her from sending hostile glares and snide comments at me across the breakfast table.

Aaren and I weren't the only ones who drank more than we should've last night. In fact, I'd say we made it out better than the rest of our company after the way they slumped into the dining room. I chuckled through a mouthful of eggs at the way Ivar's hair stuck out at odd angles, and Oswin's beard had been braided and tied off with blue bows. Who did that to him, I'm sure he would never say, but it didn't stop Axl from throwing quiet jabs at him. Von, being a lot younger than Oswin and Ivar, fared better through the evening, and according to them, even picked up a lovely lady to spend the night with. Von's cheeks reddened when his new companion was brought up, and he hid his face in a mug of juice until Ivar stopped taunting him.

"Kora has been talking up her new brew for days," Torsten said and eyed the suffering half of our company. "Is it as good as she says?"

Ivar covered his mouth, shoulders lurching at the mention of ale. Oswin pushed away his breakfast. I couldn't say I envied them; looking at Ivar's green cheeks made me feel lucky that I scraped by with a headache after my night with Aaren.

"Whatever was in it, looks like it was potent," Axl observed through an amused smile, and I wish I could've gotten a picture of it. It wasn't every day I saw Axl smile. It was like seeing snow for the first time in forever.

Torsten smacked the table, delighting in the winces and grumbles he earned from Oswin and Ivar. "Eat up, men, we've got some planning to do."

Chapter 34

Back in the meeting hall in the same seats as the day before, the strategy meeting began.

And right off the bat, I was both annoyed and fired up.

"With all due respect, Layla," Torsten began, and I knew I wasn't going to like a word out of his mouth. "I'm still not fully convinced that Markus is alive. I—"

"What is he doing then, fucking wenches from the coffin?" Oswin demanded, which sent Ivar into a violent snort that did little to rein in his laughter. I started to protest—one of those wenches was my mother after all—but a quick warning glance from Aaren shut them up. Their shoulders still shook with silent laughter, but quiet enough that I could ignore them.

Aaren leaned forward, weaving his fingers through each other. "And what evidence do you have that he's even dead?"

"I see the existence of his tomb as evidence enough," Torsten snapped.

This still didn't convince Aaren, which sent a swell of pride fluttering into my heart. Something about his taking my word over his diplomatic equal made me feel important. I did my best to send my feelings of gratitude through the rune.

"What tomb?" Aaren asked, earning him a challenging look from both Ertha and Torsten.

"Do I detect doubt in your tone, Aaren?" Torsten quipped, more amused at the challenge than offended. When Aaren replied with a cocked brow, Torsten sat back and sighed. "There is a tomb in the Fjerneda valley that is said to belong to Markus Sviker. It's called Fjellgrav, and I know it to be his tomb because I've seen his very name etched into the stone outside it."

Aaren sighed. "Then this just got a lot more complicated."

Ertha eyed him. "Or maybe Markus is dead, and your *wife* is wrong about her parentage."

270

Oh, game on, bitch.

My eyes rose to the ceiling to emphasize that the crack I had caused yesterday had yet to be repaired. Pointing my finger at the damage, I smirked. "I'll make it worse just to prove to you how right I am."

Von whistled low as the tension grew exponentially.

I thanked the heavens for Aaren and his level head. "A few weeks ago, one of my men was attacked by the mylings," he said. Our company hushed at the mention of Dagan. "Somehow, that myling implanted a piece of Markus into Dagan's body and sent him after Layla because she is the key to manipulating the curse. How could he have possessed Dagan's body if he was dead?"

Torsten rubbed the stubble across his chin, eyes going to that crack on the ceiling as he contemplated.

"How could he have conceived me if he were dead?" I added. I almost relished the glare I earned from Ertha.

"You know nothing of the spirits in this realm, girl," she spat.

Axl, to my surprise, scoffed. Aaren turned, just as surprised as I was.

"Possession of another living body requires an ancient kind of magic, one that requires both the conjuror and possessor to be alive," Axl said at a volume I hadn't known he was capable of. "Markus couldn't have possessed Dagan if he were dead."

Ivar patted him on the back. "He may not speak much, but when he does, you'd better listen!"

Axl brushed him off and muttered something about that being common knowledge.

Fiske, who had remained uncharacteristically quiet throughout the deliberation, cleared his throat. "You know the only way to be sure if Markus is really dead, right?"

"Don't say it, Fiske," Von groaned.

Fiske shrugged. "We have to go to Fjellgrav."

We ended the meeting with decision to travel to the tomb tomorrow.

Today, Aaren told me we needed to catch up on the training we had missed since being on the road. Normally, I would've groaned, but I had a lot of pent-up energy. And perhaps some aggression that needed to be released.

Aaren and I stepped out into the bright sunlight, squinting as our pupils adjusted from the darkness within the mountain. There was a small patch of space on the bank of the roaring river, a short distance away from the pub where Boden could already be seen drunkenly swaying on the porch. The rushing rapids echoed through the expansive valley, mingling with the breeze that rustled the leaves around us, as nature seemed to play us a symphony.

Sweeping his hair into a loose bun, Aaren didn't waste any time in launching his first attack. His fist connected with my gut, and I dropped to my knees when the breath fled my lungs.

"What the—"

Aaren gave me an arrogant smirk, bouncing on the balls of his feet. I fought the urge to call him a prick when his smirk grew into a teasing smile.

"I didn't even get time to stretch," I spat, finally able to push myself to my feet. I massaged the spot where he struck, knowing there would be a nasty bruise by the end of the day.

Aaren shook his head haughtily, still bouncing and warming up his joints. I didn't get to stretch, but he got to warm up. The odds were unfairly stacked. "Your enemies don't care that you haven't stretched," Aaren said, giving me just enough time to blink before he launched into his second attack, charging straight towards me.

Panic struck me, but I moved just in time, rolling on the bank and caking mud in my hair. I cringed silently—it would take me days to scrub this mud away. It was a while before I felt clean again after the trehag fight. He chuckled as I stood, examining the mud painting my cheeks from a distance.

"I'm a little offended you would rather roll in the mud than face me, *fremmed*," Aaren taunted as he circled me.

I tried to swipe some of the mud away. "You're a prick," I spat, shaking out my hands in what little preparation I could manage before his next onslaught.

"A prick with the upper hand."

I snarled, then launched into a sloppy, aggravation-fueled attack that had me back on the ground faster than last time. I growled in frustration and slammed my fist into the bank, not even caring about the splatters of mud that now freckled my cheeks.

Aaren, finding it in him to be sympathetic, strode over to me. "Alright, *fremmed*, since you look so pitiful, all muddied up like that." He offered me an outstretched hand.

Big mistake.

I drove my fist into his groin and stood, satisfied to see him drop to his knees, features pinched with pain.

"Now who's the pitiful one?" I chided, dancing on the balls of my feet. With the bit of time I earned, I could now start to warm up properly.

Aaren finally stood and let out a long, pained breath. "That was uncalled for," he hissed.

I shrugged. "You told me the cock was the best place to strike a man."

He nodded to himself, evidently regretting sharing that tip with me. "I didn't think you would ever use that against me, *fremmed*."

"Maybe next time you'll let me stretch—"

Thundering footsteps barreled towards me, then Aaren's shoulder caught me in the gut and hauled me off the ground. There was a tiny window of seconds where he held me suspended, which I took to my advantage. Maybe I was playing dirty, but Aaren started it when he punched me first.

I shoved my knee hard enough into his chest that he released me, and for the third time, I tumbled into the mud.

Aaren recovered quicker than I had banked on, so I scrambled to my feet quickly and assumed my stance.

"Is that how we're going to play today?" he asked, his tone far less playful than before. Mild fear pooled in my stomach like cement. Perhaps I had gone too far, especially since I wasn't ready to pay the price for my actions. There was something in his expression I had only glimpsed a handful of times in the sparring ring, but never this intense. His eyes darkened, and a primal shadow crossed his features. He looked almost feral.

Which meant I was screwed if I didn't get ahead of his next attack.

Panicking, I lunged forward, side-stepping Aaren as he reached for me and dove for the softer part of the bank where the water lapped. The look in Aaren's eyes didn't say he wanted to kill me, but I wasn't sure what kind of damage his dirty fighting could inflict—desperate times called for desperate measures.

My fingers dipped into the water, the cool energy sliding across my digits. There was a thrumming energy within the current, just like the waves of Kysthjem, and I tried to imagine what that energy felt like in an emotion. It wasn't anger; there was too much vibrancy in the water for rage. Perhaps it was elation, the kind I felt when I drank the right amount of caffeine. The sort of elation I felt every time I picked Lucas up for the day.

The water met me as if it understood the feeling, and that energy crept along my skin, up my wrist, and to my arms. The energy brought the water too, tendrils of cool snaking up my arms. Not only was the water on my skin, but I felt it in my veins, as if it were flushing the red blood and replacing it with cool, blue blood.

I was in control.

"*Fremmed?*" Aaren asked from a few feet away. He didn't sound fired up anymore, instead concerned by my sudden lack of assaults.

An uncontrollable smile spread across my lips as I turned. "*This* is how we're playing today."

I threw my arms out, and a thundering tunnel of water barreled towards him. Aaren could only take a single step back before the turbulent water slammed into him, his feet flying out from under his body. He flew a few feet back before thudding to the ground, coughing as the water receded.

As the water's energy ebbed from my veins, so did the euphoric high I floated on. And then my jaw dropped.

Holy shit.

I just rammed my husband with a violent tunnel of river water.

"Aaren!" I called, springing forward the short distance and kneeling before him. He rolled over and spat out water onto the mud before he clumsily brushed his stringy, wet hair from his face.

He blinked. "Ow."

At least it was better than the agonizing scream I had been expecting.

"Are you alright?" I asked, frantic now that the elation was nearly gone.

"I'm fine." His wince said otherwise.

Shit. "You're hurt."

"I'll be alright," he assured, then stood with a groan from deep in his chest.

"No, you're hurt, let me help you."

The grimace pinching his features never eased as we walked back into the mountain. Navigating the stairs was tough, but he managed to ascend them with little more than gritting his teeth and quiet groans.

When Aaren dropped onto the bed after limping into our room, he sighed in relief.

"What hurts?" I questioned, trying to fluff the furs around him.

"I'm fine, *fremmed*," he said, but I wasn't convinced. He didn't want to tell me, which tipped me off as to why.

"It's your back, isn't it?" I asked, crossing my arms over my chest. When Aaren didn't answer, I pushed him further. "*Isn't it?*"

He let out a resigned sigh. "Yes."

I hummed, waiting for him to meet my eyes, but he never did. "How can I help?"

A beat of silence passed between us while Aaren only stared at the ceiling. He needed me, I knew that was why he wasn't telling me.

Finally, he answered. "There's a bottle of oil in my pack. I need you to massage the muscles along the scar."

Obeying his instructions, I retrieved the bottle and returned to the bed, my mouth going dry when I watched him throw his shirt over his head and lie face down in the furs.

Close up, the scar along his spine looked deeper, more gnarled than it had from a distance. His shoulder blades curved to give way to the sculpted muscles of his traps and deltoids.

"This is going to hurt you, isn't it?" I asked.

Aaren hesitated, then answered, "Yes."

I dumped a generous amount of oil into my palms, letting it drip onto his back like raindrops.

"Just do it, don't give me a warning," Aaren said, voice muffled by the furs. "Rorik normally—"

I pressed my thumbs into the small of his back, meeting biting tension that fought against my touch. Aaren howled as he flinched, and I sent a silent apology through the rune. I heated my hands to help loosen the muscles, and he stilled, his back rising as he took a steadying breath, then another.

This was why Rorik was on his case about taking it easy in the ring. I hadn't realized it was because of anything other than Rorik trying to mother-hen him.

I moved my thumb along his spine, drilling small circles into his muscles. He didn't make a sound as I worked, and I dumped another hefty amount of oil into my hands before running them down his back. His muscles loosened under my touch as I dug my knuckles in, only imagining what kind of pain this was causing him.

"Why are you so ashamed of this scar?" I asked, shaking out my hands when they began to cramp.

Aaren turned his head so his carved profile could be seen. His expression was deep set, rugged, and his jaw clenched when I dug my thumbs back in. "It's an unpleasant memory," he said after releasing a quiet groan when the muscle under my thumb loosened.

"More unpleasant than the pain?"

He nodded.

"It was a hudflasker," he said after a moment of contemplation. "A shapeshifter."

I took my hands away, but he didn't move.

"I was in the woods, two years ago..."

Leadership was proving to be far more difficult than his parents had made it seem, and that day, it weighed on him more heavily than usual. The crop wasn't coming in as well as it was projected to, so he had to help devise a plan to subsidize their stores and find an alternative source of food, especially as the nights grew colder and winter drew closer. Nilsen had also had a particularly rough day, having gotten into an argument with Ingrid about the gnome infestation in the treehouse. Aaren had to act as mediator to their elementary squabble, then call in Rorik to get rid of the gnomes himself. The weight of being a leader and an impromptu father was bearing down on him, an ailment only the forest could cure.

Aaren hadn't left the village looking for a fight, but he certainly wouldn't balk if he found one.

Heading nowhere in particular, Aaren found himself close to the river and decided to follow it a few miles down to the rapids. Maybe he'd stumble upon a huldra and lose himself in a fight for a little bit. It would at least get his mind off his burdensome responsibilities.

All hopes of that dissipated when his eyes caught blonde hair. And blue eyes.

"Aaren?" Solveig's voice asked.

He blinked, pleading with himself not to believe what his eyes were seeing. Solveig was dead, had been for some time, and yet here she was, crouched on the bank, covered in mud and wearing tattered clothes. She looked like she had been in the forest for ages, wearied but still just as bright as the last time he saw her.

"I found you," Solveig said and rose from the bank. "I've been trying to get here for months. And I've finally found you." Tears brimmed in her marvelous eyes, making the blue of her irises even more stunning.

She stepped forward, and Aaren stepped back. Her face fell, eyes losing that twinkle. "I thought you'd want to see me," she said through a disappointed whimper. And damn it if the sound didn't snap something already broken inside Aaren.

It wasn't her, it couldn't be. But no matter how many times he told himself this, seeing her standing in front of him made it so difficult to believe. Every day, for weeks, months, years, he had been dreaming of her. He had no peace without her, not when her ghost continued to haunt him every time he closed his eyes. Out of all the responsibilities he had, all the burdens he carried, some days it was still an effort to think of anything else but her.

And here she was, in front of him, just like he had been begging whatever gods were left for.

Aaren allowed Solveig to take another step closer.

"I couldn't stay in Fjellhjem, not when you were here."

Another step closer, then another, and she was in front of him, blue eyes glowing and cheeks flushed despite the mud freckling her cheeks. In retrospect, it was astounding to him that he allowed her to get so close, and yet he couldn't stop her from lifting her hand, couldn't stop from nestling into the fingers that

277

cupped his cheek. He may even have touched her back, kissed her palm, sighed into her touch.

"My love," she cooed.

Something soft and wet trickled along his cheekbone, down his jaw, and when he opened his eyes, tears blurred his vision.

"I've missed you so much, *vakker.*"

A nickname he had given her because that was precisely what she was— beautiful.

Aaren hadn't realized he'd pulled her closer, that their lips were almost seconds away from brushing, but something stopped him, something cold and foreign. The pain didn't register immediately, but something warm slid down his back.

"Solveig?"

Her beautiful face twisted, the contours of her cheeks contorting into a grim smile, the resemblance to the real girl faltering.

Then the pain hit. Not pain. Agony. Raw and biting like a blade, tearing into flesh. He went to shove the thing away, the face now rippling like dough under a baker's knuckles. The real creature was beginning to show, and Aaren wasn't prepared for the horror of watching his dead betrothed's face rip away and reveal what was beneath. The hudflasker didn't let him go, though, instead sinking its claws deeper into his back and grinning as he cried out in pain.

Aaren gave one more hard shove, and the hudflasker fell away, but not before the damage to his back was done.

Blood now poured down his back, the pain excruciating as shadows clouded the edges of his vision. Moving his upper body was harder as part of his back was no longer attached to his spine. Not deep enough to cause nerve damage, he thanked Himmelfjell, but enough that fighting back would be challenging.

The hudflasker, now fully transformed to its original form, reared back for another attack, but it didn't get the chance.

He dug his fingers into the creature's throat, tips digging into the squishy flesh, but he balked when the skin rippled again. Blue eyes stared back at him again, and Solveig's blossom lips parted as he choked her.

"Aaren," she begged in a mangled groan. "Please..."

"I love you," he whispered, then ripped her throat out, tossing it into the rumbling rapids.

With his last remaining bit of strength, Aaren tossed her body into the river and turned away before she was lost to the whitewater.

It was a wonder that he made it back to the village without bleeding out.

It took Rorik and Asta two days to set him back the way he was, and even then, it took months of training and exercise to work around his new injury. While he healed physically, his heart never would.

I stared down at the scar under my hands, seeing it in a whole new light. I was almost afraid to touch it again.

"I'm...I'm so sorry, Aaren," I muttered. I didn't miss the single tear that trailed down his nose and onto the furs underneath him.

He pushed himself up, stretching his neck and softly swinging his shoulders. "Much better," he said. He didn't look any less distraught, but the mask of undisturbed leadership was sliding back into place.

We shared a quiet lunch, both lost in our own thoughts. I had no idea that scar came from something so devastating. No wonder Rorik was constantly griping after Aaren. I thought I fully understood Aaren and why he was so hardened, but knowing the story behind that scar opened my eyes to so much more. It was astonishing how he was able to keep his cool after basically strangling his dead lover, hudflasker or not. I tried to put myself in his shoes, imagining what I would've done if the hudflasker had taken the form of Mama or Granny, but the thought was unbearable.

Aaren excused himself after finishing the last of his ale, and I went to find the others, hoping to pass the time until dinner. Oswin and Ivar were face down on the bar when I left the pub, either sleeping off their hangovers or making it worse. Axl was nowhere to be found, and I caught Von pining after the girl he had met last night, pulling her into an alcove inside the mountain where she let out a pleasured squeal. I plugged my ears and moved on.

I trailed along the corridors, brushing my fingers over the cool stone as I moved. The architecture of Fjellhjem was unique—they drew inspiration from the surrounding mountains to decorate their walls and etch the stone. There were tapestries of vast mountain ranges along the halls and carvings of beautiful gorges and rivers that chiseled through the valleys. My footsteps echoed along the corridor, but the sound of voices slowed my pace until I located them in a room on my right.

"I think you are being a bit harsh, dear," Torsten advised cautiously.

"I don't think you're being harsh enough, *dear*," Ertha retorted, and I clenched my fists together, already annoyed. I wondered if she knew about Aaren's injury and how he got it.

I took the smallest step forward, creeping close to the door where the voices originated. Inside was the small library that housed Torsten's personal collection of tomes he had boasted about over dinner the night before. Pacing before the fire was Ertha, her usually pristine blonde hair disheveled, and her features were screwed tightly as she bubbled with anger.

Torsten sat in an armchair opposite the fire, reclining on an arm and rubbing his thumb and forefinger together. His expression was calm, contrasting with the way Ertha was seething.

"I'm not sure you realize how counterintuitive this is," Torsten said calmly. "There is something greater working against us, and whether it is Markus or something else, we need to keep our alliances strong."

Ertha scoffed. "We're all Fraalver; there will always be an alliance between our villages."

Torsten pressed his lips together and rubbed at his temples. "If you continue to cause such strife between us, our only alliance will crumble."

She stopped in her tracks, fists balled tightly, and I swore I could see smoke billowing from her ears. "I'm not *trying* to cause strife, Torsten! I think that it is dangerous to let someone from outside our race into leadership! Layla isn't Fraalver; she brings a threat to our village and the very foundation we were built on."

I stepped away and focused on my breathing because if I didn't, this whole mountain was going to crumble to the ground. And once it started, there was no way to stop it.

"Is she a threat to us or to your memory of Solveig?"

I could see Ertha's face harden in my mind as a tense moment of silence passed. "Do *not* bring Solveig into this, Torsten." Her voice was low and lethal. One wrong word, and Torsten could be dead. And yet he continued, unfazed.

"Ertha dear, you already have. Is that not the reason why you are so upset?"

"I never said that."

Torsten lifted his brow. "You didn't have to." I peered carefully back into the library in time to see him stand and close the short distance between him and his wife. "It's only been a few years. It's okay to hurt still." Ertha did not meet his eye when he cupped her face, though she fell into the touch, lower lip trembling as her eyes lined with silver. "But you cannot make your grief the fault of anyone else. It is not Layla's fault that she isn't Solveig, and it isn't Aaren's for putting his people first."

Ertha pulled away and turned to face the fire, heaving a labored sigh. "I just miss her so much."

Torsten brought his hands to her shoulders, thumbs rubbing in small circles. "I know, dear," he soothed. "And she is in the halls of Himmelfjell with her grandparents."

Another soft sob, and Ertha turned, cheeks ruddy with distraught tears. She pressed her face into Torsten's chest and cried, letting him run his fingers through her golden strands as he held her.

When she pulled away, she had collected herself enough to speak. "I'm sorry for my behavior."

"It's not me you need to apologize to."

I turned away when Torsten pressed a kiss to her lips, only to slam face-first into a figure shrouded in a dark cloak.

"Nosey, aren't we?" Axl asked.

Frantically pressing a finger to my lips, I snatched his hand and yanked him down the hall. When we were out of earshot, I rolled my eyes.

"I'm not nosey," I hissed. "I was just...curious."

Axl nodded sarcastically, that small flicker of a smile passing over his lips. "Yes, and I love sunshine and rainbows."

I rolled my eyes again, letting out a frustrated groan this time. "What are *you* doing here, I might ask."

He crossed his arms. "For someone who isn't nosy, you ask a lot of questions."

Chapter 35

I wasn't going to deny the trepidation I woke with the next day, especially considering we were embarking on yet another journey so soon after the last. Not to mention where we were going. It's not every day you ride off on horseback to your dead-but-maybe-not-dead father's tomb.

As I stroked Froki's mane and ignored her side eye—she seemed to be just as perturbed at the journey as I was—Torsten approached, clad in riding gear.

"We'll be on the road two days at most, but if we stick to the Lettja Pass, it'll be a day and a half," he said, tugging on his gloves before grabbing the reins and leading his horse from the stable.

"And when we get there?" Oswin grumbled, shoving extra stores of bread and cheese into his pack.

Torsten sighed. "It is unlikely we'll find burrowers inside the tomb, but draugr are most certainly guaranteed."

I shuddered at the thought.

Draugr were the resurrected corpses of soldiers, doomed to wander their tombs for eternity. Their primary intent was to protect their treasures buried within their tombs. Depending on the fortifications of their tombs and the nature of who they were before they died, sometimes draugr broke free from their crypts and wreaked havoc on whatever they could, Thea's husband being an unfortunate example. Some acted as protectors of a deceased, higher-ranking individual. In this case, that would be Markus. Either way, they were deadly.

"I am most certain Markus would've lined his tomb with his followers," Torsten said grimly and mounted his horse. "With the number of enemies made in life, I'd expect he'd want as much protection in death."

I shuddered again, blood running cold in my veins.

Unease settled in my stomach like lead when I mounted Froki and followed the group along the valley path. As much as I wanted to be right about my parentage, to know for sure that Markus was the one behind all the destruction happening to the Fraalver, a small part of me hoped we were wrong. That would mean that I didn't descend from a power-hungry madman with a breeding complex.

As my thoughts ran unchecked, my unease turned to a full dose of dread, a feeling I hadn't realized had me shaking in the saddle until Aaren spurred his horse next to mine, features heavy with subtle worry.

"What's wrong?" he asked in a hushed voice, his horse slowing its pace as the others trudged ahead.

"I'm fine," I said stiffly, trying to kick Froki forward, but she refused to cooperate. She may be my horse, but she still answered to Aaren before me. Traitor.

She knickered as if she heard my thoughts.

"You're not fine, your anxiety is making *my* heart race."

Right, the rune connection. The blessing and curse that it was.

"I'm just...concerned that we'll find something that'll make things worse," I said.

Aaren hummed in understanding. "It won't be anything we can't handle, *fremmed*. We...*you* have already come so far."

When all I could offer him was a weak smile, Aaren gave a devilish smirk. "Want me to cheer you up? You could always think of me naked."

Thankful that my cheeks were already red from the early summer sun, I scoffed and let my eyes roll. "Or *you* could think of a better fighting strategy for the next time I beat your ass in the ring."

I spurred Froki forward, hoping she would kick up dust on him.

My anxiety was gone, and I found that I preferred my racing heart to come from the uncertainty of what lay waiting in the tomb, not from the image of Aaren's naked backside in my mind. What would've happened if I had reached out and touched him instead of fleeing to the bathing room? Would he have turned around and given me a full view of his impressive length? Would he have touched me?

The images that followed those questions sent heat to every pore on my body. Suddenly, it wasn't the sun that was making me sweat. Hoofbeats passed by as Aaren pushed to the front of the group, throwing me a sly grin over his shoulder like he knew what was going through my head. For all I knew, he did.

By nightfall, the eight of us sat around the fire, picking apart small mountain rats Axl had snared. They were tough and greasy, with more bones than I could count, and I nearly cracked a tooth as I chewed a bite of thigh meat. Going hungry was favorable to digging the tiny bones out of my dinner, but I continued my labored eating with forced gratitude.

"Have you all ever heard the story of my fishermen encountering a kraken?" Fiske asked, probably trying to break the heavy silence that the crackling fire couldn't. When no one answered, he continued. "The fish were disappearing. The nets were coming up nearly empty, and as our backup stores started to dwindle, our people started to panic."

I threw the rest of my rat into the fire, giving up when my jaw couldn't take any more chewing.

"Nothing like this had ever happened," Fiske continued. "We have always been careful about overfishing, so we knew it could only be something living that was reaping our bounty. We didn't expect it to be so deadly."

A spark popped in the fire, sending a jolt of fear up my spine.

"I sent my men to find the beast and cleanse our waters. They sailed for three nights, roving our side of the Stornish sea, looking for the kraken. But there was nothing, not even a rogue wave to indicate there was something amiss. They were about to give up, to turn and head home, when the deck of the ship rumbled, shaking the sails and sending their barrels of mead tumbling.

"Men readied the sails, unable to fight the thing when they had been caught so off guard. Then eight massive, slimy tentacles wormed up the side of the ship." Fiske made a snake-like motion with his arms that cast shadows in the firelight that looked like they could've been writhing tentacles. "There was no way to fight the beast when it had already taken so much of the ship. They were doomed from the start, and the only fate that awaited them was at the bottom of the ocean.

"Wood smashed, and the hull began to snap when one lone crewman, Aymer, stepped up. Water flooded the lower decks, and the bottom of the ship gaped open to reveal the inside of the kraken's mouth. Aymer saw his only option, so he started rolling the barrels of rum into his mouth. Then he waited until one of the barrels burst, then grabbed a lantern and tossed it in, igniting the kraken from the inside."

Fiske dumped the rest of his waterskin into the fire, having filled it with rum instead of water this morning. The flames shot up into the night sky, heat affronting my face as I leaned back and marveled at the spectacle.

"What happened to Aymer?" I asked, sitting forward again, when the flames died.

"He died, sadly," Fiske answered. "He was the only casualty. We sent out a ship to look for them, and the crew was found clinging to the wreckage. The fish returned within the week."

The night drew in as Fiske finished his story, and I let out a stifled yawn. Aaren nudged my elbow, nodding his head to our tent. "Get some rest, *fremmed.*"

I was too tired to argue.

The next day, despite the lovely weather, tensions had built during the night that seemed to carry over into our ride. Oswin and Ivar started a conversation on a topic they knew both Fiske and Von would bicker about, and they did just that. The pair sat back and watched the fisherman and knife-wielder tear into each other in a volley of angry words until Aaren threatened them to be quiet.

Torsten had been correct in his estimation of travel time—we kept to the Lettja Pass as instructed, and as the early afternoon sun had me shedding my overcoat, the horses grew uneasy.

"We're getting close," Torsten said, his voice grim.

I swallowed thickly and ignored Froki's protests as I urged her forward.

The horses refused to go any further once we reached the crest of a small hill that overlooked a dense valley with a circular clearing at its center. The trees blocked the view of whatever lay in that clearing, but I didn't want to take another step until I knew what waited for us below.

"You alright, *fremmed?*" Aaren asked as he took the reins from my hand and tied Froki and his horse to a nearby tree.

I nodded, unsure if I could formulate a believable lie.

"You don't have to go," Aaren assured, coming to stand in front of me. "But I think you should."

I had fought a trehag, a hagua, survived a usett sting, gone through mylings and fenrs—how much damage could a few draugr cause?

"Come on," Aaren said, and slid his hand into mine. Normally, it would've been a romantic gesture, but it was more comforting than heart-fluttering, and I let Aaren lead me through the trees with the group trailing behind us.

When we emerged into the clearing, I had expected to see a towering temple adorned with gilded statues and a grand entrance leading into an ornate tomb. Instead, a large hole was dug into the ground, twenty feet wide and fortified with stone, with a small staircase leading down. It was a humble tomb, and poorly kept, but I supposed Markus didn't have enough living followers to maintain it. Moss clung to the stone, and the stairs started to crumble as we descended, stopping in front of the large stone door that was etched with a rune only Torsten recognized.

"It's a blood rune," he said as he examined the markings, jaw setting harshly as he contemplated it.

"Well, how do we open it?" Ivar demanded as he grew antsy and started shifting from foot to foot.

"It will only unlock if innocent blood is shed before it," Axl said from the back of the group, his face hidden in the shadows of his hood. "The life force from the blood spilled is the only thing that can activate the door."

We eyed each other, assessing just who would be the most qualified for such a task.

"Well, none of us are innocent," Oswin stated, shrugging. "Between the killing and the fucking, we'd have better luck having a myling open the damned door."

How many innocents had been slaughtered in this very spot to open this door?

The thought had me growing just as restless as Ivar, my feet growing hot as I stood over the spot where so many lives were lost.

Oswin lifted his brows, then shot Axl a considering look. "Axl, you've killed, but have you fucked? Maybe the rune will accept the next best thing."

Axl went to answer, but I didn't hear what he said because Torsten had me pinned under his gaze. "Unless..." he said under his breath, then stepped towards me. I took his extended hand reluctantly, hesitant to leave Aaren's side and stand before the door with Torsten.

Aaren barked a protest when Torsten produced a knife from under his cloak, swiftly slicing the pad of my thumb and drawing warm crimson that he smeared across my palm. I grit my teeth as the pain bit into my skin, not hearing the quiet apology Torsten muttered to me under his breath. He pressed my bleeding finger against the rune before Aaren could start swinging on him, and a warm buzzing hummed under my palm. Blood leaked from the wound and into the stone, imbuing the rune with my life force and glowing the same color as my blood. The stone peeled from my skin as the door opened, and a musty breeze tried to suck me inside.

"I thought so," Torsten mumbled and released my hand.

I turned, almost slamming into Aaren, who reached for my hand and examined the cut.

"Care to explain?" he demanded, ripping a strip of his shirt and wrapping my thumb with it.

Torsten turned from the darkness within the tomb.

"Blood runes can be tricky things. But most of them have fail-safes if the caster has any doubt in the integrity of the rune's users. Innocent blood is the primary key, but the blood of the caster can also access it." He gestured to my now bandaged hand. "Seeing as she shares blood with Markus, I suspected Layla would be the key we needed."

The musty breeze started to reek more of death the farther we descended into the tomb, climbing the stairs down, down, down until the darkness threatened to swallow us whole. I summoned a small ball of flame to light the way until we reached the bottom of the stairs, only to be led into darkness.

Aaren reached up and retrieved a dry torch, dipping it into my flaming palm before moving around the room and lighting the braziers that surrounded the walls. I shuddered as the room came into view. Carved into the green stone were man-sized niches, each holding an embalmed body. Everybody was in a different state of decay; some had flesh still clinging to the brittle bones underneath, while others were just bones with skulls forever fixed in a grimly devious smile. Each body was replete in carved steel armor, and tucked in their withered hands atop their chests were weapons of all kinds. One body's decaying fingers loosely clasped a greatsword, its hilt chiseled with runes and intricate designs crusted with rust. Another held what was once a mighty spear, reduced to dull metal and crumbling wood.

Urns and baskets filled with jewels and gold, along with remnants of rotten fruit and moldy bread, lined the carved walls. Faded tapestries hung from the cobweb-coated ceiling, and a sickly green moss covered the stone around us. The sight of the bodies wasn't what almost sent me to the floor. It was the smell. We had skipped breakfast in our haste to get on the road, and while my stomach had grumbled and whined during our travels, I was thankful there was nothing for me to gag up when the smell hit my nose.

Oswin and Ivar began hacking and coughing, slapping each other across the back and complaining of the festering odor.

"Would you two cut it out?" Aaren barked through gritted teeth. "You'll wake the dead if you're any louder."

"Who are all these people?" I asked through the hands I had covering my nose and mouth. I dared to step closer to a skeletal body tucked away in a niche closest to the entrance.

"Followers of Markus," Torsten answered, his nose wrinkled. "All laid to rest as they were in life, serving their master."

Across the room was a massive stone door with markings of an ancient language etched into the stone. Taking shallow breaths, I followed the others until I was craning my neck to take in the iron door.

"He's in there," Torsten said after reading the markings. "Or at least, he should be."

"That's deitonic language," Fiske said as he marveled at the markings. "The ancient language of the deities and their offspring. Commonly used by demigods."

Aaren cursed under his breath.

"Why would a language like that be used on Markus's tomb?" I asked in a voice that shook in the thick air.

It was Fiske's turn to curse, rubbing a hand over his bald head.

"Can someone please tell me why this is bad?"

Aaren turned to me, his face grim in the shadowed light. "It means that we could be up against something far worse than we thought."

His words barely had time to process before Torsten said, "None of it will matter when we find him entombed in the antechamber. Help me with the door."

It took all three leaders to shove the door open, and there was a bone-chilling creak that echoed into the darkness beyond. The torches lit without prompt, bathing the room in a warm glow that contrasted with the stench and green moss clinging to the walls. More bodies were tucked in the alcoves that lined the walls leading up to the dais in the middle. The dais bore a stone sarcophagus. That same ancient language was scratched into the walls, and something within me sang, almost as if the markings were whispering to me.

Something formidable thrummed in my chest as dread began to spread through my body. Our footsteps echoed through the chamber, sounding like an alarm, but my ears still rang with the ancient mantra.

Torsten ascended the dais, Aaren and I lingering close to the base. Aaren's hand gripped the hilt of his sword, and the leather groaned as his knuckles turned white with tension. Stone scraped against stone as Torsten shoved the sarcophagus lid to the side, and my hands went to cover my ears when the sound stopped abruptly, and a stunned silence filled the tomb.

"By the Gods," Torsten muttered, hands falling limply to his sides. "This...this cannot be." His face had gone sheet white in the dim light. "He's not here."

While I had expected to feel smug when we inevitably proved that Markus was no longer in his resting place, it was panic that sent me climbing the steps of the dais, temples pounding as the language still chanted quietly in my head. Peering into the sarcophagus, I examined the empty niche, counting the different cracks and imperfections in the design. Resting where Markus should be, was a small rock inlaid with yet another rune. It looked nothing like any rune I had ever seen—that number was small, but I had seen enough to know—this rune looked formidable, fearsome. The scent of death and decay suddenly wasn't coming from the bodies, but from the small stone.

I reached in and ran my thumb over the ridges of the stone before I passed it to Aaren, who had joined my side.

"What is it?" I asked as he scrutinized my findings.

"Nothing good," he replied.

Something rustled on my left, the sound like soggy flesh coming to life. I snapped my eyes in the direction from which it came. My heart jumped into my throat when I saw the closest corpse stretch its legs.

"Fuck," Aaren muttered, fingers flying to his sword and drawing it with a deadly slice.

The others readied themselves for battle below, drawing their weapons and forming a defensive circle. Saggy skin hung from the draugr's bones as it climbed from its niche, lips drawn back into a toothy, decomposed sneer. The eyes in the hollow sockets glowed a deep orange, tracking the movements of the others.

A breathy laugh rattled from its throat, and even though the axe in its hand looked dull, it still glared in the dim light.

That same soggy flesh sound came again, increasing in volume as the many draugr stirred from their eternal slumber to do the only thing they were put here for—kill.

The three of us on the dais pounded down the steps, joining the group as the draugr slowly rose and blocked our exit. They drew their rusty weapons with a chorus of scraping metal. I pulled my own sword with shaking hands, but the first draugr that was mere steps away did not attack. It sniffed, taking the stagnant air deep into its lungs before its eyes honed solely on me.

"Why aren't they attacking?" Oswin asked, knuckles white around his sword.

Something warm and wet dripped from my palm. The slice on my thumb had bled through Aaren's binding, and drops of crimson fell silently to the floor. The draugr sniffed again.

"It's me," I said, squeezing the bandage so that more blood dripped onto the stone. "They aren't attacking because they think I'm their master."

The first draugr regarded me curiously, tilting its head to the side almost confusedly.

Ivar's bowstring groaned as his trigger-happy fingers pulled at it, an arrow notched for the moment, the draugr changed their minds. Seconds went by before something in the draugr's ember eyes changed, a slight shake of the head as its sickly sneer dropped, and deadly malice filled its hollow features.

Ivar's arrow lodged in the draugr's eye, its unnatural glow dying as it fell to its knees with a sickening crunch, then toppled forward onto the ground, still. Dead, if that's what it could be called.

The closest draugr watched its comrade fall, rotten brow furrowing before a rattling battle cry echoed across the tomb.

Our formation broke when Aaren snarled, then propelled himself forward into the crowd of rotting corpses. Black ichor sprayed him as his sword sliced through the draugr's middle with deadly precision, and satisfaction glimmered in Aaren's eye when the draugr dropped lifelessly to the ground.

Whistles filled the air as Ivar took down four draugr in the span of seconds, keeping the encroaching attackers at bay so the others could execute their attacks freely. There was a nauseating squelch from my right as Oswin beheaded a draugr and sent the head tumbling to the floor. Black boot prints painted the stone in a grotesque portrait of viscera and violence. Axl and Von worked in tandem, hacking, slashing, and carving a path to the door for an easier escape.

To our misfortune, the draugr from the first chamber had awoken and stumbled into the antechamber with battle cries and clanging weapons.

A draugr wielding a rusty axe charged towards me, and I dodged its swing, turning quickly and kicking the back of its knee. There was that same, sickening crunch when it fell, and I fought the retch that barreled up my throat as the neck sprayed me with black blood. A drug-like euphoria sang through me when I threw myself into the next attack as adrenaline coursed in my veins.

The sounds of ripping flesh and dull, clashing metal rang around us, but Ivar's nearby cry of fury snapped my attention. Landing the killing blow to the draugr in front of me, I scurried away, dodging blades and rotting elbows until I caught sight of Ivar, cheeks stiff and eyes rigid as he pulled his bowstring tight around a draugr's throat. The corpse thrashed, but the string still fought against its neck, and Ivar was losing grip. I surged forward, my sword sticky in my hand, but I was vibrating with so much intensity that I didn't care. My sword arced magnificently through the air when I swung and decapitated the draugr, the head getting lost in the sea of dead. He gave me a quick nod of thanks before storming into his subsequent blows.

Trouble found me before I turned, and something hard and blunt slammed into my back. I cried out, but the pain was more manageable than the anger that crackled to life inside me. Turning, the raspy laugh of a draugr woman reached my ears, her bony, rotten fingers gripping the splintering handle of a blunt warhammer. Her arms sagged, nearly skin and bones, probably why the attack didn't deal the damage she had intended. Her brittle hair was pulled back in a loose braid, strands swaying as she reared back for another attack, but she was too slow.

I rammed my foot into her chest, relishing the sound of her breastbone cracking under my heel. She hit the floor, and I slammed the heel of my boot into her skull and watched gray matter spill and crunch. Heat licked my insides, and I watched a draugr slip on the spilled brains and slam into the ground. I drove my sword into its middle, only wrenching it free when it had stopped flailing, and the glow of its eyes died.

The tomb started to quiet as the draugr numbers dwindled, and I dropped my hands to my knees to catch my breath and avoid looking at the gut-strewn floor. The smell had increased tenfold, and I looked away from Von, who had hurried into a corner and started emptying his stomach.

"Well, that wasn't too bad," Oswin said as he kicked a head, and it flew across the stone and knocked Von's foot. It made him throw up more.

Just as Oswin's words died in the heavy air, a noise started, a soft pounding from somewhere in the tomb. I searched the scattered bodies, heart matching the rhythm of the beating until I questioned whether it was just my own chest I was hearing. But the others looked around just as I had, and the pounding was growing louder, more erratic, as if someone were trapped inside the tomb and was growing increasingly desperate to break out.

Just as soon as it started, it stopped.

Then there was another sound, like a thousand tiny rats scurrying across the floor, tiny claws biting into the stone.

The floor exploded.

Stone sprayed the air, bigger chunks raining down and thundering onto the floor. Aaren's hard form slammed into me and tucked me beneath him as a larger chunk of rock barreled toward us. He moved just in time. A second longer, and we would've been flattened.

When I crawled from underneath him, I gasped.

Hordes of bodies crawled from the sudden hole in the floor, clawing over each other as they scrambled out of the hole. Naked and unarmed, these draugr were vicious, more primal than the ones that now littered the floor. These were feral.

Their black blood was already pouring in streams as their bony hands dug into each other when they tried to slither out of the pit. When the first wave advanced in a flurry of flailing limbs, the smell nearly knocked me to the broken stone. The draugr from before smelled of decay, the kind that accompanied any dead, but the stench these draugr brought with them was overpowering. Sharp, festering death ate away at the air, permeating every tiny crack in the tomb, and it seemed even the moss tried to shy away from the filth.

Torsten led the attack, his honed sword slicing into a draugr, and the others joined in, to no avail. Just when one was cut down, four more took its place until they were piling on top of each other to get to us.

I kicked one away just as I caught a glimpse of the rotten teeth that gnashed for my throat before it hit the ground, but I didn't have the time, nor the room to swing my sword, only back away as they just kept coming. We were overrun, grossly outnumbered, and we were going to die if we didn't get out of here.

Which was going to be difficult because the feral draugr had spread far out and surrounded us.

I hacked away at one, then decapitated another, so lost in my own movements that I could barely register how much danger the others were in until harsh, biting panic flushed my system. It wasn't my panic, but Aaren's, and I searched the battle for the familiar flash of white hair. Not too far away, Fiske was staving off a draugr with his bare hands, rotting, gangly limbs held in his grip like a vice as he dug into its middle and wrenched its organs out. Something clattered against my boot, and I kicked Fiske's sword towards him when I realized what it was.

A decaying fist grabbed hold of Axl's hair, and he screamed and thrashed for the draugr that held him. He kicked another assailing draugr away, but the one that had hold of his hair bared its grimy teeth, going for his throat. A whistling arrow busted into its temple, the tip pushing through the other side. Its grip loosened, and Axl broke free to my relief.

Aaren was a few feet from Axl, trying to shake off a draugr that had latched onto his back and was trying to strangle him from behind. Thankfully, Aaren was too big, and the draugr's fingers were too weak to close his windpipe, and once he dislodged it, he swung it around his body and used the draugr like a dull machete, cutting a path through the still growing numbers.

That same, primal buzzing returned in my chest, anger and energy burning to life at the screams of my friends. I could still hear the groaning and gnashing of the feral draugrs around us, but something else filled my ears as I continued to fight, something like an ominous chorus singing a mantra into my mind. My eyes caught the ancient markings along the walls, the deitonic language Fiske had called them. The carvings seemed to pulse, sending a wave of energy and power towards me. Heat bristled at my fingertips, and sparks climbed up my spine as the hairs along my arms stood.

I found Aaren in the fighting again, now nearly overpowered by the dead. Black blood painted his hair and face. Fire now danced between my fingertips, furious flames just waiting to be unleashed, the untapping that would burn this tomb, maybe even the mountains, to the ground.

The markings pulsed again, and more heat flooded my system. Sweat beaded along my brow, but I couldn't wield the fire, the energy that was coursing through me and igniting my very being. I couldn't explain it, but something held me in an iron grip, keeping whatever was growing inside me from exploding.

Then Aaren screamed.

Another pulse slammed into me.

And I lost it.

Flames erupted and engulfed me, blazing bright and boiling the blood in my veins until I couldn't see anything, only orange and white-hot heat. A scream brewed in my chest, growing louder as I let it all go. Some screeches mingled with my own, bellows of pain from the feral draugr as I burned and destroyed and wrecked.

My senses electrified as feverish distress bled into hysteria within me, and my control abandoned me until I was unbound, reckless. Unyielding. Bodies burned and fled, but my friends were left untouched as the tomb blazed and began to crumble.

Just as quickly as it began, the markings stopped pulsating, and there was a growing silence in my head as the mantra quieted, leaving me to burn alone, destroy and burn, and burn, and burn...

And through all the burning and fire and devastation inside me, something cold snaked into me, caressing my rune and sending tendrils of ice into my veins. I let it travel up my arm and into my chest, swirling and brisk as it seeped into other parts of me, up my neck and into my cheeks, down my stomach and along my legs until even my toes prickled with ice.

The flames died, only leaving a small circle of flickering embers around me that Aaren stepped over easily. Relief made my knees weak, and Aaren caught me when they gave out. His skin was just as cold as the ice that was now cooling my blood.

I didn't feel him carry me through the tomb, nor did I hear the remaining shouts and screeches of the feral draugr that now ran about in a frenzy, trying to put out the flames that burned their papery skin. All other senses started to fade, but I could still smell the death, the rot, and charred skin. I had set the entire tomb on fire.

Just as the warm sun shone across my cheeks, everything left me, and my eyes closed, then my consciousness slipped away

Chapter 36

Kind, honey eyes greeted me when I awoke. Aaren's comforting scent filled my lungs.

"There you are, *fremmed*," his rumbling voice said, and something warm brushed my forehead.

Blinking awake, I ran my fingers over the furs, letting the sensation bring me back to life. We were in our suite in Fjellhjem, where a roaring fire crackled in the hearth and bright sunlight shone through the glass doors to the balcony. I swallowed, then grimaced at what felt like shards of glass scraping against my throat. Aaren eased me up and brought a goblet of something to my lips. The sweet flavor blossomed on my tongue, and warmth trickled down my throat. It wasn't luktrot, but whatever was in that goblet sent a rush of life through me.

"I'll admit, I was beginning to worry you wouldn't wake up," Aaren said, soaking a rag in a nearby basin and returning it to my forehead. "The dreams were too good, weren't they?"

I took another sip from the goblet before I could speak. "Oh yeah," I replied, about to weave a story of orgies and singing in the halls of Himmelfjell, when I noted the dark circles around his eyes. "Have you slept at all?"

"Here and there," he answered as he poured more drink into my goblet.

"How long was I out?"

Aaren pressed his lips together. "Two days."

I sat up abruptly, my head spinning at the sudden exertion. "You haven't slept in two days?"

"Gods, *fremmed*, you're the one who burned an entire tomb down and then promptly passed out. You shouldn't be worried about me."

He placed a supplicating hand on my arm and eased me back onto the pillow.

"What of the stone?" I asked. "The one from Markus's tomb?"

Aaren gave me a look of exasperation because I was doing anything but resting, then he replied, "In Torsten's possession. We will meet with him this afternoon."

I sighed, squirming in the furs.

"Rest, Layla," Aaren said. He pushed me gently back onto the bed.

"Only if you do," I replied, and patted the empty side of the bed next to me. Aaren eyed the empty spot, then gave me a wary look. "Don't make me beg, Aaren. I've rested enough."

A flicker of amusement flashed across his face. "This is not one of the things I want you to beg me for, *fremmed*."

I opened my mouth, unsure what to say, when he stood and kicked off his boots. As he eased into the furs next to me, he sighed almost contentedly. He fell into a lazy doze within seconds.

My strength had been nearly restored as I sat down in the meeting hall later, thanks to the broth Aaren had coaxed me to drink before leaving our room (actually, he threatened to pour it down my throat).

"We are glad to see your health is restored," Torsten said politely, like we hadn't just faced our deaths together in Markus's tomb.

"Thank you, Torsten," I said, noting the change in Ertha's expression. It was less hostile, softer, likely thanks to the conversation she had with Torsten that I had overheard. All I wanted now was an apology, but seeing as Ertha was so strong-willed—stubborn might be a better word—I didn't think I was going to get one anytime soon.

Fiske scooted forward in his chair, leaning for a better look. "That was some fire you conjured, Layla," he said without prompting. His eyes turned to Torsten with a knowing look. "With the deitonic language in the tomb and her magic..."

"I know," Torsten replied, then gave me a grave look. "Layla...I'm not sure how to put this—"

"Markus is a demigod," Fiske blurted, his eyes alight with something like excitement and dread all at once. "Which would make you a—"

"I'm a..."

What was the word? I knew it from the mythology books Lucas read to me a few months ago. It was in a Greek mythology book from the library, which mentioned Achilles and his son Euphorion...

"A legacy?" I blurted, silently pleased with myself. "But...how do you know he's a demigod if there isn't any evidence of where he came from?"

The three leaders exchanged looks, and Aaren wove his fingers through mine under the table.

"The markings in the tomb coupled with the magic he passed down to you..." Fiske rambled. "I-it only makes sense."

"That language, the markings, they...spoke to me," I divulged, squeezing Aaren's hand tightly as I spoke. "It was like they were giving me more magic."

"That's impossible," Fiske muttered, and Ertha almost squeaked as her eyes widened.

When I asked why it was happened was impossible, Torsten said, "Because deitonic language died when the gods did. It's believed to have been used by the gods to talk to their demigod children. Markus's followers must have put it in his tomb in the hopes that he could talk to the gods."

I blinked, confused. "But the gods don't exist."

"If the gods don't exist, then who was speaking to you through the markings?" Fiske demanded.

Torsten held out a silencing hand. "It doesn't matter. What we do know is that Markus may be far more powerful than we thought."

"Layla, too," Aaren said. "If what we saw in the tomb was uncontrolled, imagine what she is capable of with a little extra training."

I didn't bother hiding the surprise on my face when I looked up at him. He kept his eyes on the meeting, however, with a serious expression.

"What about the stone?" I questioned.

Torsten reached into his pocket and produced the stone that had been wrapped in a gray cloth. "With such a grim stone comes grim implications," he said as he unfolded the cloth. Unease spread throughout the meeting hall when the stone was fully displayed, that same, decaying smell prickling my nose. Fiske sat back in his chair, and Aaren's grip tightened around my hand. Torsten pushed the stone away from Ertha, who had tried to eye it curiously before he placed a careful hand over hers.

"It's a necromancy rune," Aaren said, which sent my stomach careening through my middle.

Torsten nodded. "A calling card of sorts."

Fiske swore and rubbed his head. "Why would a necromancer raise Markus from the dead?"

I shuddered, reaching forward and closing the cloth around the stone now that we didn't need to see it anymore.

"Don't know," Torsten replied. "But we best pray it was for practice and not for any nefarious reasons." Torsten's face said he didn't believe the words even as he told them.

"All necromancers are nefarious," Aaren spat. "We aren't doing ourselves any favors by assuming anything less than a necromancer's worst."

Fiske agreed, leaning his elbows on the table and shaking his head. "This necromancer is a problem, but Markus presents the bigger threat at hand. Remember, Markus is the one who sent those mylings to us, not some necromancer."

Aaren released my hand, cold air filling my palms as he folded his hands together on the table and caught the two Fjellhjem leaders in a stern gaze. "The evidence is here, *venner*. Now will you stand and fight?"

Torsten and Ertha broke away from Aaren's glare and shared a glance that exchanged silent words between them. What felt like minutes went by before they turned back to us, both stoic in their conviction.

"What do you need from us?"

Relief flooded me, and I heard Aaren release a sigh, though his posture remained rigid, and his expression was still stern. Fiske held the same pose, but I knew he was just as relieved as we were.

Now the question was—where to start?

We had accomplished our task in convincing Fjellhjem to join our ranks, but we were no closer to stopping Markus or finding Lucas than we were when we left Skoghjem. We had to focus on the most present enemies: the mylings.

"The last time we encountered the mylings in the Skoghjem, they said they were promised something," I said, remembering their icy words as they sent a chill across my skin. "If we're going to stop Markus, we need to reduce his ranks."

It wasn't searching for Lucas, but maybe if we stirred the pot enough, Markus would come out of hiding.

"What if we found out what they were promised and gave it to them first?"

Fiske cleared his throat. "And how do you suggest we find out what he promised them?"

I hid my shudder as I said, "We ask them."

My suggestion was not taken lightly.

Unfortunately, the rest of the meeting was anything but constructive, resulting in pointed fingers and some nasty words exchanged between Oswin and me. It seemed none of us were the experts in mylings like we had thought. To protect friendships and our sanity, the three leaders agreed to continue the meeting in the morning with fresher minds and better attitudes.

I excused myself from the meeting hall, mumbling that I needed a drink. Having overheard my frustrated grumblings, Fiske decided to join me, saying that he'd be there to ward off Boden should he come sniffing for more trouble.

The smell of spirits and mead wafted over us as we entered the tavern, a scent I hadn't realized I had missed until it swirled in my nostrils and made my mouth water. It wasn't the pub in Skoghjem, but it would do, especially if it meant I got to forget about the mylings and Markus and whoever this necromancer was. And forget the stirring restlessness that was growing in my veins over the last few days.

Ever since I discovered the tomb and found out that I was a legacy, the child of a demigod, something new and unfamiliar had awakened within me. I wasn't sure if it was my growing power or if the deitonic markings had unlocked something profound inside me, but I was growing restless. Restless for what, I wasn't sure, but I knew if I didn't find a way to channel whatever energy this was, I was going to burst. And I was unsure what that bursting would entail.

The barkeep handed me a tankard in passing, and I sat back to watch the revelry.

I was halfway through my mug when Fiske finally spoke. "This myling business has me tangled in knots," he said, putting his mug down and massaging a rough hand over his shoulder.

I hummed in agreement and rolled out my own neck.

"You don't suppose there is something else we could give the mylings?" I asked, leaning a little more comfortably. "Something better than what Markus promised them?"

Fiske shrugged. "How can we give them something better if we don't know what they were promised?"

I turned to face Fiske fully, the ale warming my cheeks as I drained my mug and accepted a new one graciously. "Think about it, Fiske. What do mylings want more than anything else? Probably more than whatever Markus promised them."

Fiske moved the hand that had been rubbing the top of his head to offer his palms in confusion. "Rotten things only want hallowed ground," he replied, sucking the drops of ale from his mustache after a sip. "What're you getting at, Layla?"

"What if we gave them hallowed ground?" I suggested, fanning myself excitedly as heat flushed my cheeks.

"How do you suggest we bring *all* of them to hallowed ground?"

I swallowed my mouthful and licked my lips, then gave an excited shrug. "I don't know! Isn't that for you to answer? I'm still new to this realm, remember?"

Fiske rolled his eyes and turned to face the rest of the pub again, accepting a refill with a polite nod. I watched his features shift as he thought it through, brows rising and falling as if having a conversation in his head. I noted the light, sun-kissed freckles dotting his worn cheeks, the shallow lines of his face shifting with each thought that passed through his head.

"There is a dagger," he said finally. "It is rumored that the hilt is hewn from the femur of Hel, goddess of death. Anyone who wields this dagger has the power to banish anyone straight to the top of Himmelfjell. The soul essentially skips the journey and faces immediate judgment."

Bingo.

I raised my brows expectantly, eyes going wide with unchecked enthusiasm.

"I'll think on it," Fiske said, waving his hand. "But enough of that for now, we came here to get away from that stuff." He clinked his mug against mine. "Let's drink."

And we did. A lot

Two hours and ten songs later, Fiske and I staggered about the pub, sloshing ale from our mugs and cackling with gaiety. He had slung an arm over my shoulders and swayed with the melody to an old drinking song as he slurred lyrics I'm not sure he even remembered. I closed my eyes nonetheless and tried to follow along, singing every few words I could make out.

"And she cut off his head..."

"Head."

"...and erased all her dread..."

"Dread."

"Oh, I forgot what comes next."

With a hiccup, Fiske slumped onto a wooden bench with a thud, his chin falling onto his chest. I giggled and watched his head loll to the side, followed by snores. His half-empty mug that was balanced precariously in his hand dripped ale onto the floor.

I stumbled to the bar to ask the barkeep, Josef, for a rag.

"I'll take care of it, *fruc*," he said thankfully, and instead, he slid me another mug of drink.

I took it gratefully, drinking nearly half of it before realizing it was only juice. "Josef, this is..."

Someone very tall and huge stepped up behind me, a familiar scent filling my nose. Josef came back behind the bar with an empty mug in one hand and a soaked rag in the other. I stared at him for a moment as a small, amused smile pulled at his mouth before he turned away.

"I thought you were going to bed," Aaren chided, his voice deep with exhaustion.

"I thought a woman could drink in peace without her husband sniffing up her ass!" I spat, tongue heavy with alcohol. I turned and gave his chest a drunken shove, which barely moved him. "Let me drink my ale in peace, Aaren!"

"Come to bed."

"No."

"Layla," Aaren said, still smiling, though there was no sincerity in his face. "Dearest, let's go to bed."

He reached for my arm, but I pulled it away. "No!"

Aaren's smile faded, and he sighed. Drunk and displeased, I couldn't react in time before Aaren grabbed my arm and ducked, throwing me over his shoulder as if I were a sack of potatoes. My head throbbed as I tried to regain my bearings, the ale in my stomach sloshing at this new angle.

"Thank you, Josef," Aaren said as he turned. "Put Fiske up in a room, will you? I'd hate for him to climb all that way into the mountain." I couldn't see Josef respond, nor did I care to, as Aaren pushed through the door. I fought, flinging my foulest obscenities and hammering my fists against his back, but he held steady, sometimes laughing at my more creative insults.

"You fucking asshole!" I exclaimed.

"You kissed your mother with that mouth?"

"Ugh!" I shouted. "I bet you wish I would kiss *you* with my mouth."

Aaren chuckled. "I can think of a lot of things I want you to do with your mouth."

I recoiled and made a noise of disgust. "You're such a dick! Let me go!"

I fought all the way up to our room, some of the doors opening to watch me kick and shout, but Aaren ignored them and continued to plow through the corridor. When we got back to our room, he flung me on the bed and kicked the door closed.

I crossed my arms over my chest and pouted. "I wanted another drink," I sulked, and my lower lip poked from my mouth.

"Here," Aaren huffed and placed a goblet of wine in my hands. "Go ahead, Layla, keep the party going."

I bristled with irritation, then took a long, deep drink. Aaren watched me from the fire, his arms crossed, strands of hair spilling out of the half-up, half-down braid he had it pulled into. I licked my lips and set the goblet down, stepping closer to the fire. I ignored Aaren's amused stare from under his arched brow as I lay back on the ornamental rug and stretched. My muscles ached pleasantly as the warmth of the hearth filled me. I sighed contentedly, purring like a cat in a pile of blankets.

"Have you heard of Hel's dagger?" I asked lazily, my eyes growing heavy from the alcohol.

"I have," he answered. He didn't move from his spot beside the hearth.

"Tell me the story."

He paused as if wondering if this would shut me up, then sank to the floor. "It starts with Sigurd, the leader of Fjellhjem three thousand years ago."

Sigurd, Aaren explained, was married to Lynnea, a beautiful woman who was as bright as the sky and loved by everyone. Together, Sigurd and Lynnea ruled over the mountains, long-gone ancestors of Torsten.

One day, Lynnea got sick, so sick that no physician could help her, no concoction or spell or rune could pull her from death's clutches, and within a few days of falling ill, she would perish. Sigurd, hopelessly in love with her and desperate to find her in the next life, sought an item, a weapon that would put her out of her misery yet guarantee her a safe passage to the top of Himmelfjell. His men searched and searched for such a weapon, but found none.

Running out of options, his physician told Sigurd of a sorcerer who could forge him the weapon he required, but only with the right ingredients. Sigurd found the sorcerer, a man named Raulin, who told him the dagger could be created, but it required a bone from the death goddess, Hel. Thinking he was sending Sigurd on a fool's errand, Raulin sent him away. To his surprise, Sigurd returned three days later, claiming he had retrieved Hel's femur, but never explained how he got it. The dagger was created and used on Lynnea shortly after.

"The dagger was passed down through the generations of mountain leaders. I suppose Torsten still has it. It is probably hidden away in his stores of relics."

"Did it work? Did Lynnea make it to Himmelfjell?" I asked.

Aaren shrugged. "There's no way to know. The story may not even be true."

"I think we need to find it," I cooed as I stirred blissfully on the rug.

His brows knit in consideration. "And why is that?"

I propped myself up on my elbows, cocking my head innocently. When I explained it the way I did to Fiske, Aaren went quiet for a moment and stared pensively into the fire.

"What are you thinking, Aaren?"

"I'm thinking you should drink more often."

I flushed, though I'm sure my cheeks were already red from the ale. I watched Aaren pour himself a glass of wine, but my tongue soured at the thought of more alcohol. His forearm worked as he balanced the bottle, and a thick band of muscle flexed beneath his skin. I admired his strong hands around the neck of the bottle and considered what those hands could do. Jumping at the thought, I scooted away, which earned me a concerned look.

"It's hot...in here," I stammered.

Aaren gave me a confused nod as he brought the goblet to his lips.

"I'm...I'm going to go to bed, I think," I said, trying not to look closely at his rippling forearms that disappeared under the tight cuffs of his shirt. I had seen him without a shirt countless times now that he was no longer trying to hide his scar, but I couldn't stop staring at his muscles. It was the ale, and the wine— maybe the two were mixing enough that my senses abandoned me.

"Are you sure?" Aaren asked and held up the pitcher of wine. "There's still a little left."

I shook my head. "I'm fine, I think...I don't know, I just...bed."

Aaren stood with a chuckle, then offered me a hand. I accepted it, not at all prepared for the way he swiftly pulled me to my feet. The room spun as I regained my footing, my hand gripping his bicep for balance as I looked into his face. The room may have been spinning, but his face was still, and I focused on the way his brow curved into his nose, the soft lines of his lips, counting every fleck of brown and yellow in his eyes so I didn't fall to the ground.

"*Fremmed?*" he asked, his hand clasping me at the small of my back as my knees threatened to buckle.

I didn't know if it was the alcohol or the way his eyes swam with tenderness, but something compelled me to lean forward with closed eyes and parted lips. My heart thudded excitedly in my chest, a steady yet violent rhythm that did anything but ground me in the moment.

"*Fremmed,*" he said, his face just a breath away from mine. "You're drunk."

When my eyes fluttered open, there wasn't lust or affection in his like I had hoped there would be. Instead, there was concern, and something akin to heartache. Heartache from the fact that he couldn't kiss me because I was drunk, or maybe it was because the last person he kissed was Solveig. The girl he actually wanted to kiss.

I pulled away, now thankful that I was drunk because I could blame the embarrassing flush of my cheeks on the ale, and not my lapse of judgement.

Aaren lingered by the fire as I crawled under the furs, fighting the silent tears that were threatening to break from the confines of my lashes.

Tonight, like every night, I slept in an empty bed.

Chapter 37

"Hel's dagger?" Torsten asked the next day during the strategy meeting.

Now that everyone, except for Fiske and me, had gotten a good night's rest and returned to the meeting with a fresh mind, the debate continued. Fiske, despite the raging hangover he was nursing, brought up the knife per our conversation last night. Aaren seconded the idea, giving me an assuring look, though something told me the look was for the way I almost kissed him last night. He hadn't mentioned anything about it this morning, and I was content to pretend it was a drunken mistake, and one I didn't remember.

"I understand, but how does Hel's dagger mean anything to us in this fight?" Ertha questioned from across the table.

"We give it to the mylings to offer a better option than whatever Markus promised them," I explained, keeping my voice quieter than normal so as not to anger the pounding headache beating at my temples. "With that dagger, the mylings would no longer be beholden to his promise. Instead, they would be sent straight to Himmelfjell."

Ertha's brows raised in consideration, almost like she was agreeing with me, and I nearly smiled at the notion. That was until Torsten shook his head and frowned. "As grand a plan as that is, I don't have the dagger."

"What do you mean you don't have it?" Fiske demanded, looking more pitiful than intimidating.

"I mean, Fiske, that I no longer possess the dagger," Torsten replied. "The burrowers ransacked our relic collection seventy years ago. The dagger was one of the things that went missing in the raid."

"So we steal it back," I said plainly.

Torsten scoffed, giving me the look one would give to a naive child rambling silly fantasies. "And I suppose you're just going to stroll into the burrowers' den and pluck it from their hands? Slap them on the wrist for stealing it?"

"I'll take facing a den of burrowers to an army of mylings," I spat.

It didn't take long for us to devise a plan.

The burrowers' den was only a day's journey north, and our horses were prepared by the afternoon. I opted for a quick nap before we left, as it felt like I couldn't get enough sleep between our demanding errands, deliberations, and training.

Torsten opted to stay behind this time. Only our regular Skoghjem companions and Fiske would embark in the evening. Since the burrowers were nocturnal, we planned to travel through the night and arrive by early morning, leaving us able to sneak in and steal the dagger while they slept. The last thing we needed was another attack like the one at Markus's tomb.

The energy of the company was low, seeing as two of us were still violently hungover, while Oswin and Ivar were broodily quiet over a bad game of cards last night. Axl seemed to be in his normal spirits, exuding his pensive kind of silence, but Von was abnormally quiet, his eyes falling on the reins in his hands.

"What's got you down, Von?" I called over my shoulder.

"He's upset because he couldn't get his fill from Maja last night!" Ivar cackled, momentarily forgetting his dispute with Oswin. "The butcher's daughter gave him a cold cock!" Oswin, unable to help himself, threw back his head and howled, knocking Ivar with a friendly punch.

Von grimaced. "It's not funny," he whined, and sank further into his saddle as Oswin and Ivar berated him with teases. Poor Von looked like a kicked puppy. "I love her!"

"You've known her for four days!"

"That doesn't mean it's not real, Oswin!" Von cried. "I would love her for eternity."

"Or until you finish," Ivar scoffed.

Fiske exploded into barks of laughter, followed by Ivar and Oswin, and even Axl broke into a small smile. The eruption of giggles and snorts echoed across the valley, and I sighed in relief at the break in tension. I began to giggle, my eyes flicking to Aaren, who was also smiling, his perfect teeth shining in the sunlight.

There was a clicking sound from a tree overhead that halted my laughter, the branches rustling as I surveyed the foliage. A large squirrel jumped from one branch to another. It was trying to keep up with us. It stopped for a moment and watched us with beady black eyes. Unlike the squirrels I used to see in the park, this squirrel was a light red with a brown swirl on both haunches. Tufts of hair tipped its ears, and its little nose twitched as it locked eyes with me. Small, sharp fangs protruded from its mouth as its lips pulled away to snarl at me.

"Hey, guys," I said, not taking my eyes from the squirrel. "Is that a..."

Von mumbled something else about Maja, and Oswin hooted, startling the ratato. Panicked, it stiffened, rearing back on its hind legs and letting out a frightened titter. Two others appeared, then three more, then eight more. Soon, the tree branches bowed under their weight. The clicking sound grew louder and louder as more appeared.

The laughter ceased as all attention turned to the trees, and the red fur of the animals replaced the green of the leaves.

"Von, some knife work would be great right now," Ivar whispered in a low voice.

Von moved so quickly that I barely registered the flick of his wrist or the shimmer of his dagger as it lodged in the first ratato. The one let out a small squeak before it fell off the branch. I blinked, and three more were knocked to the ground before the other ratatos could react. Then a frenzy of red fur erupted, clicking and squeaks filling the valley. Axl's horse reared and tried to bolt away from the tree that was now overrun with Ratatoskr's descendants. Axl was bucked off and tumbled to the ground, but he recovered just in time to roll out of the way of his horse, which was fleeing back up the path and around the bend. Ivar knocked an arrow, but the ratatos that darted across the tree branches were too quick for him to aim correctly. A scurry of red fur dropped into my lap, its bottlebrush tail fluffed up in agitation. The ratato clicked, followed by a shrill squeal, and pounced. Flesh buried under soft fur met the back of my hand as I swung and slapped it to the ground.

Ivar shot an arrow and pinned a ratato to a thick branch. Squealing, it scrambled to rip the arrow out of the tree, but it couldn't reach, and its squeals grew more frantic. It dangled in a fury of panicked limbs and snorts, the noises cut off by a dagger through the middle. Von surged forward on his horse and wiggled the knife out of the creature, then turned and searched for his next target.

Fiske had dismounted and was stomping the ratatos that had fallen to the ground. Aaren stood on his horse, hands grappling for the wriggling rodents and throwing them onto the ground for Fiske to take care of.

Shaking my feet out of the stirrups, I carefully braced my foot in my own saddle and rose on shaky legs. Froki did not move despite the scurrying bodies, and I caught my balance and took a shaky breath. Small, harsh teeth grazed my knuckle, and I smacked the ratato away as I reached up and hoisted myself onto a low-hanging branch. No matter how much I complained during our last training session, I was thankful for the extra upper-body exercises Aaren put me through.

Dangling for a moment, I gathered enough momentum to sling my leg over the branch and straddle it. A tiny fist grabbed my braid and yanked, but I managed to punch it away before I stood on shaking legs. As every survival instinct blared in my ears, I shuffled up the branch towards the trunk, kicking ratatos and throwing them off the branches above. The men below caught them and disposed of them.

Bark bit into my hand and cheek once I reached the trunk and pressed myself against it, the small hole above my head where the ratatos emerged just within reach. A small claw scratched the back of my hand, and I yelped, then punched my fist into the hole. My knuckles made contact with a small head, but those needle-like teeth sank into my skin deep enough to hit bone. I cried out, fighting the pain that shot up my wrist, and shimmied to the other side of the tree. Peering into the hole put me face-to-face with a massive ratato. Its beady eyes glared at me.

Before it could lunge, I stuck my hand into the hole, tapping into the pain that radiated through my wrist and up my arm. Tapped into the frustration and anger that pain stirred, letting it light my fingertips and burn. Veins of fire shot down the inside of the trunk, followed by high-pitched squalls and shrieks. It didn't take long for the flames to spread through the hollow trunk, taking out every ratato within. The tunnel inside the trunk opened to the sky, where the fire stretched high and ignited the green branches above, spreading down.

I hopped down each limb, breathing a sigh of relief when my feet hit the ground. The squeaks and squeals of the ratatos continued, and I looked up as burning rodents fled the trunk and its branches. The smell of sizzling flesh and burning wood filled the air, and I mounted Froki, letting the others take care of the rest of the ratatos.

The last one fled, and the flames nearly engulfed the entire tree.

"What the fuck just happened?" Oswin demanded, looking almost shell-shocked as he mounted his horse.

That was a great question. We had just wiped out a pack of violent squirrels, and for a second, we were losing the fight. Add this to the list of things I never thought I would do in my lifetime.

I let out a small giggle, even though laughter was what got us into that mess in the first place. But I couldn't stop my shoulders from shaking as my chuckles turned into a full-bellied laugh. Aaren's deep rumbling chuckles joined me, and mirth swirled in my chest as I watched him throw his head back and lose himself to laughter. The others began to laugh as well, and we ended the fight just as it began.

It was a much quieter ride than before though.

Morning was not far off when our horses halted at the foot of a mountain with a small sliver cracked into the base. An icy chill sluiced up my spine as I peered into the shadows. The ominous quiet both beckoned and repelled me. It was as if the silence were a sound itself.

"They live in there?" Von asked bluntly.

Aaren pushed toward the crag, his hand feeling along the entrance. "All it needs is some decorating," he joked with a sly smile.

A draft wafted from the darkness, swirling the scent of carrion and stagnant earth around us. No matter how often I smelled it, I'd never get used to the smell of rot. My stomach rumbled uncomfortably. Aaren took the first step inside, his hand on the rocky wall, our only guide since using a torch would be the same as walking in accompanied by a marching band.

The craggy corridor narrowed, and I sucked in my gut to pass through. Von unclasped his knife belt from his waist to pass, but Oswin found himself stuck in the narrowest spot, releasing a stream of quiet expletives as he shimmied through. Despite Oswin's agitation, Ivar couldn't help but point out that maybe his friend should lay off the ale, which earned him a swift thump on the head.

The tunnel emptied into a massive cavern, illuminated by a glowing blue light emitted from the veins of stone in the ceiling. It was glodstin, if I remembered the name correctly. One of Rorik's readings taught me some of the natural resources of Alveland, glodstin being one of the rarer, yet useful ores. It could be found only in caves like these and came in colors such as blue, green, orange, and sometimes red, if found near volcanic rock. I suspected this was the same kind of stone Helgi carried with her when we went to retrieve the havstok.

In the center was a small lake, large enough that it would take ten minutes to swim across, fifteen if I chose to take a break on the small island in the middle. On the small expanse of dry land in the center was a small, crumbling hut, the veins of glodstin above illuminating the tattered walls and crooked door. The lake stretched to fill the entire cavern, a small bank on the other side being the only other dry land save for the ledges and crags that held the burrowers' dilapidated shacks. A shabby little boat was moored on the other side, the only way to reach the island, should we decide not to go for a swim, which I would argue against if someone suggested it. The seemingly depthless, black water shimmered in the ceiling's blue glow, menacing and dark.

"Torsten said the burrowers keep their treasure hidden all in one place," Fiske whispered, crouching low to examine the water with a cautious eye.

"And I'd bet my left bollock that it's all in that shack," Ivar replied.

The only way to the island was that boat, and the only way to the boat was following the ledge up the side of the cavern wall, right past the burrowers' shacks and tunnels.

Von sighed in resignation as he came to that same conclusion. "We have to go up there, don't we?"

Aaren nodded with that same resignation. "It looks like it's our only option." I let out a sigh of dread. "Fiske and Oswin, you two stay here and keep watch," Aaren instructed, adjusting his sword at his hip. He was normally adept at hiding his worry, but I was learning that a gesture like that was his tell. He only adjusted his weapons when he was nervous, and it set my teeth on edge to know he was anxious enough to let it show.

With the warning to keep deathly quiet, we climbed up the first ledge, our boots barely scraping the gravel of the path. The outlines of the first ramshackle hut came into view. It was constructed from crumbling branches and moldy canvas, sturdy enough that it looked like it would collapse if someone sneezed. Something sticky had been lathered at the joints of the shack, and something told me the substance was far worse than havstok.

Aaren glanced over his shoulder and placed a finger to his lips as we passed the first shack. There was a burrower within, and I wasn't ready for what I saw when I peered in.

Lying on a grimy bedroll was a pale form curled into a fetal position. The burrower faced away from us, the thin spine that jutted from its back covered in translucent skin and cracked with blue spidery veins. Its breaths came rapidly, bony rib cage expanding against the tight skin with every breath. It was bald save for the few tufts of hair that clung to its scalp, and flakes of dandruff peppered its head. It wore a tattered loincloth that covered only what was necessary, leaving its skinny yet muscular legs on display.

My heart nearly stopped when it rolled over. A quiet whimper escaped me before I could stop it, and Aaren's calloused hand came down over my mouth.

The burrower's face was staunch white and pulled tight over its skull. Its features were stretched into a horrid sneer, and pointed teeth poked from between its thin lips. The dark circles around its closed eyes accentuated the gruesome severity of its face, and I shuddered against Aaren. The burrowers were the stuff of nightmares.

I followed the others past the first shack and further along the ledge, which now stretched wide enough for us to no longer move in single file.

We were now at the highest point in the cavern, the halfway point, with a small cluster of huts before us, and a small fire burning in the center. Axl, Von, and Ivar pushed forward and ducked behind a boulder near the beginning of the decline to the other side of the cavern. I took my first step to follow when Aaren caught my hand and wrenched me backward, tight against his chest.

A burrower emerged from a hut with a jagged knife carved of rough stone strapped to its veiny thigh. It knelt before the fire, and its rattling breath could be heard from where we crouched. Milky eyes darted around the huts, and they reminded me of Dagan's after the myling attack, but instead of emptiness, the burrowers swirled with dark, putrid life, as if scooped from the bottom of the lake below. I breathed a silent sigh of relief as it stood and shook out its long fingers before retreating into the hut.

I crept forward, eager to get away from the huts as soon as possible. Aaren followed silently behind. We began our descent down the path, but I didn't relax a single muscle until my feet hit the ground on the other side of the lake.

The boat was shabbier than it looked from across the water, and I was amazed that it didn't capsize the moment Aaren pushed it into the shallows. Seeing the condition of the vessel, Aaren instructed the others to remain on shore, then offered me his hand and helped me board. The wood in parts of the hull was rotted and slimy, and I worked not to put my full weight on the bench as Aaren paddled us across. My eyes stayed on the island ahead, knowing that if I looked over the side and into the dark waters, I would panic.

It felt like eternity before the hull nudged the shore, water splashing as Aaren exited the boat, then lifted me over the side. He carried me through the shallows and placed me on dry land, my boots staying dry while his were surely soaked through with the black water. I sent him a silent thanks through the rune, and he answered me with a subtle smile before rounding to the front of the shack.

The door was a poor fit for the frame, and flickering light streamed through the cracks. With a light push, Aaren nudged the door open, and the ancient hinges protested with a loud creak as it swung open. The shack may have been small on the outside, but the inside seemed twice as large after seeing how much the burrowers shoved inside.

Our job just became a lot more difficult.

I counted fifteen trunks before I lost count, each lying haphazardly on top of the others with their lids cracked and some of their contents spilling out. Gold and jewelry shone from the lips of the trunks, and gold-encrusted jewels littered the ground. The stash of treasure looked more like a dragon's horde than the collection of pale ground dwellers, I thought as I picked up a massive ruby from the damp ground. Small shelves lined the walls of the shack, laden with trinkets and silver goblets and bejeweled weapons fit for Fraalver royalty, if such a thing existed.

"If I were Hel's dagger, where would I be?" I questioned myself, breaking free from my jewel-induced trance.

With a grunt, Aaren flung open a trunk and dug through it, closing it in quiet frustration. "Not sure," he said as he looked around the shack cautiously. "But be careful, I'm not sure what kind of traps burrowers are capable of, but if we were to encounter any, it would be in here."

Throwing open the closest trunk, I picked up a knife that had a hilt constructed from polished wood. While beautiful and expertly crafted, it wasn't the dagger we needed, and I set it to the side, no matter how badly I wanted to strap it to my thigh.

Aaren rifled through most of the trunks while I examined the daggers that were thrown onto the shelves, though none of them was Hel's dagger. We weren't sure what the dagger looked like, so operating on intuition alone was our only hope. But unless Hel's bones were made of wood or jewel-encrusted gold, none of the daggers uncovered were hers.

"You don't think it's hidden somewhere else, do you?" I suggested, dreading the implications of the question.

I cringed when Aaren answered, "It's possible. The only other place I can think of is in the tunnels."

The tunnels we passed as we climbed the ledges. I shuddered as I remembered the darkness waiting inside those tunnels, along with whatever other horrors the burrowers chose to share company with.

Frustration edged my nerves, and I sighed, kicking the mud. Something hard caught the toe of my boot, and a dull pain arced through my foot, but I ignored it in favor of kneeling and inspecting what I found. A small wooden box peeked through the grime, and I dug my fingers in and pulled it out of the squelching muck. Mud caked the latch and, grabbing a knife from a nearby shelf, I dug the tip in and worked to clean it. It flew open after just a few seconds of picking.

Inside the box was a dagger with a clean, bone-hilted blade and a simple bronze crossguard. The blade reflected my green pupils, who marveled at the simple craftsmanship of such a legendary weapon.

"This is it," Aaren confirmed from over my shoulder. "You found it, *fremmed*."

The scabbard and clip were under the cushion the dagger rested on, and the cold bone was almost icy in my palm when I retrieved it. I secured it around my waist and stood.

"Keep it safe," Aaren said, eyeing the precious weapon at my side.

I nodded, but I barely comprehended what he said. I just wanted to get out of this stinking shack and back into the daylight.

An ear-splitting screech blasted through the den upon my first step through the shack door, and the sound blasted around the cavern like the blare of an out-of-tune brass instrument. My hands clamped over my ears, teeth gritted, and bones rattling against the shrieks as they echoed across the glowing walls and ceiling. Aaren turned on his heel and urgently searched for the source. The screeching continued to swell as something etched into the door frame above me glowed orange. It was a rune, and based on the look on Aaren's face, it was a rune we really should've looked out for. It was an alarm that activated only when something within the shack passed over the threshold. *This* was the type of trap burrowers could set—I had expected something a little more barbaric.

Something soared from high above the ledge, whistling right for us. The arrow lodged in Aaren's bicep. His skin sizzled with whatever poison the arrow tip had been dipped in. With a silent wince, he dropped to his knees, but I was able to tackle him and roll just in time for another arrow to strike where he had knelt. I shot a glance up at the ledge where a single burrower perched above us with a taut bow aimed right at us.

A powerful dose of adrenaline surged and sparked my body into action before my brain could even register it. I dragged Aaren across the mud. Quiet groans slipped from his mouth that I tried not to hear, should sympathy distract me. He struggled to gain his footing, his good arm helping to push him to his wavering feet as arrows narrowly missed their targets around us. There was a loud splash to my left, the flailing, dying limbs of a burrower sinking into the water, and just as it fell below the surface, I caught a glimpse of the fletching that marked Ivar's arrows.

Aaren dropped into the boat, features screwed together as a labored sheen of sweat covered his cheeks. The number of arrows striking the ground around us decreased, only because more were raining down on the others at the nearby shore. My feet dug into the mud as I shoved the boat off the island, then moved to swing my legs over the side, but the motion sent the crumbling wood from my grasp.

Shit, shit, *shit.*

The boat rocked as it floated towards the other shore, Aaren's cries of pain growing more desperate, and a tingling discomfort thrummed in my rune. I shook my arm out in the hopes of keeping Aaren's anguish at bay, even if it meant shutting him out completely. I couldn't get distracted—I had the dagger, which meant I needed to make it back to shore, even though to me, Aaren was more important. The rune pulled at my arm, beckoning me after the boat, as if the invisible tether between the two of us was pulled taut and ready to snap.

The burrowers above began to shoot more deadly arrows. One exploded on impact, a few feet away from me. I dove to the side, splashing in the shallows as gobs of mud rained around me.

Despite the growing danger, I didn't look away from the boat until it hit the shore on the other side, and Axl pulled Aaren out. Von took his other side. Fighting the burrowers in such a position would be a challenge, but one I had no doubt my friends would come out of triumphant. Ivar knocked off another burrower above, its gangly body splashing into the water.

Axl kicked the boat back to me across the rippling black water, but all of my hope was lost when an arrow lodged in the hull and blew it to Himmelfjell. And as the pieces of the boat washed ashore, dread sank me into the mud. My fate was sealed. If I didn't die by an exploding arrow on this island, then I would surely perish if I attempted to swim across the lake. Hel's dagger weighed heavily at my side, a grim reminder that it wasn't up to me to choose my fate. The dagger had to make it out of this cave, and I'd rather die knowing that was my purpose all along than to sit on this shore trying to make up my mind.

I sprinted to the other side of the small island, the screeching still blaring from the security rune on the shack. A harsh shiver sluiced up my spine as icy water filled my boots when I waded into the shallows. Aaren's groans had turned to fitful screams that carried over the ledges of the cavern as the sounds of swords clashed. They had reached the highest ledge and the most populated area. Oswin had disappeared from the shore at the entrance, and his shadowed form could be seen climbing up the first incline, sword at the ready. Fiske lingered near the water, head turning between the fight above and my shivering form on the island.

The tug in my rune tightened, almost pulling me into the water as Aaren screamed again. The sound sent an ache through me, the same kind of ache I got when I watched Lucas be punished in that foster home, and there was nothing I could do to stop it. The sounds of Aaren's screams and the memory of Lucas's woeful cries drove me to dive into the water, drowning out everything except the heavy dagger at my side and the biting cold of the lake.

I swam through the prickling water, and blood iced in my veins, but I kept moving, no matter how numb my fingers and toes were. When I surfaced, I was only a quarter of the way across. I would have sighed in frustration if I hadn't been trying to rally my breath for my next dive.

My lungs protested as I sucked in and held my breath to plunge under the water again. The sounds of swords continued, the guttural cackling and wheezing of the burrowers growing louder. Something large hit the water to my right, but I didn't distract myself by surfacing to investigate, even for just a second.

I should have.

I was nearly halfway across the lake when something grabbed my ankle and yanked me down. Water filled my nose, and I floundered against whatever had me. I reached above as if my desperate will alone would be enough to bring me closer to the top, but water started to fill my lungs. I kicked something hard, and whatever it was, it released my ankle. My head broke the surface, and I took in a harrowing breath. Damp, dank air greeted my airways almost maliciously, as if the cavern was mocking my struggle for breath.

"Fiske!" I cried, waving my hands in the air to the Kysthjem leader on the shore. He was preoccupied, though; his attention was focused on the others who were now descending the incline, followed by a small horde of burrowers. Aaren hadn't stopped screaming, but he at least seemed able to walk on his own. His bloody hand clung to the cavern wall as he went, grunting in pain with every step.

My chest ached at the sight of such a brave fighter losing his strength. My arms moved to cut through the water, but that thing from the water burst through the surface, limbs wrapping around me and dragging me back down. The thing let out a brief grunt before sinking below the surface, a grunt I recognized from the ledges above. It was a burrower that was dragging me to the bottom, likely one of the ones the others tossed into the lake, left for dead in the dark, unknown waters of the cavern.

I fought against the thing, feeling the hard, spindly fingers gripping any part of me it could grab hold of. We were free-falling in slow motion, and my lungs strained as the need for air grew more desperate. Fingers dug into my hair and pulled my head back as if the burrower were trying to rip my head from my shoulders. I cried out and lost precious air. Then, sharp teeth punctured the skin at my collarbone and tried to tear away at the skin as the cold water stung the wound.

The heaviness at my hip vibrated, and I grasped for the bone hilt of the dagger. The burrower's teeth sank deeper as I drew the blade. Hel's dagger sliced through the water and stabbed the burrower in the gut. It held on for a

315

moment longer, and as those precious seconds ticked away, my lungs shrank with desperation.

Finally, it let go and fell the rest of the distance to the bottom.

My chest constricted as I kicked upward, expending the last of my energy to try to reach the surface, but it seemed just as far away as when I started swimming. Shadows edged my vision as exhaustion weighed me down, slowly sending me back to the depths of the lake. I kicked again, but it was no use. I wasn't going to get anywhere without air.

I had failed.

And now the dagger would be at the bottom of the lake instead of in the hands of the mylings.

I wondered if I'd make it to the top of Himmelfjell when my lungs inevitably gave out. Would I even go to Himmelfjell, or would I wake up in my bed in Midgard, this whole thing having been a wondrous, mind-bending dream? Maybe that would be for the best—the worst I could face was a bad tip and being passed up for the psychology program. At least I wouldn't have failed as a sister.

Water swirled around me, a whirlpool surrounding me as a wave surged under my feet and propelled me up. It had gone faster than it started, and when I opened my eyes, I was on hard ground with Fiske staring at me in bewilderment. His fist slammed into my stomach, and water fled my lungs, sending me into a hacking fit as I rolled over and spat it onto the cavern floor. The fight still raged a few feet away, but I couldn't focus on anything but the frigid air now biting my lungs.

"Atta girl," Fiske said as he patted my back. I threw up putrid black water. My collarbone stung, and pain seeped into my shoulder and along the fresh scars the usett left behind.

"Thank you," I managed as I pushed to my feet weakly.

The taste of the wretched water filled my mouth as I took my first few steps. Fiske's sharp whistle alerted the others to move out. The burrowers didn't follow. Instead, they fled to the tunnels for an easier exit. If we didn't hurry, they'd be waiting for us as soon as we made it to daylight.

I squinted as the bright morning sun blinded me, but my aching lungs savored the fresh breeze. Axl set Aaren against a tree, and I scrambled over to examine him. His face was blanched, features twisted as sweat pooled along his temples. Black tendrils branched from where the wound festered on his bicep and snaked along his shoulder and up his neck. I swallowed nervously as I wondered what would happen if those tendrils reached his head.

"He's been poisoned," Axl said, darting between the bushes and gathering something in his cloak. "Nasty stuff." He returned with handfuls of purple berries. "I assume they used nightshade mixed with whatever they could find in that cave."

I watched in wonder as he shoved a handful of berries into his mouth and chewed. Then he rubbed two leaves together, creating an aroma reminiscent of Granny's Bengay. He spat the berries into the leaves and mixed them all into a sickly, purple paste. When he pressed it to the wound, Aaren thrashed. His uninjured arm swung to push Axl, who only dodged it and readjusted his grip on the medicine. Ivar held down Aaren's good arm, and Von caught his feet, despite the murderous glare Aaren had locked on them. He was feral, the pain and poison clouding his features until all he could do was scream.

On instinct, I moved on top of him, my hands gripping the sides of his face, so his eyes locked with mine and only mine. Aaren hissed through gritted teeth, and his breath came in furious spurts. Tracing a finger along his brow, I leaned in closer to keep his eyes focused on mine. My eyes were green, just like Skoghjem's; maybe they were familiar enough to bring him back, just long enough for Axl's concoction to take effect. It was a shot in the dark, but it was all I had.

Aaren stilled. His chest still heaved, but his jaw loosened, and his eyes softened enough that I could see the leader of Skoghjem behind the agony. I could see my friend, my...

"*Fremmed,*" he sighed in relief. His lids fluttered as the black tendrils receded from his neck and away from his shoulder as the poison seeped into the berries and leaves Axl still had pressed to his arm. A low hum sounded deep in Aaren's chest, his eyes deep pits of swimming honey. "My *fremmed.*"

Ivar released his hand when Axl removed the berries, which had now turned a deep gray, like a piece of moldy bread. He tossed them into the bushes and applied a fresh smear to the wound. Aaren's free hand reached up and brushed a knuckle along my cheek, lost in whatever high his relief sent him into.

"What is that stuff?" Fiske asked, nodding to the bushes of berries. He thumbed one of the leaves, then plucked a berry, examining it between pinched fingers.

"Lillaberry," Axl answered. "Coupled with godblad, they create a powerful antidote for poison."

317

Familiar, slanted writing bloomed into my mind as I remembered Asta's ledger in the medicine hut. She had made note of the berries in purple ink.

"How did you know that?" Oswin demanded as he wiped cavern dirt from his face.

Axl shrugged and threw his cloak over his head. "I like to read."

Chapter 38

Once back in Fjellhjem, Aaren slept for the rest of the day and through the night. His eyes fluttered under his lids as the tonic the physician made him drink gave him sweet dreams. I slept by the fire, letting the heat warm my face and seep into my bones. The physician cared for the bite the burrower gave me—a process that was far more painful than promised—and I was sent to bed with a tonic for pain, but it did nothing to help me sleep. I didn't know how Aaren slept on this floor every night; after the first hour, my muscles ached something fierce. I was almost ecstatic when the morning light crept through the balcony doors, and I heard Aaren stir in the furs.

"Is the floor as comfortable for you as it has been for me?" Aaren asked from across the room.

I sat up, hands rubbing my stiff back. "Hardly," I groaned and stood. "How do you sleep like that?"

Aaren chuckled gruffly. "With all the traveling I've done in my lifetime, you learn to sleep wherever you can."

The bed sank when I sat down, and Aaren closed his eyes again, brow furrowing as he fought the sleep that tried to take over him again.

"Do you remember anything?" I asked as my fingers traced circles in the furs.

Aaren dug his knuckles into his eyes, then blinked wide. "I remember finding the dagger and getting shot. Everything else is just a blur."

He blinked again. His gaze landed on the deep bite mark embedded in my shoulder. "Who the fuck gave you that?" All exhaustion abandoned him, replaced by a silent rage that rivaled the fury the poison sent him in.

"It's nothing," I said and ran a hand over the gnarly scabs along my collarbone. "Just be glad I didn't drown." That was the wrong thing to say.

"*You almost drowned?*" Aaren demanded, sitting tall in bed, face inches away from mine.

"I...may have been dragged to the bottom of the lake by a burrower," I said. "I'm fine, thank you very much." I crossed my arms over my chest. "Don't look so worried, I can take care of myself."

I was going to omit forever the fact that if it wasn't for Fiske, both me and Hel's dagger would be at the bottom of that lake. What Aaren doesn't know won't hurt him.

"Fuck," Aaren cursed under his breath and ran his fingers through his hair.

I knew that look—it was the same look I gave myself the day after I almost ran away from that foster home. Aaren was blaming himself for what happened.

I opened my mouth to reassure him, but he cut me off. "Where's the dagger?"

"Torsten has it," I replied. "It's locked up."

Aaren shoved past me as he crawled out of bed and made his way to the bathing chamber. His scar was dark in the morning light, his tight muscles rippling around it as he reached for the door. It had to hurt, but I doubted Aaren would show an ounce of pain.

"Get dressed," he instructed. "We've got work to do."

I complied, and we headed to the meeting hall where the others were waiting.

What Torsten meant when he told me the dagger was "locked up" was that it was always on his person. He claimed he'd know it was safe if it was with him...at all times.

Ertha examined it over breakfast, not taking her careful eyes off it as everyone else ate.

"Eat, dear," Torsten said, brushing her wrist lovingly.

"I will, love," she replied as she smoothed her hand over the bone hilt. I was glad to see the burrower blood had been cleaned from it. "I would just like to see it once more before we hand it over to the mylings."

The air Ertha carried with her was lighter than when we first met, and I even caught her smiling earlier in the meal. I had yet to receive an apology, though. Time was running out to get one, as we planned to leave in the morning. We weren't sure when we would see the leaders of Fjellhjem again, or Fiske for that matter, so Torsten promised a celebration tonight in honor of our departure.

To pass the time until then, Aaren and I returned to the river to train, both wary of each other's injuries. Fiske decided to try his hand at sparring with us, triumphing and delighting in besting Aaren and me, even though I reminded him countless times that he had an unfair advantage. While that may have been true, I had a feeling I still would have lost had my strength and range of motion been restored.

Aaren didn't push himself too hard, thankfully. I had used up most of the massage oil the other night, and I wasn't eager to have him relive those memories anytime soon. The three of us returned to the mountain, sore but in high spirits.

When we returned to our room, a gleaming, silver dress lay waiting for me, complete with a set of jewelry to match. I excused myself to the bathing room and donned the gown. The neckline was low, trimmed with polished stones, and the bodice was lined with shimmering lace that matched the hem at my toes. The skirts brushed the floor, just short enough that I didn't have to lift them to walk, while the back of the dress, like the neckline, dipped low to expose half of my back to the cool mountain air. After all the training I had endured over the past few months, my back looked sculpted from ivory, and I'd be damned if I didn't show it off. I braided my auburn hair into a coronet, taking a moment to flex and pose in the mirror as I admired the way the dress hugged my curves.

The meeting hall had been decorated with lively banners and arrays of food, enough to feed a small army. The halls echoed with flutes and fiddles, the sounds of merry clapping and laughter, as nearly every mountain-dwelling Fraalver came to celebrate our departure. Even Boden was present, and he stumbled across the dance floor, drunkenly searching for a dance partner. I almost felt bad for him until he grabbed a woman from behind, which earned him a swift smack to the face.

Von had found a lovely partner, not the blacksmith's daughter, according to Axl, and he twirled her around, beaming gleefully as she spun back into his arms. I wondered how long it would take for him to fall in love with her. Her brown curls bounced as they jumped, her small hands clasped in his, and her rosy cheeks glowed with warmth.

Oswin and Ivar hugged the outskirts of the dance floor and eyed a pair of women who pranced about in calf-length dresses, their hair pinned back to display broad smiles and flushed, jovial cheeks. Ivar nudged his friend forward—nudged was a generous word, shoved would better describe what he did—and the two women shouted with glee and grabbed his hand to pull him into the dance. Ivar beamed and clapped his hands before Oswin snagged him from the wall and onto the dance floor. The four of them swooped and twirled with their drinks in hand. Even Axl had emerged from the shadows; his lithe frame bobbed subtly to the beat as he watched the frivolity. Aaren, Fiske, and Torsten huddled by the food, occasionally glancing at the room between hushed whispers and bites from the array of meat and cheese laid on the table beside them.

I leaned against the wall, feeling the cool rock press against my exposed back, watching my companions and friends dance and revel in the bliss of celebration. No mylings, no Markus, no burrowers or daggers. Just dancing, laughing, and unity.

"You look lovely tonight, Layla," a soft voice sang from my left.

I turned to see Ertha, her lips painted a deep red, and her blonde hair billowed over her supple breasts. She wore a crimson dress to match her lips, and the neckline plunged nearly to her navel, exposing her sternum, which had been elegantly adorned with an array of rubies. She shimmered in the firelight, an image of pure sanguine beauty.

"Thank you," I answered, then returned my gaze to my dancing friends. "You do as well." I wasn't sure what else to say. This was new territory for me, considering this could be the first civilized conversation between us.

Ertha leaned against the wall next to me. "I would have sought you out sooner, but...with the dagger and Fjellgrav and..."

She sighed as if nudging herself on. "Listen, Layla, I'm...I apologize for the way I acted. Solveig was my first and only child, and losing her killed a part of me I didn't know I had or could ever lose." She turned fully to me. "When Aaren told us of your parentage and Markus, it...it felt like a slap to the face of Solveig's memory. And then I saw what you're capable of," meaning my magical temper tantrum and the cracked ceiling, "and it was hard for me to see that you would bring anything besides destruction."

I eyed her cautiously as she held out her hands and offered her palms to me. Without thinking, I slid my own hands into hers and let her hold them as she spoke. "What you've done for my people already has proved me wrong in so many ways. And for that, I am so deeply sorry, Layla."

I considered her for a moment, hands resting in her soft fingers. She reminded me of Sarah with the way her blonde hair framed her face, and the two favored each other in ways I wasn't sure how to describe. Interestingly enough, the way Ertha responded to me was the way I had felt about Sarah for the time she had Lucas. I hated her at first because she was the one taking care of my brother instead of me, but I had to give her credit; she was the best foster parent Lucas had ever had. I wished I hadn't burned that bridge so quickly in the beginning, now that I knew what it was like to be hated for something I had no control over. Gazing down at my hands enveloped in Ertha's, every unkind feeling I had towards her retreated.

"I understand," I replied, a forgiving smile spreading across my lips. "There's no hard feelings, Ertha." I gave her hands a reassuring squeeze. "Why don't we start over?"

Ertha smiled, relief painting her features as she nodded. "As long as you don't try to bring the ceiling down again."

We both laughed, and I relished how easy it was to do so around her now that both our defenses were down.

"Layla!" Oswin called from the dance floor, waving his arms in the air. His face was beet red from exertion, and Ivar bumped into him, both men gesturing for me to join.

Ertha chuckled. "You're being summoned," she said as I threw her an apologetic glance. "Go, love. You've earned it." She released my hands and nudged me onto the dance floor.

Oswin and Ivar were horrible dancers. Oswin gyrated off beat from the music, and Ivar threw his arms in the air as if conducting an orchestra. They both slurred the lyrics to a song the musicians were not playing, but they didn't care about the odd looks from the other Fraalver. The wine blushed my cheeks and numbed my senses when I giggled loudly. Von danced up to us with the lovely girl clasped to his arm, her red lips matching the color that smeared Von's mouth and neck. Oswin cracked a joke about how the lipstick would paint the inside of his pants by the end of the night, which sent Von into a mortified blush.

I caught sight of Axl, his hood resting at his neck as he surveyed the crowd and bounced lightly to the music. During the third sweep of his eyes, they landed on me, and his face blanched when he read my expression for precisely what it was—I was going to get him to dance. Seeming to panic as I started to push through the crowd towards him, he turned to walk off, but I was too quick. My hand caught his wrist just in time, and I offered apologies to the dancing Fraalver I shoved through as I dragged him onto the dance floor. Discomfort spelled across his face as the crowd bumped into him, but I pulled him into the little clearing our friends had made, where he was greeted with shouts of joy.

My grip on Axl's hands tightened as he tried to slip away again.

"You're not going anywhere until I get one dance from you," I shouted over the music.

"This is cruel," Axl protested as I swayed, letting the melody pick me up and carry me away.

Axl was stiff, as if even the idea of dancing locked his limbs up. I lifted one of his rigid arms and twirled underneath it, satisfied with the small smile that tugged at the corners of his mouth. I had battled a fair number of things while in Alveland, but getting Axl to dance would be my greatest victory. I held my arm up, urging him into a twirl, and grinned as he hesitantly ducked under our linked hands and pivoted on the ball of his foot. Axl's small smile grew wider, and he chuckled as we began to sway again.

A hand wove in between mine and Axl's and broke us apart. I went to protest when a woman cut in, her jet-black hair swept away from her face to reveal deep, licentious eyes. She smiled, offered me a quick apology for cutting in, then pressed herself against Axl and led him further into the horde of Fraalver. Axl seemed far more interested in disappearing with this new woman than dancing with me.

The lively music ended with an abrupt strum of the fiddles, and I clapped my hands together in excitement for the next song. Drums began, but just drums, and the Fraalver around me started moving differently than they had before. While their movements before had been lively and full of energy, now they were slower, more sensual, almost like the coiling of a snake ready to strike.

Warmth spread across my bare back, and my rune simmered as Aaren threaded his fingers through mine. He spun me to face him, my hands catching his chest before I slammed into him. A large hand found my waist, just above where my dress dipped. His hardened calluses brushed my skin, goose bumps lighting up my arms.

The string instruments entered the song with a slow crescendo, their notes carrying through the hall like a whisper in the wind. The drums intensified, battling with the strings as thunder clashes with rain, and the song began to sound like the crashing of rock and the call of the mountains. Aaren examined me, gaze leaving my face and roving over my dress, the skin over my chest heating as I felt his eyes take in every inch of my partially exposed breasts. The dress wasn't garish by any means, but the way Aaren looked at me with a hunger comparable to a starving miser, I felt almost naked.

The Fraalver around us continued their sensuous dancing, hips gyrating as the music swelled and a flute joined the mix. It sang out over the competing drums and strings, as if wordlessly telling the tale of the mountains, each note like the different peaks and dips of the range. Aaren's hand dipped lower, amber eyes catching mine as if to ask permission. When I didn't protest, his hand brushed my buttocks, bare under the dress, and I fought a shiver that tried to shake me out of his touch.

The drum sped up, something crashing like the sound of lightning striking the mountain, the flute singing louder and stronger. Aaren pulled me even closer

324

and pressed my body into his sturdy frame. He guided my arm around his neck, crouching slightly so I could reach. His fingers left my arm and traced down my side to grip my waist again. The other gyrating bodies around us brushed against me, but I barely noticed, too lost in Aaren's touch, in the pounding drums that vibrated throughout my body. My senses were overloading, drowning in his scent, the feeling of his hands roaming up and down my body, the way his eyes fluttered closed when I ground into the most sensitive part of him.

I didn't understand the sudden switch in the music, the way the dancing changed so drastically, but if there was one thing I knew for sure, it was that I didn't want it to end. I wasn't sure when my feelings for Aaren had changed to craving something like this, to wanting more than this dancing, but my body ached for him, pining and singing a song only he was attuned to hear.

Aaren's free hand found its hold in my skirts and squeezed them into his fist tightly instead of touching me like he must want to. Had he also wanted this, or was this just a product of the music and the others dancing? The whole thing seemed ritualistic, almost like he was grinding into me because he should, not because he wanted to—even though I could feel him trying to burst through his pants. The other Fraalver seemed to be just as lost in their partners, and I lost sight of my friends in the sea of writhing bodies.

Aaren's soft moan in my ear brought me back to him, away from my thoughts that were desperately trying to distract me. It didn't matter what this dance meant, or why Aaren's lips were barely grazing along my collarbone, breath pooling over the burrower's bite and the usett's sting. Warmth gathered in my center, crying out to me for friction, for touch, for...something, *anything*.

I let out a breathy sigh that got lost in the chorus of the music and the primal howls and chants of the Fjellhjem Fraalver as the drum beats grew fervently and staccato notes struck through the cavernous hall. The flute had reached its crescendo, mating with the strings and creating the most righteous sound I had ever heard. My head fell back, and the music washed over me as Aaren held onto me and kept me from collapsing onto the floor with bliss.

A sharp scream pulled me out of my euphoria.

Then there was another.

My heart stopped when a chorus of growls replaced the flute, and the sounds of swords being drawn drowned out the dying strings. I knew those growls; I had heard one rasping in my ear before I was dragged to the bottom of that dark lake.

Burrowers.

The crowd scattered as the burrowers ploughed through, swinging their jagged swords and maces and leaving a trail of blood behind them. There was too much going on to get a count on how many of them there were, but I saw enough to know that we at least weren't overpowered, not until the Fraalver who couldn't fight fled the hall.

I ripped out of Aaren's grasp, regretting not strapping at least a dagger to my leg when I dressed earlier. It seemed Aaren had prepared thankfully, and he produced a dagger that had been stashed in his boot.

Before he took off, he turned to me with a fading desire and asked, "Are you going to be okay?"

I nodded but knew it was a lie. Aaren saw it too, but Oswin's rallying war cry pulled him away. "If you're unsure, leave the hall. Go back to the room and bar the door."

Like hell was I going to do that.

But I nodded in agreement and watched Aaren dart into the crowd, knife slashing across a burrower's throat and sending it to its knees. Von pushed past me and slid a dagger into my hand as he went. I didn't miss the four popped buttons on his shirt before he disappeared.

Sending a million silent thank yous to Von for the dagger, I swung it at an approaching burrower, relishing the gnarled retch it gave when my blade buried in its chest before I kicked it off and turned to attack another. The small heels adorning my feet proved to be far easier to fight in than I had thought, and it gave me an extra edge when I landed my kicks. Maybe I'd try and find more heeled boots when we got back to Skoghjem.

The skirts gave me some trouble, though, and I scampered away to a corner for just long enough to cut the dress until it rose just to my knee, staving off a burrower with a swift punch to the nose. As I launched back into the action, Ertha herded her people to safety, her lipstick smeared along her cheek, and her curls disheveled. The ground shook as a burrower charged at her, and the hall floor split open right where its next step would land. The burrower tumbled in, and with the flick of Ertha's wrist, the hole closed, smashing the burrower within.

She led her people out of the hall, grasping for the stragglers as she pulled them to safety. Her blonde curls bounced as she moved, but her picturesque eloquence never left, despite the worried scowl that narrowed her features. Torsten and Fiske had furiously joined the fight, and I lost sight of them in a spray of blood and swinging swords.

I took down as many burrowers as I could while I wormed deeper and deeper into the fight. Oswin and Ivar fought in tandem—Oswin swung his large greatsword while Ivar launched arrow after arrow. A massive pile of bodies circled them, but the burrowers still kept coming.

A cold, pale arm snaked around my neck, the crook of the elbow squeezing and cutting off my airway. I floundered for a moment as shock froze my muscles before I fumbled for my knife. That familiar growl rumbled in my ear as the burrower laughed, the arm squeezed tighter and tighter until it felt like my trachea was ready to shatter. Another burrower sneered as it hobbled closer to help finish the job, but I swung my leg up and nailed it in the stomach with my heel. It recoiled only for a moment, but that was all I needed.

I jammed the dagger into my captor's gut and heard the squelch of blood and tearing flesh as I twisted it until the arm loosened. I ducked, releasing myself before kicking behind me, and sent the burrower onto the ground to be trampled. Now free to move, I caught the other burrower just in time. I drove my blade up through its sternum and dug it deeper as blood bathed my arm. As triumphant as I wanted to feel about such a kill, I lost hold of the dagger in the burrower's chest. I hoped Von didn't care too much about that knife.

I grabbed a sword that was clutched in a dead burrower's fingers and charged back into action, but had to rein in my sudden panic when I saw that Axl was surrounded.

Moving to help, I caught his eye, and he gave me a knowing wink. He dropped to the floor, slid underneath a burrower's legs, then delivered a swift kick to the back of the knees. It dropped, and Axl rose behind it like an executioner. With one swift swipe of Axl's sword, the burrower's head slid to the floor and tumbled into the swarm. I didn't need to worry about him as he took on the rest of them, and I turned to find my next fight.

Aaren thundered by me, ducking a stone hammer that nearly knocked his head off. He straightened and delivered a powerful kick to the chest of the assaulting burrower, where it rolled to the ground to be trampled by the horde.

"Look out!" I cried, sending a jolt of panic through the rune. Aaren whirled in time for another assailant to attack, but he had already grabbed the dagger strapped to his thigh and sank it into the burrower's groin before it could so much as swing its sword. I watched, stunned, as Aaren traced a gruesome line up its navel and to its chin. I gagged when blood bubbled into the burrower's mouth, then its entrails slipped through the slice in its abdomen.

Fiske summoned a small wave of water from one of the barrels along the wall and drowned the burrowers one by one. A gaping wound gushed on Ivar's shoulder, but he fought as if he were whole and new. The floor shook again, and cracks spread through the marble underfoot as Torsten stood near the hearth on the other end of the room, slamming boulders onto his attackers.

Time slowed as a burrower broke away from the fighting and rounded a pillar. A nasty grin spread its foul lips, and a knife glinted in the firelight, gripped in its bony, gnarled fingers.

"No!" I cried, breaking away from Aaren and shoving through the crowd, dodging blows and slashes as I went. My knees hit the hard marble as I tripped over a fallen body, and I shouted again, trying to push to my feet. But it was all too late. The burrower lunged for Torsten and plunged the knife into his back. The rocks he'd been controlling smashed into the ground, hands grasping at his chest as the burrower dug the knife further.

Grim acceptance filled Torsten's features as his eyes fell to his chest, the tip of the knife now trying to break through his shirt. Blood stained the front of his vest and painted his hands as he pawed at the wound. Burning fury clouded my vision as I threw out a hand, tapped into the fire in the hearth, and let its energy greet me like a new friend. It surged with my rage, barreling straight to the burrower that had stabbed Torsten. The flames slammed into it, smacking it against the pillar and singeing its flesh. The burrower waved its arms in the air to extinguish the fire, but I held it there and let the heat melt its flesh from the bone. I was not ashamed to say that I savored the burrower's pained shrieks.

The screeches were lost to the wave of energy that surged through the room, sending rocks flying and weapons clattering. A devastated wail rang through the hall. It would be a sunny day in Himmelfjell before that scream dulled in my mind. Another wave of energy surged as Ertha barreled through the crowd, taking out droves of burrowers that still had the gall to fight her. The power swelled inside me, and I let out a cry to match Ertha's, striking and gutting every burrower that I could reach.

It wasn't until Aaren snaked an arm around me and pulled me away from the dead burrower as I drove my blade into it one last time.

"*Fremmed,*" he said, his voice heavy with exertion, but gentle, and he ran a soothing hand over my blood-caked hair.

Something cool pulsed from my rune, dousing the flames inside me until the red I had been seeing cleared, and I could take in the carnage around me. The ground was littered with bodies, but every burrower was dead. A stuttered cry lodged in my throat as I sank into Aaren's arms, limbs now heavy with exhaustion.

Ertha had made it to Torsten, who now lay bloodied in front of the hearth, his face ashen and blank. I squirmed out of Aaren's grip and careened forward, where I fell to the ground at Torsten's side. Ertha sniffled, murmuring to him under her breath even though his eyes had gone distant, and his chest no longer swelled with life.

"My sweet," she said more clearly, tears dripping from her eyes to splash on Torsten's cheeks. "My love, my rock. Please don't leave me, you mustn't leave me now."

The hall had gone silent, not even the scrape of weapons or the roaring of the fire could drown out the sorrow that drowned the space. Silent tears trickled down my dirty cheeks as Ertha dropped her forehead to Torsten's, fingers brushing through his dark brown hair. The gentleness in her touch contrasted with the anger in her eyes, the hot, spiteful tears that spilled and dripped onto her husband's lifeless cheeks. Aaren's usually comforting heat covered my left side as he dropped to his knee next to us, but I was anything but consoled. Another person was dead. And now Fjellhjem was compromised.

Ertha straightened and pulled Torsten's limp hand to her chest. "You have to end this," she said, turning her face to me with a demanding look. "He cannot die in vain." Her eyes rose to Aaren, locking him in a gaze that could have shattered the mountain. "He *will not.*"

Aaren's face hardened as if his features had turned to stone. "This will not go unpunished," he said grimly, jaw clenched as he contained the seething anger I knew was tearing him apart inside. The rune confirmed it.

Her lip trembled, eyes still locked with mine as I fought with every bit of strength I had not to lose the grip I had on my own sorrow. "Promise me," she demanded.

Unsure how to answer, I nodded.

Ertha leaned forward and pressed a devastating last kiss against Torsten's lips. "Goodbye, my sweet." She caressed his face as if to memorize every angle and crease. Then, with a choked cry, she moved a hand over Torsten's eyes and closed them for the last time. "Safe travels."

She stood, Fiske catching her as she stumbled away and over the fallen burrowers.

Aaren watched Torsten with disbelief, losing the slightest bit of control over his anger before saying, "Until we meet again, brother. May the halls of Himmelfjell welcome you warmly." He paused. "Say hello to Solveig."

Chapter 39

As the funeral arrangements were made, Aaren managed to slip away. And since all my offers to help with the preparations were shot down, I followed him out into the warm summer night. Crickets sang pleasantly, oblivious to the bloodshed within the mountain. I stayed just out of sight and trailed Aaren along the river. He trudged into the large expanse of woods at the edge of the village, and I nearly lost him in the shadows as I tried to move soundlessly through the rustling firs. There was something about the way his steps seemed to shake the ground, the way the trees seemed to move out of his way as he ploughed forward, that made me hesitate.

He was angry, and the trees knew it.

Aaren stopped abruptly, his shoulders shaking as his hands curled into fists. Wind rustled in the trees, and the breeze carried his scent through the woods as if he were claiming it, filling it with his power until it swelled with life. Vines sprouted from the earth and crept along the fallen leaves and roots to curl at Aaren's feet and await his command.

"Why did you follow me, *fremmed*?" he asked without turning around.

Feeling entirely exposed, especially in my torn dress, I stepped out from behind the tree I had taken shelter behind. "I...I wanted to make sure you were okay."

"I'm fine," he bit, keeping his back to me. "I don't need your help."

"I wasn't trying to help, I was just worried—"

"Why are you so worried about *me*?" Aaren demanded as he turned on his heel. His features were surprisingly calm, but a disturbing shadow lay underneath. A shadow that looked like it could extinguish every star in the sky. "Worry about Ertha and the rest of Fjellhjem. Their leadership is compromised. And with Markus still at large, the mylings, and your brother still missing, I am the last person you need to worry about."

I narrowed my eyes and watched his composure slip the slightest as he listed the challenges we faced. He was shouldering it all because that's the only way he could control it.

"Aaren, you know this isn't your fault. None of it is."

That shadow behind his features darkened, but his eyes grew brighter. He looked like a creature waiting for its prey in a dark cave with the way the night illuminated his irises. "Don't tell me how to feel. You know nothing of my burdens."

But I did. I knew he blamed himself for Dagan's death, the mylings, and now Torsten's. I knew the scar along his back wasn't because of a lost battle, but a loss of his control, his restraint.

I planted my feet on the ground. "It's not your fault."

"Stop it," he warned, and I knew his thread of composure was snapping.

"It's not your fault, Aaren."

His lip curled as he gave me one last warning. "Layla..."

"It is. Not. Your. Fault."

"It is my fault! Everything is *my* fucking fault!" Aaren boomed, and the shadowy rage in his eyes exploded until they glowed like the sun. "Every decision I make ends up getting someone killed or hurt. This all rides on me. I brought us here, I should have known the mylings would hit Kysthjem, but I didn't warn them. *I* can't even take care of my own fucking village." He huffed out a breath like a bull ready to charge. "Stop trying to help me, Layla. There is nothing you can do but act as my wife for the borders."

I cocked my head as my magic crackled to life and searched for the closest energy to amplify its power. The river nearby answered my summons, curling around my insides and sending cool into my fingertips. "There is plenty that I can do if you would let me." I took a careful step forward, aware of the awakening river's energy. "Let me start by helping you."

Aaren gave an exasperated chuckle. "Go back, Layla. I am beyond help." He turned away again, and my own control faltered. The river's energy filled me up.

"Don't walk away from me," I hissed through gritted teeth. I buzzed with an overwhelming energy, and one wrong look from Aaren could send me over the edge. His back remained to me, and I balled my hands into fists as anger overrode everything else. If I didn't channel this power somehow, I was going to black out.

"Go find someone else to fix. Prove you're useful somewhere else."

What the hell did that mean?

"What did you say?" I demanded softly.

"Isn't that why you're so hellbent on helping everyone? To prove that someone would want you for *something*?"

My lips thinned as his words sank into my skin and tore me apart inside. Because, as cruel as it was, I think he was right. My whole life, no one had ever wanted me. Not to adopt, not for the psychology program, my customers barely gave me the time of day. Not even the boys in elementary school had a crush on me. Ever since I arrived, I had kept myself busy helping the village, because not only did I want to pass the time and hone my skills, but I also had a new opportunity to prove myself useful, to show that I can be wanted and needed, and maybe even loved one day.

But when I thought about it, I wasn't sorry for one second. It helped me heal from what I had endured in Midgard.

"So what?" I demanded, heels pressed into the ground, nearly shaking with energy. "It's better than running off into the woods and moping."

Aaren turned his head the slightest bit, and the vines around him stirred angrily. "Watch it, Layla."

I grunted. "We should have expected the burrower attack. Fine. However, Torsten was aware of the risks of stealing the dagger back. We all did. This isn't about you and your pity party."

"Careful, *fremmed*."

"Stop blaming yourself for this, like you blame yourself for Solveig!"

My words hit their mark.

Aaren unleashed himself.

Wind whipped around me in a cyclone of fury. My hair was ripped from its coronet until it was a tornado of red around me. I screamed angrily, let in every ounce of energy the river would give me, and allowed it to fill every cell, fuel every atom. It felt like the water had given me enough power to rival the Hoover Dam. Throwing my hands out, I summoned my own wind to slice through his cyclone to no avail. He was too strong, but I had something else in mind.

I stomped my foot, the ground trembled, and the cyclone faltered as Aaren lost his concentration. I broke free to see him stumble to the ground, his foot caught in the small divot I carved in the earth—just like I saw Ertha do in the meeting hall. The hole wasn't big enough to fall into, just enough for him to lose his footing and to throw him off balance.

Magic soared through me as I launched myself into him, palms igniting and ready to strike. A rush of wind blew over me and extinguished my flame. The son of a bitch blew out my fire. I summoned another palmful only for another rogue breeze to blow it out. His brow cocked, challenging me to light my hands again.

I did, and this time, I didn't give him enough time to blow it out.

Charging, I threw myself at him. My anger peaked when he dodged the first ball of flame I launched. After the second missed its target, I knew this was only going to end in me lighting the woods on fire, and I didn't have time to think of a new tactic before a vine caught my ankle and knocked me to the ground.

Aaren approached me, a harrowing wind stirring his white locks as the vine continued to wrap around my body. He was merely a foot away when I lit the vine in flame, scampering forward and finding my footing. I went to run, the river's energy leaching from my veins as I lost control of the fight, but hard footsteps thundered in my direction. Aaren's strong arm caught me and lifted me until my feet left the ground, and hard bark pressed into my exposed back. His hands grasped my bare thighs and kept my feet from the ground.

There was no escaping his hold. I had lost the fight.

My hands gripped the tree for balance, legs locking around Aaren's waist, should his hands decide to try and drop me.

"What are you going to do to me, Aaren? Kill me?"

His brows notched higher, the glow in his eyes morphing from anger to something I couldn't place. "After all this time, is that what you think of me, Layla? Just some bloodthirsty brute?" His grip tightened on my thighs, and his face was close enough that our noses brushed. Heat flooded my palms, searing into the tree. "Don't you ever bring Solveig into this. Do you understand?"

"Then don't ever weaponize my misfortune against me," I spat. "Do *you* understand?"

Aaren's gaze slowly dropped to my lips, and his chest rumbled with something like a growl. My palms weren't the only place where heat was now pooling. The limp dress strap across my scarred shoulder caught his attention. My rune throbbed, desire sending my heart into a violent flutter.

"You need to learn to control what you send through the rune," Aaren muttered with a lascivious look. "I can practically read your thoughts through it."

"And what am I thinking, Aaren?" I demanded, keenly aware of his calloused fingers scratching up my thighs.

Feeling returned to my legs when he released me, and I almost whined at the loss of contact. "Go back inside the mountain," Aaren instructed, and turned his back to me once again. "I want to be alone." He shot me a glance as he retreated further into the trees. "And no, there is nothing you can do to help."

I trekked back to the mountain with our fight heavy in my mind.

No matter how much I hated Aaren's spiteful words, he had been right. I had offered myself up countless times since I came to Alveland to prove that I wasn't some havoc-wreaking stranger and that I could be helpful, wanted even. And while I was trying so hard to prove that I was needed, the truth was, I didn't have to prove anything to these people. I needed to prove it to myself, just so I could believe that someone like me, an orphan who had been overlooked by adopters, lovers, teachers, and customers, could still be wanted. I needed to prove my worth so much to myself that I couldn't see that the Fraalver had already shown me. Nilsen had been the first, then Thea and Rorik, Inaborg and Börgil, and in his odd, mysterious way, even Aaren proved it. It was glaringly obvious, and I wanted to kick myself for not seeing it.

Aaren had been right, and I didn't expect an apology for it.

Just as I wouldn't give one for what I said. A truth for a truth, and I knew I had hit the nail on the head with what I said. He couldn't deny that most of the stress and pressure he felt was only from himself, from how high a pedestal he put his parents on, high enough that he would never reach it. He was a good leader, but was too blinded by misplaced guilt and self-deprecation to see it.

It drove me insane to see him beat himself up like that, which is why I wouldn't offer anything more than standing my ground. What he said was painful to hear, but it came from a place of hurt, just as my own words had, and I didn't see the need to fault him for it, especially since people had said way worse things for a lot less throughout my life. No one grew thick skin like an orphan in the public school system.

I didn't see Aaren until the sun had crested the mountain peaks and the funeral pyre had been built. Instead of the dark circles and disheveled hair I had expected, he looked refreshed, as if that release of enraged magic had restored him. I almost took a step towards him, to make amends for what went down in the woods, but I turned on my heel and sauntered away from the entrance tunnel where he had emerged, deciding to get ready for the funeral instead.

There was music and food, and everyone was dressed in their finest, but there were no cheers, no laughter, and, least of all, there was no dancing. The circumstances were too dire for anyone to summon any ounce of mirth, and I prayed that Torsten was resourceful enough to make it to Himmelfjell without the extra push a lively funeral would give. How could anyone be expected to celebrate the premature death of their leader, especially when it was at the hands of the burrowers?

Ertha had ensured that Torsten was dressed in his finest robes; the bed in which he lay was swathed in rich silk and lined with packs of supplies and baskets of food. Gripped in his stiff fingers was a shining, deadly greatsword, the hilt embedded with the same polished marble I had seen all over the inside of the mountain.

"That sword has been passed down through Fjellhjem leadership since the village was born," Fiske said. "The marble in the hilt is constructed from the first bit of rock that was ever carved from the mountain. They burn every leader with it in their hands." Seeing as swords don't melt very easily, especially with a stone hilt, that weapon must have been burned hundreds of times. And it still held a shine that rivaled any gold I had ever seen. "It represents their beginning and end."

Ertha climbed the ladder to the top and paused as she gazed into her beloved's pale face one more time. She remained stoic, her still features a testament to what was most important for a leader to possess: strength. She leaned down and kissed his brow. Hot, stinging tears welled in my eyes as she dropped the torch and set the pyre ablaze. The flames flickered across her face, and my heart ached for her. She'd already had to burn her daughter; now, her husband. All Ertha had left was her people.

People who were no longer safe as long as she remained unmarried.

Unless...

As she climbed down the ladder, the crowd dispersed to graze the food tables and mutter in hushed tones amongst themselves.

"Ertha," I breathed as I jogged to her side, noting that her makeup wasn't as pristine as it had been before, as if she'd wiped it off and started over multiple times. I pressed my lips together, my hands finding hers and squeezing. "Come to Skoghjem," I said. Aaren approached behind me, and my rune simmered. "You're not safe here anymore, not with Markus at large and the burrowers crawling through the hills." Ertha blinked, her mouth parting as if she was going to argue. "Our borders are secure, and we can muster the resources to accommodate you."

She only pulled her hands out of mine, face still vacant, but her eyes swelled with so much grief, I thought she was about to throw herself into the fire. I kept my eye on her as she turned away, walking as close to the burning pyre as she could and circled it.

As the night went on, so did the whispers, the Fraalver murmuring until the plates were empty and exhaustion filled us all.

And Ertha continued to circle as the flames raged on.

When the sun had sunk below the peaks and the pyre was barely more than embers and ash, Ertha finally halted, her makeup streaked through with silent tears. She barely gave the sword time to cool before she slid it from the ashes.

And when she turned to me, not Aaren, not Fiske, the three people who had stayed in the hall with her until the fire's dying breath. She turned to *me*.

"When do we leave?" she asked

Chapter 40

The four-day journey back to Skoghjem turned into seven days, seeing as we were now accounting for nearly five hundred Fraalver. It was grueling, and I envied Fiske, who got to mount a horse and return to Kysthjem alone. It was with a heavy heart that I bid him goodbye, unsure when we were going to see him again. In vain, I had hoped it would be soon, but I knew the circumstances would have us coming together for much different reasons than I had hoped for. In that case, I hoped it would be a long while before we met again.

Ertha was holding up better than I would have thought. Every night after the tents were erected, she would visit each fire and sit, sharing a couple of bites of dinner with each of her people and talking. I made a round with her on our second night, distracting myself with the lovely conversations and sips of stew as the night went on. The people of Fjellhjem welcomed me warmly, filling my dinner bowl with gratitude as much as they did with stew. I didn't do it to prove anything to myself—I did it because these people needed company and reassurance that everything would be alright, even if I weren't so sure of that myself.

A pining ache filled my chest when the trees of Skoghjem came into view at the edge of the horizon. Even Froki seemed relieved by the sight, and she bobbed her head and chuffed. We had been away for too long, and the first place I was going to was the pub for a hot meal and three pints of ale, minimum. Then I'd go to Thea's, of course, to see my friend, but also to grab another one of her books since I had read this one four times since hitting the road. I could recite the first hundred pages if I really tried.

The birds chirped and sang vibrantly, welcoming us home with a song that filled my soul. As we neared the edge of the village, Froki was getting harder to control as excitement overtook her, and she tried to book it straight for the stables. Rorik had already made preparations to accommodate the Fjellhjem Fraalver, and tents gathered in groups around the outside, serving as temporary lodging until we could provide them with something more permanent. Or until they could return to the mountains. For their sake, I hoped it was the latter.

When I saw the smoke rising from the pub chimney, tears welled in my eyes.

Home. I was *home.*

A group of Fraalver gathered near the border, and I smiled uncontrollably at the familiar faces that greeted us. Aaren had barely dismounted his horse before Nilsen came barrelling towards him, almost knocking him to the ground as he wrapped his arms around his brother. Aaren dropped to his knees, a hand braced behind Nilsen's head, and hugged him tightly. Something dull twanged in my chest at the sight—it was a sudden, consuming desire for that to be me, and the little boy in my arms wasn't Nilsen, but Lucas. He still, after *everything*, held so much of my headspace that it was getting to be maddening.

Everything I did, I had to remind myself that I was getting one step closer to him.

"Where's Layla?" Nilsen's voice asked, and I shook myself from my Lucas-driven stupor.

"Right here," I replied, stepping closer.

Nilsen tore away from Aaren, sprinting the short distance between us, and before his arms could wrap around me, he sent me to the ground upon impact. I laughed and gave him a tight squeeze as Aaren rose to his feet.

"Alright, *bror*," he said, and swept him off of me as I struggled to roll over. "Let her breathe, we've both been through a lot."

When I stood and brushed away the dirt, Ertha dismounted and approached.

"It's been far too long since I crossed your borders, Aaren," she said, and there was a slight shake in her voice. "Thank you." Then her gaze fell to Nilsen, who squared his small shoulders and brushed his blonde hair from his eyes. "You've grown a lot since I last saw you."

A smug look crossed Nilsen's features. "I'm a warrior now," he said proudly. "I killed a fenr and saved Layla from a huldra."

Aaren tousled his brother's hair and called for Oswin and Ivar to take care of the horses.

"Skoghjem is your home as much as Fjellhjem would have been mine," Aaren said when he turned back to Ertha, and there was a tone of sadness in his words. Ertha gave a sorrowful smile and bowed her head.

I stepped forward and reached for her hand. "Come, let's—"

A pair of rose and vanilla-scented arms slid over my shoulders and pulled me into a plump bosom.

"Gods, I missed you, *frue*," Thea's smooth voice said in my ear, and I gave Ertha an apologetic look before turning in Thea's arms and giving her the tightest embrace I could muster.

"I missed you, too."

I felt her smile against my cheek. "I want to hear all about your trip," she cooed, her embrace loosening for a second, only for her to add in my ear, "Please tell me you rode something other than that horse."

Rolling my eyes, I let out a scoff and released her, keeping her hands grasped in mine. "I finished your book. I am in desperate need of another one."

"You flatter me," she beamed, then offered me her arm. "Come, I have so much to tell you."

Thea had barely spoken a word before Inaborg dragged me away, saying she needed my help cooking dinner, considering there were nearly three times as many mouths to feed. We cooked the biggest pot of venison stew I had ever seen, bigger than even Inaborg had ever served.

The kitchen was blistering as we toiled away, the sweat threatening to drip into the stew as I stirred it. Inaborg carried her fifth serving of carrots and parsley and tossed them into the pot.

"Stir faster, Layla!" Inaborg chirped. "They're only getting hungrier."

I stuck out my tongue playfully, tasting sweat and salt.

She chuckled and went to turn away, but only made it a step before turning back to me. "It's good to have you back, *frue*," she said gratefully, almost on the verge of tears. I paused my stirring and watched her carefully as my own tears tried to wet my lashes.

"I'd better not catch you crying," I said, my voice shaky.

Inaborg let out a teary laugh, waving a hand away and turning, so I wouldn't see her swipe her apron over her eyes. "It'll save us on salt if I do."

I resumed my stirring with a chuckle.

Thea helped me pass out the stew—I pushed the cart while she distributed the bowls throughout the makeshift camp just outside the village, but still within the borders.

"Before I tell you anything, I want to know what I missed," I said as she handed the first bowl of stew to a small woman with a gray shawl.

Thea sighed. Her eyes watched the trees, following the birds as they jumped from branch to branch. "Where to begin? To start, poor Rorik was an utter mess without Aaren."

"Seriously?" I asked, surprised. "I would've thought Rorik of all people would be the best equipped to run the village."

Thea huffed contrarily. "You would think. I suppose it's hard to run a village that is being attacked by mylings left and right, though."

I froze in my tracks, nearly spilling the bowls of stew on the cart. "What?"

"There have been three attacks since you left. Luckily, no one suffered the same fate as Dagan, but it has put everyone on edge." She shook her head and reached for another bowl. "Stieg was nearly attacked. If he hadn't been so close to the border, he would've..."

She shook her head again, then plastered a strained smile as she handed out another bowl.

"Most of the hunters have been too frightened to cross the borders since the last attack."

"Is Stieg alright?"

Thea leaned forward and passed a bowl to a small girl, who displayed a wide gap where her front teeth should've been when she smiled. "Thankfully, yes," Thea replied as the little girl wandered off. "All parts are working just fine." I caught her smirk at the last bit, ignoring the mischievous glint in her eye.

"Oh, well, thank goodness *all* of his parts work," I retorted,

"You truly have not fucked Aaren?" she asked after making sure we were out of earshot before inquiring.

I laughed before I could blush. "You ask the most vulgar things."

"Layla, you read my book, you should know by now where my priorities lie."

I sighed. "No, I truly have not fucked Aaren."

Thea purred in disappointment. "What are you waiting for? You're already married to him!"

I shook my head. "I married him for the village and to reset the borders. And besides, he's my friend, I'm not sure fucking is on his mind when he thinks of me." Maybe it had been before our fight a week ago, but seeing as we hardly spoke during the journey home and he spent his nights sleeping by the fire instead of in the tent with me, I had a feeling fucking me was far down the list of the things he wanted to do to me. He'd probably be more likely to beat the daylights out of me before he ever fucked me.

But it didn't matter, because I didn't want to fuck him either. And I was going to ignore every memory of lustful thoughts my mind presented in argument of that fact. I feigned a smile as I passed out the last bowl on the cart.

"Then who are you going to fuck, Layla? You're married, the only person that could scratch that itch is Aaren."

She was right, but I didn't want to think about it.

I walked back to the house with another one of Thea's books tucked under my arm, giddy to start reading. Seeing as I was now basically celibate, Thea had better start writing a book a day with the way I was going to run through them.

Rorik and Aaren sat and conversed quietly by the sizzling fire with pewter tankards of ale in their hands. Nilsen was nowhere to be seen, but I had heard Ingrid shouting about a treehouse meeting as Thea and I passed out the stew earlier.

I dropped the book on the table and poured myself a drink from the pitcher, and drank deeply before sitting down.

"So you truly plan to hand over Hel's legendary dagger...to a group of feral mylings?" Rorik asked in disbelief. "Do you realize how dangerous an artifact like that can be in the hands of something like the mylings? Especially mylings working for *Markus Sviker*! You cannot be serious."

"It's the only option we have, Rorik," Aaren barked

"Welcome back to us," I murmured into my ale, thankful no one heard my quip.

"We need to reduce Markus's ranks, and with the draugr and the burrowers on his side, the mylings are the easiest thing to wipe out." Aaren ran his fingers over his scalp, and his shoulders tensed. A small strike of discomfort radiated from my rune. His scar was acting up. "Not to mention we now have a fucking necromancer on the loose."

Rorik sucked the ale from his mustache. "And who's to say the mylings don't just turn the dagger over to Markus?"

"By the Aesir, Rorik, they're children, do you really think they're that diabolical?" Aaren demanded, then drained his mug before refilling it. His knuckles turned white as he gripped the table.

"If Markus promised them something better, then yes, I do think so."

I blew out a breath and put down the mug that I had been hiding behind. Sliding my hand over, I brushed Rorik's and felt the tension knot through his knuckles. He was shaking, from anger or stress, I couldn't tell. I hadn't realized how much of a toll the past few weeks had taken on him, but he was wound tighter than a drum.

"Rorik," I said softly, rubbing my thumb over his knuckles. "I don't think Markus could promise the mylings anything better than a one-way ticket to the top of Himmelfjell."

The fire popped, filling the weighted silence that fell around us as Rorik's eyes dropped to my hand on his.

"This is a very, very big risk," he said through the stilted silence. "But Torsten didn't die for us not to try." I gave him a reassuring squeeze before returning my hand to my mug. "We should act tonight," he suggested. "The sooner we get rid of them, the sooner we can figure out next steps."

Next steps: to find Markus and Lucas.

Rorik lingered long enough for us to finalize our plan to return the dagger at nightfall, then he excused himself and left me and Aaren alone for the first time since our fight in Fjellhjem. The silence went from pensive to awkward. Aaren toyed with his mug, running a finger over the rim. I watched him closely, but he kept his features complex and unreadable.

"I'm sorry for what I said in the mountains," he said finally, yellow eyes rising to meet mine. There was embarrassment and guilt on his face. "It was uncalled for, and I didn't mean a word of it."

I finished my drink and licked the remaining ale from my lips, keenly aware of Aaren tracking my tongue as it swiped across my lower lip. "I did," I replied, to which Aaren's brows notched in surprise.

"You meant it?"

I nodded. "And I'm not sorry for it. The only thing I'm sorry about is that I didn't say it at a better time. You needed to hear it, and so did I."

Aaren sat back, gaze moving to the wood of the table as if he were scrutinizing the grain. "I guess I did mean one thing," he continued. He flicked his eyes to me, then gestured to our runes. "You need to figure out how to close this off. Especially during times like dancing. It was hard to discern my own emotions from yours."

The dancing in Fjellhjem where we groped and ground against each other. The dance where the music and his touch carried me so deep into euphoria, it was a struggle to claw myself out.

"What was that dance about?" I asked. "It was so..."

"Sexual?" Aaren finished for me. The blush that painted my cheeks must've been enough to answer. He chuckled. "That's what I thought the first time, too. The Fjellhjem Fraalver believe that the union of thunder and the earth formed the mountains. The drums play the thunder while the melody plays the earth, recreating the mating of the two forces. The dance is a way to pay homage to their mountains."

I cocked a brow and gave him a questioning look. "And during the dance, my emotions were that loud?"

Aaren huffed a laugh and stood. "Maybe after it's all said and done with the mylings, we can have Rorik help us dampen the attunement on the runes. Because yes, Layla, they were screaming at me."

So with my emotions overpowering his own, coupled with the dance that was supposed to be sexual in nature, not to mention the fact that he had shut down my attempts that one night in our room, all but confirmed my suspicions—the very last thing Aaren wanted to do was fuck me. And I would chalk whatever had passed between us after our fight as an act of passion, both of us so lost in our anger and the near overpowering magic that it should only be taken for what it was. A passion-driven lapse in judgment. Like a drunken one-night stand. It doesn't mean anything, but damn does it feel good in the moment.

Celibacy was going to be the death of me.

I made my rounds with Ertha again as the sun began to set, trying my best to make the Fjellhjem Fraalver feel welcome despite the circumstances. When my face started to hurt from feigning a smile, I excused myself to return to the house, but stopped abruptly at the blacksmith shop. Working alongside Borgil was a shirtless, sweaty Aaren. I bit my lip, fighting with myself to rip my eyes away from his sweat-sheened, rippling biceps as he hammered at a piece of metal at the workbench. His hair was swept up in a bun, hanging in damp strings around his face, his features set and tense in concentration.

"Hello, *frue*!" Borgil greeted with a friendly wave.

I jolted out of my trance as my brain frantically searched for words, but I couldn't speak as I watched Aaren rise from the workbench and swipe his brow.

"You alright there, *fremmed*?" he asked as he tossed the hammer in his grip.

"Uh, yep," I stammered. "I'm great, just watching you. I mean, watching you work and...what are you doing, exactly?"

Aaren and Borgil exchanged humored glances before Borgil replied. "We're working on some armor," he said. He crouched down and produced a finished breastplate from a chest under the worktable.

"Armor?" I questioned.

Aaren nodded and gestured for me to come closer. "It seems inevitable at this point, so we might as well be prepared."

I hummed in agreement. "Can I help? Please don't give me that look, Aaren. I'm bored. It's either this or I go suffocate at Harald's." Borgil gave a quiet laugh from his workstation.

Aaren considered me for a second. "You can help," he said almost resignedly. "And as you don't have any armor, you will help by making your own."

"What?" I asked. "I wanted to help polish or something, I don't know how to make armor!"

"Relax, *fremmed*."

"We'll help you," Borgil assured kindly.

Aaren stepped deeper into the forge and grabbed two large masses of metal. He tossed them in his hands before he threw them to the ground at my feet. "We'll be working with steel and leather. Can you handle that, Layla?"

I hated that Aaren knew how to twist me. All he had to do was question my capability to get me to cooperate. I could never say no to a challenge.

"Of course I can handle it," I said. Then I nearly toppled over when I realized how heavy the ingots were. Aaren watched me amusedly as I tried again.

"Shut up, Borgil," I spat when I heard a small giggle from his turned back.

"Leave him be, *fremmed*, it's not every day he has a woman in his forge."

Borgil stopped whatever work he was doing and turned, waving a hammer as he spoke. "I'll have you know, Aaren, that just last night—"

"Let's get your measurements," Aaren said and turned me away with a grin. Borgil grumbled something as Aaren led me to the fire pit, the heat sending pleasant goose bumps along my skin. Reaching behind him, he brought out a strap of leather and a sliver of coal. "Arms up."

I obeyed, and my eyes moved to the wooded roof over the forge as his scent filled my nostrils. I wasn't sure what shutting down the connection with the rune would entail, but I did what I thought would work to keep the connection closed. I couldn't have him knowing what his scent did to me. He wrapped the leather around my waist, marked it with the coal, then measured my hips before straightening.

"Keep your arms up, *fremmed*," he instructed, nudging my right bicep as he circled the leather around my shoulder.

I wasn't sure why my heart stuttered when his fingers danced across my skin and dragged the leather with it, but I focused on the slam of Borgil's hammer and let it ground me before I could be carried away into fantasies only Thea could write.

Aaren measured the length of my torso, the width of my shoulders, and my breath became difficult when his hand brushed my collarbone.

"I need to measure your breasts," he said, jolting me from my grounding.

"My…"

Come on, Layla, don't make it weird.

"Go ahead," I said, feigning the cool in my voice.

The strap cut into my shirt, the skin underneath protesting by sending tingling prickles across my chest. Aaren's brows twitched with what almost looked like surprise, and I hoped he didn't feel my heart thundering under the strap. My traitorous body reacted, and my nipples pebbled under my shirt, and it felt like eternity before Aaren marked the strap. If I didn't know any better, I'd say he lingered there for a moment longer than any other measurements, but sadly, I did know better.

The sounds of the forge came roaring back into my ears when he took the strap away, and the hammering sounded like gunshots to my temples.

I spent the next hour and a half hammering out a breastplate while Aaren critiqued and corrected the mistakes. By then, we were at each other's throats again.

"You're holding the hammer wrong," he said.

The heat stung my skin, and sweat soaked my shirt as I bristled with irritation. "There's a wrong way to hold a hammer?" I hissed, throwing the tool down.

I was thankful that Borgil had called it a day and retreated to the pub for dinner, so he wouldn't see me rip into his leader like I was getting ready to do. But then Aaren closed the distance between us, grabbed the hammer with one hand, and nailed me with a stern, but understanding look.

"Take a deep breath, *fremmed*," he said, holding the hammer away from me as if he was afraid I'd snatch it and bash his head. "It's hot, and we have not stopped since we got back." He dropped the hammer into my hand and rearranged my fingers until I was holding it correctly. "This is how you hold it. Remember that for next time."

Aaren stepped away from me and donned his shirt, then smoothed the stray strands of hair out of his face.

"Come on," he said and gestured for me to follow. "Let's get something to eat."

The pub was lively, and the food brought me back to life from the long days on the road. I had missed Inaborg's cooking, and I missed her ale even more.

Just as the sun fell below the trees, the Hem horn was blown to bring the children behind the borders. A small wave of them came from the direction of the treehouse while others trickled back in pairs, covered in dirt and giggling. It reminded me of when Lucas would come home from school with mud-stained knees and grass marks on his shirt. Sarah almost banned him from going to recess because she couldn't afford to keep buying him new clothes.

Then the moon crept above the trees, and Aaren, Rorik, Ertha, and I traipsed along the path, crossed over the border, and into the dark forest beyond. Ugleverge hooted above us, his movements a graceful flurry of flapping wings and shadows as he trailed us from the sky.

Oh, how I had missed this forest. What had only been a few weeks away felt like months, years. It didn't matter that we were on the way to deliver a dagger to a horde of cursed, dead children; I couldn't be happier to be encased in the safety of the dark branches and listen to the crickets. A breeze rustled the leaves above, and I breathed it in deeply, let it circle and cleanse my lungs.

The forest opened up into a glen, where the sparse trees allowed the moon to shine brightly, illuminating the little clusters of blue and purple wildflowers that had emerged from their winter slumber. I knelt over a bundle of blue blossoms, felt their petals kiss the tips of my fingers.

"Blamstrars," Aaren said over my shoulder, his shadow covering mine. "They only grow when there is death close by."

I pulled my hand away from the flowers as an icy chill ran up my spine.

"Hallow?"

A small girl emerged from the shadows, around five or six years old, with aged, dusty clothes and cheeks covered in a layer of dirt that masked the decay of her skin. Her eyes were a murky green, the color of dying moss, and they locked on me as she cocked her head, exposing a decaying scalp under her ratty hair.

"Hallow..."

Aaren crept soundlessly behind the girl, ready to pounce the moment the myling decided to launch into action.

"Y-yes," I stuttered, "I have hallow."

Steadying my trembling hands, I reached into the pack strapped to my side and retrieved Hel's dagger, the deadly blade shimmering in the moonlight. Something out of the corner of my eye scampered into the clearing and sent Aaren's hand flying to the hilt of his sword. Wind stirred, and caution bloomed from my rune as Aaren sent me a silent warning. The myling from the beginning, the one who spoke the night I tried to run away, emerged into the glen. His gray skin reflected the moonlight in a ghastly shimmer.

"You have hallow?" the myling asked in a gravelly voice that broke the peaceful forest night.

I studied the boy for a moment, heart growing heavier the more I considered it. How had it died, and why hadn't it been burned like everyone else? Surely it was some freak accident, perhaps its body was never found to be burned, and I prayed its misfortune wasn't the product of a neglectful household. A sick feeling sent my stomach into a tumble when the possibility of seeing Lucas among these children came to mind.

"I have something better." The blade reflected in the myling's dim eyes as I held it up, and its features glazed over with awe. Its face somehow lit up, as if a wave of life flushed its cheeks and washed away a bit of the decay caked to its skin. With a snarl, it moved to reach forward, but I withdrew and held the dagger up and out of reach. It bared its gnarled teeth and groaned, the sound like someone scraping their nails against an old gravestone. I shuddered. "I will give it to you if you vow to leave Markus's ranks. You have no place in this fight. You belong in Himmelfjell." I lowered the blade slightly, watching the myling's eyes track even the slightest of movements.

Something like a cry broke its throat as it nodded slowly. "The longer we spend here, the more our souls decay." Its eyes broke from the knife just for a moment, the briefest moment where humanity flickered across the dead features. A moment where he looked like a child again. "We vow not to take part in your fight," it said, "but a warning to you. War is brewing. And it is a war you will not win."

Aaren inched closer. "What do you know of Markus's forces?" The breeze picked up, the faint shuffling of restless vines rustling around the edges of the clearing.

The myling turned slightly, just enough to keep both Aaren and me in its sights. "He is rallying his forces, confiding in darker evils." The myling gave a slight shiver, and I couldn't imagine anything that could make even a myling shy away from darkness. "Evils that have slumbered for centuries."

"What kind of forces is Markus rallying?" I asked, hands growing sweaty around the dagger.

The myling's upper lip curled. "This is far bigger than Markus, Layla Sviker." The myling stirred, growing anxious the longer the dagger remained in my possession. I doubted it was going to divulge anything else.

I lowered my arm and tossed the dagger onto the bed of flowers in front of the myling, stepping away as if I had just thrown a starving lion its dinner. Stems snapped as its gnarled fingers dug into the flowers, pulling roots free as it held the dagger up triumphantly. Dirt and decay tainted the white, bone-hilted knife. A bone-chilling laugh rattled from the myling's throat as the battle over its eternal damnation came to a close, and the dagger drove deeply into its stomach.

That same flicker of humanity danced across its face as the iron grip of death loosened. Then it wasn't a myling in front of me, but a boy. A boy who had a sharp brow and deep-set eyes that were probably cast in shadow even in life. I wondered if he used to play Balderkrig.

His features eased, relief washing away the dead stare and sinister sneer. The boy sighed, and I momentarily forgot what I was watching. I took a step forward, the instinct to hold him overpowering my better judgement, but Aaren caught my arm, and snapped me back into sense.

"Before you go," I said as dark blood soaked through the fabric of the boy's tattered shirt. "What's your name?"

Pairs of beady eyes shone from the edges of the glen, muted rustling stirring as Aaren's vines kept the other mylings at bay.

"Finn," the boy replied, then dropped to his knees, hands stained dark crimson. "My name is Finn." The breeze picked up again, this time on its own volition, and the top of Finn's head began to flake away as he started to crumble to ash. "Good luck, Layla," he managed through a choked gasp, bigger flakes floating into the night. Finn stayed wholly still as he crumbled to dust, until every fleck of his earthly body had drifted into the moon and disappeared.

"Hallowed," a whisper said in the wind.

I hadn't realized I had been crying until Aaren swiped a thumb across my cheek, more tears trickling down my face. The dagger lay nestled in the wildflowers, and Aaren's arm snaked around my middle and pulled me out of the glen as the vines released the other mylings. They careened forward, climbing over each other much like the feral draugr had in Fjellgrav.

The first, myling, an older girl, found the dagger first and held it up for the moonlight to glint across the blade.

"My name is Agda," she said, then plunged the dagger into her chest with a sickening thud, and, just like Finn, she was just a kid. A kid with cinnamon hair braided down her back and a pouty mouth that smiled exaltedly.

And then the next myling picked up the dagger, and whispered his name—Einar. One by one, the mylings drove the dagger through their stomachs, but each one gave their name. Halvor, Irma, Nellie, Rasmus, Kaia, and I memorized every single one of them as I watched life flicker back into their eyes for just a second before they were gone. Ugleverge perched on the branch above us, watching the children that weren't his to guard anymore. The clearing clouded with ash, and when the last myling gave their name—Yngvar—and buried the dagger in his abdomen, the glen fell silent.

The dagger was buried in the dust, and when Rorik retrieved it, he paused to brush off the hilt, then offered it to Ertha. She hesitated.

"Thank you," Rorik said. "For what this has cost you."

Understanding blossomed on Ertha's face, and she pressed her lips together. Then she accepted the dusty blade.

Ugleverge followed us all the way back to the village.

Chapter 41

Inaborg set down a tray of mugs and a plate of bread with cheese as the chorus of two villages mingling echoed around us. As joyous as the sound was, I was still rattled by what had happened in the clearing with the mylings. And we had learned some new things that Rorik insisted we discuss.

"What did Finn mean when he said something about ancient evils?" I questioned, licking away the foamy ale from my lips. Again, Aaren watched my tongue as it spread the expanse of my lips. And no matter what I told myself, there was hunger in his gaze. There was no denying it. Ignoring him, I continued, "You don't think this has something to do with the necromancer?"

Rorik's chewed fingers massaged his worn brow, his dark circles more prominent in the flickering light. "If this necromancer is more involved in this plot of Markus's than we thought, then we could be in for a very long war."

Aaren nodded. "We'd be foolish to disregard the necromancer for what he is. He poses more of a threat than Markus if left unchecked."

"You don't suppose this necromancer is raising anything from the First Wars?" Ertha asked, already needing a refill.

The First Wars—the longest Chapter of Fraalver History: Volume III. That Chapter was one of the nights when I made a massive breakthrough with my magic, mainly due to my frustration. The Chapter was eighty pages long, detailing the scattered battles that occurred in the different realms against the most fearsome monsters that still dwelled and sought to destroy the realm's settlers. The most notorious monsters were known as the Drapstre, also referred to as the Killing Three, and they wreaked havoc among the realms.

The dwarf realm, Nidavellir, faced its own battles, but the Chapter only went into brief detail about them. The Fraalver and elves fought three main monsters: Ondgris, the killer boar, Morderbor, an all-powerful bear, and Darhak, a dangerous winged creature, of which most descriptions had been lost. There were smaller, less hazardous creatures that roamed the lands, but they'd been slowly picked off, some even killed by Nils and Freya, and even Aaren himself.

"We had best pray that the Drapstre stay dead," Aaren said, summoning Inaborg over for refills.

I gulped down the rest of my ale, then offered my mug to her. "So, they're really gone?" Inaborg asked as she wiped her hands on her apron and tucked a strand of hair back into her bun.

Aaren chewed on a piece of bread. "If Hel's dagger truly does what legend says, we are free of them."

The dagger rested on the table next to Ertha, and in the setting of the pub, it looked plain, like it was just an ordinary dagger that Borgil had made in his forge.

Inaborg smiled, placing a gentle hand on Aaren's shoulder. His eyes rose to meet her gaze questioningly. "Nils and Freya would be proud."

He gave her a kind smile and rubbed her hand. "Thank you, Inaborg."

I took another sip of my fresh ale, noticing the sadness that glazed Ertha's features as she watched a couple clink mugs across the pub. I was more focused on Oswin and Ivar drunkenly dancing on a table, before Inaborg snatched their drinks away and shoved them out the door. I knew the look on Ertha's face, though—it was the same look I gave every family I saw after Mama and Granny died. It was the look I gave when I saw someone with something I didn't have. For me, that was a family. For Ertha, that was her husband. And even though I knew that look, I couldn't begin to understand what she was feeling. And I hoped I never would.

"I propose a toast," Rorik began as he raised his tankard. He watched Ertha in her moment of melancholy and lifted his drink higher. "To the unity of our people."

Ertha blinked, feigning a politeness I knew only a diplomat could manage at a moment like this, and gave a soft smile that didn't meet her eyes. She raised her mug. "And to Layla. She gives me hope that we may win this war." Her gaze dropped to the table. "No matter how impossible it may seem."

I hoped I wasn't blushing, but now, on my second mug of ale, I knew my cheeks were red, whether I was flattered or not.

Aaren's mug met ours with a soft clink. "While we look to the future, we must not forget those we leave behind in the past," he said in a firm voice despite the slight grief haunting his features. "To Torsten. May he find endless ale and glory in the halls of Himmelfjell."

We all chimed our toasts of agreement, then drank until our mugs were empty, and our hearts were full.

"Now, let us celebrate this victory," Rorik beamed and rose from the bench. He gathered our mugs into his arms. "Because what is life if you don't celebrate even the smallest triumphs?" He brought our mugs to the bar for Inaborg to refill, while Oswin and Ivar snuck back into the pub by distracting everyone with a bawdy drinking song.

I joined in with the few words I knew, letting my voice carry on and mingle with my people's. Ertha smiled again, this time more genuinely, as Oswin wrapped an arm around a Fjellhjem Fraalver and sang with drunken revelry. Aaren sang too, and I could hear his voice over the entire pub, though something told me it was only because I was more attuned to hear him.

In a moment of quiet, I slipped away to the fire and let the heat burn my cheeks as I mulled over the names of the mylings.

"Finn," I whispered into the flames. "Agda."

"Viktor," Aaren said behind me, and I glanced over my shoulder to the fire's light flickering across his features. "And Tomas."

I sighed and turned back to the hearth. "Bragi."

Aaren and I took turns saying their names into the flames, giving them our own version of a Fraalver funeral. A funeral stolen from those children. We remembered every single name from the clearing that night, and my voice shook when the last one left my lips. Hot tears stung my eyes as I worked to swallow past the tightness in my throat. It only took me a minute to compose myself, but when I turned, Aaren was gone.

By the end of the night, Rorik and Ertha drank enough ale to fill a pond big enough for a Nokken to move in. Ertha stumbled about the pub, pinching Ivar's cheeks as she went for more ale, and she gave Axl a wet kiss on the forehead before stepping away to dance to the fiddle by the hearth. Axl blushed and wiped his forehead as a small smile curved his lips. Rorik, on the other hand, had passed out face-first on the bar and was snoring violently, twitching and coughing every few minutes.

Inaborg gave the last call and began putting up the chairs. I helped with the cleanup, but I had to dodge Ivar, who followed me around and begged for one more drink. Asta, who had joined the merriment only an hour ago, threw Rorik's arm over her shoulder and hoisted him off the stool. Rorik's weight didn't faze her as she dragged him through the door, and he gave a sloppy wave and a slurred good-bye as they left. He was in good hands; the person I was worried about was Ertha.

I found her by the fire with her arm slung around Von.

"Well, what are you waiting for, Von? You aren't getting any younger, *dum gutt.*"

Von shook his head. "What if she doesn't feel the same way?"

Ertha huffed, momentarily going cross-eyed. "If you love Britta, just tell her. I know the girl, she'll take kindly to that." She booped his nose. "I promise you."

Von took notice of me approaching, and though he was smiling, he gave me a look as if to say, "Save me."

"Come on, Ertha," I said, and offered her my hand. "Let me show you to your room. You're going to like it." I hoped she liked it as much as I did, seeing as it was my old room before I married Aaren.

Ertha nodded slowly and accepted my hand after planting a wet kiss on Von's cheek. I held her hand, working to keep her stable as she stumbled to the stairs and up to her room. When the door swung open, Ertha sprang forward and flopped onto the bed with a delighted giggle. Her blonde curls splayed majestically beneath her head as she rolled over with a sigh. She sang softly as she stroked a strand of hair, curling it around her finger. Her shoes hit the floor as she curled into the furs, and I poured her a mug of juice and placed it on the bedside table.

"Okay, I'm going to go," I said, inching closer to the door but still eyeing her in case she slid onto the floor. Ertha rubbed her face on her pillow and mumbled something. "Huh?" I asked, taking a step closer.

Ertha's tousled hair stuck out at odd angles when she sat up and searched the room. "Where is my Torsten?"

"Wh...where is he?" I asked, my chest getting heavy.

"Mmm," she hummed, then hiccupped. "Find him and bring him to bed."

I wasn't sure if lying would be such a bad thing at the moment.

"Okay," I replied as my lungs grew too tight for my ribcage. "I'll find him."

Ertha hiccupped again and smoothed out her hair. "Thank you." Then she nestled into the bed, and light snores replaced her hiccupping. I slid the wash basin closer to the bed, should she need it in the middle of the night, then closed the door behind me.

The last few patrons stumbled through the door while Inaborg swept the crumbs off the benches and finished wiping the tables. After she assured me she'd keep an eye on Ertha, I stepped into the soft summer night, and the sound of crickets enveloped me as I followed the path back to the house.

As I came upon the sparring ring, I was surprised to see the torches were lit. Aaren stood in the middle, shirtless and glistening, but there was someone else there I couldn't make out. Curious as to who he was fighting, I crossed the square and approached the ring, then gasped when his opponent dodged and turned to reveal a head with no face. Where its features should've been, there was only doughy emptiness, and it was naked, but lacked any anatomy other than malleable-looking limbs and a flexible torso. It looked like it had been sculpted from clay, but despite its earthen body parts, it moved with a dexterity that rivaled Aaren's.

I watched as Aaren swung his sword, jaw clenched and cheeks blown out through the exertion. His movements were unimpeded, but seeing as he was likely out here since he left the pub two hours ago, I knew he was about to push himself too far and possibly burn out. I couldn't imagine how his back was feeling.

The clay man countered Aaren's swing, but the force was enough to knock the sword out of its hand, or rather, knock the whole hand off. It thudded to the ground, and the clay man stomped. I imagined what it would be saying if it had a mouth, then grinned.

"Bested again," Aaren panted and kicked the sword away from the clay man. The thing shook its uninjured arm angrily and jabbed a clay finger at him. "It's not my fault you decided on defense instead of recovery," Aaren retorted as if he had heard what the clay man could have said. It dropped its head in resignation, and its earthen shoulders slumped as it turned to find me at the edge of the ring. It tensed, then scrambled to grab its discarded sword.

"It's alright," Aaren assured. "It's just Layla."

"What is it?" I asked, nodding to the clay figure. It bowed to me, flourishing flirtatiously.

Aaren scoffed at it. "Back off," he warned. "That's my wife."

The figure straightened and swiped a flick of dust from its shoulder like it wasn't already made of earth.

"It's a jordman," Aaren answered, smirking as it gave me a wave. "I sculpt them from the clay in the earth. They do anything and everything I say."

"I don't understand," I said as I stepped into the ring for a better look at the jordman. "I would think this is something that falls along the lines of Fjellhjem magic."

Aaren hummed. "It is. When Solveig accepted my betrothal, Ertha and Torsten bestowed this piece of magic as a gift, a welcoming, if you will." He gave the jordman a friendly look. "They make good companions, seeing as they don't speak."

The jordman's shoulders tensed and shot Aaren the finger. Aaren only chuckled. "You're dismissed."

The jordman bowed to me in farewell and stepped off the platform where it sank into the earth below.

"You summon them to train?"

"Only when I don't have a willing opponent." He crossed the ring to the table that held his shirt and a tankard of mead. I watched him take a long drink, though my eyes quickly roved the hard lines of his muscles that creased with every movement, a sight that sent an uncontrollable heat simmering across my skin. I reigned it in, hoping that would keep it from shooting through the rune.

"You could've asked me," I suggested, "I would've come out here with you."

Aaren swallowed and refilled his tankard. "No," he said gruffly. "You wouldn't be able to keep up with me tonight." I wasn't sure if he meant it as a challenge, but I took it as one.

I huffed, trying for nonchalance but bristling instead. "I'm sure I could hold my own."

"Don't hold your breath."

If that's how he wanted to play it...

Without thinking, I picked up a rock, big enough to fit in the palm of my hand, and threw it at him. It struck him in the shoulder before it bounced into his mug and splashed ale in his face. His jaw tightened, and quiet annoyance set into his features. Then he set his drink down.

"Do you really want to test me tonight, *fremmed*?" he asked, and the silent challenge caused me to falter and reassess what I had just done. It was like I had thrown the rock and awakened something far more dangerous than what I had seen before. Something primal stirred in his gaze, waiting for the right moment to strike.

He took a slow, testing step closer, and I panicked. My foot swung to kick him in the chest, and he stumbled back a few steps, then regained balance faster than he had lost it. Aaren advanced on me again, and I planted my feet, hands balling into fists as I adjusted my stance in the short time I had.

When he was just within reach, I careened forward and swung, but he dodged it. His hand closed around my fist and pulled me close to his chest. There was just enough room for me to jam my free hand into his gut, and his hold eased. It felt too easy to wriggle free and step back, but when I saw the way Aaren sized me up, I knew he had let me go on purpose. There was something different about the way he watched me. His everyday calculating look was replaced by the same look he had in the pub earlier that night. It was hunger. Instead of the regular assessments, I could see dancing behind his eyes, his gaze lingered on my heaving chest, the flush that crawled up my neck, and colored my cheeks.

"Looks like I'm doing alright," I flounced to break the tension. I bounced on the balls of my feet.

"I thought we were just warming up," Aaren said and cracked his neck as a slight grimace shadowed his features. His back was acting up just as I had suspected, but he wasn't going to stop on account of that. He looked determined to kick my ass, and I wasn't going to let that happen.

I launched forward, but Aaren read my movements and threw up a block, his forearm connecting with mine. He moved his hand inward, then grabbed my upper arm and spun. I lost my footing and slid to the ground.

Maybe he was right—the jordman was holding up better than I was in this fight. However, I was not going to give up, though a change in tactic would be helpful. I grappled for a sword that lay on the wooden boards a few inches away. Once the leather-bound hilt met my palm, I clambered to my feet, and when Aaren drew close enough to me, I seized the opportunity. My swing missed him by inches when he dove forward and spun, but I countered, and when he faltered for the briefest of seconds, he found his throat at the blade of my sword.

Aaren glanced at the blade momentarily, then smirked. A smirk that stirred a familiar desire in me that I had been trying to fight off for weeks. Aaren moved and left me exposed, and there was no time to prepare before he charged towards me, sword reared back and ready to strike. His blade slid against mine and sent sparks into the night. It would have been pretty if this fight didn't suddenly feel like a battle for my life and not a friendly spar. If I didn't gain the upper hand, I was going to panic. And if I panicked, I was screwed. I swept my foot underneath Aaren's, and he teetered, then slammed onto the wooden planks with a painful thud.

"Fuck," he groaned.

I smirked, circling him. "Are we still warming up?" I chided as he stood and shook off his small defeat.

"I'm going to make you regret entering the ring with me, *fremmed*."

He took three swift strides towards me, his fist shooting up for my face, but I caught it with both hands. But I left my chest exposed. Aaren twisted his wrist, and his fingers stretched until our roles reversed, and it was my wrists that were held captive. I tried to wriggle them free, but it only earned me a sly smile from Aaren. Then the cold metal tip of Aaren's sword traced down my neck, leaving a trail of prickled skin down my chest.

"If I were anyone else, you would be dead, *fremmed*," Aaren said in a husky voice that was riddled with exhausted exertion. The sword found the top button of my shirt and flicked it open. It clattered to the floor.

"But you're not anyone else," I said, and the grip around my wrists tightened. "So what are you going to do?"

Aaren hummed. "I can get creative." The sword flicked another button, and warm air kissed the beginnings of my breasts. If I didn't act, I wasn't sure Aaren would stop.

"I never thought creativity would ever be an attribute of yours," I teased and lifted a brow. "Since you're such a bloodthirsty brute."

He released me, but my squeaking boots gave away my next move.

I lunged, and when I saw Aaren prepare for the impact of my fist, I switched my attack and swept his feet from under him. When he hit the ground, I quickly straddled his chest and pinned his arms with my knees. I hadn't realized how hot my fingertips were until flames were practically bursting from my skin, but I couldn't figure out why. It could have been the adrenaline or the panic, but I couldn't help but think that it was the shift in Aaren. The way he looked at me was like he wasn't fighting for survival, but for sport.

I summoned a ball of blazing fire and let the flames dance through my fingers.

"Maybe so," Aaren panted, my fire dancing in his eyes. "I like to think I'm more of the quiet type. Contemplative, maybe?" His eyes settled on my lower hips, then he cocked an eyebrow.

I huffed a laugh. "Axl has you beat by a long shot. If you were contemplative, it would be because you're thinking of a thousand different ways to kill the person next to you." I crossed my arms over my chest and gave him a challenging look, which I knew he was growing accustomed to.

"There are plenty of things I think about other than ways to flay someone," Aaren retorted.

I cocked a brow. "Like what?"

"Like what you taste like."

Out of everything he could have said, I was not expecting that ever to leave his mouth.

"Wha—"

Aaren lifted his lower half, wrapped his legs around my torso, and rolled until my back pressed into the rigid boards of the sparring ring. I fought to wriggle free, which did more harm than good, considering my wrists were now pinned over my head.

"Fuck you," I hissed irritably and tried to buck him off of me to no avail.

"You want to, don't you?" Aaren asked, and the hungry look in his eyes finally solidified until it was unmistakable. It was lust, but I couldn't be sure it didn't come from me. The only logical reason for him to feel this way would be because of the rune, but from the way his eyes ate up my heaving breasts that were threatening to burst from my unbuttoned shirt, I could confidently say this was lust of his own making.

My eyes narrowed to give him an aggressively exasperated look, as if the hands pinning me didn't cause a wave of arousal that rivaled the tides of Kysthjem. "Why would you think I would ever want to fuck you, Aaren?"

He gave an indignant chuckle. "*Fremmed*, you've been sending those emotions through the rune for weeks. And since those emotions become my own once they cross over, it's been an effort not to bed you every moment of my free time."

If I had been standing, I would've been weak in the knees.

"I—" I began, but I had no clue what to say to something like that. I was so thankful when Aaren cut me off again.

"I'm connected to you, *fremmed*," he said. His face was close enough that our breaths mingled. "You can't hide the fact that what I'm saying right now isn't making you wet."

And he was right, because there was a pool of warmth gathering between my legs, and there was nothing I could do to stop it, nor could I deny it. But the moment I gave in to him, I knew everything I had been working to fight inside me would be compromised. If I gave in to Aaren, then I wouldn't be able to fight the feelings I knew I had for him, and sex with him would only make it harder to deny.

But the thought of his head between my legs turned me to jelly.

"Do you love me?" Aaren asked, and the edge of lust ebbed his voice, and the question almost sounded like it could turn into an interrogation.

"N-No," I said, and it wasn't a complete lie. I wasn't sure that I loved him, but I knew there was something more than friendly feelings between us.

Nothing about my answer changed the look in Aaren's face, but it did make him pause. His eyes went distant for a moment as if calculating what I had meant.

"But..." I stammered, watching his eyes return to mine even though they never really left. "I do...want you." Flirting was not a skill I possessed.

"No intercourse," Aaren said. His warm breath fanned over my face and sent tingles down my spine. "Sex is common amongst the Fraalver, but it holds weight when it is between leaders."

Something hard brushed my navel, and I bit back a smirk.

I went to ask why sex was so sacred when Aaren pressed a finger to his lips.

"I can explain that later, *fremmed*. But right now..."

I purposely sent a string of lust through my rune to his. His breath hitched, and his face looked momentarily troubled as he seemed to restrain himself physically.

"Fuck, right now I need to taste you."

Aaren used his grip on my wrists to pull me to my feet, then led me out of the sparring ring before I had properly gained my balance. The jog back to the house was almost frantic—an excited energy buzzed between us, and it grew harder and harder to keep my hands off of him.

My excitement died the moment I saw Nilsen standing in the doorway as soon as it opened, with his arms crossed over his chest and his bare foot tapping the ground.

"And where have you two been?" he asked stiffly with a scrutinizing look.

360

"We were trying to get in some extra training," Aaren said and stepped closer to his brother, but Nilsen took an authoritative step back.

"So I have to be in by eight, but you two can get home past midnight?"

Aaren chuckled, scooping Nilsen into his arms even though it looked like he was getting too big to be carried. "You're right. Back by eight, in bed by nine. So why aren't you in bed asleep?"

All traces of scrutiny left Nilsen's face, replaced by an innocent smile.

"Thea let you get into the sweets again, didn't she?" Aaren deadpanned.

When Nilsen didn't answer, Aaren sighed, mumbling that he would have words with her in the morning. I didn't blame her—I'd do the same for Lucas.

"Come on, *bror*, let's get to bed."

As Aaren closed Nilsen's bedroom door, his eyes flicked hungrily to mine. He nodded his head toward my room in silent command. I complied eagerly, but my mouth went dry when he closed the door behind him and eyed me from under a lowered brow.

I swallowed thickly as he took a slow step towards me. There was a momentary urge to shrink back before I realized I wasn't some frightened prey, and Aaren wasn't my stalking predator, no matter how menacing his steps towards me were.

The back of my knees hit the bed, and I bounced as I dropped to the soft mattress and waited for Aaren to finish sizing me up, like a prisoner waiting for their execution. My clothes felt too tight as he leaned over me with untamed eros swimming in his molten eyes. Suddenly, I feared for my life.

"So," Aaren said in a voice like a rumble of thunder. "Do we have a deal?"

I weighed my options as quickly as I could, my heart beating as if it were in a race against the clock. No sex, but I would at least find some release from the desire I had been swallowing for weeks, a desire I didn't dare give a name to. Something had to give—I either gave up a sliver of my pride or withstand a lifetime of celibacy.

"You have ten seconds, *fremmed*," Aaren said. "Because after that, I'm not sure I'll be able to control myself."

"Deal," I said. The very word sent a rabid flush of anticipation through me.

A wild grin spread Aaren's lips. "Right answer."

The world spun as Aaren lunged forward and positioned me at the top of the bed, wrists pinned against the furs. His lips were a breath away, and I moved to press mine against them, but he withdrew just out of reach. A devilish gleam shone in his eyes as I tried again, only to have him pull back. That gleam turned into playful satisfaction as he toyed with me, watching me silently beg. He huffed a deep grumble. His lips were seconds away from mine when he sucked my bottom lip into his teeth. I squirmed, relishing the following kiss, and my hands fought against his hold as I tried to reach for him.

I sighed into his mouth as we explored each other with our tongues, and the taste of ale and forest painted my tongue. The ferocity of the kiss sent my mind into a spiral, much like the rollercoaster Mama took me on during our trip to Hersheypark. I had nearly gotten sick on my first ride, but still insisted on going again and again. Kissing Aaren was much like riding that rollercoaster—it terrified me, but I couldn't stop, not when the first drop was so exhilarating.

I melted into him as he devoured me and claimed me for his own. His hand snaked up and toyed with the popped buttons of my shirt, then his fingers traced lazy circles against the skin on my breast. I writhed, hot need clenching me in an iron grip as warmth filled my most sensitive parts. I let out a small moan, and Aaren's lips tore away as the sound of my desire untamed him.

He let go of my wrists and clawed at my shirt, but he was too impatient to fuss with the fabric, so he ripped it from my body. My nipples peaked as the warm air kissed my skin, and Aaren's hurried lips caressed the soft flesh under my ear. Then he nudged my legs apart with his knees and settled into the cradle of my thighs. I shivered, letting him leave a delicate trail of claiming kisses down my neck and rake his teeth across my collarbone.

Even though my hands were no longer pinned, I still fought the urge to touch him, caress his head as he kissed along my skin. It felt like an admission of feelings I wasn't sure I had, even if what he was doing to me was turning every atom in my body to slush. And right now was not the time to dwell on trivial matters like the depths of my feelings. Not when the swell of desire was becoming almost unbearable.

Aaren caught my eye, his amber orbs radiating with carnal intention as his tongue flicked my nipple. I arched into his mouth, and an exalted groan sang from my throat as he circled the sensitive bud and took it into his mouth. I opened my chest to him in a silent plea, and his deep laugh vibrated across my skin. Aaren had barely made it halfway down my body, and I was already a molten puddle of anguished longing, and he knew it. I didn't want it to get to his head, but there was no stopping the second moan as he bit down on the underside of my breast. He bit and sucked my skin like a starved animal, and a delicious ache arced through my chest.

Aaren's hand snaked up to cover my mouth and muffled the pleasured, painful cries I wasn't aware I had been making. He bit me again, and I jerked, breast bouncing as Aaren released it with a pop and admired the dark purple bruise growing and glistening with his saliva.

"Mine," Aaren purred, then gave the darkening bruise a claiming kiss before moving to my other nipple.

He kissed it gently as if to apologize for what he did to the other, but I found myself missing that pleasure, edged with pain. Before I could dwell on that thought, his hand slid down my navel until it landed just above my groin. With a flick, the fastenings of my pants were undone, and he peeled the leathers from my legs. And then I was completely naked underneath him. I had never been this naked with anyone, not even with the customer I gave my virginity to.

I didn't shy away from his hungered gaze as he rose to his knees and surveyed me like a king at a feast, wondering what to eat first. Desperate for him to touch me again, I opened my legs wider. Aaren let out a sound of satisfaction from deep within his throat when his eyes fixated on the gleaming wetness that pooled between my legs. I needed him, now.

I sent the thought through the rune that earned me a hungry smile. With a sweeping motion, he threw his hair back in a bun. Loose strands fell around his face and framed the beautiful curves and sharp edges of his features. His callouses bit into the soft flesh of my thighs as he spread my legs as wide as they would go, and his tongue swiped over his lips as he muttered a breathy curse.

Something hard strained the seam of his pants, and Aaren quickly adjusted himself before he knelt. A breathless sound erupted from my lips as he dragged a soft tongue across my slick entrance. My vision clouded for a moment, the world coming in and out of focus as he gave me another teasing lick. He swore under his breath.

"Gods, you're wet, *fremmed*," he purred, then swirled his tongue over the cluster of sensitive nerves at the crown of my hips.

I couldn't keep my hips from bucking as he devoured me, but Aaren snaked his hand up and pinned me to the mattress. He sucked at the sensitive spot, flicking his tongue over me, and I whimpered when a release coiled inside like a snake waking up from a deep slumber. Aaren's short teasing licks turned to broad strokes as his tongue licked me from base to top as if eager to lap up every ounce of me. Everything else escaped me as he plunged his tongue inside, my focus only on the ministrations of his brutally demanding mouth, his coaxing tongue that caressed my sex so tenderly, yet so ravenously.

I sucked my bottom lip between my teeth as my calamitous release built more and more. It was like he knew exactly where to lick, knew the precise place that drove me crazy, banking my sanity on every kiss and expert flick of his tongue. This wasn't a matter of knowing how to please a woman, but a concern about how to please me specifically. Maybe it was the rune that attuned him to such things, or perhaps it was Aaren's own intuition that drove him to lick precisely where he needed to, but I prayed he never left my thighs. I could spend an eternity with his head buried in my most sensitive parts, writhing until the world burned to ash.

The low purrs that vibrated against me drew that coiled snake of pleasure out.

"Come for me, Layla," Aaren sighed, his mouth glistening with my arousal.

His finger brushed me, coaxed me forward, then his mouth found me again. He sucked on me and slid his tongue through my folds as his finger glided inside. Then he added another and curled them until they hit just the right spot.

With his mouth latched onto me, he met my eyes, and the snake inside me uncoiled fully, sending waves of pleasure barreling into my veins. I bowed off the bed with a cry, body wracked with relief and joy and lust, and I trembled as his tongue worked me and tossed me mercilessly over the edge. The rune burned exquisitely on my forearm and added to the euphoria of my bliss. My fingers gripped the furs underneath me, hard enough that the strands came loose, but I didn't care, not when disastrous ecstasy replaced the red blood in my veins.

As I came down from my high, Aaren placed a gentle kiss against me, and I bucked, still sensitive. He released a deep chuckle as he pushed himself up and wiped his mouth with the back of his hand.

I managed to balance on my elbows, head swimming from my release. Stars receded from my vision as Aaren stood triumphantly over me, his bulge close to bursting from his pants. I reached for him, but reddened when he backed away and clicked his tongue at me.

"Not tonight," he said, his voice gravelly. His mouth was saying one thing, but his eyes were screaming another. Would it really be so bad for us to go all the way? I was satisfied, yes, but gods damn me, I needed more.

I swallowed my disappointed whine and let my hand drop to my bare thigh, which was still slick with arousal and saliva. The bruise on my breast ached, but I didn't care—the overwhelming need for Aaren was trumping all other thoughts.

"Not tonight, *fremmed*," Aaren repeated.

He was right—I needed to learn to control what I sent through the rune.

Aaren stood and adjusted himself again before striding across the room. "Good night," he said, then closed the door behind him.

Chapter 42

Sleep evaded me that night despite the long day and my time with Aaren. I couldn't get the taste of him out of my mouth, the feeling of his hands on my thighs, his tongue licking every inch of me.

And it was ruminating like that that made me partially regret tangling with Aaren, no matter how good it felt. Sex would expose me to feelings I wasn't ready to bring to the light of day. Still, this halfway point, the limbo of passionate foreplay we could find ourselves in should we continue, could prove to be even more destructive than running away from the truths I would adamantly keep shoving into the shadows.

All of that might be true, but after last night, after the way he wouldn't let me touch him after such an earth-shattering, toe-curling, mind-bending release, I owed him. I emerged from my room stiff and yawning, but smiling nonetheless, when Nilsen greeted me through a mouthful of eggs.

"Good morning, *fremmed*," Aaren said as he scooped a helping of porridge into Nilsen's bowl.

I flattened the strands of hair that stuck out from Nilsen's head and sat down to help myself to cheese and bread. Nilsen dropped his spoon in his bowl and grabbed my arm, examining me like I was a new species of insect.

"What are you doing?" I asked, then shot Aaren a confused look. He shrugged and took a sip of his juice.

"I heard you screaming last night. I just wanted to make sure you weren't hurt," Nilsen answered. He moved to my other arm and pinched the flesh of my bicep.

Aaren choked on his juice, and red liquid sprayed out of the mug onto the table. I wanted to kick him as Nilsen released my arm and went back to his plate.

"Nightmares," I blurted as Aaren coughed again and wiped his mouth with a napkin. "I have...nightmares sometimes."

Nilsen turned back to me. "I do too sometimes. Aaren always makes me feel better." Nilsen grabbed his spoon again. "You should go to him the next time you have a bad dream."

Oh, sweet, sweet Nilsen.

Aaren coughed once more before clearing his throat and taking a deep breath.

"Are you okay, *bror*?" Nilsen asked before he shoved more porridge into his mouth.

"Fine, Nilsen, thank you." Aaren ran a hand through his hair. "Eat up, *fremmed*. We've got to get going soon."

"What for?"

Aaren pushed his plate away and combed his hair away from his face. He tied it with a strap of leather. "Rorik would like to discuss the next moves."

I cursed under my breath after swallowing the last bit of my breakfast. Days off didn't come as easily for us as they did for every other Fraalver.

Nilsen licked his spoon. "You know who would know what Markus was up to?"

I watched him curiously. "Who?"

"The huldra," he answered absently, then spooned another helping into his mouth. His next words were muffled by porridge. "Huldras may be dangerous, but they know *everything*."

Aaren and I exchanged glances.

The huldra nearly killed me the last time I encountered it—I was less than eager to seek her out again. However, she also provided me with vital information about Lucas. If we could expect the same this time—hopefully with fewer claws and less chasing—this might work.

"How do you know so much about the huldra?" Aaren questioned.

Nilsen shrugged. "You can learn a lot from the pieces of Balderkrig."

I leaned on my elbows and watched Nilsen. "Did the pieces tell you how to talk to a huldra without getting killed?"

367

Nilsen swallowed. "No, but I'm sure you could find something to offer her." He paused, then his eyes lit up. "I bet she likes jewelry!"

Aaren stared for a moment as the gears spun in his mind. Nilsen rattled on about the Balderkrig pieces for the rest of breakfast, then hurried to the treehouse.

I found Aaren in his room soon after.

"Come back for seconds?" Aaren asked as I entered, to find him pulling on his boots. I rolled my eyes as he licked his lips like he could still taste me on them.

I scoffed. "Focus," I said as I crossed the room to stand by the bedside table, just out of his reach. "What are we offering the huldra?"

Aaren turned back to his boots. His playful demeanor shifted, and his features hardened. "I have a necklace we can give her," he answered and began to lace the right boot. "It belonged to Solveig."

"You can't give that away, Aaren," I said, crossing my arms over my chest. "There must be something different we can give her."

Aaren stood gruffly. "It's collecting dust anyway."

I gawked at the piece of jewelry he pulled out of the bedside table, admiring the shimmering silver and the expertly cut emerald pendant. Its delicate chain caught on his calluses.

"It's beautiful," I breathed, lost in the deep green of the gem. I didn't want to hate Solveig, especially since I was still standing and breathing, but I couldn't help myself. She had everything I didn't—parents that loved her, sparkling beauty like the forest, extravagant jewelry that I could only dream of ever owning—sex with Aaren. I had to pick at the scraps she left behind.

"If we go before we see Rorik, we can tell him what we learn."

The woods were brighter today, with lush greens and earthy browns accentuated by the lovely spring sunlight that kissed the trees. The songbirds sang their melodies through the branches as we hiked, and our footsteps added a staccato percussion to the forest song. The heavy weight of death had lifted from the forest, and life continued with ease. I lifted my gaze to the treetops and watched the canopy drift by with every step, hoping to spot Ugleverge above us.

"So why no intercourse?" I asked bluntly. I had my reasons, but I was curious to know his.

Aaren let out an amused huff. "I've been waiting for you to ask that." Aaren helped me climb over a fallen log before continuing. "Sex is a significant value that is upheld in much of the Fraalver tradition."

"Like the dance in Fjellhjem?"

Aaren nodded. "And the role it plays in the fortification of our borders. And while the Fraalver people are free to indulge in as much of it as they want, leaders have a bit more restrictions."

I cocked a brow. "Such as?"

"Such as, it can't just be sex for the sake of sex. Think of it as a mug of ale. If it's your favorite and you love drinking it, not only will you catch a buzz, but you'll have a great time because you're drinking your favorite ale. But if it's just any ordinary ale, then you get nothing but a buzz and an okay night."

I didn't like this analogy.

"It's the same thing with the power behind intercourse with a Fraalver leader. If it isn't between the two leaders, who are true partners in love, then it loses its power. Since we can't have sex with anyone else, we might as well take what we can get from each other."

And even though I couldn't agree more, it still hurt to hear him say it.

"Besides," Aaren said, then stopped his next step and turned to face me. "I've been wanting to taste you for a long time."

I craned my head to look into his face. "And was I everything you expected?"

One minute, I was trudging over the mossy ground; the next, Aaren had me braced against a tree. A fiendish glimmer danced across his features as he brushed a finger down my neck, where invisible sparks broke out along my skin.

"You tasted," the finger dropped to my chest, tickled my collarbone, "indescribable."

He stared at my lips as his fingers played with the waist of my pants. His breath warmed my neck when he slid his hand into the fabric, and his tongue licked a clean stripe across my throat.

"Fuck," I cursed.

A deep thrum vibrated in Aaren's chest as his fingers brushed me, feeling the growing wetness.

"Just remember, *fremmed*," he whispered when his finger circled my sensitive spot. I arched, bark biting into the palms of my hands as my moan mingled with the birdsong. "Whenever you touch yourself when you're alone, I'll feel it, too." His teeth nipped my neck, and I gave a growl of pleasure.

As quickly as it had begun, it stopped. He withdrew his fingers, which now glistened with my arousal, and slid them into his mouth. He hummed sweetly as he savored my taste. Then he released me, leaving me a molten mess against the pine.

A sigh of exasperation danced on my lips as I straightened, my knees weak as I tried for my first step.

"Not cool," I said as I shook the bark and pine sap from my hands.

Aaren chuckled. "It's *my* forest. I'll do what I want."

"*Our* forest," I corrected.

Ignoring my hammering heart as I tried to recover my breath, I continued to follow him down the path. We shared small anecdotes as we went, and it felt a lot like it did before we left for Kysthjem, when we were still in the stages of getting to know each other. But this time, it was easier, especially since I wasn't having to dig past layers of his hardened exterior. The birds continued to chirp and sing as I told him about the time in third grade when I had to create a project using food. Lacking the funding for anything extravagant, I glued Froot Loops onto a poster board and created a meadow out of the greens, blues, and pinks, peppering the hills with fruity flowers. Then Robbie Coster came and ate half of my project during recess.

He got suspended for two days.

Aaren threw his head back and laughed, the glorious booming sound echoing through the forest. Unlike when Oswin or Ivar laughed, the birds did not scatter. In fact, they sang along as if they claimed his voice as their own. King of Trees indeed.

"What is a Froot Loop?" Aaren asked as his laughter died.

"It's something kids eat for breakfast in Midgard. But it's a lot of sugar."

Aaren huffed another laugh. "I've got one for you." We jumped over a babbling creek. "One time, when I was ten, I found an elderberry bush. When I pointed it out to my parents, they suggested that the pub master, Inaborg's father, make a mead out of it. Once he had begun brewing, I wanted to try it." He chuckled. "It was my bush after all, so I had the right to try the mead. Only my parents wouldn't let me. So I snuck in and poured myself a mug." He chuckled. "To this day, I have never tasted a mead like it. It had the elderberry, but he had also mixed in hints of thyme and cherry, and I had far more mead than a child should ever have.

"When my parents found out, they were livid. As punishment, I had to clean tables in the pub for weeks." He laughed. "I suppose I'd do the same if it were my child, but I hated my parents for it."

"How did you feel the next day?" I asked

"Worst headache of my life."

I joined his laughter, imagining a young Aaren stumbling around the keg room with a mug full of sloshing mead. The image alone sent me into a fit of giggles.

Taking a deep breath through my nose, I savored the crisp, invigorating air. I felt Aaren's eyes on me, though I pretended not to notice as my arms stretched in the air and opened my chest. Being outside in the wondrous air was nurturing, bringing me back to life.

A step forward, and then Aaren braced a hand in front of me to keep me from trampling whatever he had seen on the ground. He knelt and brushed away a clump of dead leaves from a spot on the earth to reveal a footprint, a clawed footprint to be exact. The outline of the foot resembled that of a human, but the ends of the toes pressed deeply into the ground, suggesting something akin to talons.

"This is fresh," Aaren said, then looked ahead for the next print. "She was here."

He shuffled leaves every few steps and pointed out the claw marks on the trees lining the path the huldra had taken. We were tracking her, and from the distant sounds of the river ahead, we were getting close.

Aaren had us crouch in the bushes lining the edge of the bank, ears straining through the rushing water for anything amiss. And as if we summoned it, a small voice called through the rapids of the river.

"Layla?" it called. It was Lucas's voice, and even though I knew it wasn't him, it sounded so real. I almost launched through the bushes had Aaren not laid a hand on my arm to ground me.

It wasn't Lucas, and we were here to interrogate the huldra, not end up as her next meal.

I cleared my throat. "Fool me once, bitch."

My brother's figure emerged from the water, his clothes the same as the ones he wore the day I took him to the bookstore. The last time I ever saw him.

"Layla, help me please." The huldra started to cry, balling its hands into fists and rubbing its eyes, the same way Lucas used to.

How could it have known he cried like that?

The huldra wailed and threw its arms out to me like Lucas used to do when he was little. His little hands would grab at my pants when he wanted to be picked up, especially when he was upset. He hadn't done that in years, but after whatever Markus might have put him through, maybe he'd want to be comforted like that again.

My poor Lucas. My baby brother. Please stop crying, please *stop*.

"Layla," Aaren said. His thumb and forefinger pinched my chin and turned my head to look at him. "He's not real. That's not Lucas." His amber eyes pulsed, and his familiar scent filled my nose, and it felt like someone had lifted a blindfold from my eyes.

The branches of the bush rustled as I stepped out, hands balled into fists as I fought the anger that was probing my magic awake.

"You're not fooling me, huldra," I hissed.

The wailing stopped abruptly, and an agitation bit into my brother's features before they rippled and transformed back to those of a woman. The same razor-toothed woman who chased me and Stieg through the forest those many weeks ago. She was beautiful, her face molded to the kind, soft features of a Balderkrig piece. Her long fingers broke the stream of water rushing past her thin legs. A tattered dress, and a swishing tail flowed behind her. Her delicate lips drew back to reveal sharp teeth, and her beauty slipped away the wider she smiled.

"I have a name," she said bitterly as she swiped a forked tongue over her sharp teeth.

"And that is?"

"Embla," she answered. Her graceful tail swirled seductively in the water.

"Okay, Embla," I said. "I have questions."

Embla took a smooth step toward us, her movements unexpectedly elegant despite her slipping charm. She didn't look as pretty as she had only seconds before. But her motions were smooth, lithe yet powerful, like the water she moved through.

"And what will you offer me if I answer your questions?"

I tensed as she took her first step onto the bank, her tail tracing small circles in the sediment.

Aaren dug out the necklace and held it up, and the emerald stones shone in the sunlight. The huldra watched it swing with her icy blue eyes that reflected the green gem hungrily.

She lunged forward with greedy hands, but Aaren yanked it away and stuffed it back into his bag. He clicked his tongue. "Not until you answer our questions."

Embla rolled her eyes and flicked sediment off her haggard dress. "I'll allow three questions." She grinned fiendishly. "Choose carefully."

Aaren and I didn't need to deliberate on what we should ask. "What do you know of Markus's plans?" he demanded.

She laughed, a chilling hiss that mixed with the rushing waters behind her. "Balance," she sneered. "It's what fuels our tree and what dwells in its foundation. He sought out the roots, bargained with fate."

Aaren went pale.

Our tree, Yggrasil. What dwelled in the roots, and why did Markus seek it out? He bargained with fate. How does one bargain with fate?

"And what of the necromancer that raised him?" I asked.

Embla turned just as pale as Aaren, and she glanced over her shoulder. It was like she was afraid someone was listening. The clouds briefly covered the sun, and the temperature dropped. Goosebumps pimpled my skin.

"We dare not speak of him," Embla snarled, her now ragged features twisting into an unpleasant grimace. Gone were the kind features that masked her unsightliness, and she looked exactly as I remembered her. "The power he summons is far more evil than that of his foot soldiers. Even my kind fears him."

I shuddered to think of a being even a huldra would fear. If Markus was just a foot soldier, we were utterly and royally fucked.

"And my brother, where is he?"

The huldra cocked her head at me, and the green of Lucas's eyes flashed in hers before she answered. "He never leaves his father's side. Wherever Markus goes, he follows."

"Then where is Markus?" I demanded as a flurry of desperation and fury roiled in my gut.

"Ah ah ah," Embla said, wagging a pointed, knobbly finger. "Your three questions are up."

Aaren grunted and drew his sword.

"You didn't answer her question, Embla," he snarled. "Answer her question, and the necklace is yours. Refuse, and you die."

Embla cackled indignantly. "You think a flimsy little sword scares me, Fraalver?"

Aaren gave a cunning snarl. Embla had just said the wrong thing.

Aaren straightened and sheathed his sword back at his side, then snapped his fingers. The ground rumbled, and the mossy bank erupted. Mud and clay sprayed into the water and over our heads as mighty roots burst from the earth and surged forward to twine around Embla's clawed feet. She watched in horror as they wrapped swiftly around her legs and snaked their way up her torso, her claws scratching and beating at the wood. It did nothing but make the roots move quicker.

"Stop!" Embla cried, and a harsh fear flickered across her face.

Aaren seemed bored when he pulled the necklace out from his pack and inspected the emerald for smudges. "Not until you answer the question properly, Embla."

The roots now enveloped her chest and slid over her jagged collarbones. They were about to wrap around her throat when she shrieked, "I can't say exactly where he is, but I'll tell you what I know!"

The roots stiffened, barely teasing the light cord of muscle at the base of her neck.

"Markus has garnered some support from my sisters, who forget just who he works for." The fear had changed her voice, and it sounded less like the water, as if the river she hailed from began to dry up and fill with earth. "The huldrafolk do not play sides in petty wars, but some of us have joined his ranks. If I tell you where he resides, I will die at his hands instead of yours."

And because of that, I had no doubt she was telling the truth. Embla was in no position to spout lies.

"Tell us what you can," Aaren said.

She swallowed, her tongue fiddling with her pointed teeth as she contemplated her answer. The tree roots held firm and groaned when she still tried to fight against them. "The death of Torsten was no vengeful attack from the burrowers. It was targeted, planned by someone from the mountains."

A fact we had suspected but had no confirming evidence to prove it. But that wasn't what she was trying to tell us. She gave me an expectant look as my eyes narrowed, reading between the lines of her words. "Are you saying he's in the mountains?"

Embla's silence was as confirming as it would've been if she said it.

That meant that Lucas was in the mountains. I had been so close to him, and yet still so far away.

"Very well," Aaren said, then flicked his wrist. The roots eased and slid away from Embla, where she splashed back in the shallows. She breathed a sigh of relief, and for a moment, she looked more human than she did when she was pretending to be one.

I threw a glance over my shoulder at Aaren, who had dropped his gaze to the necklace in his hands. He rubbed a finger over the emerald, and my own grief clenched as he tossed it to the huldra.

"Keep your head low, Embla," Aaren warned, beginning his retreat into the forest.

I didn't turn around and follow until I knew she had sunk below the surface

Chapter 43

"Markus is in the mountains," Aaren said, spinning on his heel and retracing his steps as he paced in front of the medicine hut hearth. Rorik stood by the table where Ertha and I sat, her pale fingers wrapped around a hangover tonic that smelled awful.

"That's impossible," Rorik quipped. "Wouldn't someone in Fjellhjem have come across him by now if he were in the mountains?"

Ertha gripped her mug tighter and shook her head. "Not if he is in Karridal."

Aaren nodded in considered agreement. "Seeing as he would be undisturbed there, it would be the perfect place for him to set up base."

"What is Karridal?" I asked.

Ertha sat forward, seeming to grow just as disgusted by her tonic as I was, and shoved it to the side. "Karridal is a range of mountains beyond Fjellhjem with terrain that is nearly uninhabitable. Coupled with the near rabid creatures that crawl in those valleys, most don't dare venture there."

I still couldn't wrap my head around the fact that I had been that close to my brother, even if the harshest terrain and formidable monsters guarded him. I was closer than I had ever been since I got here.

"Did she say anything else?" Rorik asked, gesturing for Aaren to sit, but he denied and continued to pace.

"Something about the roots of Yggdrasil, what was it..." I answered, trying to remember her words, but the tense energy that crackled to life in the room distracted me.

"'He sought out the roots, bargained with fate,'" Aaren quoted, his jaw ticking with agitation.

"By the Aesir," Rorik whispered.

Ertha, who had been anxiously tapping the table, froze, her eyes going wide with horror.

"What is it?" I asked urgently. I tried to catch Aaren's eye, but his back was to me as he made his umpteenth turn since the start of the conversation.

"The Nidhogg," Rorik answered with an unmistakable shake in his voice that unnerved me to my core.

Aaren finally halted his pacing when I asked what the Nidhogg was. "The Nidhogg is a serpent that resides in the roots of Yggdrasil," he explained, his features as hard as they were the day I met him. "When awakened, it will begin to destroy the roots, ripping them to shreds until the tree can no longer stand."

"But that doesn't make sense," I began. "If Markus wants to take over Alveland, why would he harness a creature that is set on destroying the tree that it is a part of?"

"You said the huldra told you that Markus bargained with fate," Ertha said, her fingers resuming their troubled tapping. "What if by fate, she meant the Nidhogg? What if Markus made a deal with it?"

Noticing the necromancer's stone from Fjellgrav in the center of the table, I picked it up and ran my thumb over the engraved rune. Aaren started pacing again, to my dismay.

"Deal or not, the Nidhogg is a creature that no one has faced before," Rorik said, his temples now red from the way he rubbed them. "And even if Markus did make a deal with it, it would be impossible to convince the Nidhogg to break it. This isn't like the mylings where we can go find something to give it that would cancel out Markus's dealings."

Aaren halted midstep, his boot squeaking at the abruptness. "There may not be something to convince it out of a deal with Markus. But there is something that could help us deal with the Nidhogg."

"Aaren," Rorik warned, "you're not talking about..."

"...killing it?" Ertha finished in bewilderment. "Are you mad?"

"I'm going to call it my budding creativity," Aaren joked, giving me a mischievous side-eye.

Rorik gave Aaren a look as if to say he'd lost his mind, and to be honest, I agreed.

"Aaren, respectfully, there's a reason no one has ever tried to face it before." Rorik made a move as if to suppress a shudder. "It can eat entire realms in the blink of an eye. You would need a mighty weapon to kill it."

Aaren crossed his arms over his chest. "And we have one." He looked right at me.

"Me?" I demanded when both Ertha and Rorik turned to look at me.

"What can Layla do?" Rorik asked, and even though I agreed with him, I took slight offense at the incredulity in his voice. I doubted I'd be able to take on the Nidhogg, but I feel like I earned enough confidence in him that he shouldn't have questioned me like *that*.

Aaren scoffed. "She is a damned legacy, Rorik. What can't she do?"

The laugh I barked was anything but amused. "I think you're putting a lot of stock in me, Aaren. I'm a legacy, which means Markus is a *demigod*. This Nidhogg is far beyond my scope of magic if it has dealings with demigods."

"I think you're selling yourself short," Ertha said under her breath as she pulled the rancid mug back towards her.

Rorik turned towards her slowly. "What did you say?" he asked.

Ertha gave him a challenging look. "Layla has faced a lot in the short amount of time she's had her magic. And walked out of those fights, more importantly. She bears scars, but not nearly as many as she should for what she has faced." She turned her attention to me. "You could be the key to winning Nidhogg's favor. Or killing it. Whichever suits you better."

Rorik muttered that he doubted the Nidhogg favored anyone other than the roots of Yggdrasil. A fair point, but one that wouldn't deter me from trying to bargain my way out of fighting it.

"With the right weapon," Aaren eyed Rorik obviously, "Layla could be the key to our success."

"If you're hinting at Quirinus's axe, Aaren, forget it," Rorik spat. He shook his head, and a few strands of graying hair fell loose. Despite the liveliness in his voice, Rorik was worn, stretched thin like the sparse leaves of winter. His laugh lines were deeper, and I was positive it wasn't because of lively nights in the pub.

"I *am* hinting at Quirinus's axe," Aaren retorted with a glimmer in his eye. "And before you say—"

"It's been lost for years," Rorik said at the same time as Aaren.

Why were the Fraalver so bad at keeping up their highly revered artifacts?

378

"I know where it is," Aaren finished. "Or rather, I know *who knows* where it is."

Rorik folded his arms over the other, nailing Aaren with a scrutinizing look. "And how do you know this?"

Instead of answering, Aaren strode to one of the many shelves of books along the medicine hut's walls and plucked one of Harald's lengthy tomes to flip through the pages. Judging by the cover and how similar it was to the last book of Harald's I had read, it was the next one Rorik was going to assign me. I thanked Himmelfjell that Aaren got to it before me.

He thumbed through it before setting it on the table and tapping a finger on the script next to a detailed sketch of an axe. From what I could quickly scan, Quirinus, the physician of Skoghjem who banished Markus and set the curse on him, feared his return, or whatever force Markus sent to the Fraalver villages in retaliation for his excommunication. That fear drove him to create and enchant a weapon capable of taking down the mightiest of creatures. It was even rumored that it could take down gods should the need arise. If Quirinus was that powerful, it was no wonder Markus was so eager to apprentice under him.

The only problem was that a few years after it was created, it went missing, and no one knew where it had gone.

Great. Another journey to find another missing artifact that may or may not help us.

Rorik snapped the book shut before I could finish reading.

"That's preposterous," Rorik huffed.

Aaren stood, a muscle ticking in his jaw. "If we find the axe, the Nidhogg is as good as dead. If it truly is lost, that is our sign to leave the Nidhogg untouched and face the consequences as is."

He made to step to the door when Rorik asked, "Where are you going?"

Aaren gave a sly glance over his shoulder. "I need to find Stieg Trohjert."

Without another word, he sauntered out of the medicine hut.

It didn't matter how many runs Aaren and I had gone on together; I still couldn't keep up with him. What was disappointing was that he was only walking faster than usual, and I found myself gasping as I tried to maintain a jog to keep up with him. The pleasant stillness of Thea's bookshop was disturbed the moment I stumbled through the door, dropping my hands to my knees as I tried to catch my breath. Thea and Stieg didn't seem to notice as the two of them were lost in the pages of one of her books, Thea's pink lips smiling as she read aloud to him. Stieg had his cheek resting in his hand, so lost in Thea's voice, I wondered if he even understood the words she was reading.

Since the Chapter they were reading was her character's passionate profession of love, I found myself wanting to fall into the story, lured into the far-off land in my mind by her soft voice, but she stopped mid-sentence.

"For Aesir's sake, Layla, you sound like a snarling hudflasker," Thea said as she marked their spot with the orange treelskere feather and closed the book. "Breathe, *frue*."

I made a gesture as if to say I was fine, but the fact that I couldn't say it should've been a testament of its own.

"I need a word with Stieg," Aaren said. His lip twitched as if he was trying not to laugh at me.

Stieg's brow furrowed in confused curiosity as he sat up a little straighter.

"Regarding?" Thea asked, looking at me as if I were the one who made the request. Finally, I straightened and gave her a pleading but apologetic look. She only crossed her arms, and Stieg's cheeks reddened at the way her posture, coupled with the cut of her dress, accentuated her breasts. I pressed my lips together so I wouldn't laugh out loud.

Aaren took a breath, whether to breathe or to calm his nerves, I wasn't sure. "Regarding a matter of Stieg's personal business that I'm not sure he would appreciate me airing out for all to hear."

Thea bristled and unfolded her arms to Stieg's disappointment. "You can't come into my shop and make demands like a brute."

Aaren was big enough that he could reach to the top of a bookshelf and brush the dust off, which he did, rubbing his thumb and forefinger together. "You might want to dust in here, Thea. Wouldn't want you to earn Harald's reputation."

Thea rolled her eyes. "Spare me your insufferability, Aaren. Why do you need Stieg?"

Aaren hid the amusement on his face, but didn't bother to block it from coming through the rune.

"Stieg, would you like me to ask for my favor here?"

Stieg looked as if he was trying to hide his worry, giving an awkward smile as if that would cover the fact that he could break into a nervous sweat any second. "Whatever it is, Thea can hear it, too."

"Fine," Aaren answered, evidently fed up now. "Stieg, we need to get in touch with the trolls."

The color drained from Stieg's face, every ounce of budding confidence dissipating in a flash. "Uh," he stuttered.

Thea scrunched her features, as if to silently demand an explanation. When no one said anything, she said, "Why would Stieg know anything about the trolls?"

Stieg sighed, spinning his stool to face her. "I'm sorry I didn't tell you, Thea." With a sigh and his gaze on the floor, Stieg admitted, "My mother was a troll."

Of all the things he could have admitted to, that was the thing I was least prepared to hear. And yet it made more sense than it should have to me.

But what did the trolls have to do with any of this?

"That's it?" she asked, confused,

Stieg met her confusion with his own, a thin line forming between his brows as he blinked. "You're not...disgusted?" he asked her.

"Layla's father is gods damned Markus Sviker," Thea laughed, to which I gave her a very friendly flip of my middle finger. She smirked, but kept her attention on Stieg. "I don't think there is anything you could do that would make me upset."

His shoulders fell as he breathed a visible sigh of relief. "You put the stars in my sky, Thea."

I went to turn away and give my friends some privacy, but Aaren had other plans. "Touching, but we are on borrowed time."

Thea groaned and rolled her eyes.

"Roll your eyes any harder, Thea, and you might find a brain back there," Aaren said.

I turned to give Aaren a reproachful look, but Thea beat me to it by chucking a book at his face. Aaren caught it with one hand and let out a small chuckle.

"You think the trolls would talk to *me*?" Stieg asked. "After my mother died, they wanted nothing to do with me. I was ostracized and sent away. My troll blood isn't enough to let me back into their good graces."

I shrugged. "You're the best plan we've got, Stieg. We need them."

Thea held up a hand to halt the conversation. "Why do you need to talk to the trolls?"

Aaren gave a quick summary of the past few hours and the new information we had learned. Stieg blew out a breath, but Thea seemed unimpressed.

"That still doesn't explain why you need the trolls," she quipped.

Aaren closed his eyes and let out a deep breath. "We need to contact the trolls because the axe is in their possession."

"How do you—"

"Because someone a long time ago gave it to them," Aaren said, dismissing any other questions, even though hundreds of them rattled around in my brain. What happened to the trolls that they would need the axe? And why did someone give it to them in secret? "Stieg, do you remember anything about where the trolls could be?"

Stieg sighed in quiet resignation, gaze dropping to the worn boards under his stool. "I was born in the hills near Klartvan Lake," he stated. "I suppose that's a good start."

Chapter 44

"You *must* tell me what happened between you two," Thea jabbed after she took a deep swallow of ale. I opened my mouth to retort, but she cut me off. "I'm not blind, *Iiue,* don't bother denying whatever happened between you two." She winked. "I have a sixth sense for these things."

I played with the handle of my mug sheepishly and shrugged my shoulders. "I don't know," I said. I tried to fight the smile that inevitably spread across my lips as she pushed me further.

"How big was it?"

I was *not* prepared for a question like that, and I nearly choked on my drink. "Oh, no, we didn't," I stammered as I wiped my mouth on the nearest napkin. Heat stung my cheeks as Inaborg's new cider burned the wrong parts of my throat. "I don't...no, I..." I took a deep breath and fanned my face. Suddenly, the pub was a lot warmer than it had been seconds ago.

"That big, huh?"

I laughed. "No, we did not have sex," I answered, though I found myself dying to tell her every detail. I smiled into my mug. "But he has a very nice tongue."

Thea squealed, balled her fists, and shook excitedly. "I knew it! I knew you two did *something!*" She flattened her hands on the table and leaned forward. "How was it? Tell me everything!"

As we finished our drinks, I recounted my time with Aaren to Thea, who listened avidly, joking that she was tempted to take notes for her next book.

"Wow," she said as she sat back with her mug clutched to her bosom. "I'm surprised Aaren is capable of that. Especially with some of the bullshit he spouts."

I dipped my finger into my ale and flicked it at Thea.

"I'm kidding!" she giggled, wiping flecks of alcohol from her cheeks. "Aaren and I may have an aggressive repartee, but he is a dear friend. He took Lars's death very personally."

As he did with Dagan's, and any other Fraalver death he couldn't somehow control or prevent.

As I finished detailing last night, Thea launched into her own recounting of her latest escapades with Stieg. My heart grew heavy with gratitude as we talked—I had never had a friend with whom I could speak to boys or tell my secrets, and I had never realized I wanted one until I had Thea to do those things with. Spending time with her filled my cup in ways no other could, and I walked back home with a smile on my face and a warm heart.

The house was empty save for the simmering embers in the hearth. I approached to coax the fire back to life, when my eyes caught the distinct markings on the stone, forever encapsulating the family story. There were Aaren's parents under the wedding branch, then their victories, followed by the addition of Aaren and Nilsen. As my eyes followed, I noticed the new carvings, the stone freshly cut and bright.

There was a female figure, me, standing under the wedding branch with Aaren. Our marriage rune was carved under the figures, and I smiled as my finger brushed that same symbol on my arm. I continued and studied the image of me retrieving Hel's dagger from the burrowers, my etching standing proudly with the weapon in her hand. The next carving depicted Aaren and me surrounded by smaller figures, mylings, who were giving them the dagger.

I studied the markings with pride swelling in my chest. In as little time as I had been in Skoghjem, I had accomplished more in a few months than I ever had in my life in Midgard. Who cared about a psychology program when I fought off an army of draugr? And burrowers. And a hagua. And a trehag. And bargained with a fleet of mylings.

I couldn't wait to tell Lucas all about it.

My elation carried me away from the fireplace and past Aaren's bedroom, where I peeked in and caught a glimpse of him by the fireplace. In his hand was a small glass of clear brown liquid, and he stared thoughtfully into the fire. Something was heavy on his mind, and it weighed his features down, and his mouth thinned to a sharp line.

Curiosity, and maybe the ale, pushed me forward, and I announced my presence with a polite clearing of my throat.

"Good evening, *fremmed*," Aaren said without turning around.

I sank to the floor in front of him and stretched before the fire. "What are you drinking?" I asked dreamily, as the fire's delicious heat kissed my exposed skin.

Aaren swirled the liquid around. "The family whiskey," he answered and took a whispered sip. "We don't touch it very often."

I propped myself on an elbow to study him closely. "What's the occasion?"

Aaren looked to his right, his jaw tightening. "I need to forget everything for the night."

My eyes dropped to the fur rug I lay on, where I took in the minute details of every strand of hair and the varying colors of the pelt. I watched Aaren as the fire's shadows licked his cheeks and danced in his yellow eyes. It was amazing the amount of sadness his face could hold when he decided to let it show. But in a way, I was glad he could let it show around me. Even if it did drop my heart every time he frowned.

The whiskey shone in the firelight as he took another sip, but it didn't wipe away the tension that set his features so sternly. But I knew something that would.

The stone floor under the rug bit my knees as I rose and placed a careful hand on his muscular thigh to test the waters. When he didn't shy away, I pushed to my feet and straddled him. When his eyes met mine, they darkened, and I smirked. He was most definitely going to forget the Nidhogg and the trolls after I was done with him.

Our lips met, and the taste of whiskey melted on my tongue, the flavor pleasant and warm, complementing his typical scent. I sucked his bottom lip between my teeth as his hands found my waist, then swept around to fondle my ass and knead the soft flesh. His shirt bundled into soft balls in my fist as my eagerness to pull him closer grew. I needed to feel him flush against me like I had been aching to feel all day. I moaned, reaching down and brushing my hand against him, palming the quickly growing length. I didn't balk at the growing size, though a touch of dulled apprehension tried to dampen my intentions. It went away when Aaren groaned, sending the deep vibrations into my mouth as his hand moved to grip my hair.

Using the base of my palm, I massaged him lightly, tearing our lips apart and placing a light kiss along his jaw, his neck, biting the salty skin and licking in apology. My own need melted between my thighs, and I ground against him to seek temporary relief from my own arousal. But this wasn't about me tonight, and I snapped back to attention and focused.

I kissed down his body until my knees met the stone floor again, where I traced my fingers up, up, toying with the hem of his pants. Aaren didn't protest; instead, he watched me hungrily as I placed a kiss on his thigh and looked at him through my lashes.

His expression was playful as he watched me and took another sip of his whiskey, sinking lower into the chair with a pleasured groan. I dug my finger underneath the hem of his pants and tugged. My mouth grew dry when his bulge sprang free, and I took in his length as if I was sizing up an enemy. Gripping him by the base, I hovered, giving his tip a playful lick. He sucked air through his teeth, and his hand found my chin and lifted my head to meet my eyes. Hungry, grave warning circled his glowing irises.

"Layla," he whispered. He gave me a look as if to ask if I was sure.

I licked my lips and looked at him from under my brow, then swatted his hand away. With a hungry flourish, I swirled my tongue over his tip. He gasped, hands grasping at the arms of the chair, knuckles growing white. I took him into my mouth, as far as I could go, my lips meeting my hand as I pumped him.

Gods, I had been waiting so long for this, not only to touch him like this, but to make him feel this. See what I could do for him besides play the role of wife. It was everything I had wanted it to be and more.

And as delightful and delectable as it was, I wanted more.

Saliva dribbled down my chin as I choked on him. His tip hit the back of my throat deliciously. I hummed, earning me another pleasured grunt. His length was considerable, but having it in my mouth was a different story. I pulled away for a moment and wiped the spit from my chin, letting out a breathy chuckle.

His thumb brushed my cheek. "It's okay, you don't have to keep going."

I shook my head. Taking a deep, rallying breath, I opened my throat and plunged him into my mouth until my lips wrapped around the base of his cock. His rumbling moans washed over me like my own waves of pleasure had just the night before. I glanced at Aaren's face, but his eyes had fluttered shut, and his tongue swiped over his bottom lip before sucking it between his teeth.

Aaren tangled his fingers in my hair, gripping the strands by the root. I withdrew to the tip, flicking my tongue over him like I was licking a popsicle before I swallowed him again, this time going deeper. I choked on a gag, but continued, and found a steady rhythm. He bucked his hips, thrusting himself deeper down my throat, and I moaned in surprise, the sound vibrating against him and sending him into a stream of expletives. And promises of what he would do to me.

"Fuck," he growled, then bucked again.

I moved my hand and fondled him, delighting as he squirmed, chest heaving. He gripped my hair tighter. Aaren thrusted into my mouth fervently, his movements losing their rhythm the closer to the edge he got. His moans grew into choppy breaths as he fucked my mouth, every delicious inch filling me until I couldn't take anymore. He cursed again, crying out my name, and the wood underneath the hand that wasn't knotted in my hair cracked under his grip. His eyes burned carnally, as if his very existence boiled down to my mouth wrapped around his cock and the release that was building inside him.

With a roar, hot seed spilled down my throat, and I swallowed, savoring the taste of him. There was a moment of breathy bliss, a moment where all Aaren could do was breathe and blink. I cooed, licking the remnants of him from my lips with a smirk and rising, my face hovering above his. Shock stunned his features, his chest swelling with overwhelming pleasure, and he reached up to wipe the spit from my chin.

He blew out a breath and pushed himself up in his chair, taking a long drink of whiskey. "Wow," he said after swallowing. "That was..."

I straightened before he could finish. My knees cracked with soreness from kneeling, and I swallowed thickly as he still painted the back of my throat. There was nothing I wanted more than to straddle him, to sink myself onto his glistening cock and ride him until the sun came up, but against every screaming instinct inside me, I walked away. There was something to be said about the power I held over him right now, and I was determined not to relinquish it over some petty lust even if it was becoming the bane of my existence.

"Good night, Aaren," I sang, and closed his bedroom door behind me.

The next morning was chaos.

Word of the Nidhogg had spread throughout the village by mid-morning the next day, and many tried to stop and question me while on my way to Thea's. I politely declined to answer, saying that I had to be somewhere and hurried along, anxious for the respite my friend's bookshop would provide.

Once I entered the shop, I rested my weight against the closed door and sank to the floor. Thea paused from shelving her armful of books to glance over her shoulder and giggle softly.

"Don't tell me you're scared of your own people, *frue*," Thea drawled and pushed a book onto the shelf. "It's not a good look."

I groaned and rubbed my eyes in exhaustion. "I don't want to be asked another question about anything." My eyes slid to the ceiling when I dropped my head against the door. "Is it bad that I can't wait to leave tomorrow?"

Thea placed the remainder of her books on the counter, locked the front door, and joined me on the floor. I thanked her, and she smiled softly. "Leading isn't easy, Layla, but what you're doing, what you've done, has been unfathomably amazing." I gave her a disbelieving look. "You've done more than most leaders have ever done for us," she assured. "Nils and Freya being the exception."

I studied the pattern the floorboards made, unable to stop the smile that spread across my lips. I didn't realize how much I needed to hear that.

"Thank you," I said, and hugged my knees to my chest.

Thea rubbed my shoulder. "When do you leave tomorrow?"

"Sunrise."

She sighed. "I wish I could come with you. After everything with Lars...Stieg is the light at the end of the tunnel. I'm consumed with worry every time he crosses the border." She sighed. "It would be nice to keep an eye on him."

I turned my head towards her as the obvious idea blossomed in my mind. "Why don't you?"

She gave a breathy laugh. "Don't be daft, *true*. Me, on a perilous journey?"

My brow scrunched. "As much as I want to promise you it won't be, I can't. But you would get some peace of mind about Stieg. Besides, it could give you some new ideas for books."

Thea mulled it over for a minute, then another, and smiled broadly. "You have a point."

Thea showed up at the stables the next morning with her riding cloak and a small bag packed for the journey, a sight that spurned Stieg into a frenzy as he tried to convince her to stay in the village. Thea, being strong-willed—some would lovingly call it hard-headed—only shook her head and slung her bag over the horse the stablehand assigned her to.

"Thea, please," Stieg begged, but his efforts were futile.

"I would rather both of us die on the road than have to endure another heartbreak alone," Thea said sternly, then locked Stieg into a stare so intense I thought the ground would start to rumble and shake.

Stieg pressed his lips together to stop himself from arguing further. How could he argue with that?

Stieg informed us that Klartvan Lake was a two-day journey west. To our quietly mumbled groans, he promised there was an inn within a day's ride where we could rest before continuing. The inn was run by a family of Andrefolk, a race of nymphs I had read about in Harald's shop, and Stieg assured us they had a few rooms they could offer us, though we would have to pay a price. Aaren packed a hefty coin purse, but Stieg shook his head, saying they wouldn't accept that.

"They're a nymph race," Stieg explained as our horses tramped through the woods. "Nymphs and huldra are distant cousins, and they share certain qualities, one of those being their love for jewelry and other fineries."

Shiny things are what he meant to say.

"I'm guessing you have something to give them then?" I asked, patting Froki's mane. As hesitant as I was to embark on another journey so soon after the first one, it was nice to be back in the saddle with her, even if she was being excessively sassy today.

"I do indeed," Stieg answered, then dug in the satchel draped over the side of his horse. He withdrew a handful of candy wrappers, the plastic papers crinkling in his palm. I swallowed my tongue and shook with silent laughter. "I'm giving them a bit of my collection of shiny paper. I'm sure it will suffice for a night."

I thanked the heavens I was behind him as I clamped my hand over my mouth.

We were out of the forest by the afternoon and crossing over the vast plains that stretched for miles and miles. As the flat terrain showed no end or inn in sight, my mind began to wander, delving into the territory of my nocturnal activities from the last two nights. I took a small breath to calm myself down before Aaren sensed what was going through my mind.

It seemed too late for that, though, seeing as he turned in his saddle with a roguish look. His brows flicked, and my heart fluttered. I wanted to grimace, but couldn't. Aaren had made me feel things so wondrously foreign to me that I saw stars. It was almost a blessing that we were already married, because I was starting to believe he might have ruined all other men for me. That didn't mean I loved him. Even though it felt like my heart was fluttering, not because of the lustful look he had just sent me, but because...

"Oh, thank the gods," Thea groaned as the outline of a surprisingly large building appeared.

As we rode closer, I could see that the inn itself was nestled in the tall grasses of the plains, with a couple of outbuildings scattered around it. Attached to the side of the building was a pen full of cows and pigs, and chickens wandered around the premises, pecking the ground at my feet as I dismounted. I absently stroked Froki's snout and whispered thank yous before Aaren grabbed her lead and tied her to the fence around the property.

The massive front door, made of dark wood, swung open as I neared it, revealing a tall, dark man standing with his arms spread wide in welcome. His limbs were slender and nimble, and taut features set in a welcoming smile that stretched to his warm, brown eyes. On his fingers were silver and gold rings, and a large gold hoop dangled from one of his earlobes, glinting in the light from the sconces outside the house. His ears were pointed like one would expect an elf's to be. Upon first glance, I knew why the front door was so large. He was taller than Aaren, with gangly limbs and a torso like a tree trunk.

"Hello!" the man exclaimed, jagged but white teeth displayed through his genuine smile. "Welcome!" He bowed low, though it barely reduced his height. "I am Erlund. Welcome to my home. How many rooms do you require?"

Stieg stepped forward, narrowly avoiding a chicken that suddenly crossed his path. "Two," he answered.

Erlund nodded, the smile never leaving his lips, and pressed his fingertips together. "And how do you wish to pay?"

Stieg opened his pack and eagerly pulled out a handful of candy wrappers. "I found these in the woods outside our village. Relics from Midgard that slipped through the cracks."

Erlund stepped forward and plucked a wrapper, a Snickers, and examined it between his pinched fingers.

"Very intriguing," he mused, placing the wrapper back and grabbing a Twix. The gold wrapper glinted in the afternoon sun, and Erlund hummed approvingly. "Very good," he said, holding out his large hands where Stieg dumped the remainder of the trash. "This will do quite nicely." He pocketed them and turned on his heel. "Please follow me!"

The warmth inside the inn beckoned me just as its host did.

"Andrefolk are known for their neighborliness. They own most inns in Alveland," Stieg said as he closed his bag. "Hospitality has become their specialty, forever serving others."

A somewhat disturbing sentiment, but with the way Erlund welcomed us so fervently, it truly was just as much a pleasure to have us as it was for us to be here.

Thea joined Stieg's side and followed the man inside, and as I moved forward, Aaren placed a hand on the small of my back protectively. I would have dwelled on the touch if the inside of the inn hadn't taken my breath away.

The interior of the large hall had a roaring hearth at the far end and a massive dining table in the center. The walls were painted a dark green, with paintings and mounted animal heads throughout the room. The paintings ranged from scenes of romance to valor to macabre defeat, each with a whorl of mysticism, as if the paintings themselves were infused with magic. Of the mounted heads, I only recognized a few, such as the farljort, tastefully decorated with a flower crown over its horned head. Much to my amusement, there was a tiny plaque in which a small stuffed ratato head was mounted, its tiny teeth bared in warning. The other creatures I had read about, but since their descriptions in Harald's books weren't accompanied by pictures like the others were, I found seeing them mounted on the walls here to be fascinating. The verbjorn was described similarly to a bear, and seeing it in front of me, with teeth snarling and glass eyes boring into me, that description had been correct. However, the fur was a lot bushier, and the ears were pointed instead of rounded, like those of any bear from Midgard.

"Erlund, who's there?" a lovely voice asked, followed by a pair of blue eyes peeking from a side room near the fireplace.

"Guests, Amara!" Erlund answered.

The pair of eyes quickly grew into a tall woman. Her skin was the same color as her counterpart's, and her curly brown hair had been tied back with a purple ribbon that matched the rest of her ensemble. Her dress barely brushed the floor, and the toes of her shoes poked out from under her skirt. A dusty apron covered her front, and a bridge of dark freckles peppered her button nose. As she emerged from what looked like the kitchen, a small boy who favored Erlund in the face clung to her skirts and burrowed shyly in her apron.

"Hello!" Amara said as she moved from the doorway. "It's such a pleasure to have you here." The little boy tugged at her skirt, then turned his head to reveal a set of pointed ears, similar to those of his parents. The small vest he wore over his cotton shirt was dusted with flour, and a smear of drying dough highlighted his cheek. Amara smiled and chuckled amusedly at his coyness, and pushed the boy forward.

"This is Jesper." The boy nodded his head timidly, then hid his face in his mother's skirts again.

With a quiet chorus of crinkles, Erlund approached Amara with the handful of candy wrappers, smiling widely.

"What are these?" Amara asked with delighted curiosity.

"Relics from Midgard," Erlund repeated Stieg's words. Relics indeed. Erlund turned to us. "I have the perfect place for these."

His long legs carried him to a wooden display cabinet with a glass lid. Opening it, he smoothed out the crinkling wrappers and placed them in the case. Amara joined his side and admired the display, and Jesper stood on his tiptoes to catch a glimpse.

Amara turned to us. "You must be very special guests.

Chapter 45

After showing us to our rooms and informing us that dinner would be ready in a couple of hours, Erlund left us to get comfortable and settle in. The room was cozy, but like in the mountains, there was only one bed. Thea bounced her brows at me when she glanced into our room, but I pretended not to notice since I was in Aaren's line of sight.

When the door closed, I sat down on the bed, bouncing a bit as I toyed with the tassel on one of the pillows. The blankets and comforter had whimsical designs stitched into the fabric with a thick green thread. On the wall was a painting of a woman picking pink flowers in an open field next to the seashore, the waters akin to the blue waves of Kysthjem.

Aaren cleared his throat as he shed his pack and placed it on an end table. With a shake of his head, he swept his silken hair into a bun and tied it, then started disarming himself.

"You're staring," he said without looking at me. "I know I'm pretty, but you don't have to make it so obvious."

I scoffed. "In your dreams, Aaren."

He turned with a suggestive look. "I don't dream about you looking at me, Layla," he said and crossed his arms over his broad chest. An air of penetrating desire filled the room, but I wasn't going to let it make me sweat. If I couldn't figure out a way to keep my feelings from shooting through my rune, then I would stop my feelings. That notion was a lot harder to put into motion if Aaren kept talking like he was.

"I dream of you doing so much more than just looking at me."

I cocked an eyebrow, challenging him. "Like what?"

One corner of his mouth lifted. "Like your pretty lips wrapped around my cock." He pushed himself off the bed and slowly rounded the corner. My heart thumped with every inch that closed between us. I held my ground as he drew closer, only moving when his hard body backed me into the wall.

"I dream about my face buried in your legs." My fingertips heated as his breath mingled with mine. He dragged a knuckle down my cheek, a soft growl rumbling in his chest. "About my tongue devouring every inch of your..."

A polite knock sounded on the door, and the air went stale. Annoyance flickered across Aaren's face when he pulled away. Cold air filled the space where he had been, and goosebumps raised on my arms. I released my breath as my heart settled, and I shook off the lustful feeling that had my limbs going molten.

Aaren opened the door.

"Hello!" Erlund said in the same manner as when he opened the front door upon our arrival. I peered around the door to find him standing with an armful of fresh towels. "These are in case you decide to visit the bathhouse around back. I would highly recommend it after a long day on the road." He extended the towels forward.

With a polite smile, Aaren accepted them and nodded. "Thank you."

As the door closed, he looked back at me with that same hunger as before, but I was determined to maintain the upper hand. I pushed past him and made sure my bottom brushed the growing hardness in his pants. Then, with a smile, I left the room and closed the door behind me.

Proud of myself, I wandered into the main hall where two girls crouched by the hearth. One was ta little older then the other, with her dark hair braided back and wearing a blue dress, while the younger one had wild, dark curls billowing around her face. The younger one wore a green smock with an ink-stained front. They huddled over a pile of ash, a small stick in the older one's hand that she used to trace small runes while the other drew polka dots and sparkles with her small finger. The two giggled before erasing their drawings and starting anew. Their drawing halted as I approached, the older one throwing me a cautious look.

"Hi," I said and took a seat at the table near the fire.

The younger one offered me a small smile. "Hi."

I crossed my legs and rested my arms on them. "What are you drawing?"

The older girl turned and straightened to her full height. Though she appeared to be about twelve, she was taller than I was. "We're practicing our runes." She gestured to the designs in the ash.

Pointing to the one closest to the fire, I asked, "And which one is that?"

The little girl jumped up excitedly. "That one is for good luck! Papa said we need it after last year's growing season."

The older girl nudged her sister as if telling her to be quiet, and the younger one complied with an embarrassed blush.

I squinted curiously, giving them the exact look I give Lucas when I could tell he didn't want to tell me something.

"What happened last year?" I asked.

The youngest girl jumped on the opportunity despite her sister's warning glance. "We had a horrible infestation of madgers. They came and ate half of our crop!"

"That sounds awful," I said, even though I had no idea what a madger was.

The older girl, now ignoring her own summons for discretion, perked up and nodded. "There are still a few out there," she said. "Papa charmed them so they wouldn't eat any more crops, but I heard him tell Mama that the charm is bound to wear off soon. Then they'll have babies, and it'll be the same as last year."

I uncrossed my legs and readied myself to stand. "Well, then it sounds like we need to get rid of these madgers." Exactly how I would've said it if I were talking to Lucas. Like when we would play our fantasy adventure pretend games together. Only now, it wasn't pretend.

The girl bounced up and down excitedly, though the older one watched me cautiously. "Why do you want to help us?"

I shrugged. "What else have we got to do until dinner?"

They didn't argue, and we headed outside.

Aurelia, the older sister, and Flora, the younger, led me to the field surrounding the inn and the outbuildings. In the field to the left of the inn were countless rows of corn with stalks that reached above our heads and swayed in the breeze. I gazed down the rows, sight trailing off as the rows did, ending in a conglomeration of green leaves and stalks. Aurelia carried a large glass jar in her hands, ready to catch any madgers we found.

"They like corn the most," Aurelia informed as she took a careful step into the rows. The wind picked up, rustling the stalks. A whisper of leaves surrounded us as my boot sank into the squishy dirt.

Mama had always dreamed of having a garden, probably not one this size, but sizable enough that she could grow us dinner. She told me that Granny had one a long time ago, and she would rifle through the berry bushes and eat until her stomach hurt. Granny promised we could have one when the season started, but she never made it to summer. Working with Aurora in the fields of Skoghjem was the closest I had ever been to having a garden. I smiled as I watched the little girls dart through the stalks and squeal with glee. Maybe I'd have Aurora help me start my own once all of this was over.

When I asked, Flora described the madgers as looking like gnomes, short and stout with little beards. However, Aurelia corrected her, saying that despite their infestation, Flora had never actually seen a madger. The real madgers looked like small, stick-thin people with yellow skin and pointed ears. They had razor-sharp nails, black eyes, and a preferred diet of corn silk.

We trailed down the rows, and I realized how hard it would be to spot yellow skin amongst the yellow corn.

"Where are you from?" Aurelia asked as we walked.

"Skoghjem," I answered, but I was more concerned with distinguishing the rustling of the leaves. It was hard to tell if it was the scuffling of tiny feet or just the wind.

Flora bounced excitedly. "I've heard of Skoghjem! It's in the forest!"

I nodded. "It is!"

Aurelia plucked a leaf and pressed the thin, silky green between her fingers. "They say that the Fraalver are in danger."

"How do you know that?"

"The visitors at the inn tell us things," Aurelia replied, running her hand over a smooth corn leaf. "Papa heard about how the leader in the mountains died."

My chest grew tight at the mention of Torsten. "Yes, the Fraalver are in danger."

"In danger of what?" Flora asked as she wove aimlessly throughout the rows and stopped occasionally to pull a stray curl that got caught on a corn stalk. "Do you have madgers too?"

I shook my head as the wind picked up. "It's complicated," I answered, because to them, it was. How was I supposed to explain to these girls that their home was being threatened by some power-hungry sorcerer who was dead, but now he's not, and now we're trying to learn more about who raised him and what

396

other nightmares he is going to commit? Children had wonderful imaginations, but I'm afraid that not even Lucas could dream up anything more absurd than the conflict we faced.

"Shhh!" Aurelia whispered and halted Flora with a firm hand on her shoulder. I followed the finger she pointed to a small, yellow figure about the size of my palm that was lounging casually on a leaf. It swung its bony leg languidly, dazed eyes drifting into the sky as Erlund's charm lured it into a sleepy stupor.

Aurelia tiptoed forward and unscrewed the lid of the jar. The madger flicked its eyes to her at the sound and pushed itself to a sitting position. It tilted its head for a better look at her, and it reminded me of a curious puppy. Or the way Lucas used to wake up in the morning with the cutest dazed look on his face.

"Be careful," Flora whispered as Aurelia drew closer, but the madger only blinked, its jaw hanging low, and a small string of drool dribbled from its lips. It was cute, but I wasn't going to let that fool me, especially after the ratato attack in Fjellhjem.

Aurelia's fingernails tapped against the side of the jar, and like a magician snapping his fingers on his hypnotized volunteer, the madger snapped awake. It lurched from one leaf to the next in a frenzy of high-pitched titters as if to taunt us.

Flora shoved forward against Aurelia's and my protests, shouting insults at the madger as she disappeared into the stalks.

"Flora!" Aurelia called, then took off after her sister.

And just like that, I lost sight of Aurelia, too.

I had always wanted to go to a haunted corn maze when I lived in Midgard, but this was not what I had in mind.

Corn stalks slapped my cheeks as I thundered down the row. I strained my ears for the rustle of leaves in between shouting their names, but all I could hear was the thundering of my pulse. The only thing that led my way was the small set of footprints pressed into the soft dirt between the rows.

"Flora!" I cried, swatting away another stalk. "Aurelia!"

I nearly toppled over Aurelia when I caught sight of her crouched in the dirt, Flora only a few feet away with her arms cradled around the madger like it was a baby doll. Dirt flecked her already stained smock—it matched the brown smudges along her dark cheeks where she must've slid through the mud. The madger tried to throw a punch, but Flora flicked its tiny hand away and chastised it.

"Flora, put it down!" Aurelia pleaded, but I couldn't help but chuckle at her horror-stricken features.

Flora shook her head and wrangled the madger back into her arms when it tried to make another escape. "He's just cranky because we woke him up."

We scouted the entire cornfield, and as the sun dipped just below the horizon, the jar was nearly full of madgers. Aurelia handed me the container, and I held it up to my face, coming eye to eye with one of the small yellow creatures, dazed from Erlund's charm. Its small jaw was slack, black eyes empty, and I smiled because it reminded me of Oswin after a couple of mugs of ale. Only some of the madgers were still charmed—the others were fighting fervently to try and break the glass with their tiny fists. One even sent me the middle finger.

"Papa!" Flora shouted as we stepped into the house. The smell of cooked meat and searing vegetables wafted around, and my mouth watered. "We caught the madgers! We saved the growing season!"

Erlund, who had been stirring a pot of stew at the end of the dining table, looked up and watched Flora as she bounced across the room. The poor madgers likely suffered a few concussions with the way she jostled the jar. Erlund knelt and took the jar into his hands to hold up to the light.

"You caught them?" he asked in disbelief as he met my gaze. When I nodded, he asked, "Why?"

I shrugged nonchalantly. "It looked like you needed some pest control."

Erlund tucked the jar under his arm and rose with a graceful nod. "Thank you, *frue*."

I nodded back with a smile and found a spot at the table closest to the pot of stew. Amara strode into the hall, followed by Thea, Stieg, and Aaren, the latter sinking onto the bench in front of me and eyeing me closely.

"What are those?" Thea questioned with a hint of distaste in her voice. She wrinkled her nose as a madger stirred, wiping the drool from its chin. Realizing where it was, it pounded its tiny fist on the glass and began to squeak angrily.

"Madgers?" Amara asked. She tenderly scrubbed the dirt from Flora's cheek before she sat. "You caught these?" When I nodded, she puffed out a breath of surprise. "You have helped more than you know."

Erlund scooped a ladleful of beef stew into a bowl and placed it in front of me. Carrots and potatoes bobbed in the brown broth, and my mouth watered as the steam rose and filled my nostrils. Amara pushed a plate of bread forward, followed by a bowl of what looked like freshly churned butter. Jesper pranced into the dining hall, wearing a different vest than he had earlier, and Amara smiled as he slid onto the bench next to her.

"Very nice dinner vest, darling," she said and tugged at the lapels to straighten the middle. She turned to Thea, who was watching with the question ready on her lips. "He likes to dress nicely for supper, especially when we have guests," Amara explained.

Thea grinned. "Very handsome."

A pleasant quiet settled around the table as we ate, Amara occasionally blowing on Jesper's spoon when he offered it to her. Aurelia and Flora chattered quietly about their new pets, as they were calling the madgers, and I caught a few words of their plan to make little clothes for them. I smiled into my stew at the thought of the little madgers wearing vests like Jesper's.

"What brings Fraalver from Skoghjem through the plains?" Erlund asked before slurping his spoonful of stew.

Aaren flicked his gaze to our host. "Just traveling," he answered politely.

Erlund brought his bowl to his lips and watched Aaren from the rim. "I can't hide that I have heard the rumors of the unrest amongst the Fraalver. Is this why you travel, half-elf?" Thea froze with her spoon halfway to her mouth, giving me a quick, cautious look. When no one answered him, Erlund continued. "If you are choosing not to answer because you are unsure what side we play, rest assured, it is not the side that jeopardizes my family."

Aaren straightened, his spoon forgotten in his bowl. "It's not just the Fraalver that are threatened, Erlund. Most of Alveland is in jeopardy."

"And I suppose you plan on stopping it then?" Amara asked as she wiped Jesper's mouth with her apron.

"Not just us," Stieg answered. "This is a lot bigger than just the Fraalver."

This gave Erlund pause, and he stopped chewing to exchange glances with his wife. He swallowed. "Meaning?"

Aaren explained as much as he could without revealing our hand, telling them that Markus was on the rise again and was raising an army of undesirables, though we didn't know who or what fought in that army. Thea chimed in and described our troubles with the mylings, and I filled them in on the burrower's attack on Torsten. When our story trailed off at our current events, Erlund blew out a breath.

"We were unaware that this was as bad as it is," Amara said and wrapped a protective arm around Jesper who had fallen into a sleepy, stew-induced stupor. "Is there anything we can do?"

Aaren flicked his eyes to me momentarily before answering. "Keep your eyes open for undesirables," he replied. "And if there is a fight, we'll need all the help we can get."

Amara threw Erlund a worried glance, though he did not meet her eye. "I do hope you can end this before there is a fight," he said.

Flora sank in her chair, eyes falling to her half-empty bowl. "I don't want to fight," she whimpered, and Aurelia scooted closer and folded her sister in her arms.

Amara cleared her throat and stood with a now sleeping Jesper clasped to her shoulder. "Come on, *barn*, let's wash up." With a snap of her fingers, Amara summoned her children to the kitchen in the back, the swinging door flapping closed behind her.

Thea watched them until they were out of sight, then said, "You have a beautiful family, Erlund."

Erlund thanked her as he tore a piece of bread. "Jesper wasn't planned," he said, then laughed. "But you know how these things go when you're in love."

I wish I did.

Thea replied with a fit of giggles of her own, very adamantly agreeing before giving Stieg a ravenous look like she hadn't just eaten two bowls of stew.

"Are the private lives of the Fraalver as free as the Andrefolk?" Erlund questioned.

The Andrefolk were very free, as evidenced by the number of their brothels.

"In some ways," Thea answered and settled into her chair. "Though I can't speak for these two," she gestured to me and Aaren. Clever. She thought she was being clever.

Erlund turned his attention to me and Aaren. "I've always wondered about the politics of the Fraalver leaders. And I suppose, while we're on the subject, the domestic lives as well. You see, I know that the marital relationship between the two forms the borders, but do the dynamics of the union determine the strength of the magic?"

I gave Erlund an amused glance. "Are you asking if the nastier the sex, the stronger the magic?"

Aaren gave a choked cough from across the table.

Erlund pursed his lips and hid the smile that was creeping into his eyes.

I glanced at Aaren, willing him to answer instead. "No," he replied and leaned forward. "There's no correlation."

"Pity," Erlund said, before turning his attention to Thea. "You say you're an author?"

Thea's response was lost in my ears, and my rune heated. A spark of pleasure shot into parts of me that only Aaren had touched. I covered my mouth with my hand to keep the moan from curling over my tongue, and Aaren gave me a knowing smirk from across the table before turning back to the conversation.

Chapter 46

Thea dropped into the chair next to mine near the fire and let out a contented sigh. Flora and Jesper sat a couple of feet away, giggling and squealing as they scribbled on scrolls of parchment. They were busy sketching their best version of a madger. Jesper held up his doodle: a skinny figure with bulging black eyes and a pink tongue sticking out of the madger's mouth, and Flora howled in delight, then added a tongue onto her own drawing.

I chuckled, turning my eyes to Thea, who watched them blissfully. Memory blended with longing painted her face as the giggles grew louder, and she smiled blissfully. "Such simple joy children have," she purred. "Sometimes I wish I could go back to that age. The age where the plainest of things brought the liveliest of pleasures."

I hummed in agreement and extended my legs. I sank lower into the chair.

"Lars and I wanted so many children," Thea shared, her voice light and melodic, as if the memory of him carried her into a blissful place, a place where Markus and the Nidhogg and the necromancer didn't exist.

I turned my head. "How many did you want?"

She chuckled amusedly. "A lot," she answered. "At least six."

"Six?!" I exclaimed and giggled at the thought of Thea corralling a herd of children. "You sure you could've handled six children?"

"With Lars, I could handle a hundred." She went quiet for a moment as she stared into the fire. A log shifted and sent a billow of sparks into the chimney. "Together, we were unstoppable."

I leaned forward, purposefully catching her eyes. "And Stieg?" I questioned.

She gave the hint of a smile, but grief weighed heavily on her features, making it look difficult to smile. "After Lars died, everything stopped. All my dreams were nothing without him. My life hit a wall. All our plans crashed and were swept away like the huldra's river. I was lost in the dark."

I knew how she felt. It was the same feeling I had felt when I lost Lucas. At least I knew he was still alive, somewhere.

Stieg laughed at the table behind us, where Erlund was engaged in a playful game of cards. The grief lifted a little from Thea's face, and the shadow of a smile brightened at the sound of his laughter. "Stieg turned on the light. All the life that I felt leave me when Lars died suddenly filled me again, as if Stieg had brought Lars back to me." She gave an impish smile. "And Stieg wants more than six children."

"Oh gods," I chuckled.

We shared a laugh, one that filled me with such fulfillment and delight that I felt light in my chair, as if I were floating on a cloud. I reached over and took her hand in mine, both of us sitting in a comfortable silence as Amara whisked her children to bed.

With a sigh, Thea said, "I suppose I should get to bed as well." Standing, she locked eyes with Stieg, who dropped his handful of cards mid-turn and quickly said good night to Erlund.

Thea blew a kiss and bid me good night.

Aaren wasn't in our room when I poked my head in, but when I spotted the towels on the bed, I forgot to worry about his whereabouts, and my body ached at the thought of a hot bath. Undressing, I wrapped a towel snugly around me, threw my hair into a bun, and tiptoed through the inn. I may as well have been walking around the inn with iron boots with the way the floorboards were creaking underfoot, but I had a feeling Thea and Steig might be otherwise occupied.

A light breeze greeted me as I stepped outside and hurried to a small, squat building with a wooden sign indicating it was the bathhouse.

As I opened the creaking wooden door, the smell of jasmine and lavender did nothing to dull the shock that froze me in my tracks. Lining the left side of the house were three steaming tubs, each with an array of soaps and bath potions of every color. To the right were benches next to a pile of hot coals, with a large tub of water nearby. Sitting on the bench against the wall was Aaren, sweaty and naked in all his glory. His head rested on the wall behind him, and he smirked at my shock, his lips curling into a knowing smile.

"Come in, *fremmed*," he said deeply. His eyes fluttered shut as the steam billowed around him. "Don't mind me."

My first step into the bathhouse was more complicated than I had anticipated. I couldn't help but balk at the sight of Aaren stark naked in front of me. All of his scars were on display, and with this new, unobscured view, he had even more than I had thought. The door swung shut behind me, and the sound rattled the sense back into me. I wasn't going to let him shake me. I was here for a bath, and I was going to take one. And I was going to ignore the remnants of that challenging look that was now simmering in his face.

The wooden planks were slippery, and the balls of my feet twisted and slid as I struggled to keep my footing. I made it to the tubs without falling and embarrassing myself, which was lucky considering the glance I threw over my shoulder confirmed that Aaren was watching me closely. I wasn't sure if it was because he didn't want me to fall or if he was waiting for the moment I dropped my towel. The fiendish look in his eyes told me it was the latter, but I didn't let it faze me as the curling steam from the bathtubs beckoned.

The warmth crept up my ankles as I stepped into the closest tub, and goosebumps dotted my skin when the heat spread up my shins. I picked up one of the potion bottles after sinking into the water with a delighted shiver and read the label.

"What does *muskler* mean?" I asked.

Aaren had closed his eyes, and he breathed deeply before answering, "Muscles."

"Oh," I said, then uncorked the bottle and poured a couple of drops into the bathwater. Bubbles emerged around me, clinging to my skin as I leaned back and breathed in the lavender and rosemary scent. It smelled like Granny's house and the potpourri she used. I hummed to myself as the water relaxed my muscles, and nostalgia began to sweep me away.

Silence settled amongst the bathhouse, drifting lazily with steam that cloaked Aaren in a veil of mist—a prince relaxing on his throne. The steam obscured my view of him, and a pool of disappointment coiled in my stomach. I wished I could gaze upon him naked and peaceful all night.

His question from the sparring ring a few nights ago echoed in my mind.

Do you love me?

No, I wasn't in love with him, but looking at him was becoming one of my favorite pastimes.

I sank deeper into the tub and let the water lap at my chin as my eyes floated to the wooden ceiling and traced patterns in the lingering steam.

"We have unfinished business, *fremmed*," Aaren said from across the room.

I pushed myself up and pivoted in the tub to rest my arms on the rim. "And that is?"

"I told you what fills my head every night. A thought for a thought. Tell me what you dream about."

My mouth went dry, and the bathwater suddenly felt cold. "Wouldn't you like to know?"

Aaren rested his arm behind him and draped the other over his groin, covering himself. I almost whimpered disappointedly. "I *would* like to know."

Challenge accepted.

I pushed myself off the edge of the tub, water dripping from my body as I rose, skin glistening in the soft lighting. A light chill swept over me and peaked my nipples, but I ignored it as I watched Aaren closely. His hand shifted over himself as he started to harden.

"Have you been dreaming of me, Aaren?" I asked with a tilted head. I traced a hand up my thigh, skin prickling at my touch.

Aaren groaned and shifted again. His hand closed over himself, but did nothing else, as if he were fighting the urge to pump himself. "Every night, *fremmed*," he groaned. He was fully hard now, and he sighed as his hand worked him once, then again when it seemed like he couldn't stop himself.

My core turned molten at the sight of him pumping himself in front of me, especially when I knew he was doing so because of me. *Me*, not the memory of Solveig or whoever else he may have lain with in the past. Aaren stroked his cock because I aroused him. I had never thought anyone could see me like this, could want me so much. But here he was, unable to keep his hands away or his honeyed words at bay because I held him in my lustful grip.

The bathwater sloshed as I took a slow step out of the tub. Bubbles clung to my breasts and covered me in a lavender cloud. Aaren bit his lip as he watched me move, resting his arm behind his head as his ministrations grew faster the closer I drew. I placed a hand on my breast, pinching the nipple between my thumb and forefinger, and let a soft moan flutter from my lips. Aaren clenched his jaw as his bicep flexed behind him.

I drew close enough to lean forward, brushing my lips against his as he let out a breathy sigh, hot breath warming my lips. His hand stopped suddenly, then grabbed my breast and kneaded with hungry desperation as he closed the gap between our lips and ravenously devoured me. His need to ferociously consume me drew a moan from my lips, muscles fluttering with pleasured delight as his hand molded my flesh down to my core. I gasped when his finger traced the small button of nerves.

He tore his lips from mine, leaving me a whimpering mess without his touch. With a strong arm, he scooped me up and laid me gently on the bench where my skin stuck to the steamed wood. He sat back, surveying me until I was almost squirming, then leaned down to tangle his lips with mine once more. His hand traced up my middle, grip wrapping comfortably around my neck, forcing me to gaze into his blazing amber eyes.

"What do you dream of, Layla?" he demanded.

"You, Aaren," I answered. "I only dream about you."

I went to reach down to stroke him, but he shifted his hips out of my reach, clicking his tongue at me. "What about me?"

He turned my head, licking up my neck and moaning greedily in my ear.

"I dream about..." My eyes fluttered shut for a moment, relishing in the sweet bliss he sent shooting down my spine to gather in my center. I dreamed about him thrusting inside me, fucking me senseless until every one of my cells imploded and my very being ended. But to want sex with him would be to love him, which I...didn't...

"I dream about your head between my legs, about your sweet tongue."

There was the quickest flash of something across his face, so fast I couldn't catch what it was before Aaren groaned approvingly. Had it been disappointment, or was I mistaking it for shuddered desire?

I wiped my mind clean, knowing the more I thought of it, the more it would distract me from Aaren's sweat-sheened body on top of me.

Aaren's teeth nipped at my ear as he lowered his hips to mine, his hardness pulsing in my palm. One arm held him up while the other left my neck, snaking down my torso to circle my sex again. Electric sparks shot through me as he ran a finger down my middle, and I arched into his touch to relieve the hot need that bubbled in my chest. I ran my hand up his length, then plunged it to the base, fingertips fondling beneath his balls, and he bucked into my hand with a bark of pleasure.

I felt concave, my center aching, almost begging to be filled as desire pulsed through me like the beating of Fjellhjem drums. Every cell in my body was empty without Aaren's throbbing cock inside me. I didn't love him, but my body sang for him the way a piano sang at the expert touch of its player. He plunged a finger inside me, grumbling with delight at the wetness within. He withdrew for a moment, flicking my clit, then added a finger, dipping deeper into me. I cried out, then pumped him harder, faster.

My body went cold when he moved away from me, but a sweeping arm grabbed me and draped me over him as he lay down on the bench. His tantalizing breath grazed my center, sending a shudder through me as I realized my mouth hovered over his cock. I had never tried a position like this, but any position other than missionary was new to me.

A devastating wave of pleasure stormed through me as his tongue traced a hungry lick on me. Awash with bliss, I sucked his tip into my mouth and swished my tongue over the head. He moaned against me, a shockwave of pleasure pulsed through me, and I licked up his shaft and wrapped my mouth around him. I was desperate to take in every inch of him; I *needed* to take all of him in.

"Oh fuck," Aaren groaned, bucking his hips and hitting the back of my throat.

His tongue drove deeper, and a hopeless need flooded me as he lapped at my folds, tasting the surge of wetness that his tongue summoned. I let out a pleasured whine as my breasts ached, and my walls clenched around nothing. His ministrations became desperate, erratic, long, broad licks reduced to short, sweet flicks as he brought me near the edge of ecstasy. I removed my mouth and pumped him, twisting my wrist with every thrust of the hand.

"Fuck, Layla! Fuck!"

He came, roaring my name as he spilled onto me and painted my breasts with his pleasure. Aaren thrust into my hand slowly, once, slower this time, then sighed. My own pleasure still writhed and gnashed inside me, though I sent a cooling wave of resignation down my body, hoping to calm my aching center. I hummed soothingly, moving to get off of him, but his hands held my hips tightly, teeth biting my buttock.

"I'm not done with you yet," Aaren said.

Before I could respond, he plunged his tongue into me with a ferocity I had never felt before. My world shattered, my existence reduced to the pleasure coiling in my stomach and the man between my legs. My head dropped, cheek resting on his inner thigh, and I cried out, the pleasure quickly uncoiling with every lick, every breath, every hum against me. My body ignited in a tantalizing flame, teasing me with heated strokes up every cord of muscle, filling every pore of my skin.

My eyes rested on his cock that shimmered with the release that also glistened on my breasts. Something was building in me, growing larger, taller, impossible to ignore. A flick of his tongue over my most sensitive spot sent me tumbling over, waves of intense release crashing onto the shores of my body. I cried, fingers gripping the inside of his thigh as I rode out the rest of my high on his tongue. All sentiments as to where we were, who I was, or what was happening in our world retreated from my mind, and all I could think, all I could feel, was this miraculous man underneath me, his silken hair splayed on the bench beneath his head like a crown. My body twitched, coming down from the most intense high I had ever experienced, and Aaren placed a loving kiss against my sex, giving me one last lick.

It was almost impossible to move after such a release, but I managed to push myself up and off of Aaren, trying to hide the wobbling in my knees. My dulled senses still felt the strike of shock when I turned to Aaren to see his hand extended to me instead of him dressing and leaving like I had expected. Hesitantly, I took it, letting him lead me across the room to the bathtub I had been in. I sighed as I sank back into the water, where Aaren climbed in himself, and guided me back until my back was against his chest.

Aaren grabbed a sponge, the carnal lust having left his eyes, replaced with a softness he usually gave Nilsen when tucking him into bed. He brushed the sponge across my chest, wiping away his release, and I shivered when his calloused hands scratched against my smooth skin, like a cat's tongue on a piece of silk.

It was amazing how different Aaren was from the time I met him. How gentle he was now when, for the longest time, I had thought all he wanted to do was throttle me. I smiled softly to myself as Aaren wet the sponge again and dripped the water across my chest.

The way he brushed my hair off my neck to run the sponge over my skin sent a warmth pooling into my stomach that wasn't because I was turned on. It was warming the way Granny's photo albums and hot tea warmed me after a hard day. It was warming the way Mama's singing voice would fill me with so much joy that I had to dance. It was warming the way Lucas's passion fueled comic book rants sent a gladdened smile to my face.

This wasn't the brute I met that night on the border.

And I was now in dangerous territory.

I wasn't sure what to do, but I ran away. I brushed the sponge away and stood up so suddenly that water spilled over the brim of the tub, but I didn't care. The mess could be cleaned, and I needed to get out of there.

I didn't look at Aaren and his confused expression as I toweled off quickly. As I closed the bathhouse door behind me, I shot "Good night, Aaren," over my shoulder and stepped into the cloudy night.

Aaren came back to the room shortly after I did, but I pretended to be asleep.

He slept by the fire again that night, rising early in the morning to tend to the horses. Sleep didn't come easily for me as thoughts rattled in my head, creating a racket I simply could not quiet.

There was a wall inside me, a wall that had been building since Mama and Granny died and had reached its peak when I slept with that customer from the bar. Behind that wall, I was protected, even if what was protecting me was the harsh truth that an orphan like me could never be loved, could never be wanted. Coming here to Alveland had started to chip away at that wall, flaking off little bits of it and turning it to dust in the night.

When Aaren hit me with that harsh truth that night in Fjellhjem, it was like he had taken a sledgehammer to that wall and started to demolish it. Because Aaren had been right, and every word of it held the almost unbearable truth I was hiding behind because it was safe. He had been right, but I was still hiding behind the rubble because it was still safer than recognizing the fact that being unwanted and not wanting anyone was easier than deciding to love and accepting love.

Because where had love gotten me before now—Mama, who was dead, Granny, who was dead, and Lucas, who had been kidnapped, and I might never see him again.

It was safer never to love anything ever again.

But it was growing increasingly complex to deny the storms that were coming to wash away the rubble of that wall. Soon, I would have nothing to hide behind because Aaren was choosing to spend his only night in a decent bed on the floor instead, if it meant that I would be more comfortable. Because Aaren made my body weep for him. Because Aaren, through all that his village had faced and would continue to face, was still adamant on helping me find my brother.

That had to mean something, but I was too scared to acknowledge it. I wasn't sure I would ever be brave enough.

When the sun finally rose, I had only been asleep for a few hours, and I gave an anguished groan as I dragged myself out of bed.

The horses were readied shortly after breakfast, and the Andrefolk family gathered outside their front door to bid us farewell. Amara gave my shoulder a brief squeeze of encouragement, wishing me luck on the journey while Jesper, in his fine vest from last night, clung to her skirts. Flora lunged forward and wrapped her arms around my legs, begging me not to leave. There were still madgers to catch, she claimed.

I knelt in front of her and grabbed her small hands. "You're going to have to catch those madgers on your own, I'm afraid," I said, swinging her arms with my hands. "But I'm confident you can. You already know how to catch them."

Flora broke into a wide grin. "I'm going to name one after you."

I laughed and hugged her goodbye.

The first half of the day dragged on as the sun beat down on us, beads of sweat gathering on my skin. The early summer warmth quickly began to feel like a mild desert heat, and it pricked my nerves, and every little thing seemed to pluck at my nerves. First, I was uncomfortable in the saddle, then it was a fly buzzing incessantly in my ear, then Aaren wouldn't stop clearing his throat, and Thea and Stieg wouldn't stop murmuring to each other.

Smaller buildings were sprawled across the plains, and I vaguely remembered Ivar saying the space between Skoghjem and Klartvan Lake was mainly filled with nymph brothels. And as we rode by the third one, the shouts and groans that could be heard coming from inside proved him right. We also passed by a few scattered Fraalver settlements, but we were too pressed for time to stop at any of them.

The grassy plains slowly turned to jutting rock, which only worked to make the heat worse and, in consequence, my irritation. When it seemed like my last nerve was spent, I kicked Froki forward, and she trotted away to give me some much-needed alone time. I relished the blissful wind that tangled my hair, the reprieve it gave me from the harsh sun. Aaren called after me, but I ignored him, pushing on until I must've been a speck on the horizon to them.

I continued to spur Froki on until we reached the base of a large hill. The hill wasn't going to stop us, and Froki kept galloping, even when the ground grew rockier the closer we drew to the top.

"Come on, girl," I encouraged as she drove us higher. Her breath came in short pants, but she still climbed and wove through the larger boulders that obscured our path. It seemed she was just as anxious to get away as I was.

Froki whinnied as we broke the crest of a hill where a massive lake spread through the valley below. The water glittered in the afternoon sun, and I pulled the reins, admiring the sparkling beauty in front of me. Muffled thuds grew louder as the others drew closer. Aaren stopped his horse next to mine.

"Feel better?" he asked over the horses' panting.

"Much," I replied now that my annoyance had begun to dissipate.

He looked over his shoulder at me, and the sun reflected brilliantly in his amber eyes. I looked away before the butterflies could awaken in my stomach.

"It's beautiful until you remember who it belongs to," Stieg said disdainfully before nudging his horse forward and leading the way down the hill.

As the hill flattened out, the lake opened wider than I had thought, yawning out a vast expanse, looking more like an ocean than a lake. The gravel path alongside the water wound around the outcrops of the shore, with some parts washed out and swampy due to an overflow from the lake. Small white lilies bobbed in the shallows, providing hiding spots for the frogs that chirped and groaned deeply, weaving a melody with the crickets that sang further up on the hill. Small trees grew sparsely throughout the path, their trunks coated in a vibrant lichen, and bunches of gray moss hung from their boughs. The scene looked like a painting come to life.

An hour passed, and we were still following the serpentine path around the lake. Thea squirmed in her saddle, clearly uncomfortable, though Stieg assured her it was just up ahead. Another hour passed, and Thea accused Stieg of not knowing where we were actually going.

"I remember!" Stieg assured, though his tone was less than consoling. "I think it's just right up..."

Stieg was cut off by something small whizzing past us and lodging in his neck. He grimaced as he pulled the needle from his skin and examined it between his pinched fingers. It was a small needle, about the size of one used to sew. A second passed before Stieg's eyes rolled back, and his body went limp. Thea gasped when he slid off his horse and hit the ground with a dull thud. She slung a leg over her saddle, moving to tend to Stieg when another needle zipped through the air and hit her, too. Barely a second passed before she joined him on the ground. Unperturbed by the sudden unconsciousness of our friends, the horses shuffled to avoid them, and Froki huffed in annoyance. The alarm rang in my ears as I attempted to dismount my horse, who didn't give a damn that I was trying to get off of her.

"Layla, wait," Aaren said in an eerily quiet voice. "Don't move," he whispered, eyes fixated on the hill to our left. "There's something up there."

411

I followed his attention to the crest of the hill and noted the swaying grasses. Then something shot towards me, a short whistle, before I felt a prick in my neck, almost like a mosquito bite. My hand moved to the side of my throat where there was a small twig lodged in my skin, but instead of pulling it out, I lost feeling in my limbs. Every ounce of strength I needed to hold myself up dissipated, sending me crumpling to the ground. Aaren's concerned face appeared over mine, a rough hand brushing my cheek as he tried to rouse me, but I couldn't keep my eyes open. Sleep was beckoning, and Aaren's amber eyes were the last thing I saw before falling into darkness.

Chapter 47

There was a deafening pounding on my head, as if little elves were in the space between my ears, and they pounded their little fists against my temples. Shifting and desperate to alleviate the throbbing in my head, I groaned at the stiffness in my body, the sound echoing around whatever room I was held in. I was on the floor, and the hard stone beneath me reeked of urine and mold. Bile filled my mouth at the smell, and I leaned over and emptied my stomach onto the floor. It only made the smell worse.

A soft moan came across the room, but I paid it no mind in my desperation to settle my stomach and rid my nostrils of the horrendous smell. When I could gag no more, I wiped my mouth, turned away from the puddle of sick, and distracted myself with my surroundings, taking in every detail.

I was in a cell. My stomach dropped at the thought of what happened that could've landed me in a cell, much less one that reeked of death and filth. Where was I before this? My rune prickled and began to fill my body with an overwhelming alarm that I knew could be coming from Aaren. Oh gods, where was Aaren? I held my rune up to the weak light coming from the tiny glass window inches from the ceiling. It glowed faintly on my skin, the alarm growing into indescribable anger and desperation, and there was nothing I wouldn't do to get out of this cell and find Aaren.

He was feeding me his emotions, wherever he was. And I didn't doubt that he would tear through these cell bars to get to me. A comforting notion, and one that I used to ground myself and block his rage. After a steadying breath, I channeled that calm I had somehow cultivated into my rune, praying Aaren would feel it and calm down.

As the anger receded, I focused on what happened.

Aaren. I was with Aaren before this. And Thea and Stieg.

The memories slowly came into focus, causing the beating drums of pain in my temples to crescendo, and as I sat back, nausea roiled in my stomach once more.

The bars of the cells were constructed from hard stone, as if they had been carved from a massive slab and hinged to the wall. The three stone walls around me were carpeted with a sickly green moss that emitted a foul stench when touched, and I scooted away, revolted. Droplets of water rained down on my head, and I realized that my clothes were drenched with dreadful brown water, the same water that pooled on the floor in the corners. Cold seeped into my bones, and I fought a shiver as I tried to focus.

Towards the back wall of the cell was a small bench, just big enough for two people to sit side by side. Dreading the pain of standing up, I crawled across the rancid floor and heaved myself onto the bench, shuffling to stand flush against the wall until my breasts pressed into the cold stone. Unable to stop the chill that spread icily through my body, I shivered as I stood on my tiptoes and peered through the little window above. I could barely see over the stone sill, staring into the murky, green, swirling water around the window, with particles of weeds and dirt flowing around the glass. Thick green algae grew on the edges of the window, and a small minnow darted by, picked at a piece of grass before flitting away.

Understanding spread through my pained head, and I swallowed past the glass in my throat.

I was *under* the lake.

I took a careful step down, my boot splashing in a puddle. The moan I heard earlier grew louder, and I turned to see Thea curled in the corner by the door. Panicked, I hurried to her side and swept a concerned hand over her brow. She was covered in a sheen of sweat, her teeth chattering with cold as her pale skin shone in the feeble light. She was burning up, likely fever-ridden from the putrid cell.

"Where's Stieg?" she whimpered, her arms wrapped tightly around herself as her whole body shook.

"I don't know," I answered solemnly and brushed a strand of damp hair from her face. "I...I don't know."

Summoning a small flame into my palm, I let it burn long enough to heat my skin, then I pressed my hands to Thea's sticky brow. She trembled under my touch.

"Hang in there, Thea, we're going to get out of here." I had no idea how I was going to fulfill that promise, but I could get creative. If only I could get a grip on the fresh wave of anger that pulsed through my rune.

414

I stood to approach the cell door and wrapped my fingers around the wet stone, then shook. A rattling echoed around the empty halls.

"Aaren?" I whispered. No reply. "Stieg?"

The answer I got wasn't what I expected or wanted. A door creaked open, followed by two sets of footsteps; then, small, stout shadows bobbed in the flickering torchlight. Two squat men were standing barely chest high to me. I would have laughed at their stature if the circumstances weren't so dire. The one on the right had a short brown beard and large ears that protruded from his tangle of brown hair. The one on the left had a bulbous nose, similar to Stieg's, and rosy cheeks. Both were clad in light armor with a crest I did not recognize—a palace encircled with a ring of seaweed—and they carried short swords at their sides.

We found the trolls, or rather, they found us.

The bearded troll held a large ring of keys that jingled and broke the dank silence of the dungeon as his fat fingers fumbled to unlock the door. Quickly sizing them up, it was easy to see that I could overpower them easily just based on our size disparity. If I could get by them, I could take Thea and find Aaren and Stieg. That was assuming they were somewhere close. With how big the lake was, who knew how big this underground place was?

The door swung open, and without thinking, I seized the opportunity and lunged. A sudden, jabbing pain pierced my thigh and stopped me just before I could push past them. The big-nosed troll snickered as its sword sliced through my pants and cut into my muscle, not enough to cause severe damage, but it stopped my unexpected and poorly thought-out escape. In my moment of weakness, the trolls moved until I was trapped between them, and seeing that I was now injured, it would be stupid to try for another escape attempt.

I snarled, but accepted defeat for the sake of a better, more thought-out plan.

The bearded troll who now stood behind me kicked in my good knee, and I dropped harshly to the floor. My wounded thigh screamed in agony at the impact. They lowered a damp bandana over my eyes and bound my hands behind me, then nudged me forward with the blunt edge of a sword. They used their swords to guide me along wherever we were going, occasionally running me into the wall and giggling when I smacked my head. After the third time, I kicked back angrily with my good leg, hoping to knock one square in the chest.

"Hey!" one of them squeaked, then batted my shackled hands with something sharp and hard. It felt like a whip, one that I had possibly missed when taking inventory of the weapons they carried. I bit down on my yelp, not wanting to give them the satisfaction.

It felt like we had been walking for nearly twenty minutes before I was told to halt. By now, the pain in my upper thigh was unbearable, and almost my entire pant leg was soaked through with blood. I could smell the coppery tang, and every step was weaker, my knees wobbling as the urge to collapse grew stronger. I hadn't been able to assess the cut before I had been blindfolded, but I knew without a doubt that it would need to be stitched.

The light glared harshly into my pupils when they shoved me to my knees and removed my blindfold. As my eyes adjusted, I gawked at the room around me.

We were in a large glass dome beneath the lake, and clear, greenish water surrounded us. A forest of water grass swayed around us, and fish watched curiously through the glass. Across the dome from where I knelt was a smaller throne constructed from the same stone as my cell, though it was cleaner and lacked the horrendous-smelling green moss. Atop the throne sat another troll, with a long, white beard that reached his ample belly, clothed in green robes to match the water beyond the glass. His deep-set blue eyes bore into me as I swayed on my knees. Nausea swelled, but I could only focus on the nailing glare from the troll atop the throne.

My rune throbbed and pulled my attention to my right, where Aaren knelt, bound like me, his white teeth dug into the dirty rag they had shoved into his mouth. His normally white-blonde hair was damp and caked with the same green moss, matching the smears of dirt and dried blood that clung to his temple. Just like me, he had put up a fight, only it looked like he had done far more damage than I had, a thought that was confirmed by the budding black eye the troll holding his bindings was subtly trying to nurse.

"Fetch the other male," the troll on the throne commanded, and the two who brought me in nodded obediently and disappeared.

"Who are you?" I demanded, and my magic seemed to crack an eye as if to inquire what was happening. The water around us seemed to stir, and the fire in the braziers behind me greeted me like an old friend.

"Careful, lady," the troll on the throne said, either unaware or unafraid of what had just awakened within me. "If you continue to speak out of turn, I'll have you gagged like him." He nodded to Aaren, who shook, spouting heated words that only came out as muffled protests. "You, Fraalver, are just how I remembered."

Aaren bit the cloth in his mouth harder, growling as his eyes blazed with fury.

I glared daggers at the troll on the throne. "Who. Are. You?"

The troll sighed, resigned to answering me. "I am Ymer, Guardian of the trolls of Klartvan Lake." He nodded his head in a mock bow. Settling into his throne again, he gestured to me. "And you are?"

I weighed whether or not to answer truthfully, but found it no use to lie. We were here to ask for help, and the trolls responded like anyone would to unwelcome guests, especially since they had been forced into hiding. As horrible as it was, I understood.

I straightened, trying to keep the shake out of my voice. "I am Layla, leader of Skoghjem." Ymer's features remained blank, but I had a feeling that the calm mask hid a nasty disdain. "We did not come here to quarrel with you, Ymer. We came to seek aid."

Ymer made a noise between a scoff and a chuckle.

"Ironic, isn't it?" he taunted. "Our people helped the Fraalver for centuries, yet when *we* needed them, they turned their backs. And now, once more, even though we have hidden our existence from your very people, you have somehow still managed to find us and demand our help." He laughed indignantly. "*How* did you even find us?"

There was a shuffling, the sound of frantic footsteps, and then a weight was thrown on the floor next to me. A harsh, pained grunt rattled through me, but I wouldn't take my eyes from Ymer as his expression shifted from ire to shock.

"Stieg?" he asked, leaning forward on his throne.

Stieg, panting, pushed himself up as best he could with bound hands. His shaggy hair was tousled, and his face was beet red and sweating, as if he had just sprinted the entire way here.

The flicker of surprise on Ymer's face dissipated instantly, and he slowly sat back, rubbing his thumb and forefinger together pensively.

"I should've known it was a crossbred mongrel like you that led these traitors here."

"A pleasure to see you too, Ymer," Stieg said through rattling breaths.

Ymer hummed with disgust, his upper lip curling under his white beard. "It's been a long time. I didn't think I would ever see you again."

Stieg bristled. "So quick to shun your own kin," he said snidely.

Ymer shot forward, anger reddening what little of his face could be seen because of the beard. He was faster than I thought he'd be, and he was upon

Stieg in seconds. Ymer struck Stieg once, sending him to the floor once more. "It is not my fault my sister decided to fuck a Fraalver and create an abomination such as you!"

I froze. Sister? Ymer was Stieg's uncle? I couldn't say I expected much from meeting with the trolls, but this was certainly nothing I could've seen coming.

"Aren't you trying to revive the troll race?" Stieg spat, squirming until he could get a leg under him and push upward. "I would think you would cling to any semblance of restoring it, me included!"

Ymer's voice dropped to a whisper as he grabbed Stieg's face in his stubby fingers and squeezed. "I'm doing just fine on that front without you, Stieg."

Stieg clenched his jaw when his uncle released his grip on his face. Heat flushed his cheeks where Ymer had held him, and I was surprised when Stieg managed to speak in a level tone. "Despite your hatred towards the Fraalver, Ymer, you're going to want to hear what we have to say."

The rage in Stieg's face matched Ymer's, and I held my breath as I expected Ymer to strike his nephew again. "Why should I listen to you snakes?"

"Because we could all die if you don't," I barked, trying to keep the pleading from edging my tone like it inevitably did.

Ymer turned his wrath to me, but I focused my attention on the water above and let its incredible energy soak into me and fill my chest. The fire behind me nudged my magic as if to remind me it was there, too. I invited the fire into my hand, and the warmth circled my palms.

"My people faced extinction when the Fraalver turned their backs on us. I don't owe you the courtesy of hearing out whatever lies you have spun."

Ymer turned on his heel and made a gesture to the troll guards, who surged forward and grabbed the rope that bound my wrists. My leg sang with rippling pain as they pulled me away, and I felt Aaren's white-hot rage strike through me once again.

"No!" I cried. "Please, you have to listen! This is about Markus Sviker!"

Ymer didn't have to bark the orders for my release before the guards loosened their grip on me, and I tumbled forward, hissing when my thigh twinged.

"What about him?" Ymer demanded over his shoulder.

I shuffled back to the small pool of blood I had left behind, swaying on my unreliable legs. It didn't take me as long to explain everything as I thought it would, starting with the mylings. With each word I spoke, my chin held higher and my voice filled with an urgent demand, eyes boring deeply into Ymer's. Every syllable left my tongue dripped with power and command; my words permeated with every ounce of magic I could convey. I spoke like the leader the Fraalver needed.

A flush of pride watered down Aaren's wrath, and I simmered inside, grateful for his silent approval.

Ymer's expression was unreadable as he soaked in my words, the silence starting to squeeze me like a hungry snake.

Finally, he leaned forward. "That is a very compelling story," he began with eyes that glimmered mischievously, "but my people are safe, undetected. If Markus were to come into power, or this necromancer you speak of, we will remain untouched."

The fire met the water inside me, and tried to mingle, but if I didn't get a handle on it, this would end disastrously.

"Do you think you will remain hidden for long?" I demanded, and my grip on the writhing power inside loosened. "Markus's evil is clever; it will root you out and find you. The Fraalver may have turned away from you before, but that doesn't mean you can ignore the thousands of deaths that will follow. Deaths other than the Fraalver. The death of your people because you were too stubborn even to listen. Are you ready to accept the responsibility for the destruction of our realm?"

Heat sparked through my palms and burned the rope around my wrists, the frayed edges brushing my skin as they fell to the ground.

"You would forsake all of Alveland," I said, and brought my hands into view. A spark of fear flashed across Ymer's face at the sight. "Watch your people perish, your kingdom crumble, all for your pride."

Ymer only snarled, any evidence of fear wiped away by the disgusted look his features had pinched into. "If Markus Sviker is here to wipe out the Fraalver, then I am going to sit back and watch every single one of you burn."

The dam inside me broke, and I lost control.

The fire from the braziers flew to my hands, curling around my fingers like snakes ready for dinner. The flames grew, climbing up my arms as I took a step closer to the throne, and there was a deafening thud that shook the glass dome above us. The water outside the throne room slammed into the ceiling and vibrated the ground under our feet. The pain in my leg was only a whisper, and I ignored the wave of warning that Aaren sent through the rune, and I glanced at him to see him watching the glass cautiously.

I wasn't going to bring the place down, but I wasn't sure I'd be able to control the water if I let it go too far.

Right now, I didn't care.

Ymer stood fiercely, the curl in his lip doing nothing to hide the fright that shadowed his eyes. The water slammed again, harder, and the flames in my hands climbed into the air. My world narrowed on the troll as the fire reflected in Ymer's fearful eyes, smiling as he darted behind his throne and took cover. He was trembling now, and there was no hiding it from the guards present. Good, let them see him cower, let them remember how he backed away from me, how he ducked behind his throne.

"You cannot hide from this Ymer," I said, my voice like a burning barrel afloat a calm sea.

"Who are you?" he asked over the roar of my fire, the angry crashing of the water.

"I'm an enemy far worse than Markus should you choose to turn us away."

Ymer considered me. "Is that a threat?" he asked, but there was an undeniable shake in his voice.

I laughed. "Consider it a mercy, Ymer. If I kill you now, then I save you from facing Markus's wrath when you turn us away." I held up a flaming hand. "You either die by my fire, or his. Your choice."

There was a moment of uncertainty on his face when he seemed to consider whether I was bluffing. When the water delivered another ground-shaking wave of force against the dome, Ymer finally emerged from behind his throne.

"If we help you," he asked with a scowl that soured his face more than it already was, "what would you require of us?"

The small victory sent a breath of relief through me, flowing into my chest where the water's energy curled inside me. It seemed to understand, easing from my hold and calming the brewing storm outside the dome. My flames shrank away as well and coiled lazily between my fingers.

"Unbind my husband, and we can discuss," I said, examining my flaming digits as if I were bored.

Ymer's snarling contempt returned, but he flicked his eyes to Aaren and Stieg, silently commanding his guards to release them. Aaren eyed the troll murderously as it unbound him, seeming to enjoy the shudder that shook the troll's body as it fumbled with the rope. He rose to his towering height, the troll coming to only mid thigh on him. I was relieved to see he hadn't sustained any injuries other than the one on his head, but upon closer inspection, there was no source of the blood. It came from someone else. I couldn't imagine what happened, especially since none of the trolls in the room had any evidence of blood on them—the troll whose blood belonged was probably unconscious somewhere.

Stieg rubbed his hands where the ropes bit into his skin, but he seemed otherwise unscathed.

"Quirinus's axe," I said coolly, "where is it?"

Ymer scoffed. "We have the axe, and I have no intention of returning it to the Fraalver." Ymer slid back onto his throne, but kept an unblinking, careful eye on me.

"We don't plan on keeping it, Ymer," Stieg reassured.

Ymer gave Stieg a disapproving look. "And what do you plan on doing with the axe?"

"Consider it a safety measure," I replied, "in case something goes wrong when we decide to pay a visit to the Nidhogg."

The trolls behind us gasped, and there was a clattering of weapons, but I didn't turn around. I kept my eyes trained harshly on Ymer.

"Markus has made some sort of deal with the Nidhogg," Stieg informed as the clanging died. "Should we find that we are unable to talk it out of the deal, we will need the axe." What was left unsaid should have been enough to imply the direness of our mission here.

Ymer's nostrils flared as he reigned in a deep breath and considered us, but I wasn't afraid. We were going to get that axe with or without permission. I wasn't going to let some prideful troll stand in the way of killing my father and or finding my brother.

"Very well," he said finally, then nodded to the trolls in the back. "Release the last prisoner, we have work to do."

It was a small triumph, but I was still unsettled.

Thea was taken to a healer after being released from our cell, and her fever broke within the hour thanks to the quick work of Odda, the troll who ran the apothecary. Her curly brown hair had been pinned back with a barrette made from fish bone, and her dark tan skin shone in the cold light of the hospital wing. The dark blue dress she wore matched the tonic she handed Thea. Odda turned on her heel and plucked herbs and small tools from the many pockets in her apron.

The apothecary itself resembled a medieval hospital ward. Beds lined one wall of the wing, each covered with clean linens and fluffed pillows. Next to every bed was a table with a box of herbs and bottles and a couple of scrolls lined up neatly side by side. Across the room were massive windows, and the water outside tinted the wing a greenish-blue hue. Thea was the only patient in the ward, and Odda seemed delighted to oblige in her recovery.

"What was the fever from?" Stieg asked as Odda toiled away and prepared to stitch my leg. She had rubbed a salve across it, and the pain eased temporarily, but I knew the stitches were going to be torturous.

"It seems it was a bad reaction to the sovngal we tip our arrows in," Odda replied, threading her needle for my stitches. My mouth went dry. "Apologies for that, I've told Ymer we shouldn't use that stuff for this very reason."

Odda settled in front of me, and my hands clenched the clean sheets when she prodded my wound.

"Hey," Aaren said and directed my attention to his face. "What was that story you were telling me about Lucas and the kitten?"

Ignoring the cold press of Odda's hands on my leg, I gave a pained smile. "Yes, the kitten," I said, though I couldn't keep the strain out of my words. "Lucas was two and our foster parents took us to a farm—Fuck!"

Odda apologized, and I tensed, awaiting the next jab.

"What was on the farm?" Aaren asked, snapping my gaze back to his.

"Um, there were lots of...ouch...animals." I took a deep breath. "And kittens. A whole litter of them."

My eyes dropped to the wound that was only a quarter of the way stitched, but Aaren moved my chin until I was looking at him and only him. The familiarity of his eyes comforted me, and I didn't feel the next jab as badly. Or the wound is stretching to close.

"And Lucas liked the kittens?"

I licked my lips and breathed. "Uh-huh. He loved them."

I smiled when I recounted that Lucas really wanted to hold one and didn't wait for someone to pick one up and hand it to him. Instead, he reached down and plucked a small, writhing kitten off the ground. Only he held the poor thing upside down, too young to know that the mews of protest were anything but joy over being picked up. Lucas was so proud to be holding this kitten that he didn't pay it any mind. Of course, I adjusted the kitten so it could sit comfortably in Lucas's small hands, but I would never forget the look on his face, the small bit of pride and excitement. It was, after all, his first time holding a kitten.

"You're all set, my dear," Odda said and moved to grab the bandages.

"I got it," Aaren said and held out a hand for Odda to drop the cloth in. Without a second glance, she complied and went back to tending to Thea.

"Thank you," I said as Aaren carefully propped my ankle atop his knee and unfurled the bandages.

Aaren gave me a small smile before his brow furrowed deep with concentration. A small troll pushed through the doors, informing us that he was there to take us to our suite. Stieg and I weren't ready to leave Thea yet, so Aaren went in our stead.

As Thea recovered, Stieg never left her side. I lingered in the hospital wing for a few more hours, and the entire time, Thea's petite hand stayed in Stieg's meaty, callused fingers as he brushed a wet cloth over her brow, eager to help in any way he could.

"I'm impressed by the architecture here," I noted, gazing out at the water beyond the windows. I wondered what kinds of creatures occupied the lake and if they were anything like the ones that dwelled in the depths of Kysthjem.

When things calmed down in the throne room—throne dome, I guess—Odda came to retrieve us and tend to our wounds. We followed her down the winding halls to the hospital wing and listened to her explain the features of the troll's secret settlement. Similar to the Fraalver of the mountains, the settlement was a series of tunnels and antechambers throughout the lake. Every troll family had a small dome they called home, all connected with long stone hallways.

As I watched the windows of the healing ward closely, I followed the larger fish that darted in and out of the lake grasses that grew in patches across the muck.

"Well, the trolls are distant cousins of the dwarves, and they are expert architects," Odda said, her voice musical yet raspy after breathing in so many fumes from the tonics and salves she had concocted for Thea. "It's passed in the blood."

She opened a small jar of oozing green slime, and I was hit with a familiar putrid smell. I fought the urge to retch. "Is that luktrot?" I asked.

Odda looked at me, surprised. "It is," she answered.

"I didn't know anyone other than the Fraalver used luktrot," I mused, wrinkling my nose.

Odda paused, slowly looking up at me. "Where do you think the Fraalver got it from?"

I pressed my lips together, embarrassed. The color started to return to Thea's face slowly, and her chest returned to a regular rise and fall since she had stopped shaking. Odda screwed the lid back onto the jar and clapped her hands, the staccato sound echoing throughout the ward.

"Alright, everyone out, my patient cannot rest with such a flurry of bodies in here. Out, out!"

Though she was small, Odda pushed Stieg and me out of the room with surprising force. We stood in the hallway, stunned and unsure of where to go. With nothing else to do but walk, we spent our first few steps in silence, and I studied the walls and the intricate stonework.

"I had no idea the trolls were related to the dwarves," I said, almost tripping since I was so focused on taking in the architecture.

"Most don't," Stieg answered solemnly. "The dwarves no longer claim the trolls as kin."

I cocked my head to the side to give him a questioning look. "What happened?" I inquired.

With a sigh, Stieg explained. "Long ago, the dwarves and trolls occupied the realm Nidavellir together. It began as a mutualistic existence, but over time, the dwarves gradually took over, expanding their empire throughout the realm. The trolls began to feel unwelcome and left to seek shelter in other realms. A few stayed, but many came to Alveland. Years after most of the trolls left, the dwarf king Ungrar Greatrock died. His son, Vorric, took the throne. Vorric had a very different opinion on the trolls, disgusted with the bloodline he shared with them."

When I asked why Vorric hated the trolls, Stieg's answer churned my stomach.

"Legend says that there was an ancient giant long ago, before Alveland even existed as a branch on Yggdrasil. When this giant died, the maggots that fed on him were given life from his body, eventually growing and evolving into the troll race over a millenia. Vorric hated this legend, but no one was sure if it was disgust or envy that the trolls, not the dwarves, fed on the giant.

"Soon after he took the throne, he ordered all the trolls in Nidavellir to be eradicated."

My jaw dropped. "He killed them? Over some legend?"

Stieg nodded. "But killing the ones who stayed wasn't enough. He hated the trolls' entire existence, the very idea of them, so he went after the trolls who fled, too."

Those were the trolls that sought the help of the Fraalver. The very trolls that lived under Klartvan Lake.

Disgust boiled inside me. How beings could commit such atrocities was beyond me. There had been plenty of cases just like this throughout Midgardian history. Untapped hatred wasn't restricted to one realm.

Still, the thought of a troll genocide made me sick—maggots or not.

"Do you know why the Fraalver didn't want to help them?"

Stieg sighed. "Vorric was a mighty king and an important ally. The Fraalver did not want to make an enemy of him. So they turned their backs on the trolls. Vorric's men were quick to reduce the troll's numbers, until they went into hiding and were not heard from or seen again."

"That's horrific," I said, hoping my words would muddle the sour taste in my mouth.

Stieg agreed as he studied the masonry. "Keeping the dwarves' craftsmanship seems to be a silent protest for the trolls. A way to cling to who they were and still embrace who they become.

Chapter 48

Thea was better by the next morning. Her rosy complexion had returned, and her eyes were bright and cheery—just like the Thea I remembered. While she wasn't as quick on her feet as she normally was, she still sidled into breakfast with a soft grin. Stieg trailed behind her, relief brimming on his face as he watched Thea flop into the chair next to me and pour herself a glass of tea.

"I'm so relieved to have you back," I beamed.

Thea sipped her tea, nodding indulgently. "I don't relish the thought of what would've happened if Odda hadn't gotten to me in time. I didn't think I was going to make it for a bit there." She swallowed and cleared her throat. "How's the leg?"

Rubbing a hand over my tightly bandaged thigh, I replied, "Better." Indeed, it was better, but that didn't stop Aaren from waking at all hours of the night to check and redress it. The lack of sleep left me in a dreadful state this morning, but I was thankful for his care.

And Aaren seemed content to only tend to me last night, carefully examining the stitches and pestering Odda for fresh bandages in the early hours of the morning, which earned him a stern talking to from the troll, but he didn't seem to care.

Thea grinned, eyes flicking between Aaren and me as if she knew he played the role of mother hen last night. "Good," she smirked.

Ignoring whatever was in her knowing look, I reached for a glass and examined a pitcher of green juice on the table in front of me.

"I wouldn't drink that if I were you," Aaren warned through a mouthful of bread.

I rolled my eyes. "And why not?"

Without looking up from his plate, he answered, "I overheard they make it from the marsh grass in the lake."

Hiding my disgust, I poured a glass despite him. Aaren didn't bother to keep the amusement out of his gaze as I brought the glass to my lips and took a gulp of the thick green juice. To say it was horrible was an understatement. The juice itself tasted as if someone had taken mud, grass clippings, and old eggs and juiced them together. The slimy texture did nothing to help the flavor, and I tried to swallow, but my stomach clenched and tried to revolt. The juice began to climb back up my throat, but I swallowed harder and more insistently, willing it to stay down as I turned my eyes to Aaren, whose lips were set into a surprised and devilish smirk.

"And?" he teased.

I gagged silently, hiding a grimace as I licked my lips. "Not bad," I answered.

Thea hummed next to me. "I'll try it," she said, then reached for the pitcher. I nudged her under the table, unable to warn her any other way as I was trapped under Aaren's knowing eyes. Thea, however, ignored the hint and took an exploratory sip. The corners of her mouth turned down, and she closed her eyes, sticking out her green-painted tongue thanks to the juice.

"That is horrible!" she exclaimed as she slid the glass away from her. "Layla, you like this?"

"She's used to swallowing things she doesn't like," Aaren chuckled, turning back to his plate.

Thea snorted, and I gave Aaren a swift kick in the shins under the table. He fought a smile as he took another bite of breakfast.

"Are we going to talk about how easily Ymer agreed to hand over the axe?" I demanded, eager to change the subject. "I can't be the only one suspicious of him."

Stieg's face fell. "If I remember anything about my uncle, it's that he never operates without a self-serving purpose."

Thea leaned back in her chair, crossing her arms over her chest. "It has to be worth the risk. Our need is far greater than any possible betrayal."

Aaren huffed his agreement.

Stieg offered placating hands. "We just need to tread carefully."

I kept his warning in the back of my mind as we entered the dome later.

Ymer was sitting atop his throne, his long beard braided down his belly. He smiled tightly, but I noted something in his eyes, something I couldn't quite place. It was a knowing look, a look that taunted me as I neared. Whatever it was that hid behind his eyes, I didn't like it, and I sent the feeling through the rune to warn Aaren to tread carefully.

"Good morning, Fraalver and Stieg," he greeted, a bite added to his tone when he spoke the latter's name. "I trust you rested well."

Aaren nodded subtly. "We thank you for your hospitality."

"Anything for our new allies." His grin was what Granny would call "shit-eating."

This was going to be a long war if this was how our alliance was going to go.

Ymer observed our group, eyes landing on Thea and looking her up and down. "You look familiar."

Thea raised a brow as if accepting this as a challenge. "Oh?" she questioned.

Ymer toyed with the tied end of his beard. "Do you have a family name, girl?"

I credited Thea for not biting something nasty back at him, though from the briefest flash of hostility across her features, I knew it was building within her.

"Forlighet," Thea answered. "My father was Arvid Forlighet."

"And your grandfather was Nanne Forlighet."

Intrigued suspicion peppered Thea's tone. "Yes," she replied. "You know my grandfather?"

Ymer sat back, painting a picture of disinterest. "Quirinus's axe came to be in our possession because of Nanne."

Holy Himmelfjell.

Everything clicked into place, and for a fleeting moment, the world made some sense. No wonder Thea and Stieg were meant for each other; they'd been tied together for decades, if not centuries. It was a match written in history and seemingly blessed by whatever fallen gods still existed.

"My grandfather was a smart man," Thea replied nonchalantly. "He saw something in the trolls that most don't."

"And that is?" Ymer asked, eyes narrowing as if he was trying to discern any underlying hostility.

"Hope," Thea answered, and her hand brushed Stieg's, light enough that it could be mistaken for an accidental touch, but I knew what it meant. What Thea saw in the trolls was what I saw in Lucas's memories. I hope that this can still end well. Ymer seemed to press his lips together, but I couldn't read his face under his beard and the years of prejudice that had aged him prematurely.

"Follow me," he said, then turned on his heel.

Accompanied by two guards, the four of us and Ymer were led down a series of narrow hallways with sharp twists and turns every few steps. The normally elaborate stonework was less sophisticated, as if the masons who built these halls had run out of time and hastily carved the tunnels out before moving on. There were no windows that opened up to the lake like in the other halls—these halls were built deeper, dug into the mud at the bottom. Sconces constructed from river rock were lit down the halls, providing a weak light to the otherwise drab passageways.

We maneuvered through the winding corridors for what felt like hours before the two guard trolls halted in front of a set of double doors, torches lit on either side. With quiet, strained grunts, the trolls pushed them open and revealed a small, dimly lit room with a dais on the opposite end. Resting atop the dais was Quirinus's axe, though I didn't have to see it to know it was there. The room purred with an unseen energy, an energy that snaked through the walls and across the stones to curl around our legs, writhe throughout our bodies. It didn't feel uncomfortable, but relatively unfamiliar, as if a sibling to my own magic. It paused around me, as if sniffing me like a curious dog encountering a lost pup from its own litter.

Shaking off the shudder that began to climb up my spine, my fingertips went static with what I thought was anticipation, but the longer I stood still, the more I realized it was the axe. Aaren was the first to move, taking slow, careful steps up to the dais and bending at the waist to examine the axe. The static crawled from my fingers and up my arms, and my power flickered inside me. The skin grew too tight for my bones as if the axe had shaken my magic awake, and it was furious. If I didn't move, I was sure it was going to claw me to shreds.

I joined Aaren at the dais, ignoring my buzzing bones, and studied the axe. It was surprisingly simple—the hilt was carved from smooth oak and polished to a shiny finish. Subtle carvings climbed up the handle to the blade that had been honed from sleek iron.

I couldn't rip my gaze from the weapon, almost drunk on the power it was pumping into my veins. It wasn't like when I tapped into the energy of the water or the fire, and formed a mutual partnership between the two forces—this was like the axe's magic was becoming my own, ingrained into every fiber of my power. The buzzing intensified, and sparks ignited my veins as my magic rewrote itself, but I didn't recoil, couldn't. Shockwaves of life burst through me when my fingers wrapped around the hilt, and the magic veiled me. It soaked my bones and coated my tongue with a metallic sting.

This weapon was made for me, and this heightened magic now singing through every fiber of my being was confirmation. Quirinus created this axe to protect from threats like Markus, threats that could bring down the very foundation of the Fraalver themselves. I was going to be Markus's—one of the biggest threats to the Fraalver ever to exist—demise. No matter who actually possessed this axe, it belonged to me.

It seemed like it had been waiting a very long time for me.

"You may use the axe, but it will forever belong to the trolls," Ymer stated, but his voice was distant in my ears. "Return it the second the Nidhogg is taken care of, and not a day later. Do you understand?"

I whirled with the axe ready in my hand, but a tug on my rune brought me back to the room we stood in and the people around us.

"You have our word," Aaren promised in a stiff voice.

Ymer sneered. "Terrific."

With the axe now in our possession, we left Klartvan Lake and traveled through the night instead of stopping at the inn. The horses carried us swiftly through the rolling fields, and we kept a vigilant eye on each horizon, unsure of an attack now that we had the axe. Once we were home, it was sent straight to the meeting hall and locked up tightly with Axl, Von, and a few others guarding the door in shifts, never leaving the door unattended.

While we were gone, Rorik had less trouble being in charge than he did before, most likely due to Ertha lending a hand to help in his leadership. And the lack of mylings.

Ertha was still the picture of beauty, but a different kind. Before she was bright and precious, like a polished gem hewn from her mountains. Now, because of the shadows that circled her eyes and gaunt cheekbones, she had a darker kind of beauty to her. It was a beauty that could be found in the first thunderstorm of summer, dark and lush and powerful.

Borgil had continued to work on the stash of armor for the village, impressively constructing sixteen pieces of armor in the few days we were gone.

The pub was just as lively as before, especially now that it was accommodating two villages. The night we returned, Aaren slid onto the bench next to me and passed me a mug of ale with a sigh.

"Are you nervous?" he asked after swallowing his first taste of ale.

"I have a feeling if I lied and said no, you would know," I said, to which he gave me an amused nod of agreement. He ran a hand over his rune absently as he watched the revelers around us. "I am nervous. Scared, even."

Aaren was quiet for a moment, his jaw ticking with tension. "I won't lie to you either," he turned his amber eyes to me. "So am I."

I raised my brows considerably. "Aaren, the brave, strong brute, is afraid?"

He smirked, then chuckled deeply. "You should know by now I'm not as hard as I seem."

There was a joke there, and I was about to say it, but something stopped me, and another brick was placed in that wall inside my chest. I was boxing myself in, even though that wasn't what I needed, or even what I wanted. I knew I could be loved, and I was learning that from the friends I had made here. I was learning to be loved, but letting myself love was becoming increasingly difficult. Especially when there was so much I could lose. Maybe after all of it, I could admit that I did love Aaren, that perhaps that wall would finally be demolished for good, and I could crawl out and love him freely. And when I learned he didn't feel the same about me, what then? There was no way to recover from that.

No, I was going to keep this in my chest and pray it wouldn't find its tipping point.

But what I noted swimming in Aaren's eyes gave me pause.

The look was undeniable, no matter how hard I tried to rationalize it.

He opened his mouth, and I could practically see the words waiting on his tongue, but someone plopped down on either side of me, jolting me from my trance. Aaren snapped his mouth shut and buried his face in his mug.

"Atta boy," Oswin joked, wiping his mouth after draining his own mug. Beads of mead clung to the scraggly strands of his beard and let out a contented sigh.

"So when are we leaving?" Ivar asked, then thanked Inaborg for refilling his mug as she passed.

"I'm sorry?" Aaren asked, his features screwed into their usual harsh expression.

"When are we leaving to kill the Nidhogg? You don't honestly think you're going to go kill it without us?"

I couldn't help but smile.

The next morning, I found Aaren near the stables, prepping Froki for me. Axl, Von, Oswin, and Ivar milled about, readying their horses in the cloudy morning sunlight. I yawned as the drowsy weather lured me into a state of fatigue, compounded by a poor night's sleep. After we left the pub last night, Aaren and I met with Rorik to figure out where exactly we would be traveling to. The Nidhogg resided in the roots of Yggdrasil, but getting there was going to be tricky.

"The doorways to each realm are like pocket doors," Rorik explained last night. "When you arrived here, Layla, you happened to find one of those doors, whether you were looking for one or not."

I asked how we would find one of those doors and how we would know if it was the right one.

"I suspect the door you came through to get here may be our ticket to the Nidhogg. If my theory is correct, these doors lead into a metaphysical hallway of sorts. If you pick the right exit, you should end up at the base of Yggdrasil."

Aaren grunted before rubbing a hand over his face. "Do you remember exactly where you were when you crossed over?"

Shaking my head, I replied, "It was months ago, and considering I didn't even know I had crossed over into a different realm, I can't tell you exactly where it is."

"All we can do is try, Layla," Rorik replied, looking as exhausted as I felt.

I snapped myself out of the memory as Aaren passed me Froki's reins. His fingers brushed mine, the rune sending me a warmth that I clung to, so my apprehension wouldn't carry me away. Aaren's rune glowed as well, but as he walked away, he flexed his fingers, as if our hands touching had shot tight discomfort up his wrist. What did *that* mean?

"Mount up!" Aaren barked before mounting his horse.

I obeyed and let Froki lead me behind the others, but I focused my attention on anything I could see in the forest and not on the Nidhogg or whatever had just occurred between me and Aaren. Birds singing, green everywhere, crunching leaves...

The Nidhogg, tree roots, Lucas, mountains, Aaren, a towering wall, a harsh scar that served as a grim reminder of a dead lover...

432

The air wasn't as soothing as I wanted it to be when I breathed in deeply. It only served to disturb me further, and I thanked the stars that Von broke the eerie quiet when he called out, "What's that?"

My heart stood still when I followed where he was pointing.

A short distance away was the small shack that Lucas and I used to play in. The same shack Rachel and I went looking for that fateful night. The shack where I came face-to-face with the fenr.

"This...," I stammered as I dismounted Froki. "This isn't right."

"What's wrong?" Rorik asked from atop his horse.

I strode to the building and placed a hand along the wooden frame, shaking my head in disbelief. "Did we cross into Midgard?"

Aaren and Rorik exchanged confused glances before Aaren answered, "Still Alveland, *fremmed*."

I shook my head again. "No, I... Lucas and I used to play in this shack together when we were younger. This is in Midgard."

"Layla," Aaren said after his boots hit the ground harshly. Then his hands were on my cheeks, steadying me with a look from those glorious yellow eyes. "We haven't left the realm, *fremmed*."

Disbelief glazed my eyes as I slipped out of his hands and ducked into the shack, looking at the small markings along the walls that now all made sense. Markus was standing above an army of mylings, and that same word was scratched underneath.

Hallow.

The mylings drew these markings.

This shack was in Alveland.

Which meant that I had been slipping between realms for years.

Alveland had been giving me and Lucas a haven for as long as I could remember, a place to shelter when things got too rough in that foster home. Alveland was our escape, and now it was my home.

I had been this close to Aaren for so long.

The sound of the fenr's growls filled my ears as the memory tried to wash me away. The brittle cold, the flash of a phone's light, the harsh aftertaste of whiskey clinging to my tongue. If this was in Alveland, that meant that Rachel was still alive.

Hot tears stung my eyes, but I quickly wiped them away when Aaren ducked into the shack, his massive body almost filling the space. His rough hand brushed mine, and when I looked up at him, there was no fighting the gratitude and...

Was this what it felt like?

To love someone because you fell for them, and not because they were born into your love?

"What now?" Ivar asked from outside, and I snapped out of my head, undeniable euphoria sending fireworks through my body. It wasn't a euphoria like I felt when Aaren made me come. This was more than physical; it lifted the fog from my mind, and there was only light and sunshine in my head.

I blinked, unsure what to make of all of it.

"Aaren?" Rorik called, but Aaren's eyes never left mine as he barked an order to search the area.

The elation that roared through my body intensified when Aaren's pupils seemed to dilate, and I knew that whatever I was feeling was being pumped into the rune, and he was starting to feel it, too.

"Layla, what're you..."

"Find anything?" Rorik called from outside the shack.

"Fuck all nothing!" Oswin called.

"Aaren, what do you—"

Harsh anger flashed across Aaren's face as he grunted and stormed from the shack, demanding what the others could need right in that second. I followed him as he trekked to his horse, which was grazing a small patch of fresh grass on the other side of the shack.

Quirinus's axe vibrated against the strap that held it to my back, humming as if in silent warning.

Then the forest disappeared.

Chapter 49

My entire body felt like it was wrapped in silk, rippling over every inch of me, catching in my fingers and toes. I felt like I was standing under a soft waterfall, or slipping beneath the surface of a still lake, with velvety-smooth water tracing circles and patterns down my skin. There was a slight tug in the pit of my stomach, like the summoning of a lost friend just out of reach. Ahead was light, warm, and bright. Everything it touched was soft as a down feather, so smooth that I could've fallen into it and never woken up again. When I was younger, I used to wonder what it would be like to sleep on a cloud. I was positive it would feel like this.

There was a hand in mine, and it was the only thing that held any mass, taking up space I wasn't willing to give. It was rough, calloused, firm, the opposite of what that light held. And it pulled me away, darkness starting to fill every crevice and space in my body. I wanted to fight, thrash against the hand pulling me away, but it was too strong, too hard, and cold doused me. I shivered instantly, hard ground meeting my knees.

I had fallen to the ground, a hand braced against the rock underneath me. The other hand remained in Aaren's, who knelt beside me, trying to rally his own recovery from the fall we both just suffered.

"*Fremmed,*" he grunted.

"I'm fine," I said as I shifted to my bottom and took a steadying breath. My hands began to shake in the cold, and I ran an anxious hand over my brow. "What was that light?" I asked, pulling my knees up to my chest and wrapping my arms around them. Quirinus's axe pressed uncomfortably into my spine, and I wished I could shed the strap and chuck it across the stone.

Aaren stayed crouched before me, though his eyes surveyed our surroundings. "I don't know," he answered. "But I think we're in the right place."

Underneath us was jagged black rock, similar to hardened lava. For all I knew, it was. To our left was a large crevasse, with massive wooden tendrils that wove themselves over and around the entrance of the rock. The wooden tendrils thickened as I traced them higher, but they disappeared into the low-hanging fog. They were the roots of Yggdrasil, or at least some of them. And the entrance they presented was the way to the Nidhogg.

I swallowed, my throat bone dry. Behind us was a vast expanse of sea, and a cloudless, gray sky meeting the horizon. Strength slowly returned to my legs as I stood, a dull ache radiating through my healing stitches and old wounds. I hoped the fall didn't hurt Aaren's back, considering the fight we might be walking into. I watched the sea, curious to know what else was out there, if anything. If we were at the base of Yggdrasil, then there may well be nothing out there. I assumed this was like launching into outer space and looking down at the earth.

"We should wait for the others," I said, eyeing the entrance crowned by the roots.

Aaren didn't say anything, just kept looking at me with a frustratingly unreadable expression. I started to pace, and Aaren followed my every step.

"Layla, I..."

"They'll be here soon," I said, more to assure myself than anything else.

"*Fremmed...*"

Every lonely second that ticked by instilled another ounce of dread in me. I made several turns in my pacing, sure that if I kept going, I'd wear treads into the rock under my feet. That feeling of warmth from the light was gone, and so was the foreign feeling of what I thought could've been love; all I was becoming was dread, panic, and fright.

"Listen to me, Layla, please..." Aaren began.

"No, they'll be here any minute. We need to be ready."

"They're not coming," Aaren tried, but I wouldn't listen, letting my anxious pacing turn into frantic sprints across the jagged rock. My breaths came in short spurts, and I couldn't get a solid breath.

"Layla! For the fallen gods' sake, *listen to me!*"

I spun on my heel. "*What?*"

The look in Aaren's eyes was almost helpless. "They're not coming. We have to do this alone."

Heavy stones sank in my stomach. "We're going to die," I whimpered.

"No," Aaren said and shook his head. "Not today."

"How do you know?" I asked frantically, taking a small, pleading step closer to him. "We have no help, just you and me against one of the most dangerous creatures in all of Yggdrasil. How are we going to be okay?"

"*Fremmed...*"

"No, how are you so sure? What is that look on your face? How can you be so calm in the face of our demise?"

Aaren looked to be shaking with whatever he left unspoken.

"Aaren!" I exclaimed. "How?"

"Because I love you, Layla!"

Everything suddenly went deathly still. "You...you what?"

"I love you, and you should know by now that love makes any Fraalver bond stronger. Especially magically." Thunder clapped above us.

"I don't—"

"I. Love. You."

And then that wall in my chest exploded.

It was so painful, and so liberating, and confusing, and agonizing, and orgasmic, and everything I felt flew into my steps as I bounded towards Aaren. Whatever it was that was coursing through me was inside Aaren, too, and he met my strides with the same ferocity. Neither of us balked when the distance between us grew smaller and smaller, and then his shirt was balled in my fists until my wrists were destined to snap.

And then our lips crashed calamitously together, delicious and sweet and haunting. It was a kiss of passion, of remorse, of desperate, hot need, because now the wall was down, and I couldn't hide anymore, wouldn't hide because I *loved* him.

I loved Aaren.

I forfeited every ounce of myself to him, and power whirled through me, intertwining with his as our lips danced and nipped together. Fire and ice battled under my skin as Aaren deepened the kiss, his tongue swiping over my bottom lip as his hand gripped my cheek. He held me like he would be lost to the wind without me, as if every breath we shared were his last. And for all we knew, they could be.

His lips seemed to whisper every victory, every regret, every sin, every moment of his life into me, and I drank it like a tankard of my favorite brew. The rune heightened my senses to him, and not only could I feel his emotions, but I could see them, as if they were playing through my mind like a picture show.

There was Nilsen across the table with a smile as they battled it out in Balderkrig. Then I saw his father, nearly identical to Aaren, hands balled into fists, teaching him how to throw the perfect punch. It was the exact technique he had taught me. Then there was his mother, bright and shining like the afternoon sun through the trees, and then Rorik, spouting some rambled advice in the safety of the medicine hut.

There were flashes of battle and blades and victory and scars, as the memories of Aaren's triumphs flashed by.

Blue eyes blinked through my mind, curtains of blonde hair framing them as the girl they belonged to smiled, proudly displaying the small gap between her front teeth. Her blonde curls cascaded behind her as she bunched up her skirts and started to run down the village path, beckoning Aaren to follow. Her image rippled, growing fuzzy and unclear, and then Aaren let out a rattling scream, dripping with grief and despair that tore apart the light of the forest until all I could see was darkness.

I fumbled through the shadows, the sounds of the village surrounding me, but I couldn't see, couldn't move. Panic tried to strike through my chest, but I felt nothing, because all sensation had left my limbs, and I was numb, so agonizingly numb.

Something whispered to me, *hallow*, and firelight flickered into view. It was the night I came to Skoghjem, my shaking figure curled at Aaren's feet, and Nilsen shouting his desperate pleas of my innocence. Then we were in the medicine hut, where I was in bed, arms crossed over my chest, and after all of that darkness, after being numb for so long, all I could feel was anger and hatred and spite. And even though I despised those feelings, I wasn't numb anymore, so I clung to them so that I could stay afloat again.

And then we were fighting in the ring, and I watched myself purge Markus, and the anger eased. A slight shimmer of light and warmth filled me. I saw Dagan die again and felt the regret and shame as word came of Kysthjem's attack, as everything started to slip through the cracks, every bit of control winking away like dying stars.

I walked down the aisle in Thea's dress, and for a moment, there was Solveig again, her blonde hair braided down her back, and the gap in her teeth showed as she gave me a delighted smile. I blinked and there I was again, scared and so desperate to prove myself.

Our time in Kysthjem passed, and every memory that blinked by, that light grew and grew until I was warm, complete, and happy. Until Aaren and I fought in Fjellhjem. And suddenly that numbness tried to come back, fighting tooth and claw to seep into my skin and weigh me down until I sank below the darkness again.

But there I was, writhing under Aaren's touch and singing his name, and training with him, and that same, unfamiliar feeling from the shack returned, filling my veins and continued to grow as the memories up until the current day ended, and I came back into myself.

It felt like the world ended when our mouths finally parted.

"*Fremmed*," he whispered in a husky breath. "Layla."

"Aaren," I cried, feeling the hot tears flowing freely down my cheeks.

There was a presence I hadn't felt until it was leaving my mind, and I let out a choked sob as understanding dawned on Aaren's features. Just like I had lived through his memories, he had mine, experiencing every loss, every heartache, teasing and fighting, nights in the bar, days with Lucas. Mama and Granny's deaths. Aaren had lived it all inside my head.

His hands found my face again, and silent tears spilled down his own cheeks as he wiped away mine.

"Layla, I have fallen so desperately in love with you," Aaren admitted. "I wanted to hate you, with all my being, I wished I could."

I know, I thought. *I felt it. Lived it.*

"I tasted you and realized I had been starving," he continued. "I couldn't hate you even if I tried, and gods *fremmed*, I tried." I laughed, and it released some of the tension in me. "Seeing everything you went through to get here, how many times you had only been just an arm's length away..."

He kissed me again, deep and slow.

"I love you, Layla Sviker. With all of your power and might and stubbornness. You took my shadows, my darkness, and planted a forest in it."

If Aaren hadn't been holding me up, I would have crumpled to the rock. I pressed my forehead against his.

"I love you, too, Aaren," I said. "Wholly, with all of your scars and losses, victories and battles. I don't care if you win, lose, or draw. I love you with every breath and every ounce of my evil blood."

Aareen chuckled, then kissed me again until our breaths were ragged and lips raw. When we finally pulled away from each other, I took a deep breath.

"I guess we're doing this alone," I said, turning to glare at the dark tunnel.

"No," Aaren said, his thumb brushing my rune. "Together."

He turned to face the tunnel, extending his empty palm to me. When my skin met his, my magic flickered to life, thicker and more potent than ever.

Chapter 50

Aaren and I were more attuned to each other than ever. Somewhere in the feelings I had been holding back was the final key to fully attuning to one another, and now every touch, every breath between us was electric. Not only were *we* more connected, but so was our magic, as if whatever bond that was now wide open between us now served as a channel for power.

Now fully equipped with my magic, Aaren's, and the power that the axe channeled into me, I wasn't afraid to walk into the roots. Instead, I was buzzing so fiercely I was sure I was leaving behind scorched footprints along the scattered twigs on the floor.

The passage before us ended in unnerving darkness, the sound of a hollow wind echoing throughout. I summoned a dancing flame, grateful for the small release of my power it gave me, and illuminated the stone walls with thick roots woven throughout. Hard, carved wood met the buzzing palms of my hands when I brushed a root, shivering as the weight of the place sank in.

How many could say they'd been to the roots of the world?

I just hoped we made it back to tell the story.

Wood splintered under my skin, and I recoiled, shining my flame over the root I had been following. The wood ended in a sharp spike, as if massive jaws had snapped it in half, and the other half had fallen to the stone in splinters. It reminded me of a timeline that had been cut short, ending prematurely. What happened when this branch fell? Or rather, what didn't happen?

Deeper and deeper we walked, encountering more and more broken roots, gnawed on by the relentless jaws of the Nidhogg. Every step deeper elicited another shudder down my spine, another wave of power I had to try to tame with little success. Aaren wove his fingers through mine and siphoned some of the power from me. I sighed as it took the edge off, but it was temporary and bound to come back with a vengeance.

The mouth of the passage opened up onto a massive cavern, the only light coming from the flame in my hand. The light only reached so far before darkness swallowed up the rest of the room. And whatever lay waiting in that darkness.

There was a great, sweeping sound, and something sighed; then a deep rumbling filled the cavern, vibrating the heels of my boots. The presence filled the dark cave, as if its very existence was enough to take down the entire place. It could. And it would if we didn't play our cards right.

"I know you're here, King of Trees," a whispering, husky voice said. It didn't frighten me, and my magic rose in challenge. "You bring his blood with you."

I swallowed.

"Layla, daughter of Markus."

The thing moved, a swishing, slithering sound across the stone floor. Blood roared in my ears, and even Aaren took a cautious step back. Suddenly, there was a whoosh, a sweeping exhale, and the shape of an enormous head was illuminated in the fire that blew from its mouth. The trail of fire hit a towering pile of wood, the remains of some of Yggdrasil's destroyed roots. It erupted into writhing flames that licked the ceiling of the cavern.

The Nidhogg turned, and every muscle in my body froze, and a shred of doubt dampened my confidence. The Nidhogg was a deep, earthen brown with lighter specks lining its back that complemented the roots it chewed. Its head was crested with brittle branches that wove through each other in a deadly crown, some of the branches growing thick, hardy vines among them. Ridges scaled down its back like large rocks, and its underbelly was crusted with dirt and twigs. It looked like a massive snake bore a forest along its body, though the forest was knotted and bare, almost desolate. Its green eyes locked on us, and it snarled to show rows and rows of sharpened teeth. Not to mention it was massive.

"Why have you come to the bottom of the world, Layla Sviker?"

I straightened, holding my chin high. "I hear you have made a deal with my father," I said firmly, holding the Nidhogg's eyes as it shifted across the stone floor.

The Nidhogg laughed, a hollow booming that rattled the walls of the cavern. "Perhaps I have," it replied. "Perhaps not. I am surprised you ask about my dealings and not about your brother's. Lucas?" Hearing my brother's name spill from the Nidhogg's slithering tongue sent a barreling rage igniting through my neurons.

"Where is he?" I demanded, and there was a deep, cell-melting fire burning through me. I would give it two minutes before I inadvertently burned everything in sight.

The Nidhogg slithered closer to me, and Aaren stepped protectively to my side, his own precarious anger rising to meet mine.

"Markus speaks to me," the Nidhogg answered. "I've known about Lucas for a very long time. But..." it gave me a sportive look, "I've known about you for even longer." I narrowed my eyes at it in question. "Oh yes," it said, cocking its head. "He fears you, Layla Sviker. He fears the power he unwittingly gave you."

I took a deep breath. "If Markus is afraid of me, then why did you strike a deal with him? Why not wait to make one with me?"

The Nidhogg hummed low. "There are many things you will never understand, Layla Sviker."

I opened my mouth to ask another question when the Nidhogg reared back, *tsk tsk tsking* me. "I would like to hear from the King of Trees," the Nidhogg said, turning its deadly attention to Aaren.

"How kind," Aaren sneered, and the Nidhogg growled quietly. "Is Lucas Sviker still alive?" he asked in a harsh, biting tone.

The Nidhogg sneered. "How selfless of you to ask about her brother and not about your fate. Or the fate of your village."

Was that a threat?

I started to shake, anger and power crawling up my throat and soaking every muscle fiber.

"The brother lives." It gave a menacing side eye. "For now."

That was two threats, and if the Nidhogg was making them on behalf of Markus, then their deal was confirmed. The only thing left to do was to reap as much information from it before we killed it.

"But these trivial matters should be the least of your worries," the Nidhogg warned, though it was more taunting than cautious. It slithered even closer to me and dipped its head again, its hot breath now puffing nearly inches in front of me. Expecting the smell to be foul and reeking of death, I was surprised when all I smelled was the earth and the scent of split wood.

"Do you mean the necromancer?" Aaren asked.

"Ah, yes," the Nidhogg hissed before pulling back and snaking away to gnaw on a branch. "The necromancer. The one who gave Markus a second life, only for him to squander it on mylings and hubris." It spat the last bit out as if Markus's actions left a sour taste in its mouth. "And wouldn't you know, only a fortnight ago, your father paid me a visit."

"To strike a deal," I affirmed, but only grew confused when the Nidhogg gave a shake of the head.

"On behalf of the necromancer." Twigs dropped from its mouth as it spoke. "He asked me to fight with them. To destroy the realms to create one divine realm."

How could the necromancer even be capable of such a thing? Even with the help of the Nidhogg, could they really bring down the entirety of Yggdrasil?

"And did you agree?" Aaren pressed.

The Nidhogg laughed again, and this time, it was flecked with pride. "I ate all of Asgard. Of course, I agreed."

I had learned many jarring truths today, but this one almost sent me to the stone floor. Asgard existed, and the Nidhogg destroyed it.

"Why?" I asked, voice shaking, not with fear, but my slipping grip of control.

The Nidhogg rose so it towered over us, its body expanding slightly as if it was broadening its chest in pride and vanity. "My purpose is balance. I eat the roots of Yggdrasil to maintain that balance. Once a branch or realm becomes too powerful, it must be reset. Everything must exist in equilibrium." It rose and snapped a root in half. "Otherwise," a massive boulder thundered from the cavern ceiling where the root was, "chaos will ensue." It chewed the root pensively, sinking to watch me carefully. "I am not evil, Layla, I stand for judgment."

"If you stand for balance, then why did you agree to help Markus?"

The Nidhogg sighed as if suddenly bored with the conversation. "Each branch of Yggdrasil has grown to pose a threat to my beloved balance. The dwarves and their greed for treasures that promise them power, the Midgardians and their weapons of mass destruction," it dipped its head, staring at Aaren and me from under its brow, "even Alveland and the Fraalver threaten that universal equilibrium."

The Nidhogg was morally neutral, blind to the nuances of right and wrong. Markus and the necromancer's plan would create a balance in the realms, one united realm with an equal balance of power. But what the Nidhogg was looking past was the intention behind that plan, the reality of that united realm: the necromancer ruling as the supreme leader. There would be no balance, only chaos.

I sighed dreadfully. "You must know why we're here then."

The Nidhogg nodded slowly, inching closer. "To bargain with me, but seeing as there is no way you can convince me out of my decision, I suppose you're here to kill me."

When I didn't respond, it reared back and rose to reveal its full height. The rooted crown atop its head brushed the ceiling of the cavern. "I'm sure you will prove to be an honorable opponent," it said, baring its teeth. "But I do not plan on dying today."

In an instant, it struck. Aaren and I darted away from each other, and I tumbled forward, splinters embedding in the skin of my palms. Whirling around, I stood in time to dodge another strike. Stone crunched behind me when I moved, and my magic buzzed excitedly as I reached back and retrieved the axe from my back.

Aaren drew his own sword, battle-ready malice glazing his eyes when he charged. The Nidhogg redirected its attention to him and gave a deafening hiss that filled the cavern. The axe thrummed in my hand, and I darted forward, swinging a powerful arc over my head. It slit through the Nidhogg's scales, but just as red blood oozed from the wound, it disappeared in a blink as the scales mended back together.

This all-powerful axe, the very weapon we retrieved for the sole purpose of slaying the Nidhogg, couldn't even scratch it.

What the fuck.

Out of the corner of my eye, the Nidhogg struck, knocking Aaren to the side with a pained grunt. I launched into movement and swung the axe before the Nidhogg could rear back to make the kill. The blade caught a cluster of vines hanging from the Nidhogg's crown, and it recoiled and roared angrily at the destruction of its macabre regality.

Aaren jumped to his feet, swaying a little as he regained his balance. Fury blazed across his face, a dangerous smile that curved his mouth as his brow hooded his eyes. His magic curled inside me and surged as the discarded roots scattering the floor shook, then fused and twined together. The Nidhogg only watched as its foe took shape, growing to meet its height and brilliance. When

445

Aaren blinked out of his concentration, a wooden Nidhogg stood before its original, sizing it up with malicious intent.

A strike of brilliance hit me like a lightning strike, and I lunged forward, throwing my hands in front of me and summoning a furious stream of flames at the wooden Nidhogg. It caught fire, burning disastrously as our creation came nose to nose with its opponent.

The Nidhogg recoiled, baring its teeth at the blazing replica of itself. With an effortless flick of Aaren's wrist, the fire snake struck, but its target dodged to the right. Our snake ducked, slithered to wrap around the dark body of the Nidhogg, and squeezed. I sent a tunnel of power to Aaren in case his magic began to falter, then watched the flames climb up the Nidhogg's body with a satisfied smile. The twisting, brittle branches that crested its head lit in a spectacular display of burning grace, and the Nidhogg let out a bone-shattering roar as its macabre grandeur turned to ash.

It was furious now, and the rage drove it to brave the flames of our burning snake. The Nidhogg snapped its jaw around the snake's coiled body, ripping shreds of vines apart until the flames faltered and it could gain the upper hand. Another enraged roar, and the fire snake exploded into burning vines and ash that rained down around us like snowing defeat. Then it locked its sights on Aaren and struck.

My heart caught in my throat the moment the Nidhogg hit Aaren and threw him to the side like a ragdoll. He slid and a jolt of pain rang through my rune, but he was up again before I could take a step, sword drawn and daring the Nidhogg to tread closer. It did, and laughed when the blade couldn't even draw blood. Aaren sprinted away to avoid another strike.

"I am unending," it said, as it rose to full height again and bristled audaciously. "I cannot be defeated."

The Nidhogg was quick, but Aaren was quicker. I lost sight of their attacks, the sounds of Aaren's frustrated grunts, and the Nidhogg's arrogant laughter going quiet in my ears. Something was pulsing, something ancient and powerful. And it was starting to fill me with more power than I was capable of holding. The sounds of battle went nearly silent, and that same familiar chanting began in my head. The chanting I had heard in Fjellgrav was accompanied by a surge of power that almost caused me to set the entire place ablaze.

Somewhere in the base of Yggdrasil were markings of deitonic language, and it was screaming at me.

I came to for a moment, realizing minutes had passed, and Aaren was sorely losing this battle. Strands of bloodied hair clung to his brow, and a deep gash opened a streak of crimson across his shoulder. But he kept fighting, and no matter how hard he seemed to be losing, he never lost his strength.

There was another pulse of power as the chanting got louder, and the axe in my grip hummed vibrantly, as if it were singing the words of ancient music in my head. My rune burned too, as if all three sources of power were finally meeting and preparing for the fight that could bring down the world.

I needed Aaren to take the edge off again. I needed to share this power that was going to consume me, or we truly would destroy each and every realm we had ever known. I needed him, the duality of our powers, I need him, I *need* him, *I need him...*

Aaren felt it, the tunnel between us widening, and magic sluiced through it like a swelling river in a hurricane. Another wave of power from the chanting surged into me and flowed straight into Aaren, who was siphoning more than I knew he could handle. Only a few seconds, and the flow ebbed, and Aaren turned to face the Nidhogg with a wrathful smile.

The Nidhogg, puzzled by the abrupt pause in combat, reared back and cocked its head to the side, watching curiously. It reminded me of a curious puppy sniffing a new playmate.

"You cannot be giving up now, King of Trees. We are just getting started."

"If you want balance, Nidhogg, I'll give you balance," Aaren challenged. "Now!"

I flung out my arms, blasting a whirlwind of water out of my palm and letting it swirl around the Nidhogg's head. Aaren unleashed his wind, and it clashed with the water to brew a brilliant storm that raged around the Nidhogg. Neither of us faltered as it lashed out, roaring and shaking and cursing.

The fingertips of my free hand itched as static buzzed along my skin, and more power writhed to be unleashed. Obliging the demands of my aching magic, I threw out my other hand, breaking cracks in the stone floor and launching boulders at the Nidhogg. It thrashed in protest, still trying to break free from the hurricane, but I hit it again and again until its body was nearly buried under hard stone.

A hard line of fire broke free from the storm, rocketing straight for me and singeing the skin along my hands. I screamed, and my concentration broke, then my magic balked for the briefest of seconds. That hesitation weakened Aaren's hold on the storm, and that was all the Nidhogg needed to break free and barrel towards us.

I jumped and barely missed the next stream of fire that spewed out. Hard stone slammed into my shoulder as I fell, and pain arced through my body. But it didn't stop the pulsing or the chanting, and I stood only a moment later, ready to charge like an outraged bull. Aaren siphoned more magic as it reached its peak inside me, and I sent him a silent thank you.

"Markus believes you possess a higher purpose that he can control, Layla Sviker, but I don't listen to trivial absurdities like destiny." The Nidhogg reared back once more, and I craned my neck to take it in, almost reveling in its majesty. I truly hated that we had to kill it—the Nidhogg truly was a force that no one should reckon with and could have been a formidable ally if we could have convinced it. I sincerely hoped this was the right thing to do.

"You cannot destroy fate, Layla," the Nidhogg said, and it was right. But if the fate of our realms rested in the Nidhogg's forsaken balance, then we were going to rewrite it.

"Give my regards to the gods," it said, and Aaren gave a fierce shout as the Nidhogg's yawning maw opened wide and swallowed me whole.

Chapter 51

I don't remember exactly what it felt like to be swallowed, but one thing that would never leave my mind was the smell. While the Nidhogg only ate the roots of Yggdrasil, it still reeked of rot. Granny used to have a compost bin out in the backyard that she would throw her banana peels and eggshells into to make the fertilizer for her garden. The smell reminded me of throwing away potato peels on a hot summer night, where the soil had been fermenting in the heat all day.

No other thoughts came to me other than "Holy shit, the Nidhogg has swallowed me." The eater of realms ate me. I wondered what kind of balance eating me would bring to the realm.

Down I went through the slimy passage of its throat, mucus and saliva coating me as I moved. My fingers were gripped around something hard and wooden, something that vibrated anxiously in my grasp. The axe sent a stunning wave of energy up my arm, shaking me from my stupor. I was in the Nidhogg's throat, and in seconds, I would be in its stomach, and I would be doomed.

I could still feel the passage between Aaren and me, but it was closing quickly, like the connection between us was pulled taut. Despite the hot breath and roar that shook the Nidhogg's gullet, the chanting still thundered in my mind, loud and fierce and strong.

My toes dug into the squishy walls of the Nidhogg's throat and lodged me in place. The muscles of the esophagus pulsated and tried to push me further down, but I fought with gritted teeth, the now-angry power inside me quieting my protesting muscles. A rush of air blew past me and sent flecks of saliva smacking into my face as the Nidhogg coughed, another feeble attempt to dislodge me. But I remained locked in, beginning to sing the chant as the axe swelled in my grip.

Another contraction in the throat pushed me an inch further down, and bile lapped at the sphincter muscle between the throat and the stomach. The smell was almost overpowering, and I worked to keep my breathing steady, my limbs firm, my mind present. My muscles twitched again, and I writhed, restlessness now coursing through me. My skin stretched taut over my muscles, bones eating away at my fascia, and I shook, as if my skeleton was trying to break free. Strength and spirit flooded me as I chanted louder and louder, my voice leaving me only to make room for more power. I became the words I sang, strength rising with every flick of my tongue, every intonation of my vocal chords.

The axe was slick in my hand when I gripped it tighter, pushing it into the Nidhogg's throat with enough force to slice a deep wound. A ringing screech blew through its windpipe, deafening me as blood spurted from the slice and coated me in dark crimson. It started to close up, and the axe began to slip from my fingers. The Nidhogg's stomach bile was about to brush my boots.

Another dose of power, from both the chanting and the axe, sizzled in my veins, and I screamed until my throat was glass, and my lungs felt like they were shriveling up. I sliced at the throat again, but it did nothing but coat me in more blood and summon the angry torrent of bile.

I had maybe a minute if I was lucky, but I was only succeeding in slicking myself up for the descent into the Nidhogg's stomach. Anger soaked my chanted words now, furious that this venerated axe was doing nothing to hurt the Nidhogg permanently. What was the point? Why did we travel all the way to Klartvan Lake to retrieve it if making menial cuts was all the axe could do?

It sent another angry pulse through my arms, as if answering my anguished plea. Shockwaves coursed over me, and my skin was growing too tight for my bones, and it all clicked. It wasn't about the axe itself—it was about who possessed it. The axe was just a weapon; what mattered was what it was imbued with. Magic, a force so powerful that it could take on something like the Nidhogg down if in the right hands.

And I knew without a doubt that it belonged to me.

Pulse after pulse of energy filled me, and I cried louder, voice rich in power and anguish and euphoria and bloodlust. The chanting and axe infused me, remade me, like my DNA was being rewritten with the crackling flame of magic. And just when I thought I couldn't take it any more, Aaren sent me one last wave, and I exploded.

The splintered vines embedded in my palms pulsed and broke free from my skin. Tendrils of Yggdrasil sprouted from my hands and curled around my fingers like a snake coils around a tree branch. Then the vines thickened and grew away from my hands to press into the sides of the Nidhogg's throat. Magic pulsed again, then the vines responded and ripped into the flesh, closing in around me. The Nidhogg let out another harrowed screech, but the vines had done their damage. As the wood tore a hole through the Nidhogg, warm light seeped in. The Nidhogg fell to the ground with a thud, and the vines held open the wound for me to crawl out and slide to the stone floor with a squelch and an exalted, deep breath.

My blood was still humming with magic, but the chanting quieted, and the connection between Aaren and me widened again. He channeled another dose out of me as I took a deep breath, and then I felt his arms cradle me to his chest.

"Oh, *fremmed*," he sighed heavily. "Thank the fucking gods." He brushed a sticky strand of hair out of my face.

"Holy fucking Himmelfjell," I breathed, the angry roaring in my ears dying as my heart began to settle. I was alive, and I had just killed the Nidhogg.

"Layla Sviker," Aaren said, almost like a curse. "Fate Slayer."

I gave an exasperated chuckle. "Doesn't quite roll off the tongue like I want it to."

Aaren helped me to my knees, where my stomach churned at the sight of the brutalized Nidhogg. Its head lay in a growing pool of blood, teeth bared and dead eyes staring right into my soul. My soul felt like it had been ripped to shreds and made in the image of power.

I hadn't killed fate; I became it.

I glanced around the cavern in search of the markings of deitonic language, but found none to my surprise. Where did all that power come from if there were no markings?

"Are you okay to move?" Aaren asked, and I nodded, letting him help me to my feet.

"Let's get back," I said. "If I don't get this stuff off of me, I'm going to rip my skin off."

Chapter 52

The portal back to Alveland reappeared when we emerged from the tunnel as if it had been there the whole time. I didn't question it, not when my skin was sticky with the Nidhogg's viscera.

To my disappointment, there was no warm light when we went through the portal this time. But the group was right where we had left them, albeit most of them were sitting on the forest floor, picking apart leaves as they anxiously awaited us. I dropped to the ground upon arrival, brushing off leaves that clung to my skin as Rorik came striding toward us in four brisk steps.

"What happened?" he stammered, but he took one look at the blood coating me, the static air of power that clouded me and Aaren, and he fell silent.

"It's done," Aaren said. "The Nidhogg is dead."

Rorik blinked disbelievingly, but Oswin and Ivar scurried to their feet and howled victoriously. Ivar went to wrap me in a hug, but paused when he saw the state of my clothes.

"We tried to find the way you took," Oswin spilled. "We checked every nook and cranny, Von even scaled four trees!"

I gave a breathy laugh, but only one thing was on my mind at the moment.

"Bath," I said, pushing through the crowd of men. "I need a bath."

They parted as I walked to the borders, and I didn't slow down until my boots hit the dirt path.

Oswin and Ivar arranged a celebration, and while the idea of a celebration was nice, I just wanted to go to bed. The enormous expenditure of magic I had absorbed and dispelled today left my soul weary, and I wasn't sure a night's rest would be enough to recharge me. But the thought of a full mug of ale and a suckling pig sent me to Thea's to borrow a dress.

She had a bath waiting for me in her cellar home, and I didn't care that I was stark naked in front of her; I was just eager to scrub my skin until it bled. Of

452

course, Thea prevented that, but she gave me the spa treatment I needed to feel clean. She scraped the grime and dried blood from under my fingernails while I rinsed my ears and scrubbed my scalp. I didn't necessarily feel like a new woman when I rose dripping wet from the tub, but it was enough that I didn't feel like I was going to hurl every time I got a whiff of myself.

Thea pinned my hair into wooden curlers and listened to me recount the battle, and I had to admit, it sounded pretty badass. I had, after all, just killed one of the most powerful beings on Yggdrasil.

"You never told me about the deitonic language," Thea cooed as she began to remove the curlers from my hair. "And you say it gave you magic in Fjellgrav?"

"It didn't give me power, more like it...amplified my own?" I replied, unsure of how to describe it.

Thea paused, a pink wildflower intended for my hair in her hand. "That doesn't seem possible," she said, confusedly. "Deitonic language is supposed to let the gods communicate with their demigod children. But the gods are dead, if the Nidhogg was telling the truth."

The truth that it had eaten Asgard? How could I ever forget that?

I gave her a considerable look in the mirror. "I don't know what it was then. I can't explain it."

"Hello?" came Stieg's voice from the stairs.

I glimpsed him in the mirror, frozen on the last step with a hand shielding his eyes in case one of us wasn't fully dressed.

"Hello, my love," Thea purred, and Stieg peeked through his fingers. "Come to keep us company?"

"Um," Stieg stuttered, then his cheeks reddened. "Well, I—"

"Ah," I said and rose from my seat. "That's my cue."

I gathered my things and clomped up the stairs, hastily sliding on my dress and sandals in the shop before making my way to the celebration.

The music had started by the time I reached the square, and my stomach roared at the sight of the spread Inaborg had set up. There was, in fact, a pig, and Kare stood by the fire and spun the spit where it was skewered. Sofie passed him an ale, and he planted a grateful kiss on her forehead. Aurora helped Inaborg arrange the trays of vegetables while Borgil and Randolph chatted and laughed close by. Asta had somehow roped Harald into a dance, and I smiled as I watched the eccentric author prance around the square, stepping his own moves into the dance instead of following the choreography of the others. The kegs could see Oswin and Ivar, and Axl clung to the shadows, though his face was more visible through his hood than usual.

I gladly watched the revelry with a chest warm with bliss as Fjellhjem and Skoghjem Fraalver mingled, danced, drank, and ate.

This was why we killed the Nidhogg. This was why I would go to battle again and again.

If only Lucas could be here to see this.

"Here," a gruff voice said behind me. I turned to see Aaren approach with a plate full of food, but it wasn't the bread and cheese that made my mouth water. It was the way his green coat hugged his arms, the way his chest stretched the cotton shirt underneath. It was the way his hair had been pulled back into his usual do. The way his scent filled my nose and stirred excitement in my stomach. But most importantly, it was the way his eyes shimmered in the firelight, so familiar and deep, and now that I could love him, fully, wholly, I dove into them, showering myself in the warm sunrise of irises.

"Thank you," I said and popped a grape into my mouth.

I turned and watched Von sweep Britta across the dancefloor, both rosy-cheeked and beaming.

Thea and Stieg joined us, both in high spirits from whatever I had walked away from earlier.

"When do we give the axe back?" Stieg asked and took a sip of ale.

Never, I wanted to say. At the end of it all, it belonged to me. "As soon as possible, I suppose."

Stieg shook his head. "I'd say hold onto it a little longer. Let Ymer squirm for a bit."

Thea thumped him on the chest, rolling her eyes. "We made a promise. Just because he is your bitter, estranged uncle, doesn't mean we can't be true to our word." She settled against his chest, crossing her arms over her own. "The alliance is strained as is, no need to poke the verbjorn."

Stieg chuckled, his lips spreading to reveal his crooked teeth. "Care to dance, milady?" he asked, smoothly spinning Thea to hold her flush against his chest. I had to give him credit—Stieg had charm. Thea smiled and gave him a loving peck before she followed him onto the dance floor.

When Aaren stepped closer to me, heat rushed across my skin, and desire pooled in my stomach.

A pensive quiet settled over us, where we watched the celebration. I smiled warmly as Stieg, with white knuckles, dipped Thea, and her brown curls swept the ground. He pulled her up and brushed a featherlight kiss across her lips. Oswin and Ivar clapped and stomped their feet, coming up with lyrics to the melody that played. Even Nilsen was allowed at the celebration, and he darted in and out of the crowd, giggling and chasing after Ingrid, whose blonde braids trailed behind her as she moved.

Ertha stood stiffly on the sidelines of the movement, watching politely. Her eyes were so lost in the dancing that she didn't see Rorik as he approached, clicking his heels as he halted in front of her. Startled, she clasped a thin hand to her chest and chuckled as the color returned to her face. Rorik bowed his head slightly, and Ertha watched in surprise as he offered her his hand and gazed at her from over his palm. She hesitated for a beat, then she lightly placed her hand in his and allowed him to pull her into the square.

Rorik was the first man she'd danced with who wasn't Torsten.

"Did you mean it?" Aaren asked suddenly, and I turned to him, confused.

"Mean what?"

Aaren turned to me, longing, holding his features in a desperate vise. "Did you mean what you said about me when we thought we were going to die?"

I laughed, and the intensity in his face eased, but he was unblinking as he awaited my answer.

"I did," I said, holding his gaze. "I meant every word."

Aaren offered me his hand, and I slid my fingers into his. "Come with me."

I put down the plate of food, and we slipped away under the cover of darkness. Leaves crunched under our feet as we dove into the forest, and I listened for the soft hoot of Ugleverge in the sky.

We wove throughout the branches, giggling like two teenagers who had just snuck out of their parents' houses for the night. Sapling trees swatted our shins, and I laughed when Aaren tripped over a fallen log and toppled onto a bed of leaves. He pulled me down with him, leaves replacing the wildflowers in my hair, and I savored Aaren's deep, rumbling laugh.

He bolted to his feet, then took off into a sprint, and I protested, bunching my skirts into a hand before following him. The night was warm, and the fireflies flew lazily around the forest, lighting my way back to him.

He had stopped in a clearing, the moon above us shining a cool light over the marriage branch above. My heart fluttered.

"What are we doing here?" I questioned as Aaren pulled me under the branch and held me at arm's length. His rune arm snaked over mine, aligning our marks.

"I love you, Layla," Aaren said, and my insides went molten.

He loved me, and I loved him.

When the realization struck, my chest went concave.

"I stand before you, tortured by the mere possibility of loving you, half anguished, half hopeful. Would you do me the honor of consummating our marriage, *fremmed*?"

A relieved smile broke on my lips, but my throat was too tight to say anything. I gave Aaren a frantic nod, managing a "yes," and Aaren's eyes glimmered. Something primal had awakened in him, and coupled with the surging passion coursing between the two of us, I was in for something I knew I couldn't prepare for.

"I'm not sure I'm going to be able to contain myself once I start," he warned, glowing with that feral energy that was seeping through my rune. "The magic that is summoned in this is ancient."

"I'll be okay," I assured, my desire quenching the apprehension that was trying to take form. I placed a hand over his rune as my need shaped itself into an insatiable force. "You don't know how long I've been waiting for this, Aaren."

Aaren fell apart. "Oh fuck, *fremmed*," he breathed, and he brought his lips to mine, skipping the pleasantry of softness as he devoured me. Our mouths danced in unison, welding together as if his lips were made for mine. The hand on my cheek brushed a strand of hair from my face while the other tangled in my hair.

The freedom was intoxicating, the light of his love shining through me like a stained-glass window in a church, painting my soul with the spectacular colors of his forest. *Our* forest. He kissed me deeper, and it was wondrous, devastating, and breathtaking. Everything I had ever dreamed it would be, everything I had ever wanted.

I allowed my hand to wander, fingers trailing down his torso and playing with the loose buttons of his shirt. Smooth skin met my fingers, and I relished the carved muscles of his chest as I traced small circles over his abdomen. That skin was mine, the stony muscle was mine, and the thumping, thriving heart underneath belonged to me.

With a growl, Aaren's hand moved from my hair to grip my breast, kneading it hungrily as his lips left my mouth and nipped at the soft skin below my ear. I leaned my head back to give him easier access and moaned as his tongue trailed down my neck and bit the flesh of my breast.

Aaren looked at me from under his brow, nothing but desire dripping from his stare as he took the ribbon from the front of my dress between his teeth and pulled. My corset loosened. His fingers wormed under the laced fabric and pulled it away to expose my peaked nipples to the warm air of the forest. A gentle breeze kissed my skin as he took one in his mouth, flicking his tongue over the top and sending a shock of pleasure down my spine. I held his head to my chest, head thrown back in exhilaration as he sucked and nipped at me.

He groaned, delicious vibrations dancing across my chest. Hours could've passed, and I wouldn't have known because I was so lost in the moment, so lost in him.

Aaren.

My husband.

His hands gripped my waist, and his strong fingers dug into my hips as he moved to the other breast and repeated his ministrations. It was amusing to see how much I had changed since our first encounter. My first time having sex left me with nothing to be desired, but after Aaren, there was so much I wanted, so much I needed to feel. I was willing to give this man, this Fraalver, every inch of my body, every cell and pore and neuron. It all belonged to him.

Gripping his chin, I pulled Aaren up to my mouth, crashing our lips together, and kissing him like my life depended on it. He claimed me, soaking me up like the warm, summer sun. My hand left his chin, snaking down his chest, lower, *lower*, until it grazed his pulsating bulge, hopelessly trying to break free from his pants. I palmed him, and heat flooded my core as he moaned melodically. Aaren's forehead dropped to my shoulder as I rubbed him again, his cock throbbing against my hand, and he bit my collarbone and begged me not to stop.

His chest rumbled when he moaned and pulled away from me, bracing his hands underneath my bottom and guiding my legs to wrap around his middle. Placing both hands on his face, I showered him in desperate kisses as he moved, only stopping when my back was firmly pressed against the coarse bark of a tree.

I nearly crumpled to the ground when he released my legs. Warm air enveloped me when Aaren tugged my dress off, and left me utterly naked in front of him, bare to the trees and the glen, and the moon. I leaned back and let the bark press pleasantly against my skin, savoring how natural this felt. How natural it was to be laid bare in the place that rebirthed me, shaped me from the angry, exhausted waitress into the leader and lover I was now.

Dipping his head, Aaren's lips brushed mine, barely touching me before they trailed down my neck, my collarbone, kissing each breast, licking down my navel, until his warm breath wavered over the crown of my hips. He massaged my thighs. Calluses bit into me as he lifted my leg and draped it over his shoulder, drawing his mouth closer to me. I shivered when he placed a gentle kiss on my inner thigh. He smiled against my skin before kissing the other. Aaren's tantalizing breath alone was enough to ignite me, to send me reeling, and I gripped the tree trunk behind, grateful for the bite of the bark that brought me back to reality if only for a moment. I moaned in anguish and squirmed with anticipation as he continued to kiss me everywhere other than where I needed him to.

Amber eyes locked onto mine as his fingers parted me and he slid his tongue up my middle. I threw my head back when ecstasy cascaded over me, the bark tattooing my palms as I gripped the tree, unsure whether my knees would be able to hold me up by the end of this. His tongue circled the sensitive bundle of nerves, and I cried out, and wove my fingers through his hair, lost in his expert strokes. His tongue flicked before his lips wrapped around my center and sucked, as if he were eating a ripe piece of fruit, and he was determined to consume every drop.

"Fuck, Aaren," I cried, and gripped his hair.

That primal, thrumming energy intensified, and his hands moved to grip my thighs, holding me in place. Aaren's pace quickened, and he devoured me ravenously like I was his last meal. My knee began to buckle as he continued, bringing me closer and closer.

The world shattered into a million pieces, edges of the universe circling my vision as a million stars and swirls danced over my skin. Aaren moaned against me, the throes of rhapsody flooded through our runes, only serving to keep his pace steady. One climax wasn't enough for him, and Aaren kept working no matter how sensitive the first left me. His tongue lapped and sucked and licked and devoured until I was nearly ruined, begging and crying and groaning as I peaked the next climax. My knees did collapse this time, but Aaren caught and held me until I could steady myself again.

He smirked, lips glistening with my release. The sight sent me into a renewed frenzy, and I pushed forward and guided him to the ground.

A light fog had formed around the wedding branch, veiling us in moon-kissed bliss.

Aaren's fingers fumbled with his pants, a feat that took too long for my aching body to wait for. Buzzing with the high of my releases and whatever power we were conjuring, I straddled him and reached between my legs to stroke him. He shed his shirt, leaving him bare beneath me. A brush of my lips over his left him groaning for more, but instead of complying, I kissed the scar on his shoulder, then the one across his chest, licking the clumped tissue bunched under his ear.

Gods, I wished I could kiss every scar away, take away every reminder of the battles he'd fought, the wars he'd waged. Starting with the one on his back.

I stroked his length and brought my lips back to his, relishing in the moan he sent into my mouth before bucking his hips into my hand. My thumb circled his tip and rubbed the sensitive nerve underneath. He bit my lip in answer as if pleading with me to sink just an inch lower.

"I've been wanting to feel you for so long, *fremmed,*" he groaned, rubbing a hand over my cheek. "But I fear being inside you might be the end of me."

"You are endless, Aaren," I breathed. "Feel me."

Wrapping his arm around my middle, Aaren flipped us, his cock grazing my stomach as he hovered over me. He looked at me for a moment, with amber eyes aglow with passion, lust, and love. Then he gave me a tender kiss. And without taking his eyes from mine, he slid into me.

I roared as he filled me, at the heavenly sensation of his skin, flushed and sheened in sweat, pressed into mine. I had waited so long to feel him, to have him fill me up, and I could've screamed with elation if I wasn't already groaning with pleasure.

"Are you okay?" Aaren asked breathily, swiping away a strand of hair that had matted to my face in the warmth.

I nodded, adjusting. "Don't stop," I whispered.

"Are you..."

I didn't let him finish before my hands found his backside, fingers digging into his flesh and shoving him in further. Aaren's moan thundered through the clearing. His forehead dropped to mine as his breath came in short spurts when he pulled out to the tip, then slammed into me. His hands caught my shoulder as the force shoved me up. His thrusts grew quicker, and I raked my nails down his back and savored every buck and shift of his hips. Hot breath coated my neck as he buried his face in the crook, perfect teeth biting my skin as his pleasure built. I wrapped my legs around him to give him deeper access.

Another climax stirred within me, that same sleeping snake that had awakened the first time I had tangled with Aaren. It coiled loosely and writhed lazily as his thrusts grew faster, harder.

I whimpered at the emptiness he left when he suddenly pulled out.

"Don't worry, *fremmed,* I'm not done with you."

Aaren looped his arm under my back and, with a sweeping motion, then flipped me so that my belly pressed onto the leaf-strewn forest floor. I rose to my hands and knees as he braced my hips, sliding into me once again, this time deeper than he had been before. I threw my head back and groaned, the sound sending him pounding into me with more ferocity, more desperation.

The fog around us thickened, static with energy that crackled and sparked with every thrust, every moan, every breath.

Aaren's hand slinked around me, finding its target between my legs. A finger circled that sensitive spot that had been left aching by his tongue, and my mind and body collided. The snake within me had uncoiled and was now rearing its head, ready to strike. Aaren's thrusts became more erratic, sloppy, and his grip on my hips tightened, shoving me forward and backward, my movements controlled by him. All my senses went quiet, every sense except the ones that tuned me into his movements, his lustful thrusts, and passionate groans.

The snake struck, and I cried out in ecstasy, euphoria flushing my system and sending more stars erupting in my vision. My walls tightened around him, and it was enough to send Aaren barrelling over the edge after me. He spilled into me with a roar that reverberated throughout the clearing, throughout the forest, the celebration likely hearing his cry of pleasure.

A wave of energy erupted, sending a shockwave of blue light spreading rapidly through the clearing and into the forest. Leaves blew away from us, and the crickets stopped singing for a moment, aware of the power that radiated from our joining.

Our marriage was consummated correctly, and the borders were thoroughly restored.

With a sigh of exalted pleasure, Aaren pulled out of me, pausing to admire the scene before him. The sight of me bent over before him, my sex gleaming in the moonlight.

"I could stare at that forever," Aaren said and placed a kiss along my spine. "That tight little thing coated in me."

I cooed, every word I had ever known lost in the hazy void of pleasure.

I had just had him, and yet it hardly did anything to quell my need for him, my undying desire to have him live inside me. I shoved my hips back, wiggling my center over his already hardening cock.

"*Fremmed*," Aaren's gravelly voice breathed, but we both knew there was no use in fighting it.

His fingers brushed the edge of my entrance.

"I can't have enough of you," he sighed, sliding the first knuckle of his finger into me. I whined.

"We want to make sure the borders are extra protected, right?" I quipped, tightening around his finger as it slid deeper into me. Aaren pulled me up until my back was flush against his chest, his cock brushing the smooth skin of my ass.

His nose brushed the skin behind my ear, and a hand snaked up my chest and wrapped around my throat. "We have training tomorrow, *fremmed*. I want you to still be able to walk."

I wiggled my hips against him, and he moaned.

"You're going to regret that," he whispered in my ear.

With a soft shove, I landed back on my hands, crying delightedly when Aaren pounded into me once more.

Chapter 53

That day after the celebration, I visited the bookshop, immediately ignoring Thea's knowing look. When I didn't reciprocate the look, her eyes rolled to the ceiling.

"I'll ask you again, how big was it?"

"How did I know you were going to ask that?" I sighed, sitting down across the book counter from her.

"You didn't answer my question, *frue.*"

My eyes dropped to the book before me, the bindings fresh. Her newest novel is ready to be checked out and read. I traced my finger over the new spine and evaded the question, though I had been anxious to tell her. I mumbled something under my breath.

"What?" Thea questioned. She leaned in closer.

"As endowed as any character you've ever written," I answered, thumping the new book with a knuckle. Thea squealed and slammed her hand on the counter before demanding every detail.

After spending a couple of hours with Thea, I went to meet with Rorik, hoping he had news about what Markus's next move would be.

"Nothing," Rorik said as I closed the door to the medicine hut to find Aaren lounging by the windowsill. "I have absolutely nothing."

Pulling out a chair from the table scattered with bottles and caked ointments, I sank into it, discouraged.

"Do you think it could be worth another conversation with the huldra?" I proposed, even though it was shot down as soon as I asked. A coil of desperation gripped my insides as, like the thousand times already today, Lucas came into my mind.

Aaren eyed me when he felt that desperation.

Rorik groaned. "The unfortunate reality is that despite the work we have done, we are at square one once again. There is nothing to go off of." Rorik dropped into the chair in front of me. "At least when the mylings were here, we knew something about Markus's plan."

The latest events had begun to take a serious toll on Rorik, and not just in appearance this time. He was moodier, drained, and whatever work he had produced over the past few weeks was sloppier than usual. The state of the table before me was evidence of that. I knew Rorik enough to know that a messy table indicated a troubled mind. It was certainly too much for Asta, who seemed to avoid the medicine hut since our return, just because of its state.

Things weren't easy for any of us, especially after what we learned from the Nidhogg.

Asgard existed, which was a truth that kept all of us up at night, especially the questions that followed. Rorik and I had spent days poring over books and scrolls, searching for any implication of the fallen gods. According to the many tomes we read, gods cannot be killed. But if Asgard was destroyed, where did all of the gods go?

Especially since they seemed to speak to me through the deitonic language.

As gripping a question as that was, there was still Markus and the necromancer to address, and with no word or inkling of what they could have planned, Rorik was right—we were at square one.

I reached across the table and found Rorik's strained fingers, wrapping them into my palm. "Take a rest, Rorik," I said, and squeezed his fingers reassuringly. "You're run down, take some time, we can come back to this."

Aaren pushed himself from the windowsill and strode across the room in four graceful steps, halting in front of a shelf neatly lined with small glass jars. The hut was silent as he plucked a jar and grabbed a mug from the table, then stepped to the fire to pour some water from the already steaming kettle Rorik had placed there when I arrived. Uncorking the jar, he tapped a couple of leaves into the water, swirled them around, and put the jar in front of Rorik.

"Here, my friend," he said, watching as Rorik inhaled the fumes delightedly.

Rorik placed his hand on the side of the mug and glanced over his shoulder at Aaren. "Your mother used to make me this tea," he said as a weight pulled down his features, showing his age more than before.

A shadow crossed Aaren's face.

"Rest, *venn*."

A flick of his head was the only summons I needed to follow Aaren outside, where the warm sunlight kissed my face. Summer was in full swing, and since our return, there had been nothing but sunshine, flowering buds, and newborn forest creatures roaming the woods. It was a wonder how such beauty could persist in such dire times.

"He's fading," Aaren said, the warm weather taking little effect on the harsh lines that had etched themselves into his brow. "And without any leads, we're sitting ducks."

Leaning against the wooden exterior of the hut, I sighed. "I don't suppose we can just walk into Karridal guns blazing, can we? "

Aaren scoffed. "If he's even still there."

His hand dropped limply at his side as he closed his eyes and breathed in the summertime. My fingers wove through his, the moment demanding only solidarity. Aaren's eyes remained closed, but his answering squeeze told me enough.

"I told Oswin and Ivar I'd join them in the pub," Aaren said before peeling his head up and giving me an assessing look. "I think I need it."

I chuckled. "At least some things are back to normal."

I kissed Aaren goodbye outside the medicine hut and headed towards Thea's.

When she wasn't in her shop, I turned on my heel and decided I'd join my friends in the pub. Besides, Inaborg had been brewing a new honey ale for the last week, and the thought of it teased my taste buds. And I had a feeling that if I didn't get there soon, Oswin and Ivar would drain the keg before I got even a drop.

My hand had just brushed the door handle of the pub, the sounds of merriment spiking my thirst, when someone called my name.

"Hey Nilsen," I smiled, trouncing down the pub steps to see him.

"There's a tree house meeting today," he said, getting right to the point. "They want you to come and talk about the Nidhogg."

The feeling of cotton filled my mouth, growing more intense the longer it took for me to taste the new ale.

"I don't know, Nilsen, it might not be a story for children..."

"Pleeeeaaasseee!"

I sighed—I couldn't say no to Nilsen just like I couldn't say no to Lucas. "Fine," I said, crouching before him. "But you owe me an excellent game of Balderkrig."

Nilsen bounced excitedly and agreed to my terms.

"Lead the way, kid," I said.

Nilsen took off into a sprint.

Swearing under my breath when he disappeared down the path, I took off after him, the summer heat working against my angry lungs. He ignored my plea to slow down and the worried looks of the Fraalver that slid out of my way.

I tried to track his darting figure as he leapt into the forest, weaving through the bramble and slapping ferns out of his way. My breath rattled through my throat as I continued to follow, and I seriously considered just going back to the pub and drowning in ale with my friends. Out of the corner of my eye, I saw Stieg trekking in the opposite direction with a pack at his side. He smiled humorously.

"He went that way!" he called, pointing left.

I redirected and caught sight of Nilsen's white-blonde hair as he ducked through a bush. A few seconds later, I burst through that same bush, brushing away leaves that had snagged onto my shirt. Thankfully, Nilsen had stopped at the treehouse ahead, and the notches in the tree had already started to form.

"If you're going to defeat Markus, you need to work on your stamina, Layla," Nilsen chuckled, then began to climb.

I almost threw him the middle finger, then realized he wasn't Aaren, no matter how much he resembled him in looks and attitude.

My breath only returned when I dropped to the floor of the treehouse just above the trapdoor, chest concave and heaving as the children gathered around me. Some watched me confusedly as I sat up red-faced and sweaty, while the others giggled quietly.

Ingrid swallowed a laugh and held her chin high. "Hello, Layla, Fate Slayer."

"Hi," I said, waving a sweaty palm at them. *Some Fate Slayer*, I thought to myself with a silent chuckle. I couldn't even keep up with Nilsen. Sometimes, it was a marvel to me how I had managed to kill the Nidhogg.

"You are here to speak of the Nerdhosh."

I bit my lip to hide my smile. "Nidhogg," I corrected. "What would you like to know?"

Ingrid perched herself next to Nilsen, who lingered near the window. "Tell us about the fight. What did the Nishag look like?"

"Nidhogg," I said again. "It was massive. Big enough to fill up the meeting hall."

Gasps erupted from the group, followed by shouted questions about what its scales looked like, whether it had horns, and whether its teeth could rip through stone. Ingrid, frustrated at the loss of order in the treehouse, stuck two fingers between her teeth and whistled. The noise died almost instantly, and some children even clamped their hands over their ears.

When the treehouse was quiet enough that the sound of rustling leaves outside could be heard, Ingrid gestured for me to continue.

"Its scales were impenetrable. Nothing could cut through its armor," I said, watching the shocked gazes of the children now enraptured in my words.

"How did you kill it then?" Nilsen asked.

Excellent question, Nilsen. It swallowed me, and I grew vines that tore it apart from the inside of its gullet. How was I supposed to say that to a group of children, some of them even as young as five years old?

"We killed it...from the...inside," I said, and knew it was foolish of me to think I could outsmart these kids.

"It *swallowed* you?" Ingrid demanded, losing grip on her steely demeanor, and I caught a glimpse of the child beneath the facade she put up.

"Uh," I stammered, but was interrupted by the shiver that ran through me at the memory of the slime that had clung to my skin. I had been quick to shake away this feeling over the past few weeks, but recounting the fight brought it back anew.

Nilsen stood from the windowsill, shocked. "You went into its stomach?!"

466

"N-No," I managed, hands beginning to shake as I felt the walls of the Nidhogg's throat tighten around me, or maybe it was the walls of the treehouse that were closing in. I didn't know, but the urge to flee was becoming insistent.

There was no way I could think up an appropriate way to say what happened when there was a swell of more questions, begging me for every gruesome and vile detail. And with every second, every demanding question, the air got heavier and began to reek of the Nidhogg's saliva and bile, the reek of Granny's compost bin.

It was just compost, I told myself.

And the roaring sound wasn't the Nidhogg's rattling battle cry, but the sound of the blood rushing in my ears, the children barking their desperate questions.

I slammed my hand over my rune, feigning surprise. "Oh, that's Aaren, he needs me for...leader things."

Nilsen narrowed his eyes as he caught me in my blatant lie. I didn't let him call me out, though, and I flung the trapdoor open to clamber down the trunk. I barely gave the notches time to form before I shoved my feet into them, then slid the last few feet to the ground. The painful bark ate at the skin of my palms, but it brought me back to reality, back to the forest that sang with summer.

I needed a drink, and I needed one now.

Chapter 54

With the borders fully restored and Quirinus's axe still in our possession, life in Skoghjem had lifted a bit. In the mornings, I resumed training with Aaren, and we reviewed the basics, reassessing my form and addressing the techniques that had faded since our last sparring session. We worked on building more strength in my core and upper body to add more power into my swings, and afterwards, we worked on wielding our magic together, finding creative ways to attack the practice dummy and the jordmen that Aaren conjured.

In the afternoons, I helped Inaborg in the pub and, occasionally, Aurora in her fields. I even powered through a couple of hours here and there, helping in Harald's shop, where he had me shelving dusty books and keeping logs of which titles were checked out.

With more instruction, I finished my piece of armor, but before I helped make more, Aaren and Borgil encouraged me to try again. And again. By the third attempt, it was still far from perfect. Aaren helped me with my next try, smoothing out the metal where I accidentally dented it and fixing every other mistake. As the finishing touches were added, the piece was almost pristine. I didn't trust myself to make another one, so I provided other help by keeping the fire blazing, handing them tools, and tanning the leather. After two weeks, Aaren, Borgil, and I had made enough armor to cover a small army, but we continued to work through the evenings to make sure every last Fraalver had something to wear, whether they were going into battle or not.

My nights were spent in the pub with my friends or playing Balderkrig with Nilsen. I had finally become a worthy opponent. Most games were close ties, only sheer luck dictating the winners instead of strategy. Then I would slide into bed next to Aaren, our days ending in nights of passionate lovemaking, exploring, and basking in each other's desires and filling our lustful needs that had so long been ignored.

One night, after a long day of training and helping around the village, I sat down for a drink alone and watched Oswin and Ivar get into it over a card game.

"Want some company?" Ertha asked as she slid onto the barstool next to me.

"Sure," I said, sipping on the honey ale. Inaborg did a wonderful job on this brew—it may have been her best one yet.

Ertha nodded a thanks as Inaborg slid her a mug, and she tapped on the ceramic, eyes darting between me and her cup. Her lips pursed as she sensed my mood. "What's on your mind?" she inquired, taking her first sip.

"Just...trying not to catastrophize at this point," I replied. "We're no closer to finding Markus. Which means we're no closer to finding my brother." I sighed and dropped my head into my hands. "You would think after everything we've done, there would be something we could go off of."

Ertha considered this, then nodded in agreement. "I know the feeling."

"You do?" I asked, trying to keep the bite from my tone.

She scoffed. "You mean the feeling that every second you sit around, the more you fail your people?"

Yeah, she knew the feeling exactly.

"It's a leader thing, Layla. I'd hate to lie to you and tell you that the feeling goes away, because it doesn't." Ertha raised her brows into her mug as she took a sip. "It comes with the territory."

I dropped my head onto the bar and sighed. Being a Fraalver leader was sometimes for the dogs.

"There's something else," Ertha said, and I could feel her eyes watching me as I sat up. "What else is bothering you?"

There was something familiar about the way she asked me—it was the same way Mama could tell I was hiding something from her. Ertha eyed me with the same scrutiny, too, and while my instinct was to shy away, I couldn't help but fall into it because I hadn't seen that look, heard that tone in so very long.

I blinked, about to lose myself to nostalgia, when I stirred myself to answer. "I'm...scared that killing the Nidhogg hasn't helped anything. All it has done is put us at risk of more destruction."

It was a thought I had been having for weeks since the battle, and one that spurred me into a whirlwind of what-ifs and catastrophizing that only a nasty bout of sparring could clear away. Aaren was happy to oblige, and considering the way we beat each other senseless, because he was having the same thoughts.

"But you killed it," Ertha said finally, her face set sternly. "Can you bring it back to life?"

"No."

"Can you go back in time and not kill it?"

"No."

Ertha pressed her lips together and gave me a knowing look. "You made your decision to kill it. Stand by it. Make it the right one." If she had resembled Mama before, she now reminded me of Granny, with her blunt certainty and stern gaze. "Your people look to you for guidance. They don't need someone unsure of herself. It breeds uncertainty, and they can question your authority when left unchecked. Why did you kill the Nidhogg?"

I chewed my lip. "Because Markus had recruited it to fight with him. But the Nidhogg agreed because it thought that Markus and the necromancer were better for the realm, that they would create more balance."

What if the Nidhogg had been right? The Fraalver, though small in number, was a powerful and influential group. What if, in taking down Markus and the necromancer, it unbalanced the scales and wrecked Yggdrasil in other ways? If we as a race remained unchecked, what kind of colossal damage could we cause in the long run? In killing the Nidhogg, Aaren and I took on the responsibility of judgment, a role neither of us was qualified for.

"The Nidhogg was blind to who Markus and the necromancer are. It wanted a unified realm, and it saw that it would get that by siding with them." Ertha turned on her stool to face me fully. "It didn't care what would be sacrificed for the sake of that unified realm. A unified realm could mean wiping out every race except one. There would be balance because there was nothing to challenge them."

Kill the Nidhogg and face unchecked forces that could and would throw off the balance of the realms or lose the very realms themselves. Lose the entire gods damned tree.

"But..."

"No," Ertha said and held out a finger to hush me. "You create balance within the realms without sacrificing what is important. Unification and collaboration. That's what will bring balance, not some moody snake with a taste for roots. It is up to you, Layla, and to us, to make sure that happens." She drained the rest of her ale and pushed it forward for a refill. "Do you hear me, girl?"

I knocked the rest of my ale back and sat up straight. "I hear you, Ertha."

Chapter 55

Aaren's calluses bit into my hips as I straddled him, matching his rhythm as he pumped inside me. I threw my head back and moaned as wondrous pleasure soaked my veins. His palm slapped against the meaty flesh of my bottom, a simpering pain tingling pleasurably across my skin as his pleasure thundered in his chest.

"You sing so pretty for me, *fremmed*," he gasped, ecstasy edging his irises.

His biting voice broke in my ears as my walls contracted around him. Pleasure blinded me.

Aaren grunted, and his fingers felt like they had melted into my skin as he thrusted into me harder. His eyes fluttered shut, mouth parting blissfully as he spilled into me with a groan.

Aaren's soft, relieved sigh fluttered through my ears and caressed the roughest parts of my mind. He eased my head as much as he did my body. I bent over and grazed a loving kiss across his lips before moving off of him, reveling at the beautiful sigh that escaped him.

He rolled over and wrapped me in his embrace, his fortified muscles encasing me in security. I hummed and closed my eyes as his rhythmic breathing began to lull me to sleep.

"What do you think about taking a scout run back to Fjellhjem?" Aaren droned as sleep blanketed his voice.

I rolled in his arms, and my nose brushed his. A soft chuckle rumbled in his chest as he pulled back to level me with an assessing look. "Go back to Fjellhjem?"

Aaren adjusted his head on the pillow, tucking a stray hair behind my ear. "We're out of leads, *fremmed*. The best thing we can do is look for him in the last place we know he was."

He propped his head up with a hand. I couldn't help but admire the cut of his shoulder that led into the dip of his collarbone. My hunger for him was insatiable. I just had him, yet I wanted him again. He seemed to share that sentiment, seeing as he had taken me three times just that day. I had never known pleasure like what Aaren showed me, and it was addictive.

"As right as you might be, I would rather endure a week at Klartvan Lake with Ymer than travel back to Fjellhjem."

Aaren chuckled. "No, I'd take the horrors of Karridal over a day with Ymer any day."

Shortly after, I fell into a dreamless sleep, content to stay nuzzled into Aaren's smooth chest. I breathed in his scent, let it fill my nostrils, and swirl in my head. That familiar scent I had been trying to place since the moment I met him. Leather and forest, two complementary scents that struck a chord of nostalgia in me.

Leather. Granny had a leather couch that I would curl up on and watch movies with her. It was on that couch where I saw Mama crying into Granny's lap after Dallas left her. When she found out she was pregnant with Lucas. But it wasn't Dallas. It was Markus.

It was all part of his twisted scheme.

Granny stroked Mama's hair, muttering kind words that I now knew were promises that weren't going to be kept. Promises that Granny had no right to give. Because they'd both be dead within two years of that night. Promises I had to let go of when our caseworker brought me to Granny's house that last time. And while files were being sifted through and belongings were being hauled out, I curled up on that leather couch, breathed it in deep, and committed it to memory.

Aaren smelled like that couch. And his forest. *Our* forest.

The forest scent that gave me so much comfort when Lucas and I would go to that shack when things got rough. That little haven, covered in moss and leaves and filled with the same forested scent that clung to my husband.

He smelled like home. *My* home.

I curled in closer to him, earning me a sleepy groan when he pulled me flush against his chest.

The bedroom door opened, followed by small, frantic footsteps to Aaren's side of the bed. Cracking my eyes open, there was a flash of his white hair, identical to Aaren's, and a stuffed ratato tucked under the arm of the small shadow. The dying embers in the hearth cast just enough light to see Nilsen and the quiet tears streaming down his face.

"Aaren, wake up," Nilsen's strained voice squeaked as he started to shake his brother. "Please, please, wake up."

I was the first to sit up and reach across the bed to wipe a tear from his cheek. My whispered words of assurance stirred Aaren, who rolled over and croaked, "What's wrong, *bror*?"

Nilsen let out a pained sob. "I couldn't breathe. I couldn't breathe." He wiped his nose, throwing himself into Aaren's arms. "I saw mountains and dead people and huldras. And I couldn't breathe!"

Nilsen tucked himself into Aaren's bare chest and shook with frantic sobs. Aaren stroked his hair, turning a concerned look to me, but I could only blink away the sleep and silently ruminate over his words.

Mountains, dead people. Huldras. All things that shared a commonality.

Markus.

It didn't tell us anything we didn't already know, but there was something off about it all.

I suggested that Aaren should sleep with Nilsen for the rest of the night, and he agreed. His sleep-addled face was cut with concern as he threw back the covers, scooped Nilsen into his arms, and brought him back to bed.

Exhaustion quickly took over before I could ponder anything more, and I fell onto the pillows, sleep overtaking me almost immediately.

Moments later, I knew what Nilsen meant by he couldn't breathe.

That familiar, crippling weight slammed into my chest as the mare dropped onto me. Beady orange eyes shimmered in the darkness, but I wouldn't let myself panic as I struggled to breathe. I opened my mouth to struggle through a question, but the mare shushed with a cold hand that muffled my words.

"Discretion, Fate Slayer, or I won't tell you what I have to say."

The discomforting shiver the beady eyes sent through me did nothing to dull my curiosity, and I stilled, breathing harshly through my nostrils.

"A pleasure to see you again, Layla Sviker," the mare greeted like an old friend, one that may or may not want to kill me.

It removed its hand from my mouth with a quiet hiss. "Where is Lucas?" I gasped. It may have moved its hands from my mouth, but its weight was still just as crushing as it was the first time.

"The boy lives with him, tucked close to his side." The orange eyes blinked. "But I am not here about the boy, but the water."

I narrowed my eyes, trying to discern the mare's shape in the darkness. The embers had died completely, and shadows blanketed the room. "The wa...the water?"

"Like the water it dwelled in, it opened its mouth and out flowed the truth, right into your betrayed blood's ears." It rasped a rattling laugh, vibrating on my chest. I gulped another breath of air. "And now he moves for the sea."

An icy cold hand, or maybe a paw, scratched at my forehead, holding tight as I wrinkled my brow. Then the fiery eyes faded, and colored light splashed into the room.

Every inch of darkness washed away as sprawling cliffs tumbled before me, and a roaring sea lapped at the roots of the bluffs. I took a moment to sigh as the breath returned to my lungs, and the salty air sent life back into me. Wind whipped my hair, and I gazed out to the horizon as storm clouds churned and brewed thunder. Lightning struck in the distance. I was on the cliffs of Kysthjem.

There was a shout, and I turned, the one scream turning into a chorus of shrieks of fright and panic. A frenzy of chaos confronted me as I pounded closer to the noises. Crashes and bangs mingled with horrified cries and a sickening laughter echoed throughout the village in front of me. I dashed forward, sprinting to the collapsing buildings, dodging fresh debris and mangled pathways. So much progress, all of their rebuilding, crumbling in front of them once more. It was enough to break any spirit. Fraalver pushed past me, or rather, they moved through me like a knife through softened butter.

I wasn't really here; it was just a vision.

A deafening blast sounded, followed by frantic screams and pleas for help. I tracked the sounds and came to the open square in the center of the village, which was now in ruins from the thundering blast. The meeting hall doors hung by their hinges, and a draugr filled the entrance with the cuff of Fiske's shirt clenched in its rotting fingers. I gasped as the draugr shook Fiske's collar and began to turn purple, the tighter the fabric cut into his windpipe. His thrashing did nothing to ease the draugr's hold, and it let out a rattling, dead cackle as it surveyed the destruction that ripped across the reviving village.

There was a sound so damning, it ripped my eyes away from Fiske and the draugr for the briefest moment. On the other side of the square, Helgi wailed and called her husband's name, rearing back like a bull about to charge.

The draugr, with lips rotted away in a permanent, deadly sneer, laughed again. Then snapped its fingers. Before Helgi could so much as think to take another step, it disappeared, taking Fiske with it. Helgi dropped to her knees, tears streaming down her dirt-clouded face as her village crumbled around her.

The vision didn't so much fade as it popped like a bubble in my mind, and released me back into darkness. The weightlessness in my chest told me that the mare was gone, and so was Fiske.

The cold wood met the soles of my feet as I kicked back the covers and scrambled for the door. As I wrenched Nilsen's bedroom door open, I wished I could take a moment to admire the two sleeping brothers, both with the same dreamy look on their faces, but Fiske had been taken, and Kysthjem was once again in ruins.

"Aaren," I whispered frantically. "Aaren, wake up."

His brow furrowed when his eyes fluttered open to see me before him, in the same state Nilsen had been in just minutes ago.

"It's Fiske," I managed to whimper. "He has Fiske."

Chapter 56

"Fuck," Rorik cursed as he rubbed his wearied eyes. I noted the grime that caked underneath his fingernails, remembering the clean, groomed man I had met when I arrived. "I suppose we got what we wanted, though. We now know his next move."

I paced the medicine hut as we waited for the others to respond to the summons we had sent out. Aaren had Nilsen tucked close to his side. Ertha had arrived within minutes and took up a spot in the chair by the fire in shock. Oswin and Ivar arrived shortly after, followed by Stieg and Thea, then Von and Axl. The medicine hut was grim; not even the cheerful crackle of the fire could break the heavy silence that weighed on the shoulders of the occupants.

My stomach swirled, and nausea pooled into my gut. Unsure whether it was the experimental meat Inaborg had served tonight at the pub or the undeniable dread that was permeating every cell of my being, I sank lower in my chair and tried to hide the hand I placed carefully over my abdomen. It couldn't have been the meat—I had thrown up twice this morning, too. I was thankful my retching didn't wake up Aaren, but the sour taste that coated my tongue followed me late into the morning. I would have pondered the source of my sickness further, but Aaren awoke with a need to bury his face between my legs, and I forgot all about my nausea.

Unfortunately for me, it was back and ready to tear my guts apart.

"Nilsen, what did the mare show you?" I asked, trying to keep the shake out of my voice.

Nilsen rubbed a balled fist over his eyes. "I saw mountains...and a river, a big rushing river."

The tension in the room grew, tightening in my chest like a constricting snake. There was no sound except for the fire in the hearth, and even the flames were receding into a frightened silence.

"Did you see the inside of the mountain?" I probed.

Nilsen nodded. "Yes." His eyes went distant as he recalled the memory. "It was a cavern. There were pillars of rock and carvings in the ceiling."

"Did you see what one of the carvings was?" Ertha asked, having stood up without me realizing.

Nilsen's eyebrows knit together as he tried to recall. "There was a carving of a man in a chariot..."

Ertha gave a choked gasp, and her hands flew to her mouth. "No," she whimpered through her clasped fingers.

My heart stuttered in my chest because I knew exactly what this meant.

"He's in our mountain," Ertha muttered. "Markus is in Fjellhjem."

Time seemed to stop, but not for Aaren.

"Oswin, Ivar, ready the horses," he barked as he led Nilsen out of the medicine hut. "Axl and Von, round up as many able bodies as you can." As we passed the blacksmith forge, he instructed Borgil to distribute the armor we had made over the last few weeks.

It was all happening. Everything we had waited for and prepared for was actually happening. I didn't think any of us would actually need the armor I had spent hours watching Aaren and Borgil craft. That day seemed too far away to me then, and I had been clinging to that tiny kernel of hope that it would never come. I hope that Lucas would come back to me without having to fight Markus, and I hope that my father would crawl back into his tomb without another sound and stay there. Wishful thinking when there was a necromancer behind it all.

I hurried to keep up as Aaren swept Nilsen onto his hip and carried him to the house. Neither brother uttered a word to me before Aaren tucked Nilsen back into bed, and I lingered near the fire because I was unsure what else to do. Aaren brought more silence with him when he returned, choosing to pace by the hearth instead of speaking. I sat down at the dining table and reached for an apple I had no intention of eating.

"It's finally happening," I muttered, and Aaren paused his pacing to kneel in front of me. "After all the searching, all the fighting. After everything..."

"That's right, *fremmed*," Aaren said as he reached for my hand and slid his thumb over my knuckles. "We're going to bring Lucas home."

Most of the village had woken up to Aaren's barking orders, and the preparations for the sudden journey were finished in an hour.

"Promise me you won't get yourself killed?" Thea prodded before wrapping me in a tight hug. "I don't need my best friend impaled on a spike before I can finish my book on her."

477

I pulled away. "You're writing a book about me?"

Thea's eyes shot to the wooden slats above and bobbed her head consideringly, then shrugged. "More like a sexy retelling of your love story." I raised my brows, frowning to hide my smile. "What? I was running out of stuff to write about! Don't give me that look!"

I squeezed her hand. "I promise I will be back to read every word."

Thea smiled, though it didn't reach her eyes, and concern lingered at the edges of her features. There was no lying to her; I wasn't sure if I *would* make it back. But these feelings accompanied every journey out of the village, feelings that I had hoped I could slowly grow accustomed to. Instead, the thought bubbled in my stomach, along with the hasty breakfast I had inhaled before leaving the house.

"Please be safe," Thea said, and tried for her normal playful smirk, but the underlying plea in her tone didn't escape me. Her evident worry was what told me I wasn't the only one who felt like this journey would be different from the others, for more reasons than the obvious ones. My stomach somersaulted.

I pressed my lips together, knowing that if I opened my mouth, only a choked cry would come out.

I didn't bother fighting the heavy sense of foreboding twining through my body as I left her bookshop. It was undeniable, and the more I tried to tolerate it, the more an uneasy feeling opened up in my chest. It yawned wide, then crawled into my throat. And there was my breakfast. I bent over and threw up along the side of the path, praying none of the Fraalver milling about decided to turn down this way. My body wracked with every violent retch, and I was sure by now I was going to throw up my liver if I kept heaving.

"Are you okay, *frue*?" a voice asked, then a hand brushed on my back while another moved my braid out of the way.

Spitting bile onto the ground, I straightened and wiped my mouth. Rorik stood behind me, his features already darkened with worry.

"I'm fine," I answered. "Just...stressed. I have a bad feeling about the journey. Something feels different from the times before."

Rorik nodded. "Nerves," he said. "Understandable. You've been through a lot these past few months." He gestured down the path. "I can give you something for the anxiety if you'd like."

I agreed and let him lead me the short way to the medicine hut. Rorik set to work browsing the shelves and cabinets, plucking jars and bundles of herbs, and placing them on the table. He dropped a couple of pinches of dried leaves into the mortar, then drizzled a bit of lilac liquid, and crushed it with the pestle. After adding a couple of additional ingredients and stirring them together, he poured the mixture into a small cup and passed it to me.

"I'll put the rest in a bottle for you to take with you," he informed as he turned away from me.

I knocked back the brew like a shot, and coolness spread through my middle as it took effect. For the first time in what felt like days, I wasn't nauseous. It seemed I had forgotten how nice a calm stomach felt.

"Thank you," I said, reaching for the bottle he handed me and pocketing it. "I already feel much better."

Rorik smiled politely. "Layla, may I ask a favor?"

"Anything," I answered.

"Might I obtain a small sample of your blood? I have a...hunch, and I would like to inquire about it further, but I would need a small bit of your blood to proceed. Just a few drops, I assure you."

I frowned. "Is there something I need to be worried about?" I asked, and the incredible feeling began to take hold as a hot intrigue slithered in. Such an odd request set my nerves on end despite the swirling peace in my gut.

Rorik shook his head and waved the worry aside. "No, no, I just had an idea on the borders. I was thinking of experimenting with a bit of blood magic. Not unheard of, but a bit rare when it comes to protection spells. Just a drop will do."

Still hesitant, I offered my palm to him. Reluctance only intensified as he pulled out a small paring knife, and I almost ripped my hand away as he pricked my finger, then squeezed. Three beads of blood trickled into the vial Rorik held underneath my hand, the *drip, drip* sound exaggerated by the weighted silence between the physician and me.

"Thank you, *true*," he said as he corked the vial. "This will do quite nicely."

He helped me bandage my hand and followed me through the door.

Chapter 57

We headed to the coast first, a decision made at Rorik's urging. He insisted that, despite the accuracy of the mare previously, we had no way of knowing if it was a trick. Things could've changed between now and the last time the mare came, he had said. For all we knew, Markus could have recruited the mare folk and sent one here to lead us astray and knock us off his path.

Our company was far larger than it had been before, numbering nearly three hundred Fraalver, Skoghjem, and Fjellhjem folk combined. Ertha rode by my side the majority of the journey, but there was something about her that sent caution through my mind. There was something behind her eyes that hardened her perfect features, a deadliness that sent a strike of fear through me when I first glimpsed it this morning. There was cruel, unspeakable rage lingering under her skin, an anger that could rattle the earth with one misplaced look. Ertha was going to explode soon, and I looked forward to when she did.

There were no breaks on our way to the coast, and we rode throughout the night and day, desperately trying to ignore the wearied exhaustion that plagued all of us. I took a few swallows of Rorik's brew throughout the ride to keep the queasiness at bay. As the sea came into view by sunset on the second day, I nearly collapsed in relief on Froki.

My relief was short-lived, and Rorik's tonic did nothing to stop the frenzied panic that flooded my system.

The scene before me was gut-wrenching. Nothing could have prepared me for the destruction I saw, not even the myling attack from a few months ago. That attack was merely a scratch compared to the havoc that now spread across the coastal plains. Not a single building survived, save for the meeting hall in the center of what was once the square. Every building was in smoldering ruins. Plumes of smoke billowed from the piles of rubble, and my boots crunched over the soot-crusted grass after dismounting. The destruction of the already fragile village hammered a rusty nail into my heart, and despair seeped in like poison to a wound. I was eager to escape the crippling havoc that had wrecked Kysthjem, so I dismounted Froki and began to follow the path on the outskirts of the village. I couldn't escape it; however, the disastrous reality confronted me at every turn as I wound over the battered trail and stepped over fallen beams and shattered windows.

The air was thick with smoke that created a heavy haze around us, and I took shallow breaths as I moved. Something large and dark lay on the path in front of me, and I tripped over it before I could stop myself. Gravel carved through my palms when I caught myself. Aaren halted behind me, gaze frozen on the form on the ground. I recovered and wiped my hands on my pants, wincing at the stinging as the pebbles fell away from my cuts. Aaren crouched over me and rolled the thing over, a frightened gasp rolling off my tongue.

It was Isak. He was dead.

My face fell as I took in his unseeing eyes, akin to his brother's those weeks ago. Blood caked his temple that matched the crimson on his shirt, and I clamped my hands over my mouth to muffle the rising scream in my throat. Another friend lost at the hands of my father. Another Fraalver I couldn't save.

We needed to burn him soon—he needed to see his brother again.

I backed away as fear, anger, and despair roiled inside me. How many more had suffered this fate?

I met Aaren's eyes and knew he was asking himself the same question.

I waved a hand over Isak's face to close his eyes before stepping away quickly. The sight of Isak, dead in front of me, was the spark that spawned a wildfire of rage through me. Another few steps, and we encountered several more bodies, all carved up with multiple stab wounds and gashes, each with the same empty eyes. One man's mouth had opened into a silent scream, permanently freezing his features in fright. I turned away because I was unable to look at any more bodies.

A relieved sigh slithered across my tongue when we made it to the square, and there were no bodies to be seen. The meeting hall, surprisingly, stood firm, though the wood had massive scorch marks along the sides and entrance. How the building wasn't engulfed in flames was beyond me, though I suspected a hefty dose of Fraalver magic had been at play.

I hadn't taken another step into the square before the door to the meeting hall burst open, and Helgi pounded down the steps with her arms spread wide. Streams of tears flew down her face as she came closer. I embraced her, only to feel the violent shake of her form as she sobbed into my shoulder. Tears stung my own eyes.

"They took him," Helgi wept into my shoulder, which was now soaked with her despair. "They took my Fiske."

481

"I know," I said. "We're going to get him back." As I said, I sent a silent prayer that I was right.

Over her shoulder, I saw a cluster of Fraalver in the meeting hall, all huddled tightly and watching from within. Markus had dwindled their numbers, just as he did with Ertha's people. He was knocking us off, one by one.

Axl and Von helped erect the tents throughout the square and beyond while Oswin and Ivar concocted a stew large enough to feed our people and Helgi's. Aaren secured the perimeter and stationed a watchman every few feet, establishing a rotation of every three hours.

Helgi hadn't left the far window that overlooked the cliff and the sea beyond, her glassy eyes reflecting the crashing waves and milky foam. Ertha and I sat with her in silence, unsure what else to do but hold space.

"I'm so sorry to hear about Torsten, my dear Ertha," Helgi finally said after what felt like an hour had passed. "Your strength is ever enduring with the amount of loss you have faced."

Ertha extended her hand to Helgi's and gave it a reassuring squeeze. "He rests with Solveig now," she said, and smiled when her touch was what could pull Helgi's eyes away from the window. There was something about the way the two women held each other's gaze, a look of silent solidarity that I was in no position to share. Whatever history they shared aside, they had both lost their husbands to some capacity and were left to lead their people—or what was left of them—on their own. I wanted to share in that solidarity, but it wouldn't be right. I had Aaren still, and the entirety of my village was still alive and breathing. So I sat back and kept my gaze on the floorboards at my feet.

"Do you think you can tell us what happened?" Ertha asked, and Helgi sighed.

"They came out of nowhere," she began in a teary voice, pausing as her lip began to quiver. "We were so prepared after the mylings, and so careful. The borders were more fortified than ever." She quickly explained that Isak had been dabbling in a few spells that would strengthen the borders and the loopholes they were finding in the magic. Similar to what Rorik had told me he was working on before we left.

"But they came from underground," she muttered, and her voice now shook with anger. "Our borders weren't fortified under the earth, and they used that to their advantage." And they weren't prepared because Kysthjem's borders would not need to be fortified underground. Each Fraalver village's borders are designed to protect against its specific environmental dangers. Fjellhjem would need underground border protection because it faces enemies like the burrowers, but not Kysthjem, which is precisely why the burrowers worked alongside the draugr in this attack. Helgi said they started in the sea cave in the cliffs below and dug underneath the village.

If the draugr were able to take down the Kysthjem borders, they could take down Skoghjem's. And neither I nor Aaren were there to stop it.

"They tore down everyone in their path," Helgi continued. "Leif, Marsy, Freida..." Her voice tightened. "Isak."

This time, I did grab her hand, holding it tightly as she lost her battle and let her tears flow freely.

The waves at the base of the cliff flooded my mind, probing me as if to ask if it could come in. I hadn't realized how angry I was getting until the water demanded an invitation, but I pushed its energy away and tried to calm down.

How much more devastation did Markus have to bring before I could take him down? Dagan first, then Kysthjem and Torsten, then Kysthjem again. Isak. And Fiske.

Oh gods, Fiske.

What kind of unspeakable horrors was Fiske enduring at this very moment? If he was even alive to endure them...

The water probed me again, this time more insistently, demanding an answer.

Unsure how long I could deny it, I bid the women farewell and hurried onto the beach.

The sun was starting to sink low in the sky when Aaren came to find me on the beach where I was wading in the shallows and letting the waves swirl through my veins. My feet had sunk deep into the sand, dwarfing me compared to Aaren as he approached.

"There you are, *fremmed*," he said as he rolled up his pants legs and stepped into the water. "There should be some stew left for you. Are you hungry?"

My chest warmed at the question despite the incredible energy that was working to tame the heat in my fingertips.

"I'm alright," I said as I dipped my fingers into the water.

When I didn't say anything more, Aaren asked, "Everything okay, *fremmed?*"

I faced him, but it only put me eye level with his lower chest. Aaren grabbed me by the underarms and hauled me from the sand, then placed me gently back in the water. I stood a little taller now.

"Did Helgi tell you that the burrowers helped dig underneath the borders?"

Aaren pressed his lips together and nodded grimly.

"Should one of us go back to Skoghjem in case Markus decides to strike while we're away?" I asked.

"No," Aaren replied sternly. "I'm not letting you face your father alone. The burrowers won't be able to dig underneath Skoghjem. There are too many roots. Besides," he brushed a knuckle along my cheekbone, "Rorik wove enchantments between the tree roots as an extra safeguard. We needed it after Nils and Freya died."

"But Aaren—"

"I said no, Layla. The day that I am not there to fight by your side is the day my heart stops beating." He laced his fingers with mine. "I'm going with you to Fjellhjem. Not just for my village, but for everything he has put you and your brother through."

I craned my neck to gaze into his face, the ferocity and passion that etched his features. There was no doubt in my mind that Aaren would rip the realm apart for me. It felt foolish of me to think he would ever concede to going home while I faced my biggest demon.

Aaren stooped and kissed me lightly, and the water's energy receded as if it was trying to give us privacy. I was thankful for its retreat, and I invited the warm flush that snaked through my body. I opened my mouth and gave him silent permission to deepen the kiss when there was a slight sound from the top of the cliffs. Our lips parted, and I squinted for a better look.

Oswin stood at the edge, waving his arms frantically as the waves drowned out his shouts.

Aaren and I hurried from the water and darted across the beach, cursing the squishy sand that impeded our speed. My pulse throbbed through my neck as we ascended the steep path, and my legs screamed fiercely when I dropped to the ground at the top.

"They brought an army," Oswin shouted like we weren't standing right in front of him.

"Who?" Aaren demanded, but we both knew the answer already.

Oswin swallowed grimly, and my heart bottomed out in my stomach. Aaren pushed past him, his strides carrying him in a sweep of power that sent the air into a static frenzy.

"Prepare for a battle," he said to Oswin over his shoulder. "Have Helgi hide her people who are unable to fight, gear up the rest. If this army is big, we're going to need all the help we can get."

Nearly tripping over myself to keep up, I followed Aaren into the village and through the panicked Kysthjem Fraalver who were fleeing for the beach. He veered around a corner, then another, and my mouth went dry when we emerged at the edge of the village.

Axl stood watch a few feet away, knuckles white around his sword as he watched the army at the crest of the hill. A spread of rigid draugr lined the horizon, awaiting the order to attack. Burning acid rose in my throat as I scanned the lineup and noted the different stages of decay each draugr was in. Some were more decomposed than others, and they looked as if any movement would disintegrate them. That would help, but it wouldn't be enough, especially when most of them wielded fresh blades, upgrades from the rusty weapons the ones in Fjellgrav had.

"How many are there?" I asked.

His face was pale. "At least five hundred," he answered, and my heart sank deeper until my nausea returned to full force. "All dead followers of Markus."

I swore under my breath and wrangled my nerves as they frayed out of control. I took a swig of the potion Rorik made me. Five hundred against our three hundred prepared soldiers, and whatever number of Kysthjem Fraalver that volunteered to fight. Manageable, but that wasn't accounting for whatever surprises that army could have in store for us. For all we knew, Markus could be in that very crowd. The thought lit my senses, and an angry flash of anticipation struck me.

We shouldn't have come here. We should've gone straight to the mountains, just our small group, so none of my people would have to face this slaughter.

Ertha's words rang in my mind, and they gave me a reprieve from the stiff dead awaiting us atop the hill. Maybe we shouldn't have come here first, but if we weren't here, Kysthjem might have been wiped off the map. We were going to lose a lot of people, but it was better than losing Helgi and the innocents who were now fleeing to the sea cave.

Aaren's magic stroked mine through the rune, the caress so similar to the way he held me at night as we drifted off to sleep.

"They could strike at any moment," Axl said.

"Let them," Aaren growled, jaw ticking with a brewing, unbridled anger. "I've been itching for a fight for a while now."

Chapter 58

The pile of bodies towering before me was far bigger than it was the last time Kysthjem had a funeral. With the draugr army lingering on the edge of the village, and no guarantee any of us would survive to burn our dead from the burrower attack, we hurried to gather the bodies and set them ablaze.

Except for the Fraalver that stood guard and watched the waiting enemy, the rest of us gathered in the square in worried silence. I scanned the faces of the dead, naming each of them that I knew, remembering the faces of the ones that I didn't. At the very top was Isak, eyes now closed, black hair matted to his forehead. I wished we could have prepared the bodies before rounding them up and making them more presentable for their last minutes in this realm.

Helgi approached the pile, one hand woven with Ertha's, and the other gripped a lit torch. My throat tightened when I saw the sorrowful lines etched into her features, the deep shadows circling her eyes that the torch only made darker. She met my gaze, then gave the slightest of nods, a silent command for me to join her and Ertha. I took a hesitant step forward, then Aaren entwined our fingers together.

The heat of the torch in Helgi's hand fanned across my face when we joined her side. And together, the four of us stood in front of our people—the only remaining leaders of the Fraalver. I prayed there would be five of us when this was all over.

"It may seem like the end," Helgi said in a voice that made me question the grief that weighed her shoulders. It was steady, strong, and commanded the crowd like the wind through sails. "It may seem like we have lost everything, but we haven't." Her knuckles cracked as her grip tightened around the torch. "But until the waves stop crashing, the trees stop growing," she glanced at Ertha, "or the mountains stop rumbling, this isn't over.

"Markus Sviker may destroy our homes, try to kill our spirit, steal away our loved ones..."

Helgi swallowed angrily, and her brow scrunched with fury.

487

"But he will never take away who we are at heart. We are persevering. We are strong. We are the sea and the trees and the mountains.

"We are the Fraalver."

She thrust the torch high into the air. "Say their names."

A man who stood a head taller than the others said, "Ari."

"Evin," another voice said from within the crowd, followed by "Raynor," "Annika," and "Karsten."

Fraalver voices rose and melded together, playing a symphony of grief and memories of their dead. I yelled Isak's name into the echoes, then followed it with Dagan, Torsten, Finn, Agda, and every other myling name I could remember. And as the voices shouted and wailed, one name was the clearest of all.

"Fiske Sjøbrytt!"

Once one shouted it, everyone did, until the chanting in the square was the name of the stolen leader, the Fish King.

"Fiske! Fiske! Fiske!"

Helgi's torch blazed. "To Himmelfjell!"

Then she set fire to the bodies.

There was no time to lose. Once the bodies finished burning, we all set to work.

I helped Helgi set up an infirmary in the meeting hall while Aaren distributed weapons and armor to the willing Fraalver fighters.

The Fraalver choosing to fight were equipped with the weapons and small pieces of armor we had made in Skoghjem. There wasn't enough for everyone to have a full set of armor, so we split the pieces amongst them, some wearing shin guards and breastplates while others donned bracers and helmets.

Aaren had donned thick metal bracers and an iron breastplate that hugged his chest in every way it should. I took what little time I had to admire the way it fitted him. He was the picture of deadly grace, a soldier of death ready for the reaping. My knees grew weak at the sight.

I, on the other hand, couldn't help but tremble as I suited up, strapping the breastplate Aaren and I had made to my chest and breathing as deeply as I could.

The straps cut into my skin, and I squirmed to adjust, but it was no use. I went to blame the armor for my discomfort, but it had been tailored almost perfectly to me by the very hands that strapped it to my chest. The armor wasn't the reason for my discomfort, but admitting it to be anything else was a weakness I didn't want Aaren to see.

As if reading my thoughts, Aaren said, "Do not be afraid."

"I'm not afraid," I said, hoping for the briefest moment that I would believe it.

"You know you can't lie to me, *fremmed.*"

I sighed as Aaren finished buckling a bracer around my forearm, the armor protecting the very thing that made it so impossible to lie.

"You're right," Aaren said, grudgingly. "You're not afraid. How could you be when you have faced so much worse than what is on that hill?"

"What're you getting at?" I asked snarkily as the fear got the better of my nerves.

Aaren shrugged and began working on my other hand. "You've fought a trehag, a hagua, an army of draugr far more deadly than those out there. Burrowers, for Aesir's sake, Layla, you killed the fucking Nidhogg." He finished buckling and placed my hand on his breastplate, right over the spot where his heart was. I cursed the metal, wishing so fervently that I could feel the beating underneath.

"What I'm trying to say is that the army out there is nothing compared to the battles you have already won. There is nothing out there that is worthy of challenging you with the strength you bear. The magic that lives in your blood."

"My blood is the reason we're in this mess," I said dejectedly.

Aaren shook his head. "I'm not talking about the blood Markus gave you. I mean the blood that came from your mother. Markus may have given you magic, but your mother showed you how to handle it. What to do with it. It's the reason why it hasn't corrupted you like it has your father."

He placed his hands on either side of my face. "Now, I'll ask you again, Layla Sviker. Are you ready?"

With only a small bit of trepidation swirling in my chest now, I nodded with a mostly restored confidence. Aaren placed a kiss on the top of my head. "Good girl. Let's get to the battlefield.

Chapter 59

Aaren and I stood side by side at the base of the hill with our army crowded behind us. I shifted my weight from heel to heel as Quirinus's axe pressed tightly against my back. I was far enough away from the water that it didn't rise to meet my magic, but there was still a buzzing that didn't emanate from the axe or Aaren. It was the earth under my feet, waking up and stirring to nudge my power. This energy was different from the others I had felt before. It was unhoned, raw, and it rubbed against my senses like a cat's tongue against my skin. Unlike the wild, untamed magic of the water, the earthen energy was pensively ferocious, as if biding its time and waiting to strike like an angry snake.

I nudged the energy through the rune, and Aaren tensed next to me as it crept into his body. The air became alive with power as we shared our magic, electricity crackling in the air as if a thunderstorm was brewing in this very spot. The hair on my arms stood on end, and I shivered as it filled me almost to capacity.

Ertha and Helgi gathered on either side of us.

"He won't get away with this," Helgi spat at the draugr lining the hill.

The ringing power around us intensified when Ertha clenched her fist, and the earth rumbled softly. "Let's send him back to Hel."

The two women exchanged devious smirks. "It's good to fight with you again, *frue*," Helgi said to Ertha. "Let's make it the last time."

"Enough with pleasantries," Aaren grumbled. "Let's go fuck up some draugr."

Ertha grinned. "With pleasure."

Then the ground rumbled again, louder this time, and the waves in the distance roared. Wind gathered amongst our army, smelling of leather and rain-kissed leaves.

"Ivar, on the mark!" Aaren barked.

"Archers!" Ivar commanded, and there was a scraping of wood as arrows were notched in their bows. "Aim!"

This was it. After those arrows were fired, there was no turning back. We had seconds to change our minds. To turn away and figure out another way to take down the army. But every second spent standing idly by was more wasted time. I couldn't take any longer to find Lucas.

"Fire!"

Arrows whistled through the air in a deadly arc, almost every single one of them meeting their mark. The first line of draugr collapsed, but the next one stepped forward to take their place. Ivar commanded another attack of arrows that yielded the same result, but this time, a large draugr that stood in the center line barked a guttural command, and the undead army marched forward.

A synchronized battle cry exploded behind me, male and female voices clashing together in a roar like no other.

"Forward!" Aaren bellowed.

The hill's incline was slow and gave us enough time to gain speed before clashing with the draugr, but it hid the rest of the army.

The ground shook, and the waves crashed, and the forest-scented wind blew, and all I could feel was the rising heat in my fingertips and the buzzing axe strapped to my back. The draugr had barely made it a quarter of the way down the hill when the four of us stopped, and time seemed to still. I was so filled with power that it made my skin crawl, my teeth rattle, and my heart skip, as if I had taken a volt of electricity to the heart.

"Let go, *fremmed*," Aaren urged as we pushed forward, drawing closer and closer to the dead.

But I couldn't. There was something in me holding onto the magic.

"For Fiske!" Helgi shouted, and the waves were almost deafening now.

"For Torsten!" Ertha echoed, and the ground shook so fiercely that the charging draugr stumbled.

"Let go, Layla!" Aaren yelled, and there was a moment where everything went wholly still and silent.

"For Lucas," I whispered, and then unleashed.

Fire and wind and vines and rock flew up the hill and mowed down every draugr we could see. Waves of energy burst from us as we led our people into battle, and I drew the axe. It sang with power, and a vicious grin spread across my lips as we crested the hill.

Helgi peeled away and began her retreat to the infirmary, leaving Ertha, Aaren, and me to lead the attack.

My magic-fueled high diminished when I saw what was waiting for us on the battlefield.

It wasn't a draugr army numbering five hundred. It numbered two thousand. We just happened to pick off five hundred of them with our initial attack—over a thousand draugr to our three hundred fifty barely armored Fraalver.

The first strikes of my axe slid effortlessly through the draugr, and we cleared the front row in a matter of minutes. The archers dispersed to the edges of the battle, attacking with a barrage of arrows and sending draugr to their knees to be knocked over and trampled. I let out a warcry, and my voice carried through the chorus of clashing weapons and shouts of victory and defeat. A rallying cry met mine, and the following line of draugr were flattened.

Despite my successful attacks, dread weighed my movements, and I became sloppy, slicing through draugr with an abandon similar to a child with a wooden sword. I sustained a couple of nicks and bruises, but nothing substantial enough to excuse my lack of strategy. If it weren't for the earth thrumming power into me, I would burn out quickly.

Aaren moved flawlessly beside me, slicing through one draugr, then two, spearing them on the end of his sword before shaking them off and stomping on them. I almost gagged when I saw their brains crushed to mush under the cracked skulls, but I turned away in time to see a draugr charge me with its spear raised to impale. I ducked, and the axe sang as it caught the draugr's legs, where it cut cleanly through them. The draugr paused, and surprise cleared its murky, dead eyes, before it toppled to the ground. Aaren did me the favor of stomping on its head.

The battle roared across the plains like a gale of death, but it wasn't the sound that tried to derail my concentration. It was the smell. Every single draugr was decomposed to some degree, and the smell was evident. It was what I expected a mass grave to smell like—rot mated with the sweet smell of wet earth. It was a smell I would carry with me for the rest of my days, but I feared those wouldn't be much longer.

We were fighting well, but not for the numbers we were facing.

Axl moved to my right, hacking and slashing as Oswin came to Aaren's left. We were a line of deadly precision that tore down the draugr with an ease that was waning, but enough to get the majority of our army over the hill.

"Look out!" a frenzied voice called, and I turned on my heel in time to see a shortsword-wielding draugr advance, jumping just in time to miss its swing. In an instant, an obsidian-encrusted knife embedded itself in the draugr's forehead, the milky white leaching from its dead eyes. I turned for a microsecond and caught a glimpse of Von as he tossed a dagger in his hand and readied to strike again. He nodded briefly, then turned and sliced into the abdomen of another assailing draugr.

"Keep moving!" Aaren shouted from a few feet away. His preternatural coolness smothered my panic at the numbers, and I was able to regain my concentration, and I sent him silent praise through the rune. Not a single soldier would catch a single glimpse of doubt on Aaren's face. This would end with us on top, and he wouldn't have it any other way. Aaren would fight until he was down to three soldiers. He would not end this battle until he won. Or it killed him trying.

A larger corpse charged me, and I dropped to the ground, sliding between its legs. Dirt caked against my scalp, but I didn't care as I watched Aaren finish the attack. He whirled, strong hands grabbing the draugr's sword arm and distracting it long enough for me to rise and hold the other arm. The draugr's head spun on a swivel as it realized the position Aaren and I had it in.

Aaren bared his teeth as strays of sweaty white hair clung to his brow. Then he pulled the draugr's arm. I grit my teeth at the sickening crack that ran down the draugr's limb, and I braced my foot against its leg for better leverage. Another crack, then the squelching of tearing flesh, and I thudded to the ground with the draugr's torn arm still in my grip. It whirled on me, now missing both extremities as Aaren held the other. I backed away as it laughed viciously, as if the loss of a limb would do nothing to stop it from tearing me to pieces. It dropped to its knees, gnashing yellow, rotted teeth. My foot smashed into the center of its face and drove its nose bone deep into its brain, then rolled away before it could collapse on top of me.

Aaren pulled me up before he fell into his next attack.

By now, my magic had hit full capacity, but if I didn't use it carefully, I would hurt someone I knew. The earthen magic didn't seem to care, though, and the ground shook under my feet with every step.

"Behind you, *frue*!"

I whirled as Ertha darted past me, clad in her shining gold armor. Her blonde locks were twisted into braids and pinned in a coronet atop her head, and that growing fire beneath her features had reached its peak. Teeth bared in a deadly grin, she swung the massive silver greatsword, the ceremonial sword of Fjellhjem, and sliced it through a draugr. She adjusted her grip, and with one hand, she wielded the heavy blade while the other clenched into a fist. The earth shook, sending a strike of discomfort through me as the earth's magic branched away and met her whim. The ground fissured as she summoned chunks of rock from the dirt and pelted them at the draugr.

Ertha gave me a wink, then disappeared deeper into the battle, but her lethal attacks could still be heard from where I stood. The ground continued to shake.

Bodies fell all around me, and the rotten stench was overwhelming, but we had made substantial progress across the field. I squeezed the handle of the axe, the hilt sweaty in my grip, but I was bristling with so much power that it didn't matter.

In an effort to take the edge off, I shot flames at the closest draugr, careful not to hit any of my soldiers.

There was a blood-curdling scream in the distance, followed by a rattling shout.

"No!" Ivar boomed, and ice filled my veins.

I followed the direction of the sound and wrenched the axe free from a remarkably fresh draugr. I caught sight of Oswin's bald head in the distance, then a flash of white blonde pushing through to him. I carved my way through the battle, working in tandem with Ivar to keep the attacking foes at bay as Aaren knelt with his hands pressed to Oswin's abdomen. Another blink and I realized Aaren was holding two sides of a gaping wound closed, blood spurting through his worried fingers.

Oswin let out a weak cry as Aaren dug a shoulder under him and brought him to his unsteady feet.

"Get him out of here," Aaren ordered, sliding Oswin onto Ivar's shoulder, then turning to rip out the throat of an oncoming draugr. "Take him to Helgi in the meeting hall."

I tried not to think of how many already occupied the makeshift cots we had assembled in the meeting hall. Of how much blood already stained the floors.

As Ivar disappeared below the crest of the hill, Aaren wiped the blood from his hands, making a kill every few seconds as he surveyed the fight around us.

The ground shook again, and I was swelling with my magic, but no matter the progress, no matter the number of kills, the uncertainty that wove through Aaren's brow and wound along his features only confirmed my fears.

We were losing, and this battle wouldn't last much longer.

Aaren moved to me, snapping the neck of a draugr that tried to strike him, and slid his blistered palms across my cheeks. I didn't care about the cut of his calluses or the streak of Oswin's blood that now stained my cheek; the look in his eyes sent a ringing dread through me that blanketed all my other senses.

"You need to get out of here," he breathed, watching over my shoulder. He let go of me for a moment to rip the head off of a heavily decayed draugr. It dropped to the ground just as the earth shook again.

"No," I argued, "I'm not leaving."

"I'm not losing you, Layla, I can't."

Another draugr charged us, and I spun, kicking it onto the pointed end of Axl's sword. He kicked it off effortlessly, then turned to swing at another. I shook my head defiantly and blinked away the image of Axl's bloody face. Not only could I not leave Aaren, but I couldn't abandon my people, my *friends*, on this battlefield. Not when Axl's face was so bloody that he was nearly unrecognizable. Not when Oswin had been almost gutted. Not when the battlefield was littered with so many Fraalver bodies, it made my head spin.

"This isn't going to end well, *fremmed*," Aaren said, and the shake in his voice rattled me to my very being. "Get on Froki and go to Fjellhjem. If anyone is going to walk off this battlefield, it's going to be you."

Von's knife flew right past our faces, barely nicking my ear as it landed in the unseeing eye of an approaching draugr.

"This is the wrong time for a heartfelt moment, you two!" Von barked as he pushed past us to retrieve his dagger.

I shot a flame over Aaren's shoulder and took down a group of three draugr that were hellbent on ripping Axl's arms off.

Aaren shook his head, then kicked a draugr in the chest. "Why are you so gods damned headstrong, Layla?" he demanded. "You *have* to make it to Fjellhjem. Do it for Lucas."

I wanted to hate him for knowing how to twist me. But it was true. I was on this battlefield for my people, my friends, and my husband, but most importantly, I was here for Lucas. Everything I had ever done here was for my brother.

It would all be in vain if I didn't make it to Fjellhjem.

"Aaren..." I pleaded, and hot tears stung my eyes. The battle around us seemed to quiet as I conceded to the desperate, horrific truth of it all. I needed to leave the battlefield. Leave Aaren behind.

"It's alright, *fremmed*," Aaren said and pressed his forehead to mine. "I'll be waiting for you at home."

My throat was too tight to say anything, my lip quivering too fiercely to form any comprehensible words.

There was a horn in the distance, loud enough that the fighting paused for the briefest of moments. Aaren and I peeled away from each other to follow the direction of the sound, then I gasped.

At the treeline was a massive army clad in armor shining so brightly I couldn't see who wore it.

A wild grin spread across Aaren's face. There was a figure at the front lines of the army that stood taller than the others. I squinted to focus on the crooked nose and shaggy hair.

It was Stieg.

And next to him, a little shorter, stood Ymer, wearing heavy iron armor.

Sweet, delicious relief blew through me like a tidal wave as the troll army blew the horn again. And when the trolls began their march toward the undead army, the draugr turned and stormed towards them.

"Perfect," Aaren mumbled, then knelt to the blood-soaked ground.

His fingers dug into the dirt, body going so rigid he could have been carved from stone. I felt the strain on my end of the rune, and my own muscles clenched as his veins glowed with magic that started to shake the ground. It was a different shaking from Ertha's—hers was shattering and unyielding—the shaking Aaren caused made it seem like the very dirt was alive.

I sent him more of my power, sourcing it from the earth, only for him to return it, imbued with might and a lust for battle. And when Aaren let out a mighty grunt, the ground underneath his fingertips cracked, then fanned out like spidery veins all the way towards the cliffs. Mounds of earth emerged and morphed to grow necks and shoulders, limbs that reached down and grabbed the discarded weapons of the dead.

Hundreds and hundreds of jordmen emerged, and Ertha whooped from a few feet away. Our new, earthen soldiers thundered toward the distracted draugr that were too busy battling the trolls to pay them any mind.

The draugr army was surrounded, the trolls on one side, the jordmen and Fraalver on the other, now that our numbers had increased to match theirs. Finally, it was a fair fight.

There was nothing left to do but keep fighting now. With a better handle on the power coursing through me, I wielded each element, interchanging them as if it were a dance amongst nature. Aaren and I fought in tandem—if it wasn't our blades complementing each other's attacks, it was our magic. When I shot flames at one draugr, his wind would carry it over to the next and engulf it in hungry fire. When a draugr swung for the killing blow, Aaren would block, while I sliced it in half. Every movement was synchronized, every magical whim attuned to the other's. We were a well-oiled death machine together.

Boulders flew across the battlefield as Ertha slammed them on the remaining droves of draugr, their numbers having dropped drastically to my exhausted relief. It didn't stop them from fighting until their last...breath? The thing about summoning an army of the undead was that they wouldn't tire and would fight until their second death came for them.

Jordmen clashed and exploded into bits of clay and dirt as swords and warhammers bombarded them. Aaren glided around me, the tip of his blade gutting three draugr in one swing. Entrails spilled out of their middles, but they pushed forward with sinister cackles bubbling from their rotten throats. Axl swept between two of the draugr, grabbing their insides from behind with a squelch that sent my stomach into somersaults. He whirled to wrap the guts around their necks and pulled, sending them careening back and slamming onto the ground, where he stomped their throats.

Von picked off the remaining one with a knife to the head.

The trolls had permeated the draugr's remaining line of defense and slowly picked them off one by one. I caught a flash of Ymer in a whirl of knives and fury as he hacked away at the decrepit legs of the assailing corpses and drove his blades deep into their skulls.

Aaren grunted, wrestling with a particularly large draugr, weapons flung on the ground next to him. The draugr's rotten breath blew the flyaways from Aaren's brow, and I gasped when the deceptively strong draugr grabbed a fistful of Aaren's hair and pulled. I threw myself forward when the draugr's gnashing teeth came dangerously close to Aaren's neck, grazing his Adam's apple. Dipping around a scuffle between Von and a corpse with sickeningly rotting jowls, I kicked Aaren's sword just within his reach, then came behind his attacker.

The scalp of the draugr tried to break free from its skull when I tangled my fingers in its hair and wrenched it back. Sword already in hand, Aaren delivered a clean slice across its neck, strings of decayed muscle and tendon severing from the neck and head. The body fell limp for Aaren to shove off of him while the head hung loosely in my grip.

I spat out bile when I tossed it to the side, stomach churning violently.

Slowly, the sounds of battle died as the last of the draugr fell. The field was littered with the scattered bodies of draugr and Fraalver alike. Limbs and pieces of jordmen were dispersed throughout the sprays of mud and puddles of blood. A couple of them wandered around with bloodied blades in hand as they searched for their next target. The surviving Fraalver, led by Ertha, combed through the bodies and finished off any draugr that moved.

Aaren flicked his sword, flinging drops of congealed blood onto the speckled earth.

"You alright, *fremmed?*" he asked when he strode to me and scrubbed at the dried blood along my cheek. I assured him that I was fine, but that didn't stop him from searching me for injuries.

"Thank the gods we arrived because I started to believe we'd never see the axe again."

Ymer wove around the bodies with a smug scowl.

My gaze dropped to the axe in my hands, heat growing in my chest at the thought of giving it up. When I looked up again, Ymer was in front of me, nearly untouched save for the large abrasion slashed across his features.

I bristled, searching for anything to say that wasn't the nasty thoughts roving through my mind, especially since Ymer and his army had just saved our asses.

"All it was doing was rotting in a room," I said, unsuccessfully keeping the bite out of my tone.

Ymer scoffed and pulled a cloth from within his armor. He began to clean one of his knives. "Be that as it may," he held the knife up and watched it glint after its new polish, "that was not our bargain. And seeing as I just had to move *my* army to come to *your* aid, I think it's safe to say you are in debt to me."

Aaren grumbled next to me.

"What was that, King of Trees?" Ymer pried pompously.

Aaren swallowed, a muscle rippling in his jaw. "We thank you for your help, Ymer." It was all he could get out—if he said any more, our alliance with the trolls would be over. I'm sure Ymer wouldn't take kindly to a swift punch to the face. I felt Aaren's patience run paper-thin as Ymer raised his brows expectantly in silent request.

"Just take it back," Aaren bit and gestured for me to drop the axe at Ymer's feet.

The axe seemed to protest the exchange, but I buried my animosity deep inside and handed it back to its undeserving owner.

"Thank you for your cooperation," he nodded, turning on his heel. "We can discuss the manner of the rest of your debt at another time. My army requires tending, and" he threw an assessing look at the ruined battlefield, "you have a lot of cleaning up to do."

I threw up my middle finger at Ymer's back, and Aaren chuckled.

There were pounding footsteps to our right, and then Stieg whooshed past, slowing down too late and having to follow up to meet us.

"Thank the Aesir you're okay," he panted, dropping his hands to his knees. "I left for Klartvan Lake as soon as you left Skoghjem, and I convinced Ymer to come because I just had a horrible feeling and..." He dropped to the ground. "Oh, Yggdrasil, I can't breathe."

Aaren dropped onto a cleaner patch of grass next to Stieg and propped up a knee. "And we are far more in your debt than we are in Ymer's." He patted Stieg on the back and smiled widely—a light contrast compared to the gore and mud clinging to his face. "I suppose you'll have to tell Thea when you get back. Make sure she gives you the hero treatment."

The two of them broke into delighted chuckles.

The lightheartedness only lasted until we were in ear shot of the infirmary.

Oswin's screams could be heard from the square, loud enough that I grit my teeth against the sound. My ears were still ringing from battle, but Oswin's screams rattled me more than anything I had heard all day. I pounded up the steps of the meeting hall where the injured were being treated. Aaren and Stieg were close on my heels.

Blood was everywhere when I stepped through the tall doors of the hall, and Oswin was splayed across a cot, ashen-faced and coated in sweat. A ghastly wound opened his abdomen, and the coppery tang of fresh blood wafted through the air. Helgi knelt before him and applied pressure while Ivar dabbed the sweat from his brow. Ivar offered Oswin encouraging words, but there was no mistaking the shell shock on his face. I navigated around the bloody rags that littered the floor and sank to my knees at Oswin's side.

Aaren rounded the cot and, to her relief, took Helgi's place, holding the wound closed. "Fetch me the medicine pouch," Aaren instructed calmly, and Helgi complied, the blood on her fingers staining the treated leather sack.

"It's not much," she said as she dropped the bag at Aaren's knees. "Isak kept his stores in the medicine hut. It was all burned."

Aaren dug one hand through the sack and grumbled frustratedly as he pulled out vials of empty tonics. When the sack was nearly empty, Aaren cursed.

"I'm sorry, venn," he said to Oswin, who yelped when Aaren shifted the wound to reach behind him and retrieve a needle and thread. "This isn't going to feel good." He glanced at Ivar. "Grab him a drink. It's all we have to numb him."

Ivar retrieved his waterskin, which I knew to be filled with ale, and poured some of it into Oswin's waiting mouth.

"Hold him steady."

Nothing could have prepared me for the deep gash along Oswin's gut. Crimson ran everywhere, staining the cot and dripping onto the floor below. It wasn't deep enough to reveal entrails, but it would be deadly if it weren't closed. Aaren threaded the needle and leaned forward, using one hand to prod the wound.

Oswin bucked against Aaren's touches and twisted free. He moved as if he meant to slide to the ground, but merely budged an inch before Aaren practically tackled him and pinned him to the cot.

"I said hold him!" Aaren barked.

Stieg ran to take my place, and I moved around to the other side and leaned over the wound. Aaren caught my eye and sighed, "I need you to hold him closed."

Warm, metallic blood soaked my hands when I placed them on both sides of the wound and pushed them closed with a horrific squishing sound. Oswin squirmed again and begged to be left alone, to let him die in peace, but Stieg and Ivar held him still. Those desperate pleas and bellows bounced off the walls of the meeting hall, but I let them distract me from the warm viscera at my fingertips. The back of my throat activated, acid burning, and I fought tooth and nail to keep whatever was in my stomach down.

"It's okay, Oswin," Ivar said nervously, his eyes avoiding Aaren's working fingers. "Once this is done, you can have all the ale you want."

"Hey, they might even write a song about you," Stieg offered with a strained smile.

A sound like a chuckle bubbled from Oswin. "I'll h-hold you t-to that."

Minor relief settled into me. At least he was still coherent.

Aaren stuck the needle through.

Oswin screamed again, thrashing about, only for Ivar and Stieg to put more weight on him so Aaren could concentrate.

"Shall we sing *now*?" Stieg suggested and gave Ivar a pleading look.

Ivar gave Stieg a look like he had bats crawling out of his ears, then paused to consider. Stieg raised his eyebrows as if to urge him to start, beginning to hum a deep, soothing melody.

Ivar finally complied. "Oh, Oswin, so fair, with the reddest of hair..."

"I'm b-b-bald you asswipe," Oswin stuttered before groaning when Aaren stuck him again.

"I was talking about your beard, shit for brains," Ivar bit back.

Stieg cleared his throat and continued with, "Drinker of ale, and skin so pale..."

"He is good with a sword, so much he's adored," I sang, concentrating on the wound and wincing at my lyrics.

Ivar chuckled. "He's not great with the ladies, he's been single since his eighties..."

"F-fuck you," Oswin breathed.

Aaren smirked as he worked, his nimble fingers dancing expertly. He was over halfway down, the wound still oozing, but tapered. I adjusted my hands.

501

"What an excellent fighter, you'll find none any mightier..."

Oswin coughed. "This is a horrible song."

Ivar scoffed, for a moment forgetting that his friend's entrails were threatening to burst from his middle. "I'd like to see you sing one better, Os."

When the gash was closed, Aaren leaned back and rolled his wrists, tissue caked underneath his fingernails. He examined his work through heavy-lidded eyes and blew out a breath.

"All done," Aaren said and gave Oswin a friendly pat on the cheek.

I wiped my hands on one of the few cloths that wasn't soaked with blood.

"How do you feel, Os?" Ivar asked, releasing his arms.

Oswin let out a pained puff of air. "N-not great, a-asshole."

Ivar broke into a grin. "He'll be fine."

I would've felt more relief if my own fatigue hadn't fully hit me like a bag of bricks, and I stopped fighting it. My shoulders slumped as my limbs grew heavy, and I leaned back on my hands to wearily watch Stieg and Ivar fuss over Oswin. Helgi brought over a basin of fresh water and began to clean the freshly sutured wound, dodging a blow from Oswin as he groaned painfully and swung on instinct.

"Give him more ale, he'll be fine," Aaren told them, then helped me to my feet. "Come along, *fremmed*," he sighed. "Let's get you to bed."

My eyes closed before I had even kicked my boots off.

I had never slept harder than I did that night, curled into Aaren's embrace in the tent at the edge of the village. The fatigue in my muscles hadn't left when I awoke the next morning, but it had eased enough that I would be able to ride all day. However, I would be sore and *very* stiff. My entire body was full of knots that threatened to snap with any wrong movement.

I rolled over onto my other side, yawning, but it was cut short when I flexed my ankles. My calves screamed as pain contorted my legs into a vicious cramp. I shot up, grasping at my leg and desperately trying to rub some relief into it, but my fierce kneading and massaging were no use. My arms complained from the movement, and within a minute or so, my whole body had awoken, twisting itself into pained knots, and I groaned with discomfort. I wished I had been able to stretch before the battle yesterday, but as Aaren had said before, your enemy doesn't care whether you've stretched or not.

502

Aaren stirred next to me, and his honey eyes glimmered in the morning light as they fluttered open. He gave me a dreamy smile, but then chuckled.

"Battle not treat you as well as you had hoped?" he joked when he pushed himself up.

"Fuck this hurts," I groaned.

Aaren's fingers brushed my seizing calf muscles, which my fingers were desperately trying to work. "May I?"

I nodded, and he kicked the covers away to dig his fingertips into my flesh until the muscles eased. I protested at first, biting on a knuckle as he massaged me, but when the dull, aching pain started to recede, I sighed.

Aaren moved, throwing my leg over his shoulder until my thigh was flush against his torso, and a whole new arena of pain sparked along my hamstrings.

"Breathe out," he said, then leaned forward. My hand clamped over my mouth as my muscles strained against the stretch, a million tiny tears erupting in my muscles. "Good girl, you got it. Just breathe through it, *fremmed*," he purred, then pushed it farther before kissing my shin and releasing me.

We had barely made it through the second leg before Aaren gave in to the arousal the stretching stirred. I bit my lip to keep my pleasured cries to a minimum as he plunged into me, but I was unsuccessful, so Aaren placed a hand over my mouth to remedy that.

We had just finished when Aaren's back began to twinge with pain, though he assured me through gritted teeth that he was fine. Retrieving the fresh bottle of oil from his pack, I worked it into the muscles along his spine before letting him move an inch from the bedroll.

When the pain eased, we both dressed and emerged from the tent, greeted by the bright morning light. The village had become a small war camp, and Fraalver milled about, still tending to the wounded that couldn't fit in the meeting hall. Ertha was found in front of the food tent, hunched over a massive steaming pan that simmered over a crackling fire.

The small gash across her cheek had closed and welted slightly, but she was in high spirits as we approached. "Glad to see you two in one piece," she said as she wiped her hands on the front of her dress.

"You're awfully chipper this morning, *frue*," I said, noting the flush in her cheeks and receding dark circles.

Ertha shrugged and smirked. "It's been nice to win something for once," she replied, handing out a bowl of food to a passing Fraalver.

I couldn't argue with her. For me, winning the battle put me closer to Lucas. For Ertha, it was one step closer to avenging Torsten.

Chapter 60

Froki stepped over the bodies that littered the field before us, weaving in and out of drying pools of blood and piled weapons. I couldn't stare at the wreckage for very long before my heart started to snap in half in my chest. I hadn't realized just how many of our people fell, most of them familiar faces from my own village or Fjellhjem. Some of them I had shared a campfire meal with during the journey back to Skoghjem after the attack. More of my people were dead, and the grief was almost unbearable.

No matter how many victories we secured, it all still felt like a failure.

Helgi had arranged for the remaining, able-bodied Fraalver to embark into the field and pick out their dead for the mass funeral that night. Everyone who fought and fell would be going to Himmelfjell today.

Given the loss of life and the fragile state of Kysthjem after the battle, we decided a small traveling group would be best to continue on our way to Fjellhjem.

Ivar elected to stay with Oswin while he healed and would return to Skoghjem when the others were ready. Our company consisted of Aaren, Ertha, Von, and Axl, with me as the fifth member. Small, but easier to slip into Fjellhjem unnoticed. As we rode, I found that I missed the giggles and howls of Oswin and Ivar cracking wise. Lacking his regular entertainment as well, Von had fallen into an abnormal silence, keeping his eyes on the reins in his hand, only breaking to polish the knives strapped to his chest occasionally. An overall foreboding kept the silence thick, dense, as if the air had been sucked out of the world and replaced with an angry, somber smog.

My stomach had settled for the time being, though the nerves hadn't gone away. My senses were on high alert, twitching at every snapping twig, hackles rising at every shadow that dared cross my vision.

If it weren't for Aaren, I would have been reduced to frightful tremors by the end of our ride that evening.

He gave me a quick kiss on the forehead as he helped me off of Froki before helping Von and Axl pitch the tents. I noted the clearing we were in, and the memories of that night made me wary of every sound. This was where we camped the night the fenrs attacked, and the sight of furry, bloodied bodies was still just as fresh in my mind now as they were the night it happened.

Ertha milled about the clearing in the valley, collecting a small bundle of firewood in the crook of her arm.

"Want some help?" I asked.

She nodded, and I set about picking up sticks and fallen branches, cradling them in my arms as we moved. Wandering to the stream's edge, I peered into the bubbling water and studied my distorted image. The evidence of battle was bleak. I was pale, and dark circles had begun to ring my eyes from exhaustion. I had slept well for the past few nights, but according to the reflection that stared back at me, it wasn't enough.

Ignoring the almost unfamiliar face in the water, I instead watched the little fish dart in the shallower waters, while the larger fish fought the current in the center of the stream. This was the same stream Fiske and I had fished, and the thought sent heaviness to my stomach. No, it was rising in my stomach, getting lighter, and burning, and—

I retched into the stream. The fish fled further upstream. My abs were already so sore from the battle that another round of vomiting might send me toppling over the edge of misery.

"Alright there, *frue*?" Ertha called, setting her bundle of wood onto the bank and kneeling next to me.

"I'm fine," I answered through a shudder. I was more frustrated than anything else. I just wanted to stop vomiting. "I guess I'm not as cut out for war as I thought I was."

Ertha sighed. "Not many are. Have you been sleeping?"

I nodded. "I've been sleeping alright."

Ertha cocked a brow. "And you're still unwell?" I nodded. Ertha hummed in contemplation, her eyes falling to the stream and the returning fish. "When was the last time you bled?"

"What does *that* have to do with anything?" I asked as I ignored the knowing concern in Ertha's wrinkled brow. When she said nothing, I sighed and replied, "It...it's been a while." I had lost track around the time of the Nidhogg. Things just got so crazy after that that I didn't really pay attention to my cycle.

Ertha's brows shot to her hairline. "I think you and I both know what this means, Layla."

506

I shook my head, waving the assumption away and hoping the breeze would carry it off to crash into the mountains above. "No," I snapped. I pushed myself off the ground. "No, Ertha, it's just nerves. I'll be better once all of this is over. Really, I'll be fine."

Ertha kept her stare on me, reluctant to let the notion drop. "Just watch yourself, *frue*. I'd hate for this to be worse than what you may think it is."

I paused, about to say what was really going through my mind, but instead I turned, throwing a frustrated "thank you" over my shoulder. I scooped up my bundle of firewood and trekked back to camp.

As much as I had hoped I could leave that conversation in that clearing, it followed me all the way back to camp.

Axl had snared a few rats that we ate around the fire, spitting out bones and murmuring. The heaviness still lingered, and no one decided to break through it. I stewed throughout dinner as I silently mulled over Ertha's theory. And no matter how many ways I tried to explain everything away, her words kept coming back to me.

After the sun had set, we retreated into our tents. The crickets' song blended with the swish of leaves as the evening breeze snaked through the valley. I curled into Aaren's warmth to find solace from my racing thoughts. His body heat seeped through my pores and wrapped my bones until his forest and leather scent blanketed my mind.

My nausea was gone, and I felt a little more invigorated after eating, but the thought of tomorrow lingered in the forefront of my mind. I tried to think about seeing Lucas again, bringing him back to the village, watching him play with Nilsen, and being a kid again. But all I could think of was the looming doom and uncertainty of what awaited in that mountain.

I refused to entertain the possibility that Lucas was dead, even though it had become an infuriatingly persistent thought over the past few weeks. No, Lucas couldn't be dead, but if he wasn't, what kind of torture had he endured since his capture? Had it been physical, body-breaking torture, or had Markus spent the last few months bending his mind and manipulating him into some altered state of thinking?

The mare's words rang through my mind suddenly, which brought another mountain of questions I needed answered.

Like the water it dwelled in, it opened its mouth and flowed the truth...

The only significant body of water I could think of was Klartvan Lake. If I were speaking honestly, despite coming to our aid yesterday, I wouldn't put it past Ymer to sell us out to Markus for the sake of his foolish vendetta against the Fraalver. The traitorous troll must have given us away after we didn't bring the axe back right away. Then he showed up to the battle to save face, put on a show for the sake of maintaining this false alliance with us. And get the axe back. Unlike the few trolls I had met, Ymer was spiteful. And this explained the knowing looks I noticed him giving us after we started the alliance. He knew as soon as he made the deal with us that it would be short-lived. Maybe that's why he made it in the first place.

I had to be careful thinking like this. If I get myself too riled up, I may accidentally burn our tent down.

I rolled over to tell Aaren, but stopped when I met his sleeping features instead of his blinking eyes.

He stirred in his sleep, features screwed as if his dreams had just darkened. I admired his carved face, with its strong jawline and dark brows that contrasted with his platinum hair. We would be lucky if our children favored him. I snaked my hand down to rest over my navel, wondering if there really was life growing within. There couldn't be, I begged to Himmelfjell itself that there wasn't. Not when, just tomorrow, I would face the biggest fight of my life. I couldn't die tomorrow with an extra life in my womb today.

Settling my thoughts away from the darker, more pressing matters, I imagined what would happen when we brought Lucas back to Skoghjem. Life would go on as usual. I would help Inaborg in the pub and Thea with her writing. Aaren would train Nilsen and Lucas to be fighters, and Stieg could take them out to find treasures in the woods. Perhaps Stieg would finally learn what those shiny wrappers were truly intended for. Maybe in a few years, Aaren and I would have children, and they could play with Thea and Stieg's.

I smiled at the wonderful life I had built in my mind.

But it couldn't happen now, no matter how desperately I wanted it.

And sadly, it wasn't over after Markus. We still had the necromancer to deal with. This was just the first battle of many. We had a long time to go before that dream could be fulfilled. And I battled the harrowing thought that I may *never* have that life. After all, everything was riding on our fight the next day.

I cursed myself for letting my thoughts wander into the darkness again.

Aaren groaned and jerked, now overtaken by a violent nightmare. I placed a gentle hand on his shoulder and shook gently.

"Aaren," I whispered. "Aaren, you're having a nightmare."

He lurched forward and searched the tent with wild eyes. Clenched muscle met my fingertips when I placed my hand on his arm, listening to his ragged breaths as they slowed.

"I'm alright, *fremmed,*" he said when his breath returned to normal, and his head dropped back to the bedroll. His jaw ticked when he closed his eyes again, as if the horrors he faced behind closed lids were enough to keep him awake for eternity.

"What were you dreaming about?" I asked as I rubbed a hand over his chest in soothing circles.

Aaren swallowed. "I get nightmares after big battles. It's just the way my mind processes what happened." I nodded, ready to brush it off when his following words made my heart stutter. "Only this one was different," he said. His head rolled so that his honey eyes could hold me in a fierce stare. "Battle used to be just that. A fight to win. Another victory to add to the history books. Now every battle is so I can keep you safe." Aaren sighed, his eyes somehow hardening into solid amber. "And every loss weighs so much more than before."

Every troubled thought I'd had before dissipated from my mind, and all I could feel was an odd sort of anguish that sank my heart into the pit of my gut. The place where a child may or may not be growing.

I grappled with the idea of mentioning Ertha's assumption to Aaren, but how could I put something like that on him? I couldn't tell him something like this when I wasn't even sure if it was true, especially when just the memories of battle were giving him nightmares that rivaled the horrors of a mare. He worried about me enough as it was; I didn't need to give him another reason for his nightmares to return.

Aaren draped an arm over me and pulled me in close, resting his chin atop my head.

"You need to rest," he rasped in a voice heavy with sleep.

"I know," I answered as I traced troubled circles on his chest. "I know."

"There's something you're not telling me."

I sighed and replied, "You're right." And no matter how much it killed me, I said, "I don't think I'm ready to tell you."

Aaren's silence filled the tent like a heavy fog as I waited for his response. His chin brushed the top of my head when he nodded. "And I wouldn't expect you to tell me until you are ready, Layla."

My throat tightened as he placed a kiss on the crown of my head.

With those words, Aaren gave me a handful of his control. His beloved, sacred control.

"I love you, Aaren," I said through tears that were of no use fighting.

Aaren placed a tender kiss on my lips. "I love you too, Layla. And nothing could stand in the way of that. Not Markus, or the necromancer. Not even death itself."

When Aaren kissed me this time, I lost myself in his touch, in his homely scent that brought me back to the towering oaks and soft leaf-strewn earth of our forest. His fingers massaged the sore flesh of my bottom, aching after so many days in the saddle. I snaked my arms around him and ran my fingers along his spine, feeling the gnarled flesh cascade down to the curve of his bottom.

Aaren let out a pleased growl when I slung my leg around his waist, opening myself to him.

"Eager, aren't we?" he grinned against my lips.

I didn't care to search for a retort, especially when his hand grazed over my breast, and goosebumps broke out along my skin. Power seemed to snap to life in the air of the tent, a static buzzing sending the hairs along my arms to attention.

Aaren gave a claiming growl as his fingers trailed down my chest and danced across my navel. Ice doused my excited fire as I found myself wanting to shrink away from that touch, to shove his hand away from the place his child could be growing inside me. It felt unfair to bring him so close to something that could be ripped away so easily.

And so soon.

Aaren gave me a concerned look, one that I wiped off his face when I wrapped my fingers around the bulge in his pants. Another ounce of Aaren's control slipped when his hand gripped the roots of my hair, pulling my head back to expose my throat, where he nipped and licked and sucked. The other hand slid from my navel to between my legs, where he parted me and traced a finger over the delicate nerves.

He gave me a reprimanding nip to my neck when I let out a moan, my hips rocking on his fingers when he plunged one inside me. Delicious relief spread across my scalp when Aaren let go of my hair to tangle his lips with mine. He cursed against my lips when I slid his pants down and grasped him. A bead of arousal had formed, and I rubbed it away as I brushed the nerve underneath the head of his cock.

There was something to be said about the way Aaren crumpled in my touch. About the way he melted against me into a beautiful, sopping mess of desire. Aaren, the unyielding warrior, turned helpless in my hand. I may have killed the Nidhogg, I may be the daughter of one of the most powerful beings in Alveland, but having Aaren's manhood in my hand, hard and willing for me, was my most remarkable feat.

The ferocity in his kiss when our lips met again sent me spiraling down a tunnel of pleasure; the only grip on reality I had was my grip on his cock. I pumped him, unable to fight the smile as he bucked into my hand with a hungry growl. Our once delicate kisses turned devouring as my need to taste him became overwhelming. And I was on the brink of lustful oblivion.

Aaren's fingers curled inside me, my harrowed moan lost on his lips. With each ravenous kiss, a new breath of life was exchanged. Every breath was like a tempest of spirit reveling through me, lighting every ounce of passion until I was sure I would burn alive.

My mouth broke from his to plant soft kisses on his jawline, his neck, to trail my tongue all the way down his chest and his abs, until I was poised over his cock. I licked my lips. He kicked his pants the rest of the way off, and I grabbed him by the base, fingers grazing his balls.

There was a moment of pause, a beat of pleading that flashed across his features as I held his gaze, breath fanning over his hardness. When my tongue licked across his smooth tip, the look of helplessness that soaked his irises before they closed was devastating. With every lick and suck of my mouth, a little more of Aaren was forfeited to me, willingly given if it meant that I wouldn't stop. It was delicious and desperate and intimate, and every bit of him, every second of this, was mine. All mine.

"Gods, *fremmed*, your mouth is catastrophic," he gasped as he threw back his head.

My lips closed over him, plunging him down my throat, and he cried out, a beautiful sound that I ingrained in my brain forever. I bobbed my head and licked up the saliva that dribbled onto his base. Then he met my eyes and watched as his cock slid in and out of my mouth.

Aaren's fingers grappled for my chin and pulled me up, his cock slipping out of my mouth to my disappointment.

Our lips connected once more. His tongue made a wistful swipe across my bottom lip before his strong hands slid down my body and directed my thighs to straddle his face.

Suddenly, I was at *his* mercy, our possession of control an ever-changing volley between the two of us. And just as Aaren was willing to give every ounce of himself to me, I was ready to sell my soul if it meant that I could feel his warm breath and disastrous tongue against me for eternity.

Calluses bit into the soft flesh of my bottom, and his breath grazed over my center, planting a soft kiss on my inner thigh. Then he swiped his tongue across me. I arched back, hands bracing his thighs as he worked me. I felt the pleasure everywhere—in my vertebrae, my taste buds, in every bit of buzzing, exposed skin. Aaren flicked the sensitive bundle of nerves, then wrapped his lips around it. My senses dulled, only tuning me in to him. His tongue swiped me over and over again, licking every inch of me until I was a crumbling mess of pleasured ecstasy atop him.

Aaren's hands crawled up my spine, fingers splayed across my back to keep a better grip on me as my legs started to wobble. My fingers roved along his thigh and quickly found their mark. I wrapped my fingers around his length, pumping him with a heightened vigor as my edge grew closer. Aaren groaned, the vibration against me releasing a flurry of hungry butterflies fluttering through every cell. My walls tightened and ached for his length inside me, begging for the delicious release he coaxed me so close to.

"I can never taste enough of you," Aaren murmured against me, licking me as if I were his favorite dessert that he hadn't eaten in years.

His hands slid from my back and clenched the crease where my thighs met my hips to hold me in place. I couldn't take it anymore, not when his insistent tongue pulled me closer and closer until suddenly, every bit of my existence shattered, the pieces of me crashing down and imploding. Aaren gripped me as I rode out my release into oblivion, writhing until I was utterly hopeless.

Just as I recovered, Aaren shifted me off of him and then moved to kneel behind me. I braced on all fours as anticipation ate me alive, and every second that ticked by without him inside me was a second closer to my self-destruction, my calamitous end. I sent my hips back, begging him to fuck me. And with a hungry growl, he grasped my hips and slammed into me.

I cried out, my palms sweaty as they gripped the bedroll underneath them. He gave me no time to adjust before he hammered into me with an unchained, primal desire. He groaned, the steady rhythm of his thrusts barely skipping a beat when he reached forward and grabbed a fistful of my hair. Pleasure soaked my bones, and he dove deeper into me, whispering love and praise that sent me further toward the edge of release.

He released my hair and keeled forward, fingers circling my sex and coaxing moans from me that I knew were far too loud for discretion.

"Quiet, *fremmed*," Aaren warned, then slammed into me again.

It was no use, though, because his next thrust sent stars to my vision, and the moan that tumbled from my lips was my demise.

Aaren pulled me to my knees, my back flush against his sweat-damp chest. He thrust up into me, one hand snaking around us to circle my sex, while the other climbed up my chest and wrapped around my neck.

"If you so much as make one more noise, Layla, not even the fallen gods will be able to help you."

His teeth bit my earlobe as his finger continued to circle me, but this time, I caught the moan in my throat and swallowed it.

"That's my good girl," he said.

Then he pulled out and flipped me, the strands of fur along the bedroll tickling my skin. I slammed a hand over my mouth when Aaren ran his tongue over my center again, and lapped up every bit of me before throwing my leg over his shoulder and entering me again.

My rune burned, sending wondrous heat all across my body as time escaped me and everything outside of the tent faded from reality. My whole existence was reduced to the slapping of skin, the smell of sweat, and the sound of gasps.

And Aaren above me, his heavy-lidded eyes lost in the rapture of sex, the euphoria of his thrusts, the pleasure coursing through the rune and exchanging between the two of us. His release was mine, and mine was his until it all just became one.

Then we exploded, and it felt like everything ceased to exist altogether. I bathed in the pleasure that flowed so freely between us, fibers of contentment weaving around my muscles and circling my cells until I felt nothing but delight and relief.

Aaren's thrusts slowed, sweat-sheened brow dropping into the crook of my neck as he caught his breath and peppered soft kisses along my skin as he pulled out.

Aaren's nightmares didn't return that night, and we both slept soundly until morning.

Chapter 61

I may have slept well, but it did nothing to remedy the fact that I may be riding through the mountains to my death. And it did nothing to help my stomach, considering the first thing I did when I woke up was flee the tent and empty my guts in the stream again.

After a breakfast of leftovers from last night, I downed the rest of Rorik's tonic with a silent prayer that it wouldn't wear off before we faced Markus. My stomach was still gurgling when we mounted the horses and began to follow the trail, but at least I wasn't vomiting.

Yet, the anxiety smacked me like a warhammer before curling around me like a steel coil. There was nothing that could distract me from the throat tightening, spine tingling snake of apprehension that had begun to nibble at my nerves, and suddenly, I couldn't breathe, couldn't move. The trees around us closed in, and no matter how much I tried to convince myself that they were the trees of Skoghjem, that I was really just back home and safe and secure, the fright still blared sirens through my head. It was deafening, and unsure what to do, I slid silently from Froki's back and fled into the trees, only stopping when my boot caught on a root, and I slid to the ground.

"Layla!" Aaren called from behind me, confirming my suspicions that the tree root had moved at my husband's command.

My breath came in short, erratic puffs as Aaren approached, swiping away tears I didn't know were trickling down my cheeks.

"Calm down, *fremmed*," he hummed as he tucked a strand of hair behind my ear. "*Breathe*, Layla." When I still couldn't control the air coming into my lungs, Aaren tapped my shoulder. "Count the taps, *fremmed*, count with me."

He tapped once, and I counted out loud, following the sequence until he had tapped ten times.

"Good," he said. "Now backwards."

I counted backwards, and when Aaren continued his tapping, he only tapped nine times.

"Backwards, again."

This went on until we had reached three taps before my breath mostly returned to normal, and my heart slowed its rhythm, stalling from the vicious pounding to a slower, dull thump.

"Are you ready to tell me what's wrong?" he asked.

That was a loaded question to say the least.

I took a deep breath and admitted, "I have a bad feeling about this." The bitter taste of mountain rats lingered on my tongue and waged a battle with Rorik's tonic. The taste was winning, and my stomach rumbled again. "I just don't think this is going to end well."

He gave me a look that said he felt the same, which did nothing to erase the unease that was creeping back with every second.

"I know," Aaren answered. "I don't like it either. But one word from you, and we can head back to Skoghjem. We can find another way to get Lucas back."

I shook my head quickly. "No, we're this close. We can't turn back now."

Even though everything inside me was screaming to turn around and flee.

Aaren studied me with soft eyes, mouth turned down in a contemplative scowl. "Is that all that's bothering you?" he asked, knowing I bit my tongue on what I really wanted to say. "Have you sat with it long enough to tell me?"

Pressing my lips together, I shook my head. "I can't," I replied. "Not yet."

I couldn't tell if it was a case of selfishness or self-preservation, but I didn't regret it. It would only keep both of us safer if this conversation were saved for after we killed my father. I couldn't risk letting anything get in the way of our mission. Find Lucas, kill my father.

Aaren wiped another tear from my cheek, his hand lingering along my chin where my lip trembled.

"Whatever is in that mountain isn't anything you aren't ready for, *fremmed*," he said.

"But what if one of us doesn't make it out? What if I lose you?"

Aaren tilted my chin up to him. "Then I will see you in Himmelfjell. I'll be waiting for you in those grand halls with a mug of ale." His eyes dropped to my lips, and he smiled. "I expect you to have the best time at my funeral. And dance like you did at Dagan's."

I laughed through the tears, running through the fuzzy memories of that night, how I danced with Aaren and Thea as the funeral pyre blazing in the square. The night Markus took control of me, Aaren followed to keep me within the safety of the village, and what I would give to go back to that night.

"Here," Aaren said and pulled the dagger from the holster at his side. "Since we had to give the axe up, take this. It's not as powerful, but it'll get the job done in a bind."

The cold, harsh metal bit into my hand. My reflection gazed at me from the blade. Wrapping my fingers around the grip, it melded to my hand perfectly, strange since it was Aaren's. Unless, in making it for him, it was also made for me. Funny thing, Fraalver blacksmithing.

"Thank you," I breathed.

"Anything for you, *fremmed.*"

A thought that had never occurred to me ran through my mind. "I've never asked," I began. "You call me *fremmed*, but what does it mean?"

Aaren cracked a smile as he answered, "It means stranger." He chuckled. "Because when you got here, that's what you were. A mysterious, lively, caring little stranger that I fell in love with."

We mounted the horses again, and continued to Fjellhjem.

The late afternoon greeted us with warm temperatures and a welcoming breeze, all elements for a wondrous afternoon, if we weren't headed straight to our doom. Froki stirred uneasily as we moved along the mountain path, as if she sensed the evil that encroached as we drew closer. I sensed it too, unable to shake the feeling of being watched. It was like every rock and crevice in the mountains around us had a pair of beady eyes staring at us. For all we knew, we *were* being watched.

Aaren didn't bother to hide how on edge he was. As soon as we mounted the horses again, his spine stiffened, shoulders unmoving. Watching him was enough to set my teeth on edge, and worry wormed back into my stomach in no time. Aaren knew something was amiss, and the truth that I hid from him was beginning to eat at him as much as it did me. He hadn't witnessed my incessant vomiting. I decided to keep that hidden from him, first out of desire to hide my weakness, now to prevent my condition from affecting his decisions. But I was beginning to fear that my not telling him would distract him just as much as the truth itself.

The mountains stretched higher into the sky, their roots digging deeper into the earth, and the trickling stream widened as rapids began to take form. Once I could hear the whitewater roaring in the distance, I knew we were getting close. Ertha suggested we stop just outside the village and move towards the sprawling valley on foot so as not to draw attention. In case any threats were lingering outside the mountain entrance.

Von and Axl tied their horses to a cluster of nearby juniper trees, and I dismounted Froki with a heavy heart. I didn't know if it was the veil of darkness that came out of the mountain or if I was worried about leaving her tied to a tree where anything could find her, but leaving her behind sent a wave of sorrow through me that quickly drowned any fortitude I had tried to muster during the ride. I dropped my forehead to hers, scratched the side of her face, and she snorted somberly, chewing on the bit in her mouth.

"I'll be back," I murmured, and Froki blinked. Even she knew that might not be true. But I couldn't help but keep lying, because it was the only thing moving me forward. Froki chuffed before I kissed her snout and turned away.

Following Ertha, we avoided the outskirts of the village, though it seemed empty and quiet. Instead, she pointed out a small path on the side of the mountain, barely big enough to walk comfortably on.

"I used to use this path to sneak out to the pub when I was younger," she recounted, breaking the tension for a moment. "It's a bit perilous at night, though."

It was perilous *now*; I couldn't imagine it at night. My fingers clung to the stone face for balance as we inched forward, fighting the urge to look down. Understanding my obvious trepidation, as I'm sure it was readable *without* the rune, Aaren reached forward and wrapped his hand around my belt to ensure that if I slipped, at least I wouldn't fall.

We climbed for what felt like hours, finally coming to a level crag no larger than the room I had at the inn. We crammed ourselves onto the outcropping, each of us hugging the rock. Von had gone pale, and he kept his eyes to the sky. It seemed he disliked heights just as much as I did.

Ertha shimmied and turned to face the rock, and I was astonished when she closed her eyes. Perhaps it was because of her territory and her familiarity with the path, but no amount of bribing could get me to close my eyes. She placed her palm flat against the rock. There was a pause only long enough for a breath, then the stone under her palm cracked to form the shape of a small door. Axl, having unknowingly leaned on said door, toppled backwards with a groan. I clamped a hand over my mouth, genuine laughter bubbling in my chest for the first time in days. His bottom half jutted from the entrance, the top half lost to the darkness in the tunnel.

"Ow," he said bluntly, sunlight shining on his face as he sat up and dusted off his arms. He took the arm Aaren extended to him and bristled. "A warning would've been nice, Ertha."

Ertha smiled defiantly. "And where's the fun in that?" She flicked her eyes to Aaren and me. "We're going to need light."

Aaren held out his palm where a small, leafless branch grew from the center, and handed it to me. A snap of my fingers and a little flame flickered, lighting the branch and creating an impromptu torch.

Ertha instructed us on which way to turn and what walls to cling to as the path inside had different spots where the floor had fallen out. The torch only illuminated so much, and Von tripped countless times, blaming it on broken spots in the floor. Axl just said his boots were too big for him, to which Von tried to throw a small punch, unsuccessfully, thanks to the tight walls of the tunnel. It seemed almost feverish, the lightheartedness of it all, especially right before whatever was going to happen inside the mountain. As grim as it was, I appreciated it.

The tunnel ended abruptly with another stone wall carved with minor runes and symbols. With a sad, reminiscent smile, Ertha traced her hand over them. "Torsten and I put these here, right after we were married. Just in case someone found their way through this tunnel." Then she smiled at the floor. "And then he fucked me right there."

Von jumped, dancing on the balls of his feet as if standing on that spot would infect him with something.

Ertha turned to flatten her hand against the stone as she did outside, but instead of pushing it open, she cracked it, then peeked into the hallway beyond.

There was a pause where the dusty air was suddenly alive with crackling, unkempt energy from each of us, just waiting to be unleashed. "It looks clear," Ertha whispered, then pushed the door all the way open. The hall was empty, not even a shadow on the wall from the nearby brazier save for our own. Pressing against the wall and letting our shadows vanish, we moved forward. Our footsteps were nearly silent in the echoing corridor.

The hall rounded, and a familiar small alcove opened up. I remembered hiding in this spot, listening intently to a conversation I wasn't supposed to hear.

It was the small, personal library Ertha and Torsten kept, the same library where they debated whether to trust me. I peered in and stared at the exact spot Torsten had stood in front of Ertha, where he held her against his chest, the place where he kissed her. The hearth was barren, all except for the charred logs from the fire that night. Most of the books were torn to shreds, pages trampled and stomped in a mockery of the knowledge they held. It was hard to imagine a burrower ripping the books apart with its pale fingers, and it only served to make me angrier.

Ertha glanced inside. A somber shadow crossed her face when she beheld the destroyed room. She merely blinked, then whispered, "This way."

The alcoves leading into other empty rooms increased, their doors hanging ajar and displaying the ransacked interiors. Stone beds were overturned, goblets and pitchers smashed, and the pages of more shredded books lay plastered to the stone floor. There was an odd smell in the air, like smoke and mold, and it wended through the halls to fill every brick in the stonework. There were draugr here. Enough of them for their stench to permeate through the mountain.

I didn't want to see the bedroom Aaren and I had stayed in during our visit, but there was no fighting the urge to look inside when we passed. The once-beautiful room was now in ruins. The elegant balcony doors had been shattered and rested on busted hinges, and the lovely ornamental rug had been shredded, the center stained with a dark crimson. I prayed that crimson didn't come from Fiske.

Aaren didn't show the resignation he sent through the rune, followed by the angered rush of energy that surged up my arm. I slipped my hand into his, embracing his anger that was now mingling with my own.

The library, our bedroom, the ruined halls, the reek of draugr, I used all of it to channel into my chest to dig into my magic and stir it to life. My magic curled and churned, twisting awake and furious at its arousal. I shook my shoulders as it electrified my atoms and begged to be let loose.

There was a scuffling ahead, then the shadow of a hunched figure crept across the wall in front of us. We retreated into a room, but left a small crack in the door where we watched a burrower pass, a torch in one hand and a small rough stone axe in the other. It grunted as it moved past, its creamy white eyes swimming brainlessly.

A few minutes ticked by as we waited in case the burrower decided to turn around and come back our way. After five minutes, we slipped out of the room and continued to sneak through the halls.

As we drew closer, my gut clenched, and I wished we were able to pick up the pace before anticipation burned me more than it already had. My senses were alight with it, heart beating a tattoo of anxiety and a readiness I had never known before now. I had waited months for this very moment, and with every fleeting second that passed, it felt like it was growing farther and farther away. I withdrew Aaren's dagger from my side to give my fingers something to hold instead of flexing and sweating like they were at my side.

The hallway opened up to the cavern outside of the meeting hall, which was guarded by two burrowers, their translucent skin shimmering in the light of the torches clutched in their spindly, clawed fingers. Aaren knew just as much as I did that every second was precious, so he wasted no time as he soundlessly slipped his fingers into his pack and retrieved two throwing stars, fanning them out with a quiet, metallic sound. He flicked his wrist and launched the stars into both eyes of the burrower on the left. Black blood oozed from the sockets, and the burrower dropped to the stone floor with a throttled gargle.

Alerted by its fallen comrade, the burrower turned, slack-jawed as it pounded over to investigate. Von pounced on the opportunity, rolling forward and crouching, his boots muted against the stone. Within seconds, he was behind the burrower. He grabbed the few strands of hair the burrower had and pulled to expose its neck. The burrower gagged on dark ichor when Von slid his dagger across its throat, then let it drop to the ground. Its long, pallid fingers coated with dark blood as it pawed at its throat, but its choke quieted in a few seconds, and it went still.

Well done, Von.

It was a little victory, giving only enough relief to keep my heart from bursting through my chest at the sight of the double doors leading into the room that was once the meeting hall. My pulse hammered in my wrists, neck throbbing with that same angry beat vibrating through my body to create an arrhythmic symphony of fright.

Nothing stood between me and Markus, nothing but that door ahead of us.

My rune prickled with a wave of calming warmth as we crossed the entry hall on muffled footsteps. I didn't need to turn to know that Aaren was at my back, but I couldn't let anything distract either of us, especially if what was behind the door was just as bad as my guts were telling me. So as much as it hurt me, I did my best to shut down the connection between us, ignoring Aaren's questioning look as I braced my hand against the cold, brass door.

There were only two hopes I could cling to in the brief moments before I pushed this door open and faced my father. The first was that if either Aaren or I perished, at least we had the venerated halls of Himmelfjell to look forward to.

I would climb to the highest peak of that heavenly mountain and wait for Aaren if that was what it took ever to see him again. That was the only promise I would die with should that be my fate.

The second was that no matter what waited behind that door, none of it mattered. Because Lucas was there waiting for me. If I died today or lived to be eight hundred years old, my brother would no longer be in Markus's clutches. Lucas was in there, and when I opened this door, he wouldn't be some lost memory, some phantom shadow that escaped me in my dreams and resided in the recesses of my mind. When I opened this door, he would be my brother again.

With a deep breath, I pushed the door open.

The meeting hall looked the same as it did the last time I was here. There was a roaring fire in the massive hearth across the room, and the carvings on the ceiling hadn't changed or been defiled by Fjellhjem's new occupants. The blatant familiarity, coupled with knowing who roamed these halls, felt like a formidable insult to Torsten's memory. An insult to the Fraalver themselves. The fact that Markus worked so hard to infiltrate the villages of my people, all efforts made and lives lost to prevent it, all for him to worm his way into their mountains, was loathsome. Right on cue, my blood began to boil, and my fingertips lit with heat.

Before I could take in any more of the room, a movement in the corner caught my eye. It was Fiske, bound and gagged with a face battered almost beyond recognition. His clothes were bloodied and covered in dusty earth as if he had been thrown in a dirt cell after enduring whatever beatings they had put him through. The firelight flickered off his sweat-sheened bald head, and his features were screwed in a brutalized wince, teeth biting into his gag as a wave of pain seemed to blow through him. He hadn't noticed us yet; his eyes were fixed across the room. Specifically, in the center where the large table was. The same table where we had all our meals and meetings during our stay here. Another mockery of the memory of what this great mountain once was.

Then came the hissing, unbridled rage that lit every fiber of my being when I saw him.

Him.

My *father.*

Markus looked exactly like Lucas. I realized now, after seeing my father for the first time, that Lucas didn't favor a speck of my mother. It was all Markus. Something tried to convince me that there was still some of Mama inside Lucas, deep, deep down, but staring at my father from across the room, noting the uncanny resemblance, dispelled that desperate belief. His light brown hair and pointed nose were almost identical to Lucas's, and as I examined his green eyes, I realized what parts of him were clear in my own appearance. Curved jawline, firm cheekbones, full lips, dimpled chin. It all came from him. And I hated every single piece he gave me.

Six draugr huddled around the table near him, poking and prodding a writhing form atop the stone surface. A harsh screech rattled from the thing on the table that echoed across the hall, but none of the things reacted. It was as if they were so accustomed to screams that whatever had made the sound was simply a source of background noise to them. There was another scream when one of the draugr dug its rotted finger into an open wound along the thing's abdomen, cackling as the sound grew louder, more pleading, the deeper the finger went. I squinted for a better look and choked on a gasp at the familiar cascade of hair and twitching tail.

Like the water it dwelled in, it opened its mouth and out flowed the truth, right into the betrayed blood's ears.

It was Embla, the huldra.

The water wasn't Klartvan, it was our own river in Skoghjem. Ymer didn't give us away, Embla did. They had captured and tortured her into revealing our secrets, what little of them she actually knew. The poor huldra was splayed across the stone table, brutalized and covered in deep wounds, bits of her skin peeled back and nicked. My stomach turned over at the sight. Embla's mouth had fallen slack, and she sucked in ragged breaths between screams, her chest rapidly jumping to bring in precious life as the spirit slowly ebbed from her eyes.

Though the entire scene before me was enough to throw me into a blind fit of agonizing, brutal fury, it was seeing Lucas a few feet away from the table that stirred the darkest monsters that resided in the depths of my being. There wasn't a scratch on him, and seeing him untouched was what frightened me the most. What had they done to him that I couldn't see? He sat on the stone floor, tracing patterns into the ash, swiping it clean, then drawing again. His hair had grown longer, and it brushed his shoulders as he reached forward to sweep the ash. Perhaps it was the fact that his image had slowly faded in my mind over the few months we were apart, but he had grown a bit more into his features, and his limbs seemed a little longer. As my brother was growing up, I had missed it. I had missed precious moments in Midgard, and Markus had stolen the rest from me.

"It is quite the honor to finally meet you, Layla," a smooth, silken voice said.

Lucas's eyes rose to meet mine, curiosity and something like confusion spelling his features. "Layla?" he asked.

Fiske's muddled shouts sounded from the corner.

I didn't want to take my eyes off Lucas, but I whipped my head to the table, gaze connecting with Markus as he straightened and adjusted a black leather vest that covered an equally black shirt. His long hair had been pulled back from his face, though the rest draped over his shoulders and stopped at his collarbone. With his face entirely in the firelight, he looked a little more haggard than he had before, his features worn and etched, though still handsome nonetheless. He hardly looked like he had been dead for hundreds of years. And yet he didn't look like he was alive.

Markus looked over my shoulder at my friends behind me. "And I see you've brought guests. I am quite ecstatic to meet your husband." A wicked grin broke the oily stillness of his face. "My son-in-law."

A nasty shudder sluiced up my spine at his words, because the thought of any form of familial tie sent a sick roar through my nerves. I chanced a glance at Lucas, where the curiosity had been wiped away by betrayal that sank deep into my chest. His brow furrowed.

"Husband?" he mouthed. His lip curled angrily, and one eye squinted as anger overtook the rest of his face. He abruptly turned back to the ash pile and swiped it clean aggressively. Something in me lurched, pushing me forward to go to my brother, to explain and tell him how sorry I was for how long it took for me to get to him, but Markus's grim sneer rooted me where I stood.

"You've been quite busy, Markus," Aaren snarled as he met my side. The wrath that draped his every syllable commanded the room, every draugr now carefully watching us with rotted hands on the rusty hilts of their swords. Aaren's power was practically dripping off of him, and I opened the rune the slightest bit. My power, that was starting to claw at its confines, charged through the opening like a bull free from its stall.

"I might say the same for you as well," Markus replied as he rounded the table. "Killing the Nidhogg must've been a difficult feat to accomplish. Which is why I needed to find you, that I bring you...", his mouth twisted into a nasty grin as he gestured to the stone walls around him, "...home."

"Home?" I asked.

"Well, not home as in here at Fjellhjem, but home to me." He pointed to Lucas, who was now refusing to lift his head. He always did when he was upset. "Bring you home to him."

My eyes narrowed. "What do you mean?"

"Isn't that what you've always wanted? For your family to be reunited?" Markus's tone was inquiring, almost teasing. Like my misfortune was some joke to him. I went to retort, but Markus continued. "To be honest, Layla, I wanted the three of us together. Because I am a demigod, and you two are my children. Imagine the power we could grow, the tides we could turn."

"And the realms we could destroy?" I demanded. "Because that's what the necromancer wants, right? To wipe out every single realm on Yggdrasil except the one he builds?"

"*He* is just a means to an end," Markus spat.

"And who is *he*?" I demanded. Aaren stirred next to me as the air grew more static. He was having trouble containing himself, his control slipping through his fingers the longer the power ate at us. We didn't have much longer until Aaren had no choice but to unleash himself.

Markus clicked his tongue. "So eager for all my secrets, aren't we?" He shook his head. "No, this isn't about him, I'm afraid. This matter is a bit more personal. This is about you and me, Layla. Father and daughter. A reunion of sorts."

A cursed reunion.

I took a step further into the meeting hall against my better judgment.

"You have my attention," I said.

"Splendid."

Lucas shuffled to his feet and dusted his hands on his pants, something I had tried to teach him not to do for years. Silver tears blurred my vision because I was so eager to hold my brother after so long, to smell his scent, to feel his warmth. I held my arms out for him. Gods, all I needed was to hold him. Everything would be solved if I could touch him again, hear him talk about his comic books, and see him scribbling in his sketchpad. He didn't move to come to me, though, instead walking to Markus and standing tall next to him. Lucas's chin raised confidently as Markus tittered proudly. Father and son, side by side.

I couldn't understand how this could've happened, even though it had been a fear of mine since I married Aaren instead of running off to look for Lucas. I was his sister. I took care of him all those years when no one else wanted to. For so long, we only had each other. A situation created by the man whose side Lucas chose to stand by. The man who caused all of this. And Lucas still chose him. The dagger in my hand may as well have pierced my heart.

"Lucas?" I gasped, tear after tear silently dripping down my face. My arms were still spread wide, but emptiness and cold created a void in my embrace.

Lucas only looked at me through arched brows and scrutinized me. "No," he said, keeping his head high, jaw set. Just like his father. Oh gods. This was all my fault.

Markus shook with laughter. "Apologies for the disappointment, Layla dear, but Lucas is more my son than your brother. He answers to me. Unlike you, I didn't abandon him to go fall in love."

My mouth hung open heavily as every emotion sang a deafening symphony in my head. "That is not what happened, and you know that, Markus."

He flourished. "Tell him that."

I took a step closer, but Lucas backed away and slid closer to his father. I halted, despair erasing every ounce of strength in me. My power responded with a furious hiss.

"Lucas, I looked for you. I never stopped. It's just taken me this long to find you."

Lucas considered me for an angry moment. "Then who is he?" he asked and shoved a finger at Aaren next to me.

"He..." I stammered.

Markus's lip curled. "He's the one whose bed she decided to warm instead of finding you, *gutt*." Markus spat on the ground. "Whore."

Aaren snarled, and overwhelming energy cascaded from him. The others behind me stirred, with the sound of a dagger being drawn and the leather of a sword hilt being gripped.

"I...Lucas, I've done what I could. I promise, I haven't stopped looking for you since the moment you went missing."

Lucas shook his head. My magic coiled like a hot spring at the sight. "No, Layla," he said then, and everything inside me turned to stone. "You're not taking me."

Markus laughed brazenly. "He knows his loyalties well," he cooed, flicking dust from his shirt.

"Fuck you," I hissed.

"Always the fighter, just like your mother."

"Don't you *dare* speak of my mother."

Markus cocked a mischievous brow as a smirk pulled at a corner of his mouth. "You're mother fell in love with me twice. As two different men. And she served her purpose when Lucas was born and was no longer necessary." Drops of water dripped from the end of my pointer finger as I tried to rein in the control that was quickly slipping away. I could hear Aaren's breathing next to me as his restraint grew paper-thin with every second that ticked by.

"So I removed her from your life," Markus said.

The roaring in my head silenced, everything inside me going wholly still. I was sure my heart stopped beating as his words echoed in my mind. I couldn't feel Aaren's magic or my own anymore, nor could I think of my raging heartbeat or the flames that had ignited and were now dancing between my fingers.

"You...you..."

Lucas lost a moment of his composure as he looked up at Markus, eyes wide and distant.

"Dad?"

Markus ignored him, his eyes stuck tauntingly on my trembling form. "Yes, Layla. I killed your mother. And your grandmother when you were in her care. I needed Lucas to be easily attainable when I was ready." Markus chuckled again and held up his hand to examine his nails. "I hadn't taken into account the fact that you would go into your grandmother's care, so I had to compromise. Then I lost both of you somewhere in Pennsylvania."

"All of this for what? So you could gather more and more power to give to some necromancer?" I demanded.

Anger flashed across Markus's face, and his composure slipped. "I serve no one!" Heat flashed in his eyes. "Lucas is my key to break free from the servitude my debts hold me in. His life force and his potential magic will give me the power to break these chains."

Markus's brow arched. "And you, Layla. You complete us. I need you just as much as I need him.

"When I sired you, I thought you were to be the one to liberate me. But when you were born insignificant and female, I left." Markus laughed, and it sounded so much like Lucas's. "Then I sired Lucas, my one male heir, and I couldn't take any chances. So I took him, but when you followed him here, something told me you had a bigger role to play. My suspicions were confirmed when you purged me all those months ago."

His brow lowered and his eyes darkened. "I made a mistake abandoning you, Layla." He extended his hand to me. "Join me, daughter. Make our family whole."

The choice I never thought I would face. Join him, be a part of my missing family, or die taking him down.

"You know how this is going to end if you refuse me."

I grit my teeth, lip quivering. "We may share blood," I trembled, flames simmering beneath my skin just as they filled my palms, "but you will never be my father."

Markus grinned crookedly. "Then you won't be my daughter for very long."

Aaren growled, and I met his eye for the briefest of moments.

It was all we needed.

We unleashed ourselves.

Power like I had never known before zipped through me and into Aaren, then back to me in an electric display of static power.

My friends broke formation; Ertha moved to the corner, where Fiske writhed, while Axl thundered past Markus and wrenched Lucas from him. Von leapt forward and closed the gap between him and the draugr that surrounded the table, then sliced into them before they could even unsheathe their weapons.

I pounced, sheathing the dagger and aiming both hands at Markus as a blazing stream of fire shot from my skin. With the flick of his wrist, my father effortlessly threw up a shield of water that extinguished my flames in seconds. I didn't let it faze me in the slightest because he killed Mama and Granny. He had stolen my brother. He was playing with my people's fate like it was a coin to be tossed to the wind.

Nothing was going to stop me from annihilating him.

Markus waved his hand, and there was a thundering crash as pieces from the ceiling above rained down, pelting us with rocks and pebbles that stung like riding horseback through violent rain. Aaren snatched me by the arm and yanked me just in time for a gargantuan boulder to smash where I had been standing.

Lucas shouted in the distance as Axl carried him out of the hall, limbs thrashing and flailing as he begged for Markus to save him. He wouldn't, of course, when I was standing in front of him.

Ertha had successfully released Fiske, who shook life back into his limbs. His movements were stiff, and the grimace on his face was nothing but agony. Yet he stood, squinting through swollen eyes and gnashing his teeth through brutalized lips as he bellowed a war cry.

Aaren summoned a blustering gale and sent it over Markus, who faltered on the balls of his feet. It was the first moment of weakness, so I launched into motion, mustering the strength to move a handful of the smaller boulders to charge toward him. He recovered too quickly and smashed them as they collided, and bits of rock sprayed around the cavern. Ertha appeared next to me, then stomped her foot onto the floor. It cracked, then yawned into a gaping chasm that would have sent Markus tumbling into had it not been for the fallen piece of ceiling he summoned to catch him.

There was a ringing clank of metal and the sound of footsteps.

"No," I breathed when I turned to face the door.

Spilling from the opening was an army of draugr and burrowers, numbering fifty to each one of us. However, there were more than I could count at the moment, and only a small handful were charged. The rest stayed to the sides of the cavern, like they were watching a wrestling match and placing bets on who would reign triumphant. They were going to fight in waves, tire us out before finally killing us. It was all a sick game of my father's, delighting in every chance to torture us. And seeing as this fight would make or break us, it was his last chance to play.

Von, Fiske, and Ertha were now preoccupied with the oncoming slaughter of the draugr and burrowers, leaving me and Aaren to face Markus on our own.

I glanced at the fire in the hearth and almost grinned as an idea took form. I turned my attention to the fireplace to prod the flames to awaken them to my bidding. They were more than eager to respond; a large tunnel of fire erupted from the opening and curled until it took the shape of a flaming copy of the Nidhogg. The flames were antsy, begging me to sink their burning fangs into my father. A cry ripped through my throat when I threw my arms forward, all thought and feeling lost in the exertion, in the anger, in the exchange of power between Aaren and me.

The flaming Nidhogg surged forward with a delighted roar, but my hands met resistance, like trying to put two magnets of the same polarity together. My hands were one magnet, the snake the other.

"Layla, look out!" Aaren barked.

I dove just in time for the Nidhogg to spin and spit a raging tunnel of fire towards me. It took me only seconds to return to my feet, searching for the lost control of the fire and cursing when the magic protested my touch.

Markus had taken control of it.

"Oh fuck," I cursed again, dropping my hands and abandoning the plan.

The fire snake stormed forward, hissing horrifically, the sound like crackling fire and fierce, angry electricity. I took off in a sprint and leapt out of its targeted sight as it struck. I backed away across the floor and dodged the hailing footsteps of battle going on before me as another wave of creatures surged forth on my friends.

Fiske took the small break in the fight to summon a cannon of water at the snake that doused the back half of it. The fire snake hissed again, a sound that vibrated in my bones and rattled my teeth. The fire was furious, not because Markus told it to be, but because of the sudden change of hands. It didn't like being tossed between wielders like hot coals.

I scrambled to my feet, lifting already exhausted arms and barrelling a boulder-sized ball of water at the flaming serpent. Fiske turned his attention back to the oncoming assault of burrowers, and I refocused my attention to hone it in on my stolen magic. Smoke hissed as my water collided with it and sent the snake into oblivion.

The remaining flames from the hearth retreated as if to hide from the battle.

"Quite impressive," Markus called from across the cavern. "It's a shame to see such power go to waste."

"Fuck," I hollered, shooting a boulder at him, "you!" He dodged the assailing earth with frustrating ease.

My breath was sharp in my lungs, and my magic flinched when the fire refused to meet my summons again.

"You certainly have fucked *him*," Markus retorted in a biting tone. "Tell me, Layla, when did you decide you loved him, before or after you gave up on Lucas?"

I hammered a fireball at him, unsure what else to do as my anger overcame my better judgment. "When did you decide to kill Mama? Before or after you fell in love with her?"

Markus descended on his rock with a biting sneer on his face. "It was my plan all along, Layla. Love was just another obstacle that stood in my way." He stepped down from the boulder, still halfway across the cavern. "It seems you were too weak to overcome it." Markus flicked his hand, and the ground shook, something growing deep within the chasm Ertha had created. "Maybe the power of being married to a Fraalver leader got to your head." He chuckled. "I understand the allure of power. It's impossible to ignore." The floor on the lip of the chasm crumbled as a massive stone hand slammed down. "Too bad you'll never get to really feel the full extent of the share I gave you. It's intoxicating."

The stone hand held tight to the mouth of the chasm, then the shape of a head hewn from stone emerged. And as it rose to full height, I knew all hope was lost.

To my left, Aaren was summoning vines from the open earth within the chasm. The thick, wooded tendrils climbed up the giant, digging into the rock and crumbling chunks of it away. The giant opened its mouth and howled, a sound that halted the fight around us momentarily as it rang through the cavern. The draugr and burrowers lining the walls cowered for a moment, flinching at the harsh resonance of the rock giant. Ertha looked ready to join our fight, but changed her mind when a draugr almost whacked her with a dull warhammer. Besides, rock against rock likely wouldn't work, and the irony wasn't lost on me. It was like a twisted game of rock, paper, scissors.

The giant came from Markus's power, and I supposed the only thing that could take it down was his own magic. The same magic that flowed in me. The same magic that was now tethered between Aaren and me.

Gritting my teeth, I planted my feet and invited Aaren's magic to fill the empty spots where I had been drained. A renewed vigor buzzed within me as his power struck. Deeper stores of my power rose from the depths as his magic curled around mine, stroking it, teasing it, almost like our energies were mating and becoming one. An untamable humming vibrated in my chest, and I grew hot, beads of sweat pooling along my brow.

The feeling inside me was akin to the one I experienced after my first drink of ale. Light and heady and almost bubbly. The ground shook again, but it didn't distract me from the feeling that was pooling in my stomach, the weight that was growing pleasurably. It wasn't a tipsy feeling anymore, but that sweet feeling that accompanies arousal, that fiery delight that ignited in me every time Aaren and I tangled. It was no longer my power and his power, but just power. That delicious, burning heat engulfed me as Aaren and I became one united entity.

The rock giant hesitated with a balled, stone fist frozen in the air. Its stone eyes watched as a clump of rock crumbled from its arm and disappeared into the chasm behind it. In the giant's moment of hesitation, I got a good look at the brilliance behind the enchanted stone. If Lucas had a pen and paper, he'd be able to capture its essence brilliantly.

If I ever got that side of my brother back.

I had never seen Lucas look like the one he had given me. A look laced with venom and an abhorrence that was reserved for one's darkest enemies. Had I become Lucas's darkest enemy? In my time of growth and prosperity, had I neglected Lucas so much that he had molded into the sickly, malevolent copy of our father? After everything we had been through in the foster home, all of the fighting I did to keep him close, and I still ended up as the enemy.

Just like the day at the park. It wasn't Stephanie and her nasty words that hurt Lucas, but my own. Isn't that what happened here? It was our father, who, despite all the havoc he had wreaked in our lives, had rescued Lucas from the foster home and brought him to a better place. Not what I had always planned. I fell in love with a stranger, grew into the most powerful being in Alveland aside from Markus, and found my brother, albeit a few months later than planned.

No matter how hard I tried, it was never good enough. Not when it came to my brother.

Today was the day I changed that.

I clenched my fists, unable to keep in my fury any longer.

Throwing my hands forward, I roared, releasing every ounce of power and magic I had ready and launching it at the giant. The rune sang between us as Aaren gave a rallying cry, and his own reserves of magic soared until the giant couldn't fight our chaos anymore. I yielded, sending my power back to the depths to recover, and there was a beat of calm while the giant stood still.

There was a deafening crash, and the stone giant burst into millions of pieces, raining boulders and earth onto the cavern floor and smashing the battling draugr and burrowers to a pulp.

It didn't stop the next wave from coming to attack our friends. Taking a quick moment to survey the fight, I spotted a flurry of blonde hair as Ertha whirled about, smashing rocks onto her attackers and slicing into them with weary ease. Von, visibly tired, swept his foot underneath a burrower and knocked it onto its back. Fiske, still bloodied and bruised, knocked two draugr's heads together, and smirked as they toppled to the floor.

Still fighting strong, but they weren't going to last much longer.

Aaren saw it, too, and he puffed out a breath, his chest heaving.

Markus, for the first time since the fight started, looked concerned. It only manifested on his face for a moment before that disturbing mask of nonchalance fell back into place. He clapped his hands twice, and the fire in the hearth huffed with renewed life, then broke free from the confines of the fireplace. Individual bursts of flame broke away and took shape, molding into flaming fenrs that snarled and gnashed their fiery maws at us.

Aaren cursed under his breath, puffing a stray strand of hair out of his face.

The fenrs charged, their barks and howls echoing throughout the chamber, but it did nothing to staunch the fight off to the left. Fiske panted after felling another burrower, his face bleeding freshly from old and new wounds.

Ertha's blonde hair was covered in dirt and matted to her head, but she lifted a weary arm to summon another boulder. No matter how exhausted she was, her magic never faltered. She flicked her wrist and opened a small chasm big enough to fit three burrowers, who fell unknowingly inside. Another flourish of her hand, and the chasm closed again and crushed the burrowers inside.

Axl had reappeared and fought alongside Von. They stood back to back, a hurricane of swinging blades and side kicks as they mowed through the new opponents, yet more streamed through the door.

The fenrs were upon us before I could blink, and I extinguished the closest with a wave of water.. Aaren blew a breath and summoned a deadly wind that overpowered the angry flames of the next fenr, but they continued to spawn from the fire in the hearth. They were storming toward us in droves, too many for the both of us to take them all on.

Aaren and I took turns staving off the closest fenrs that scaled the chasm to get to us, each expenditure of magic taking more and more from us. My stores of power were depleting with every attack, and my chest ached as it felt like I was starting to take more than there was to give. As I slashed through a fenr with a blade of clear water, Aaren braced his fingers in his mouth and whistled over his shoulder.

The battle to our right halted for the briefest moment, long enough for Ertha to glance over her shoulder and nod in understanding. The distraction cost me, and white heat blazed the skin of my forearm as a fenr latched on and shook. My feet fell out from under me, and the hard ground met my side. I cried out as the fenr's flaming jaws tightened, then dragged me toward the chasm. I reared my foot back and kicked, but my boot only met emptiness that singed the leather. And still, the fenr continued to drag me. Aaren howled from a few feet away as flame caught him, too, overpowered by the wolves now that the end of our defense had faltered.

My fingers brushed the stone, grappling for purchase on any lip of broken floor I could feel. The closer I got to the chasm, the louder Aaren's screams echoed in my ears, and I waited for the moment they stopped, praying I'd be thrown into the abyss before that time came. Instead, a shadow crossed over my head. The fenr's paws were grazing the jagged edge, but I looked to where the shadow went, and gasped as a massive boulder slammed Markus to the side. He flew feet first into the air before smacking onto the stone.

Ertha shouted triumphantly from a distance away, then returned to her own attack.

The fenr that had hold of me vanished into smoke. I scrambled to my feet to see Aaren covered in scorch marks, charred bits of skin peeking through burned scraps of his clothes, but when I went to move to him, he gave me a silent warning. There was a bigger problem at hand, and it was now recovering from being smacked by a boulder.

Markus stood and roared with an anger that rivaled my own. What a pathetic coward, hiding on the other side of the chasm to remain untouched.

"Scared of your own daughter, Markus?" I taunted.

My father gave me a look hewn with malice.

I had to get across the chasm. And I knew just the way to get there.

Shooting Aaren a look, I backtracked away from the edge and prepared to run. Without question, Aaren knelt, channeling deep into his magic.

Then I started to run.

Right for the edge.

A friendly gust of wind whipped my braid, kissing my cheeks as it propelled me forward, and sent me straight across the abyss to the other side. I landed with a thud, my scorched boots denting the stone. Aaren followed and appeared by my side.

I hadn't closed the connection through our rune yet, and I wasn't sure I was going to. Nothing could distract me. Not when the atrocities Markus committed against me, against my family, were so disastrous.

Vines broke through the floor as Aaren's magic coiled around, itching to manifest in more vicious ways instead of the curious greenery growing around us.

Now closer to Markus, I could see the faults in his face. There was a deep scar running along his jaw, and there were still indications of decay that the necromancer hadn't been able to erase. It still didn't make him look any less like Lucas. Markus surprised me, though, when his eyes softened, the brutal sneer leaving his lips flat.

"Your eyes," he sighed somberly. "They're the same as your mother's."

My throat tightened as a wave of emotion rolled over me. Standing before me was my father—the man I had cursed a million times into my pillow in a fit of unfair rage. The man I had begged the heavens would return to us and take us away from the foster homes. The man who lived on forever in my mind as a legend, a myth, the only evidence left behind that he had even been here was me.

"I am proud of you, Layla," Markus said, voice softer than before. Paternal, everything I had ever dreamed it could have been. "You have surprised me at every turn. You're more like me than you think." He chanced a step closer, hands lifted as if I were a scared deer searching to flee. "I've only ever wanted us to be a family."

"It's not true, *fremmed*," Aaren pleaded.

"It is," Markus continued. "When you were born and I left your mother, I couldn't stay away. But Midgard was not where I belonged, and I couldn't stay."

"And what about Granny, was she just collateral to you?"

Markus shook his head, taking another careful step towards me. Aaren gave a warning snarl.

"Your grandmother was an unfortunate obstacle I had to face. I don't regret it. I needed your brother. The only thing I *do* regret is that I never gave you a chance. And you had to suffer because of it." Markus smiled. "And now you're here. Think of all we could do together, Layla, everything we could accomplish."

Aaren went to protest, but his words got lost in my ears as something painted my mind. It was an image of the three of us—me, my father, and brother—traipsing through the woods of Skoghjem. Lucas gripped a bow in his hand, keeping his footsteps light and his sight honed on a short distance ahead. A small rabbit nuzzled the dry leaves, nose twitching and whiskers flicking.

Markus whispered something in Lucas's ear, and my brother's brow hardened as he drew back the bowstring. The arrow struck, and the rabbit fell lifeless to the ground.

"Excellent job," my father beamed as Lucas darted away to retrieve his kill.

The image changed to the three of us sitting before a fire in a small, humble shack. There were Balderkrig game pieces sprawled before us and empty dinner bowls stacked on the hearth. Markus sat next to Lucas with a devilish grin on his face. He whispered something, then Lucas made his move, his piece successfully snatching my Balder.

"That's cheating!" I exclaimed, slapping my hand on the table.

"Let your brother win for once, Layla. You win every time," Markus said, and Lucas stuck his tongue in my direction. I returned the gesture, and a small smile spread across my lips as Markus's voice brought me back.

"Isn't this what you've been dreaming of for years, Layla? Your blood family back together?"

My eyes dropped to the floor as desire nudged my heart. He was right. I *had* wanted this for years. For us to be a complete family. It was the only thing I ever asked for when I blew out birthday candles or when it came time to write letters to Santa in grade school.

A small vine curled around the toe of my boot, stroking the leather lovingly.

"Layla," Markus said, and extended his hand.

Aaren had been watching me closely for the time we stood there. And finally, I met his eyes. Those warm, honey eyes.

It had been all I wanted, but not anymore.

Aaren gave me a nod.

Then I fired a blast of water at Markus, knocking him back. It enveloped him, trapping him in a swirling flood. He tried to kick forward, propel himself to the side, and break free, but I moved the water with him to ensure he stayed within the bubble.

Suddenly, there was silence, and all clanking of weapons and hollers hushed, both friend and foe stopping to watch from the other side of the chasm.

Aaren, barely having caught his breath, waved a hand at the water, the sounds of fresh ice cracking as the water froze and trapped Markus inside. I watched Markus's frozen form glare from within the icy blue as I set the block of ice down on the stone floor. And when I approached the hardened wall of ice between us, I spat in his frozen face.

I was his usurper.

His downfall.

I was his daughter.

And as I foolishly let my guard down, ice erupted around us and Markus sprang free. He didn't need any time to recover before he wrenched forward and snagged me around the neck, his breath steaming against my skin.

I always thought one day I'd be able to hug my father. This wasn't exactly what I had in mind.

Aaren lunged forward, but Markus hummed his disapproval before he threw out an arm. The vines Aaren had left behind whipped forward, snaking up his legs and around his waist. He drew his knife to hack at them, but they were too fast, and they locked his arms to his side. My heart sank when I saw his throat bob. For the first time, Aaren was at a loss, lacking even a hint of a plan. A leader with no power. No control. The only thing he had craved so desperately. Something he had lacked since the beginning of his leadership. He had no control over his parents' dying or being thrust into power. No control over Markus and the attacks on his people. No control of my fate that was now held in the hands of my deranged father. He couldn't save me.

We were at the end.

"You're fucking pathetic," I spit, the sides of my throat constricting as Markus's hold around my neck wrenched tighter.

"And you're out of time, *daughter*." Markus's breath came as a hot cloud against my ear, and I shuddered to feel the life that filled his dead lungs. Then he inhaled deeply. "You smell like her, too. Your dear mother." He sighed again, then pressed a kiss to my temple. "You've caused me a lot of trouble, Layla. I'm going to enjoy killing you." He dragged the tip of his dagger down my cheek, the searing point sending a chill shooting down my spine. "You and the babe that grows in your belly."

Oh gods.

It couldn't be true.

I carried Aaren's child.

Emotion welled inside me, filling the space where my baby grew in my womb. I mourned the life I wouldn't be able to give this child, the life that would be so rich with love and nature and friendship. I mourned the life I couldn't have with Aaren, the life I so desperately pined for, the one I never thought I'd want but now ached the loss of. All the laughs I would miss out on, the loving embraces, the joy. That life that was so close to being mine, and it was slipping away with every breath I took, every vine that twined around Aaren. That life was so clear and vivid once, now veiled by the scraping of my father's knife against my skin, the warm breath in my ear.

Aaren dropped to his knees, helpless in the vines that no longer listened to his magic. It wasn't his fault. None of this was his fault, even though he would inevitably blame himself.

Markus reared back his hand, and with a furious laugh, he sank the dagger deep into my stomach.

Chapter 62

The pain didn't register at first; just the mere shock of being stabbed rang in my head. All I felt in the moment was Markus's fist over my abdomen, his dull laughter echoing throughout the cavern in my ears. And the seething anger that poured into my vision. There was only red, burning because of everything my father had done. He had tried to destroy my village, steal my brother, attack us countless times, and kill my unborn child. He killed me. I knew I was dead the moment his fingers wrapped around my neck.

Aaren roared, an overpowering guttural cry that shook his body and sent everything around him careening. A wave of energy erupted from him, one that broke the vines that restrained him and sent splinters exploding into the air. He stayed on his knees, unable to rise as the dagger dug deeper and deeper into my gut. His hard fist pounded against the stone, knocking every enemy in the room, except Markus, to the ground, pinned to the stone. Another pound on the floor, another wave of energy, and they dissipated, dissolving into ash.

Then the pain hit. The sharpest strike of lightning shot up my middle, and spread its branches across my body, and lit every cell on fire. I cried out for my life as it was ripped away from me, from the child I could have had, from the one I could have lived with, Aaren. Strength drained from me as the blood flowed from the wound, painting Markus's hand in the life he gave me. His child's life.

Every inch of me dulled. The color left my skin as the pain shook me, took over everything that I was. I wasn't a wife, a sister, a student, or a friend anymore. All I was was pain. Markus let me crumple to the floor and stain the stone with red. I had just enough strength to roll over, to push myself up with shaking arms.

Markus crouched in front of me, so he could watch the light leave my eyes.

"I am inevitable, eternal..." he spat. Aaren roared again, sending the earth into a violent tremble as another wave of power erupted. "I am your father..."

"And I am your daughter," I coughed. Copper coated my tongue as blood blended with bile and surged up my throat. My father's eyes widened, his following words mangled in his throat. A strangled gasp ripped through him, and his eyes dropped to the dagger I had buried in his gut.

"And you are dead."

I twisted the dagger to let his blood stream out and mix with mine, creating a gruesome puddle of familial ties. Markus gagged, his tongue rolling out of his mouth as crimson bubbled in his throat. His hands fumbled for the knife in his abdomen, the exact spot where he had punctured me.

I felt no remorse as I watched my father writhe. Every gram of humanity left me as I relished his pained groans and pleas for relief. Desperation soaked his features because this time, there was not a necromancer to revive him, no second chance at life.

I was his end.

His hopelessness had his hand brushing my cheek, pleading with me. "Layla," he gasped, mouth gaping like a fish out of water. He said my name as if he were the one who gave it to me.

"I'm your father, Layla, please."

"Not anymore."

Summoning my remaining strength, I dug the dagger as deep as it would, and sliced it up his chest and to his throat, nearly breaking him in half.

Markus's eyes went blank. Every bit of power and magic and energy bled out of him. And I watched with what little joy I could muster.

Markus collapsed, dead.

All remaining strength expended, I dropped the rest of the way to the floor, feeling my blood pool coldly around me. My skin chilled, and blood loss sent me into tremors. And then Aaren was there by my side, sliding my limp form into his arms as I wheezed what little breath I could hold in my lungs because they were slowly filling with blood. Tears dripped like rain from his face and onto my cheeks. He was painting me in his sorrow.

I closed the rune for good because the last thing I wanted was to share this pain with him. And when he realized what I had done, Aaren gave a choked sob.

"Don't shut me out, *fremmed*," he begged, running a devastated hand over my blanching cheek. Over the constellation of freckles that were slowly fading.

With the last few drops of life I had left, I brushed a strand of hair from his face and gave my best attempt at a shaking smile. The corners of my mouth twitched. It was all I could give.

"No, Layla," he begged, dropping his forehead to mine.

"I-It's not y-y-your f-fault," I stammered, but my words gurgled because there was more blood than air in my windpipe.

Aaren pulled me closer, rocking me in his arms. "Somebody do something," he cried. "Please, someone do something!" His heart was breaking in his chest, and I couldn't do anything to help. All I could do was die.

The blurred forms of Fiske and Ertha materialized, but there was nothing they could do either.

I dropped my hand limply onto Aaren's rune and traced my finger over it.

"K-keep the forest g-growing," I whispered, knowing Aaren would understand. I wanted to cry, wrenched my gut to form the sob, but I was too pain-addled to feel the full force of my emotions.

And as I took another breath, I breathed out the rest of my life.

***

Hard ground slammed into my back and knocked the wind from my chest. I gasped, eyes flying open. I focused on the sky above me, but the trees obscured the gray, overcast oblivion beyond. Dead leaves brushed my fingers, and my temples pounded. A dull ache throbbed in my lower abdomen. I winced as I brushed my fingers over the spot. It was tender to the touch. I wasn't nauseous anymore, thank the Aesir, and my movements were unimpeded from the exhaustion I felt before.

I blinked, feeling my face returning. Pushing myself up, I grimaced as the throbbing morphed into dreadful pounding when it spread throughout my head, a bunch of small fists beating against my skull. My vision steadied, and I took in my surroundings.

I was in a forest, tall, strong trees stretching before me. I wasn't in *my* forest, though. This place was darker, more sinister. No birds sang in the canopy, and a heavy fog settled amongst the desolate trunks. The air was not crisp and earthy as I had come to know. No, this was heavy with musk that smothered my nose and lungs as if it was trying to suffocate me. The air made me feel like I was drowning, gaping like a fish out of water.

Where was I?

I wracked my brain, trying to remember what exactly happened, how I ended up here. Wherever here was. What did I remember?

There was a pounding, a shadow of a figure coming into focus as it beat its fists against the stone where it knelt. There was a shimmer of white hair, a wave of ferocious energy radiating from the figure. It threw its head back and howled, and my stomach twisted when the dull pain became sharper, as if someone had plunged a knife into me.

Someone *had* put a knife in me. My father. And the figure screaming in my mind was Aaren, my...husband. Oh gods, he was my husband. Every memory of our time together came flooding back, spinning in my head as if someone had pressed fast forward on a television in my mind.

Suddenly, I remembered everything, and I dropped to my knees, wondering how I was even alive after such a fight, after Markus had sliced me open with his dagger. How could I have arrived here, wherever 'here' was? It wasn't Skoghjem, I knew that immediately. It wasn't any of the surrounding forests; nowhere was this dark and desolate. Only one forest came to mind, one I had only read about. The idea struck me with a pang of fright, strong enough to send me fleeing the clearing with my heart hammering in my throat.

I halted before the base of a thin tree, small enough to climb, but tall enough to see above the canopy. I hoisted myself up onto the first branch, the pain in my stomach radiating and mingling with the ache in my head. I climbed another branch, then another, my efforts drowned out by the panic and toil in my mind. I prayed I was wrong, begged the gods that I wasn't where I thought I was.

I steadied myself, gripping the top of the tree with a fist tight enough to break a hand. I swallowed when my suspicions were confirmed.

Before me was a vast expanse of trees, the same cloud of mist hanging over the entire forest and the cleared patches beyond. And far, far off in the distance, was a lone mountain that pushed its peak into the sky, high enough that clouds gathered around.

My throat stung, the name of the mountain clear in my head.

It was Himmelfjell.

And I was dead.

Book two in the Realms Trilogy is already in the works — and the world you just stepped into is about to deepen, darken, and unravel in ways you won't see coming.

A Battle Between Realms

Coming Winter 2027

Acknowledgements

Firstly, I would like to thank Alexis and Leah, my first beta readers. They believed in it through every draft and revision, and I am so thankful for our taco runs and unhinged brainstorming sessions in the car while listening to Hozier. Thank you, and love you both.

A special thank you to Mariyana, who designed the cover and vine pattern, and provided the feral screaming to every spicy scene I wrote. She is one of the unhinged beta readers featured on my Instagram for her hilarious doodles and comments. Not only did she make me kick my feet and scream delusionally, but she also gave me what it took to push through the tough drafts and doubt. Thank you, Squiggy Bean, I love you bunches.

Thank you to Courtney for being my rock through all of the editing and publishing. If it weren't for her as my coach, unofficial agent, and shoulder to cry on, this book would not be in your hands. Through imposter syndrome and more self-doubt, this woman has helped me with so much more than just putting this book on shelves—she helped me decide that this was my forever. Thank you, Court. You are so special to me, and I'm happy you came into the bookstore that day. (Also, check out her book *Uncaged*; it is a whirlwind of a read.)

Collins, you made the first draft possible. Without your help and devotion to my dream, my words would not have made it out of our shared Google Doc. You are amazing, and thank you again.

To my Autumn, thank you for your insanity. Obviously, it helped with the book, but you keep me on my toes and make work worth going to.

Special thank you to my other beta readers: Lizzie, Liza, Dani, Deana, Alison, Cody, Asia, Christin, Reagan, and Jane (the other unhinged beta on my Instagram). Thank you for helping make my dream a reality.

To Dusty, thank you for reading the second draft in a day. I'm not sure how you did, but I'm still impressed, and I'm very excited for you to read the final product.

To my Mama, thank you for...everything. Thank you for reading this book eight times to ensure every i was dotted and every Oxford comma was in place. Thank you for making sure my voice was strong and whispering so that I could scream. The pen awaits you, too, Mama. It's your turn.

And finally, thank you to my sparky. To name off everything he has done for me and the book would be pointless, because behind every word of this book is my brilliant man. Every tear I shed over this book was wiped away by his hands. There isn't much more to say other than I love you and thank you.

Darby Cox is an author located on the coast of North Carolina. She has a passion for all things writing and all things fantasy. When she isn't writing her novels, she spends time reading, working her three jobs, and camping with her fiancé.

Instagram: @authordarbycox
TikTok: @darby.cox